ALSO BY MARY MACKEY

A GRAND PASSION
THE LAST WARRIOR QUEEN
McCARTHY'S LIST
IMMERSION
THE DEAR DANCE OF EROS

ook is a work of fiction, not of history. Except for a few well-known
ters such as Sarah Bernhardt and Lee Strasberg, names, characters,
and incidents are either the product of the author's imagination or
ed fictitiously. Any resemblance to actual events or locales or persons,
or dead, is entirely coincidental.

Copyright © 1988 by Mary Mackey
All rights reserved including the right of reproduction
in whole or in part in any form.
Published by Simon and Schuster
A Division of Simon & Schuster Inc.
Simon & Schuster Building
Rockefeller Center
1230 Avenue of the Americas
New York, New York 10020
Simon and Schuster and colophon are registered trademarks
of Simon & Schuster Inc.
Designed by Bonni Leon
Manufactured in the United States of America
1   3   5   7   9   10   8   6   4   2
Library of Congress Cataloging-in-Publication Data
Mackey, Mary.
The kindness of strangers / Mary Mackey.
p. cm.
I. Title.
PS3563.A3165K5 1988
813'.54–dc 19
87-34931
CIP
ISBN 0–671–62710–4

THE

KINDNE

OF

STRANGERS

MARY MAC

SIMON AND SCHUSTER
NEW YORK LONDON TORONTO SYDNE

ACKNOWLEDGMENTS

I owe a special debt of gratitude to novelist Sheldon Greene, who read every version of this novel in manuscript. His suggestions and criticisms were invaluable. Special thanks also to Peter Hobe, who corrected my German, to my editors, Patricia Soliman and Patricia Lande at Simon and Schuster, and to Valerie Miner, Sue Schweik, Madelon Spregnether, and Angus Wright.

PLAYA AZUL, MEXICO

1976

The helicopter crawled slowly across the great red dish of the setting sun. Everything was blood-colored—the waves, the clouds, the foam—nothing looked real, or normal, or solid. The helicopter labored on, buzzing and bucking slightly, grinding its way from the fiery rim of the sun to its more fiery center, and then, suddenly, just as it was laboring out the other side, its motor coughed, skipped, and gave out. It fell of course, not as a pelican dives or as ocean things fall back into the sea, but as man-made things fall—violently, crazily, as if felled by the fist of some vengeful god. Yet before that fist could strike again, suddenly and miraculously, the motor coughed back into life, the blades started to revolve, and the crippled shell of metal with its precious human cargo climbed back into the sky.

Inside there was terror and confusion. Mandy was shaking so hard she couldn't think. The whole cabin was a mess from the sudden plunge, and if they hadn't all been buckled into their seats, they would have been part of it. For a second no one could move or speak.

Mayumi sobbed softly, hands over her face. Kevin was bleeding from a cut that ran all the way across his forehead, but they were all alive and no one seemed seriously injured and it was a miracle.

Ted threw back his head and laughed. His pale blue eyes sparkled, and he looked drunk with relief. Mandy opened her mouth to say something to him, but no sound came out. She leaned forward to hug him, to kiss him, to celebrate their reprieve, and the tips of her fingers had just touched his shoulders when the motor stopped again for the second and final time. . . .

Fire blossomed out of the cockpit, exploding, consuming, taking on a life of its own. The smell of burning things poisoned the air and black smoke gagged them. Oil and gasoline exploded; the sick-sweet smell of burning flesh and metal filled their nostrils. The fire had a taste of its own, bitter as all the things each of them had left undone.

Fire—that had tongues but no voice.

And they fell . . . and they fell . . .

Viola Kessler woke with a start, sat bolt upright, and clutched at the arm of her seat. Her heart was beating wildly, and for a few seconds she didn't know where she was or who she was, only that she was a nameless, frightened old woman, lost somewhere on the edge of sleep.

She looked down the long, dark aisle at the tiny pools of light that fell over the orange seats, at the black portholes, at the stewardess standing nonchalantly near the rest-room door, whispering in rustling Spanish to a slim, prosperous Mexican who looked as if he might be a Pemex engineer from one of the big refineries near Villa Hermosa.

Her memory came back. Of course. She was on a plane, heading across the Caribbean to Playa Azul, Mexico, to visit her granddaughter, Mandy, who was making a movie. The plane was beginning its descent. No doubt the change in altitude had startled her out of her nap.

She closed her eyes again and tried to remember her dream, or rather nightmare, but as usual she couldn't. It had been something about fire, but what exactly? Opening her eyes, she drummed her fingertips impatiently on the plastic knobs that controlled the air and overhead light. It was annoying not to be able to remember. You'd think that after over sixty years of having the same recurrent dreams, she would have been able to remember at least one of them, but she never could. Whenever she dreamed of fire there was always a veil that shut her off from the content. All she knew was that she always woke with her heart beating a mile a minute. Not that she didn't have any number of perfectly good, completely rational reasons for being afraid of fire. After all, thanks to the Fascists, she had had two theaters burned out from under her, one in London and one in Berlin. She had lived through the Blitz. She had lost people she loved to fire, and nearly died from it herself. Joseph had burned to death and so had her mother.

She put her mother quickly out of her mind. She wouldn't think of Mama's death. For over sixty years she had been running from the memory of that first fire, and she didn't intend to start analyzing it this late in life. Leave psychoanalysis to the younger generation. Her phobias were part of her, and she was more or less resigned to them, and besides they probably made her a better actress. After all, what was art without neurosis?

Joseph was another matter. After all these years, the thought of him still brought a twinge of pain, but it was a bearable twinge. His face floated out of the past: curly black hair hanging in a shock over his forehead, hazel-brown eyes, a square chin and stubborn mouth. She felt the stirrings of old lusts. Joseph had been such a brilliant playwright, and such a wonderful lover, and she'd been so crazy about him. He had taught her most of what she knew about acting; nothing in her life had ever matched up to those years they'd spent together in Berlin.

That was the trouble with a good memory. It made you a fast study, but it played hell with your life. Normal people probably couldn't even remember ten lines of Shakespeare, much less the minute details of something that happened half a century ago. When you were old you were better off thinking about the good parts of life: like the command performance she had once given for the Prince of Wales or that honeymoon in the South of France with her second husband, Richard, when they had made love so passionately that they could barely stagger down to dinner in the evenings.

She yawned and stretched. Now those, she thought with a grin, were memories worth having. Brushing a strand of hair off her forehead, she picked up the open script that lay on the seat beside her, turned on the overhead light, and resolutely set about learning her lines. The script was a dog-eared copy of *A Long Day's Journey Into Night* that had accompanied her all the way from London—O'Neill's last play and in her opinion his best. In six weeks she was opening at the Carlyle Theater in the role of Mary Tyrone, the drug-addicted mother. Of course at seventy-five she should have looked far too old for the part, but the pleasant fact was that she didn't. Her high cheekbones, smooth skin, and large brown eyes made her look like a much younger woman, and given the right makeup, a little bit of color in her hair, and suitably low-key lighting, she could still give Hepburn a run for the money.

She turned the page, read for a few minutes, frowned, nibbled at the tip of her pencil, and then threw the script back down on the seat impatiently and picked up a magazine. Mandy's face looked back from the Cinema section of *Time*, surrounded by her friends, the whole pack of kids airbrushed to a glossy perfection. She inspected Mandy's face, seeing it with secret grandmotherly pride, as she always did, as a younger version of her own: the same unruly blond hair (hers was gray of course by now, but it had once been blond as flax), the same small determined chin and turned-up nose that had been the despair of Viola's youth and which now, by a miracle of genetics she couldn't begin to comprehend, were Mandy's trademarks.

She was just beginning to reread the article when the seat-belt signs suddenly blinked on. Viola put away the copy of *Time*, obediently fastened her belt, and turned her mind to Mandy, who would be waiting for her at the airport in Playa Azul. Mandy had been on location in Mexico for the past seven weeks, shooting the movie *Atlantis*, built around a group of five young actors whom the press had recently taken to calling "The Lang Gang." The Lang Gang had already made one successful film together and were generally considered to be the hottest group to hit the screen in decades, whatever that meant.

Still Mandy was good; there was no doubt about it. *Variety* had singled out her performance in *The Plunge*, calling it "brilliant," but of course Mandy would turn in a brilliant performance. She came from three generations of great actresses. "Brilliant" huh? How about radiant, electrifying, the best young actress since Evelyn Nesbit?

She chuckled at her own prejudice. Ostensibly she was flying to

Playa Azul to take a vacation and add some new seashells to the collection on her coffee table, but the truth was, she would have cheerfully paddled across the Atlantic in a canoe to pay Mandy a visit. If there was one secret and quiet passion left in Viola's life beside acting, it was her granddaughter.

Outside, the earth was rushing up to meet the wheels of the plane. She saw the lights bordering the runway, a shadowy fringe of palm trees, and in the distance the yellowish glow of Playa Azul. Settling back, she closed her eyes and tried to think of something else. She never particularly liked landings and takeoffs, having once read that most airplane mishaps took place at such moments, and she had even been known to surreptitiously mumble a prayer to herself if things got too bumpy. On this occasion she tranquilized herself by contemplating the question: why was Mandy wasting herself in film when she could have been acting on the stage? The beauty of this question was that it was impossible to answer, and thus a perfect way of forgetting that you were plunging toward the earth at some three hundred miles an hour encased in a nine-ton metal cage.

The wheels made contact with the runway and the plane taxied to a halt. Viola relaxed, opened her eyes, and looked out the window. How odd, she thought. Two Mexican soldiers were hurrying toward the plane accompanied by a tall woman in a pair of baggy white shorts and a straw sombrero whom she realized with a start was none other than Jane Crews, the director of *Atlantis*.

"Your coat, señora."

"Thank you." Viola held it in her lap as the air-conditioning hissed to a stop. There was a moment of silence in which she considered half a dozen possibilities for Crews' mysterious appearance with the soldiers, none of them good. The plane began to empty. Getting to her feet, she threw her coat over her arm and hurried toward the hatch. By the time she got down the steps, Crews was waiting for her, flanked by the soldiers. She looked grim and awkward.

"Hello, Miss Kessler," she said solemnly, reaching out to grasp Viola's hand. She was a tall, rather intimidating woman in her mid-forties, with short brown hair, a sharp nose, and a way of standing with her feet apart that always made her look as if she were on the verge of issuing marching orders to an invisible army. Pressing her lips together firmly, she pushed her gold-rimmed glasses up on her nose and frowned. "I hate like hell to tell you this," she said bluntly, "but your granddaughter may be in some trouble." Tact, Viola remembered, had never been Jane Crews' strong point.

"What kind of trouble?" Viola put her flight bag down on the ground, not able—or rather not wanting—to understand the implications of Crews' peculiar greeting. Around her she could smell the balmy odor of a tropical night. The air was damp and thick, so full of suspended drops of water that her cotton slip was already clinging to her legs.

Crews cleared her throat. "We've been shooting for the last few weeks on a small uninhabited island about sixty miles southeast of here. I was having everyone—cast, crew, the works—ferried out to that godforsaken hunk of coral by helicopter, which was probably a mistake in retrospect, only there was nowhere to land a plane and it was too long a boat ride, not to mention that we had maybe ten tons of gear." Crews gasped for breath and plunged ahead. "Anyway, the airlift was going fine until this afternoon. We quit around three-thirty, four at the latest, and I headed straight back to Playa Azul with the footage to put it on the 5:20 flight to L.A. The second copter came in about an hour after I did. The third copter—well, the long and short of it, Miss Kessler, is that the third copter hasn't shown up yet."

"Just how late is it?" Viola demanded.

Crews inspected her watch. "As of ten minutes ago it was two, maybe three hours overdue, and it doesn't take three hours to go sixty miles."

Viola felt a wave of panic that left her sick. "Who was on the third helicopter?" she asked in as calm a voice as she could manage. Let it have been the crew on that downed helicopter: gaffers, electricians, grips, anyone but Mandy.

"All of them," Crews informed her grimly. "The whole gang— Kevin, Peter, Mayumi, Ted and"—she paused—"Mandy, too, I'm afraid. I had these copters checked and rechecked. I never imagined that there'd be any problem and . . ." She stopped painfully in mid-sentence as Viola exploded with questions.

"Why did you leave Mandy behind? Why didn't you take her with you?" Viola knew it was an unreasonable question, but she couldn't control her fear. She imagined a helicopter on fire, falling out of the sky, its blades freezing against the sunset. She saw flames blossoming from the windows, an explosion, Mandy burned as Joseph had been burned, Mandy terrified and dying, and all her love not able to save Mandy or put out a single flame. Stop it! she told herself sharply. Don't even think such thoughts. But the old terror of fire rose up in her throat, nearly choking her. She felt her hands tremble and her mouth go dry. Taking a deep breath, she willed her heart to stop pounding. Mandy couldn't have been killed in such a horrible, senseless way, and yelling at Crews wasn't going to make her come back any sooner. Digging her nails into the palms of her hands, she squared her shoulders and forced herself to ask in a calm, practical tone, "If they did go down, where would they be?"

"The currents are bad around here," Crews said somberly, "so they could be almost anywhere. I've had my two copters flying between the mainland and the island since around six-thirty, but it's dark now, and so far we haven't found a trace of them."

"Have you called Hermann and Kathe?" Viola picked up her shoulder bag and set it down again. The inside of her mouth tasted like copper and her brain buzzed with a thousand plans. She tried not to think how Kathe was going to take this news. Kathe was more terrified of flying than Viola was of fire, and the very idea of Mandy being in a helicopter accident would be a nightmare for her.

"I tried about half an hour ago, but I couldn't get through. Their service said they were off camping in Wyoming. We've called the relatives of the others. The Mexican government's flying in a search team from Vera Cruz. So far we've managed to keep the fact that a planeload of film stars is missing out of the news, but who knows how long that can last." Crews paced back and forth. There was sweat on her forehead and her jaw was set. "Damn it, if this had happened during the day we could have found them in no time, but the Mexicans just aren't set up for night searches. Dope runners and smugglers, yes; they're experts on that around here, but searching for wreckage in the dark in over hundreds of square miles of ocean—forget it."

"Maybe they made an emergency landing." She wanted to beat her fists against the side of the plane. She wanted to grab Crews by the collar of her Hawaiian shirt and shake her until she admitted that this was all some kind of terrible joke.

Crews shook her head. "I've thought of that, but it doesn't seem too likely. There aren't many of those damn islands anywhere within a reasonable range of here, and they're pretty barren, and a helicopter on one of them would be a cinch to spot, even at night. Still I suppose there's a vague possibility." Crews swung her arms awkwardly and bit her lower lip thoughtfully. "Well, hell yes, I suppose they *could* have set down by some rocks and more or less blended in. There's no moon tonight, and they'd be hard to see if they were in the shadows, and if the radio was broken, there'd be no way they could contact us."

"You haven't found any sign of a crash?"

"Not even an oil slick."

"Well, there you have it," she said sharply. "An emergency landing." Viola felt the hollow desperation of her own words, but Crews seemed encouraged, or at least she pretended to be for Viola's sake. Shouldering Viola's flight bag, she escorted her to the baggage claim, brushed aside the customs officials, retrieved Viola's luggage from a large, battered cart, commandeered a rust-pocked taxi, and heaved everything into the trunk.

"You're staying at Las Tres Palmas across the bay. Nice place, not first-class, but nothing is in this town." Crews squared her shoulders. She was the director again, in control. "Try to get some sleep, Miss Kessler, and if anything turns up, I'll call you right away."

She paused and they looked at each other for a moment, and Viola felt the last bit of hope drain out of her. Mandy, she thought, am I being punished for the sin of taking too much pride in you, for thinking of you as my own younger self? She felt another irrational burst of anger, as if Mandy were being a disobedient child, hiding herself on purpose to worry all of them.

Shaking Crews' hand for a second time, she climbed into the stuffy cab, feeling the age in her bones, the terrible fatigue of impotence and fear.

It seemed like a long ride to Las Tres Palmas, although in reality it was probably less than ten kilometers. They drove through the center of town down a cobblestone street, past a market and plaza. On any other occasion she would have been fascinated by the small stands selling papayas and mangoes, the trucks strung with red and green lights, the lacy iron bandstand overgrown with bougainvillea, but this particular night she saw none of the quaintness of Playa Azul. Closing her eyes, she leaned against the back of the seat. She hated waiting; she hated not knowing; she hated not being able to do anything useful. The image of the burning helicopter obsessed her. It drove her crazy to sit back like an old lady while Mandy was in trouble.

She fought to put her anxiety about Mandy into some kind of reasonable perspective, but it kept coming back, making her feel ill. Opening her eyes, she looked out the open window of the cab at the dark sweep of the ocean that lay just beyond the edge of the headlights. A spitting sort of rain was beginning to fall, and there was obviously nothing anyone could do until morning except keep searching and monitoring the shortwave bands in case a fishing boat picked them up.

She stared at the back of the driver's head and then out at the Gulf again. At night the water would be pitch black, full of sharks maybe. All at once her courage gave out, and she began to cry uncontrollably in great, gulping sobs. Mandy, she thought, Mandy darling, where are you? She hid her face in her hands. Mandy, sweetheart, don't be dead, please don't be dead. Because without you, I won't want to live either; because without you . . .

The cab driver looked at her in the rearview mirror. "You okay, señora?" he asked in a concerned voice.

"Yes." She bit her lower lip and proudly forced herself to stop crying. "Yes, thank you." She blew her nose, and wiped her eyes, but she knew if she looked out at the ocean, she would start again. What could she do to distract herself?

Opening her purse, she began searching through the contents. Finally, in a corner of an inside pocket she found what she had been looking for: a small pearl button backed with gold. She held the button in the palm of her hand, feeling its cool circumference. On the surface it wasn't much, but she had carried it with her for over sixty years now. She touched the iridescent bit of pearl with the tip of one finger. Half good-luck charm, half talisman, it had accompanied her all over the world, gone onstage with her every time she'd performed in the last half century.

Shutting her eyes, she closed her fist around the button and tried to remember a time—over sixty years ago—when everyone she loved in the world had been safe, happy, and alive, but in her grief over Mandy she had forgotten an elemental truth: memory is never merely a distraction.

Memory is a fire storm that sucks everything to its center.

BOOK
ONE

FIRE

1

NEW YORK
1912

It was Christmas Eve, vaudeville was in its heyday, and the stage of the Dionysia Theater at Forty-third and Sixth Avenue looked as if all the animals in Noah's ark had escaped to celebrate the occasion: camels with green wreaths draped around their necks lolled and chewed their cuds indifferently under the hot lights; ostriches paraded their finery, reaching up long, naked necks to nip the tails of the six rare pink Amazonian cockatoos—insured by Lloyd's of London, it was rumored, for a thousand dollars each; kangaroos in red and gold boxing gloves tugged at the ropes that restrained them, threatening to plunge into the audience at any minute; in the great tank that stretched 120 feet from one side of the stage to the other, swans and pink flamingos swam beak to cheek with 115 of the most beautiful chorus girls in New York, the latter decked out in filmy pseudo-Egyptian costumes that would give the critics something to fulminate about in tomorrow's reviews.

"Nothing could be neatah than to imitate Aidah." Annie Bern—the

great, the inestimable, the very, very funny Yiddish comedienne—
was singing a parody of Verdi in an accent that was pure Bronx, and
the audience was lapping it up, even though most of them had never
gotten any closer to opera than the outside of the Met.

Viola and Conrad Kessler opened the edge of the curtain cautiously
and put their heads together to stare out through the minuscule
crack. It was forbidden—absolutely and positively forbidden—for
actors to watch the show in progress, but Viola was so obsessed with
the theater that she was willing to watch anything that moved across
a stage no matter what the consequences, and Conrad was hopelessly
in love with a small blond chorine named Betty Norman who was at
the moment rising like a plump Venus out of the tank.

Conrad inspected the wet drapery that clung to Betty's ample
figure and shivered. "She's beautiful," he muttered in a low, awestruck voice.

"I like the kangaroos better," Viola observed in a brisk whisper,
tugging impatiently at one of her long blond braids. She was a pretty
child, with dark brown eyes, a turned-up nose, and strong, slender
legs, one of which sported a skinned knee from some tomboyish
prank. At the age of eleven, she was a harsh critic of second-rate
acting, having witnessed all too much of it in her time. She worshiped
Ethel Barrymore and longed to do serious theater, and as for Betty
Norman, the less said the better.

"She's an angel," Conrad sighed.

Viola gave her braid another tug and shook her head. "For gosh
sake, Con, don't be a sap. Bern has got about four hundred times as
much talent in her little finger as Betty has in her whole body. Mama
could act circles around her; even Papa has more stage presence; the
elephants are turning in a better performance for heaven's sake." She
giggled and then cast a wary look over shoulder. The whole idea of
watching the show was Conrad's, but she had to admit that the
danger of being caught by the stage manager added an extra thrill.

"You're still a kid," Conrad said with disgust. "What do you know?"
He was a tall, thick-set boy with brown hair and sensible gray-blue eyes
that completely misrepresented the sentimentality of his nature. Like
his father, Conrad was a romantic at heart, always taking up causes and
abandoning them, passionate about everything—traits which should
have made him a good actor but, alas, didn't.

Viola snorted at the insult, which she wasn't about to take seriously. Ever since she could remember, she and Conrad had been buddies, playing together in a hundred cheap hotels and boarding-houses, acting with Mama and Papa on makeshift stages in mining camps and small-town theaters. In the last year alone she had played Juliet to his Romeo, Wendy to his Peter Pan, Gretel to his Hansel, and now, just because of some third-rate chorus girl, Conrad had suddenly defected and had begun to lead a secret life of his own. Viola looked out at Betty, who was simultaneously chewing gum and singing at the top of her lungs, and wrinkled her nose in disgust.

"So *meine Kinder*," a familiar voice suddenly intruded, "I catch you peeking out the curtain again. How many times do I have to tell you?" Viola and Conrad turned guiltily to find their father regarding them with an attempt at stern disapproval. Dietrich Kessler was a remarkably handsome man in his mid-thirties, a German of gentle disposition and mediocre talent who some fourteen years ago had caused a brief sensation in Paris by eloping with Sarah Bernhardt's talented protégée, the young Alsatian actress Yvette Boulay. He had once been possessed of a fine tenor voice, but a good decade of overwork had worn it away, leaving him with not much more than the ability to play the violin, walk to the correct part of the stage, and come in on cue.

"Go put on your makeup and quit the fooling around," Dietrich said with another lame attempt at sternness. Viola fought the desire to grin and tried to assume a suitably abashed look. Her father never did have the heart to scold them, but if he wanted to pretend he did, she was willing, as usual, to go along. "And tell your mama I need her to tie my tie."

"Yes, Papa," Conrad and Viola chorused obediently. At that moment the curtain came down on Annie Bern's extravaganza and everything backstage became chaos as over sixty animals were wrangled, pulled, and pushed out the service door into the three large horse-drawn vans that were to take them back to the Bronx Zoo. A stocky young man in baggy pants, a ragged cutaway, a dented top hat, and a large red nose hurried past them muttering to himself. He was the next act—a fellow named W. C. Fields who had been billed as a silent juggler. Viola grinned. Silent, huh? From the curses this

Fields fellow was uttering it was a good thing he wasn't talking to the audience.

Dietrich looked at Fields and then at the large gold pocket watch that Viola had personally redeemed from Mr. Kowsky, the pawnbroker, only yesterday. "There goes the filler act," he said. "He juggles for ten minutes and then we're on. Move, *meine Kinder*. Move."

Five minutes later the entire Kessler family could have been found in their dressing room in a huddle, arms intertwined, foreheads barely touching, hugging one another with all their might and wishing each other luck without mentioning the word, for, like all actors, they were a superstitious lot.

"Merde," Mama called out gaily. Her face was so beautiful that Viola never got tired of looking at it, sweet and gentle, with soft brown eyes and a rosy, playful mouth. Mama laughed and kissed everyone: Viola and Conrad on their noses, Papa on the lips. *"Merde* to all of you, *mes petits choux."*

"Break a leg!" Conrad yelled.

The four of them laughed and embraced again. Never mind the spotted mirrors, the peeling paint, the cobwebs on the ceiling; never mind that this was only another dreary dressing room in another anonymous theater: for a few seconds even the walls seemed to glow with love.

Papa stepped back and straightened his false mustache. "What was der motto of der Three Musketeers?" he demanded cheerfully.

"All for one and one for all!" they chanted.

"Right." He nodded with satisfaction. *"Schön gut!"* Lifting his hand, he pointed dramatically toward the door. "Now let's go out there and knock that audience dead."

Some twenty minutes later, Viola stood onstage performing the climax from the popular melodrama *The Lion's Cage*. Papa was now the villain, Mama the much-beleaguered heroine, Conrad the young hero, and she herself a little girl about to be thrown to the lions.

And lions there were, three real ones concealed at present on the other side of the set, snaggletoothed, too old to do anything but sit around looking like large, flea-bitten cats behind a fine invisible mesh screen that blocked off half the cage, creating the illusion that anyone tossed within ten feet of them would be in imminent danger of being instantly torn to shreds.

"Don't harm my little girl," Mama was pleading, clutching Viola to her, her whole body quivering with emotion. Even though the lines were trite, there was something about the force of Mama's acting that always made the hairs stand up on Viola's arms. Mama looked more beautiful than ever tonight, Viola thought proudly. Her long reddish-blond hair was done up on top of her head, and her dark eyes shone with a passionate desire to protect her baby, as if the danger to Viola were real instead of the sentimental fantasy of some theatrical hack in New Jersey. Lifting her face, Yvette allowed two tears to roll down her cheeks. Viola forced herself to stay in character, although she had a sudden urge to reach up and comfort her mother.

For eighteen straight nights Mama had cried on cue. How in the world did she do it? Was it something a person could learn or just a talent she'd been born with?

"Spare my baby, spare my helpless child."

"Your prayers come too late."

"Alas, is there no one who will help us in our hour of need?" Yvette gave Viola a covert nudge. Carefully disengaging herself from her mother's skirts, Viola turned a pathetic look on the audience. No matter how often she saw it, that bank of expectant faces, turned toward her like flowers about to be watered, gave her a thrill. Tonight there were some five thousand spectators. As Viola stared at them she had the momentary impression that there were invisible strings connecting her to everyone: to the ladies in their jewels, the men in their dark suits, even the poor immigrant families in the balcony. The energy of the people in the theater seemed to multiply, cresting over her, and she felt wonderfully powerful. Pity me, she told them silently. I'm a little girl who is about to be torn apart by lions. And silently the audience told her that they did pity her, that even in this silly melodrama she had somehow touched their hearts.

Papa, the villain, gave a particularly nasty laugh. Lightning suddenly flashed, startling the audience into a long "Oooh," and the stage began to revolve slowly, bringing up a dark, blasted heath on which the lions' cage was improbably perched. Viola noted with pleasure that for once everything looked formidably realistic. New York, wonderful New York. What a relief it was to be playing here again after almost a year of being booked into places liked Topeka and Boca Raton. The Dionysia wasn't one of those little hick theaters where you had to use painted lions and cornflakes for snow. Papa, who always loved gadgets, had explained that the stage was a marvel of technical innovation, constructed by the late mad inventor Steele Mackaye, jammed with all sorts of odd and wonderful machines. At the moment, for example, a "nebulator" was generating great puffy clouds of fog that added to the eeriness of the scene.

Papa suddenly lunged for Viola, snatched her out of Mama's arms, and staggered with her toward the lions' cage.

"No!" Mama screamed hysterically.

"Yes, madame," Papa countered with equally evil hysteria. "Become my bride or I will toss your dear and innocent child to the lions." One of the lions opened his mouth and yawned, exposing a set of toothless gums. Viola bit her lip so as not to giggle. "What say you to that, my beauty?"

"Never!" Mama proclaimed.

"Then," Papa thundered, "to the lions with her!" Suddenly above the stage fiery titles sprang to life—another invention of Mackaye's. Burning cheerfully, the three-foot-high letters informed anyone who might have missed the fact that EVIL IS AT HAND.

Swinging Viola up in the air as if she were a sack of flour, Papa tossed her into the lions' cage. The effect on the audience was electric: men rose to their feet; women shrieked; a lady in what was later referred to as a "delicate condition" fainted dead away and had to be carried out of the theater. Before it could become embarrassingly apparent that the lions had absolutely no interest in Viola, the curtain fell.

The applause was tremendous. Yvette, Dietrich, Conrad, and Viola linked hands and walked out through the curtain. Flowers rained down around them, and a man in a silk top hat thrust a huge box of chocolates into Yvette's arms. What a silly play, Viola thought, and yet people liked it so much. As she took her bows she remembered the story her mother had told her of James O'Neill, the great actor who had played the Count of Monte Cristo every night for almost twenty years. Twenty years from now when she was thirty-one, would Papa still be throwing her to the lions?

"Bravo!" the audience shouted. "Bravo."

The Kessler family bowed and smiled. It was honest work and they needed the money, but—as Mama always said—if you really cared about the theater, it wasn't enough.

But at that very moment better things were at hand. Shortly after the final curtain, Viola returned to the dressing room to find everything in a state of excitement and turmoil. Mama was clutching a yellow Western Union telegram and waving it over her head.

"Bernhardt's forgiven me!" she called out as Viola came into the room. She kissed Viola and Conrad, and then she pulled off Papa's fake mustache and gave him a kiss too. "She's coming to New York this spring to open at that new theater down on Forty-seventh and Broadway and she wants *me* to act with her again, in *Phèdre, mes enfants,* in *Phèdre!"* *Phèdre* had been Mama's greatest triumph before she left Paris to marry Papa. She seized Viola and Conrad by the hands and danced around the room with them. "Who has ze luckiest maman in the world?" she demanded.

"We do," they chorused.

Papa took the telegram, read it, and a slow smile spread across his face. "I never thought the old witch would change her mind." He winked at Mama, opened his violin case, took out the battered old instrument that had accompanied them on so many tours, and launched into a polka. "So dance," he said. "We will celebrate Mama's return to the legitimate theater, *Ja?"* And they danced like happy fools until the stage manager came down, pounded on the door, and told them that if they didn't stop making so much noise, he was going to fire the lot of them.

Five months later, on a spring evening in late May, Conrad and Viola sat in the Palace Theater as Mama and Sarah Bernhardt performed the climax of *Phèdre.*

"Je m'en mourrai plus coupable!" Bernhardt intoned passionately. She turned and swept regally past Mama, her long white and gold robe billowing out behind her like an exclamation point.

"Translate, for Pete's sake," Conrad whispered, giving Viola a dig in the ribs. "I never can remember what they're saying up there." Viola could tell he was nervous tonight. Watching Mama act with Bernhardt was like watching her walk over Niagara Falls on a tightrope: you always knew she'd be good, but you couldn't help worrying that she might lose her balance.

Viola leaned over and put her mouth to Con's ear. "Bernhardt's just about to reveal to Mama that she's in love with her stepson and—"

"Quiet please!" A large lady in a black silk taffeta dress turned a glowering look on them and placed one gloved finger to her lips. Viola sank guiltily back into her seat. The lady was right. This was Bernhardt's last performance in New York and they had no business talking, not even in whispers.

Onstage, Mama and Bernhardt were building up to the climax. Pulling out her handkerchief, Viola dabbed at her eyes, feeling moved, confused, and not a little silly. She had seen this play twelve times in the past four weeks, and she still cried like a baby. Well, it was no wonder, really. It was said Bernhardt could move an audience to tears simply by reading from the phone book. Now, as Phèdre, her voice was molten gold; every subtle range of emotion registered, flooding the auditorium with such nobility and suffering that, even though most of the audience couldn't understand French, there wasn't a dry eye in the house.

Viola translated Phèdre's confession silently to herself, moving her lips to catch the rhythms of the original. Someday, she promised herself, she'd do *Phèdre* in front of adoring fans; someday she'd be up there making the ladies cry into their pocket hankerchiefs. Meanwhile, she had a lot to learn. Offstage—Mama had confided—the "Divine" Sarah was a sixty-eight-year-old woman with a tubercular knee, so lame she had to hang on to ropes to make her exits and entrances, but once she stepped out in front of the footlights, Bernhardt was . . . Viola searched in vain for some adjective adequate to describe what she was witnessing. She didn't know what Bernhardt was. She only knew that in the last month, watching her and Mama perform, she had found out more about serious acting than in all the rest of her life put together.

The play went on for another half an hour, until Hippolytus was killed by his own horses and Phèdre committed suicide. When the curtain came down at last, Viola and Conrad clapped until their hands were raw. The houselights came up slowly. Around them people stretched and got to their feet.

"Are you Mademoiselle Kessler?" a high-pitched voice inquired in perfect French. Viola looked down and saw a small boy standing in the aisle, dressed in a red-and-blue livery with a little box hat perched on the side of his head. "Because if you are, Madame Bernhardt requests that you call on her in her dressing room, *toute de suite.*"

"*Toute de suite,* huh?" Conrad said. "My French isn't as good as yours, Vi, but I think that means now."

"But that's impossible. He must have the message wrong." Viola felt a sudden burst of panic. Mama had said she should study Bernhardt's technique, but meeting Bernhardt face-to-face was quite another matter. Bernhardt had had Napoleon III's cousin as a lover; Victor Hugo had knelt at her feet; she had once been the most beautiful woman in all of Europe, and at the present moment she was without a doubt the most famous actress of all time. Even Mama was afraid of her. Viola looked down at her wrinkled white-and-blue dress, her new black leather patent boots that only a few hours ago had seemed so fine. She wasn't dressed properly; there was a hole in the tip of one of her gloves. Bernhardt would probably speak to her in French and she wouldn't understand a word of it. She looked at the exit and then back at the boy, torn between the desire to escape and a curiosity so intense it gave her chills.

Conrad was examining her with a concerned expression. "You aren't going to get stage fright at this late date are you, sis?"

"Con, what in the world could Bernhardt want with *me?* I'm nothing, nobody."

Conrad put his arm around her shoulders. "Go on," he said encouragingly, "go see what she wants. Don't be afraid. Mama probably just asked her to have a word with you. After all, Mama used to be her favorite."

"But why me, Con? Why not you? You're the oldest."

"Because everyone knows that you and Mama are the talented ones in the family." Viola tried to deny it, but he stopped her with a wave of his hand. "Vi, I've got two left feet; I say my lines with all the conviction of an off-duty cop acting in a church play. I've known for years I don't have much talent, and I don't particularly care. Papa and I admitted to each other long ago that we were just the backdrops for you and Mama. But you've got the stuff real acting is made of."

"Con . . ."

"No more excuses." Conrad smiled encouragingly. "Look here, I'll make you a deal. It just so happens that I have thirty-five cents in my pocket. You go see Bernhardt and afterwards I'll take you over to Rector's and buy you a *baba au rhum* with vanilla ice cream."

"Really?"

"Yes, really."

Somehow the idea that Conrad was behind her made all the difference. Viola felt the panic subside. What had she been making such a fuss about anyway? So what if Bernhardt had a reputation for being something of a dragon? So what if even Mama was afraid of her? Bernhardt was a famous actress and this was a great chance to see her up close. Impulsively, Viola threw her arms around Conrad and gave him a passionate hug. "Con," she said, "you have to be the best brother in the world."

He pushed her away, embarrassed. "Say there, don't get mushy on me. I figure it's worth thirty-five cents just to get a firsthand report of what Bernhardt's dressing room's like. They say she bathes in milk and sleeps in a coffin quilted in pink satin." Conrad grinned and gave her a brotherly pat on the arm. "Now get going, Vi, and if you see a big black box or a lot of empty milk bottles lying around, try to remember it, will you?"

Ten minutes later Viola stood in front of the door to Madame Bernhardt's dressing room having second thoughts. The gold star nailed into the wood was bigger than both of her hands put together. All up and down the hallway baskets of roses and gardenias were stacked in careless heaps—obviously the overflow from the evening's tributes. Viola took a step forward, raised her fist to knock, and then lowered it abruptly.

What was on the other side? Viola's imagination, always fertile, began to run wild: maybe Madame Bernhardt would be stretched out in her coffin; maybe she would be sitting hand in hand with the famous skeleton that adorned her drawing room in Paris. Viola had read somewhere that she liked monkeys. Maybe there'd be a whole troupe of them in there, running wild, or maybe there'd be dogs— big, mean ones that would lie at Madame Bernhardt's feet snarling and showing their teeth.

The thoughts were so silly that she couldn't believe she was having them. She was just nervous. Still, there was no reason not to have a look. Bending down, she placed her eye to the keyhole and was disappointed to discover that all she could see was a piece of blue velvet, which appeared to be hanging on the back wall. Inside there was a murmur of low voices. All at once footsteps came toward the door. Panicked, she tried to stand up but she was too late. The door opened suddenly and she lost her footing, stumbled forward, and half fell into the room.

"Who are you?" a voice said sharply in French. Blushing furiously, Viola tried to straighten her hair and rearrange her dress. A middle-aged woman in a white apron and a black high-necked dress was staring at her suspiciously.

"I'm Viola Kessler."

"Who?"

"Viola Kessler, Mrs. Kessler's daughter." Tears of humiliation sprang to her eyes, but she fought them back bravely. "Madame Bernhardt sent for me."

"Who is it, Marie?" someone called from the next room. At the sound of the words a shiver of excitement went through Viola's whole body. There was no mistaking Bernhardt's voice.

"Put yourself together, child," the woman said, "and I'll announce you properly. I'm sorry I was so sharp with you. I had no idea you were Yvette's daughter. You really shouldn't have been peeking in the keyhole, you know. So many strange people try to get a look at Madame." Turning in a flurry of skirts, she was gone, leaving Viola to try to regain her composure as best she could.

Quicker than she would have thought possible, the maid was back. "You may go in now, mademoiselle," she said, holding open the door. Taking a deep breath and squaring her shoulders, Viola bravely stepped across the threshold.

It was the room that drew her attention first, an amazing room that seemed no more to belong to the Palace Theater in New York City in the year 1913 than a cave from the *Tales of Ali Baba*. Over the walls—which were probably ordinary enough in themselves—someone had hung great swaths of blue-and-gold brocade. Towering tropical plants were massed between oversized vases of camelias and orchids. At one end of the room a vast mahogany wardrobe disgorged costumes onto the Persian rug: Hamlet's black doublet, Joan of Arc's penitent's robe, a cardinal's red silk cape, hats, shoes, walking sticks, pink silk umbrellas—the profusion was dizzying to look at. To the left of the wardrobe was a gigantic gold-framed pier glass, a Louis XVI dressing table littered with tubes of greasepaint, and a rack of wigs, each neatly labeled.

"Whatever are you staring at, *mon enfant?*" Madame Bernhardt said. She lay on a blue satin couch dressed in the most exquisite robe Viola had ever seen in her life. Made of white satin, the robe was trimmed around the neck, wrists, and hem with egret feathers. It was a robe designed for a young, romantic woman, but the face that looked out from the feathers was anything but young and romantic. It was a strong, tired face—familiar and strange at the same time: curly hair piled high on a delicate head; a long nose, flared at the tip, and eyes like no other eyes on earth—dark, slightly sunken, weary and mysterious eyes that at the moment were fixed directly on Viola.

"I'm sorry, madame," Viola said. "I didn't mean to stare, but I was thinking . . ." She stopped suddenly, horrified at what she had been about to blurt out.

"Thinking what?"

"That you didn't look as bad without your makeup as I thought you would." That sounded awful. She floundered on. "That is, for a woman as old as you are, you don't look so old because you don't have wrinkles to speak of, that is . . ." She stopped, paralyzed by embarrassment.

Bernhardt laughed. "Blunt little thing, aren't you?"

"Yes, madame." She hung her head, bit her lower lip, and wondered if it were possible to will oneself to disappear. "I'm sorry."

"Don't be sorry. I've been flattered by the experts for fifty years. You'd be surprised how pleasant it is to hear the truth once in a while. So, Miss Kessler, I look like an old wreck, do I?"

"Oh no, madame." She was horrified that she could have implied anything of the sort.

Bernhardt smiled, displaying a row of perfect teeth. "Do you know who was just here? Mr. John Singer Sargent, the famous painter, asking me for perhaps the tenth time to sit for a portrait. Mr. Sargent said to me—with a perfectly straight face—that I had the skin of a thirty-year-old. Well, do I?"

Viola looked at the fine wrinkles around Bernhardt's mouth, the lines under her eyes, the small rough spots on her cheeks. Her skin was faintly purple, like faded lavender. There was a sense of ruin about her, as if a work of art, carved in painted marble, had been carelessly left out in the weather to crack and fade.

"Well?"

She wanted to say what Mr. Sargent had said, but she was gripped by an irresistible honesty. "No, madame," she whispered.

"What?" The word exploded into the room and Viola cringed inwardly.

"No, madame," she said in a voice that was much firmer and louder than she had intended it to be, "you don't look thirty. But you do look pretty good for sixty-eight."

Bernhardt guffawed. "You're just like your mother—smart, too impulsive for you own good, and honest to a fault. Come over here and let me get a better look at you." Viola took a few steps closer. "So you want to be an actress?"

"Yes, madame, with all my heart."

"Why?"

Viola wrinkled her forehead and thought it over. This was a question no one had ever asked her before. "I don't know. I just want to. I've always wanted to act. I've never even thought of doing anything else."

"Good"—Bernhardt nodded approvingly—"that's the right answer. People who think they know why they want to act never have much success. If you'd told me you wanted to be famous, I'd have politely shown you the door. The only thing worth knowing about acting is that you have to be addicted to it the way Musset was addicted to poetry or Coleridge to laudanum. Well, well." She tilted her head, examining Viola in a way that made her acutely uncomfortable. "Yvette's claims seem to have been founded on more than mere motherly prejudice. You aren't bad-looking, which is an asset but not an absolute necessity. The essence of theater is, after all, illusion. A few years ago—with this same wreck of a face—I played Joan of Arc—a girl of nineteen—convincingly, so I'm told. It was all accomplished with makeup and lighting." Bernhardt sat up and swung her legs over the side of the couch with a grimace of pain. "Create a good enough illusion and you can convince an audience of anything. Remember that; it's the only piece of wisdom I'm handing out today." She gestured toward the wardrobe. "Bring me Phèdre."

"I beg your pardon, madame?"

"The Phèdre costume, over there."

Relieved that it was the costume Madame Bernhardt wanted and not Phèdre herself, Viola hurried across the room, scooped the gold-and-white robe up in her arms, and brought it back to the couch.

"Do you see a pair of scissors anywhere?" Bernhardt picked up the robe and began pulling at one of the buttons.

"No, madame."

"Never mind." Bending down, Bernhardt took one of the buttons in her mouth and, to Viola's astonishment, bit it off. "Surprised you, didn't I? Not exactly the dignified way for a great lady of the theater to go about detaching a button. Ever hear the story of the time at a banquet in my honor in Paris when I poured a bottle of wine over my head to demonstrate to a friend that my hair was naturally curly?" She smiled, and Viola found herself smiling back. Bernhardt held out the button.

"Here," she said.

"Madame?"

"The button; take it; it's yours."

"But why are you giving me a button?"

"Let me see," Bernhardt said. "I suppose at this point I should give you a long speech pointing out that the button symbolizes the power of illusion, the hard work it's going to take you to become an actress, the trials and tragedies along the way, the sacrifices, all that, but let's just say I want you to have it because"—she paused for a moment—"because, for one thing, you're Yvette's daughter. Yvette was the most talented girl I ever had in my troupe, and she made a mess of her career by running off with your father when she wasn't all that much older than you are now, so let's say I'm giving you this button to remind you not to do the same." She held out the button again, and Viola took it from her.

"Thank you, madame."

"You're an interesting girl." Bernhardt pursed her lips thoughtfully. "All that white-blond hair, eyes like a raccoon—you'll probably end up with the men at your feet. And you're so impulsive—much too impulsive. It's the temperament of a born actress, our curse really. Frankly, you remind me all too much of myself when I was young. Despite the briefness of our acquaintance, I keep having an urge to warn you."

"Warn me of what, madame?"

"Never mind. The illusion that you can prevent young people from making their own mistakes is one of the afflictions of old age. You can go now." She waved dismissal. "I promised your mother I'd have a talk with you, but now my leg's hurting and I want Marie to come in and rub it with ether and that's not a pretty sight." She settled back on the couch and then sat up again suddenly. "Oh yes, I nearly forgot—tell your mama for me that a man is going to contact her in the next few days."

"Who, madame?"

Bernhardt laughed. "You'd like to know who, wouldn't you? And so will she no doubt. But let's just say a man. That makes it all the more mysterious and perhaps will give your papa something to think about. Wicked of me, isn't it?" Bernhardt sighed, settled back down on the satin couch, and stretched with catlike grace. "But I just can't completely forgive Dietrich for stealing Yvette away."

A week after the last performance of *Phèdre*, the Kessler family sat around the remains of their dinner, cracking hazelnuts and drinking cold lemonade from the heavy china cups provided by Mrs. Kreuter, their landlady. Mama was especially pretty that evening: happy with the good reviews she had gotten for her part in *Phèdre*, red-cheeked from the unseasonably warm weather, a little plump from several months of regular dinners, and bursting with energy. Viola watched her admiringly as she sat on the sofa in the parlor of their rented suite, combing out her long reddish-blond hair and joking with Papa. The two of them were playing chess, and Mama—as usual—was losing badly.

"Look at your queen, Yvette."

"What's wrong with my queen, Dietrich?"

"You just put her in front of my castle."

"So?"

"So this." Papa picked up his castle, swooped down on Mama's queen, and removed it from the board.

"Oh *mon Dieu!*" Mama shrieked in mock horror. She threw down her hairbrush, stood up, and tried to retrieve her piece, but Papa held it high over her head. "Give it back, Dietrich. *Donnes-moi la reine.*"

"Never, my proud beauty." Papa laughed his villain laugh.

"Please." Mama jumped for the queen but Papa only held it higher. Laughing, they grappled like two silly children.

"Make her pay a forfeit," Conrad suggested, closing his copy of *Swiss Family Robinson.*

"*Wunderbar,* a great idea. You pay a forfeit, Yvette, and I'll give it back to you." Chess as played by Mama and Papa had rather elastic rules.

"What kind of forfeit?" Mama threw herself back down on the couch, breathless, her dark eyes shining with mischief.

"I know," Viola said, munching on a hazelnut, "have her recite 'The Jabberwocky.' "

"Not 'The Jabberwocky.' " Mama threw her hands up in mock horror.

"In the style of President Wilson," Conrad suggested with a fiendish grin.

"*Sehr gut.*" Papa tucked the red queen in his vest pocket, sat down, and began to fill his long-stemmed German pipe with tobacco. "Mama will recite 'The Jabberwocky' in the style of our new President and then I will return her queen. Yes, Yvette? You agree?"

"*Ma foi,* do I have a choice?"

"Nope," Conrad said, "no choice, Mama."

"Not a choice in the world, Mama," Viola agreed.

"Come over to my side, children, and I'll bake you a cake, *au chocolat,*" Yvette pleaded in mock desperation. "I'll even darn your socks."

"You can't cook, Mama," Conrad pointed out. "Remember that time in Colorado when you tried to make eggs and nearly started a fire?"

"And you can't sew either," Viola said, "so don't try to bribe us with that."

"They're right, Yvette," Dietrich observed, complacently puffing on his pipe. "Except for the fact that you're a joy to look at, can act like an angel, and are ridiculously lovable, you're absolutely useless."

"I know when I'm outnumbered." Mama leaned over, snatched Papa's reading glasses off his nose, and put them on her own. "Ladies and gentlemen, behold your President." She stood up, snatched a sheaf of unpaid bills from the table and held them in front of her, and suddenly she was lean, scholarly, shy Woodrow Wilson making one of his famous back-of-the-train speeches." 'Twas brillig . . ." she intoned solemnly.

"What about those 'slithy toves,' Mr. President?" Conrad heckled, waving the nutcracker.

". . . and the slithy toves did gyre and gymble in the wabe." She paused and looked over the rims of her glasses with the pained tolerance of an educated man who is being harassed by his inferiors. "Beware the Jabberwock," Mama thundered, and then she broke down in helpless giggles. Falling on the couch beside Papa, she laughed so hard her face turned red, and Viola, Conrad, and Papa laughed with her. It was a simple moment, full of good-natured family teasing, not out of the ordinary at all, yet for the rest of her life Viola remembered it. She remembered the way her mother looked, her beautiful face as open and innocent as a great flower; the way Papa leaned lovingly over her; the feeling that she and Conrad had of being part of their parents' love.

A minute passed—perhaps two—and then there was a brisk knock on the door.

"Oh dear." Mama scrambled to her feet, picked up her hairpins, and began to jam them randomly in her hair. "Not a visitor, not at this hour. Conrad, Viola, throw those magazines somewhere out of sight."

Quickly grabbing the magazines and newspapers that littered the rug, Conrad and Viola obediently tossed them behind the sofa. Viola scraped the hazelnut shells into the palm of her hand and deposited them in her pocket. Seizing Papa's gutta-percha raincoat, a pair of Conrad's socks that had been drying in front of the window, and Viola's overshoes, Mama thrust them into the bedroom and shut the door on them. The Kesslers were used to cleaning house in this abrupt fashion, and over the years they had gotten it down to something of a science.

The knock was repeated. "I'll get it." Papa put down his pipe, donned his suit coat, and walked to the door, managing somehow to assume an aura of respectability on the way. As she settled into a chair and picked up her embroidery, Viola wondered what the person outside the door would have thought if he or she could have seen the Kesslers as they'd been a few minutes ago—laughing like a pack of idiots.

"Good evening." The voice was cultured, almost British, with the rounded vowels and definite consonants of a trained actor. "Is this the Kessler residence?"

Viola looked over the top of her embroidery and saw a most remarkable man standing in the hallway. He wasn't merely tall, he was gigantic—six four or six five at least—and nearly as wide as he was high. White-haired, dressed in a blindingly white summer suit with white gloves and white spats, he looked like a giant iceberg cut adrift. This man could have sunk the *Titanic*. She bit her lower lip to keep from grinning and went back to her embroidery, trying to look as indifferent as possible, consumed all the while with curiosity.

"Are you, by any chance, Mr. Dietrich Kessler?"

"I am," Papa said.

"Permit me to introduce myself. My name is Harrington, Kenneth Harrington. I do a bit in the way of theatrical directing. Perhaps you've heard of me?" The man extended his hand and Papa shook it. Viola felt a thrill go though everyone in the room. Mama's face suddenly went red and then white. Viola gave Conrad a secret look of amazement. Heard of him? Why everyone in New York knew who Kenneth Harrington was. Harrington had been one of the most famous Shakespearean actors of the 1880s. In fact, there were still a number of people who claimed if you hadn't seen Harrington do *Lear* then you hadn't seen *Lear* at all. At present, he was the owner and manager of The New Globe over on Forty-seventh Street, a perfect replica of Shakespeare's original theater, right down to the flag on the turret.

"How do you do, Mr. Harrington," Papa said with what Viola thought proudly was admirable aplomb. "Won't you come in?"

"Thank you." Mr. Harrington entered the room and stood in all his glory waiting for an introduction.

"This is my wife, Mrs. Kessler," Papa said, "and my two children, Violetta and Conrad."

"A pleasure to make your acquaintance, Mrs. Kessler," Mr. Harrington said, ignoring Viola and Conrad but beaming at Mama. "In point of fact, Mrs. Kessler, it was to make your acquaintance that I took the liberty of calling on you."

"Oh?" Mama said.

"I don't like beating around the bush, Mrs. Kessler, so if your husband will excuse me, I'll be direct. I saw you playing Oenone in *Phèdre* and I thought you were superb. It's hard to stand up to Bernhardt—believe me I know, having once had the pleasure of playing Polonius to her Hamlet—and you did not only a credible job but a brilliant one."

"That's what James Gibbons Huneker of *The Sun* said," Viola piped up impulsively. "He said, 'The pretty and talented Mrs. Kessler bears watching,' and James Gibbons Huneker's the very best critic in all of New York."

"Viola"—Mama blushed with embarrassment—"please . . ."

"No," Mr. Harrington said, "I beg you, Mrs. Kessler, don't reprimand the child. I quite agree with her—and with Mr. Huneker for that matter, although I must say it's rare I'll admit to having the same opinion as a critic. The pretty and talented Mrs. Kessler does bear watching or—more to the point in my opinion—she deserves a debut at The New Globe."

"Whoopie!" Conrad yelled.

Mr. Harrington paused and smiled at Conrad, then turned back to Mama. "I know this must seem rather abrupt, but I assure you I'm in earnest." He cleared his throat and smiled the famous, winning smile that had made him a matinee idol of the 1880s. "How does the part of Lady Macbeth strike you, Mrs. Kessler?"

"Am I to understand that you're offering me the role, Monsieur Harrington?" Mama stuttered.

"I am indeed."

"Snap it up, Mama," Viola advised.

"Enough, *meine Kinder*." Papa shrugged helplessly. "I apologize, Mr. Harrington, for the rudeness of my children. They tend to cheer their mama on as if she were a one-woman baseball team."

"An excellent attitude in children, if you ask me. Enough to make me consider having some myself sometime." Mr. Harrington beamed at Mama from the white heights of his suit. "Well, Mrs. Kessler, I realize that I've sprung this on you with no preface, but I'm faced with a play to produce and, to be quite frank, at the moment I'm without a Lady Macbeth. We don't open until the fall season, but I'm anxious to get the rehearsals under way. Should you be so good as to accept the part, I would be more than happy to see that your expenses were paid up until that time, after which, of course, you would receive a suitable salary to be agreed on at some later date. Without placing undue pressure on you, I'd like to know if you're at all interested."

"Why yes," Mama said, "yes, I'm very interested indeed. Thank you, Mr. Harrington. This is so sudden, so . . ."

"Good," Mr. Harrington said briskly. He shook Mama's hand and then Papa's. "We can work out the details later." He paused. "Ah, I suppose I should warn you before you fully commit yourself that Julia Marlowe was originally slated to take the role of Lady Macbeth, but considerations of health have forced her to cancel. Miss Marlowe's alter essence"—he smiled at his own wit—"Mr. E. H. Sothern will be performing the ambitious Macbeth so you may have to work your way through some rather unfair comparisons from the critics, Mrs. Kessler."

"I'll take my chances, Mr. Harrington," Mama said weakly. She looked pleased and rather stunned.

Julia Marlowe and E. H. Sothern! Viola could hardly believe her ears. Marlow and Sothern were simply the most famous Shakespearean actors in the country. To American audiences Marlowe and Sothern *were* Shakespeare, and now Mama was being offered a chance to step into Julia Marlowe's shoes.

"Good-bye, then," Mr. Harrington said, shaking hands again all around. His gloved palm was smooth and cool against Viola's fingers. Mr. Harrington is destiny, she thought, come knocking at our door.

It was a silly, melodramatic thought, the kind that would occur only to a romantic young girl, but it turned out to be accurate. On the Friday after Labor Day, Mama opened at The New Globe, performing a Lady Macbeth so chillingly ambitious and icily sensual that the critics ran out of adjectives to describe her. Viola always remembered that hot September night as her mother's finest hour: Yvette took ten curtain calls by herself, a string of borrowed diamonds glittering around her neck as she bowed and bowed. And later, the diamonds still glittering, she and Papa went to a party where she was congratulated, petted, and made much of by the Vanderbilts, danced the fox-trot with a real U.S. senator, and was introduced to Ethel and John Barrymore, who paid her the compliment of saying her Lady Macbeth was one of the best they'd ever seen. It was —or rather it should have been—the launching of a whole new career for her.

Three happy weeks passed, four—a whole month of packed houses and rave reviews that Viola carefully cut out and pasted in her scrapbook—and then came the night of October 5.

"Lo you," the lady-in-waiting cautioned, putting one finger to her painted lips, *"here she comes!"*

On the stage of The New Globe, Mama, dressed as Lady Macbeth, suddenly appeared out of the shadows carrying a lighted taper. A wig of dark hair hung loosely down her back; her long gauzy nightgown floated from her shoulders like a trail of fog. Behind her, her own shadow was projected ten times life size, huge and distorted like the body of a giant ghost. Mama placed the taper on top of a low stone wall, then reached out into the air, her fingers trembling; dipping her hands into an invisible basin, she rubbed them together with frantic haste.

"Out, damned spot! out, I say! One: two: why, then, 'tis time to do't." Mama's voice had an eerie quality, like the swinging of a rusty gate. Sitting in the balcony next to Papa and Conrad, Viola shivered. She had gone over Mama's lines with her a hundred times, and she knew perfectly well that this was only a play like any other. Still, it was so terribly convincing.

"Hell is murky!" Mama turned to the audience, her lips trembling. She rubbed her hands together again, trying to wash off the invisible blood. Her eyes were wide open and sightless; she spoke Shakespeare's lines as if she were dreaming them, as if she had invented them out of some wicked, secret nightmare. It was a wonderful, frightening performance.

"Here's the smell of the blood still: all the perfumes of Arabia will not sweeten this little hand." Mama lifted her right hand toward her face, and took a few steps backward as if recoiling in horror, and as she did

so she must have brushed against the lighted taper. For a moment nothing happened. The fire, they later realized, must have started at the back of her gown, out of sight of the audience or the other actors, and was well under way by the time anyone noticed it.

Mama finished speaking, turned to exit, and for the first time the audience saw the flames running up the back of her gown, small and ragged like a rim of tiny diamonds. Before anyone could say anything, the flames doubled in size. There was a collective gasp, the sound of eight hundred people coming simultaneously to the same realization, then an uproar.

"Yvette!" Papa was on his feet, yelling out Mama's name.

"She's on fire!" the woman next to Viola screamed. "My God, someone *do* something!"

It all happened so fast that there was probably nothing anyone could have done to avert the tragedy, but for the rest of her life Viola wondered why it took so long for the people in the wings to realize what was going on. Onstage, the other actors—who couldn't see the flames from where they were standing—turned toward the audience in confusion, but Mama was so caught up in the character of Lady Macbeth that she didn't even appear to hear the shouts of "Fire!" She took two more steps forward, crossed into a draft, and her filmy gown, catching the breeze, billowed out behind her. So suddenly that it was almost impossible to believe, the yards of gauze burst into flame. For a split second Mama kept on going, as if still not understanding what had happened, and then, as the flames rushed over her bare arms, she screamed.

"Jesus!" Mama screamed, and beat at her dress as the fire engulfed her. Viola stared at the stage in horror, unable to take her eyes off the terrible sight. Mama turned toward the stunned audience as if begging for help, a human torch, flailing at the fire that was consuming her, and then—realizing perhaps that it was impossible to put out the burning gauze without help—she did the worst possible thing she could have done. She ran—not toward the other actors who might have helped her—but toward the side of the stage where she normally made her exit. The actors made a futile attempt to come to her aid, but they were too far away. Mama took a half dozen steps, stumbled, and fell.

At that instant help came at last. Rushing out of the wings, a stagehand pulled off his coat, threw it over her, and beat out the flames. Picking Mama up, he staggered to his feet and glared at the actors and then at the audience. He was a small, burly, redheaded Irishman.

"Yer fools," he yelled angrily. "All o'yer." And then the curtain suddenly came down.

Backstage, Papa knelt beside Mama, holding her head in his hands and talking to her as they waited for the ambulance. The front of his formal white shirt was smeared with soot and his face was unbearable to see. Mama lay inert on the boards, a limp bundle covered by two coats. The charred wig had been removed and Papa was stroking what was left of her long reddish-blond hair, repeating her name over and over. She was covered from the neck down; the flames hadn't touched her face. "My beautiful girl," Papa kept saying, "my darling *schönes Madchen.*"

Dr. Moberly carefully turned back the edge of one of the coats and inspected Mama's burns. Witnessing the accident from the audience, he had rushed backstage to offer his services.

"Easy now, Mrs. Kessler," Dr. Moberly said soothingly, as if Mama could hear him. When he turned back the second coat, exposing Mama's legs, Viola gripped Conrad's shoulder and averted her eyes, unable to look. She concentrated on Mama's face instead, telling herself that Mama looked fine, that she would be all right. The pain of thinking anything else was so terrible, she couldn't bear to entertain it. She felt her whole body shaking and she was seized by a sudden impulse to cry and laugh and pray all at the same time. Biting her lower lip, she forced herself to think of Papa and Conrad instead. This was no time to break down or faint.

"How bad is it, Doctor?" Papa asked in a tone of voice Viola had never heard him use before. He curled Mama's singed hair around the palm of his hand and there was a blankness in his eyes, as if a light had been put out. She wanted to throw her arms around Papa's neck, to kiss him and comfort him, but she forced herself to stand quietly beside Conrad.

"It's difficult to say, Mr. Kessler." Dr. Moberly gently replaced the coat. "She's been badly burned."

"But she wasn't on fire that long," Conrad protested. "Mama has to be okay. She couldn't have been hurt all that much in a few seconds."

Dr. Moberly shook his head gravely. "Unfortunately, it takes only seconds. I had a little boy come into the hospital just a month ago—bent over the candles on his birthday cake and was severely burned before his mother—who was sitting right next to him—could put out the flames." The doctor touched the charred edge of Mama's gown. "It was criminal to let her wear this costume around a lighted candle."

"But is she going to get well?" Conrad persisted desperately.

"I wish I could say yes, young man, but there's simply no way to tell. One consolation is that your mother probably isn't feeling any pain. When the burns are this extensive, the skin simply stops functioning as a sense organ."

Papa grasped at the reassurance. "It doesn't hurt her then, my Yvette isn't in pain?"

"Probably not, although I'd like to get some morphine into her as soon as possible."

"Thank you." Papa pumped the doctor's hand. "Thank you, Herr Doktor."

Dr. Moberly seemed taken aback by this demonstration of emotion. "There's always the danger, of course, that she'll go into shock." He got to his feet. "Keep her warm and don't move her. I'm going to see if that ambulance has come yet."

They waited for a long time—how long Viola was never sure. She was dimly aware of people milling around in the background, of the cast and crew trying not to stare, but mostly she was aware of Papa, bent over Mama, trying to get her to speak to him. Finally, shortly before the ambulance arrived, Mama opened her eyes.

"Yvette." Tears streamed down Papa's cheeks and lost themselves in his mustache. At the sight of Papa crying, Viola broke down and began to cry too.

Trembling, she knelt beside her father. "You're safe," Papa said to Mama. He kissed her lightly on the cheek. "My beloved wife." His voice broke and he shifted into German, caressing Mama with it.

"We're all here," Papa said. "You'll be fine."

"Dear Jesus, Dietrich," Mama said in a voice so normal it was profoundly unnerving, "I should have been playing Joan of Arc." She tried to move her arm, and her face was suddenly contorted with terrible pain. Viola felt a chill move up her spine. Dr. Moberly had been wrong; Mama was feeling everything. "It hurts," Mama said. She tried to smile bravely, but the smile was lost in a grimace of anguish. "How can it hurt so much?"

"Hell and damnation." Conrad beat his fist on the floor.

"Don't swear, Con," Mama said, and then she shuddered, and closed her eyes.

They took her to the hospital, where she lived for six more hours, and for six hours Papa sat beside her, kissing her burned hands, begging her to be brave, and telling her that the doctors would make her well again. On October 6, 1913, at four o'clock in the morning, Mama died at last, mercifully released from the pain that had never stopped for a moment.

For almost a year after Mama's death, the three of them struggled on, but without her the simple fact was that the Kesslers didn't have an act. The theaters got smaller and smaller, the bookings fewer, the money dried up. That next summer Papa fell ill with a mysterious wasting disease that was finally diagnosed as tuberculosis, Conrad went to work as a clerk in one of the big department stores, and Viola stayed home to play nurse. It was supposed to be a temporary retirement from the stage, but it took Papa seven years to die, seven years during which Viola tended to him faithfully, sang him the old songs, and brought out Mama's picture when he grew feverish and begged to see it; seven years in which she never once put on greasepaint or stepped in front of an audience. From 1914 to 1921 she saw only three plays, all of them from the balcony. If anyone had asked her if she was still an actress she would have said bravely that she never thought about such things; that acting belonged to her childhood; that she was happy with her life and never thought of changing it.

But it wasn't true. She never stopped longing to return to the stage. She missed the crowds and the applause, the smell of greasepaint and dusty scenery, the gossip of the actors, the excitement of waiting up all night for reviews. The love of the theater was in her blood; it burned in her and obsessed her, and at night she dreamed of standing on a stage again, and often she awoke with the applause of a great, phantom audience ringing in her ears. Whenever this happened she would get out of bed and splash cold water on her face and tell herself sternly to forget about such things, but the next morning she was always sad, and a small, still voice inside her whispered that something vital was missing from her life.

BOOK

TWO

BERLINER
WEISSE

3

BERLIN
1921

The crowd swirling up one of Berlin's main streets slowed down for a moment as it passed the pretty young woman who was standing on the corner across from the Kaiser Wilhelm Memorial Church eating a Bockwurst on an onion roll. The girl, who was obviously a foreigner, was dressed in a black skirt and blouse that made her look as if she might be in mourning, but even so male heads kept turning in her direction like compass needles jumping to the north. Stray wisps of curly white-blond hair framed the girl's cheeks with a glowing, sensual halo; her eyes were mahogany brown; her breasts lush, her waist slender, her legs long and coltish, her feet small, with high arches and delicate ankles. She was, in short, a beautiful sight—a fact not lost on most of the Berliners who passed by her on this cold winter morning.

Viola, in turn, was pleased by the sensation she was causing, but she didn't know how to acknowledge it, so she kept on eating the Bockwurst while she tried to figure out what to do next. She had just arrived in Berlin and she had no idea where to go to find the theaters, but if the Berliners liked her this much on the street, then surely they'd like her on the stage, so in a sense, just standing here on this street corner, she was already launching her career. The thought made her feel quite optimistic, which was a good thing because her shoes were leaking and a cold wind was blowing, and if she didn't find some warm place to sit down, she was probably going to turn into a block of ice. Taking another bite of Bockwurst, she stepped back to get a better perspective on things and collided awkwardly with a portly gentleman in a dark suit, smearing the mustard all down the front of his jacket.

"I'm sorry," she apologized. Pulling out her handkerchief, she made an ineffectual dab at the mess. Her ears burned with embarrassment. "I'm so clumsy sometimes, I—"

"A pretty girl never has to be sorry," the man interrupted in a heavy Hungarian accent. He winked, smiled, and tipped his hat, and she noticed suddenly that his lips were painted bright red. Then he was gone, lost in the eddying crowd that surged up and down the Kurfürstendamm.

Putting her handkerchief back in her purse, she stubbornly contemplated her sausage, which was lying in the gutter in half an inch of cold, dirty water. Admiring comments from strangers might be flattering but—like dreams of becoming the toast of the Berlin theatrical world—they didn't fill the stomach. She licked her lips, savoring the last traces of the mustard, and wondered if there was any use fishing the Bockwurst out of the water and trying to eat it. Conrad had insisted she take every penny he had when she left Munich, but even so she had to be economical if she didn't want to find herself sleeping in the Tiergarten tonight. Her last real meal had been dinner two days ago, and she had been too excited to eat—a fact that she now regretted, to say the least.

On the other hand, she obviously wasn't the only one who could use a meal. A few yards away a small boy, dressed with shabby respectability, was eyeing the half-submerged Bockwurst with quiet desperation. The boy rubbed his hands together, trying to keep warm, and perched on one foot and then the other like a stork. His coat was miserably thin and one shoe was tied up with a piece of rope to keep the sole on. His father was out of work no doubt—everyone in Germany seemed to be out of work these days.

She looked at the pinched, chilled face of the boy and her hunger turned to pity. Once or twice, during the worst part of Papa's illness when Conrad was out of work and money was hard to come by, they had lived in the slums of New York, but she had never seen anything there to equal the postwar poverty of Berlin. There seemed to be only two kinds of people out on the street this afternoon: rich foreigners swathed in furs and jewels buying up everything in sight, and unemployed Germans leaning up against the sides of buildings or standing on corners with their caps in their hands, begging for a pfennig. Except for stores that catered to the foreigners, the shop windows were almost empty: tailors were offering colored dickeys as substitutes for shirts, bakeries sported cakes made out of half-rotten potatoes, and as for what was in her Bockwurst, Viola realized suddenly, it was better not to speculate.

She made a decision. Motioning to the boy, she pointed to the sausage, indicating, You can have it if you really want it. The boy's eyes gleamed with joy and desire. Instantly he threw himself to his knees and snapped up the remains of the sausage, shoving it into his mouth like a hungry dog.

"Vielen Dank, gracious lady." The boy clicked his heels together politely and then turned and ran, his tattered coat fluttering out behind him like the wings of some small, ungainly bird.

Taking a firm grip on the battered suitcase that contained all her worldly possessions, Viola stared up and down the busy street, past the swirl of people and motorcars, wondering which way to go next. She didn't know a thing about Berlin except that somewhere there was a street called Unter den Linden that had been featured in a popular vaudeville song ten years ago, but that didn't particularly intimidate her. She had spent most of her childhood in strange cities; Papa was dead, Conrad was in Munich making money, and she had no more responsibilities to anyone but herself. She had one suitcase, three dresses, about fifty dollars' worth of marks, and a dream that had been percolating inside her for the last seven years. The dream was to become an actress again, and if that was impossible or unrealistic or foolish, then the sooner she found out, the better.

She walked a few blocks, feeling the energy of the crowd surge up around her. On the corner of the Tauentzienstrasse two women in short silver skirts and garish yellow leather boots strutted back and forth accosting passersby, their laughter echoing over the noise of the traffic. She watched them, entranced, wondering if they were prostitutes. She'd never—not to her knowledge at least—seen what the newspapers always euphemistically referred to as "the ladies of the night."

"Lost?" She turned to find herself being examined in a friendly way by a short, slender young woman who wore a bright red beret pulled down over her ears in a comic fashion—presumably to keep out the cold. The woman's eyes were tiny and dark. Her black hair—from what Viola could see beneath the beret—was cropped close to her head like the fur of a small animal. In her arms she balanced a pile of books that threatened to tumble to the sidewalk at any minute. Viola caught a quick glance at some of the titles: *The Interpretation of Dreams, Leonardo da Vinci: A Study in Psychosexuality, The Incest Motif in Poetry and Legend, Three Contributions to the Theory of Sex.* . . .

As Viola read the last three titles, her eyebrows shot up. Sex seemed to be high on this stranger's reading list. The young woman followed her glance. Shifting the load of books with mild embarrassment, she shrugged her slender shoulders.

"Don't let the books fool you." Her voice was cheerful and full-voweled and she had a slight foreign accent. "I'm not one of the girls in the high boots across the street. My name's Jeanne Dufour and I'm a student at the Berlin Psychoanalytic Institute, and I thought you looked like maybe you were lost." She smiled a lopsided, rather endearing smile. "I know how it is. I got lost in Berlin myself when I first came here." She extended her hand and Viola shook it.

"How do you do, Miss Dufour." Viola found herself smiling back. "My name is Viola Kessler, and I'm not so much lost as overwhelmed." She caught at *The Theory of Sex*, which was about to take a dive to the pavement, and Jeanne gave her a brisk nod of thanks. "I just got here today, from New York by way of Munich. You see, I'm an actress and"—Viola took a deep breath and plunged ahead, throwing modesty to the winds—"I'm starting a new theatrical career here in Germany. I'm going to work with Eric Stern."

Jeanne pursed her lips in a silent whistle of admiration. "Say, you must be pretty good if you're going to work with Stern. He and Max Reinhardt are the most important theatrical producers in the world, or at least that's what the Berliners claim. Are you famous or something?"

"Actually," Viola admitted, suddenly feeling slightly sheepish, "the truth is, I haven't been on a stage for seven years." She felt that this needed more explanation, so she continued. "My mother, who was an actress, died just before the war, and then my father got sick and I had to take care of him—not that I begrudged him the care. He was a wonderful man, but when he died this fall I decided to come to Berlin and resume my career—"

"Why?" Jeanne interrupted.

"Because I'm obsessed with the theater. It's the great love of my life." Viola felt a little taken aback by so many questions from a complete stranger.

"But why did you choose Berlin?" Jeanne persisted. "I'd think New York would be a better place to be an actress. Say"—she examined Viola with interest—"you aren't on the run from the law or anything, are you?"

"Of course not. What an idea! I came here because of Uncle Otto."

"Uncle Otto?"

Viola looked around, trying to find some way to extract herself from this conversation. "Uncle Otto is my father's oldest brother. He owns a brewery in Munich, and when my father died, he sent my brother and me some money to come visit him. When we got here it became pretty clear that Conrad—that's my brother—was probably in line for the brewery, and I didn't want to go back to the States without Conrad, and I'd always wanted to go back on the stage so . . ."

"So you wrote to Stern," Jeanne prompted, "and told him you were coming to Berlin to join his company?"

"Not exactly."

"No?"

"Stern doesn't know I exist yet," Viola admitted, "but he will, I promise you."

Jeanne laughed, and the stack of books did a midair twist, coming down—by some miracle—intact. "That's the spirit," she observed approvingly. "When I first arrived at the Psychoanalytic Institute no one knew me either, so I sat down in front of the door for three days

and refused to move until they took me on as a student. Actually"—
she laughed with infectious good cheer—"Karl Abraham said they
should have taken me as a patient. Listen, I know I've asked you no
end of personal questions, but that's my nature. Not only am I
naturally nosy, but I'm studying to be a psychoanalyst, and we have
to listen to at least one confession a day or they put us to scrubbing
floors at the hospital. Besides, you're an unusual person. I knew it the
minute I spotted you giving your Bockwurst to that kid."

"You followed me!"

"Four blocks. You're a fast walker. But then when I see a woman
tossing her breakfast to a hungry urchin, I figure she's worth the
effort. And don't try to tell me you wouldn't have eaten that sausage
just because it fell in the gutter, because I saw the longing look you
gave it. You stared at that sausage like it was Valentino."

Viola found herself liking this Jeanne Dufour very much. She took
a chance. *"Vous êtes française, n'est-ce pas?"*

"Mon Dieu"—Jeanne's whole face lit up—"someone else in this
godforsaken Teutonic world who speaks French and with a Parisian
accent, no less. I thought you said you were an American."

"I am, but my mother was French."

"What luck! It makes me homesick just to hear you. I haven't had
anyone to speak French with in six whole months who was capable of
speaking a sentence without mutilating the language out of recognition." Jeanne made a face. "Ugh, German! I have a German boyfriend,
a painter named Friedrich, but it hasn't made me love the language
any better. You always have to wait until the end of the sentence to
find out what kind of verb they're going to spring on you. Just
listening to them talk is like eating an endless sausage."

Viola laughed and made another attempt to catch Jeanne's books.

"Thanks." Jeanne settled back and casually scratched her nose with
the side of her arm, an operation that demanded considerable
dexterity. "Listen, I'm taking you under my wing." Viola tried to
protest, but she silenced her with a shake of her head. "You can't go
wandering around here like some kind of female Candide, you know.
Berlin is a strange place—sort of a combination between paradise and
a cesspool, and if you don't have someone to show you the ropes,
you could end up in the Landwehr Canal."

"Don't worry, I can take care of myself." Surely Jeanne was

overstating the case. Viola noticed that the short-skirted pair across the street had finally snagged a customer—a thin man in a checked jacket. It might be a bit decadent to see things like that going on in broad daylight, but there was nothing particularly dangerous-looking about the scene. She wondered if Jeanne was the sort of person who was given to unnecessary panics.

"The police pull a body a day out of that canal," Jeanne observed matter-of-factly. "Suicides, murders, political assassinations—it's hard to tell the difference around here, but let's not talk about that because it's all too grim. Let's talk about where we're going to have lunch."

"Thanks but I'm not hungry," Viola lied proudly, thinking of the diminishing number of marks in her purse.

"Ha, an unlikely story. Come along." Jeanne nodded at a large, barnlike building across the street. "We'll go to the Cafe Schiller and I'll treat you to some Havelaal, that's green eel—don't make a face like that, it's not really green. Max, the owner, just serves it with a dill sauce. It's the house specialty."

"Thanks, but I have to find a place to stay and . . ." Viola hesitated. Her mouth was watering but she was too proud to impose on a total stranger.

"Come on. I don't know much about you, but I can tell we're going to be friends. I believe you can tell whether you're going to like someone or not in the first five minutes and the rest is all rationalization. Besides, after all the stuff they've put me through at the Psychoanalytic Institute, I know pathology when I see it, and it's my professional opinion that you're not schizophrenic or even particularly neurotic. Unresolved Oedipal problems maybe—we all have those—but nothing a couple of years on the couch wouldn't cure." She laughed as if encouraging Viola not to take her seriously. "The fact is that I liked you before you ever spoke a word, and I'm probably going to try to convince you to take a room at Bluebeard's, so if it's the idea of me treating you to lunch that's bothering you, you can pay me back after you get that acting job with Stern."

"What's Bluebeard's?" It was a little disconcerting to be inundated with so much friendship, but Viola found herself warming to Jeanne. She suddenly realized that she had been feeling terribly lost and lonely ever since she said good-bye to Conrad in Munich.

"Bluebeard's is what my friends and I call the boardinghouse we live in," Jeanne explained cheerfully. "It's a joke you see, because the rooms are all the size of closets and the rumor is that Herr Meckel, our landlord, has several wives stashed away on the premises in various stages of moral decay. Now come on." Jeanne rearranged the books once again and started across the busy street. "Besides," she called out over her shoulder, "you have to see the Cafe Schiller. It's probably the center of . . ." The rest of her sentence was lost in the roar of a truck that splashed by, inches from Jeanne's right hip. Startled, Jeanne jumped back and her books went flying all over the Kurfürstendamm.

"The center of what?" Viola yelled, rushing forward to help her. Together they scrambled to retrieve Jeanne's books and notes.

"The center of the world," Jeanne said gaily, apparently undaunted by the sight of her entire education lying in mud. "Intellectually speaking, of course. More so than Paris even, although I hate to admit it." She struggled to her feet, clutching the weighty brown and black volumes. "In Paris they feel, but in Berlin they *think,* and the Cafe Schiller's where most of the thinking around here goes on. All the intellectuals without a pfennig to their name go there to get warm. Max is too softhearted to throw them out, you see. He's kind of an anarchist, or maybe a Dadaist. I never can keep the labels straight. Anyway, Max's green eel may not be the best in Berlin, but believe me it's the cheapest."

The Schiller was a big, overheated place, furnished with dozens of small wooden tables; an assortment of badly matched, rickety folding chairs; several huge, provocative Dadaist posters announcing the end of the world, and a modest set of fly-specked engravings of German poets which seemed to have been left over from a previous owner-ship. At the tables men and women of all ages appeared to be locked in intense discussions, pounding their fists emphatically, shaking their heads, leaping to their feet as if about to commit homicide. Fragments of their shouted conversations assaulted Viola from all sides, along with huge clouds of cigarette smoke.

"Fool!"

"Idiot!"

"Your ideas about psychics stink! Galileo would roll over in his grave!"

"How many times do I have to say it—the meaning of Dada is that it *has* no meaning!"

"You call a building without bathrooms a *building?*"

"Richard Oswald isn't a filmmaker, he's a pornographer!"

A large black dog barked over and over again like a broken record; waiters in grimy white aprons threaded their way through the mob toward the kitchen, yelling out orders as if the cook were deaf. On their arms they balanced tin trays of beer, bread, and a dark liquid that vaguely resembled coffee. One of the trays crashed to the floor with a noise so loud it put Viola's teeth on edge.

"Wonderful, isn't it?" Jeanne yelled. She pulled Viola toward the back of the cafe where half a dozen people sat silently engrossed in games of chess. The din was a little less deafening here. Relieved, Viola sank down into her chair and looked around at the tumult.

"What's wrong?" she asked Jeanne. "Why is everyone yelling?"

Jeanne grinned. "Why you poor little country bumpkin. They aren't yelling, they're discussing—coming up with the great ideas of our times, creating new art forms, solving all the world's problems— or at least that's what most of them think they're doing."

"Oh." Viola stared at the patrons of the Schiller, feeling acutely uncomfortable and very out of place. She was briefly tempted to wander toward the ladies' room and escape out the back door.

Jeanne shrugged. "I can see that I'd better give you the lay of the land before you stray into the lions' den and get eaten for lunch." She leaned forward and put her chin on the palms of her hands. "Now the first thing you have to understand is that the Schiller is divided up like a big meat pie. Most cafes in Berlin attract just one group. The Coq d'Or and The Russian Tea Room, for example, attract mostly Russians. The Romanische Cafe next door is the place where the writers congregate. You want to talk philosophy, you go to the Red Lantern; right-wing politics, the Cafe Spree; left-wing, the Spartakus Cafe in the Nollendorfplatz. Following me so far?"

"I think so."

"Good." Jeanne took a cigarette out of her purse, lit it, and inhaled deeply.

Viola sat back against the wooden chair and began to relax. Since Jeanne was so good at explaining things, maybe she could explain how to find Eric Stern.

A waiter appeared and Jeanne gave him an order for two coffees and two plates of Havelaal. "Now what you have to understand about the Cafe Schiller," Jeanne continued, "is that it's different. *Everybody* comes here—poets, actors, chess nuts, philosophers, political types, the whole works. It's the only place in Berlin where an out-of-work anarchist is likely to rub elbows with the conductor of the Berlin Philharmonic—only sometimes the elbow rubbing gets a bit out of hand, if you know what I mean, so the various groups have more or less divided the place up between them. Over there, for example"—Jeanne pointed to a group of men near the door—"is the table where the Expressionist painters sit. My boyfriend, Friedrich, joins them sometimes. George Grosz and the rest of the New Objectivists sit on the other side of the room, for obvious reasons."

The reasons weren't at all obvious to Viola, but she nodded as if it were all perfectly clear. Jeanne went on to point out the other tables: the section where Gropius's Bauhaus students gathered to argue architecture; the musicians' table where at present Busoni and Schnabel (two famous pianists who Viola, to her chagrin, had never heard of) were having coffee.

Filmmakers, poets—as Jeanne spoke, the geography of the Schiller slowly began to emerge out of the chaos. Lang, Sternberg, Kollwitz—Viola tried to commit the stream of names to memory, but she was appalled by her own ignorance. She thought of the public libraries where she had done most of her reading, of the dramatic poems of Browning she had consumed with such pleasure. New York—and maybe all of the United States—was stuck in the nineteenth century while Berlin was hurtling toward the future at a hundred miles an hour. She felt a stab of panic. Her whole education was obviously fifty years out of date. How in the world was she ever going to catch up?

"And over there," Jeanne was saying, "is where the theater people sit."

"What?" Viola suddenly stopped worrying and snapped to attention.

Jeanne grinned. "I thought that would wake you up. The theater people, you know—actors, playwrights, producers, and the like. Bertolt Brecht comes in sometimes, as does Erwin Piscator and a pack of Communists, and they sit around all night yelling at each other about the use of theater as a means of mobilizing the working classes. Joseph Rothe used to join them, but he and Brecht had a big fight because Joseph didn't have enough political consciousness or something of the sort. By the way, do you have any particularly rabid political beliefs, because if you do, now is the time to lay them on the table. If you're a fan of that bastard Scheubner-Richter, for example, this friendship is going to be over before it starts."

"I never heard of him," Viola admitted. "In fact, I don't know a thing about politics. I've been too busy taking care of my father to pay any attention to who gets elected to what office."

"You poor, naive little thing." Jeanne shook her head. "Politics isn't just who gets elected to what—not in Berlin anyway. It's an ongoing war, and sooner or later you're going to have to take sides whether you want to or not."

"You make German politics sound like a fistfight."

"Oh it is." Jeanne nodded. "The Germans are completely insane on the subject. Some night when you're in the mood for a very bleak conversation I'll make an attempt to explain the whole mess to you, but on your first day I think we should stick to more pleasant topics. Now where was I?" She inhaled thoughtfully and blew a lazy smoke ring. "Oh yes. I'd just mentioned Joseph. Joseph's out of town at present, but if you move into Bluebeard's you'll get to meet him. He's quite a sexy guy and a very talented playwright, but watch out"— Jeanne lifted her eyebrows and made a little French *moue* with her lips—"because Joseph, *cherie*, runs through women like water. Not that I know firsthand, but the walls at Bluebeard's *are* thin."

"Does Eric Stern ever come here?" Viola scanned the theater people intently, even though she didn't have the faintest idea what Stern looked like.

Jeanne shook her head. "No. You'll probably have to corner him in his own lair over at the Kallmann Theater. Hilde Krauss used to take lessons at his acting school before the war, so maybe she can still remember his daily routine. He's something of a creature of habit, I hear. Hilde lives at Bluebeard's too. She's a cabaret singer and she's a little . . ." Jeanne paused uneasily, as if holding back something unpleasant. "She's just a little odd, that's all. But you'll get used to it. I like Hilde; everyone does. That's the problem, actually. Well, hello. Look what's arrived."

Jeanne's last words were either directed at the plates of Havelaal the waiter had set down in front of them or at three young men who had just walked in the front door—it wasn't clear which.

Viola looked at the eel, steaming hot next to a blob of green dill sauce, and her courage left her. Hungry as she was, she couldn't bring herself to taste it.

"Get going on that eel," Jeanne advised, "because here comes Friedrich, and he'll eat it off your plate. Friedrich's saving all his money to buy a new easel—claims he's going to paint the picture of the century—and since he doesn't have any money anyway, he has a tendency to gobble up whatever's handy."

Viola stuck her fork in a piece of eel, lifted it to her lips, and discovered it was delicious. In less than a minute she had cleaned her plate.

"Good work"—Jeanne chewed and swallowed her last bite—"and just in time too." She wiped her mouth and flashed a sweet, slightly coquettish smile at the three young men who were looking around the Schiller in an aimless, somewhat hungry fashion.

"Was ist los, boys?" Jeanne called out over the din. She turned to Viola. "They're all housemates of mine, from Bluebeard's," she confided, "and completely crazy, all three of them. Wait a minute, and you'll see what I mean."

"Jeanne." The men hurried over and one of them kissed Jeanne on the lips with an enthusiasm that made Viola blush to the tips of her fingers.

"This is my boyfriend, Friedrich Hoffman." Jeanne laughed, coming up for air. "Friedrich, this is Viola Kissel."

"Kessler," Viola corrected.

"Kessler," Jeanne said, "forgive me. I have a terrible time with last names. Anyway, Friedrich, Viola's an American actress and she's come to Berlin to work with Eric Stern."

Viola was so pleased at hearing herself called an American actress that she blushed again, this time with pleasure.

"Sehr erfreut." Friedrich clicked his heels together and bowed from the waist but there was something about the way he did it that let you know that he thought all this German politeness was a bit silly. He was a small, intense man with a large nose, black hair, and piercing eyes that made him look a little like a hawk.

Viola reached out to shake his right hand and discovered to her dismay that it was missing.

"Oh." She blurted out the words impulsively before she thought: "I'm so sorry. What happened to your arm?"

"I lost it during the war." Friedrich smoothly offered her his other hand. "Careless of me, wasn't it?" He smiled, but there was an edge of anger under the joke that made Viola uncomfortable.

"Now don't start pitying him," Jeanne warned, "or he'll start in on how Germany was stabbed in the back at Versailles. Besides, he was left-handed in the first place so it hasn't affected his painting in the slightest. And as for everything else"—she pulled Friedrich to her and kissed him again—"everything else is quite intact." Friedrich's pale face colored, and he laughed a pleased, masculine laugh of satisfaction.

"Let me see, where was I? Oh yes, introductions." Jeanne pointed to the tallest of the three men. "This is Hermann Lang, he's a filmmaker."

"A would-be filmmaker," Hermann corrected with a modest grin. "No relation to the famous Fritz Lang." He was a big man, flat-nosed, strong and athletic-looking, with a shock of copper-colored red hair that had already begun to show signs of thinning, although he couldn't have been more than twenty at the most. Not particularly handsome, Viola thought, yet there was something good-natured about his face that was appealing. She shook Hermann's hand, noting the strength of his grip. He was the kind of man who made women feel secure, she decided—the good-natured, honest kind who often got lost in the shuffle.

"And this is Richard Stafford, our token Englishman. Richard's a composer. In fact, if you decide to take a room at Bluebeard's, Richard will keep you up nights banging on Herr Meckel's piano."

"How do you do," Richard said in English. "It's really not as bad as Jeanne claims, because I compose only in the afternoons when everyone else is out." He was the best-looking of the three, blond and sweet with a round baby face, a slender nose, and innocent blue eyes.

"If you'd only write something *harmonious*," Jeanne sighed, "instead of all that horrible atonal stuff."

"On a piano as out of tune as Herr Meckel's, harmony is impossible." Richard smiled at Viola. "I've been thrown into my life's work by the lack of a good piano tuner," he quipped. He pulled out a chair and sat down next to her. There was something soft about him, a passive handsomeness that she wasn't completely sure she liked. She grinned at the thought. My, she'd gotten picky. Three men and not one of them to her taste. There must be something in the air of Berlin that made a female feel independent.

"Buy us a beer, boys," Jeanne suggested. "Viola's moving into Bluebeard's with us, and I think we should all celebrate."

"Wait a minute . . ." Viola protested.

"Of course you're moving in." Richard waved to the waiter and held up five fingers for five beers. "It's the best deal in Berlin. Besides, one of the inmates just skipped out without paying his rent, so there's a room free."

"Give in gracefully," Hermann advised Viola. "When Jeanne makes her mind up about something, there's no use trying to resist her."

Why not throw in her lot with these people? Where else did she have to go? Impulsively, Viola decided to accept. "You win," she laughed. "Bluebeard's, here I come!" They drank another beer apiece and then another. Time passed, it grew dark outside, the noise in the Schiller turned to soft cotton in Viola's ears, and she found herself laughing and joking with these four strangers as if she'd known them all her life. They were all so witty, so eccentric. They reminded her of the actors she had known as a child. She suddenly realized how starved she had been for this kind of companionship.

"Had enough to drink?" Richard inquired suddenly.

Viola realized that she had indeed. It was an odd, giddy feeling. Great vistas of opportunity seemed to be opening up in front of her. "Yes," she mumbled fuzzily. "In fact," she giggled, "I think I'm drunk."

"Good," Jeanne said. "Then it's time to rent you a room at Bluebeard's. That way you won't notice the mice."

"Mice? What mice?"

"The little mices that run up and down your nose at night."
Hermann ran his fingers up and down her nose.

"Don't pay any attention to Hermann." Jeanne got to her feet and
hooked one arm under Viola's. "He's always kidding."

Richard retrieved her suitcase from under the table and the four of
them walked her to the trolley stop, deposited her in a seat, and sat
down around her. As the trolley rattled through the streets of Berlin,
they talked about mutual friends, about Joseph, who was out of
town, and Hilde, whose new lover was a baron of some kind. Viola
let their words drift over her like the humming of summer bees. It
was warm on the trolley, and there was something comforting about
being with these people—as if they had already become part of her
family. At last the trolley stopped on a street near the canal. They got
out and walked for about two blocks.

"Well here it is, in all its glory." Friedrich stopped and pointed to
a large brown house, badly in need of paint, that sprawled on one
corner like a gigantic, exhausted dog. "Bluebeard's."

"Ah," Viola murmured giddily, "how opulent. A palace from *The
Arabian Nights*."

Later—thanks to five beers and a bad case of exhaustion—she
wasn't able to recall much of what came next. She dimly remembered
meeting Herr Meckel—a walruslike man with a tiny mustache—and
renting a room for a sum so modest she could hardly believe her luck.
Then Jeanne helped her unpack—an operation which took only a few
minutes.

When she was finally alone, she took off her shoes and dress,
slipped on her long flannel nightgown, and put Conrad's picture on
the dresser next to the silver-framed photo of Mama and Papa that
she had taken with her when she left New York. As she looked at the
photos she felt a sudden wave of loneliness. It was so odd to be on
her own. All her life there had been someone else to care for,
someone else to worry about, and now there was only her.

Viola Kessler. Viola Kessler. She said her name to herself twice,
feeling a little silly. Picking up her purse from the chair by the bed,
she took out the pearl button Bernhardt had given her and contemplated it for a moment, remembering how as a girl she had longed to
perform *Phèdre* before an audience of adoring fans. Why was she so
obsessed with the theater? Other women seemed content with their

homes and families; why was she different? She often felt as if her life would be meaningless if she couldn't act. Had Bernhardt felt that way? Had Mama? Was it a disease to love an art so much, or was it a sign that you had the calling?

Stowing the button safely back in her purse, she climbed into bed. Tomorrow she would begin to examine her life systematically; tomorrow she'd start getting to know herself. It was going to take time to get used to so much freedom, but how exciting it all was, what an adventure. In some ways her life as an actress was just beginning, and if she hadn't been so exhausted, she would have stayed awake all night just to savor it.

"Du bist ein Arsch, Friedrich!" The curse rang through the house, sending Viola bolt upright in bed, clutching at the covers. For a moment she didn't have the slightest idea where she was, and then it came back to her: she was in her room at Bluebeard's. She grappled for the electric light chain, and as she pulled it there was a sound of something being dumped into the hall. A woman laughed.

"Leave his junk alone, darling, and come on in to bed." The German was clear and fine, like a piece of crystal, but there was something crude about the way the unseen woman emphasized the word *bed* that made even Viola—who was rather naive in these matters—understand that sleep was the last thing on her mind.

"My room isn't his studio!" It was the same masculine voice that had awakened her, a loud, firm bass that echoed through the thin walls like grand opera. There were more crashes and thumps, as if furniture were being moved, then the sound of running feet, and a loud moan of agony as someone caught sight of the destruction.

"You crazy maniac!" a second male voice yelled.

"Crazy, huh? Watch this." Another thump.

What in the world was going on? More intrigued now than frightened, Viola reached for her robe, threw it over her nightgown, and walked over to the door. The wooden floor was cold under her bare feet.

"I write in this room, get it? I *write* in here." More crashes.

"You're desecrating my art." The second man's voice, hysterical and vaguely familiar. That would be Jeanne's boyfriend, Friedrich, Viola decided, the one-armed artist.

"I'm not desecrating your lousy art. I'm evicting it."

Pulling open the door, Viola found herself face-to-face with Friedrich, clad in a pair of striped pajamas. Friedrich's face was livid with rage; he was so angry that he didn't seem to notice she was there. At his feet lay a pile of paintings, tossed every which way. Viola inspected the top paintings with curiosity and was disappointed to see that they were mostly ugly splotches of black and gray—disturbing profiles of men with egg-shaped heads; a woman whose whole face was an enormous screaming mouth; a forest of ugly, twisted trees. There was something amateurish and disconnected about it all, as if the paint had been thrown at the canvas by an angry child.

"You philistine." Friedrich pointed at an invisible enemy who had evidently disappeared into the room next to Viola. A laugh emanated from the room and echoed down the hall, hearty and clear as a breath of fresh air."

"Philistine?" a voice said. There was no anger in it now, only amusement. *"Gott im Himmel,* the man's actually called me a philistine. I should die. I should fall down on the ground and slit my throat in shame. A philistine? Oh it's too good."

Stepping into the hall, Viola closed the door behind her, and as she did so a man emerged from the room next door carrying a large canvas. The man—who was in his early twenties—was dressed in gray slacks, a black leather jacket, and a small woolen cap that would have looked ridiculous on anyone else. He was a little under six feet tall, with curly black hair, wide shoulders, and a firm, square chin.

Noticing Viola, the man stopped laughing. "Well, well," he said, "what have we here?" His eyes were nothing spectacular—a sort of cross between brown and hazel—but there was energy and intelligence in them. He looked her over approvingly, and Viola looked back, meeting his glance straight on. For some reason she didn't feel the least bit shy.

"You bastard!" Friedrich yelled.

"I've been away for two weeks and he's been using my room for a studio," the man explained matter-of-factly to Viola as if they were old friends. He lay the canvas carefully on the hall rug. "I've told him a hundred times not to do it, but as soon as I'm gone he creeps in with his lousy paints. Claim's the light's better in my room. Not that any of the light ever gets into Friedrich's paintings." He took a step forward, swayed unsteadily, and grasped for support. His hand briefly brushed against Viola's arm and then found the doorjamb. She realized suddenly that he was drunk. "Welcome to Bluebeard's, whoever you are," he said, attempting a bow that nearly sent him flat on his face. "You definitely improve the scenery."

"Joseph," a female voice complained impatiently from the room behind him.

"Duty calls." The man smiled. "Sleep dwell upon thine eyes, peace in thy breast. Would I were sleep and peace, so sweet to rest." He stepped back, closing the door behind him.

"Rotten bastard," Friedrich mumbled.

She turned to him, consumed with curiosity. "Who was that?" she demanded.

"Joseph Rothe." Picking up the nearest canvas, Friedrich launched into a long series of complaints, but she hardly heard him. Her arm was still tingling from the touch of Joseph's hand, and she was trying to convince herself that he had really quoted Shakespeare to her—not some trite lines that anyone would know—but two lines out of the very heart of *Romeo and Juliet,* and he'd quoted them, she realized suddenly, in flawless English.

She rehearsed the lines in her mind, blushing when she got to the rhymes "breast" and "rest." She suddenly became self-conscious. Good heavens, what must the man have thought about her standing around like this in the hall in her nightclothes?

Fleeing back into her room, she slammed the door shut, feeling embarrassed and foolish. Taking off her robe, she climbed back into bed, vowing to be polite and distant tomorrow in case he had gotten any mistaken ideas about her. After all, they were sharing the same house, and it wouldn't do for him to think . . .

For some reason, she couldn't finish the thought. She turned over on her side, then onto her back, and finally onto her other side. It was stuffy in the room and she couldn't seem to relax. On the other side of the wall some disturbing noises were starting up. Boots dropped to the floor, bed springs winced, a woman sighed softly. As she listened the noises began to form an unmistakable pattern. A realization slowly dawned on her. Joseph and the woman were . . .

Oh no, they couldn't be! She was embarrassed and then intrigued.

She lay motionless, her arms stiff at her sides, almost afraid to breathe. How interesting. Didn't the two of them realize that she could hear them? She suddenly remembered something Jeanne had said about the walls of Bluebeard's being like paper.

Sigh and creak; creak and sigh. The bed next door developed a musical rhythm and there was a soft, sensual rustling like dried leaves. On the other side of the wall, the woman moaned and began to pant.

"Do it to me," she said, "don't stop. Do it; do it. *Ja, ja,* oh that's good; oh, that's very good." The bed banged against the wall, right beside Viola's head.

Viola felt the blood rush to her cheeks. Her whole body tingled now, as if she had climbed into a warm bath. In her ignorance she imagined that this was simply due to intense embarrassment. Pulling one of the heavy feather pillows over her head, she tried to muffle the sound of the woman's sharp little cries and the thump of the bed slamming against the wall, but it was useless. There was a frenzied creaking and more moaning, and then sudden silence.

"Ah," the unseen woman sighed, "that was nice." There was a long pause. "Got a cigarette?" A match rasped against the plaster. Burrowing under the pillow, Viola shut her eyes, but it was a long time before she managed to go to sleep.

The next morning, breakfast at Bluebeard's brought more surprises. The first was a bouquet of violets, emerging gallantly from the neck of a beer bottle. The purple-blue petals caught the sunlight, luminous and translucent, casting small blue ovals on Herr Meckel's stained tablecloth, turning a collection of sticky cups, clogged salt shakers, cracked milk pitchers, and greasy plates into a spring still life.

"Hello there," Jeanne said cheerfully, lifting her coffee cup in partial salute. "I've got quite a day ahead of me—an exam on schizophrenia designed to drive the examinee stark, raving mad." She grinned and dabbed at her lips with the edge of a much-mended napkin. On the other side of the table, framed by a large, dusty philodendron, Hermann Lang, the big, redheaded filmmaker, was sitting in his shirt sleeves, reading the morning paper out loud to a young woman in a bright yellow kimono. An elderly, heavyset German matron, her hair wound in curling papers, shuffled in and out of the room in a pair of men's carpet slippers, clearing off the dirty plates and replacing them with their slightly less dirty cousins. Probably one of Herr Meckel's wives, Viola decided with a feeling of satisfaction that she had at last managed to figure something out about the place.

She sat down at the table and contemplated the room for a moment: the peeling pink-and-gold wallpaper, once elegant; the moth-eaten blue velvet curtains; the mixture of heavy Teutonic chairs clustered around the cheap deal breakfast table. Obviously the Meckels—like so many Germans—had fallen on hard times.

"Well," Jeanne prompted, "go ahead."

"Go ahead and do what?"

"The violets."

Viola stared at the bouquet, still not understanding. "What do you want me to do, eat them?"

Hermann stopped reading and looked up from his paper. "The girl's too shocked to take it all in. And who can blame her? Here she is in a city where half the population's starving—without much more than a few marks to her name—and some fellow's already given her violets." He ran his hand through his hair so that it stood up in funny little tufts on the side of his head. "I'd like to claim it was me, of course, but no such luck."

"Are you saying those violets are for me?"

"They certainly aren't for one of the Frau Meckels, darling." The woman in the yellow kimono smiled and took a long, sophisticated drag on her cigarette. She was a lanky brunette with severely bobbed hair and makeup that was somewhat astounding at this hour of the morning: heavy, plum-colored rouge; eyebrows plucked and drawn back in again; a small, pretty mouth refashioned into a perfect cupid's bow, and on one cheek a beauty spot shaped like a heart. "My name's Hilde Krauss, by the way."

"Viola Kessler." They shook hands.

"Pleased to meet you." Hilde blew a long, slow smoke ring. "Always pleased to meet Americans because Americans have so much *joie de vivre*." Hilde's French accent was so terrible that Viola had to bite her lip to keep from laughing. "I had an American friend before I met Baron von Lenau—my present patron." Hilde waved away the smoke as if consigning her American friend to some kind of archive. "I met the Baron at Leda and the Swan—the cabaret where

I sing. The Baron"—she pronounced the title with an heroic attempt to make it sound English—"is rumored to be the late Kaiser's illegitimate nephew. At present he's involved in the international fur trade—a man of aristocratic taste and great generosity." She blew another smoke ring, and contemplated Viola with patient good cheer. "You are going to read the note aren't you, darling? I mean Hermann and Jeanne and I are simply *consumed* with curiosity."

A piece of yellow paper with Viola's name on it stuck out from under the bottom of the beer bottle. She retrieved it and held it for a moment, not daring to open it. A sudden suspicion formed in her mind: the violets were from Joseph Rothe. She felt her hands trembling. What a ridiculous reaction. She hardly knew the man and she certainly didn't have the slightest reason in the world to imagine that he would send her flowers. Since Hermann had disclaimed all connection with them, the violets were obviously from Richard, the young English composer. Having decided that it was Richard who had given her the flowers, Viola felt a distinct sense of relief and then a sharp, irrational pang of disappointment.

"Well, go ahead," Jeanne urged with a knowing smile. "Open up the note before Hilde explodes with curiosity."

Viola unfolded the paper briskly. A few lines were scrawled in English in a bold, definite hand:

> Dear Miss Kessler,
> Sorry about all the noise last night. My most recent play just died in Munich after one performance at the Elf Scharfrichter, and I was mourning for it in my own peculiar fashion. I can't remember what I said to you, but I hope it wasn't too terrible. You looked quite beautiful in that ridiculous flannel robe with your hair all down around your shoulders like Ophelia.
>
> Joseph Rothe

Viola felt a sudden burst of joy that was all out of proportion to the occasion. So Joseph Rothe had thought she looked beautiful, had he? She felt unreasonably pleased by the thought. Reaching out, she stroked the violets delicately with the tip of one finger, feeling the coolness of the petals, the slender, furry stems. Violets, Viola. Surely it wasn't by chance that he had picked violets as a peace offering.

"Well, *who* are they from, darling?" Hilde asked, with a fleck of impatience in her voice.

"Joseph Rothe," Viola said. "An apology for waking me up last night."

Hilde tapped her cigarette ash into her coffee cup and shrugged her narrow shoulders in a weary way that seemed to indicate she was unbearably bored by the news that it was only Joseph who had sent the violets. "Rothe makes a scene like that about once a month. The rest of us are completely used to it by now. Rather like living near a train track, if you know what I mean. The trains roar in and out, and after a while one ceases to notice."

Jeanne grinned. "You're here less than twenty-four hours and Rothe is already on the scent and closing in." She looked at Viola with sudden concern. "Watch out for him, Viola. He's a real wolf."

"Sure"—Viola tried to smile but her lips felt stiff—"thanks." It was as if someone had poured a bucket of cold water over her head. She tried not to show her disappointment. So Joseph Rothe always made scenes like the one last night; so he always made advances to pretty girls. Well, what had she expected? Love at first sight? She'd heard him on the other side of that wall. What kind of fool was she anyway to think that a man like that could possibly be sincere? She mentally gave herself a good shake. Straighten up, Viola, she told herself briskly, be sensible. She was just lonely; she missed Conrad and she was feeling down and a little vulnerable, but she'd soon change all that.

"Don't worry about me," she told Jeanne firmly. "Like I told you, I can take care of myself."

"Good," Jeanne said, "then I'm off to my exam." She picked up her beret and books, grabbed a piece of bread, and hurried out the door. There was a moment of silence, and then Hermann retrieved his paper and began to read to Hilde again. The news had a foreign, unfamiliar ring to it: a wealthy industrialist named Walter Ratheneau had been appointed German Minister for Reconstruction; in Munich a group of Socialists who called themselves Storm Troopers were accused of attempting to terrorize their political opponents.

Unlike the news itself, Hermann's voice was soothing. Viola filled her cup with the thin, chicory-flavored coffee and went about making plans. In the first place, she was going to be careful about getting to

know Joseph Rothe—violets or no violets—and in the second place
. . . She took a long drink and almost choked. Good lord, that stuff
was foul. She gritted her teeth and took another drink, remembering
that breakfast came with her room. Today was the day she had to find
Eric Stern and convince him to let her into his company, and that
wasn't something she could do on an empty stomach.

According to Jeanne, Hilde Krauss would know where Stern was
likely to be this time of morning. Viola ate two pieces of dry bread and
a bowl of cold porridge as Hilde sat about doing her nails, bent
forward, completely absorbed in her hands, a look of blissful concentration on her face. The equipment—brushes, polish, remover, orange sticks, tiny gold scissors, cotton balls—was detailed and
elaborate, a small arsenal, fortified against every possibility.

Viola hoped Hilde's memory would prove equally well stocked.

Two hours later Viola was lying in wait for Eric Stern on the steps
of the Kallmann Theater. When she caught sight of him striding
toward her, her heart fell. He was short, stocky, with a tremendous
aura of vitality; square-faced, stubborn, proud, and fierce—altogether
not a man to be trifled with.

"Herr Stern?" she said boldly.

"Yes?" Eric Stern came to a full stop and turned abruptly, his
expensive English overcoat billowing out around him like a cape. He
glared at Viola with what she hoped was interest. "What is it?"

Viola's mouth went dry. Thanks to detailed directions from Hilde,
she had managed to waylay Eric Stern on the steps of his own theater,
and now all she could think of was how famous he was and how
insignificant she was. Although a small man, he seemed to peer
down at her from a tremendous height: Eric Stern, producer, actor,
who at present raced neck and neck with Max Reinhardt for the title
of most influential theatrical director of the century; Eric Stern, who
had banished the heavy, cumbersome sets of nineteenth-century
German drama, who had staged performances in circuses and
cathedrals, who had almost single-handedly given birth to the
modern theater.

"I'm Viola Kessler," she said more loudly than she'd intended. She
hoped the name Kessler might ring a bell with him. Her mother's
death had been such a famous tragedy.

"So?" he said, lifting his bushy eyebrows. The name had obviously rung no bell. "What do you want?"

"I want to act in your company, Herr Stern," she said bluntly. She knew she should have led up to it somehow, but diplomacy wasn't her strong point, especially when she was nervous. "I'm an actress, from America. A good actress."

"You are, eh? What kind of experience do you have?"

"I spent twelve years in vaudeville."

"Vaudeville?" He spat out the word with contempt. "A refuge for jugglers and trapeze artists. What was the last *real* play you were in?"

"*The Lions' Cage.*"

Stern looked at her blankly, obviously not recognizing the title. "*The Lions' Cage*, eh? When was that?"

"About eight years ago."

"What!"

"Eight years ago," Viola admitted. She knew she should lie, but she couldn't bring herself to do it. "In 1913."

Stern's look of interest changed to one of contempt. "You were a child star and you haven't acted since, is that right?"

"Yes, but I'm sure—"

"Look, Miss Whatever-your-name-is—"

"Kessler," Viola supplied.

"Look, Miss Kessler, over the years my company has contained some of the most gifted actors on the continent—Gertrud Eysoldt, Alexander Moissi—not to mention a fine technical and directorial staff. We're a collective effort, and we're not set up to train amateurs. Acting is an art, not a hobby. I don't understand why you young girls can't get that through your heads. It takes work, dedication, guts. If you're really serious about wanting to refurbish your career, then take classes at my Theater School, but until you know your way around the stage, don't waste my time."

Tears stung Viola's eyes, but she held them back, too proud to cry in front of him. A cab approached the curb, and she saw that he was going to get in and leave. A feeling of desperation seized her.

"I'm not an amateur, Herr Stern," she pleaded shamelessly. "I'm Yvette Kessler's daughter. Surely you've heard of Yvette Kessler—the great American actress who died at the height of her career." It was terrible trading on Mama's name like this, but she didn't know what else to do. Impulsively, she planted herself in front of Stern so that he would have to walk over her to get to his cab. Stern came to a sudden stop, obviously furious, but she didn't care. She knew that if he got away she'd never have another chance. "I've been acting since I was hardly old enough to walk. If I had enough money, then of course I'd be happy to go to your school, but I need a real job or I'll starve. I have talent, Herr Stern. I promise you, you'll never regret giving me a chance to prove myself. And I admire you immensely. The way you bring psychological depth to your characters, the idea you have that the theater expresses a collective will—you see, I've read about your work."

"Get out of my way!" Stern thundered. He tried to walk around her, but Viola anticipated him. It was ridiculous, like a game of basketball, but she hung on, refusing to give up.

"Please let me audition for you," she begged. "I've got a wide range—comedy, tragedy. Please, Herr Stern. I know you like to discover new talent and, believe me, I'm as new as they come."

Stern tried to take another step forward, and she blocked him again. "*Fräulein*, you're insane. You shouldn't be on a stage, you should be in a mental institution. Step aside, damn it. I'm a busy man and I don't have time for games."

"No," Viola protested, "please, Herr Stern, you don't understand. I've come all the way from New York to join your troupe. It's the only reason I'm in Berlin."

"Go home!" he yelled. "The theater is full of pain and hard work. You don't need it."

"But I do need it," Viola cried passionately. "The theater is everything to me. It's all I've ever wanted to do with my life."

"I asked you to step aside, but you're deaf, yes? So now I must take action." Placing his hands in Viola's armpits, Eric Stern swept her off her feet and set her to one side. Viola was so shocked that she was rendered temporarily speechless. Stern tipped his hat. "*Auf Wiedersehen, Fräulein*," he said, sarcastically, as he disappeared into the cab. He stuck his head back out the window and glared at her. "If I see you anywhere near this theater, I'll call the police. Do you understand? Go away. Go back to America where you belong."

Half an hour later, having partially recovered her powers of speech and locomotion, she went to the main post office and sent a long cable to Sarah Bernhardt, reminding her that she was Yvette Kessler's daughter and begging Bernhardt to recommend her to Eric Stern. The cable—composed in complete sentences in Viola's very best French—cost a fortune to send, and as Viola counted out the marks to the postal clerk she realized that she probably wouldn't be able to afford to eat, but, at the time, such petty sacrifices seemed irrelevant. She told herself—with a fine appreciation of the drama of her situation—that she wanted to be an actress more than she wanted food, and then—more realistically—that after the way Stern had treated her this morning, a recommendation from Bernhardt was her only chance to get a job with his company. Surely the letter would come soon, she told herself.

Meanwhile, she would have to look for work elsewhere.

Max Reinhardt's Deutsches Theater was located on a quiet side street. Constructed with a Greek exterior, the building was said to symbolize Reinhardt's constant search for simplicity and proportion—two qualities that had made him one of the most highly respected directors in all of Europe.

With the feeling that she was about to tread on sacred ground, Viola cautiously tried the stage door. Open, what luck! Turning the knob, she stepped inside, expecting to be stopped at any minute, but her luck held: there was no one in sight, only a few flats of scenery propped up against the wall and a coil of rope dangling next to a fire bucket. About twenty yards ahead, on the famous revolving stage—which critics had dubbed one of the miracles of the modern theater—she could make out a series of white stairs and severe columns positioned in rhythmic patterns so their shadows crossed and interlocked geometrically.

She paused for a moment, drinking in the atmosphere, thinking how long it had been since she had been backstage. She remembered the cockatoos and camels of the Dionysia, the stagehands calling to one another as they hoisted scenery into place. This theater, in contrast, was almost unnervingly quiet, but she could imagine what it must be like on an opening night when the seats were filled and the curtain was about to rise. What she wouldn't give to be in front of an audience again.

She closed the door silently behind her and took a few steps toward the stage.

"Just where do you think you're going?" a voice bellowed out of the shadows.

Viola was startled, but she kept on walking.

"Hold it, hold it right there!" A man in a black sweater bounded into sight waving his arms. He had a large nose, dark circles under his eyes, two prominent gold teeth, and a stocky, bulldog-like body. Striding up to Viola, he blocked her path and looked her up and down.

"Who are you?"

"Viola Kessler," Viola said boldly. "I've come to audition for the play."

"For which play?"

"All of them," she said confidently. *"Danton's Death, Orpheus in the Underworld, A Dream Play,* even *The Sunken Bell* if Herr Reinhardt's casting that one this early in the season." She planted her hands on her hips and looked the man square in the face. She'd spent much of her life outwitting stage managers, and she wasn't about to be intimidated. "Maybe you could tell me where the auditions are being held. It's awfully quiet around here."

The man's face softened. "Need a job, don't you?"

"Yes," Viola admitted, "I do."

"Well, *Danton* and *Orpheus* are already cast and the auditions for *Dream* are closed." He shook his head. "This is a repertory theater, not some second-rate cabaret. Even the extras have to work their way up. Herr Reinhardt almost never uses anyone except his own students, and when some actor from the outside does audition, it's by invitation only."

"But I have an invitation," Viola insisted.

"Oh you do, do you? From whom?"

"From Herr Reinhardt himself."

The man laughed. "Nice try," he said, "but Reinhardt's in Stockholm. Do you realize that you're the nineteenth out-of-work actress who has tried to pull this trick in the last month?"

"I'm that unoriginal, am I?" Viola couldn't hide her disappointment, but it wasn't easy. She had hoped to at least get a chance to audition.

"Sorry," the man said, "I can see you need the work, but there just isn't any to be had. Why there are actors waiting in line just for a chance to mop this floor." He took her by the shoulders, steered her gently out the stage door, and closed it firmly behind her. Viola heard the click of the lock slipping into place. For a moment she stood looking at the door, wondering if he might relent and reopen it. Well, that was that. No use brooding. Sitting down on the steps, she opened her purse and took out the list Hilde had helped her make up last night. There were forty-nine active theaters in Berlin, and sooner or later she'd land a job in one. Too bad they were scattered all over town and she didn't have enough money to take streetcars, but that couldn't be helped. She was young and strong and walking wouldn't do her any harm. She'd find work somewhere—it was merely a matter of making the right connections.

Rubbing the backs of her legs briskly, she examined her shoes, wondering how long the soles would hold out.

The hall smelled of stale cigarette smoke and mold and the stage was nothing more than a wooden platform. Overhead the pennants from the last beer festival drooped in dusty splendor and the floor was littered with cigarette butts, but the Kesslers had played in worse places and Viola wasn't intimidated.

"To the Winter Palace, comrades!" she yelled with what she hoped was revolutionary fervor. The play she was trying out for was about the Russian Revolution so she tried to think of snow and ice and endless steppes, all of which was fairly easy since it was so cold in the hall she could see her own breath.

"Enough," the director called out. His face was pinched and his eyes glowed with a missionary-like intensity. Leaning over, he conferred in whispers with a tall, thin woman. Viola watched the two of them hopefully. She had been to sixteen theaters in the past week and a half, and this was only the fourth time she'd made it onto a stage.

The director straightened up. "Sorry," he said, "you just won't do."

"Why not?" Viola walked to the front of the platform, dizzy with fatigue and disappointment.

"You don't look right for the part," the thin woman observed, "you're not working class enough."

"But all my family ever did was work!" Viola protested.

"You look like an aristocrat," the director said. "Sorry, it can't be helped." He turned to a pale, dark-haired woman in a stained green-and-gold skirt. "Next," he said.

Every bone in Viola's body ached. Slowly she left the stage, found her coat, and put it on. Her fingers felt numb, and she dreaded the long walk back to Bluebeard's through the snow. Up on the platform, the woman in the green skirt was saying the lines Viola had just spoken. Her voice trembled and Viola could see she was shaking.

No matter how bad off you were, someone always had it worse. Viola swallowed her own disappointment and wished the woman in the green skirt luck.

The Arizona was one of the best small theatrical cabarets in Berlin. Famous for its cowboy-booted waitresses, its murals of the Grand Canyon, and its corral-shaped stage, it had been the cradle of some of the more outrageous productions of the postwar period. The owner, George Freund, was a short, chubby, square-chinned German who had a passion for everything American, including ice water, which he served in large mugs to everyone who walked through the door.

Leaning up against the bar, George contemplated Viola with interest. He looked a little ridiculous in his ten-gallon white cowboy hat and hand-tooled boots, but Viola was in no position to laugh. When he heard that she was an actress from New York, George had invited her in to audition, and she was so grateful she could have kissed him.

"So what can you do?" George asked.

"Anything," Viola assured him, "anything you want."

He gestured toward the stage. "Give me a sample."

Viola walked up onstage, feeling strangely light and happy. She knew just the thing to please George—a play called *Stampede* that the Kessler family had performed to enthusiastic audiences from Boston to Denver. It wasn't much from an artistic standpoint, but it had a great monologue in the first act, complete with a lot of Western slang that Viola prayed she could translate into German.

Taking a deep breath, she turned to face George and launched into the monologue: *"The sky goes on forever in these parts, clear out to the Indian Nation, but if a gal ain't careful some cowpoke will stake a claim on her and tie her down . . .''* She went on, extolling the beauties of the West, turning in a good performance if she did say so herself. George seemed pleased, and when she got to the end he even applauded.

"Great," he said enthusiastically, "wonderful."

Viola was elated. "Then I have the job?"

"What job?" George raised his eyebrows. "Who said there was any job?"

Viola couldn't believe it. "But you said you were looking for an actress."

"Did I say an actress? I meant a singer. I'm thinking of making this an all-American place, not just Western, but Northern, Southern, Eastern"—he waved his arms—"New Orleans, Chicago, Kansas City, very gay, very exciting. I may remodel, give up my Stetson, and wear a gangster suit like your Mr. Al Capone."

"I can sing," she insisted. He'd liked her performance, he had to hire her.

"Yats?"

She realized he was trying to pronounce the word *jazz*. "Sure," she said desperately. "I've been singing jazz all my life."

George thought it over and then shook his head. *"Ja,* but you aren't Negro. Berlin audiences want Negro yats singers like Josephine Baker. The Negroes seem mysterious and exotic, whereas you seem— pardon me—quite talented but almost German."

Viola stalked off the stage and seized her coat. "You idiot," she yelled. "Why the hell did you tell me to audition if you knew you wanted a Negro jazz singer?" Slamming the door behind her, she walked back out into the Kurfürstendamm fuming with disappointment and fury.

The next cabaret was the size of a hotel room. It had black and silver walls, fake palm trees, and a stage shaped like a roulette wheel.

"So you want to act at the Monte Carlo," the owner said. He was an aristocratic-looking man who affected a small white pipe and gold earrings.

"Yes," Viola said staunchly, "I do."

"Tried any of the other cabarets?"

"A few." Twenty-eight to be exact, but there was no use letting him know that she'd already been turned down twenty-eight times.

"We don't pay our girls much."

"It doesn't matter," Viola said bluntly. "I'll take anything."

"You aren't bad-looking," the owner said. "Nice legs."

"Thank you," Viola said through gritted teeth.

"Get up onstage and take off your clothes."

"No," Viola said stubbornly. She folded her arms across her chest and glared at the man. The memory of George still rankled and she wasn't about to make a fool out of herself twice in one afternoon.

"Do you want this job or don't you?"

"I want it, but not enough to strip."

"All the girls in the cabarets strip. Even Josephine Baker dances with only a string of rubber bananas around her waist. Why should you be different?"

"I'm a serious actress, and I'm tired of being compared to Josephine Baker."

"Then go do Goethe for Reinhardt and don't waste my time."

"Tell me the truth," Viola demanded, "are there *any* acting jobs to be had in Berlin?"

The owner smiled. He had very small, clean white teeth. "Not if you won't strip," he said cheerfully.

That afternoon Viola finally faced the truth: she was not going on the stage—at least not in the near future. Fine. Then she would wash dishes, wait tables, scrub floors if she had to. Sooner or later that letter from Bernhardt would come. Sooner or later, she'd get a break; meanwhile, if she was going to survive, she had better start looking for any kind of work.

Clutching at her coat, she plowed through the icy wind toward the Cafe Schiller.

Max was sympathetic but discouraging. "The dishwasher is my brother-in-law," he explained, "and the waiters are all relatives. If I fired one of them to hire you, my wife would put an ice pick through my heart."

"I could sweep the floor," Viola pleaded.

"My aunt does that. She's an educated woman—has a doctorate in philosophy, speaks five languages." Max ordered her a plate of Havelaal. "It's on the house," he said. "Sorry I can't give you a job."

She ate the Havelaal gratefully. It would have been even better with a cup of coffee, but she no longer had the money for such indulgences.

"Sorry."
"No work here."
"We want someone older."
"Someone younger."
"We're not hiring at present."
"Check back next week."
"We can't afford to pay the help we have."

Every day of that endless, bitterly cold winter Viola went out looking for work, but there seemed to be no work of any kind to be had. The weeks passed with no word from Bernhardt. Conrad sent her money, but it disappeared in no time, and she couldn't bring herself to beg him for more. By mid-February she was reduced to pawning the only thing of value she owned: the silver frame that had contained the photo of Papa and Mama—but that money too came to an end all too soon.

It was the end of April and the linden trees were putting out their buds, thick and fat as babies' thumbs. This was the month the birds returned to Berlin: mallards, wood thrushes, magpies, nightingales, grebes; the month the city threw off the grimness of winter and suddenly burst into life. But for Viola spring might as well not have come at all.

She sat in the front parlor of Bluebeard's, forced into a new respect for the power hunger could exercise over a person's life. She was wearing her best brown wool dress, wearing it without pleasure or hope, feeling thin, pale, dull-haired, and filled with an entire winter's worth of desperation—an impression of her that Hilde's friend, the Baron von Lenau, obviously didn't share.

"Such a charming girl." Baron von Lenau bowed over Viola's hand, kissed it, and then turned it over and kissed the palm. "Such lovely blond hair, such remarkable eyes." The Baron's lips were damp and flaccid, like the lips of a small dog. Viola flinched self-consciously and tried to cover her aversion with a smile. She was dizzy from hunger, discouraged, and on the verge of a breakdown, but she still had enough sense to realize that she could hardly expect the Baron to take her to dinner if she let him know that his touch made her nauseous.

The Baron drew back and contemplated her with the kind of look that a man might give a fine horse that he had recently purchased. It was a look obviously not meant to be unkind, but it shamed Viola to the core. For a fleeting moment she wished with all her heart that he was at least handsome, but he was a thin, rather goatlike man with a small mustache, dressed in a beautifully cut English suit, soft-faced and harmless-looking, with a small potbelly and a head as shiny as a well-waxed kitchen floor.

Ordinarily she wouldn't have cared—bald or fat, tall or short, it would have been the inner person who mattered to her. She was, after all, an actress who had been trained to be sensitive to the most subtle currents of the human soul. But tonight it was different. Tonight she wished with all her heart that the Baron von Lenau looked like Valentino.

"Miss Krauss says that you have agreed to give me the pleasure of your company for the evening," the Baron said smoothly.

Viola nodded, already feeling humiliated. Her fear had grown as her money had trickled to an end and finally run out. Yesterday, badly frightened, she had finally given up all hope of finding a job and faced reality: she was starving—not metaphorically, but quite literally. For forty—no, make that forty-one—days she had existed solely on two slices of bread a day, a bowl of porridge, and as many cups of coffee as she could force herself to swallow, and now it was the end of the week, her rent was due again, and soon she would not even have breakfast—not to mention a place to sleep. She had passed a bad night, full of hungry nightmares. This morning, in desperation, she had confided in Hilde, and Hilde—having grown tired of the Baron—had generously suggested that Viola "take him over."

"Pretty girls in Berlin all come to this in the end, darling," Hilde had said bluntly, "unless, of course, they have rich families like Jeanne or they're simply terribly talented."

As Viola watched the Baron lower himself onto the sofa beside her, Hilde's words rang in her ears, making her so miserable that she could hardly keep from crying. She mustn't have any talent. Why had it taken her so long to see that simple fact? If she'd been talented, surely someone would have given her an acting job. It didn't matter that she was obsessed with the desire to act; it didn't matter that she would have given her right arm to be on the stage. She was a fool, laboring under the delusion that she had some special gift. Stern had been right: she didn't belong on the stage; she belonged in a mental institution with people who thought they were Napoleon and Jesus Christ.

The Baron cleared his throat and put his arm around her waist. His touch was odd and boneless, and his hesitation grated on her nerves like chalk dragged across a blackboard. She gritted her teeth. In Berlin these days perfectly respectable women sold themselves all the time.

"We'll go to a revue at the Apollo," the Baron was saying, as he tentatively fondled one of her breasts. She shuddered. The Apollo was an infamous theater where nude women dressed in laurel wreaths cavorted on white plaster horses. "And then I'll take you out for a nice lobster." She thought of the lobster dripping with butter, of fresh bread, green salad, wine and pastries.

The Baron stood up and offered her his arm.

Viola got to her feet, reached out, and froze. She simply couldn't go through with this. Impulsively, she gave him a shove. "Go away," she said.

He looked at her, not understanding. "What did you say, my dear?"

"I said go away."

"But Miss Kraus lead me to believe . . ."

"I don't care what Hilde lead you to believe."

"I beg your pardon?"

"Just go away." She put her hands on the front of his white formal shirt and pushed him toward the door. "The bargain basement's closed down. The deal's off." She knew she was raving at him in English, but she didn't care. "I'd rather *starve* than let you touch me." The whole situation suddenly seemed ridiculous, like one of those melodramas she and Mama, and Papa, and Conrad used to do together. She planted her hands in the Baron's soft belly and pushed him hard.

"Don't hurt me!" he shrieked, and to her surprise he turned and ran out the door.

The thought of the dignified, potbellied Baron—the Kaiser's illegitimate nephew no less—flapping down the steps of Bluebeard's, dragging his gold-headed umbrella behind him, was too much. Falling into an overstuffed chair, she began to laugh with hunger and helpless hysteria. A real flesh-and-blood baron and she let him get away. Hilde would never forgive her.

"Quite a performance," a voice said. She looked up and nearly choked with surprise. Joseph Rothe was standing in the doorway, hands in his pockets. "I presume that was your meal ticket that just went running out the door?"

"Yes." Something had snapped inside her; she was beyond shame. She tried to keep a straight face but the effort was too much. She began to laugh again, and then, in the middle of it, to her surprise, she began to cry.

"What's wrong?" There was concern in Joseph's voice, as if he might really care somehow, and that—for some ridiculous reason—only made her cry more. For months she had been avoiding Joseph, taking Jeanne's warning to heart, yet she was acutely aware that he had had no more women in his room since that first time—at least none that she'd heard—and that he spent most of his days at his typewriter. Maybe he was a good man after all. The idea that she might have misjudged him and been rude to him for no reason made her infinitely, foolishly sad. Salty tears ran down her cheeks and dripped into the corners of her mouth; her heart felt heavy and waterlogged. Joseph came over to her and put his hand on her shoulder. There was something in the gesture that reminded her of Conrad and that, too, made her cry. "Come on," Joseph said in a friendly way, "what's wrong?"

"Everything." Viola knew she was making a spectacle of herself, but she just couldn't stop crying.

"Everything, huh? Sounds pretty serious." She looked up, thinking that he was making fun of her, but there wasn't a hint of mockery in his eyes. The words came pouring out:

"I came here to work with Eric Stern but he treats me like I've got a bad case of the plague. I cabled Bernhardt for a recommendation months ago, but she hasn't answered. I've tried and tried to get a job, but I can't even qualify to wash dishes in this town and . . ."

"And you're hungry," Joseph supplied.

Viola stopped abruptly. "Why no," she said with quick pride, "what makes you think that?"

"I've watched you eat breakfast. Richard left some crusts this morning, and when you thought everyone else was gone, you picked them up and stuffed them in your purse."

"I got those crusts for the birds," she said defensively. "I walk to the Spree every morning and feed the ducks."

"The ducks, eh?"

"Right."

"Stubborn, aren't you." A statement, not a question. "Proud too. Impulsive, from what I've seen. An altogether difficult woman."

She suddenly felt angry. "Are you through listing my character defects?" She got to her feet. "Or are there some you've overlooked?"

Joseph put out his hands in mock supplication. "Hold on there. Don't get me wrong. I *like* difficult women."

"You do?" She was confused again. She suddenly became intensely conscious of how very handsome he was.

"Yes, I do. For one thing, they make the best actresses—a fact that I, as one of the great unsung playwrights of Germany, am bound to appreciate. In fact, I like them so much that even when they aren't the slightest bit hungry, I usually insist on buying them dinner. Of course, unlike our friend the Baron, I don't present a bill afterward for services rendered. No, I consider a difficult, stubborn woman's difficult stubborn company quite payment enough. Gives me a whetstone to sharpen my wit on, you see. A playwright needs to keep his wit well honed. So, how about it?"

"What are you talking about?" Viola stared at him, confused by the rush of words, not able to tell if he was joking or serious.

"My dear Miss Kessler, do I have to get down on my knees and beg? I'm inviting you to dine with me."

"To eat?" She suddenly felt the saliva rush to her mouth.

"Lung soup, if you can stand it. It's all I can afford, but it's hot and filling."

"Why me?"

Joseph gave her a look that was admiring and absolutely serious. "Because," he said quite frankly, "I've been wanting to talk to you ever since you moved into this place, but I get the feeling you've been avoiding me. Right?"

"Right."

"Ah, honesty"—he grinned—"one of the prime characteristics of stubborn, difficult, talented women. An admirable trait, but one that rather sets a man back on his heels." He took her hand and she felt a tingling sensation that rushed from her palm all the way up to her arm. A warning bell rang at the back of her mind, but she was too hungry to pay attention to it twice in one evening.

Several hours later—after a hearty dinner of lung soup, rye bread, and beer—Viola sat in Leda and the Swan, a small, smoky cabaret on the Friedrichstrasse, watching Joseph's most recent play being performed on a stage the size of a pocket handkerchief. Viola remembered being refused a job at the Swan. The cabaret was unforgettable, crowded with round lacquer tables decorated with green swan-shaped lamps. Strange birds flew on the painted walls, and over the bar a forest of plaster trees reached out fingerlike twigs to embrace large womb-shaped nests. The trees gave Viola an eerie feeling, as if they were trying to talk to her, but what was going on on the stage gave her a stranger feeling still.

"We're here to shock you."

"Amaze you."

"Disturb you."

"Daze you."

Four actors stood in four colored spotlights wearing animal masks—fox, hyena, vulture, bear—chanting a brilliant litany of eroticism and artistic passion. The animals linked arms and began to dance to a slow jazz beat, twisting sinuously. Behind them, on some kind of semi-transparent screen, hand-tinted images were suddenly flashed: a woman's bare breast, a child holding a bouquet of yellow flowers, a giant eye (which looked suspiciously like Joseph's), an Indian god dancing on an immense pink-and-white lotus blossom.

"Only beauty exists."

"Only art."

"Only the pulses of the human heart."

"Reality is an illusion."

"A delusion."

"A pain in the brain."

Joseph leaned forward, an unlit cigarette dangling from his hand, following the action onstage with complete concentration, moving his lips silently along with the actors. Viola looked at him with new respect, not unmixed with awe. Onstage the lights flashed, strobing in time to the music. It was hard to believe that Joseph had actually conceived all of this.

The play progressed hypnotically. Viola felt herself nodding over her beer, lulled by the music and movement. Then suddenly, without warning, there was an explosion that made her almost jump out of her skin. People screamed and rose to their feet in panic. For an instant the entire cabaret was filled with smoke and the smell of gunpowder, and then—to Viola's surprise—Hilde Krauss appeared out of the chaos and began to sing one of the "gutter songs" that had made the cabarets of Berlin famous all over Europe:

"WHO NEEDS LOVE?
IT'S ONLY PAIN
SO MUCH LOSS
SO LITTLE GAIN."

Hilde straddled a chair, threw back her head, belting out the words in a husky voice. Her upper body was encased in the briefest of black lace corsets; fishnet stockings covered her long, slender legs; on her head, perched at a rakish angle, was a silk top hat.

"I'M TIRED OF PROMISES
I'M TIRED OF SIGHS
IF YOU WANT ME, JUST TAKE ME
WITHOUT ANY LIES."

The applause was tremendous. People stood on tables, stamped and whistled and tossed napkins into the air. Hilde was snatched off the stage and carried around the cabaret on the shoulders of four men. Joseph was forced to stand up and take one bow after another.

"A great play."

"Marvelous."

"So original, Herr Rothe."

The audience crowded around Joseph, shaking his hand, patting him on the back. Viola stood to one side, surprised by all the attention he was getting. She'd had no idea Joseph was so well known.

"Well," Joseph said, after all the patting and congratulating was over, "how did you like it?" He sat back down at their table, lit his cigarette, and took a nervous puff, and she realized that he was waiting for *her* opinion.

"I liked it a lot." Such a bland, simple thing to say. She considered telling him that it was the most original, confusing, disturbing play she had ever seen, but suspected it wouldn't be altogether a good idea. There was something about Joseph's play that had made her understand that underneath that competent exterior of his there were some very human emotions: fear, self-doubt, confusion, and a passionate longing for something she couldn't quite put her finger on. And how could you say something like that to a man you hardly knew?

Joseph took a long drag on his cigarette and looked at the painted birds on the walls. Then suddenly, without warning, he reached out, took her hand, lifted it to his lips, and kissed her fingertips. "You know," he said, "you're very beautiful." She stared at him, speechless. She could feel her whole body trembling. Joseph kissed the inside of her wrist and slowly raised it to his face. She could feel the warmth of his skin, the slight prickles of his beard. His fingers were threaded through hers, strong and blunt, and she could sense the pulse racing through his wrist. A kind of sexual, emotional dizziness overcame her. "You glow with light," Joseph said, "do you know that? You radiate it." He kissed her hand again. "Do you have the slightest idea how much I'd like to make love to you?"

His voice trailed off, and she looked down, embarrassed and surprised by the intensity of her own desire. He had promised he'd present no bill for this evening, and she knew he meant it, and yet . . . why not admit it? She was tempted. Suppose she lost her virginity to this handsome, brilliant playwright. Would that be such a disaster? *Why not?* an impulsive voice whispered inside her. *After all, this is Berlin. The old rules don't apply here.*

She thought about how much he attracted her, and then she thought about how he had "mourned" the failure of his last play—the woman in his room, the bed thumping against the wall. The memory of those intimate noises was sobering. After what she'd heard, how could she believe he was sincere even for an instant? She must be out of her mind to consider such a thing. The man obviously went around collecting women like they were stamps.

She jerked back her hand as if it had been burned. "Don't say things like that," she told him sharply. "You hardly know me, and besides, Jeanne says you're a wolf." The words seemed to blurt themselves out of their own accord. She shut her mouth, horrified at her own tactlessness.

Joseph guffawed. "Jeanne says I'm a what?"

"A wolf." She felt herself blushing furiously but it was too late now to take the words back. "She says you make advances to every woman you see, that you're a nice enough guy but unreliable. I'm sorry. I know that's a terrible thing to tell you, but that's what everyone says about you. I suppose if I were more polite, I'd just say that I'm not attracted to you, but that's not the truth. I am attracted to you, you see . . ."

"Well that's good news."

"No it isn't. I am attracted to you, I admit it—a lot to be honest, but I don't have very much experience with men, and I certainly don't intend to start off by being one of the crowd. I don't want to be collected or—as Victorian as it sounds—trifled with. I can hear through that wall, you know."

"Oh my God"—Joseph choked on his cigarette smoke—"you are a strange, unusual woman."

She stood up, feeling upset, foolish, and embarrassed beyond belief by the whole situation. Here a man had made her the first proposition she'd ever had in her life, and she'd responded with a sermon. Not that she didn't mean every word of it, but she wasn't a prude and why couldn't she have done something more sophisticated like flutter her eyelashes and tell him that she bet he said that sort of thing to all the girls. Hilde would have fluttered *her* eyelashes, you could bet on that. But no, she had to get up on a soapbox and play for the balcony. "I guess you better just take me home," she said, feeling perfectly miserable but too proud to cry.

"Now hold on a minute." Joseph took her wrist and pulled her gently back down into her seat. "Let's talk this over."

"What's there to talk about?"

"Us."

"What us, Joseph?" She bit her lower lip, confronting him bravely, but her voice shook. "Didn't you just hear what I said? I don't trust you. I know that's not the kind of thing you're supposed to tell a man the first time you go out with him, and I'm sorry, but that's the way it is."

"At least give me a chance to be honest with you."

"Very well." She settled warily into her chair. She could hardly refuse him that. Let him be honest with her.

"In the first place"—Joseph took another puff on his cigarette as if trying to calm his nerves—"you're right. I have had a lot of women in my life. I'm a man with a past you might say. You see"—he looked at her almost pleadingly—"I spent time during the war at the front as a medical orderly in a military hospital. It was horrible—we didn't have enough bandages, morphine, food. We operated without anaesthetic. I suppose I could tell you I got hardened to it, but the truth is, I didn't. I actually saw one of my best friends die. Casper Eugen was his name. A big, gentle guy who'd had a passion for bicycle racing in civilian life. We'd grown up in Freyburg together, gone to the same high school. They brought him in with a stomach wound from a land mine, and I was the one elected to pick the shrapnel out of him because all the real doctors were busy trying to save people who had a better chance of surviving. I guess it was about then that I started to think of life as something quick and cheap, to be grabbed while you still had both your arms and legs."

Joseph took another nervous drag on his cigarette. "On top of all that, I'm an artist. I'm passionately involved in my work, virtually to the exclusion of everything else. Writing a new play isn't just a job like being a bank clerk or driving a truck. It's not a profession, it's an obsession." His eyes glowed for a moment, and his face was suddenly illuminated. "The creative act is the most pleasurable thing I've ever experienced. It's the only thing I've found that makes life make any sense. When I was fourteen I had a kind of spiritual crisis—I'd been suspended from school and the doctors had decided I had a heart murmur, which turned out to be a misdiagnosis, but anyway sports were out, so for weeks I lay in my room looking at the ceiling wishing I was more like my brother Hans, who was well on his way to becoming a textile engineer. Then, one day, I began to write. I put my words into the mouths of strangers. I began to recreate the world the way I wanted it to be, and in the process I found myself. I know this may sound overblown to you, but I assure you to this very day that I get a sense of being God when I write a new play—no, let me take that back—not a sense of being God but of *imitating* Him. I create an entire universe, you see. Are you understanding any of this, or do I just sound like I'm raving?"

"You sound a little crazy but I think I understand." She leaned forward, moved by his frankness, thinking that Joseph was the most amazing man she had ever met, that he was saying what she had thought a thousand times and had never been able to put into words. "When I'm on stage, performing, I feel the same sense of creation."

"I knew that as an actress you'd understand." Joseph put out his cigarette and paused for a moment, as if reluctant to go on. "But for me at least," he said at last, "all this has had its consequences—in the personal realm. I have to admit to you that I've had an unfortunate tendency to see other people—women, to be more specific—as secondary somehow—good enough for an evening or even a few months, but placed against the pleasure of writing a play, they've mostly been, well, light entertainment."

The words "light entertainment" made her sit back again, sobered.

Well, what had she expected? He'd said he'd be honest, hadn't he?

"Don't look at me like you're giving up on me. Because I'm not done yet." Joseph leaned forward and took back her hand. "What I'm trying to tell you is that I feel different about you. I have ever since that first time I saw you in the hall. I won't say it's love at first sight, that's too old a chestnut. I don't believe in it, and I wouldn't even use it in one of my plays. But you're the first woman I've ever met who makes me feel like I feel when I'm writing. This isn't some kind of whim. I've been watching you for months and it hasn't changed. I feel calmed in your presence and excited at the same time. I suspect that we mirror each other emotionally, that we're twins under the flesh somehow. I know I'm starting to sound like a poet who's gone off the deep end, but I want at least a chance to see if there can be anything serious between us. And I'll confess something else to you. I don't have any idea how to go about it."

He shrugged and looked at her helplessly. "It's ironic, really. I've picked up so many women in my life, handed them so many good lines, and now when I want to do it for real, I feel as tongue-tied and foolish and awkward as a sixteen-year-old kid." Joseph abruptly lifted her hand to his lips and gently kissed it. "Just give me a chance, please. That's all I'm asking. I'm not denying that I have a rotten reputation"—he kissed her hand again—"but I'll live it down." The blood beat in her wrist and temples and she suddenly felt drunk with beer and joy and apprehension. She knew she should draw back her hand, but she couldn't bring herself to do it. "Will you give me a chance, Viola?"

"I'd be out of my mind, wouldn't I? I'd be doing just what Jeanne and Hilde warned me not to do."

"Yes, but you'd never regret it."

"I don't know." She was moved and confused by his declaration. He was so handsome, with those hazel-brown eyes and that shock of curly black hair hanging down over his forehead, so intelligent, and sensitive, and overwhelming in every way she had ever imagined. If only she could be absolutely sure that this wasn't merely another play he was writing with her cast temporarily in the role of leading lady. He lifted her hand to his lips, turned it over, and kissed her palm with such passion that it left her breathless and shaken.

"I suppose I should warn you," he said softly, "that I don't know how to do this sort of thing slowly."

True to his promise, Joseph was not a slow man. Viola was never sure exactly how long it took him to change her mind about him, because once she let him touch her she began to lose all sense of proportion. Falling in love with him was like taking a sudden plunge off a sheer cliff. It left her breathless, confused, and excited. It was one of the most unsettling things that had ever happened to her, and she was alternately elated and frightened, wary and obsessed, never sure from one moment to the next whether she wanted to throw herself into his arms or pack up and leave Berlin altogether.

"You have the most amazing eyes," he said to her on that first night when he took her back to Bluebeard's. "They look like caves." They were standing outside her room in the hall saying good night.

"You certainly say some strange things." She laughed nervously, so conscious of the nearness of him that she felt slightly panicked.

"Dark caves." Joseph smiled ironically. "Caves a man could get lost in." He pulled her to him, put his hand under her chin and tilted her face toward his, and kissed her suddenly on the lips. Taken by surprise, she started to pull away but the kiss was so sweet that against her better judgment she lingered, intrigued, wondering what he would do next. What he did next was to keep kissing her, thoroughly and completely, pressing his mouth to hers until she was breathless and weak in the knees.

He drew back suddenly. "Good night," he said softly. "I'll pick you up tomorrow at six for another round of lung soup. Meanwhile, sweet dreams." And then he was gone, with his door closing behind him.

Good heavens, Viola thought as she staggered into her room. I feel as if I've just been run over by a freight train. She listened to him on the other side of the wall, taking off his shoes, climbing into bed, switching on the lamp. What was he doing over there? She suddenly realized that if she could hear him, he must be able to hear her. Sliding cautiously between the sheets, she lay there holding her breath, trying to put her thoughts in order, but they refused to be arranged in any sensible pattern.

Well, she thought, one thing is certain. I definitely *won't* have dinner with him tomorrow night. All of this is happening much too fast.

But when tomorrow came, her resolve had weakened.

"My mother died of tuberculosis when I was sixteen," Joseph informed her. "I have a passion for amateur ornithology. My father doesn't approve of the kind of life I'm leading. I play the guitar and sing German folk songs—off key, of course. I'm not much of an athlete myself, but I love to watch the six-day bicycle races. My favorite color is blue. I abhor politics, belong to no organized religion, and—"

"Why are you telling me all this?" Viola interrupted, tucking her hands into the sleeves of her coat to keep them warm. They had finished dinner hours ago, and now they were walking the streets, talking aimlessly, or rather Joseph had been talking and she had been listening.

"I'm following the five-hundred-thousand-word rule," he said soberly.

"Never heard of it."

"No? Well, a famous philosopher once wrote that before you begin a serious relationship with a woman you have to exchange at least five hundred thousand words before you get down to more essential matters." He grinned. "I think I have about two hundred thousand more to go. Care to hear about the job I once had feeding the python at the Berlin Zoo?"

She laughed. "You're the strangest man I ever met."

Joseph lifted his eyebrows. "I'll take that as a compliment and for revenge I'll tell you about—"

"Stop," she begged.

"Sorry," he said, "but the word *stop* isn't in my vocabulary." She had the impression that he wasn't joking.

When he brought her back to Bluebeard's that evening, he kissed her in the hall again, but this time he didn't stop there. Pushing open the door to her room, he guided her inside, still kissing her, and kicked the door shut behind them. Almost before she knew what was happening, he had set her down on her bed and was touching her breasts, slipping his hand inside the bodice of her brown wool dress. His palm was rough and warm, and she could feel her nipples harden under his touch. It was an amazing sensation and she felt drunk from it, dizzy, excited, as if she might jump out of her skin. He smelled of smoke and wine and wool and sweat, and his mouth tasted like honey and salt, and for a moment she wanted to close her eyes and let him do whatever he wished.

Joseph cupped her breasts in his hands. He ran his tongue around the insides of her lips. "A true actress feels passion," he murmured.

"What are you talking about?" She pulled away from him.

"A real actress can burn an audience to ashes." He leaned forward and kissed her again. "You don't understand this yet, but I'm going to teach you. Love is the best teacher any actor can have."

"You must be crazy," she said, not sure whether to be amused or offended. "How can you kiss me and make speeches at the same time?"

"I am crazy," he said, stroking her hair, "completely, totally crazy." He slipped his hand inside her dress again, and she was once again embarrassed by the fierceness of her own desire for him. She had never been so attracted to a man. It was like an addiction: the more she fought it, the stronger it got. She knew that this was the moment to ask him to stop, but when she opened her mouth all that came out was a small moan of pleasure.

"I'm not going to make love to you tonight," he said, slowly withdrawing his hand, "even though you're very lovely, because it's still too soon and if I do, you'll wake up thinking you've done something terrible, and I don't want that." He sat back and smiled at her. "Besides, I don't think it would make you trust me."

"I wouldn't let you make love to me," she said shakily.

"Oh no?"

"No."

He kissed her again and slipped his hand back into the top of her dress. "Are you sure about that?"

She wanted him to go on touching her, she wanted him to stop, she didn't know what she wanted. "Joseph, what are you doing?"

"Asking for an honest answer."

She began to laugh helplessly. "You're impossible."

"True," he admitted with disarming honesty, "but I have one great virtue."

"What's that?"

"You're probably not going to believe this, but I love you."

"You don't mean it. You told me less than two days ago that you didn't believe in love at first sight."

"Well, I was wrong." He stood up. "God, it's hard to leave you, but one of us has to have some sense. Will you have dinner with me again tomorrow night?"

"No." She shook her head. "This is all too fast, it's insane, imprudent, it's . . ."

"Overwhelming?" Joseph supplied.

She nodded. "You said it."

"Good." He smiled. "That means you'll have dinner with me. Trust me, I know the signs. I'll knock on your door around six." He paused. "Unless, of course, you decide to knock on the wall before that."

"Knock on what wall?"

"The wall that separates our rooms. Whenever you want me, any hour, day or night, all you have to do is knock." He laughed. "You have power, do you know that? Do you know what it means for a woman to have power over a man? No? Well you will, I promise you." And then he was gone, closing the door behind him.

Viola sat on her bed, staring at the closed door. What in the world was she doing? She must be having a nervous breakdown. And yet . . . she thought of Joseph's hands on her breasts and felt such a strong wave of desire that it made her tingle down to the tips of her toes.

The sensation alarmed her. Leaping off the bed, she dragged her suitcase out of the closet and began piling her clothes into it. This infatuation with Joseph Rothe was definitely getting out of hand. If she couldn't be sensible, well then she'd go back to Munich until she returned to her senses. If she called Conrad from the station, he'd wire her the money for a ticket.

And yet when she got her suitcase packed, she didn't have the heart to leave, so she started unpacking again. She put her dresses in the closet, lined her shoes up under them, arranged her underwear in her dresser drawers. What was she doing? She didn't know. She felt nothing at all like her ordinary self.

Climbing into her flannel nightgown, she lay down on her bed and folded her arms stubbornly across her chest. I must have drunk too much beer, she thought. I'll go to sleep and in the morning all of this will be clear. I'll be rational. I'll know exactly how I feel about him.

She closed her eyes but her mind skittered from one thought to another restlessly. Opening them again, she sat up and did a very silly thing: leaning over to the wall that separated her room from Joseph's, she gave the cold plaster a long, passionate kiss.

Sometime around three in the morning, she was awakened by the sound of Joseph's typewriter. She lay in the darkness, listening to the incessant clicking of the keys and the muffled ring of the carriage bell, wondering what he could be writing at such an hour.

At a little past eight a knock on the door startled her out of a deep sleep.

"Who's there?"

"It's me, Joseph."

Throwing on her robe, Viola staggered to the door and opened it. Joseph was standing in the hall, holding a sheaf of paper. There were dark circles under his eyes, his hair was mussed, and he was wearing the same shirt he had had on last night.

"Hello," she said, completely nonplussed by the sight of him. "You're certainly up early."

"Let me come in," he begged. "Something wonderful has just happened. A miracle." He waved the papers in the air and did a strange little dance on the hall rug. "A revelation from the gods, a gift from the muse." His eyes were bright with excitement and insomnia. "And I have you to thank for it."

"You really have gone crazy. Come in before the men in the white coats get you." She stepped aside and he entered with an explosion of masculine energy.

"You," he said, "are an inspiration. What do you think I did last night? I wrote, that's what I did." He paced from one side of her room to the other. "For months I've been blocked. I've been sitting in front of that typewriter, feeling all washed up, without an idea in my head, but last night it came to me, or rather *you* came to me, not you in the flesh—although I admit I would have enjoyed that—but your essence, your shadow-self, your *akashic* body, as the Hindus say."

"Joseph," she interrupted, sitting down on the edge of her bed. "It's eight A.M., I haven't had my coffee yet, and I have no idea what you're talking about."

"Of course you don't. No one does, because what I'm talking about is totally new. I just wrote it." He sat down beside her. "Here." He handed her the manuscript. "Look at this."

She inspected the pages with curiosity—a dozen or so, typed single-spaced. "It looks like a play."

"It's more than a play. It's you."

"You're making another of your German jokes, right?"

"No I'm not. This is your unconscious self captured right here on paper."

"My 'unconscious self'?" She tapped her foot impatiently. "What does that mean?"

"I'm sorry," Joseph said. "I know I'm going too fast. I forget that you don't know the jargon. Jeanne could probably do a better job of explaining this because I'm more interested in the practical applications of modern psychology than the theories, but let me make a stab at it." He stood up and walked across the room. "Your unconscious self is more or less that part of you that lives in your dreams, the part you forget when you wake up. Are you following me so far?"

Viola nodded, still dubious. "I think so."

"Good." Joseph frowned and looked thoughtful. "For reasons which I personally consider foolish, most playwrights down through the ages haven't considered that part of human beings a proper subject for the stage, but since the war that's changed—at least in Germany. But the change hasn't been easy. You might think of it as the difficult birth of a new way of looking at the world, and it's made for some nasty battles between writers, directors, and actors. At present there are more or less two camps—one that thinks that the theater should be realistic and another that thinks the theater should be the stuff of dreams."

"And which one are you?"

"A dreamer, definitely a dreamer."

She leaned forward, fascinated. "And why is that?"

"Because German reality stinks. Because in my opinion politics is a trap that will lead us into another war. Because the right wing and the left wing in this country are Siamese twins. Because things are such a mess that the redemption of the individual is the only hope I have left." He suddenly broke into a smile. "Just listen to me. I sound like a manifesto. I didn't come over here to lecture you. I came over here to ask to you to read for me." He sat down and pointed to the first page of the manuscript. "Start here."

"You can't be serious."

"You want to act, don't you?"

"More than anything."

"Well, I wrote this for you and about you, so read it."

She stared at him, hoping that she'd understood him correctly, but afraid that perhaps she hadn't. "Joseph, let me get this straight. Is this an audition?"

"No"—he shook his head—"because you don't need an audition. The truth is, you already have the part. That is if you want it."

"You're joking."

"No, I mean it."

She gripped the manuscript so hard that her knuckles turned white. "Are you telling me that you're actually going to let me act in one of your plays?"

"I'm not going to *let* you, I'm going to *beg* you. Of course just because I've written this thing doesn't mean it will ever get produced, but I have a pretty good track record along those lines, and if I can scare up enough cash to stage it, I want you in the lead."

"Why me?"

"If you had any idea how spectacular you are, you wouldn't even bother to ask that question. And I don't mean simply beautiful. You are beautiful, of course, but this isn't merely some shoddy seduction technique on my part. I have an exceptionally good eye for spotting talent in actresses. In fact, I'm somewhat famous for it."

"And you see talent in me?"

"Absolutely. I realize that I haven't actually seen you onstage yet, but quite frankly you strike me as a human explosion waiting to happen. I predict that you are going to be capable of moving audiences. In five years, maybe less, you're going to be famous. In fact, with a little luck, we're both going to be famous. Now read."

She picked up the pages with unsteady hands and gazed at the lines, so excited about the prospect of actually appearing on a stage again that she could barely make out the words. She read them and reread them, but they didn't make much sense to her. There was a character called The Girl who kept uttering lines like *a flight of birds touches the vanilla of my palms oh jasmine come the blue air bend of ecstatic falling mighty aristotle on your gray wings,* and so on with no punctuation. Sadly disappointed, she handed the play back to Joseph, wondering once again if he were quite sane.

"I'm afraid I don't have the training for this," she said bluntly. "And besides, it's garbage. There's no logic to it."

"I'm not surprised. In fact, I expected you'd react that way, but that's easily fixed." He put his hand gently over her eyes. "Close your eyes," he commanded.

"Close my what?"

"Close your eyes. I'm going to show you how to do this."

"Right now, before breakfast?"

"Right now, this afternoon, tonight, for months if it takes months." He took both of her hands in his. "There's no one but you who I'd let touch this part, and you can do it, I promise you. I know it must seem strange to you, but trust me. Now close your eyes."

Feeling suspicious, she closed her eyes. The touch of his hands sent a shiver up her spine.

"What do you see?"

"Nothing except the insides of my eyelids. What am I supposed to see?"

"I'm going to take you on an imaginary journey. All you have to do is relax."

"Being told to relax always makes me tense."

He chuckled. "I know what you mean, but give it a try. Imagine you're going down a long, dim flight of stone steps. On either side of the steps there is a row of torches."

She opened her eyes. "Are you trying to hypnotize me?"

"No, no, nothing of the sort."

"Where did you pick up this technique?"

"I made it up from all sorts of things—yoga, Tibetan Buddhism, mesmerism, Freud, Jung, Rimbaud, Quevedo, Gurdjieff, St. John of the Cross."

"I've never heard of any of those people except Freud."

"I'll lend you some of their books. Now close your eyes and relax. See those stairs and at the bottom see a dock and a boat floating on an underground river."

She closed her eyes. "What kind of boat? Be specific. A freighter? A tanker?"

"A gondola, padded with black velvet. Don't be so literal, just imagine yourself climbing in. Take a deep breath, now another. The boat begins to rock you. It begins to float down the river."

Viola tried to imagine the gondola and succeeded. There was something particularly lulling about the image. She imagined herself stretching out on the black velvet cushions, trailing her fingers in the warm water.

"How do you feel?"

"Not bad."

"Where are you?"

"Far away." Something strange was happening. She had a sense of casting loose from her physical body. Her mind seemed to flow into its own thoughts, gracefully and easily. The imaginary boat floated on through the darkness, and she floated with it.

"Now I'm going to say the lines from my play and I want you to repeat them after me."

"Why not?" She felt strangely amiable and dreamy. This was certainly a relaxing method of acting.

"A flight of birds touches the vanilla of my palms oh jasmine . . ."

"A flight of birds . . ." she repeated. She was surprised to hear her voice tremble with passion. *"Oh jasmine come the blue air bend of ecstatic falling . . ."* The words meant nothing—or at least nothing in the ordinary way—but as she said them she was seized with an irrational desire to weep. Suddenly she understood what Joseph was doing. He was training her to do what Bernhardt had done: move an audience to tears by reading anything, even the phone book. She hadn't known until this second that that kind of performance could be learned.

Opening her eyes, she jumped to her feet, scattering the pages on the floor. "I understand!" she yelled happily, throwing her arms around his neck. "You're a genius! Thank you, thank you." Without thinking, she gave him a kiss full on the lips.

He caught her around the waist and pulled her close. "You're going to be a wonderful actress."

"Like Bernhardt?"

"Better than Bernhardt. I knew it from the first moment I laid eyes on you." He kissed her again and again, until she was breathless. "I never doubted your talent, not even for a second."

"Will you teach me more?"

"Everything I know."

She closed her eyes and shuddered with pleasure that came from two things—from his touch and from a sense of her own power as an actress. The future, which had seemed so dreary only a few days ago, suddenly seemed to open up in front of her. She imagined herself acting in his plays; she imagined herself in his arms.

"Kiss me again," she demanded. She felt reckless and happy and intoxicated.

"Liebling," he said, "I'll kiss you for the rest of your life if you'll let me." He embraced her and lay her back gently on the bed. This was the edge of the cliff they had been dancing on for the past two days, the place she had wanted to be and was afraid to be, both at the same time. Joseph moved his tongue slowly over one corner of her mouth. His lips were strong and forceful and she could feel his whole body poised behind them, dark with desire and tense as a bow. The kiss went on and on, like a piece of music, full of such variations and surprises that she felt moved, stunned, and amazed.

Leaning back, he cradled her face in his hands. His eyes were so gentle, the browns in them as soft as smoke. She could never remember having been looked at before with such gentleness. "I want to do more than kiss you. Do you want me?"

"Yes," she said eagerly. "I do."

"I won't ever hurt you, I promise." His voice was husky and quick. "I'm supposed to be a writer, but I'm out of words." He kissed her again. "Do you trust me?" he asked, and there was such love and concern in his voice. "Do you trust me, *Liebling?"*

"I trust you, Joseph." Her mind was in a whirl and she felt an ecstasy of excitement.

Joseph held her for a moment, cradling her like a child. He kissed her eyes and her neck, and then he carefully reached behind her and began to unbutton her nightgown. She shrank back, suddenly shy, and he paused, but she didn't want to stop him anymore, and she knew this suddenly with perfect clarity. It was like a revelation to know how completely she desired him, like a piece of music played inside her brain, and her spine arched to the tune of it, and she turned toward him, pulling him closer, as if she were casting herself into a deep pool.

Joseph kissed her again and again until she couldn't think, or move, or resist. One button, then another, then her robe and nightgown cast aside on the floor, and him undressing himself, kissing her all the while, the thoughts floating through her mind, the fear and nervousness disappearing with each kiss, until she didn't know or care anymore what he was doing, but only wanted the kissing to go on and never stop.

She felt him lift her in his arms, and she closed her eyes, and then the cool sheets were on her back and he was on top of her, still kissing her, warm and quick and strong, and his skin felt better than anything she had ever felt in her life. He bent forward and brushed the tips of her nipples with his tongue and she felt a surge of happiness. "How sweet," she murmured. She was astounded to discover that she could lie in front of him naked and not feel any shame.

"My love," he said. "How very beautiful you are." He ran his hands over her hips and thighs and breasts. "All curves and circles, all grace."

She touched the hair on his chest, the muscles in his arms, she felt the strength and power of him. So this is what men are like, she thought with amazement: thick-boned, slim-hipped, heavy, strong instead of subtle.

With exquisite slowness, Joseph drifted down her body, kissing each rib, kissing her navel, and her stomach and the inside of her thighs, kissing the turn of her ankle and the bend of her foot, glorying in every inch of her. His tenderness gathered around her like a warm cape. She closed her eyes; she rose and fell with him. She moved toward him and with him, saying his name over and over again.

And then she lost herself, and was obliterated; and he lost himself and was obliterated. And together they disappeared into that dark void that lies at the root of passion.

On the stage of Eric Stern's great Kallmann Theater the sack of Troy was being reenacted, complete with burning buildings, butchery, and mass panic. Greek invaders in golden helmets fought savagely against the defending Trojans. Women stood on top of the thirty-foot walls throwing papier-mâché beams down on the attackers and screaming curses. Five real riderless horses reared and stampeded, children wailed, the audience applauded, and Viola was having the best time she'd had in years.

She was only a Trojan slave girl, without any important lines, only one of twenty, but she was as happy as if she'd been asked to play Helen. Throwing back her head, she took a deep breath of the artificial smoke. Just to stand on a stage again was intoxicating.

Glaring at the great wooden horse, she yelled enthusiastically at the Greeks, and silently thanked Bernhardt. After nearly seven months without word, the letter of recommendation had finally arrived. Sarah Bernhardt had recommended Viola Kessler to Eric Stern in the strongest possible terms.

Stern had called her the next day and gruffly offered her this part. It was nothing, only a walk-on—or to be more exact, a scream-on— but it was a beginning. She was getting paid, she was eating regularly, she was acting for the first time in nearly nine years.

And she was in love.

My God, was she in love.

Never mind the inflation and the threat of war; never mind that the mark now stood at an incredible 1.3 billion to the dollar; never mind that the German economy was collapsing around her like the fake walls of Troy. She saw everything in Berlin in gold this summer: the water in the Spree, the iron arches of the Friedrichstrasse Railroad Station, the dome of the Reichstag, the faces of total strangers in the Cafe Schiller. Everything glowed like the separate petals of one immense sunflower, the center of which was Joseph Rothe.

Stern could rage at her all he wanted, she didn't care.

"Athena curse you!" she yelled at the actors who were playing the Greeks. Not a great line, and it was all she could do to keep from laughing as she said it. She shook her fist, and managed to look

appropriately grim, but it wasn't easy. It helped to know that better parts lay ahead of her. Joseph was finishing up his play, looking for a producer. She might be a slave girl now, but in a few months she'd be doing some real acting.

"Athena strike you blind, you Greek dogs!" The walls of Troy were falling into carefully orchestrated rubble. The war was almost over.

Sometimes she felt so happy it was almost shameful.

6

BERLIN
1923

In the Alexanderplatz the matronly two-ton statue of Berolina pointed a dimpled copper arm at the Niebuhr Hotel—a seven-story structure of brick and marble, adorned with so many coats of arms, turrets, cornices, nonfunctional balconies, miniature Corinthian columns, canopies, and other baubles that the avant-garde architect Walter Gropius regularly brought his students here to impress on them how truly terrible German architecture could be. This particular morning, however, there were no architectural students on the sidewalk outside the Niebuhr, no one much to speak of in the whole Alexanderplatz for that matter—which was unusual, to say the least, on a busy Saturday afternoon only seven weeks before Christmas when ordinarily the stores would have been seething with shoppers.

There were no shoppers because there was nothing to buy, and even if there had been anything to buy, there was nothing to buy it with. The mark as of ten minutes ago had been selling at 630 billion to the dollar. This morning at 10:00 A.M. a loaf of bread had cost 32 billion marks, a liter of milk 25 billion, a pound of meat somewhere between 40 and 50 billion. Add to this a sudden cold snap, rumors of riots and pogroms that had been circulating for over a week, the recent arming of the police with machine guns, and the simple fact that simply to travel from one streetcar zone to another took more money than most people could comfortably carry, and the emptiness of the Alexanderplatz suddenly made sense.

For a long breathless moment the only human figure in the square was Berolina, standing on her granite pedestal, and then suddenly a streetcar clanged up past Loeser & Wolf's tobacco shop and discharged four men and three women. Two of the men were carrying heavy burlap sacks slung over their shoulders, one of the women was in white, crowned with a coronet of red and gold chrysanthemums. Laughing and talking, the seven people wandered toward the Niebuhr Hotel. Halfway there, just opposite Berolina's pedestal, one of the men paused, knelt down, opened a battered violin case, pulled out an instrument, and began to serenade the woman in white, who blushed and laughed, removing the last doubt that this was indeed a wedding party.

"Play some dance music," Viola begged. She threw back her head and laughed again, and her hair tumbled down her shoulders, raining pins onto the cobblestones. Her white dress, borrowed from Jeanne for the occasion, fluttered in the wind as she stood on the sidewalk, ignoring the cold, feeling buoyed up on the breeze, as if with just a little more effort she could have left the ground entirely and floated up over the newspaper kiosk to shake Berolina's outstretched hand. She was so happy, happier perhaps than she had ever been in her life, intoxicated with love and with the utter folly of getting married. She danced a few steps to the tune of Richard's violin and then stopped, laughing and out of breath. Her body was awkward, five months heavy with child, but the sense of lightness persisted.

"*Love me little, love me long,*" Richard sang, gleefully bowing out the notes of the old English tune, " '*tis the burden of my song. Love that is too hot and strong fadeth soon to waste.*"

"Not this love, Richard," Joseph protested. "This love is as hot and strong as they come, and it isn't showing any signs of fading. In fact"—he patted Viola's round stomach proudly—"it's more or less on the increase, wouldn't you say?"

"Joseph!" Viola protested.

"My dear Frau Rothe." Joseph caught Viola by the waist and gave her a kiss—not a formal kiss but a good hearty one that set Hilde and Jeanne to applauding.

Richard launched into another wedding song. The violin quivered in his hands and the music was sweet and lively. Hilde and Jeanne joined hands and began to dance sideways down the street, and Hermann and Friedrich danced after them, pirouetting clumsily under the great heavy bags of money they had lugged all the way from Bluebeard's. The money was for beer to celebrate Viola and Joseph's marriage—performed not more than a quarter of an hour ago in the rectory of a nearby church by a dour Lutheran minister who had taken one look at Viola's protruding belly, cleared his throat disapprovingly, and run through the ceremony so fast that Hilde, at least, claimed he had left out the line about "love, honor, and obey"—which as far as Hilde could see put Viola in an excellent position to do whatever she wanted to with Joseph for the rest of her life.

At the front steps of the Niebuhr Hotel they stopped, laughing and out of breath.

"Speech, speech," Hilde said. "Someone make a speech."

Hermann and Friedrich lowered the money bags to the pavement. "I think we should just go inside and buy some beer," Friedrich said, "go inside, get drunk, and try to forget that our friends here have just gotten married at one of the worst possible times in recent German history, get drunk while we still have enough money to do it. If we stand here another twenty minutes, these marks"—he pointed to the two huge bags—"won't even buy three rounds."

"Speech first," Hilde said, not to be turned aside. "This is an important moment and I think it should be immortalized."

"You win," Hermann said. "I'll make the speech. Let me see." Hermann cleared his throat and looked at Viola and Joseph with a beaming acceptance. "How to begin? Well, first of all let me say that we all know that you two truly love each other because—"

"Because," Hilde interrupted with a grin, "the walls in Bluebeard's are ever so thin. I'm surprised you never knocked down the one between your rooms, actually. A year of walking back and forth— Herr Meckel may have to charge you for extra wear on the carpet."

"Hilde, please," Hermann protested, "let's keep this on an elevated level. Now where was I? Oh yes, we know that you both truly love each other and we wish you the greatest happiness. Frau Rothe is— as we all are aware—a famous actress."

"Famous?" Viola protested gaily. "I'd hardly say famous. Eric Stern gives me five roles in a year and a half, all of them walk-ons or bit parts with maybe six lines—a slave girl in *The Fall of Troy*, a part in the chorus in *Oedipus Rex*, a woman-crushed-in-the-crowd in *Julius Caesar*, one of Job's daughters—and then Joseph here drags me from one cabaret to another to chant about inner illuminations or sends me out on the Kurfürstendamm to play Freud's first patient."

"Which you did to perfection," Joseph said encouragingly.

"For which," she continued, "we earned maybe a dollar and sixty-five cents, American. Famous? Let's be realistic, Hermann. My name isn't exactly on the lips of everyone in Berlin."

"It will be." Hermann nodded sagely. "You're on the brink of international fame, believe me. And so is Joseph."

Joseph snorted.

"So," Hermann continued, "I propose a toast to you both—eternal love, eternal happiness, great artistic collaborations, and the sense to know when to play for the balcony and when to keep your mouths shut."

"Hear, hear," Jeanne, Richard, Friedrich, and Hilde cheered furiously.

"And now," Hermann said with a dramatic flourish, "on to the next item of business—the wedding present." He extracted a long white envelope from the pocket of his jacket and handed it to Joseph. "From the five of us to the two of you."

Joseph opened the envelope and stood for a moment, staring at the contents, a look of disbelief slowly spreading over his face. Reaching inside, he took out two blue pasteboard train tickets and handed them wordlessly to Viola. At the top of the tickets were stamped the words BERLIN-MUNICH-BERLIN.

"My God"—Viola turned the tickets over and then back again as if she were afraid they might melt in her hands—"these are first-class tickets. They must have cost a fortune." She looked at her friends, so touched by the gift that she was suddenly at a loss for words. She had wanted Conrad to be at her wedding so much; his absence had been the only cloud on the day, and now she would get a chance to visit him in Munich and introduce him to Joseph. "Thank you," she managed to say at last.

"Look"—Joseph cleared his throat—"I know this isn't exactly a diplomatic question to ask when receiving a wedding gift, but where the hell did you people get the money for all this? The last I heard the lot of you were living on potatoes and Meckel's ersatz coffee." He faltered uncomfortably. "I guess what I'm trying to say is that—"

"Don't give it another thought," Hermann interrupted. "The fact is, we took up a collection. My own small contribution, for instance, came from vampires."

"Vampires?"

"From the money I finally got from working on *Nosferatu*—Murnau's vampire film. A year ago it would have amounted to maybe five hundred dollars, American, but by the time it reached me I calculate that it paid for about twenty-five kilometers of your honeymoon."

"Actually," Jeanne observed, "the truth is, we all put in something but Richard came up with most of the cash."

"Please." Richard made a modest gesture of dismissal.

"Richard claims he sold one of his atonal compositions," Hermann said, "but none of us believe him."

"Actually"—Hilde grinned—"we suspect he robbed a bank."

"Or has his own printing press," Jeanne added.

"Or that his money tree came into bloom," Friedrich observed, hoisting the burlap sack back on his shoulder.

"All we know for sure," Hermann continued, waving Joseph and Viola toward the canopied entrance of the Niebuhr Hotel, "is that Richard here absolutely insisted that you both go first-class."

Conrad leaned down from the top of a pile of lumber that was part of the unfinished Deutsches Museum of Science and Technology— the pride of Munich, located on Kolen Island in the middle of the Isar River. "Come on up here, Vi," Conrad urged.

Viola shaded her eyes with her hand and peered up at her brother, admiring him from all angles. During the years he had spent with Uncle Otto in Munich, Conrad had changed from a stocky American boy into a slender, rather handsome German. His dark brown hair was clipped stylishly short, he had lost weight, and he was dressed in a brown suit and fur-collared overcoat that gave him the air of a Bavarian count out for a winter holiday. Uncle Otto's brewery was obviously prospering despite the inflation, and although she had no plans to ask Conrad for money, it was comforting to know that if she and Joseph needed help after the baby was born, help would be there.

"Up you go," Conrad said cheerfully. Viola grabbed his hand and climbed carefully up the pile of boards, balancing the new weight of her stomach in front of her as if it were a tray of delicate pastries. At the top she stood for a moment looking at the construction site—the beams and concrete, bricks and empty window frames, rolls of electrical wiring, bags of plaster—that would someday be the new museum. Several hundred yards away she could see the Isar swirling deliriously around the far edge of the island against a backdrop of November sky so blue and intense that it looked like a huge silk bedspread.

She examined the buildings on the opposite bank, trying to pick out the Schauspielhaus, a commercial theater where Joseph was at this very moment meeting with two wealthy backers who just might be convinced to stage his latest play. She smiled, amused at herself. Joseph, always Joseph, running through her mind like the words to a song she couldn't stop singing. You'd think that after having practically lived with him for the last year, she wouldn't be acting like a new bride, but she was and there was nothing she could do about it. She thought of him this morning, getting up from the big four-poster rosewood bed in Uncle Otto's guest room, his hair messed from sleep, pulling on his clothes in a hurry the way he always did, and a rush of love ran through her, so strong that it almost made her dizzy. Someday, she supposed, she and Joseph would settle down and become bored with each other the way married people always seemed to, but for now . . .

"Thomas Mann," Conrad was saying, "lives over there, and those two domes belong to the Frauenkirche, and . . ."

"Never mind the scenery," Angela yelled up from down below, cupping her hands to her mouth, "show her where the . . . is going to be."

"The what?" Conrad yelled back.

"The . . . sics lab."

"The physics lab?"

Angela nodded vigorously. She was a stocky Bavarian girl with large features who wore her brown hair pulled back in a tight coronet of braids. From the heights of the lumber pile, Viola stared down at her, thinking how deceptive Angela's simple appearance was. When Conrad had first introduced her to Viola at the train station, Viola had taken one look at Angela's bulky gray coat, sensible shoes, and rather bedraggled hat and decided she must be another in the endless line of German middle-class girls reduced to poverty by the inflation. Nothing could have been further from the truth. Angela was actually exceptionally well-off. Her father, Conrad had proudly informed Viola, was none other than Gottfried Wolter, owner of the largest construction firm in Munich, the same firm that was building the Deutsches Museum. According to Conrad, Angela was something of an eccentric: determined, blunt, absolutely indifferent to her appearance and mordantly intelligent.

"And over there," Angela called up to them, "Papa's building the aviation exhibit." Viola examined the blank, muddy space, trying to imagine what it would look like filled with planes, and wings, and motors.

Conrad beamed proudly. "What a memory that girl has."

"Photographic," Viola agreed.

Conrad smiled again, his gray-blue eyes radiating a prosperity and happiness that was so rare these days that it flapped around him like a colored flag. He took Viola's arm carefully, and turned her toward the opposite bank of the Isar. "Now if you look right between those two buildings, you can see part of Uncle Otto's brewery."

"Where?"

"There, between those two buildings, the big yellow monstrosity with the two turrets."

"I thought that was a castle."

"Uncle Otto has feudal aspirations." They both laughed.

"He must be raking in money," she said, leaning forward to get a better view.

"The brewery's thriving," Conrad agreed with a touch of something uneasy in his voice. "Taking in trillions, actually. Just last week Uncle Otto set aside a whole room on the ground floor just for counting and bailing money. Everyone in Munich needs beer these days. It's the politics, you know. Beer and politics"—Conrad gestured expansively—"are an old Munich tradition. Ever since the French invaded the Ruhr in January, we've been having politics like we haven't had politics for years and the beer halls are buzzing. Over there"—he pointed across the Isar—"in the Octoberfest, the Socialists are drinking dark beer and plotting to overthrow the Nationalists; in the Löwenbräukeller the Nationalists—a nasty lot—are drinking lager and plotting to overthrow the Socialists, the Jews, and the whole Weimar Republic."

"Sounds like a mess."

"Oh it is," Conrad agreed soberly. "Speeches, marches, posters plastered up all over the place faster than the police can rip them down. Everyone knows it's just a matter of time before something snaps and we have the 1918 revolution all over again."

"And all these plotters drink beer?"

"Every mother's son of them—by the keg."

"So Uncle Otto's prospering, then?" Viola shifted her weight uneasily and took another look at the brewery, the glint of its yellow turrets, the chilly sheen of its windows.

"Cleaning up, making a fortune." Conrad bit his lower lip the way he always did when he was uncomfortable with something. There was a long silence between them.

"How do you feel about it, Con?" Viola said at last.

"About what?"

"About making so much money off of . . ." She paused, not wanting to hurt his feelings yet knowing that it had to be said. "How do you feel about making so much money off of so much misery?" There was another long pause, so long that she wondered if she'd offended him.

"Not so good, to tell the truth," he said at last. He looked at her as if grateful for an opportunity finally to say what was really on his mind. "Oh the brewery keeps us all afloat and it's saved us from the worst effects of the inflation, I can't deny that, but there's something crazy about what's happening here. Uncle Otto ignores the crazy part, of course. He goes to the brewery every morning at the same hour like clockwork. He treats the world around him like it was that giant glockenspiel in the Marienplatz—wound up, full of precision gears, and guaranteed to go on forever. But I don't think things *are* going to go on this way much longer. I think sometimes I should get Angela out of here, marry her, and take her to the States before something really terrible happens. The problem is, of course, that she'd never leave her father. She adores him."

So Conrad intended to marry Angela—not a surprise really, but how like him to announce it in such an offhanded way. Viola felt a smile spreading over her face. She wanted to hug Conrad, kiss him, jump up and down on the lumber pile. So what if the beer halls of Munich were filled with plotters and there were reports of riots in Berlin? Happiness for Conrad filled her, healing everything else, making the real troubles of the world seem distant and unimportant. She reached out impulsively, put her arms around her brother, and gave him a hug. "I wish you both joy, Con. I wish for you and Angela"—she tried to think of the very best thing she could wish for her brother at this point in his life—"I wish for you the kind of love Joseph and I have."

Wednesday dawned cold and gray, with a spitting of sleet mixed with rain and a sense that something was wrong. When Conrad returned from the brewery for dinner at Uncle Otto's apartment on the Widenmayer Strasse that evening, he reported that there were strange things going on in the city.

"The Nazis are marching everywhere." Conrad helped himself to the sauerbraten, and then paused, fork in midair, a worried expression on his face. "I just saw about a hundred of Herr Hitler's Stosstrupp assembling over by the Torbräu tavern."

"They're always assembling," Uncle Otto observed disinterestedly through a mouthful of potatoes, "it's just more comic opera." Uncle Otto was a tall, dignified, handsome man in his late fifties who had been lamed in his youth on a vacation to Austria when he had tried (and almost managed) to outski an avalanche. Viola often imagined that—except for a crooked right leg—he looked as Papa might have looked if he had lived to a healthy half a century. Sometimes when she was with her uncle she experienced a pang of loneliness, and she had wondered more than once how Uncle Otto felt about his wild younger brother, Dietrich, the black sheep of the family who had played the violin and sung so beautifully. Someday, she promised herself, she'd get up the courage to ask him about the days when he and Papa had been boys.

"Hitler," Conrad was saying, "shouldn't be underestimated."

Viola realized that she'd lost track of the conversation. "Who's Hitler?" she asked. The name had a faintly familiar ring to it, but since she rarely read anything but theater reviews, she couldn't place it. News in Germany was so depressing that she had gotten into the habit over the last few years of avoiding it as much as possible.

"Hitler's some kind of Bavarian patriot, I think," Joseph offered. "A troublemaker, wants secession of Bavaria from the Weimar Republic or something of the sort."

"A fool, but more or less harmless," Uncle Otto observed, taking a sip of water. Uncle Otto made beer by the vat, but he never drank it except in the line of duty. "A tiny little Austrian with a mustache who runs around in a trench coat snapping a rhinoceros-hide whip and trying to stir up trouble, but he's so vulgar he can't get anyone to take him seriously."

"Well, Uncle Otto," Conrad said, "excuse me for differing, but it seems to me a lot of people are taking him all too seriously these days. That Stosstrupp of his is full of all sorts of thugs just waiting for a chance to smash some heads."

"What's the Stosstrupp?" Joseph asked, leaning forward and putting his elbows on the table. Uncle Otto took a bite of sauerbraten and chewed it methodically.

"It's a private army of sorts," he said, swallowing, "only without guns. The chorus of the comic opera, that's what the Stosstrupp is. They even wear costumes—gray tunics, black belts, swastikas, and nasty little death-head symbols on their ski caps. Every time I see one of them, I expect to hear an aria."

Joseph and Viola laughed, but Conrad didn't. "Angela thinks they're dangerous," Conrad said, "and so do I. With all respect, Uncle Otto, you take this Hitler fellow too lightly."

"Nonsense," Uncle Otto laughed, "he's a petty demagogue, like one of those snake-oil salesmen I've read about in your American author, Mark Twain." He nodded kindly at Viola. "Snake oil to cure all the ills of Germany. Who but a fool would buy it?"

Viola sat up in bed, turned on the light, and looked around the guest room apprehensively. "Joseph," she complained, "I just had a terrible nightmare." Her heart was beating wildly and the palms of her hands were clammy with sweat. In front of her, the rosewood posts of the bed gleamed reassuringly, and the big family Bible on the dresser cast a neat black shadow against the blue-flowered wallpaper. She smelled the peaceful odors of furniture polish and cut flowers. Everything was orderly and quiet. Taking a deep breath, she tried to convince herself that what she had just experienced had only been a dream, but the fear was raw and hard to put away.

"What kind of nightmare?" Joseph asked, peering up at her sleepily from a tangle of sheets and blankets.

She frowned, searching her memory for some clue, but there was only a blank space where the dream had been. "I don't know." She smiled sheepishly, feeling silly. "I can't remember. It was something about fire, I think."

"What about fire?"

"I'm not sure."

Joseph struggled to an upright position and pushed his hair out of his eyes. "Ah"—he grinned—"I knew it."

"Knew what?"

"You're having an attack of nighttime restlessness and you're about to ask me to go out for ice cream and pickles. I've been expecting this for weeks."

"I don't want pickles."

"Sauerkraut?"

"You're not taking me seriously!"

"*Liebchen*, I am taking you seriously." He put an arm around her and began to massage the back of her neck. "Suppose you tell me what's wrong."

She tried to smile. "I know it sounds foolish, but that conversation we had with Conrad and Uncle Otto at dinner this evening must have upset me, because I woke up with the feeling that something dreadful is going to happen."

"Like what, for instance?"

"War, revolutions, earthquakes"—she laughed uneasily—"mad dogs, tornadoes, volcanic eruptions." She shook her head. "I'm being pregnant, aren't I?"

"Very," Joseph said gently. "But there's a cure."

"What is it?"

"The same as the cause." He bent over and kissed her lightly on the shoulder. "That is if you're in the mood." He followed the curve of her neck with his lips.

"Mmm." She closed her eyes. "That feels good."

"Love is the world's best sleeping pill." He began to unbutton her nightgown. "In India there are famous sages who boil roots into a potion that brings nirvana. *Soma* they call it, but what do they know? Nothing."

"Nothing," she agreed, slipping back into his arms.

"Passion brings tranquility. That's why it was invented." He licked her earlobe. "Your skin tastes good—like honey; no, like ginger; no, make that well-aged sherry. It's a taste that puts life in order."

She laughed and opened her eyes. "You pick the oddest times to lecture on universal truths."

"Philosophy should only be discussed in bed." He kissed her lightly on the lips. "Don't you agree? What man could take Kierkegaard's concept of dread seriously in the presence of your breasts? If Nietzsche had been given a glimpse of your thighs, do you think he'd have wasted his time dreaming up a Universal Will to Power?"

She smiled at him, comforted and amused. She felt smoothed, and coddled, and loved, and precious. It was miraculous how Joseph's touch could make her anxiety disappear. Languidly, she let him undress her. Joseph pulled back the covers and examined her admiringly. Her breasts were firm and brown-nippled; her belly a smooth, tight globe.

"The more pregnant you get, the more beautiful you look."

"Really?" she murmured.

"Really. Like one of those fertility statues from the Stone Age. Come here, my lovely Frau Rothe." He pulled her toward him and kissed her and then moved behind her. For a few moments he lay there, rubbing her back with strong, sure hands, finding every tight muscle, tracing her spine, kneading her like bread. She relaxed and then she grew tense with a new, sweet tension. Her nipples tingled and she felt desire for him, not the swift, sharp desire she had felt before her pregnancy, but something vast and fertile.

"I love you," he whispered. Carefully he slipped between her legs, and covered her back with his body. "Close your eyes. Float away. Let me take you where there aren't any bad dreams."

She closed her eyes, remembering the boat he had once told her to imagine, the black boat with the black velvet cushions. He was that boat, she thought dreamily, and she was rocking in him, floating down a dark river.

Reaching over the globe of her belly, he touched her lightly, feathering her with his fingers, coaxing her to orgasm. She held back as long as she could, enjoying the sensation of being poised on the edge of such sweet pleasure. Clenching her fists and closing her eyes, she moaned Joseph's name. The invisible river she was floating down grew swifter: there were rapids, sudden plunges, irresistible currents, and then her body coiled, and arched, and warm waves of release washed over her, and she had no worries anymore, no anxieties, only deep sleep with the warm rhythm of her husband's breath gently rising and falling against the back of her neck.

She woke up Thursday morning cheerful and optimistic, but as the morning progressed the sense of impending disaster began to build again. This time she kept it to herself, but the more she tried to ignore it, the worse it got. Restlessly she finished her breakfast, restlessly she went through the motions of getting dressed to go out. By noon she had begun to feel as if an invisible, gray tension were bleeding out of the very stones of the city, flooding the Marienplatz, coating the curbs and lampposts outside the city hall, transforming the double domes of the Frauenkirche into two deflated balloons. It was her imagination, of course; she knew that, but she couldn't shake the uneasy feeling that something terrible was about to happen.

Actually, when she looked around the city objectively, she had to admit to herself that there was nothing particularly out of the ordinary—at least nothing she hadn't already seen in Berlin a hundred times. True, every blank wall in Munich seemed to have been covered with giant posters—half announcing a speech that evening to be given by Bavarian Prime Minister Kahr in one of the city's largest beer halls, and the other half touting a similar event in another (even larger) beer hall on the Stiglmaierplatz, where the Nazis were proudly proclaiming that "our Führer Adolf Hitler will say a few words to us," but there were no signs of the private armies of thugs that Conrad had claimed to have seen in the streets, and the blue-uniformed policemen were smiling and directing traffic as usual, as if the only danger in the offing was that some rich Munich businessman might exceed the speed limit.

There were a hundred other things to do in Munich that Thursday besides worry about politics. Joseph had appointments with several producers, Conrad wanted to give Viola a tour of the brewery, and Angela had arranged a farewell lunch. In the evening *Fidelio* was being given at the National Theater, there was a light comedy on at the Schauspielhaus, two chamber music concerts were scheduled, and Brecht's *Drums in the Night* was still playing to full houses. After making return reservations on the train to Berlin for the following day at two, Viola and Joseph counted up their marks and wavered between Brecht's play (which they had both already seen) and the comedy—a brilliant little piece called *Tennis Anyone?* The comedy won and they went to it that evening, walking through the quiet streets of Munich to the old Schwan Theater. During the play Viola began to feel silly that she could have been so worried, so silly, in fact, that after the performance, when Joseph met some old friends, she told him to go off and have a drink with them.

"I'll take a cab back to Uncle Otto's," she insisted as they stood on the steps of the playhouse. "I'm tired, but there's no use for you to go home so early."

"I don't know if that's such a good idea." Joseph examined her with tender concern.

"It's only a fifteen-minute drive."

One of Joseph's friends—a tall fellow with a small mustache—slapped him on the back. "Give in to her, Rothe. If my wife offered to take herself off and let me go out on the town with my buddies, I'd leap at the chance."

"I'll be fine," Viola insisted. "Really."

Joseph's other friend examined Viola admiringly. He was a lean would-be playwright who wore a black beret. "Quite a woman you have there," he told Joseph. "Most independent."

"Well," Joseph hesitated. A cab pulled up to the curb, and Viola got in, settling the matter.

"I'll see you later," she said, waving to Joseph.

Joseph leaned in the window and kissed her. "You're looking at a man who's going to miss you," he said.

"It's only for a few hours."

"I'm your Siamese twin"—he grinned—"connected at the heart."

"You're a very sentimental fellow, did you know that?" She smiled back, pleased.

"All writers are sentimental, sickeningly so. It's an occupational hazard. Besides, this is our honeymoon. I'm supposed to be acting like a fool about you." He kissed her again.

"Where to?" the driver asked impatiently.

"Fifty-six Widenmayer Strasse." Viola laughed.

"He's jealous," Joseph whispered. "Every man who sees me kiss you is racked with jealousy. I'll be back early."

"Come home anytime you want. I'll be asleep."

"It's disconcerting to have you be so trusting," Joseph whispered, "and even more disconcerting to know that you have every reason. Where is the Joseph Rothe who used to cut a swath through the ladies? Tamed, utterly domesticated."

He kissed her again and waved to the driver to pull away from the curb. Everything looked perfectly normal; there was no way that either of them could have known that while they were watching the play the world as they knew it had changed profoundly.

An hour earlier convoys of heavy trailer-trucks had braked to a halt outside the arched gate of the Bürgerbräukeller, disgorging hundreds of uniformed members of the Stosstrupp Hitler. Armed with machine guns and bayoneted rifles, the troopers charged into the garden of the beer hall where Bavarian Prime Minister Kahr was speaking.

In the vestibule of the hall, Adolf Hitler had heard the sound of their boots pounding on the gravel. Taking out the silver-plated watch he had received as a gift from an admirer of the Nazi philosophy, he had checked the time. Good. He nodded and smiled to himself. Everything was going according to plan. There was even time to finish his beer. Taking a final swig, he wiped the foam from his mustache, put down the glass mug, extracted a Browning revolver from the pocket of his coat, and opened the outer door.

"Set up the machine gun," he commanded the waiting troopers. As four of the troopers set up the machine gun, the rest formed a protective wedge around their leader. Hitler inspected them with satisfaction: high black boots, steel helmets, the glint of rifle barrels. This was the way loyal Germans should look. This was beauty, power, and death.

"Now!" he commanded.

The great double door of the beer hall was jerked open, and the Nazis began to beat and kick their way forward through the densely packed crowd. There was panic: people screamed, benches were overturned, beer mugs were shattered. At the podium, Prime Minister Kahr stopped in mid-sentence and gazed in horror at what was happening.

"Order," the chairman of the meeting begged, ringing his bell, "order, please," but there was no order. As the Nazi troopers advanced the audience was thrown into confusion. Some tried to take shelter under the tables, others fought their way toward the exits only to discover that those, too, were guarded by armed troopers. Nazi sympathizers, who had been concealed in the audience, stood up and put on swastika armbands; they pulled grenades and pistols out of their pockets.

"Quiet!" Hitler yelled. Reaching the front of the room, he climbed up onto a table and fired a shot at the ceiling. There was a sudden terrified silence. He leaned forward, pale and sweating, a little man in a wrinkled black morning coat. "The national revolution has begun!" he screamed in a high voice. "I declare the Bavarian government deposed!"

"Surely you can't be serious," Prime Minister Kahr yelled back at him.

Hitler pointed his gun straight at the Prime Minister's forehead.

"The revolution," Hitler yelled, "cannot be stopped!"

* * *

By the time Viola got into the cab in front of the Schwan Theater, the beer-hall revolution had been going on for over an hour, although most of Munich was not yet aware of it. Prime Minister Kahr was being held hostage, several of the main streets were blocked, and the Nazi troopers, flushed with their success, were out settling old scores. Equipped with rifles, machine guns, and grenade launchers, Hitler's private army was on the rampage: terrorizing Socialists, Communists, and Jews, destroying businesses, smashing windows, looting and beating under the direction of Field Marshal Hermann Göring. Fifteen years later there would be another time of broken windows and violent death that the world would know as Crystal Night, but this was the prelude, the first time the Nazis showed their true colors.

What Viola saw that night changed her forever. At first there was only silence—an eerie silence of deserted streets without so much as a pedestrian in sight. She leaned back and kicked off her shoes as the cab glided beneath dark arcades of leafless linden trees, wondering idly where everyone was, too tired to give much thought to the matter. In Berlin at this hour there would have been activity everywhere, but perhaps in Munich people went to bed early on Thursday nights.

For blocks she saw nothing out of the ordinary: a dog ambled slowly along; the silhouette of a white cat appeared and disappeared; leafless trees and steep-pitched roofs dozed in the oily quiet of streetlamps. In fact, they were almost to the Marienplatz before the terror began. At first it was nothing particularly frightening, only a burst of loud, drunken singing coming from somewhere up ahead. Pulling into an alley, the cab driver quickly shut off his engine.

"What's going on?" she asked, jolted out of her nap.

"Who knows"—the driver shrugged—"but when I hear singing I wait. The last time I tried to drive through a pack of those idiots, I got all my windows broken."

"Who do you mean? What idiots?"

"Take your pick, madam." The driver relit his cigar and sat back. "Communists, Nationalists, Socialists—window breakers all of them, especially when they're drunk, and on my salary I can't afford to go around replacing things. I have a family to support. Do you have any idea what it costs just to buy gas for this cab?"

The singing grew louder and Viola began to make out the words of the Nazi *"Sturmlied."* Suddenly a truck came careening around the corner, full of troopers—twenty or more of them singing drunkenly at the top of their lungs. She saw the metal helmets, the gleaming rifle barrels, the long gray overcoats, the silver death heads, the swastika armbands. On the side of the truck was a sign that read *STOSSTRUPP-HITLER MUNICH.* As the truck sped recklessly down the street, one of the troopers lazily aimed his rifle at a streetlamp and shot it out. There were bellows of laughter from the truck, and then it disappeared and the street was empty again.

Viola stared out at the empty street, shaken by what she had just witnessed. What a crazy thing to do. Broken glass lay shattered on the cobblestones. Suddenly she was very, very frightened.

"What's going on?" she begged the driver. "I'm a stranger to Munich and I don't understand. Tell me what's happening, please."

"How can I tell you what I don't know?" the driver said in a frightened voice. Cautiously he inched the cab back out into the street, looking anxiously over his shoulder. They drove in silence toward the Marienplatz. Less than five minutes later Viola heard more noise: singing, cheering, yelling. Suddenly the driver slammed on the brakes so hard that she was nearly thrown out of her seat.

"Damn," he said, jamming the cab into reverse.

Viola picked herself up and felt her knee for a bruise. "What's wrong?"

"More trouble up ahead."

"Can we get around it?"

"Maybe, who knows."

He drove down a side street, stopped, turned around, drove down another, but the sounds seemed to be coming from everywhere. Giving up, he plunged ahead and soon they found themselves in a huge crowd that was yelling pro-Nazi slogans and pushing and shoving to get sight of the carousing, singing Storm Troopers. Women waved Nazi flags and red-white-and-black banners; some of the men carried burning torches. As the cab edged through the crowd Viola tried not to look at their faces. Their eyes were bright and fanatical, and in the flickering light there was something ghostly and terrible about their enthusiasm. Surely all these Germans couldn't believe in Hitler, surely they were being deceived.

"Germany is reborn!"

"Heil! Heil Hitler!"

Climbing down from one of the trucks, a band of Storm Troopers began to methodically smash shop windows with their rifle butts. The sound of breaking glass seemed to drive the crowd wild. Bystanders joined in. Viola saw men grabbing meat from a butcher shop; bottles of spices and jars of honey were smashed on the cobblestones. Suits and dresses were ripped, thrown in a pile, and set on fire.

"*Alle Juden raus!*" the crowd chanted. "All Jews out on the street!"

"Hang the Communist women by their hair!"

The cab was forced to a stop and people jumped on the hood to get a better view of the Storm Troopers. She saw hands, and feet, and legs, a swarm of people pouring over them like ants.

"Get us out of here," Viola begged the driver.

"I can't," he yelled.

The windshield cracked; the car rocked from side to side; the roof buckled and appeared to be about to collapse. Terrified that she was going to be crushed, Viola struggled with the door handle only to discover that it was jammed. Throwing herself against the door with all her weight, she hit it as hard as she could, and it gave suddenly, spilling her out on the street under the feet of the crowd. She tried to struggle to her feet, but people ran over her as if she weren't there. Someone stepped on her hand; she was kicked in the ribs, in the head. For a second all she could do was scream, but then some instinct for survival took over. Biting her lip against the pain, she fought her way to her feet, clawing at the door of the cab. The crowd caught her and swept her away as if it were a river and she were a twig, pulling her off toward the Marienplatz. Swimming and pushing her way to the edge of the mob, she collided with a metal lamppost and clung to it. Men and women rushed past her, and then, suddenly, she was alone, bruised and bleeding on an empty sidewalk.

For a second she simply held on to the post, too stunned to move. The cab was nowhere in sight. She realized dimly that she must have been carried several blocks by the crowd. In front of her was a dark side street. Letting go of the lamppost, she fled into the shadows, trying desperately to escape from what appeared to be an entire city gone mad, but things only got worse. Up ahead, on Altheimer Eck—a short, narrow, cobblestone street—the Nazis were busy destroying the offices of the Socialist *Münchener Post*. As Viola turned the corner a heavy metal filing cabinet flew through the air and landed on the cobblestones in front of her, spewing its contents into the gutter. Everything was being thrown through the windows: desks, boxes of type, composing stands, chairs, reams of paper, books, pictures of Social Democratic leaders, bottles of ink. Putting her hands over her head, she retreated in panic. The Nazi Storm Troopers, fortunately, were too busy to pay any attention to her. Gathering up the remains of the newspaper office, they swept files and broken furniture into huge piles, doused them with gasoline, and lit them. The fires rose into the air with a great roaring sound, sucking up dust and scraps. Viola ran past the bonfires toward the safety of the shadows, but there was no safety anywhere. The heat from the flames frightened her to the point where she could barely think. A terrible vision of her mother's death rose before her, and for a moment she was convinced that she was going to die the same way.

Flames licked at her dress and smoked filled her throat and stung her eyes. She collided with a Storm Trooper, and he pushed her roughly away with a curse; she fell, skinned her knee, got up, and stumbled forward past the last fire as a small rain of cinders stung her face and burned holes in her skirt. She was never exactly sure of what she did next. She knew only that she ran, hardly conscious of what she was doing or where she was going, until at last she found herself alone again on a dark side street. Sitting down on the curb, she put her face in her hands and shook with fear and horror. In the distance she could still hear the singing and the crash of breaking windows.

Time passed, and she grew a little calmer. Getting unsteadily to her feet, she checked herself over once again to make sure that she wasn't on fire. Her dress was a mess and ashes clung to her legs and arms in a gray smear, but except for that she seemed to be intact. For a second she stood, bracing herself against a wall, convinced that she wasn't going to be able to go another step. The noise of breaking glass grew louder; it was only a block away now, maybe two at the most. She had to get out of this part of town before the crowd came closer.

Plunging forward into the darkness, she hurried toward Widenmayer Strasse through small alleys and obscure streets, passing through the deadly calm of that half of Munich which was too frightened, too cowardly, or too indifferent to protest what was going on in the center of town.

The walk seemed to take hours, and when she finally arrived at Uncle Otto's apartment building, her stockings were in shreds and her feet were raw. Limping up to the door, she pounded on it with both fists. "Joseph, Conrad, Uncle Otto!" she yelled. "Let me in! Joseph, can you hear me? It's me, Viola. Please, somebody, hear me! Let me in!" Suddenly a small square of light appeared in one of the upper windows. Looking up, she saw Joseph looking down at her.

"Vi," he yelled, "thank God! I've been worried sick about you."

"Joseph"—she felt like weeping with relief—"are you safe?"

"Yes, yes, of course. I'll be right there." His head disappeared from the window, and the shutter closed, and she was in darkness again. She waited for an eternity, and then the huge door slowly creaked open and Joseph stood in the entryway flanked by Conrad and Uncle Otto.

"Vi," Conrad exclaimed, obviously shocked by her appearance, "how did you get here? What happened? Joseph says the streets are full of Nazis. He was in the center of some kind of demonstration, and he's been frantic about you. You look terrible. Are you hurt?"

"If she's hurt," Joseph said grimly, "someone's going to pay for it." He took Viola in his arms and kissed her protectively. "I never should have let you go home in that cab. There's been a revolution." He looked incoherent and excited. "Did anyone hurt you, *Liebling?*"

"No, no one hurt me, but it was terrible. You should have seen the hate on the faces of the mob; they wanted to kill all the Jews. They were crazy—like wild beasts." Throwing herself into Joseph's arms, she buried her face in his shoulder.

"There, there," Joseph said soothingly, stroking her hair.

"I want to leave Munich," she said fiercely. "Take me away from here, Joseph. Not tomorrow—now—right this minute."

"Vi," Conrad said, "I know you've just been through hell, but try to get ahold on yourself. You can't leave tonight. The trains aren't running."

Uncle Otto took her arm. "Come inside," he said quietly, "and have some beer. You look like you could use it. Tomorrow this will be all over. Politics is the curse of Bavaria. Munich is like Mexico or some little country in South America. You just have to learn to live with whatever happens." He guided her up the stairs to his apartment, sat her down in a comfortable chair, and rang for the maid.

Viola's hands shook so hard that she could hardly hold the mug of beer Uncle Otto forced on her. "Promise me we'll leave tomorrow," she demanded.

"I promise," Joseph agreed.

But that next afternoon they didn't make the two o'clock train to Berlin. Shortly before they were scheduled to leave, there was a violent clash between police and Nationalist demonstrators in the Residenzstrasse. Hermann Göring was wounded, Hitler injured, and fourteen members of the Stosstrupp killed outright. The general opinion, after the smoke cleared, was that Munich—and Germany for that matter—had seen the last of the Nazis. Hitler was soon in jail, and by the end of the next year historians like Viscount D'Abernon were identifying him in footnotes as "a political figure who, after leading an insurrection in Bavaria in 1923, faded into oblivion."

Yet neither Viola nor Joseph ever forgot the night of the beer-hall revolution. Viola's encounter with the bonfires of the *Münchener Post* marked the end of her political innocence, and in many ways the end of her youth. She was—as the leftists of the era liked to put it— "radicalized"; overnight she became an ardent anti-Nazi. Also, for the first time she realized how precarious her happiness with Joseph was and how easily it could be destroyed. She never felt totally secure again, and that insecurity, combined with a sense of the mortality of love, fueled something in her acting that transformed it.

For Joseph, too, the night of November 8 was the seed of an artistic transformation. The work he began on the day they returned to Berlin from Munich belonged to a whole new order. Never again would he write a play without political implications, never again would he simply retreat into aesthetics and leave the world to take care of itself. In the middle of the Munich riots, fighting his way back to the Widenmayer Strasse, not sure if Viola was dead or alive, he had realized that silence in the face of evil was wicked. Among the broken glass and looted shops, he had found his voice, and the result was an outpouring of creativity that refused to be silenced.

The critics soon agreed that Joseph Rothe's new political plays were, nearly without exception, works of genius, and it soon became equally obvious that, given the deteriorating situation in Germany, they were very dangerous plays to write.

7

BERLIN
1925

"Let me confess my sins." Viola knelt on the stage and faced the audience with a bowed head, clasping her hands in front of her, resisting an urge to tug at the hem of the short black skirt Joseph had insisted she wear for this part. There was a hum of interest from the crowd, the kind of noise she had come to recognize over the past two years as a mixture of arousal, anticipation, and incipient trouble, as if a herd of restless animals were on the brink of a stampede. *"I am Mary Magdalene."* She lifted her head and revealed a painted face, haunting eyes outlined with black mascara, lips painted blood red, a cascade of blond hair. *"I'm a woman of Jerusalem, and I have been wicked and selfish."* Her voice was clear, bell-like. It trembled with power, always poised on the brink of breaking, yet she pushed it forward, out into that black sea of unarticulated faces. Inside she felt the strength of Joseph's words rise in her.

"What are your sins, my child?" a hollow, disembodied voice inquired from someplace above and behind her.

"I have sold myself to strangers," she told the voice. The secondary lights on stage dimmed and went out, leaving her in the pool of a single blood-red spot. Behind her images were suddenly projected on a screen—not the surreal images Joseph had been using in his plays three years ago, but stark, realistic photos Hermann had taken in the streets of Berlin only last week: the first was of a twelve-year-old prostitute standing in the rain on the Kurfürstendamm bargaining with a heavyset, greedy-looking man in a Mercedes.

"I have not fed the hungry" (a slide of two starving children searching through garbage), *"nor tended the sick"* (a slide of an old woman lying on a bench in the Tiergarten while people passed by with averted eyes). *"I have tolerated the persecution of the innocent without speaking a word"* (slides of Jewish stores with their windows broken out, slides of prisoners staring out through the bars of their cells). *"I have given no hope to the hopeless"* (slides of unemployed men standing in front of a shut-down factory), *"I have tolerated violence and stupidity without speaking up against them"* (slides of the Nationalists at one of their torchlight rallies; slides of a street fight between the Communists and the Nationalists).

There was another hum from the crowd, angry this time, a kind of dull, hostile drone of agitation that snapped Viola out of character and brought her back to the danger of her situation. She tried to ignore the reaction she was getting, but it wasn't easy. There was always trouble when she performed in Joseph's plays, so much trouble in fact that the first thing she did when she entered a new theater was to plan her escape route. But tonight the trouble was probably going to be worse than usual, especially given what was about to happen on the platform behind her. She braced herself, trying to act over the top of the restlessness of the crowd, thinking that it was a miracle that she'd managed to get this far—especially with those pictures of the Nazis that Joseph had insisted on using to accompany her last two lines.

She took a deep breath and continued. *"I have committed the greatest sin of all, the sin of apathy."*

"Apathy?" the disembodied voice said with a tinge of surprise. *"You're kidding."* Suddenly the curtains at the back of the stage drew back with a snap, exposing a half-naked man hanging from a cross, wearing a gas mask. *"The only sin you can commit in Berlin is the sin of*

not having any money.'' Music suddenly exploded from two loudspeakers in a syncopated jazz beat and fake gold coins rained down on the stage.

"Blasphemers!"

"Bourgeois idiots!"

"Jews!"

The audience was on its feet in an instant, yelling, hurling things at the stage. Viola ducked rotten eggs, tomatoes, a dead rat. A small rock hit her a glancing blow on the forehead; she stood up, hands on her hips, faced them down, and tried to deliver her last line, but the din was too great, Kicking off her stiletto heels, she beat a quick retreat into the wings, grabbed her coat, and made it out the stage door just as the first of the rioters vaulted over the footlights and was coldcocked by the boxer whom Joseph—with unusual foresight—had hired to play the part of the gas-masked Christ.

"Joseph, we've got to talk." Viola sat down wearily on the worn plush of the sofa, took one-year-old Kathe in her arms, and began to nurse her. The baby, dark-eyed and fragile, snuggled against her breast, her tiny high cheeks pulled into triangles as she sucked hungrily, oblivious to everything else. Viola looked at Kathe with protectiveness, love, and a small stab of envy. How long had it been since she'd been able to forget herself that completely? "I'm worried," she said, instantly feeling a stab of guilt. She hugged Kathe closer and waited for a reaction from Joseph, but none seemed to be forthcoming.

On the other side of the room, Joseph stood with his back to her, wearing the blue cable-knit sweater she'd made for him last Christmas when she'd still been waging a campaign to get him out of baggy gray slacks, lumpy green sweaters, and his beloved black leather jacket. His broad shoulders were squared stubbornly and she could feel the resistance in him, the same resistance, no doubt, that had gotten him expelled from the Freyburg Realgymnasium when he was fourteen and had continued to get him into trouble ever since. Viola pressed her lips together, feeling a brief burst of irritation at this new proof of his obstinate, good-natured, almost adolescent assurance that he was always right—so devastatingly attractive when you adored the man and so completely maddening when you tried to have a serious argument with him.

"Relax," Joseph said at last, picking up a ball of paper and tossing it idly against the wall. "You worry too much." He turned and smiled at her, one of those comforting smiles that never failed to make her feel she was being silly, the kind that made his hazel eyes open up for a moment like doors into some warm, safe place, and for a moment she was caught up in it, reassured and disarmed. Then she looked down at Kathe and the fear came back again.

"Joseph," she begged, "please listen. You know I hate the Nazis as much as anyone; you know I believe public protest against them is vital, but the reaction to your play is getting worse. Last night the audience wasn't just throwing tomatoes—some of them were throwing rocks."

Joseph shrugged and turned toward her slightly and she saw, against her will, all the things she had come to love so much about his body: the strong bluntness of his hands, the freckles on his wrists, the handsome completeness of this man that made her desire him at the most inappropriate moments, made her want to agree with him even when she knew he was wrong.

"Vi, you told me yourself that they were just tossing pebbles."

"Pebbles this time, rocks the next." Viola felt herself getting not just irritated but angry, an all too familiar emotion these days. Talk to Joseph about any other topic and he'd listen, but try to tell him that these new plays of his were dangerous, that the reaction of the audience scared her, that she was constantly nervous and on edge because of them, and he instantly moved to change the subject. She remembered that there had been a time when the idea of getting angry with Joseph had seemed completely preposterous, but now it was all she could do to keep her voice civil.

"I could have been hurt, Joseph. You don't go onstage; you don't see those faces. Half the people in the audience don't just dislike what you've written, they hate it with a passion. It doesn't just inspire them to reevaluate their politics—which I know is what you intend— it inspires them to murder."

"Don't get melodramatic, Vi." Joseph threw another wad of paper at the wall, avoiding her eyes.

"I'll be melodramatic if I want to." She heard the nagging edge creep into her voice and wished she could soften it somehow, but the problem was that she had tried being soft, tried reason, tried gentle persuasion, and he still hadn't heard her. "I'll rave, Joseph," she threatened, "I'll cry, pull out my hair, do a complete reprise of *The Lions' Cage* if it will wake you up and make you see what's going on. You're putting both our lives in danger." She groped for the words that would make him hear her. "This is Berlin, remember? For the last six months the Communists have been calling you a right-wing deviationist; the Nationalists—in case you're unaware of the fact—are passing out nasty little pamphlets suggesting that you're corrupting German morals, in league with the Jews, and probably personally responsible for inspiring high school students like Paul Krantz to run amok and shoot their girlfriends. Dear God, Joseph! People wind up dead on a regular basis for doing a lot less than you've been doing lately."

"I've only been telling the truth." Joseph squared his shoulders again obstinately and brushed his long, dark hair off his brow with the weary gesture of a man who is being more than patient in the face of his wife's unwarranted hysteria. "Of course I don't want to put either of us in danger, but I think you're overestimating the problem." He smiled encouragingly at her. "You have to remember that you're performing in plays, sweetheart, not running for the Reichstag. You talk as if you're going to be the target of a political assassination, as if no other playwright in Germany were saying these things. You're frightening yourself unnecessarily. Look at Piscator and his proletarian theater. He's twice the radical I am."

"That's just the problem." If Joseph could be stubborn, so could she. "Piscator and Brecht are clearly Communists—or in the case of Piscator I suppose you'd say he's something along the line of an anarchist. Whatever political labels you want to stick on the two of them, they're clearly outside the pale. But you've managed to stay in the mainstream somehow; you're not so far left that people can predict ahead of time what you're going to say, so you offend everyone."

Joseph grinned one of those rash, cheerful grins that under any other circumstances would have had her laughing. "Then I must be doing something right."

"Doing something right isn't always the best way to survive. What kind of political work are we going to be able to do from a hospital bed? The first duty of anyone interested in keeping Germany from falling into the hands of Hitler and his friends is the duty to stay alive." She bit her lip, sorry for taking such a harsh tone with him, yet driven to the limits of her patience. She felt torn between her duty to Kathe and her duty to protest the growing Nazi terror; torn between her loyalty to Joseph and common sense. Why couldn't he just admit there was a real problem?

Joseph's grin disappeared and was replaced by a frown. His full lips tightened ominously. Picking up another ball of paper, he bounced it off the wall. There was a long, uncomfortable silence between them. "I'm not the kind of person who can just sit back, Vi," he said at last. "I see this country being overrun by the worst elements in German society; I hear lies every hour of every day. What do you want me to do? Be complacent? Write nice, entertaining drawing-room comedies that will bring in lots of money so we can eat three square meals a day? I admit the security would be nice for you and Kathe—for me, too, for that matter—but the price is too high. I'm completely incapable of keeping quiet when I have something impor-tant to say, you know that. I'm not good at compromise; I've never been diplomatic. As much as I love you, I can't let you or anyone else convince me to stand back and become a spectator. You may be willing to retire into your private life, but I'm not."

"Joseph, that isn't fair. I've put my body on the line for my political convictions almost every night for the past two years. I believe what you believe—that it's criminal to keep silent in times like this." She shook her head, frustrated, not knowing what to say or how to say it. She had fallen in love with Joseph partly because of the strength of his convictions and his uncompromising honesty, and now that same strength and unwillingness to compromise were driving her away from him. She had always thought of herself as impulsive, but Joseph was twice as impulsive as she, rash and passionate and wonderful, and so stubbornly in the wrong at present that if it hadn't been so dangerous, it would almost have been admirable. "Joseph, you're an absolutely brilliant playwright—"

"Thank you."

"And I admire you more than I've ever admired any man in my life, but"—Viola steeled herself and said what had been on the tip of her tongue for months—"I just can't do this anymore."

"Can't do what anymore?"

"Act in your plays."

He turned a puzzled, betrayed face to her, and there was so much hurt and disbelief in his eyes that she almost took back her words, but somehow she managed not to.

"You aren't serious." He made a move as if to put his arm around her and she edged away, knowing that if he touched her, he could convince her to do anything.

"I am serious, completely serious. I'll campaign, stuff envelopes, write speeches, keep the books, paint protest signs, sew flags, go door to door and beg people to wake up and see what's going on, but I'm not acting in your plays anymore, Joseph—at least not as long as you go on writing things that provoke riots. Oh it's exciting, I admit it, exciting and crazy, and exhilarating, like getting drunk all the time, or taking some of that cocaine Hilde's always fooling around with, but I just can't do it anymore." She looked down at the child nestled in her arms, the tiny fragile bones of the baby's hands, Kathe's small pink fingers spread across her breast, and another wave of protectiveness washed over her. "I've got Kathe to think of. What would happen to our daughter if one of those rocks connected with my head?"

"Are you telling me that you're giving up acting, Vi?" Joseph took a few agitated steps across the room, very nearly knocking over his guitar. "Are you telling me that? Because if you are, I don't believe it for a minute. You're better than just a good actress, and you know it. You make those plays of mine come alive for the audience." He paced back to her and stood so close that she could smell the familiar odor of the soap he used to wash his hair. For a moment she was lost in that sensation of intimacy that always overtook her when she was near Joseph, and she was seized by an irrational desire to end this quarrel by standing up, closing her eyes, and putting her head on his shoulder. "I *need* you," Joseph pleaded. "Doesn't that count for anything?"

"It counts for a lot, Joseph." She was determined not to weaken, knowing that if she gave in to him now, they'd just have to go through all this again. "Knowing that you need me is what's kept me going for all these months, even though I've understood all along how dangerous it was for me to go onstage and say the words you kept putting in my mouth, but now . . ." She stopped, unable to continue.

"Now what?"

"Now I'm going back to Eric Stern. Wait, Joseph, listen, please." She put out her hand to draw him back to her again, but he was already halfway across the room, his face red with anger, standing beside the easy chair with his fists clenched at his sides. "Just hear me out, that's all I ask. Stern's written to me twice in the last month alone, offering me parts."

"Parts in *real* plays." Joseph kicked at the pile of books that was serving for their end table, sending one to the floor in a puff of dust. His eyes were hard now, glittering and unfriendly.

"I didn't say that."

"But you thought it." He was badly hurt, lashing out at her in unfair ways. She understood, but it was more painful than she'd imagined it would be.

"Joseph, your plays are the real ones. Stern does revivals—*Oedipus Rex, A Doll's House, The Oresteia*—you're a genius and he's a museum curator. I know that. But if I act in his plays, I won't have to duck out the back door of the theater every night; I won't have to go onstage wondering how long it's going to take one of those maniacs to take a shot at me. Maybe you think it's cowardly to want to stay alive, but I don't. We have a one-year-old daughter, Joseph. Don't you think we owe at least as much loyalty to her as we owe to Germany?"

"It sounds like you've been planning to spring this on me for a long time." Joseph sat down on the edge of the chair, planted his hands on his knees, and looked at her as if she were a total stranger. "Well, I suppose that's your right. You're a free agent, after all."

"Joseph, please, don't talk to me about free agents. It isn't a matter of money. You know that under ordinary circumstances I'd be happy to starve with you for the next twenty years while we got our careers off the ground, but I can't stand the sort of life we've been leading. You're made for combat, I'm not. I feel fragile and vulnerable when I'm up there in the spotlight, and I worry about Kathe all the time, about who'd take care of her if I got hurt. I want a safer life. Is that such a terrible thing to ask for? Stern saw me in *Gas Mask* last week and was kind enough to say that my Magdalene was amazing. Next to Max Reinhardt and Leopold Jessner, he's the most important producer in Germany—maybe in the world for that matter—and he's offered me the part of Ophelia in his new production of *Hamlet*. How could I turn something like that down?"

"Out of loyalty to me," Joseph said through tight lips, "that's how."

"Joseph, please don't make it sound like I'm deserting you. I'm not asking you to stop writing controversial material. I'm just asking you not to expect me to martyr myself." She leaned forward, cradling Kathe in her arms. "Please try to understand how I feel. If you want to go on putting yourself in danger because you believe that's the only way you can fight the Nazis, then that's your right. It scares the hell out of me, I admit that, but I understand and I'll give you whatever support I can short of appearing in your plays. All I ask is that you let me do what I need to do."

"If you aren't with me, then you're against me."

"What the hell does that mean, Joseph? That sounds like the kind of slogan you'd expect some second-rate street-corner preacher to come up with." Joseph got up from the chair, picked up his jacket, and slung it over his shoulder. "Where are you going?"

"Out."

"Joseph, be reasonable. Talk this out with me. At least try to understand."

"I do understand, damn it." Joseph bent down and kissed Kathe on the forehead. "I understand that you don't want to be in my plays any longer, that you're quitting me when I need you, that you find money and fame just a touch more attractive than commitment and truth."

He was gone for hours, and when he finally returned, sometime after three in the morning, he fell asleep on the sofa.

That night was particularly bad for Viola. For hours she lay awake, missing Joseph, wondering if she had made the right decision. She wanted comfort, but there was no one she could talk to. Jeanne, Hermann, Robert, Hilde, even Conrad, could never understand what went on between her and Joseph, for the simple reason that there was no way she could ever explain to them that odd mixture of love and anger and hurt and desire that pressed against the base of her throat whenever she thought of him.

She was still awake when he returned, and the fact that he made no move to come into their bedroom cut her to the quick. It took her several hours to face the fact that for the first time in their married life he wasn't coming in to sleep beside her. The sun was already up and the sky developing a gloomy gray tinge when she finally went quietly over to Kathe's crib, picked her up, brought her back into the big double bed, and fell asleep with the baby curled in her arms. When she woke again Joseph was gone, leaving behind a dirty coffee cup and a plate of half-eaten toast.

That morning she went to the Kallmann Theater and told Eric Stern that she had decided to accept the part of Ophelia. Then she spent the afternoon going from store to store, standing in endless lines to buy the things Joseph liked to eat: fresh rye bread, the first asparagus of spring, two tiny precious lamb chops that cost a fortune. She knew as she stood in front of the stove cooking the chops in the heavy iron frying pan Jeanne had given her for Christmas that she was offering Joseph a bribe, creating a chance for both of them to pretend that everything was fine and all was forgiven, and a black, hopeless panic seized her. What if he was so angry that he left for good? What if he could *never* forgive her? Viola tried to imagine her life without Joseph and failed utterly. There was no question in her mind that she loved him as passionately and completely as she could ever love a man, and yet surely loving someone didn't mean you had to completely sacrifice yourself.

Viola turned the chops back and forth until they were browned to perfection. She cooked the asparagus and made a sauce for it out of the last of the butter, laid out the rye bread on a clean white napkin, and then sat and waited, but Joseph didn't come home at his usual time. She passed the first hour alternating between anger and fear, and then, realizing that she had to do something to calm herself, she sat down and began to memorize the part of Ophelia.

> HE IS GONE, HE IS GONE,
>
> AND WE CAST AWAY MOAN.
>
> HE WILL NOT COME AGAIN . . .

Viola read the lines twice, translating the German back into the original English, and then put her head down on the table and sobbed uncontrollably for a few minutes. When she stopped crying she felt a little foolish that Shakespeare's words could have moved her so much—a little foolish and very lonely. Yet, at the same time, a stubborn conviction rose in her that she really was doing what she had to do.

When Joseph finally appeared around ten o'clock, he was half drunk and formidably polite. Eric Stern was not mentioned but his presence loomed over the evening like a dark cloud. They exchanged a few casual words, Joseph ate the cold food, complimented her on it, and then sat down at his typewriter and worked like a demon until the small hours of the morning.

That night, to Viola's intense relief, he didn't sleep on the sofa, but in some ways he might as well have. By the time Joseph finally came to bed he was so exhausted he fell asleep immediately. Viola lay beside him, feeling the anger in his body, the stiffness of his backbone, the crouched, defensive way he curled into himself, and she had a sense of broken rhythms, as if the music between them had gone off key and out of tune.

A week later Viola stood on the stage of the Kallmann Theater doing a run-through of Ophelia's mad scene. In her hands she clutched a bouquet of wilted flowers; her hair was hanging around her shoulders in a wild mass of curls, and she was wearing a plain white shift. Eric Stern watched her from the front row, his foot tapping impatiently on the red-and-gold carpet.

"White his shroud as the mountain snow . . ." she moaned in a singsong voice, handing a battered handful of weeds to the actress who was playing the Queen. *"There's fennel for you, and combines; there's rue for you and—"*

"No!" Eric Stern thundered, jumping to his feet. "No! No! No! That's not it at all. Ophelia is mad, insane, out of her mind with grief. You're playing her like she's got indigestion."

Viola turned and stared at him in astonishment. He couldn't be serious. "But I thought . . . "

"Don't think. Act."

"I am acting, Herr Stern." She felt angry and embarrassed, and if she hadn't fought so hard with Joseph to make this change in her life, she would have walked out of the theater. She confronted Stern proudly. "Exactly what do you expect me to do with this part?"

"Make it live. Make Ophelia a woman of flesh and blood, not a department-store mannequin."

"I was under the impression that that was exactly what I was doing."

"Well you were wrong." Stern stalked up on the stage frowning. The other actors parted in his wake. He circled Viola, muttering to himself, and then came to a stop in front of her. His jaw was set stubbornly and his eyes glinted with aggression. Viola was reminded of a bulldog. "What," he bellowed, "were you thinking of?"

"I beg your pardon, Herr Stern?" She'd be damned if she'd let him make her flinch. Yelling at his actors was one of Stern's major amusements, and she wasn't going to give him the satisfaction of seeing how much it bothered her.

Stern cast his eyes up to heaven. "I ask her a simple question, and she doesn't understand? Why, God, am I given fools to work with?" He lowered his eyes and glared at Viola. "I asked you what you were thinking about when you were saying your lines. You were thinking about something, *Ja?* That pretty head of yours wasn't completely empty, I trust."

"I was feeling Ophelia's emotions."

"You were *what?*"

Viola took a deep breath and told herself to be patient. Stern was a very famous director who got amazing results from his actors. If he wanted to act like a Prussian military officer chewing out a new recruit, then there was little she or anyone else could do about it. The fact that he was yelling at her was probably a good sign. He rarely yelled at actors he didn't like, he just fired them. At least he wouldn't order her to scrub down the stage with a toothbrush. Or would he? She wouldn't put anything past him, not once he got into one of these artistic temper fits.

"I was feeling Ophelia's emotions," she said evenly. "You see, Herr Stern, before I go onstage I always put myself into a slightly altered frame of mind."

"What does that mean?" Stern snapped.

"It means that I go into a light trance. It's a difficult technique to explain, but the gist of it is that I imagine I'm the character I'm portraying, and then I summon up that character's emotions from my subconscious." From the look on Stern's face, she had the distinct impression that she wasn't explaining this very well.

"And then?" Stern prompted.

"Well, then I simply draw on those emotions as I act."

"Russian garbage!" Stern exploded. "Surrealist trash! Who taught you this so-called technique?"

"My husband."

"God," Stern moaned, "do you hear that? Why do you give me such trials. Am I Job?" He turned back to Viola. "On this stage," he said, shaking his finger in her face, "we use technique, not feeling. We don't mesmerize, we *imitate*." Stern's face was so red that she wondered if he were about to have a stroke. He put his hands behind his back and paced from one side of the stage to the other, walking around the other actors as if they weren't there. Viola waited for the next explosion with as much calm as she could muster. Finally his pacing brought him back to her. "Do you have any idea what a real madwoman looks like, Fräulein Kessler?"

"Well, yes, I think so."

"You *think* so, do you? Have you ever seen a madwoman? I don't mean some poor, dazed soul but a full-fledged maniac? Ever seen one of those, eh?"

"Actually," Viola admitted, "I haven't."

"I thought so!" Stern said triumphantly. He took her by the arm. "Well, come along and I'll show you one."

"What?"

"I'm taking you to a madhouse—or a mental hospital, if you prefer the euphemism. When one of my actresses plays a starving woman, I make her go hungry for a week; when she plays Camille I take her to the tuberculosis ward to watch the beauties there cough their lungs out; when she plays a prostitute"—he smiled wickedly—"well, I leave that to your imagination. Now come along."

"You mean right now?"

"Of course right now. Do you want to wait until you're too old to play Ophelia?"

"But"—Viola was completely nonplussed—"but I'm not even wearing my shoes."

"Put them on," Stern thundered, "or don't put them on. It doesn't matter. Dr. Grunberger won't mind."

"Who's Dr. Grunberger?"

"The madman in charge," Stern said briskly. "Who else?"

The Feher Asylum was hardly a madhouse. A red-brick structure set in the center of a vast, rolling park on the outskirts of Berlin, it looked like a first-class hotel. Stern, who had obviously been there many times before, parked his car in the center of the gravel driveway, strode into the reception hall, and demanded to see the director, Dr. Grunberger.

"Yes, Herr Stern," the red-cheeked young nurse said. "Right away, Herr Stern."

When Grunberger appeared, Stern pumped his hand, asked after his family, and introduced him to Viola. Grunberger was a tall, slender man with stooped shoulders and tiny gold-rimmed glasses. Viola was relieved to see that this director—whom Stern had described as a maniac—looked awkward, birdlike, and not at all sinister.

"We have about a hundred patients," Dr. Grunberger said pleasantly as he led Stern and Viola through the grounds toward the west wing. "Some of them seem as sane as you and I do, at least at first glance, but"—he smiled at Viola—"on more intimate acquaintance their problems become apparent. Take that lady." He pointed to an old woman in a blue dress who was sitting primly on a bench reading a book.

Viola inspected the woman and had to agree that she looked perfectly normal. "What's wrong with her?"

"Senile dementia," Dr. Grunberger said. "You'll notice that she's holding that book upside down."

In the second story of the west wing there was a ward for seriously disturbed women. Viola's first impression was of a large sunny room full of tables and chairs. There were plants at the windows, pictures on the walls, and even a radio. It took her a moment to realize that the tables and chairs were bolted to the floor, the plants and pictures behind wire mesh, and the radio in a kind of protective cage. Half a dozen women walked or stood or sat, gazing off into space. They ranged, she calculated, from about eighteen to sixty. She stared at them with curiosity, feeling a little frightened.

"Are they violent?" she asked Dr. Grunberger.

Stern guffawed and tapped the ends of his fingers together. "Ha," he said. "You see. Already questions occur to you."

"No," Dr. Grunberger said, "we keep the violent ones on another ward. These women do violence only to themselves."

"They're suicidal?"

"Many of them are, unfortunately."

Viola looked at the women, none of whom seemed to be noticing her presence. She wondered if they were accustomed to being stared at like circus animals, or if they were so disturbed that she didn't seem real to them.

"I suppose you'd like Fräulein Kessler to talk to one of these ladies?" Dr. Grunberger said to Stern.

Stern nodded. *"Ja,"* he said. "Let her have a dialogue with the shadow side of the human soul; let her see how she likes it."

Dr. Grunberger led them over to a table where a young woman was sitting looking at her hands. The woman had a pretty face and long red hair, but when she looked up her eyes seemed frozen in a permanent squint.

"Clara," Dr. Grunberger said gently, "this is Fräulein Kessler. Clara Hameister, Fräulein Kessler."

"Hello," Clara said to Viola. "I was expecting you. Have a seat."

Viola sat down, feeling a bit confused at the idea that Clara had been expecting her. Clara bit her lip and looked at the two men uneasily.

"Rapists," she said, "all of them." She lowered her voice. "They send their signals through the clouds. I've asked and asked to be put someplace where I can't see the sky, but they say it isn't good for me. That's only an excuse though. At night they write messages in the clouds and by morning they've been engraved on my breasts— obscenities, execution orders."

Viola stared at Clara, fascinated and horrified. She felt pity and wanted to do something to help this girl, but she didn't know how to begin.

"Since you're so interested in feelings," Stern said, "why don't you ask this lady what she feels."

How could he be so callous! Viola was appalled. She hoped Clara hadn't heard the suggestion, but evidently she had.

"How do I feel?" she looked at Viola. "I feel like there's electricity in my head. It hurts so much. I feel like they've made me drink poison. My soul aches like it's been bitten by some venomous insect." She clutched at Viola's hands. "Please help me, please take me away from this place." She began to cry; tears dripped down her cheeks. "Please save me, please."

"Now, Clara," Dr. Grunberger said gently, detaching her hands from Viola's, "you shouldn't upset yourself this way."

"Look at her," Stern said, "if you can stand to. This is what's at the center of madness. Not indigestion, not a little middle-class misery, but the most terrible pain a human being can experience. I suppose you think I'm a monster for showing you this?"

"Yes, I do," Viola said angrily. "I've never seen anyone react so unfeelingly. How can you stand there and study that poor woman like she's some kind of insect?" She didn't care what Stern thought of her; she didn't care if he fired her on the spot.

"What you don't understand," Stern yelled, "is that I'm teaching you compassion."

"Compassion! You call this compassion?"

"Yes," Stern said, "I do. One madwoman reaches no one, but you can reach thousands. Show the audience what insanity is like. Play Ophelia. Not a pretty Victorian Ophelia with flowers in her hair, but a *real* Ophelia."

"No," Viola said. "I'll never use her pain. It's obscene." But it was too late. Clara's tragedy had entered her, and when she stepped out on the stage to say Shakespeare's lines, she said them knowing what madness was.

On the opening night of *Hamlet* the Kallmann Theater was packed with the bland, mildly bored faces of rich Germans and jaded foreigners. In the middle of Ophelia's mad scene, Viola broke down and wept.

"*There's rosemary, that's for remembrance,*" she said, "*pray, love, remember . . .*" Her voice broke; she remembered Clara. She remembered Joseph, who perhaps—like Hamlet—no longer loved her. She remembered that madness was pain, and she wondered if perhaps she was really going mad.

The audience sat, mesmerized. When she left the stage, after struggling through the final lines that preceded Ophelia's suicide, the crowd applauded for ten minutes until the actor who was playing the King walked to the front and begged them to stop so the play could continue.

No one who saw Viola Kessler come into her own as an actress that evening ever forgot it. The next morning every critic in Berlin was proclaiming that Eric Stern had found himself a new prodigy.

BERLIN
1927

Eric Stern and La Belle Margarete
Berliner Börsen-Kurier, September 12, 1927

Today, in front of the Wittenberg Cathedral, Eric Stern once again made theatrical history with a production of Faust *that left this critic shuddering with the conviction that the Devil was indeed abroad in Germany buying up souls.*

In the past several years, as most of the public is no doubt aware, Stern has gravitated toward some of the most colossal productions of the present century, staging an adaptation of Dante's Inferno *in the salt mines of Salzburg, transporting his company to Rome to perform* Antony and Cleopatra *in the Colosseum, involving virtually the entire village of Kahlenberg in his monumental reinterpretation of* Everyman, *but* Faust *is by far and beyond in a category by itself.*

The reason is simple, blond, and stunningly talented. I speak, of course, of Viola Kessler, Stern's gifted protégée who has turned in not merely another of her superb performances, but who has created out of some mysterious inner place of her own what I can only call the most moving, appealing, completely Aryan Margarete to appear on the German stage since Goethe first conceived her in the mad torment of his genius. . . .

Oh no, Viola thought with irritation, they always ruin it somehow. She took the review and folded it in half quickly without reading the rest of it. The word *Aryan* had a nasty taste to it that gave a bitter flavor to all the good things Rudolf Hausmann had said about her, not to mention that he was about to launch into more of that mystical Nazi mumbo jumbo that always set her teeth on edge. "Mad torment of his genius" indeed. Goethe would probably throw up if he read that line.

Stuffing the review in her purse, she looked through the dirty haze of the Cafe Schiller's front window at the pawn-shop clock across the street and realized with mild annoyance that Hilde was over forty-five minutes late. Well, that wasn't surprising, really. Hilde had sounded nervous last night when she'd called and asked Viola to meet her at the Schiller, and when Hilde was nervous she had a way of arriving so late that most people gave up on her and went home. Viola allowed herself to speculate again on what might be upsetting Hilde and once again came up with half a dozen possibilities, all equally probable: maybe Hilde was broke and needed money, maybe she was having another affair with a married man and wanted a shoulder to cry on, maybe she had lost her job at Leda and the Swan, maybe Hilde was—God forbid—pregnant.

She ran through the list of disasters and then gave up and reconciled herself to the fact that she'd just have to wait for Hilde to arrive to find out which of them it was. Picking up her coffee cup, she looked around the Cafe Schiller, thinking how long it had been since she'd taken the time to drop by. At the various tables the intellectual arguments were going at full volume as usual—painters berating poets, poets cornering musicians. There were street philosophers, poor students, a smattering of tourists, and the inevitable half a dozen chess players moving through their endless games as if they lived outside of the flow of time in some world of perpetual slow motion. The air was still smoky, the noise from the kitchen deafening, the posters on the walls flyspecked, the green eel hot and cheap, but something had changed since the days when the whole gang from Bluebeard's spent their afternoons here.

It took her several minutes to put her finger on the difference: maybe it was just her imagination, but the conversations at the battered wooden tables seemed more bitter than they'd been six years ago; there was something fanatical in the air, something dark and a little frightening, as if a bad spirit were loose in the place.

That was obviously ridiculous. The Schiller had always been a place for heated confrontations. She shook her head, thinking that probably it was her own mood that was making things in the cafe seem so ominous this afternoon. She had to admit that cheer and optimism had definitely been in short supply in her life lately. She took another sip of bitter black coffee and thought of Joseph, of the steadily deteriorating state of their marriage. Coldness—she thought—ice, the freezing down hour by hour of the best between us until there's hardly anything left but habit. She bit her lower lip and took another sip, remembering that she'd resolved to look on the bright side of things today. After all, she'd just gotten back from Wittenberg to rave reviews. She was a success, right?

There was a newspaper on the table next to her. Viola picked it up, turned to the back page. Usually she forced herself to read the important political news first, but this morning she was in the mood to lose herself in trivia—not an easy thing to do when a group of Nazis had just been acquitted of political murder in Vienna, and Hitler's buddy, Gottfried Feder, had just published a new program for National Socialism. Still, it was possible to find parts of the world that were going about their business untouched by such things. In Magdeburg the first German Dance Congress was being held, while in the United States, Babe Ruth was still hitting home runs for the New York Yankees, the fox trot had become the latest dance craze, and the deepest well in the world had been sunk in Orange County, California.

Viola experienced a moment of nostalgia for the peace and quiet of the States. Her German friends were always complaining how ridiculously naive Americans were, how they kept their heads stuck in the sand like ostriches and didn't even seem to notice that the world was going to hell around them. They were right, of course, but still sometimes she missed that blind optimism. She wondered what it must be like to wake up each morning isolated on the other side of the Atlantic Ocean with nothing more than baseball scores on your mind. Opening to an inside page, she discovered an article on the new Nazi theater that had recently been founded in opposition to the liberal Berlin Workers' Theater. Nazis everywhere.

"Viola, *Was ist los?*" It was Hilde, coming across the room dressed in a tight purple dress and red scarf that was causing every male head on the premises to swivel in her direction—except, of course, the heads of the chess players, who stayed hunched over their boards like large, hairy dogs pointing birds.

"Hilde, how are you?" Viola embraced her, trying not to wrinkle up her nose at Hilde's perfume, which was, as usual, completely overwhelming. In honor of the new *garçonne* style, Hilde had bobbed her hair so short that it clung to her head like a cap, giving her the appearance of a sleek, rather glamorous seal. Her nails were painted gold and green, and she had outlined her eyes with some kind of sparkling metallic mascara. All this at ten in the morning. Viola grinned, thinking how much work it must be for Hilde to put her face together.

"Well." Hilde settled down at the table, spread her legs cabaret-style, exposing a rather formidable expanse of black stockings, and waved to the waiter. "Well, well." She seemed nervous and at a loss for words. "Well, well," she said again, "it's been a long time, hasn't it?"

"Since Friedrich's last show," Viola agreed, wondering what had Hilde so on edge. "March, I think it was."

"Weird paintings Friedrich does." Hilde pulled out a long ebony cigarette holder, stuck an expensive Russian cigarette in one end, and lit it with a small gold lighter decorated with a double-headed eagle—all of which, as far as Viola was concerned, practically constituted a public announcement that Hilde had snagged herself some rich Russian lover. "But then Friedrich's a weird guy all around." She inhaled the smoke and looked at Viola uneasily. "How's Joseph?" she said abruptly, apropos of nothing.

"Fine," Viola lied. "Working hard."

"Working hard, huh?"

"Writing a new play called *Penguins.*"

"Penguins are cute." Hilde took another quick drag on her cigarette, not meeting Viola's eyes. "Ever see the penguins at the zoo? They have blocks of ice for them to slide on." Hilde laughed nervously. "I like penguins."

"Actually, there aren't any real penguins in Joseph's play."

"Oh." Hilde was obviously disappointed.

"It's a parody of National Socialism."

"Oh." Hilde looked around uneasily. "Do you think that's a good idea, darling? Considering the present political situation? I mean, the Nazis *are* represented in the new government, which means they must have more popular support than bears thinking about."

One of the most surprising things about Hilde was how she could suddenly drop the femme-fatale routine and become a completely rational human being. "No"—Viola looked down at her coffee cup, at the wet rings on the table, and tried to make her voice sound moderate—"no, I don't think it's a very good idea—or rather it's a great idea, a noble idea, and Joseph, as usual, is doing a fantastic job of putting it all together—but it's about as safe as sleeping in a tiger's cage. But then"—she forced herself to smile—"you know Joseph."

"Right." Hilde nodded. "I know Joseph. Right." There was something in her voice that made Viola do a double take. "That is to say . . ." Hilde stuttered to a stop and looked at Viola so guiltily that it was impossible to pretend not to notice. Under her thick makeup her face turned lobster red. "Uh, Viola . . ."

Viola had a sudden premonition of what was coming next. Odd thoughts ran through her mind: she could put her hand over Hilde's mouth, get up and walk out of the cafe; she could—

"I'm not very good at keeping secrets, darling." Hilde tapped the end of her cigarette holder nervously against the edge of the table and a snake of gray ash tumbled into her coffee cup. "And besides, I thought you should know. I mean"—Hilde leaned forward, radiating embarrassed sincerity—"I mean, it's always seemed to me really rotten that the wife is always one of the last to find out."

"Hilde"—Viola took a deep breath and tried not to jump to conclusions—"what the hell are you trying to say?"

"It's about Joseph." Hilde stopped and stared at her helplessly.

"What about Joseph?"

"Forget it." Hilde reached for her purse. "It was a stupid idea to come here this morning. I'm stupid, darling, I admit it. Let's just forget—"

She put her hand on Hilde's arm, drawing her back down into her chair. "Hilde," she said in as level a voice as she could manage under the circumstance, "it doesn't take very much imagination to figure out what you've been trying to tell me for the last ten minutes, so let's just get it out in the open. You've been sleeping with my husband, right?"

"Good lord no!" Hilde looked at her with real horror. "I'm your friend. Friends don't sleep with other friends' men—unless the friends kind of turn them over to them the way I turned the Kaiser's illegitimate nephew over to you that time you were hard up for a hot meal." She laughed nervously. "Good lord no, I wouldn't do a thing like that."

"Well, what in the world is it then? Come on, Hilde, spill it."

"Joseph kind of . . ."

"Hilde"—Viola leaned forward—"if you keep stopping in mid-sentence like this, I'm going to scream. This isn't one of Hermann's movie serials, continued next week and all that. I'm going crazy trying to figure out what you're going to tell me. Have a little mercy."

"Joseph asked me to go to bed with him but I didn't." The words tumbled out of Hilde's mouth, and she gave Viola a look of distressed horror, as if she couldn't believe she was actually saying them. "I absolutely swear I didn't go to bed with him."

"So what did you do, Hilde? What's all this about?" Viola felt herself getting hurt and angry, both at the same time, and yet part of her wasn't surprised. That was the worst of it really—that Joseph had asked Hilde to sleep with him and it wasn't even surprising. "Tell me what the hell you did—that is if it's anything that can be said between adults."

"You'll be angry." Hilde looked at her again with helpless guilt.

"Good lord, Hilde, my imagination is running wild. What the hell did you do with Joseph if you didn't sleep with him?"

"Kissed him."

"Kissed him? That's all?"

Hilde nodded, the red on her face taking on a purple hue that very nearly matched her dress. "I swear to you, Vi, that's all I did. I just kissed him, like a sister, I swear, and I said, Joseph, I said, you're married to Viola, who happens to be one of my best friends, so it's out of the question, and then he said that you wouldn't care, and I said I'd heard that from lots of married men but I never thought I'd hear it from him, and, oh, Vi, darling, it made me so sorry to hear him say that. He looked hurt and angry when he talked about you, you know how men are in that state, like whipped dogs or something."

Hilde gulped in some cigarette smoke, coughed, and tapped her green-and-gold nails on the rim of the table like a drummer without a drum. "Look, Vi, I'll be straight with you. I don't have any morals, really. I haven't been able to afford them since I was maybe fourteen. But somewhere under all this trashy flash—yes, I know I look trashy, darling—I still believe that marriage is special, maybe the ideal state." She looked up at Viola, almost pleading. "You can laugh if you want."

"I'm not in a laughing mood, Hilde."

"I don't want your marriage with Joseph to fall apart." Hilde put one finger in a wet ring on the table and moved the water in small curls on the shiny surface of the wood. The two women sat for a minute in silence. "When Joseph was talking to me I could tell he loved you a lot but that something was terribly wrong between the two of you. I could tell if it wasn't me he was going to sleep with, it was going to be someone else soon—that is if it hadn't already been." Hilde looked up at Viola and shook her head grimly. "Maybe I should have kept my mouth shut, but I had to warn you. I've slept with lots of married men, Vi, and I know all the signs. Something's really wrong. Forgive me if it hurts you to hear that, darling, but you've got to do something about Joseph, and I'd say you'd better do it pretty fast."

In 1906 Eric Stern had taken over a run-down gymnasium next door to his grand Kallmann Theater and rebuilt it, converting the shabby, drafty building into a walnut-paneled chamber theater with a small, elevated stage, the merest suggestion of a proscenium arch, and acoustics so good that they rivaled the famous ancient Greek theater at Epidaurus. The Stern Chamber Theater, which seated only three hundred, had all of the intimacy and none of the disadvantages of a private living room. It was a place of experiment and artistic innovation, a place where young playwrights could test their material on some of the best-informed, most critical audiences in the history of the theater. It was from here that the last five winners of the coveted Schröter Prize for Drama had been selected, and yet it was never an easy place to launch a production.

Eric Stern might have believed in innovation in theory, but in practice he was fiercely protective of the little building, determined to make sure that nothing but the best plays were ever seen on its stage. His interest in the place was so intense that it had become a joke to the actors and actresses of the lavish Kallmann Theater next door. There was even a story—apocryphal no doubt—that one afternoon when Max Reinhardt showed up unexpectedly in the middle of a rainstorm to have a look at the new facility, Stern had met his arch rival at the door, embraced him like a brother, and then ordered Reinhardt to remove his rubber overshoes so that he wouldn't drip water on the rug in the lobby.

Twenty-four hours after talking to Hilde at the Cafe Schiller, Viola sat nervously in a front-row aisle seat in the empty Chamber Theater longing for more coffee but knowing if Eric Stern caught her with a cup anywhere within a hundred-meter radius of the rose-colored velvet upholstery he would go berserk. She crossed her legs, uncrossed them, and then crossed them again, feeling the smoothness of her silk stockings and wondering—for perhaps the hundredth time that morning—if she was overdressed. She had learned from long experience that when you wanted to ask a favor from Stern, it paid to appear as feminine and sweet as possible, but not too feminine or too sweet or he would get distracted and wander off into sarcasm and the kind of vague, double-edged compliments that only a man who had been faithfully married to the same woman for over forty years could possibly have thought appealing.

"Ah, Fräulein Kessler, good morning." Viola started, jarred out of her reverie, to see Stern hurrying down the aisle like a human dynamo, his short stocky legs pumping with the energy of a rider in one of Berlin's famous six-day bicycle races. She stood up, still slightly intimidated in his presence, but Stern, as usual, didn't notice her feelings—in fact it was probably safe to say that Stern didn't notice anybody's feelings unless they were stage center muffing a line. Bending down, he swooped over her hand in a perfunctory kiss, and then gave her one of the you-are-doing-well smiles he reserved for actresses who had just gotten good reviews. "I saw Rudolf Hausmann's piece in the *Berliner Börsen-Kurier*." Stern bobbed his head up and down, and his small, dark eyes gleamed with satisfaction. "Wonderful, wonderful."

"Thank you, Herr Stern." Viola shifted her weight uneasily from one leg to the other, not knowing quite how to bring up the topic she wanted to discuss with him. She was all too well aware that Eric Stern usually gave people a maximum of about three minutes before his attention darted off to something else. She couldn't risk being too blunt, but there was no time to waste.

"A pity Hausmann's mind is cluttered with all that Nazi garbage about Aryan purity, but a good review's a good review, eh?" Stern pushed up his shirt sleeves—he never wore a jacket except on opening nights—and cleared his throat. "So," he demanded suddenly without preface, "out with it."

Viola was taken aback. "Out with what, Herr Stern?"

"Out with whatever it was that prompted you to ask to meet me here this morning. It's not for love you want to see me, *ja?* So what is it? More money?" Stern made a gesture as if to turn out the pockets of the jacket he wasn't wearing. "You're a brilliant actress, Fräulein Kessler, even if I—who trained you—do say so myself, but money is scarce these days." Viola bit her tongue, restraining herself from reminding Herr Stern that he had just spent a small fortune on a new set of curtains for the Kallmann Theater. "In my *Faust*"—Stern frowned—"you've become a star, so you could leave me for telling you I can't pay more. You could go to Reinhardt or Jessner, *ja?* But I believe you won't." Stern gave her a clipped, businesslike nod. "I am your Stanislavsky, Fräulein Viola Kessler. I've taught you how to express yourself onstage; I have given myself to you, *mit Herz und Seele*, and so I think you'll stay with me."

"Of course, Herr Stern. I couldn't imagine leaving. You are"—she paused, wondering how thick to lay it on—"the theatrical genius of the century."

"Of course I am." Stern nodded cheerfully. "Of course."

Modesty, Viola thought, was definitely not one of Stern's virtues. "And I have no intention of asking you for more money."

"Ah, good." Stern was obviously relieved.

"But I do have a favor to ask."

"A favor." He lifted his eyebrows. "What sort of favor?"

"It's about my husband, Joseph Rothe. He's just finished a new play."

"Penguins," Stern said unexpectedly. "Heh, you're surprised I know the title, aren't you?"

"Yes, I am." Viola looked at him, amazed. She had had a complete speech prepared, but she couldn't remember a word of it. Stern slapped his lips together as if savoring a juicy bit of meat.

"So you asked to meet me here this morning so you could beg me to let Herr Rothe put on this new play of his in my Chamber Theater, fully aware, of course, that this *Penguins* is a satire on National Socialism, and that any theater that presents it has a good chance of being torn apart by Herr Hitler's thugs, yes?"

"Yes, Herr Stern, that is . . ." She stumbled awkwardly to a halt and her heart sank. So Stern already knew about Joseph's play, and had already decided against it. She thought about how much it would have meant to Joseph to have one of his works done in Stern's Chamber Theater—not that Joseph would have ever admitted to wanting such a thing. Joseph was forever saying that he didn't need any official stamps of approval from Berlin's theatrical establishment, but if *Penguins* could have been performed on this stage, it would have been one of the turning points of Joseph's career and maybe a turning point in their marriage as well. If she could have convinced Stern to back *Penguins,* then maybe Joseph would have seen that she was still behind him, that she hated the Nazis as much as he did, and had never meant to betray or abandon him.

"Do you think, Fräulein Kessler," Stern thundered, pointing toward the stage, "that I would ever endanger one square meter of this theater?"

"No," Viola said unhappily. "I suppose not."

"Wrong! The fact is"—Stern surveyed her with satisfaction, obviously delighted to have shocked her—"the fact is, I was going to ask *you* to approach your husband about doing *Penguins* in the Chamber Theater. I've read the manuscript, you see." He lifted his hand. "Don't ask me how I got a copy. My lips are sealed. Let's just say that I have connections and your husband has friends. It's an amazing piece— funny, witty, devastating. Only a fool would refuse to produce it."

"But the Nazis?" Viola stared at him, still not quite able to believe he was serious.

"The Nazis made a mistake recently, a bad mistake." Stern tapped the tips of his fingers together and frowned ominously. "They bothered my wife. A pack of the little cowards knocked her into the gutter when she was out shopping, called her obscene names. We're Jewish, as you know."

Viola was beginning to understand.

"The only thing I care more about than this theater is Greta. So go home and tell your husband I want *Penguins*." Stern strode forward, seized her hand, and shook it as if the two of them had just concluded a deal. "There's only one thing I require, but I require it absolutely— don't mention to Herr Rothe what happened to my Greta. I want to keep her out of this. Let him believe you convinced me to give him a break. Let him believe I've been aching to raid his talent for years— which, by the way, is true. Agreed?"

"Yes." Viola pumped his hand, almost too happy to speak. "Yes, thank you."

Stern dropped her hand and stepped back. "Tell Herr Rothe that he has my word that we'll do a good job with his play. Tell him that I'll personally see that *Penguins* gets the kind of publicity we usually reserve for Ibsen and Sophocles. And tell him that he doesn't have to worry about the Nazis giving us any trouble."

"Why not, Herr Stern."

"Because"—Stern smiled wickedly—"I have decided to declare the opening night of *Penguins* a benefit for the pension fund of the Berlin police."

"Joseph." Viola draped her coat over the back of a chair and stood for a moment in the center of the room, not knowing how to begin. At the table, Joseph was typing, his fingers moving in a steady rhythm, as if he hadn't noticed the fact that she was home. "Joseph, I've got something to tell you."

"What's that?" Joseph lowered his head and went on typing, his back squared against her like a wall. How good they'd gotten at ignoring each other.

"I've convinced Eric Stern to do *Penguins*."

The typing stopped and Joseph turned to her with a look of incredulity. "Did I hear you right?"

"Yes, you did." Viola wanted to run to him, hug him, but she was suddenly shy, as if he were a stranger instead of her own husband. "I've persuaded Stern to do *Penguins* in his Chamber Theater, that is"—she hesitated, suddenly conscious of the possibility that Joseph might be too proud to accept—"that is, if you'll let him."

"Let him? Of course I'll let him. My God." Joseph got up from his typewriter. "This is certain, not just a possibility? Not just some whim of his? I mean, does Stern have any idea what *Penguins* is about?"

"It's a firm offer. He's already read the play in manuscript."

"And he's willing to take the risk?"

"More than willing—eager."

"Vi, my God." Joseph's face was suddenly suffused with joy. He caught at her hands and impulsively kissed them. "Thank you. *Penguins* in Stern's Chamber Theater, and you convinced him! How the hell did you do it?" He reached down, lifted her face to his, and gave her a long kiss, and she had a sense of relief and at the same time she felt sad that it had taken this to get him to turn to her again. "Vi, *Liebling,* thank you."

She had bought him, but what did that matter? He was kissing her as if he meant it for the first time in months. She closed her eyes and tried to convince herself that Joseph loved her as much as she loved him, but bleak thoughts kept haunting her: What if Hilde hadn't asked her to come to the Schiller yesterday morning? What if she'd never talked to Stern or Stern had turned her down? Would Joseph still be kissing her? Joseph drew her closer and she could feel the gratitude in his body, the warmth of his skin, the fresh smell of him that she'd missed so much over the last few months.

"Thank you Vi," he whispered, "thank you." But she didn't want to be thanked, she realized. She wanted to be loved—not because she was good at arranging his career or doing him favors; not because she did or didn't do what he wanted her to do. She wanted Joseph to love her the way she loved Kathe—freely and completely, just because she existed. But was that even possible with a man? Did men ever love without tangling it up with conditions and theories and God knows what else?

She kissed Joseph back, grateful that the coldness between them had thawed, yet at the same time dissatisfied. For a moment she had an irrational urge to push him away, an urge so angry and sharp that it frightened her. What in the hell was wrong with her? For months she'd been waiting for Joseph to care about her again. She must be half crazy even to think of pulling back.

Impulsively, she threw her arms around Joseph's neck and drew him closer. Joseph mistook her ambivalence for passion and kissed her harder. For a long time they stood toe to toe, hip to hip, locked in a mutual misunderstanding. Then Joseph ran his hand down her back and up across her shoulders and put his lips against her ear. His breath tickled like feathers and she felt annoyed and stimulated both at the same time.

"Vi," Joseph whispered, and she knew it was an invitation. For a moment she felt her body recoil from his again, and a stubborn part of her whispered that he had no right to come back to her this way, under these circumstances, so suddenly, as if all it took was a few words to heal the hurt between them, and then she thought again of Hilde's warning, and she knew that if she didn't let Joseph make love to her now, she would tear a new rift between them, one so wide that no amount of favors from Eric Stern or anyone else could ever mend it.

"Vi?"

"Yes," she whispered, "yes, Joseph."

He picked her up in his arms and carried her toward the couch and she felt suddenly cold, like a log or a piece of wood, as if all her flesh were bark, sharp and scaly and numb. Settling her down on the cushions, Joseph slowly unbuttoned her blouse, running his hands over her silk stockings, kissing her neck and ears. A good lover, admirable technique, but then he'd had a lot of practice before they were married, and who knows how much since. Now that was a nasty thought. She had no proof that he'd been seeing other women.

She tried to still the chorus of unspoken accusations, but it was impossible. The voices whispered to her, undermining her, making her awkward and cold in his arms, but Joseph didn't seem to notice, or if he did notice her coldness, he chose to ignore it. Slowly he caressed her, over and over again, rubbing her gently, kissing her arms and wrists, her mouth and cheeks, not insistently, not forcing himself on her, just touching her and touching her until, despite herself, she began to feel desire.

When the desire came it was like a hunger, quick and sharp and surprisingly strong, pulling her toward him, making her forget everything except the fact that she wanted him. She gasped for breath, opened her eyes for a minute, looked over Joseph's shoulder, and saw all the familiar things in her life in an unfamiliar way: sunlight from the garden was streaming through the tiny, leaded panes of the windows, moving across the leaves of the ivy like a clear, luminous liquid; the books on the floor glowed in blue and red rectangles, and even the dust on the rungs of the chairs seemed soft and illuminated. Amazing how desire transformed things; amazing, she thought, how it could lead you back to love even half against your will.

She watched her own anger dissolve with a mixture of amusement and growing humility and an intimate tenderness came over her. What did it matter that they had disagreed or fought or tormented each other? What did it matter if she'd bought Joseph back by persuading Eric Stern to do his play? She felt suddenly foolish for having demanded such purity from Joseph. So what if his love had a price? She should be grateful it was one she could afford.

Joseph gently lay her on one side and clasped her in his arms, and the last bits of resistance in her dissolved. She felt her spine relax, and the tension go out of her throat and hands. Her body and heart opened to him, and for no particular reason she remembered some tulips she had seen once in one of Hermann's films, hand-tinted, captured in slow motion, the petals folding slowly back like dozens of lips on dozens of mouths, the stems swaying and turning toward the light, quiet explosions of gold and red and in the center a perfect white-starred stamen.

Forgiveness of the body, she thought, is the only kind worth having. And then for a long time she thought of nothing at all.

Penguins opened on January 14 at the Stern Chamber Theater. As the curtain rose an actor dressed as an emperor penguin waddled up to a table, mounted it, and stood awkwardly, waving his stubby wings at the audience. Reaching into the pocket of his long, shabby overcoat, the penguin extracted a small revolver.

"The revolution cannot be stopped!" the penguin screeched in a high voice, firing a shot at the ceiling. A rubber sea gull was catapulted out of the gun barrel. At that precise instant a large white polar bear emerged from the wings riding a unicycle. Careening up to the penguin, the bear dismounted, rose to its full height, and slapped the hysterical bird in the face with a large, wet flounder.

The audience roared with laughter, applauded, gasped for breath, beat their hands on the arms of their seats, and stamped their feet. "More!" they begged the bear. "More!" The policemen of Berlin and their wives were having an evening to remember.

But there were some in the crowd that night who were not amused. In the back row two ominous-looking men in dark suits sat grimly watching the stage and taking notes.

Two months later, several weeks after the opening of *Penguins,* the seven members of the Schröter Prize committee sat around a long walnut table in the west parlor of the Niebuhr Hotel making their yearly decision. Or perhaps it would be more accurate to say that the seven were trying to make their decision, since for the last five hours now they had been exhausting themselves by arguing acrimoniously, hurling charges and countercharges until at the present moment they sounded more like a disgruntled lynch mob than an assembly of the most important scholars and theater critics in Germany.

"I protest the nomination of Joseph Rothe," Rudolf Hausmann thundered, pounding his fist on the table so hard that the water splashed out of the glass next to his elbow. Hausmann's bald head glowed a dangerous shade of red and there was a look in his close-set blue eyes that would have reduced half the producers, playwrights, and actors in Berlin to abject terror had they had the misfortune to witness it. "I protest it, and I protest it again. This isn't an artistic decision, gentlemen. As I said at the beginning of this meeting, when Rothe's name was first introduced, *Penguins* isn't a play, it's a tract, three acts of pure political rabble-rousing, three acts of shameless—"

"Please, Herr Hausmann." Professor Holl, chairman of the Schröter Prize committee, hunched his shoulders awkwardly, like a large crane caught in an invisible cage, cleared his throat, and adjusted his gold-rimmed glasses on his nose with a trembling index finger.

"Please, Herr Hausmann, the question has been called and we must proceed to take the final vote."

"I don't care if the damn question has been called," Hausmann persisted. "For over twenty years I've been a theater critic in this city. In 1912 I sat on the committee that awarded Reinhardt Sorge the prize for *Der Bettler*. I'm not against theatrical innovation, I'm not even against politics on the stage, but *Penguins* is a cheap parody of German values and I won't have my name associated with it."

"Cheap? It's absolutely brilliant," a bass voice declared from the far end of the room.

"Herr Wulf, please." Professor Holl spread his long thin fingers out on the table as if wishing he could climb under it. "Please, don't argue with him."

"It's in my nature to argue," Wulf snapped. Professor Holl sank back down in his seat, looking abashed. Johannes Wulf was the oldest of the seven committee members, the uncrowned king of the Berlin critics. Plays had closed on a single prejudicial adjective carelessly spilled from Wulf's pen. Productions costing trillions of marks had never seen public performance because Wulf hadn't liked the dress rehearsals. "Hausmann, here," Wulf said, "is a fool. He doesn't know talent when he sees it. His mind is rotted with pseudo-Nietzschean garbage. Not to mention that he himself has the sense of humor of a penguin."

Rudolf Hausmann got slowly to his feet, fists clenched at his sides. "I don't have to take this, Wulf, not even from you."

"Ah," Wulf observed, tapping his pipe against the cut-glass ashtray, "so now we have a penguin in revolt, flippers flapping, Nazi philosophy hanging out of its mouth like a dead fish. What an enlightening sight. Rothe was right. The whole flock should be shipped off to Antarctica until it cools down."

"Gentlemen," Professor Holl begged, "if we could just get on with the voting."

"I'm resigning from this committee," Hausmann yelled. He picked up his glass of water as if about to throw it in Wulf's face, then reconsidered and took a long drink. Slamming the empty glass back down on the table, he glared at the committee. "If you award Rothe the Schröter Prize, I won't be responsible for the consequences."

"Is that a threat, Hausmann?" Wulf took a long puff on his pipe and leaned back in his chair. "Are you trying to convince us that penguins have teeth after all?"

"Shut your mouth about the damn penguins, Wulf, and take what I said any way you want. I just won't be responsible, that's all." Rudolf Hausmann picked up his papers, stuffed them in his briefcase, and stormed toward the door, slamming it behind him. There was a moment of silence.

"Well, gentlemen," Professor Holl said at last, "I believe the question has been called." He looked down the table at the remaining members of the committee. "In consideration of the circumstances, it would seem best if we, uh, took a secret ballot." There were grunts and nods of agreement, and Wulf was heard to mutter his approval.

Looking relieved that he had finally discovered something the committee could agree on, Professor Holl extracted a piece of paper from his notebook and nervously tore it into six equal squares. Walking the length of the table, he handed one square to each committee member.

Ten minutes later the reporters gathered outside the front door of the Niebuhr Hotel were informed that the Schröter Prize for Drama had been awarded to Joseph Rothe.

Jeanne, Joseph, Richard, Hermann, Friedrich, Hilde, and Viola were all drunk—gloriously, happily drunk; silly drunk; drunk at that stage where even the most sedate people sing songs, pound their feet on the floor, and cackle good-naturedly at each other.

Viola lifted the heavy pewter mug to her lips, took a long drink of beer, and smiled a benevolent, drunken smile at Joseph, who was sitting across the table with one arm thrown around Hermann's shoulder, wearing the suit he had rented to receive the Schröter Prize earlier that evening—a rather spiffy-looking black affair with a formal shirt that made his shoulders appear square and powerful.

Here's to the good times, she thought, *Prosit*. She tilted her stein of beer and took another gulp of the bitter, cool liquid. Drinking deeply, she settled forward on her elbows, feeling satisfied. She and Joseph weren't doing badly these days, no, they weren't doing badly at all. For the past few months—ever since *Penguins* had proved such a success—it had been like old times. They were sleeping in the same bed, making love to each other again, really living together instead of merely politely sharing the same lodgings. Not only that, Joseph was working on a new play called *Berliner Ballade*, and from what she had seen of it, it was going to be very good indeed: music and dance instead of brickbats; entertainment instead of social sermons. A play no one would want to throw dead cats at—a play you could act in without checking your life insurance policy beforehand—and he was working up the nerve to ask her to be in it. She could have saved him the trouble because she knew this time, well beforehand, she was going to say yes, but she enjoyed the courting dance men always did when they wanted something from a woman—be it sex or agreement—all the fuss and movement that reminded her of the mating rites of the ducks along the Spree or the peacocks in the zoo.

My God she was drunk, rambling on to herself like this. Let's hear it for happiness, she thought giddily, and if I live to be a hundred I'll always remember this particular evening when I was young and in love and as perfectly content as a woman can be.

In the center of the table Joseph's prize money lay in a sodden pile. Having finally come to the end of his song, Joseph picked up one of the bills and contemplated it with glassy-eyed appreciation. "This is a lot of money," he said. "But who knows"—he tossed the wet bill casually into a puddle of beer—"tomorrow or next week or next year all this pretty paper could be rubbish again." His face was flushed with enthusiasm and there was a brilliant, drunken look in his eyes which Viola recognized as the first symptom of a full-blown obsession. Resting the palms of his hands on the table, he leaned forward with that old seductive grace of his, and Viola could feel everyone at the table—herself included—nod toward him like snakes around a snake charmer's flute.

"*Berliner Ballade* is a great play, my friends," he announced. "It's light and funny with a nice, well-hidden backbone of social commentary. It combines everything—music, poetry, crazy sets, film, great characters, a plot with popular appeal. I've revamped all the major roles, thrown out those boring middle-class puppets that have been tormenting me since before Christmas, and created an entirely new cast of thieves, beggars, prostitutes, murderers, and political agitators. And you know what? It works. Finally it works." He pushed back his chair and surveyed them all with cheerful arrogance. "Six weeks ago, as you may remember, I was on the verge of throwing the whole thing away. But today—well today what I've got is a wonderfully entertaining piece of theater." He spread his hands and paused dramatically. "There's one catch."

Here it comes, Viola thought, the sales pitch. Joseph, dear Joseph, you could have made a fortune selling lightning rods.

"What catch, darling?" Hilde asked, rocking forward drunkenly. Hilde was even more resplendent than usual this evening, decked out in gold stockings, gold shoes, and a gold dress so tight that she seemed to have been electroplated into it.

"Why it's obvious." Joseph leaned toward her with inebriated enthusiasm. "Stern won't touch the play—at least not in this form. I've already showed him the revised manuscript and he said that even though I'd just become the critics' fair-haired darling, *Berliner Ballade* was too commercial for the damn, sacred precincts of that Chamber Theater of his. No comic opera and cheap music-hall culture on his stage, the man told me, so after buying enough beer to ensure that we all have epic hangovers, we'll just have to use what's left of my prize money to produce it ourselves."

"We?" Richard pretended to clear wax out of his ears. "I know we're friends and all that, my dear fellow, but surely you don't expect *me* to traipse around the stage singing."

"No." Joseph was suddenly serious. "I don't expect you to sing, Richard, I expect you to write the music—not that atonal crap you keep turning out, but something with a beat that the audience can hum."

"But I can't," Richard protested. "I appreciate the offer, truly I do. Here you are, Joseph Rothe, the Schröter Prize winner asking *me*, England's most unknown composer, to work with you, but alas, Rothe, I'm just not *capable* of writing popular songs. Believe me, I've tried, but I'm unlyric to the core. If I tried to set this *Berliner Ballade* of yours to music, it would come out sounding like a chorus of ruptured hyenas."

"Good." Joseph grinned. "I knew you'd agree." He wheeled around and confronted Friedrich. "And you," he said, "are going to paint outrageous Expressionist sets that will make the audience feel like there isn't a right angle left on the face of the planet—you know, the kind with trees that look as if they're about to reach down and join you in a dance routine—all in bright colors of course—reds and maybe clear yellows."

Friedrich pressed his lips together and stared stubbornly at Joseph. "I don't paint to order, Rothe. I'm an artist, not an illustrator."

"You'd have a free hand." Joseph's voice took on that soft, persuasive tone that Viola knew so well. "Thousands of people would see your work; there'd probably be write-ups in all the major papers. When you consider how many people go to the theater, it makes a show in a gallery look like nothing in comparison. Do those sets for *Berliner Ballade* and you could become famous overnight."

"Well." Friedrich's pale face flushed and two purplish-red spots appeared high on his cheekbones like circles of rouge; he was obviously seriously tempted by the prospect of instant fame. "I don't know. I'd have to think it over."

"Good," Joseph said, "and while you're thinking, let me know how much money you need to buy the canvas and when you intend to start painting." He peeled off one of the larger bank notes and tossed it in Friedrich's direction. "Use this for the paint and tell me if you need more."

Friedrich's hand shot out. He clasped the bank note lovingly, rolling it between his fingers, and his thin lips curled in a smile. "You're a convincing man, Rothe."

How well Joseph played this game: assembling his team, silver-tongued, not to be resisted, always aware of the large and small desires that could be used to tie people to him. Viola found herself admiring him and at the same time feeling just a little nervous. In a minute he would be done with the others and it would be her turn.

"I suppose I'm next on this list," Hermann was saying. He leaned back and ran his fingers through his hair until it stood up on either side of his head like a pair of red fans and he grinned good-naturedly at Joseph. "I think I heard you say the word *film*; if you want to put together a film to go with this new opera-play of yours, I'm your man."

"Good"—Joseph smiled happily—"I was hoping you'd say that. As for Hilde and Jeanne"—he turned in their direction—"Jeanne can do the publicity and I want Hilde to play Zu-Zu, the exotic dancer. We'll stand you in front of a screen, Hilde, and project your image behind you ten times normal size. You'll have a chance to drive all the men in the audience wild. How about it?"

Hilde laughed a quick, husky laugh and the coins on the bodice of her dress rattled together cheerfully. "Ten times my normal size, eh?" She winked at Joseph and then at everyone in general. "Sounds marvelous, darling."

"Then, of course, there's Vi."

"What about me, Joseph?" Viola said. She suddenly felt dead sober and more than a little frightened.

Joseph leaned forward, his eyes shining. "You know what I want. I want you to take the lead role in *Berliner Ballade*. I want you to play Maria. Please. I'm not just asking you this time, I'm *begging*. This play is made for you. You're a wonderful actress—you can sing, you can dance, you make the air come alive around you when you walk on a stage. There's no other woman in Berlin who could bring to the part what you could bring to it."

He had her down so well: her professional pride, her vanity, her ambition, her love for him. He knew how to weave it around her like a net. What he couldn't know was that the fish had already been caught long ago.

He reached across the table and took her hand. She felt the strong, familiar pressure of his palm.

"Yes or no, Vi?"

"Yes," she said. Almost involuntarily her hand closed around his, and she felt such a mixture of fear, desire, and unbounded love that it made the very last shreds of reason and caution evaporate. "Yes, of course. I've been waiting for weeks for you to ask me."

Joseph jumped to his feet, leaned across the table, and gave her a kiss that took her breath away. She laughed, lifted her stein, and toasted him. "To *Berliner Ballade*," she said gaily, relieved beyond words to have finally given up struggling against him. "*Prosit!*"

"*Prosit!*" The seven of them drank and drank again, and Viola's "yes" hung on the air, putting everyone in the best of moods. Hilde told off-color stories, Jeanne sang French drinking songs, and even Friedrich joined in the general good cheer.

By the time they finally staggered to the streetcar stop in the early hours of the morning, they had named the new production company *Berliner Weisse* after Joseph's favorite drink: a noxious combination of semifermented beer and raspberry syrup that was sweet and very intoxicating.

Over the next three months the seven of them drew closer and closer as *Berliner Weisse* bonded them into a kind of friendship that not one of them would ever experience again in their lives. Later, each would look back on those weeks of creating Joseph's play together and long for them the way other people longed for their college days or the honeymoon nights of a passionate marriage.

In the mornings they would all meet in the Cafe Schiller: Hermann, bleary-eyed, ready to regale them with a description of the footage he had shot the previous day; Richard spreading out sheaves of indecipherable music among the bread crumbs and puddles of coffee; Friedrich loaded down with beautiful watercolor sketches of sets; Jeanne bearing black leather account books and publicity posters; Hilde, Joseph, and Viola reporting on the progress of the rehearsals, and Kathe—everyone's pet—eating sweet buns and looking on with her great, silent dark eyes as plans were made and discarded at a rate so furious that sometimes they felt as if they were all passengers on a runaway locomotive.

"I've got a new version of the script," Joseph announced one afternoon as Viola walked in the door of their apartment. It was late March, the snow had melted off the chestnut trees, and the first ducks had returned to the Spree. Joseph stood by the open window, balancing a large brown folder on the palm of his hand as if it were a tray of sweets. He pushed his hair back out of his eyes and thrust the manuscript at Viola with an elated smile. "All of Act Two is better, much better. Here, have a look."

Berliner Ballade had started out as the story of an immoral but rather likable charlatan named Martin Straub who turned every disaster Germany had experienced over the past ten years to his own profit: stealing medical supplies during the war and selling them on the black market; seducing rich women during the inflation by pretending to be a medium and then converting their pet poodles into a popular brand of knockwurst; running a house of prostitution disguised as a church; making a fortune by convincing gullible Berliners that he could teach them how to fly.

As Viola scanned the new pages she felt a stab of anxiety; the changes were so good and yet . . . she read on and her apprehension grew. She turned another page and bit nervously at her lower lip. As much as she wanted to convince herself that she was imagining things, it was clear all the revisions were moving in one direction. "Why have you suddenly decided to change Straub from an embezzling bank clerk to a failed artist from Vienna?" she asked.

"I thought that was obvious."

She shook her head. "That's just the trouble—it's *too* obvious. Penguins were one thing, but Straub is so much like Hitler that the Nazis are going to go wild when they see him up there selling poodle meat."

"It isn't all that provocative, it's funny. Look how it's written."

She looked at the lines again and had to admit they were indeed funny. "I'm sorry." She sat back and took a deep breath, wanting to tell him what she thought, but not wanting to start a fight. "I just worry about the direction the play's taking."

"No one else in the cast is worried, sweetheart."

He was right about that, no one was, or if they were, they weren't saying anything. The actor who was playing Straub—a slender, dark-haired fellow named Erwin Reiter—had taken it upon himself to grow a little brushlike mustache that gave him an uncanny resemblance to a person Viola preferred not to think about.

She read the manuscript again and then reread it for a third time. When she thought about it there was only one of the additions she really wanted Joseph to cut—a new song-and-dance number called "Let's Find Someone to Hate." Straub—who had formerly delivered a comic monologue on poodle knockwurst—now sang it in the second act, on the occasion of deciding that he should go into politics:

> LET'S FIND SOMEONE TO HATE
> A WHOLE GROUP OF PEOPLE
> A GOAT WE CAN SCAPE
>
> THEN WE CAN TAKE OVER THE GOVERNMENT
> BY FORCE
> OF COURSE, OF COURSE

BY THE TIME THEY REALIZE
IT'LL BE TOO LATE
OH LET'S FIND SOMEONE
ANYONE (IT'LL BE SUCH FUN)
OH LET'S FIND SOMEONE TO HATE!

She read the words of the song over to herself and knew it was useless to suggest that it be deleted. It was in the perfect place, and the actress in her told her that if Joseph took it out even she would miss it. Maybe she was exaggerating the danger. She certainly hoped so. If she wanted to go on living in harmony with Joseph, she had better hold her tongue and keep her fears to herself.

Less than forty-eight hours later, Richard set the words of "Let's Find Someone to Hate" to one of the best tunes he was ever to write in his life. From the moment it was played at rehearsal the song ran irresistibly through everyone's head. You could hear the actors humming it in their dressing rooms, the janitors whistling it as they swept out the theater, and even Viola found herself singing it.

Still, for all its political overtones, *Berliner Ballade* was a comic opera, and it probably would have come off without much trouble if it hadn't been for Friedrich.

From the time Joseph had handed him the money that night in the beer hall until well into the middle of the summer, Friedrich had been holed up in an unheated warehouse planning, sketching, and painting night and day. Each morning he showed up at the Cafe Schiller white-faced and specked with paint, looking exhausted but being surprisingly friendly, as if this project had somehow allowed him to capture a peace of mind and a sense of self-respect that had hitherto eluded him. During the weeks he worked on the sets he was, to the considerable surprise of everyone else in Berliner Weisse, a changed man: social, enthusiastic, and even warm—or as close an approximation to warm as Viola had ever seen, and so obviously happy that she felt guilty about all the hours she had spent disliking him.

For weeks, then, it seemed that work on the scenery was progressing better than anyone could have anticipated, but when Friedrich finally had the sets brought to the theater for the first dress rehearsal it was immediately clear that something had gone wrong.

"What the hell is this stuff, Friedrich?" Joseph asked. He had been sitting in the empty auditorium, waiting for the curtain to open so he could see the sets for the first time as the audience would see them. Now he was up out of his seat, walking down the aisle with a look of disbelief on his face.

Onstage, the faces of the actors registered similar shock. In place of the cheerful sketches Friedrich had shown them, there were vast expanses of canvas full of some of the gloomiest images any of them had ever seen. The hospital where Straub got his start on a life of crime looked like a Babylonian temple, complete with high columns, windows shaped like sets of teeth, and a door so malevolently tilted that Viola couldn't walk through it without shuddering.

"What the hell have you done, man?" Joseph came to a dead halt and stared at the set as if by looking at it hard enough he might make it go away.

"What do you mean what have I done?" Friedrich laughed nervously. He was very dressed up today, more dressed up than Viola had ever seen him: his jaw shaved to a blue sheen, his short black hair slicked down against his skull, wearing a shiny blue suit that he had obviously purchased for the occasion. How much he must have looked forward to this moment, she thought. She examined the hospital set again and felt a stab of pity. It was so completely wrong.

Friedrich squared his shoulders and confronted Joseph defensively, looking almost pathetic in all his finery. "I've finished the sets for the play, that's what I've done."

"The sets for the play? But what happened to those sketches you showed me? The ones with all the color and movement? My God, Friedrich, why didn't you paint the scenery from those sketches like we agreed?"

"The sketches were trite"—Friedrich waved grandly at the stage—"mere shadows of these. They lacked Teutonic force. As a serious artist, I saw that early on, so I abandoned them for something more Wagnerian."

"Wagnerian?" Joseph looked at the columns and windows with the expression of a man who had just found ground glass in his bratwurst. "Are you telling me that you painted *Wagnerian* sets for *Berliner Ballade?*"

"Of course. Why? Is there a problem?"

There was so much of a problem that Joseph obviously didn't know where to begin. "Let's see the sets for the other scenes," he said lamely. He sank down into a front-row seat and stared despairingly at the stage. "That is if you're up to it. And let's try them with the lights so we can get the full effect."

"Of course, no trouble at all." Friedrich beamed. "Coming right up." He turned toward the wings and waved at the three stagehands imperiously. "Set up Scene II, boys."

The houselights dimmed, pulleys creaked, and the hospital set was lifted into the air to be replaced by the Church of the Ladies of the Night where Hilde was supposed to do a comic dance with a purple fan while singing a slightly off-color song entitled "Feathers of Fun."

"Oh my God." Viola heard Joseph's voice emerge from the darkness. "I don't believe it." One look at the set for Scene II and she didn't believe it either. Five giant bleeding Christs hung suspended over her head, their mouths twisted in agony.

"I couldn't dance under those guys," Hilde whispered. She let her purple fan sink limply to the floor and contemplated the Christs with fascinated horror. "Good heavens, darling, I couldn't even *breathe* under them. What could Friedrich have been thinking of?"

"Well," Friedrich called out, "what do you think of it?"

"Amazing," Joseph said. There was an ominous tone to the comment that Viola recognized as a sign that he was near his limit.

"Glad you like it." Friedrich's voice was uncertain, filled with pride and bravado. "What's next?"

There was a long silence. "Give me the backdrop for 'Let's Find Someone to Hate,' " Joseph said at last.

While the stagehands were moving in the new set, Viola and the rest of the cast wandered off the stage and sat down in the auditorium as if they had all simultaneously arrived at the hope that perhaps things wouldn't look so bad from a distance.

"I want to close the curtain on this one." Friedrich walked to the front of the stage and stood in a spot of green light, which did nothing at all to improve his appearance. He folded his arms across his chest and shot them all a look of hope mixed with defiance. "I want you to get the full effect."

The curtain was duly closed. In the cool darkness of the theater, Viola took a deep breath and crossed her fingers. Surely at least one of Friedrich's sets would be appropriate.

Joseph motioned to the pianist in the orchestra pit, sitting in lone splendor at the battered grand piano that Richard had donated to Berliner Weisse. The pianist was a thin nervous man whom Viola once calculated earned approximately a stein of beer per hour accompanying them. "Play," Joseph ordered.

As the pianist struck up the opening chords of "Let's Find Someone to Hate," the curtain rose grandly on what proved to be the last disaster of the afternoon, a set so ludicrously wrong that it provoked guffaws from the cast and a moan from Joseph.

"Jesus," Hilde said in a loud voice, "the man's lost his mind."

Viola bit her lower lip to keep from laughing. She closed her eyes and opened them again, but the set was still there. For some reason no one could ever understand, Friedrich had evidently decided to paint a series of heads all over the backdrop—terrible disembodied heads with screaming mouths and wide, terrorized eyes. Many years later, when she saw some of the art that had been done by the prisoners in Treblinka, she realized with a shudder that Friedrich's dark visions had been accurate after all, but in the summer of 1928 there was no way to see this, and she—along with everyone else who looked at the set—was provoked into helpless laughter by the melodramatic excess of it all.

"Bring up the houselights," Joseph yelled. "No one could act in front of that *dreck.*" The houselights came up suddenly, leaving them all blinking and rubbing their eyes. "It's terrible, horrible, I can't believe it." Joseph paced up to the front of the theater and confronted Friedrich. "What in the world were you thinking of when you painted that stuff?"

"Of the play, of course, the scenes, the acts. . . ." Friedrich's face was pale with humiliation and disappointment.

"Well," Joseph said bluntly, "maybe you were thinking of the play and maybe you weren't, but I have to level with you—it just doesn't work. Any fool can see that it's too damn depressing. Three days of rehearsing in front of those sets, and the cast would be so damn demoralized that *Berliner Ballade* would be about as funny as a funeral. You'll just have to do it all over."

"Do it over?" Friedrich took a step back, as if he'd been physically struck. "You can't be serious. It took me *months* to paint those sets."

"Tough. You'll just have to do the next batch faster."

"That's out of the question."

"Listen, Friedrich. I happen to be the director of this play and when I say your sets stink, they stink."

Friedrich's face hardened. "The problem with you, Rothe, is that you don't have any taste. This"—he gestured angrily at the set—"is *art.*"

"The hell it is. It's shit."

"Shit?"

"Shit."

Friedrich clenched his fist at his side. "You're doing this to humiliate me. I see it all now." He stared out at all of them, a small man standing in a spotlight whose whole body seemed hunched forward with anger. "All of you are against me."

"You're crazy," Joseph said.

"Crazy am I? You don't deserve these sets, you philistine!" Wheeling around, he stalked upstage, seized an iron batten, and began to methodically demolish the set, ripping up the faces, splintering the wooden frames. Viola made a move to stop him but Hilde grabbed her arm.

"Forget it, darling," Hilde whispered. "If Friedrich wasn't doing this, then we'd have to do it for him. Let him have his tantrum."

Friedrich swung the batten wildly and the set crashed down around him; soon there was nothing left but a pile of torn canvas. Panting, he dropped the iron bar on the ground and turned to face them again.

"I'm not making any new sets for your damn, perverted little left-wing sideshow, Rothe!" he yelled. His voice echoed eerily in the half-empty theater. "Not now, not ever. I'm an artist." Friedrich drew himself up in a way that would have been funny if there hadn't been such a look of hate on his face. "I'm a man of soul, of taste, and you're just a poor, pathetic hack." He smiled a bitter, triumphant smile. "In case you don't get the full picture, let me remind you that this play of yours opens in less than a week. Since I'm not doing new sets and I know you don't have the money to pay anyone else to do them, you open without any scenery. Now that *is* a problem, isn't it? Well it's not my problem, Rothe. Not anymore."

Friedrich turned toward Viola and Hilde and clicked his heels in a sarcastic parody of politeness. *"Auf Wiedersehen,* gracious ladies," he said. "Don't bother to see me to the door. I think I can find my own way out."

There was a moment of stunned silence, broken only by the sound of Friedrich slamming the stage door behind him.

"My God." Erwin Reiter, who played Straub, tugged at his mustache and gave Joseph a look of pure panic. "What are we going to do?"

"I don't know." Joseph paced to the lip of the orchestra pit and back again. "I suppose I could sue Friedrich for breach of contract or something, but the catch is that—as you all know—no one in Berliner Weisse has a contract." He ran his fingers through his hair. "Jesus, this is a disaster."

There was no use rehearsing any more that morning. The play was doomed, anyone could see that. For almost an hour the entire cast sat around in a pall of gloom, trying to figure out some kind of solution to the problem Friedrich had dumped on them, but outside of robbing a bank no one seemed to be able to come up with any practical suggestion for raising the money to hire someone to paint new sets. Around noon Jeanne showed up with the new publicity posters and two wicker baskets full of lunch. One look at their faces and she knew something bad had happened.

"What's wrong?" Jeanne exclaimed, hoisting the wicker baskets up onto the stage. "You all look like you've just been invited to a funeral."

"Your boyfriend's run off with the sets, darling," Hilde sighed, and looked morosely at the feathers on her fan, which seemed to have gone limp with despair like everything else, "and we're in a real pickle."

"To be more exact," Joseph said grimly, "he smashed up one of them with a batten about an hour ago, but that doesn't matter because they were all wrong anyway." Joseph looked at the stage and winced. "They're like something out of a bad dream, Friedrich's own personal nightmares running amok."

"*Mon Dieu!* So that's why he wouldn't let me look at them. I suspected that something strange was going on when he spent so many hours barricaded in that warehouse, but I didn't dare ask him what he was doing. It was like living with Van Gogh, except that he was so terribly cheerful. I suppose I'm lucky I didn't end up with one of his ears." Jeanne joined them in the first row of seats. "I'm sorry," she said. She sighed, ran her fingers through her hair, and looked around the theater as if new sets might materialize out of the shadows. "How rotten of Friedrich to put us in such a situation. I wish I could say I'm surprised."

Viola, who had half expected Jeanne to defend Friedrich, was relieved.

"What are we going to do?" Jeanne asked.

"I haven't the slightest idea," Joseph said.

There was a long silence. Finally Jeanne cleared her throat. "Have any of you ever tried free association?" They all looked at her blankly. "It's a psychoanalytic technique," she explained. "We use it at the Institute to open up the subconscious. The idea is simple. I say a word, and you say the first thing that comes into your mind. For example, I say 'blue' and you say 'ocean.' I've always thought it might be a good way to solve problems, because when you do it you think of things that you'd never think of under ordinary circumstances."

"I'm desperate enough to try anything," Joseph said gloomily.

"Good." Jeanne stood up. "Let's give it a try."

"Do we all have to lie down on a couch?" Richard asked.

"No, *cheri*, all you have to do is relax. Look, here's the plan. I'll say a word and you just tell me the first thing that comes into your head. Ready?"

Viola nodded along with everyone else, wondering if this would do any good. Probably not, but it couldn't hurt to try.

"Sets," Jeanne prompted.

"Friedrich."

"Rat."

"Hanging is too good for."

Jeanne grinned. "I detect a bit of hostility here, my friends. Let's try it again. 'Stage.' "

"Bare."

"Embarrassment."

"Major problem."

They went on for five or ten minutes like this, getting nowhere. "Play," Jeanne said. Viola could tell she was getting discouraged.

"Not happening."

"Closing."

"Sophocles."

Everyone looked at Joseph.

"What did you say?" Jeanne looked confused.

"I said 'Sophocles.' " Joseph stood up and contemplated the stage. "My God, why didn't I think of this before! I've been blind." Joseph's entire face changed. He pushed his hair off his forehead and something quick and hard and brilliant glowed in his eyes again. "The more I think about it," he said, "the more I realize that we don't *need* Friedrich's sets."

"You're kidding, darling," Hilde said. "You've finally cracked under the pressure."

"No," Joseph said, "I'm not kidding. I'm completely serious." He took in the entire cast with a sweep of one arm. "It's you people, it's the actors who make a play, not sets."

They tried to object but he waved them into silence. "No, listen. Think about it. Sophocles and all the other great Greek dramatists didn't use sets. Shakespeare's plays were originally performed on a bare stage."

Viola began to see his point.

"Suppose"—Joseph paced in front of the first row of seats enthusiastically—"suppose we included some sort of note in the program telling the audience that they were about to witness an experiment in . . . what could we call it?"

"Nothingness," Reiter suggested.

"No, too negative." Joseph frowned and looked at the stage again, at the bare back wall hung with ropes and peeling plaster. "I've got it. We could call it 'classic minimalism.' That way the fact that we're fresh out of scenery will look like an intentional artistic concept instead of a last-minute disaster."

"Do you think we could get away with it?"

"What choice do we have, Vi? Friedrich's got us over a barrel. Either we pretend we meant to do it this way all along or we close the show." Joseph paused, cleared his throat, and looked at the cast uneasily. "I suppose the only real question is, are you all willing to take the chance? I know most of you have your own reputations to protect, and I don't expect you to relish the prospect of walking out there on an empty stage."

Erwin Reiter tugged at his mustache. "Straub's the best part I've ever had." He paused. "I'd be a fool to throw it away, so you can definitely count me in."

"Me, too, darling," Hilde said. "I never much liked scenery. As far as I'm concerned, it's only something to trip over." One by one, the rest of the cast expressed their willingness to go on with the show.

"And you, Vi?"

"I'm with you all the way, Joseph."

"Really?"

"You bet. Now lean your face over here so I can give you a kiss to seal the bargain." Joseph leaned over, and there, in front of everyone, she kissed him—a quick, hard, sweet kiss that spoke volumes.

A week later *Berliner Ballade* opened with no scenery. Using only Hermann's film as a backdrop, Viola, Hilde, Erwin, and the rest of the cast gave a performance so funny and brilliant that no one missed the canvas and paint. There were twenty curtain calls that night, and by the next day anyone in Berlin who had a serious interest in the theater knew that "classic minimalism" was the only topic worth discussing.

But some members of the audience had not been amused. They had sat in the back row and in the balcony, watching grimly and taking notes.

Friedrich stood in his room at Bluebeard's with his back to the door, painting furiously. The room, which had once belonged to Joseph, was flooded with early morning light, but as usual none of it was getting into the painting. The canvas that Friedrich confronted with such fierce intensity displayed only a huge eye, vast and bloodshot, with tiny wormlike lashes and a drooping lid.

Jeanne looked at the painting and shuddered. The sight of it made her even more sure that she was doing the right thing. "Friedrich." She took a few steps into the room and waited for him to stop painting long enough to acknowledge that she was there.

"What?" He turned around and stared at her like a man who had just been jerked out of a deep trance. His face was drawn and paint-spattered, and he looked terrible, as if he hadn't been eating or sleeping.

"I can't see you anymore," Jeanne said bluntly. She was sorry to say it, but she never had believed in working up to things gradually. Let the break be clean and clear. How many mental patients had she seen who had gone insane from double messages?

"You can't see me?" Friedrich repeated. "Just what does that mean?"

"It means we aren't going to be lovers anymore." She shook her head. "I'm sorry," she added gently.

He paled and put down his brush. There was something ominous in his eyes that she found unsettling; involuntarily she took a step backward. "Why?" he demanded. "I thought we had a convenient arrangement. Give me one good reason for this humiliating little scene you've sprung on me."

Jeanne shook her head. "Friedrich, I'm not springing anything on you. Look at yourself. You've changed. Since you pulled that dirty trick with the scenery you've retreated into some kind of shell. You're bitter, you brood. You're rough with me in bed—so rough that once or twice lately it actually hurt. You act like everyone's your enemy. I hate to say this, but if you came to us at the Institute, I'd say you were on the verge of some kind of paranoid breakdown. I've tried to talk to you about this, but you won't talk, and I can't take it anymore. I want a lover, not another patient."

"You dirty little French bitch," Friedrich said in a low voice, "I might have expected this. Who is he?"

"What?"

"Who's your new man?" He took a step toward her, and she backed up, frightened.

"I don't have a new man. *Mon Dieu*, haven't you heard anything I said?"

Before she realized what he was up to, he reached out and grabbed her arm. "You're lying," he hissed through clenched teeth. He squeezed her arm until it hurt. "You French bitches will do it with anything that moves. The whole race is decadent, immoral, disgusting."

"Friedrich, let go of me!"

"Go ahead, yell," he said. "There's no one here this afternoon except the two of us." He pulled her so close that she could smell the odor of cloves on his breath. "Do you know what I should do with you? I should throw you down on the floor and fuck some sense into you, but you're not worth it." He glared at her and she tried to glare back, but his grip hurt and she was terrified by the hatred she saw in his face.

"Let go of me, Friedrich. You're acting crazy."

"Shut up." He shook her until she was breathless and in tears. "I'll get you for this someday," he hissed. "Do you understand? I'll make you pay for this."

"Stop," she begged, "stop it, please."

He pushed her away from him roughly, and she stumbled, hitting her elbow on the doorframe. "Get out," he said coldly.

Fleeing into the hallway, Jeanne went to the phone and called Viola.

"Can I stay with you and Joseph for a few days, *cherie?*" she asked. Her voice was trembling, and she could hardly hold on to the receiver.

"What's wrong?" Viola asked. "You sound terrible."

"I just broke up with Friedrich and he's acting like a madman about it." She lowered her voice to a whisper. "The truth is, I'm afraid of him."

"Come over right now," Viola said. "You can stay as long as you want."

Jeanne stayed with Viola and Joseph for over a week, until Hermann called with the news that Friedrich had moved out of Bluebeard's after destroying every one of his paintings.

"He threw them in a pile on the front sidewalk," Hermann told Viola, "tossed gasoline on them, and set them on fire."

"Where has he gone?"

"No one knows," Hermann said, "but we're all glad to see the last of him."

10

1928

On a clear, crisp morning in early October, Viola and Joseph were sitting in the dining room of their new apartment silently drinking coffee, eating buttered toast, and going through their mail at the leisurely pace of two people who were so in harmony with each other that speech was irrelevant. Things had changed a great deal in the last few months and all for the better. At the beginning of 1928 five men had dominated the German stage: Max Reinhardt, Eric Stern, Leopold Jessner, Bertolt Brecht, and Erwin Piscator. On August 13, after the opening of *Berliner Ballade*, Joseph's name had been added to the list. Joseph's joking promise that the members of the Berliner Weisse would become famous overnight had proved more accurate than any of them—Joseph included—could have ever imagined.

The success of *Berliner Ballade* was, in short, the reason she and Joseph had the time this particular early fall morning to sit about in lazy splendor in a room full of brand-new furniture playing with their daughter and reading their congratulatory letters from perfect strangers. Those pages Joseph had spent so many hours rewriting had not only made them famous, they had made them comparatively wealthy, and wealth—Viola had quickly discovered, somewhat to her chagrin—was something she took to without putting up much of a fight, especially since it seemed to give her so much more time to be with Joseph and Kathe.

She took another sip of sweet, milky coffee and replaced the letter she had just read on the pile to her left. Then, tearing the crust off a small piece of toast, she dangled it in front of Kathe's mouth.

"Voom, here comes the airplane in for a landing."

"Voom," Kathe echoed. She broke into giggles and clutched at the toast with two chubby hands. "Give it to me, Mama."

"Come and get it, *mein kleiner Vogel.*"

Kathe's small dark brows met in a frown and she assessed Viola with the air of a highly intelligent elf who had just been radically underestimated. "I'm not a 'little bird,' Mama. I'm four and a half going on five."

"Pardon me, Fräulein." Viola grinned. *"Verzeihung,* I forgot your advanced age." She handed Kathe the toast with mock gravity. "Your breakfast, gracious miss."

Kathe grabbed the toast, stuffed it sideways in her mouth, and chewed it with obvious enthusiasm. She was such a beautiful child, with Joseph's thick black hair, and dark brown eyes that reminded Viola of her own, only with something quicker and more impulsive in them that was bound to get her into trouble someday. Kathe swallowed the toast and the small brown mole disappeared for a moment into the hollows of her cheek like a tiny brown animal drawing its head into its den. Yawning contentedly, she went back to the picture book that lay on the table beside her, a sumptuously bound edition of *Grimm's Fairy Tales* illustrated by Fritz Kredel, which Richard had presented to her when he dropped by yesterday afternoon.

Viola took another drink of coffee and slid the tip of her finger over the pile of letters to her right, looking for something interesting to read next. On the other side of the table Kathe turned a page in her book and a gold coach, pulled by four great white horses with golden tails and hoofs, jumped into the spot of sunlight in front of her.

Viola sighed a small sigh of resignation. Sometimes she wished the gang didn't keep giving Kathe such expensive presents. In the last three months the child had been moved into an apartment in one of the best districts in Berlin, placed in an excellent private nursery school, and had—at a conservative estimate—at least half a dozen new dresses bought for her. Was all this attention going to spoil her?

She looked at Kathe bent over her book, sucking thoughtfully on a lock of her hair, and decided if spoiling was taking place, there was, thank heavens, no sign of it yet. Besides, it was hopeless to try to keep Hilde and Hermann and the rest of them from giving her gifts. No doubt when they married and had children of their own, they'd buy them stuffed toys and picture books, but at present—like it or not—Kathe was the group mascot.

Picking up a large brown envelope, she slit it open with the blade of her silver butter knife and unfolded the letter inside. Even before she read what it said, it struck her that the paper was odd. Most people who wrote fan mail did it on pretty, scented cards or creamy formal stationery; Germans were always so careful to make a good impression. But this letter was scribbled in watery black ink on a piece of cheap yellow notebook paper.

Your play is a dirty piece of shit.

She stared at the scrawled message with incomprehension. The words were quick and vicious, like a sudden punch to the face.

Get out of Berlin you dirty Communist bastard and take your bitch with you. We're watching you; we know where you live you filthy . . .

There was more: horrible obscene threats of violence to her and Joseph and Kathe, crazy diatribes on *Berliner Ballade* and everyone in it, but she couldn't bear to read further. There had been threats before, but nothing like this. Whoever had written this was badly disturbed—no, not just disturbed, insane. Surely no one could seriously propose doing this kind of harm to another human being. Angrily, Viola took a drink of coffee, thinking that she was a different woman than the one who had fled to Eric Stern three years ago. With Joseph's help she'd found the courage to put her political beliefs into action. She was proud of the two of them for speaking out when so many Germans had been cowed into silence, and she'd be damned if she'd let some anonymous threat come between them. Impulsively, she crumpled the letter into a ball and dropped it into the wastebasket, feeling as if she were disposing of a poisonous snake.

Joseph heard the noise of the paper being crumpled and looked up from the article he was engrossed in—a pleasant, laudatory piece on Berliner Weisse that had just appeared in a small newspaper of the arts called *Berlin at Night*.

"Didn't like that one, eh?"

"No." She quickly picked up another envelope, hoping he wouldn't ask any questions. Perhaps it was only a cruel joke. The threat rolled through her mind so obsessively that she could hardly concentrate on the next letter, which, when she was finally able to devote a little attention to it, seemed to be from an elderly lady named Frau Werfel, who had particularly loved one of Richard's tunes.

In the wastebasket the crumpled piece of hate mail lay on top of a discarded apple core. Viola turned her head. She wouldn't look at it again. She'd forget all about it.

She took another quick drink of coffee, put Frau Werfel's letter on the already-read pile to her left, and went back to the stack on her right. The sun was still shining as brightly as it had been shining five minutes ago, but she couldn't shake the impression that there was something dark in the room now, something heavy and brooding that was casting a cloud over everything.

Stop it, she thought. Just stop it. And perhaps she could have stopped it, even forgotten the letter in the wastebasket and the threats it had contained, if at that moment she hadn't looked at the pile of unread letters and seen, three from the bottom, another long brown envelope, and on it, her own name—VIOLA KESSLER ROTHE— scribbled in watery black ink.

HITLER

AT THE SPORT PALACE

Nov. 16 8:00

LOYAL GERMANS HEAR YOUR FÜHRER!

The posters appeared overnight: plastered up on walls with a crude white glue that oozed out from under the edges, tacked to trees, wrapped around lampposts with short twists of wire. A whole forest of swastikas stretched the length of Unter den Linden up the Kaiser Wilhelm Strasse. Viola threw another handful of stale bread crumbs to the ducks swimming at her feet and tried to ignore the black and red rectangles but even here, on the banks of the Spree, you couldn't get away from the omnipresent signs.

"It must have taken an entire army to put those things up," Jeanne said wearily. She sat down on one of the wrought-iron benches, drew her coat closed, and contemplated the river with a look of misery so complete that Viola impulsively sat down beside her and put her arm around her shoulder. For a few minutes they sat in silence. Out on the river the ducks battled over the crumbs.

"What's wrong?" Viola asked at last.

"Nothing." Jeanne tugged her wool beret down over her ears as if trying to hide her entire head in it. She was looking tired—lusterless, almost ill—and there were dark circles under her eyes. Avoiding Viola's glance, she retrieved her purse from under the bench, a black leather affair that looked large enough to double as a small suitcase, fumbled around in it, and extracted a pack of French cigarettes. "I've been doing a lot of publicity for Berliner Weisse—not that I'm complaining, in fact that's the only thing I'm doing these days that's any fun—but on top of it I'm working too hard at the Institute." She struck a match, lighted her cigarette, and inhaled in a quick, nervous way that wasn't at all characteristic of her. "I'd almost decided to do my thesis on the mass psychology of political movements." Jeanne grinned with a weak attempt at humor. "After all, you have to admit I'm in the right place at the right time to do the research, but"—she hesitated, staring at the cigarette in her hand as if reluctant to continue—"there are problems."

"What sort of problems?"

Jeanne sighed wearily and gave another tug at her beret. Her face looked pinched and cold. "Some of the Jewish professors are leaving. The best ones, naturally. That's the way life is. Sooner or later the best always leave."

Viola didn't know what to say. They sat for a moment watching the ducks dive for the last of the bread crumbs. The green and blue necks of the mallards sparkled in the cold gray water like spots of paint.

Jeanne took a long, slow drag on her cigarette. "I ran into Friedrich the other day," she said, flicking a few centimeters of ash onto the sidewalk.

"Did he threaten you again?"

"No, nothing like that." She turned to Viola. "He's joined the Nazis, did you know that? Become a member of the local *Ortsgruppe*. I've never seen anyone undergo such a change in my life. You remember how he always dressed as if he'd found his clothes in a pawn shop?"

Viola nodded. "I think he did, actually."

"Well, now he goes around wearing a brown shirt and spouting the most amazing nonsense about discipline and sacrifice for the cause. It seems the Nazis have adopted him as their pet artist. They even let him paint a big portrait of Hitler for that speech at the Sport Palace, some monstrous thing the size of the Eiffel Tower that's supposed to hang behind the podium inspiring the faithful." Jeanne blew another stream of smoke in the general direction of the ducks. "It's unbeliev-able really. Friedrich's like a man who's undergone a religious conversion, and he's gotten so fanatical. Not that he was ever what you could call mentally flexible even in the best of times, but now . . ." Jeanne rolled her cigarette nervously between her fingers, and Viola noticed that her nails were bitten down to the quick. "Actually that's why I asked you to meet me here today, Vi. I wanted to warn you about him."

"Warn *me* about him?"

Jeanne nodded. "Yes. Our encounter wasn't pleasant. He was nasty to me. Polite but nasty. He made some ugly comments about the 'Jewish practice of psychoanalysis' which I'll spare you, all but told me I was a fool to stay at the Institute, and suggested I take the next train back to France where I belonged, and then he got on the subject of Joseph and you, and it was, well"—Jeanne took another quick, nervous drag on her cigarette—"it was frightening."

"Did he threaten us?"

Jeanne nodded. Throwing her cigarette into the river, she watched it as it sank in a small sizzle of steam. "I've never seen anyone put out so much pure hatred in such a short time in my entire life. He said that Joseph had humiliated him publicly and tried to wreck his career, that both of you had plotted against him, but that he was going to take care of that."

Viola thought of the brown envelopes lying in the top drawer of her desk. So Friedrich had joined the Nazis and was out for revenge? Interesting, very interesting indeed. That certainly explained a lot. She tried to remember if Friedrich's handwriting looked like the handwriting on the hate letters, but without success. As far as she knew, she'd never seen him write anything, and besides he would no doubt have taken the trouble to disguise it. Still, after what Jeanne had just told her, it seemed a good bet that Friedrich was behind the threats. She didn't know whether to be relieved or even more upset than she'd been before. Friedrich was a dangerous man to humiliate, that was obvious, but surely he wouldn't actually do them any real harm. After all, they'd been friends.

"I've come to a conclusion," Jeanne said abruptly. "I'm going back to France."

Viola turned to her, startled beyond words. "But what about your work at the Institute? What about Berliner Weisse?" It was ridiculous, of course, but she found herself suddenly feeling abandoned. Even though she'd always known Jeanne was French, she'd never imagined her leaving Berlin. In some foolish way, she supposed she had always counted on them all growing old together, tottering out to the Spree in their mid-nineties to throw crumbs at the ducks.

Jeanne shrugged. "The Institute's falling apart, Berliner Weisse doesn't need me anymore, and I want out of Germany. It's too ugly here, too crazy." She embraced Viola and kissed her on both cheeks. "I'll miss you terribly, Vi. I really will. I wish I could convince you and Joseph to come with me."

"There's not a chance of that, Jeanne. Joseph's already working on a new play." Viola picked up her purse and made a small production of buttoning up her coat, afraid if she tried to say anything else, she might actually burst into tears.

A spark of interest appeared in Jeanne's eyes. "A new play, you don't say? What's it about?"

Viola fumbled with her top button, not meeting Jeanne's eyes. Her fingers felt clumsy and cold, and suddenly she felt as if she'd give anything to be sitting in the Cafe Schiller over a hot cup of coffee. "I don't know if I should tell you. Joseph asked me to keep it a secret, but since you're leaving, I guess you might as well know. It's not a comedy. It's a serious piece called *The Wailing Wall*, an attack on anti-Semitism, you know, all that 'master race' garbage."

"*Mon Dieu.*" Jeanne reached out and put a hand on Viola's shoulder, horrified. "You're both crazy. I mean neither of you are even Jewish, Vi." She looked around uneasily, but the only thing within a hundred yards was the ducks. "You can't take chances like that, not so publicly, not now. The Nazis got over eight hundred thousand votes in the last election."

"I used to worry a lot about things like that," Viola confessed, "but lately I've stopped. I decided the day I went to Stern and asked him to do *Penguins* that politics would never come between Joseph and me again. The stakes are too high. Besides, speaking may not be safe, but someone has to do it." She tried to smile. "I admit that I'm still scared, but I go ahead anyway."

"Vi, Vi"—Jeanne patted her on the shoulder as if she were a small child—"you've got to look out for yourself better. And remember what I said about Friedrich. I mean it; he's not a man to be underestimated."

A week later Viola, Joseph, Hermann, Richard, and Hilde went down to the train station at nine in the morning to see Jeanne off to Paris. It was an emotional parting, full of cheerful promises to write and visit, but it left a sad feeling in its wake. As they sat in the Cafe Schiller afterward drinking coffee and eating green eel, no one had much to say. Despite the fact that all five of them were now successful, famous, and even more or less well-off, it was clear that Berliner Weisse was falling apart. That morning there wasn't one of the group who didn't secretly long—at least for a moment—for the old days at Bluebeard's when they all had been young and poor and the world had seemed so much more simple.

Three nights later the phone rang in the box office of the Neues Theater.

"Hello, you Jewish bastards," a male voice said, "we've got a little present for you."

"A present?" the ticket seller said. She was only seventeen, just out of school.

"A bomb."

"Oh my god!"

The man on the other end of the line laughed nastily. "Have fun looking for it, and I hope it blows you all to bits."

The show was halted immediately and the theater evacuated. Fortunately, no bomb was found, only a briefcase full of some of the ugliest anti-Semitic propaganda Viola had ever seen in her life. There were many ironies to that particular evening, but the one she remembered the longest was that the phone call had come at the exact moment Erwin Reiter was in the process of singing "Let's Find Someone to Hate."

Sundays in Berlin tended to be quieter than other days, especially in the early mornings when half the population was at home sleeping off hangovers and the other half was in church. The cobblestones in the streets always seemed to glisten more brightly on Sundays, the birds seemed cleaner and better behaved, and what little traffic there was in the neighborhood moved at a measured rate, as if honking horns and speeding trucks were under a temporary ban. At least that was Viola's impression on this particular Sunday in December as she made her way at a leisurely pace toward the park with Kathe, carrying a bottle of milk, two sandwiches, and a wool blanket in a net bag.

Kathe was going skating in the park this morning, and she was very excited by the prospect, having just received a new pair of skates as a pre-Christmas present from Hermann—a lovely set of white-and-red high-topped girls' skates with glistening steel runners. As the child ran along ahead with her precious skates slung over her shoulder, the runners caught the sunlight and were transformed for an instant into two bright bands that made Viola squint and shade her eyes.

"Look, Mama, I'm Sonja Henie!" Sonja Henie, the blond Norwegian ice-skating champion, had recently become Kathe's idol. In fact, Joseph had observed only yesterday that if they could flood the dining room and freeze it into a rink, Kathe would be more than happy to skate to meals. "Here I go!" Kathe lowered her little head with determination, crouched down, and catapulted herself onto a small patch of ice on the sidewalk, sliding wildly on the soles of her leather shoes, arms flailing. To Viola's immense relief, she reached the end without falling. Giggling and red-cheeked, she looked back to see what Viola's reaction was going to be.

"Good job." Viola tried to sound as approving as possible on the grounds that Kathe should be encouraged to take reasonable risks, but privately she felt a little anxious. The child was so completely fearless; someday she was going to break an arm or leg out of sheer physical exuberance.

"Want to see me do it again?" Kathe walked back to the edge of the ice and prepared for another reckless glissade.

"Only if you can promise me Fräulein Henie won't fall on her fanny."

"Oh, Mama," Kathe giggled, "you're silly."

"Suppose I slide on the ice instead of you, gracious miss?"

"Oh no, Mama." Kathe shook her head gravely. "You're too old. You'll break."

"I'm not old. I'm only four and a half going on five."

"No, Mama." Kathe shook her head vigorously. "*I'm* four and a half going on five."

"No, *I* am." Viola laughed and Kathe laughed with her. This was an old game, dating back to when Kathe first learned to talk, a game in which Viola became the little girl and Kathe the mama, and it never failed to amuse both of them.

"A very tender scene, Frau Rothe." Viola turned, startled at the interruption, to find a middle-aged man standing behind her flanked by two younger ones. All three men were large and heavy, with hair clipped close to their heads, military style. They were dressed in nothing that would indicate they were Nazis, yet she knew at a glance they were. Her first impulse was to grab Kathe's hand and run, but Kathe was ten yards or so away sliding happily on the ice, and even as Viola had the thought the men moved between her and the child, not in any subtle way but as if daring her to try to push past them.

She looked at the slippery patches of ice that would make running so difficult, at the vacant windows of the surrounding buildings, at the long empty streets, at the three strangers who stood between her and her child, and a kind of cold terror spread over her—not for herself but for Kathe—and she knew that the men could sense it and that it amused them, and she felt angry that they could be amused at a mother's fear. She remembered the hateful letters stuffed into the bottom drawer of Joseph's desk, the terrible descriptions of violence they had been threatened with, the sick details born of sick minds that she and Joseph had managed to convince themselves were only idle threats. And now here she was, alone with her child on a deserted street, and these men had her cornered. What a fool she'd been not to be more careful. For a moment she felt nauseous and powerless, as if somehow she was the one who had betrayed Kathe into this danger, and then she got hold of herself. I can't panic, she thought. I'm weaker than they are; there's no way I can fight them off if they want to hurt us, but maybe I can talk them out of whatever it is they have in mind. It was a fragile hope, but she clung to it.

The men stood looking at her with a sort of bland indifference, as if they did this sort of thing all the time. One of them took a handkerchief out of his back pocket and blew his nose. The noise seemed unusually loud.

"Who are you and what do you want?" She fought to keep the fear out of her voice, sensing that these men were like cats playing with a mouse, waiting for her to squeal and run so they could strike, and that when and if they did strike, the blow would be quick and ruthless.

"Oh it doesn't matter who we are, Frau Rothe. It's you who matter." The man who seemed to be the spokesman for the group smiled an unpleasant smile full of crooked teeth. He was taller than the rest, with large, beefy arms and a florid face. With a shock Viola realized she had seen him somewhere before, but where? It seemed an important thing to remember, as if by knowing she could somehow stop this nightmare from unfolding. "We know all about you, you see, dear lady." The man beat his gloved hands together to warm them and looked at Viola with the sort of casual, benign interest people usually bestow on distant acquaintances, and she suddenly had the feeling that she couldn't possibly be hearing him right, that he couldn't be saying what he was saying with such an ordinary expression on his face. "We know where you live," he continued. He held out his hands and inspected his gloves, as if trying to decide if he needed to buy another pair. "We know where you perform your stinking Communist play, where you shop. We even know where the little one over there goes to school, the route you walk every morning to take her there; we know your dentist, your doctor, your green grocer, what time you eat, what time you sleep, what time you and your filthy husband screw." The man with the crooked teeth suddenly gestured at Kathe. "Pick up the child, Franz," he commanded.

The man called Franz took half a dozen quick steps along the sidewalk, bent down and picked Kathe up under the arms, swinging her lightly, as if she were a stuffed doll. He was about Joseph's height, dressed in a leather overcoat, blunt-fingered and dark, with small wolfish eyes and badly pocked skin. "Hello, little girl," he purred in a heavy Swabian accent, "want to go for a ride?"

"Please," Viola begged, "don't let him hurt her." There was no pride left in her now, only panic. "I'll do anything you want. Please. She's just a little girl."

"Children have such pretty faces," the man with the crooked teeth said. "Don't you agree, Frau Rothe?"

"Yes," Viola said. "Yes, of course." She hardly knew what she was saying. Kathe was looking at the strange man with a puzzled expression on her face.

"Who are you?" she asked, sucking dubiously on her lower lip. "Are you a friend of Mama's?"

"Yes," Franz said pleasantly. "A very old friend. Would you like to go for a ride like an airplane?"

Kathe looked at Viola for permission. "Tell her yes," the man with the crooked teeth said in a low voice. "Tell her it's fine."

"Please," Viola begged, "don't hurt her."

"Just tell her it's fine and that we're your friends; tell her now and quit stalling."

"It's fine, honey." Viola nearly choked on the words, but she forced herself to say them somehow. "This is a friend of ours." She bit her lip to keep from crying out a warning, bit it so hard that later she realized she'd drawn blood.

Kathe's face relaxed. "Oh." She put her arms trustingly around Franz's neck. "Then it's okay." There was something about the fact that Kathe had decided to use an English word at that moment that made Viola want to break into tears.

"Here we go." Franz suddenly turned Kathe over, grabbed an arm and an ankle, and then—to Viola's horror—he began to swing the child's body in a long, dizzy circle, bringing her head within inches of the pavement. "Now you're an airplane, little girl. Round you go."

"Oh my God, please tell him to stop."

"You should get out of Germany, Frau Rothe," the man with the crooked teeth observed calmly. "Children have such pretty faces and such tender little heads. Like eggshells."

Kathe laughed happily. "Look, Mama. I'm flying." Franz swung her harder, taking her closer and closer to the cobblestones until it seemed to Viola that there was no chance that Kathe's head wouldn't strike them. Impulsively, she clutched at the man's coat. "We'll go"— she was hysterical now—"I promise. Joseph and I will leave. Only tell him to stop. Please tell him to stop."

"I think the little girl's had a long enough ride, Franz," the man with the crooked teeth called out cheerfully.

Flipping Kathe up into the air, Franz caught her neatly in his arms, as if she were a ball, and deposited her back on her feet. Kathe stood for a moment, dizzy and laughing.

"That was fun." She smiled at Franz. "Can we do it again?"

Franz shook his head. "Afraid not. Maybe some other time." He stepped aside. "Good-bye," he said.

"Good-bye." Kathe gravely reached out and shook his hand. *"Auf Wiedersehen."*

"We know where you live." The man with the crooked teeth put one finger under Viola's chin and lifted her face to his. His eyes were small and pale and she could see a trace of lust in them. "Remember that, my pretty little Frau." And then they were gone, all three of them, turning into an alley, leaving the street empty and peaceful again, wrapped in its Sunday morning silence.

Viola stood for a moment, too stunned to move. Then she ran to Kathe, knelt down, and threw her arms around her. She felt the rough wool of the child's coat and inside it Kathe herself warm and alive and safe. Grasping Kathe to her, she hugged her and hugged her. She began to sob, great shameless sobs that caught in her throat and made it impossible for her to speak.

"What's wrong, Mama?"

Viola pulled her closer. "My Kathe, my *kleiner Vogel.*"

"I'm not *little*, Mama," Kathe protested, wiggling impatiently in her arms. "I'm not *klein* at all."

Half an hour later Viola sat in the living room of her own apartment listening to someone pounding on the front door. The dishes in the china closet rattled and the chain to the bolt danced up and down as if it might snap, but it didn't matter if the bolt itself broke, Viola thought, with the lucidity of the completely irrational, because it wasn't holding the door closed anyway. A bureau was now performing that function, as was a bookcase, a table, and the big stuffed chair that Joseph liked to relax in after he finished writing for the day. Viola could feel the pain in her back and arms where she had strained to drag the furniture to its present position. In the dim light it looked like a pile of boulders with unnaturally sharp, square edges, a great insurmountable heap that would hold out against anything.

On the sofa near the window Kathe lay asleep, thumb planted squarely in her mouth, her face flushed with the healthy color of childish dreams. The apartment was dark, the curtains drawn, windows shut and locked, dark and safe like a cave. I'm standing guard over her, Viola thought stubbornly. She realized that she was probably half hysterical with fear, but all she could feel at present was a simple determination not to let anyone into the apartment.

The knocking grew more impatient. "Vi," a familiar voice demanded, "let me in. Vi, pull the bolt for Christ's sake. What have you got the bolt thrown for in the middle of the day?"

"Joseph? Is that you?" She went over to the door and tried to lean her ear against it, but the furniture was in the way.

"Of course it's me," a muffled voice said from the hallway.

Convinced, she began to pull at the heap of furniture, breaking her nails, skinning her arms and elbows. The table fell to the floor with a loud thump, legs up like a dead horse; the bureau tilted dangerously and she caught it; drawers slid out, socks tumbled onto the carpet. Grabbing the chair, she lugged it out of the way and then shoved the bookcase to one side. She could feel sweat dripping off her neck and falling in sticky drops down her back. Shoving the last of the books into a messy heap against the wall, she threw back the bolt and opened the door.

Joseph was standing in the hall dressed in his new overcoat, white silk muffler wrapped jauntily around his neck, looking worried and annoyed and then, when he caught sight of her face and the pile of upended furniture, startled. "My God, Vi"—he stared at the room, and then back at her, his face pale with puzzlement—"what happened?"

"Some men almost killed Kathe." She was amazed how easily she was able to say such a terrible thing. Wiping her hands on her skirt, she motioned for him to come inside.

"What are you talking about?" Joseph took off his coat, unwrapped his muffler, and draped them both carefully on the back of a chair. His steps were cautious, the kind of steps people took when visiting invalids. He thought she'd lost her mind, of course. That was natural. Under the circumstances, she wished she *had* lost her mind.

Viola took a deep breath, knowing she needed to explain as quickly as possible but hardly able to bring herself to conjure up the scene again. Her throat felt dry and sore, and her head ached, as if she'd spent the afternoon in some beer cellar drinking cheap lager. "We were on our way to the park." She stumbled over the words; her tongue felt swollen. "And some men came up and one of them took Kathe and swung her up in the air as if he was going to knock out her brains, and she didn't even know what was happening, and she kept laughing, and the other man kept telling me we should get out of Germany, and. . ."

The words poured out of her as she told Joseph as best she could what had happened to her and Kathe on their Sunday excursion to the park, told him all at once in a grand, disorganized irrational sweep, getting the end before the beginning: the three men, the threats, the danger, her fear, the empty street, the ice.

"My God," Joseph kept saying, "my God." He switched on the light and contemplated the sleeping child and the heap of furniture. "You must have gone almost out of your mind."

"Yes, I think I did." Her knees suddenly felt as if they were attached with rubber bands, and she had the odd sensation that she might actually faint.

"Do you want me to hold you?"

"Yes, please."

He put his arms around her but she still couldn't cry. She steadied herself against him, glad for the support. The smell of him was comforting—wool and skin and something else she could never identify. She let herself sink into it, trying to convince herself that now that Joseph was here everything would be all right.

"The bastards," he said. She could feel the anger swelling in him. His heart was beating faster and there was something tight and hard about the way he was holding her, as if he were afraid someone might try to pull her out of his arms.

"I know I should have gone to the police, but once I got here I was afraid to take Kathe back out on the street again. So I waited." She felt herself starting to tremble. The relief of not having to deal with all this by herself was incredible.

"You should have called someone, Vi."

"The phone wasn't working. I thought at first they'd cut the lines, but then I remembered that phones in Berlin go dead all the time." She was beginning to feel almost sick with the aftershock of it all. "Could we sit down?"

"Yes, of course." They sat at the dining-room table. Around them Joseph's new play lay piled in heaps. She put her hands together, but the trembling wouldn't stop.

"Who were they, Vi?" Joseph pushed his hair out of his eyes and gave her a look she'd never seen before, a look of love mixed with protective anger. Taking her hand, he squeezed it hard, lacing his fingers through hers. "They were Nazis, of course. We can take that for granted, but did you recognize any of them?"

"I don't know for sure." She hesitated. "Actually, I do think maybe I've seen one of them before."

"Where?"

"With our old buddy Friedrich."

Joseph's eyes narrowed dangerously. "Friedrich?"

"It's just a hunch. I could be all wrong. I think I vaguely remember seeing one of them in the Cafe Schiller. It struck me on the way home—an image of him sitting at one of those artists' tables in the corner talking to Friedrich."

"Damn it." He dropped her hand.

"I could be wrong. I'm not sure."

"But of course Friedrich's behind this!" Joseph got up and walked angrily over to the far side of the room. "It all makes sense now. Friedrich's never forgiven me for throwing out those rotten sets of his." He walked back to the table, bent over, and gave Viola a fierce, quick hug. "I should have taken those letters more seriously. You kept warning me, and like a fool I ignored you."

"It isn't your fault."

"The hell it isn't."

"Joseph, please."

But he was past listening to her. "Do you think I can look at our child and think that she was almost killed by a pack of Nazi scum and not feel that it was my fault? Do you think I can come home and find my wife terrified and not think it was my fault?" He seized a pile of pages from his new play and threw them angrily on the floor. "I've been wrapped up in this trash, sitting here indulging my damn artistic sensitivity while the two of you were in danger. Well, never again!"

The pages from the half-finished play fluttered into the corners of the room. "What do you mean 'never again?' " Viola asked anxiously.

He picked up the cup of cold coffee and drained it, wiping his mouth on the back of his hand. His chin was set stubbornly and everything about him suddenly seemed square and solid. "I mean I'm finding Friedrich and having this out with him. I mean I intend to drag him over here by the collar and have him apologize to you and promise that he'll never sic those bastards on us again."

"But, Joseph"—she was horrified—"that's crazy. It's too dangerous. Friedrich isn't just an ordinary person anymore; he's a high-level something or other in the Party."

"Vi, I don't give a damn."

She knew he hated being told what to do; she knew his pride made it almost impossible for him to take a sensible route if anyone suggested it to him, but she couldn't stop herself. This time he *had* to listen to her. He could get hurt, badly. "You didn't see those men today. I did. And I'm telling you, they aren't to be trifled with."

"They don't scare me, Vi."

"They should. Please, if you love me, don't even think of going after those thugs. We should call the police."

"The hell with the police. They can't do anything. I'm going out right now and put a stop to this shit." He picked up his coat, and she realized that she wasn't going to be able to stop him.

"Please don't go," she begged. She would have given anything to have been able to sound feminine and vulnerable at that moment, but she couldn't of course. She might be able to act on stage, but when it came to Joseph she could only be herself, and that was the curse and the joy of their marriage. She was strong enough to take almost anything, and they both knew it.

Joseph put on his coat. "I'll call Hilde and Hermann and Richard to come stay with you." He seemed calm now, like a man who knew exactly what he had to do. It was that kind of calm that got men killed, Viola thought, the kind that sent them into battle singing patriotic songs when any woman in the same situation would be flat on her belly in the nearest ditch avoiding the bullets.

"Joseph, please."

"I'll be back in an hour, maybe less. Since he stopped hanging out at the Schiller, Friedrich is always at the Cafe Romanische or in the Tiergarten this time of day. The man's like a clock. I'll only be an hour, two at the outside. I promise." He bent down to kiss her and she turned her face away, angry with him for putting himself in such danger. Hadn't she been through enough today without him adding to it?

"Good-bye," she said coldly, thinking that, as much as she loved him, he was an impulsive fool.

Friedrich sat on a bench in a deserted part of the Tiergarten looking at some sketches for a new portrait of Hitler. They were fine, strong sketches, some of the best he'd ever done, and he was proud of them.

"Do you really like them?" he eagerly asked the man in the dark suit who sat to his right.

"Yes," the man in the dark suit said. "You've caught the Führer's strength and compassion perfectly. The Party will be delighted." He nodded to his friend in the leather overcoat. "Don't you agree, Franz?"

Franz picked up the sketches, held them close to his pockmarked face, and inspected them critically. His eyes were wolfish and sharp. "They're too small," he objected.

"The final portrait will be larger," Friedrich explained. "These are only preliminary studies." He was reaching for his sketches when a shadow fell across the paper.

"Friedrich, you bastard." Joseph Rothe stood before them, his face flushed with anger. "What the hell do you mean by terrorizing my wife and child?"

Friedrich paled slightly. "I don't know what you're talking about, Rothe."

"Shut up. I don't want to hear your lies. I want you and your criminal friends to stay away from Viola and Kathe. Do you hear me?"

"Very impressive," the man in the dark suit said, "but very, very stupid." He nodded. "Now, Franz," he said.

The last thing Joseph remembered was something cold and hard slamming him with sickening force on the back of the head.

He came back to consciousness facedown in the trunk of a moving car with a gag stuffed into his mouth. His hands were tied with electrical wire, and there was another loop around his legs. Joseph tried to breathe, but the trunk was suffocating, reeking with the odors of exhaust and gasoline; he tried to yell, but the best he could produce was a muffled moan.

The car lurched from side to side, throwing him against the metal struts. He had been hit on the head and was still dizzy from the blow, but some survival instinct made him notice the roughness of the road. They must be going down a country lane. When they stopped he would try to break away and make a run for it.

He was furious at himself for underestimating Friedrich. Vi had been right. He should have taken Richard and Hermann along with him instead of confronting the bastards alone. It had been a stupid thing to do.

The car lurched to a stop, throwing him sideways. Sickening pain spread from his neck down his spine and he saw dancing lights.

"Pull him out," he heard a voice say. The trunk lid flew open, and the man in the leather coat grabbed him and dragged him out into the freezing air. Cutting the wire that bound his feet, the man stuck the barrel of a pistol into the small of Joseph's back.

"March," he commanded. They were in some kind of forest. The trees were shadowy and immense and the air smelled of pine sap. It was overcast and snowing, with a cold, cutting wind. Joseph staggered down a twisting path, his head throbbing horribly with every step he took. He was frightened by the thought that they were probably going to take him somewhere and beat him senseless.

Friedrich and the man in the dark suit walked ahead, carrying large brown cans. The cans struck Joseph as ominous. He couldn't imagine what they were going to be used for. After about five minutes, they reached a small clearing.

"Put him there," the man in the dark suit said, pointing to the center of the clearing. There was something oddly matter-of-fact about the way he spoke, as if he'd done this all a hundred times before. "Cut his hands free."

Joseph was surprised. He hadn't expected to be untied. The man they called Franz handed his revolver to Friedrich, pulled a knife from his pocket, and cut the cords that bound Joseph's hands.

"We want you to be able to run," Friedrich said, "but not quite yet. If you start running too soon, we'll shoot you. Do you understand?"

Joseph tried to yell something at Friedrich but the gag was in the way.

"He understands," the man in the dark suit said. Bending down, he did something to the top of one of the cans. Picking it up, he handed it to Friedrich. "I think you should have the pleasure, Hoffman."

Friedrich stood for a moment holding the can, as if planning his next move. Then, swinging his arm in a wide arc, he threw something on Joseph. Joseph gagged and choked. His eyes stung and his skin burned and for an instant he couldn't breathe. Friedrich threw on more of the liquid. It had a thick, petroleum smell to it. With horror, Joseph realized it was gasoline. Suddenly he understood what Friedrich was going to do.

"No!" he yelled, but the gasoline-soaked gag muffled all sound. He turned to run, only to find Franz's pistol jammed in the pit of his stomach.

"Not yet," Franz said. "We want you to enjoy this."

Joseph froze, knowing that if he took another step, Franz would shoot him in the stomach. He tried to think of something to do, but he couldn't think of anything. Reaching into his pocket, he felt for a weapon, but all he had was his wallet. Franz stepped aside.

More gasoline rained over him, drenching him to the skin. Friedrich put down the empty can and picked up a full one. Dropping his wallet to the ground, Joseph slowly edged away from it. If Friedrich did what he thought he was going to do, then there'd be no way of identifying his body, and Viola would need to know . . .

The thought of Viola and Kathe was painful. For a moment he was filled with a dizzy, overpowering love for them, a love so intense that it overcame his fear. More gasoline rained down on him; he reeked of it; it dripped off his clothes and formed puddles in the snow at his feet. At last Friedrich stopped. Putting down the can, he reached into his coat and pulled out a small box of matches.

Joseph saw everything: he saw the match being dragged along the side of the box; he saw it burst into flames. Friedrich held the match upright, savoring the moment. Then, walking up to Joseph, he held it out to him.

"Let's see how fast you can run, Rothe," he said as he tossed the burning match straight in Joseph's face. There was a burst of light, a terrible searing pain. For a second Joseph held his ground, too shocked to move. Then he turned and ran. He got almost to the edge of the clearing before what was left of him fell twitching into the snow.

All afternoon Viola waited for him to return. By dinnertime she had begun to panic, and shortly thereafter Hermann, Richard, and Hilde began to panic too. Conversation lagged and they avoided each other's eyes. Richard, who usually talked nonstop, fell silent and began to drink one glass of Moselle after another. Hilde ran out of amusing stories about her many lovers and suddenly lapsed into a nervous fit of chewing her fingernails. Even Hermann, who was more patient than the rest of them, grew increasingly restless as the hours passed, shifting uncomfortably in his chair and casting covert glances at his watch.

Where was Joseph? Why hadn't he returned in an hour or two as he had promised? By nine o'clock it was clear that they couldn't go on avoiding the topic so they began to speculate on his whereabouts. Maybe he'd gotten himself lost; the slums of Berlin were, after all, a famous maze, and Joseph had absolutely no sense of direction. Maybe he'd run into Eric Stern and was at this very minute sealing a deal to put on *The Wailing Wall* in Stern's Chamber Theater.

For over an hour they made up stories to comfort her and each other, but their laughter was hollow and their stories had the ring of bad fiction. At ten o'clock no one could stand the waiting any longer. Putting on their coats, Hermann and Richard went out to look for Joseph, leaving Hilde to comfort Viola, but as far as Viola was concerned, there was no comfort in Hilde, or in anything else for that matter.

From the moment Hermann and Richard walked out the door the night got worse and worse until it became the most terrible night of her entire life. It stretched on forever, monotonous and terrifying. She couldn't read to distract herself, couldn't go for a walk, or think, or eat, or even be more than barely civil to Hilde.

A dozen times she ran to the door, sure she had heard Joseph's footsteps on the stairs, and each time it was a false alarm: a cat, a neighbor coming home, or merely the creaking of the wooden stairs in the winter cold. Finally, exhausted and terrified, she fell asleep in Joseph's chair, hugging his white silk muffler to her chest as if it were a talisman that could bring him back to her.

At about seven in the morning a car stopped on the street outside and a door slammed. Viola was awake in an instant, confused, not quite sure how she had gotten in the chair in the living room. Gray winter light was coming in the windows, bluish and pregnant with the hint of a snowstorm in the offing. On the sofa Hilde lay curled in a warm pile, snoring softly, her stockings and shoes in a heap on the rug.

Viola sat up, and all the worry of the previous evening hit her suddenly in the pit of the stomach. Getting unsteadily to her feet, she looked around the apartment—at Joseph's muffler, crumpled and warm from her body, at his typewriter, his blue sweater hanging on a hook by the door—and she felt such a sense of love, and loss, and nostalgia that she wanted to cry out in pain.

Bending down, she began to pick up the pages of his new play, stacking them neatly back on his desk as if somehow, by putting his workplace in order, she could lure him back to it. The dining-room table was a mess: empty wineglasses from last night, stale cigarette butts tossed carelessly into coffee cups, dirty dinner dishes, crumbs from the spice cake Hilde had brought from the bakery around the corner. Kathe would be awake soon, wanting breakfast.

She was just carrying the dirty dishes into the kitchen when another car stopped outside and another door slammed. Viola froze, listening as the front door opened, listening as someone began to climb the stairs. Was that Joseph's step? Yes, it was. Oh my God, it was!

She turned, full of joy, throwing the dirty dishes down on the table, thinking only that he had come home at last and that all her worry had been foolish, thinking with the instant vanity of a beautiful woman that she should have taken time to comb her hair.

Hilde heard the crash of the plates and sat up, startled. Her face was pale, spotted with rouge; her mascara had bled off her eyelashes and lay under her eyes in black rings that gave her the air of a sleepy raccoon. "What is it?"

"It's Joseph!" Viola was already halfway across the room; she could hear the familiar cadences of his feet on the landing, and in the split second before she threw open the door to greet him she thought how happy she was to have him back, how angry she was that he'd been gone so long without sending word, how unreliable he was, how very much she loved him, and how if he ever did anything like this again she'd insist—absolutely insist—on going with him.

"Joseph!" She threw back the bolt on the door, ran out into the hall, and stopped dead.

"Hello, Vi," Hermann said. He looked terrible: his round face drawn and strained, his copper-red hair lusterless. Climbing the last of the steps, he stopped in front of her, avoiding her eyes.

Viola stared at Hermann blankly, unable to take in the fact that he wasn't Joseph.

"May I come in, Vi?"

"Oh." She realized that she was blocking the door. "Yes, of course." She moved aside, so disappointed that she wanted to cry but too proud to show it. Hermann came into the apartment, sat down in the overstuffed chair, and ran his hands through his hair, sending it up into fans on either side of his head, but instead of looking comic, as he usually did, he looked grim.

"I'm afraid I've got some bad news for you, Vi," he said. "So maybe you should sit down."

"What kind of bad news?"

"Joseph's dead."

Her mind simply refused to hear what he had said. "Why didn't he come home with you?"

Hermann shot her a look of pity that chilled her to the core. "He's dead, Vi. My God, I hate to be the one to tell you this, but someone had to. Richard's down at the morgue with his body. The police fished it out of the Landwehr Canal early this morning."

No, Viola thought, this can't be true. I'm still asleep. This is a horrible dream I'm having. She felt irrationally angry at Hermann for coming into her dream with such an awful message. She opened her mouth to tell him this, but no sound came out. On the other side of the room Hilde was crying, her tears running down her cheeks in long streaks of mascara.

"I brought you this," Hermann said. He delved into his back pocket and took out a gold ring and a wallet. Viola reached out and took them from him, still unable to speak. Everything in her denied that this was possible. She opened the wallet and found Joseph's identity papers, a picture of her and Kathe taken last spring sitting in front of the monkey cage in the zoo, Kathe making a funny face like a monkey. There was an old, well-worn photo of Joseph's parents standing stiffly in front of an elaborately carved sideboard, two tickets for a play they had both been wanting to see, a bundle of marks. She put down the wallet and picked up the ring. Inside two sets of initials were intertwined: JR & VK.

She held the wedding ring in the palm of her hand, feeling the cold weight of it, and she knew at last what Hermann had been trying to tell her: Joseph was dead. Oh my love, she thought. How could you leave me like this? She thought of his face and his hands and the smell of him; she thought of her life stretching on now without him, long and unbearable, and of Kathe, who would grow up without her father. Opening her hands, she let the ring drop to the floor and then she began to cry. She felt an arm around her shoulders—Hilde's probably or maybe Hermann's, it didn't matter. Joseph, she thought, I love you. There are so many things I wanted to say to you, and now it's too late.

"Vi," Hermann was saying, "Vi, listen. There's something else you have to know. Joseph, you can't—that is you won't want . . ." He stumbled to a stop and fell silent. When Viola looked up from her tears he was staring at her with such pain and pity that she almost pitied him in return.

"What is it, Hermann? What else do I have to know?" She was amazed that she could talk, amazed at the strength of her voice.

"Joseph was burned," Hermann said. "I didn't want to tell you, but Richard insisted. When the police found his body it didn't have any features; they had to identify him by the ring and wallet. Whoever killed him must have put the wallet on him for that purpose because it was the only thing on his body that wasn't charred. Richard thinks they wanted us to know he was murdered."

"Oh my God," Hilde said, "shut up, Hermann."

Hermann ignored her. "Richard and I have already arranged for a closed coffin, Vi, and we both think it would be best if you didn't try to see him."

This new horror was too much to bear. She imagined the flames licking at Joseph the way they had licked at Mama. She saw him turning in agony, screaming and crying out for her. "No!" she cried. "Tell me that isn't true, Hermann!" But she could tell by his face that it was true, and there was no escaping it.

Sitting down on the couch, she put her face in her hands and wept for Joseph's pain and for her own.

A month after Joseph's funeral, at eight-thirty in the evening, three hundred people sat in the Neues Theater watching a remarkable performance. The stage was bare except for Viola, who stood alone in a pool of light, proud and self-contained, dressed in red velvet, her blond hair tumbling in a crazy mass to her shoulders, her eyes burning with her own private grief. For four weeks all performances of *Berliner Ballade* had been suspended. Tonight was the first time the theater had been opened since Joseph's death. This was a memorial performance, one that Viola had stubbornly insisted on giving after the first bitter wave of her grieving had passed. No one in the audience knew what it was costing her to appear tonight, yet everyone sensed the force that radiated from her—a searing, comic, bitter force that was unlike any acting any of them had ever seen.

"What does it take to seduce a woman?" she demanded. *"What does it*

take? Go on. Don't just sit there. Tell me." Her body was tense and coiled. "I'll tell you what it takes—it takes greed and lies." She was Maria, the heroine, whom Straub, the charlatan, had first raped, then forced into a life of prostitution; she was the conscience of Germany. Stretching out her arms, she drew the audience to her. She was aware of her power over them; she played them out and reeled them in. She was beautiful and hypnotic.

"What does it take to seduce a whole nation?" Her voice was molten silver.

In the entire theater there was only one person who was not moved. He sat in the last row of the balcony wearing a dark suit. At his feet was an ordinary shopping bag. Without looking down, the man reached out cautiously with one foot and shoved the shopping bag under the seat next to him. He looked cautiously to the left and then to the right. Good. No one had noticed him hide the bag. The man relaxed. In precisely one minute and fifteen seconds he would get up and leave.

Viola was standing with her hands planted on her hips. Her head was thrust back and there was a strange, sad smile on her lips. "It takes the same thing to seduce a nation as it takes to seduce a woman." She paused and shrugged. "How do I know? Experience, my friends. In the end, all seductions are the same. In the end, it's always the lust for power that rapes a country and rots a soul." These were Joseph's words: bitter, comic, accusatory. As she said them she felt him standing beside her, urging her on.

On the word soul the orchestra launched into Richard's famous "He's Made a Bargain With the Devil." The entire stage was suddenly flooded with light, and Erwin Reiter appeared, dressed as Straub in a white tuxedo, twirling a white cane.

"He's made a bargain with the devil," Viola sang.

"With the devil," Reiter sang, "it's true. So keep your mouth shut and I won't bother you."

"But if you object to his methods, he has a taste for retaliation."

Reiter twirled his cane and tap-danced over to Viola. "I only act in the best interests of the nation."

In the balcony there was a slight disturbance. The man in the dark suit got up and excused himself, pushing his way past people's legs. The woman who had been sitting beside him noticed that he had left his shopping bag behind. She concluded from this that he must be coming back.

"*Looting, killing, intimidating.*"

"*My dear, your tone is rather grating.*"

The music swept on and Viola began to lose herself in it.

"*Laws?*"

"Made to be broken." Reiter took her by the hand and began to waltz her around the stage.

"*Democracy?*"

"*Only a token.*"

"*What about the Jews, Straub?*"

"*The Jews were born to lose.*"

"*Doesn't anyone care?*"

"*Don't make me laugh.*"

The next line was Viola's, but she never got to say it, because as she opened her mouth there was a violent, fiery explosion. The orchestra crashed to a halt, and for an instant audience and actors froze in terror. In the balcony there was chaos. Several seats in the back row no longer existed and the remains were burning in flames so hot that people sitting on either side were screaming in pain. Bodies lay in the aisles, charred and burning. Gobs of some kind of sticky molten chemical had been thrown into the faces of the living, sticking to their flesh, blinding them so that they groped in panic, stumbling back into the center of the fire even as they tried to escape it. A few people had enough presence of mind to try to wrap the burning victims in coats to smother the flames, but it was useless.

Fed by gasoline and other chemicals, the fire rose straight up with a roar, doubled and doubled again. Within seconds the flimsy carpet began to burn and the tinder-dry wooden rails of the balcony burst into flames. Almost before anyone had time to realize what was happening, the fire leapt the gap between the balcony and the stage, turning the curtains into a raging holocaust. Roaring, the flames were sucked up into the fly space, into the flats of scenery covered with volatile oil paint, into the greased ropes and the exposed electrical wires. As the fire leapt for a second time the audience down below turned and ran, screaming, for the exits.

"Stay calm!" Reiter yelled, running as close to the front of the burning stage as he dared. "Stop pushing! You have to leave in an orderly fashion! Don't panic! Ladies and gentlemen, *please*, I beg you . . . !" His words were lost in the screams of the crowd.

"Fire!"

"Help!"

"Fire!"

They pushed and shoved; they stumbled over each other. Women and children were knocked to the floor and trampled. People crawled over each other, yelling and cursing. The lucky ones ran toward the main entrance and staggered out onto the street, clothes torn, bleeding and dazed. The unlucky ones ran for the emergency exits and discovered to their horror that they wouldn't open. Screaming in terror, they pounded on the heavy wooden doors, begging to be let out.

The fire spread with incredible rapidity, leaping again, climbing the wooden walls of the theater. As the air grew superheated, clothing burst into flames; women flailed at the veils of their hats and at their skirts. The screaming and cursing turned to moaning. Turning away from the useless emergency exits, the crowd stampeded back toward the main entrance. Burning rubble began to fall from the balcony, blocking the aisles.

Viola stood like a statue where Reiter had left her, paralyzed by fear, unable to move so much as a finger. In the flames that licked at the burning curtain she saw her mother dying again, turning in torment, beating at the flimsy gauze of her dress; in the flames she saw Joseph burning beyond recognition. The fear went on and on. The muscles in her back contracted, her hands went cold, she all but stopped breathing. She had the sense of looking down a long, dark tunnel. By the time Reiter gave up trying to calm the panicked audience, Viola Kessler no longer existed. Only the fear of fire existed.

Reiter grabbed her hand. "They aren't listening," he yelled at her. "We've got to get out of here!" A huge scrap of burning curtain fell to the stage, sending up a fountain of sparks. They were completely cut off from the crowd now, walled in behind a ring of fire. Viola looked at Reiter as if she had never seen him before. "Vi, what the hell's wrong with you?" he yelled. "Are you crazy? Move!"

Suddenly there was a thunderous crash. A six-foot iron batten careened down from the fly space, missing them by only a few feet, digging a large chunk out of the soft wooden floor. Heavy metal spotlights tumbled to the stage; burning tangles of electrical wire rained down from above. Grabbing Viola around the chest, Reiter dragged her toward the stage door, cursing.

The stage door was open. Still holding on to Viola, Reiter stumbled through it, gasping for air. His lungs burned, and for a moment he couldn't see anything but more smoke. Staggering a few steps more, he emerged into the cold, freezing air of a Berlin night.

Outside of the theater it was a scene from hell. Badly burned people lay in the street moaning in agony. Mothers screamed for children who were still trapped inside. Survivors with blackened faces and torn clothing stared in dazed horror at the burning theater. A brigade of men was making a pitiful attempt to throw snow on the blaze.

Stumbling across the street, Reiter nearly collided with Hilde and Richard and Hermann. Hilde was crying, and Richard was trying to comfort her.

"Erwin! Viola!" Hermann yelled. "Thank God. Are you two all right?"

"We're fine," Reiter coughed. Staggering to a stop, he sat Viola down on the curb and propped her up against a lamppost. Her body was limp and doll-like. "I think she's in shock," he yelled to Hermann. "Come here and see what you can do about it."

Hermann ran over to Viola and knelt in front of her. "Vi," he said, "Vi, can you hear me?"

She opened her eyes.

"Vi, are you hurt?"

She opened her mouth but no sound came out.

"Vi, are you in pain? Are you burned?"

She shook her head slowly, not trusting herself to speak. Her eyes smarted, and her lungs felt as if they had been filled with hot sand. Slowly she began to come back to her senses. The tide of fear began to recede.

"I'm sorry," she mumbled, feeling ashamed.

"Vi." It was Hilde. "It's all right, darling. It's all right. You're safe." She held Viola, rocking her, soothing her. Viola trembled, buried her face in Hilde's shoulder and began to cry in great, childish sobs. Hilde went on comforting her, and gradually she grew calmer.

Finally, with Hermann's help, she got to her feet. Leaning on him for support, she stood watching the fire. Pump trucks had arrived, but they were too late. Flames danced into the air, crackling horribly, turning the water to steam before the fire fighters could get close enough to be effective. Windows exploded; doors turned into sheets of flame; the roof began to collapse.

Half a dozen more people escaped through the stage door, and then with a roar the entire Neues Theater turned into a giant torch that lit up the Berlin skyline, and—despite the fire trucks, and the water, and the heroic efforts that saved the neighboring buildings—no one else made it out alive.

When the smoke cleared Berlin fire inspectors determined that over forty people had perished. They also determined that an incendiary bomb had been the cause of the fire, and that every one of the emergency exits had recently been nailed shut.

BOOK THREE

—

THE

ARENA

12

LONDON
1932

"Erpenbeck is like all Germans—he's infected with Hitlerism."

"He jolly well deserved to be hissed off the stage."

"You don't understand." Viola put down her glass of champagne and looked at the earnest circle of humorless, disapproving British faces. She had just completed her London visit by giving the last of five successful performances of *Hedda Gabler* to these same people; they had applauded her, thrown her bouquets of flowers when she took her final curtain call, and now suddenly, here at the cast party, they seemed to have undergone a metamorphosis—and all because she had objected to the fact that stink bombs had recently been thrown at the visiting German actor Karl Erpenbeck.

"Erpenbeck may be a German, but not all Germans support Hitler. Hitler lost thirty-four seats in the Reichstag in the November election, and, according to my friends in Berlin, the Nazi Party is so in debt that Goebbels has been sending his Storm Troopers out into the streets with tin cups to beg for donations."

"Rubbish. Every Kraut adores that little Austrian Caligula."

"The Communists have been fighting the Nazis in the streets; the Socialists loathe Hitler; the Social Democrats and the Catholics all have their doubts. The problem is that the parties of the left and the center can't seem to unite to resist him. They're too busy fighting each other." Viola realized that she was up on a soapbox again. It was incredibly frustrating to try to explain German politics to anyone who hadn't lived there. The situation was changing so fast that she could hardly keep track of it herself.

"My dear, the fact remains that Erpenbeck shouldn't have been allowed to appear on the stage—not in any civilized country." Lady Cecily Dockett, Viola's hostess, waved one graceful hand in the direction of the ceiling. "The vulgar little Nazi should be hung from the rafters if you ask me."

"But as far as I know, Erpenbeck *isn't* a Nazi." Viola picked up her glass of champagne and confronted Lady Dockett with polite obstinacy. Four years of living in Paris had made a difference in her. She was more self-confident, less likely to cave in to other people's opinions. She had worked with some of the best playwrights of the century, shared the stage with Katharine Cornell and Lynn Fontanne, built her reputation play by play, part by part, touring until she was exhausted, putting herself into her characters until she sometimes felt as if she hardly had a personal life. She had raised Kathe on her own, supported herself, learned to deal with loneliness and pain, and all of this had made her stronger than she would have believed possible a few years ago. Not happier—those years with Joseph had been the best of her life—yet there was something in her these days that made her more sure of herself, more steeled to petty annoyances, an undertone of grief that, despite her best resolutions, she couldn't seem to shake. It was a grief that brought strength with it and—although she never would have chosen it—she knew it had tempered her. She was thirty-one years old and almost no one intimidated her now, not even Lady Dockett.

"Don't you see—when you run an actor off the stage because of his political views, you're doing exactly what the Nazis do. You become no better than they are." She knew she should drink her champagne and be quiet, but diplomacy had never been her strong point. "You have a democracy here in England; you have laws. Once you start breaking those laws, you begin to undermine the very fabric of your own society. I know from bitter experience what it's like to live in a society where terror and intimidation have replaced due process."

Lady Dockett smiled a strained, slightly condescending smile, and her lovely painted lips curled into a perfect bow. Her evening dress was a tube of slick green silk topped by ample bare shoulders blossomed out like the petals of some large, exotic flower. "You Americans are so attached to that Bill of Rights of yours. Freedom of speech is a dangerous thing if you ask me."

"But you have the same tradition," Viola insisted passionately. "You British have always tolerated eccentricity and differences of political opinion. Look at Hyde Park Corner."

"Look at it indeed." Lady Dockett sighed, and the two tall, horse-faced gentlemen on either side of her exchanged significant looks.

"I don't want to put myself in the position of defending Hitler"— Viola wondered if there was any way of getting past those polite exteriors—"but you have to see that there are parallels to what he's doing and what that crowd at the Shaftsbury Theater did to Erpenbeck. I lived in Germany for years before I moved to Paris, and it taught me that if you try to fight the people you hate by becoming like them, then you lose. Violence leads to more violence, and before you know it innocent people are being killed." She thought of the burning of the Neues Theater, of Joseph going out to get revenge, of the folly and waste of it all. After all this time the memory of Joseph's death was still unbearably painful.

She gave herself a brisk mental shake. How many times had she promised herself that she wouldn't get off on this train of thought? Sometimes she still missed Joseph so much that she wondered if she were quite sane. She leaned toward Lady Dockett, wanting to make her understand the price violence extracted, yet knowing it was hopeless. "There are ways to resist that are fair and effective and ways that aren't, and hissing Erpenbeck off the stage just wasn't ethical."

"Bravo," a familiar voice said. "Don't try to argue with her, Cissy. When Viola Kessler takes a cause to heart, you might just as well give in gracefully."

"Oh hullo, Richard." Lady Dockett peered over Viola's shoulder with a surprised expression on her face. "Whatever are you doing here? You're perfectly welcome, of course, but I thought you rather avoided these rituals of high capitalism."

Viola turned around to find herself facing Richard Stafford, resplendent in white tie and evening dress. "Richard, my God." She choked on her champagne with surprise and went into a sudden fit of coughing. "What are you doing here?"

"Upscale slumming," Lady Dockett said, laughing prettily.

Richard flushed slightly. "Actually, Vi," he said, shooting an annoyed glance at Lady Dockett, "I heard there was a chance you might be here tonight, so I thought I'd pop by and see if you still remembered me."

"Remember you!" Viola managed to stop coughing and catch her breath. "Of course I remember you." She was delighted to see him. "I didn't know you were in London, or I would have looked you up. Last I heard you were in Majorca." He was different than she remembered, slimmer, with less of the look of baby fat about him, lean and clean-boned. It was a shock, really, to see how much he'd changed. She realized suddenly, to her embarrassment, that she'd been staring at him. "It's good to see you," she said lamely.

"Good to see you too," Richard said. "You look splendid—thinner and more soulful, but not a year older."

"Such flattery."

"Ah, but it's the truth. You're as beautiful as ever, Vi." They stood looking at each other, neither of them knowing what to say next. Lady Dockett and her friends had moved on, and so for the moment they were more or less alone.

"I heard you decamped to Paris and were sharing a flat with Jeanne," Richard said after an awkward silence.

"I roomed with her for a while, but I have my own place now."

"How's Kathe?"

"Wonderful. She's nearly nine, you know."

"Nine, not really." Richard laughed nervously and tossed his blond hair out of his eyes with a gesture that reminded Viola achingly and inappropriately of Joseph. "That just doesn't seem possible."

"Time flies." Viola could hardly believe she'd said something so trite. The surprise of meeting Richard had obviously turned her into an idiot. The problem was that she was feeling all sorts of things, not any of them particularly suitable for the occasion. The memories were almost overwhelming, so much so that she felt a little giddy. She recalled Richard giving Kathe a book of fairy tales; scribbling the music for "Let's Find Someone to Hate" on his napkin; standing beside her at Joseph's funeral.

"Ah well." Richard cleared his throat and pulled at his tie with delicate, musician's hands. There was something sweet about him and at the same time something definitely masculine. It was a mildly unnerving combination. "To tell the truth, old girl, I could have gotten in touch with you ages ago, but I never did."

Viola felt a little hurt. So he'd known where she was all this time and never come forward. "Why not, Richard?"

"Well, frankly you've become so famous that I was intimidated." Richard grinned. "It took me a rather awkwardly long period of time to work up my courage, Vi. I mean, suppose you just stared through me like I was a windowpane or something? I'm a proud little monster, you know, and I couldn't have taken that."

"Richard," Viola said bluntly, "you're crazy. Why would I stare through you? You're my friend. You were part of Berliner Weisse. Do you think I have so many friends that I just toss them away?"

Richard laughed. "Snap at me again, Vi."

"What?"

"Snap at me again. It puts me at ease." He took the champagne glass out of her hand and drank it all in one gulp. "Lord, you haven't changed a bit, have you?"

"I should hope not."

"Let's get out of here," Richard proposed suddenly. "I hate these functions, God's truth, Vi. I wouldn't be caught dead in one of these outfits except for the chance of seeing you again. Let's go back to my place and have a drink and tell each other lies about all the great things we did when we were younger."

"I can't." Viola was flustered. She retrieved her empty champagne glass from Richard and shook her head. "I'm the guest of honor."

"Never mind that." Richard had his arm hooked under hers and he was already pulling her to the door. It was a familiar, brotherly gesture that was somehow inordinately comforting. "Cissy is undoubtedly too snockered by this time to notice whether you're here or not."

* * *

Richard's flat proved to be a modest enough place, filled with objects that seemed to have been grabbed at random out of totally different worlds. The mugs—into which he poured warm beer strong enough to stand a spoon in—were cheap pink and white affairs with chipped rims and patched handles that appeared to have been bought for a few pence at a secondhand store. Richard's furniture, what little there was of it, was overstuffed, tattered, and unfashionable: a great red chair of worn plush with one leg missing, a monstrosity of a couch that made a noise when you sat on it, a deal table with a mismatched leaf, and a set of listing, crowded bookshelves that seemed to exist primarily to bear witness to Richard's ineptness as a carpenter.

On the other hand, as Viola wandered around his living room she discovered that the much-mended tablecloth was of the finest Brussels lace, the curtains real velvet, and his wineglasses Waterford crystal. A massive, expensive-looking grand piano sat in one corner, polished with such loving care that she could see her reflection in the tilted lid, but most surprising of all was a small watercolor over the fireplace, an exquisite seascape, caught at sunset, the color of the sky and ocean blending in fiery reds and golds against a background of bruised plum and gray. Viola looked at it from several angles, not quite believing her eyes, but the signature was unmistakable.

"Richard."

"Um?" Having discarded his coat and tie, he was setting out frayed plaid napkins and cracked plates with a look of intense concentration.

"Is this really an original Turner?"

Richard cleared his throat uncomfortably and unwrapped three mildly stale rolls from a packet of brown paper. "Oh, you spotted that, did you?"

"It has to be a copy."

"Yes it does rather, doesn't it?"

"But it's so good." She inspected the thin line of the horizon, the barest suggestion of waves. "The original would cost a fortune."

"Have some beer." Richard hastily handed her a mug, slopping foam and lager onto the table. Picking up one of the napkins, he dabbed at the mess, then wadded up the wet square of cotton, stuffed it into the pocket of his trousers, and sat down across from her, cradling his own mug in his hands. "I've become a Socialist," he announced.

"A Socialist?" Viola tried not to look too surprised but she couldn't help it. The Richard she remembered had always been completely indifferent to politics. She and Jeanne had even teased him about it from time to time. True, he had written the songs for *Berliner Ballade*, but Joseph had supplied the lyrics. Back in Berlin, Richard had been the aesthete of the group, pounding on Herr Meckel's out-of-tune piano for hours at a time, unaware of what he wore or ate, much less who was running the government. On the rare occasions when he had come up for air, he had seemed so young, like a delightful child— "our little British Candide," Joseph had once jokingly called him.

"We've had no end of unemployment since the American slump— especially among the miners." Richard drank his beer and made a face, as if he had encountered something bitter. "You've no idea what kind of lives those fellows lead. Barely scraping along from one day to the next, and the children are enough to tear your heart out, poor ragged little mites."

This was indeed a different Richard. Viola looked at him with new respect; there was maturity in his face, a kind of solidness that hadn't been there before. For the first time he looked like a man to her instead of a boy. She realized suddenly that she was actually finding him attractive. Ridiculous. She hadn't found a man attractive in years—not that she hadn't had the chance. There were always men interested in her, even if she wasn't particularly interested in them, but sitting across from Richard, her hand nearly touching his arm, she felt something different: a tingling at the base of her spine, as if she were coming alive again. Being with him reminded her of Joseph. It must be lust by association, she thought. The idea that Richard was some sort of stand-in made her feel both amused with herself and slightly uncomfortable.

"I've been giving them pods of money, actually," Richard was saying.

"Who?" She really should pay attention. It was hardly polite after all these years to sit here drinking his beer, lost in her own private memories.

"The miners, Vi. Like I said, the relief subsidies they get don't begin to be enough, especially with as cold a winter as we've had this year."

Viola looked around the apartment, not sure she'd understood him. "But, Richard, where do you get any money to give them? You must be constantly strapped to make ends meet."

"Oh, I make a bit from my music." Richard smiled and drank off his beer noisily; reaching for a stale roll, he ate it with a hearty indifference to manners. She could see that he was doing his best to be proletarian, and for some reason she found that rather touching.

"You're still writing popular songs?" She tried to remember if she had heard something he might have written but nothing came to mind. Still, she spent so much of her time working that she was hardly up on such things. "April in Paris"? "Smoke Gets in Your Eyes"? "Night and Day"? She ran through a list of the few tunes she could remember but none of them seemed to possess that combination of maniacal wit and lyricism that had been Richard's specialty when he was composing for *Berliner Ballade*.

"No." Richard looked down at his hands, not meeting her eyes. "Not popular songs. Actually, I'm back at the keyboard doing my bit toward the progress of cacophony. Or to put it another way, I've undergone a reconversion to the atonal. I've been having quite a run of success, you know. Public concerts and all that."

"That's great, Richard. Have you played Albert Hall yet?"

Richard grinned a mischievous, self-mocking grin. "Not quite yet, Vi, but it's definitely in the works. Right now I'm packing in enthusiastic audiences of from ten to twenty people, getting rave reviews in little publications that perish the next day or next week—in such rapid succession that, to tell the truth, I sometimes feel as if I've put a curse on the poor beggars."

"And that sort of thing brings in money?"

"In its own modest way."

There was something about Richard's tone of voice that just wasn't convincing. Viola suddenly remembered the cracks Friedrich always used to make about Richard having a money tree somewhere. Well, if he had some source of income he was ashamed of, she wasn't about to pry. Still, it was intriguing. She tried to imagine him running guns to Africa or smuggling diamonds to South America, but it was hard work. Somehow Richard just didn't seem like the type who could keep a secret long enough to pull off a shady deal. On the other hand, all that aside, it was really quite wonderful to be here with him. Just listening to the familiar sound of his voice made her feel as if she were nineteen again, back at Bluebeard's sitting at the breakfast table, waiting for Joseph to come bounding through the door, bareheaded and full of life, bringing her a bouquet of spring violets.

These memories were getting out of hand. She really had to get a hold on herself.

"The problem with coming to London on tour the way you do is that you never really see it." Richard poured himself some more beer and launched into another roll, blessedly unaware of what she had been thinking. "Oh you see the official spectacles all right—the changing of the guard, the Tower, and all that, and maybe coming into town on the train you get a glimpse of the slums, some old lady hanging out her wash in carpet slippers or something of the like, but what you don't ever get to see is the real contrast between the rich and the poor, the class divisions, the country estates of My Lord Such-and-Such"—he gestured grandly in the general direction of the fireplace—"and not half a mile away the colliers' row houses, stinking with coal dust. I take it from what you were saying to Cissy that you haven't gone right wing in your old age, so perhaps you'd be interested."

"Of course I haven't gone right wing," she was a little upset that he could imagine such a thing, "but I'm not a Socialist, Richard. To tell you the truth, I've spent the last four years in something of a muddle—politically speaking."

"What sort of muddle?" Richard leaned forward, obviously interested. She wondered fleetingly if he might try to convert her to socialism.

"Well," she said, sipping at the beer, "it's not easy to explain. The fact is, I've always had trouble trying to decide what comes first—my acting and my family or some kind of commitment to political issues. On one hand, there's always been a problem of time—once you get involved in politics, there really isn't room for anything else, and for a performing artist that can be fatal. And then, to be frank, there's the danger. For quite a while, when I was living in Germany, I was against the Nazis but afraid to expose myself to them onstage—

mostly for Kathe's sake. Then Joseph convinced me to go ahead and speak out, so I did and you know what happened—he was murdered, the Neues was burned. I left Germany running scared. I moved to Paris, took refuge in my career. Politics was like a hot poker and I was terrified to touch it. I felt so much hatred for the Nazis that I was afraid of becoming bitter and fanatical."

She paused and stared at the seascape, lost in thought. "I told myself that I was an American, not a German. I told myself that as long as Kathe was dependent on me, there was nothing worth risking my life for. But I remain divided. I haven't joined any political parties, but always in the back of my mind I keep thinking I should be doing something more. Oh, don't get me wrong. I haven't abdicated entirely. When Hermann did that anti-fascist documentary film a few years ago, I sent him quite a bit of money, but of course the Nazis have made it impossible for him to show the thing in Germany." She smiled uneasily. "I suppose I'm part of that hopeless middle-of-the-road majority. It's not very exciting, or very romantic, but I have time for my acting and my daughter and I feel safe—although a bit guilty, which is why I suppose I end up making speeches at chichi cast parties about respect for the law and due process."

What was left of the evening was taken up with Richard's explanation of the sorry state of the British economy. Later, back in the privacy of her hotel room, Viola thought what an oddly impersonal conversation it had been to have with a friend you hadn't seen for four years, and she couldn't help wondering if there had been some tension lurking under the surface that had made it as impossible for Richard to be intimate with her as it had made it for her to be intimate with him.

She spent most of the winter and spring of 1933 in Paris, rehearsing for a run of the first French production of Lorca's *Blood Wedding* and devoting what little spare time she had to Kathe, who, blossoming late into the world of childhood diseases, managed to contract both measles and mumps. It was a spring of long cold rains, of flowers blooming in profusion in the Luxembourg Gardens, of sudden, bitter upheavals in distant countries. Famine stalked the Soviet Union, banks failed in the United States, but from Viola's perspective the worst news was the burning of the German Reichstag and Hitler's subsequent election as Chancellor of Germany.

Given the international situation, Kathe's illnesses, and a work schedule that sometimes left her so dizzy with fatigue that she was too tired to do anything but take off her makeup and fall into bed, she spent very little time thinking about Richard, but when she returned to London for a few weeks at the beginning of the summer, it occurred to her that she should look him up.

It proved to be a happy decision. Richard was delighted to see her, warmer than he had been at their last encounter, funny, witty, mercurial, an altogether delightful companion. For ten days she spent all her spare time following him about, renewing their friendship, enjoying his company, frankly fascinated by his intimate, eccentric perspective on British life, and then, on a warm, sunny Sunday four days before she was scheduled to return to Paris, she discovered something so unexpected and unsettling that for days afterward she had the feeling that she had run full tilt off a cliff. To put it in the simplest terms possible: Richard Stafford was not what he seemed.

"Richard."

"Mmm?"

"It says here in the guidebook that we're only five miles from Sanford Palace." Viola was sitting in a battered, nondescript car beside Richard watching the narrow country roads unrolling between the hedgerows like dusty brown ribbons. This morning, at the ungodly hour of four-thirty, she had—at Richard's insistence—ushered in the summer solstice at Stonehenge, sitting groggily on the main altar with him drinking cold tea as he expostulated with almost maddening cheerfulness on Druids and Thomas Hardy. Now they were on their way to Bath to see the Roman ruins—that is if Richard's car survived, which from the sound of the motor seemed increasingly unlikely.

"Sanford Palace, eh?" Richard surveyed the landscape with a quick, uneasy turn of his head and went back to his driving. The road took a sharp left-hand turn, and then bent suddenly to the right, as if inviting crashes between cars and trucks. An orchard appeared; cows lay in the fields chewing their cuds among the daisies.

"Well?" she persisted.

"Well what?" Richard kept his eyes on the road. He was dressed in his usual proletarian uniform this morning: a well-worn, slightly patched blue shirt, scuffed shoes, dark pants, and a tweed jacket that was either the same one he had worn in Berlin five years ago or its twin—all of which should have made him look dowdy and puritanical, like the other British Socialists she had met, but which in Richard's case only managed to give him the air of an English lord about to set out on a fishing trip.

"Aren't you going to suggest we see Sanford? God knows you've taken me to every other attraction within a day's drive of London."

"Isn't worth the effort," Richard said quickly. "Boring old pile of rocks." He grinned at her winningly, tie loose at his throat, blond hair blowing in the wind, the perfect picture of relaxation if you didn't notice his hands, which were clutching the steering wheel so hard his knuckles had turned white. She suddenly had the sense that something was making him uncomfortable. Feeling a bit uneasy herself, she once again sought refuge in the guidebook.

"It says here that Sanford Palace has one of the finest formal gardens in England."

"Roses," Richard said, taking the next corner a little too fast, "acres of roses, all thorny and full of aphids and so damn rare that when one of those blasted bushes dies every retired British colonel who ever dug in the dirt holds a special wake."

"Sounds beautiful, actually."

"You'd be bored stiff. Believe me."

"It also says that Sanford Palace was a gift to the first Duke of Sanford from Queen Elizabeth I." She put her finger on the print to steady it as the car continued to bounce along over the ruts. "*A massive, H-shaped structure of honey-colored stone whose foundations were laid in the year of the Armada,*" she read out the description in a passable British accent, but Richard stolidly ignored her, keeping his eyes glued to the empty road as if he expected a bus to appear around every bend. "*Sanford Palace, with its symmetrical east and west fronts and perfectly proportioned windows, is one of the most outstanding examples of Tudor architecture still in existence. Of special interest are the Great Hall, with its famous collection of eighteenth-century tapestries, the Chinese rooms . . .*"

"Filled with exquisite silk hangings and the famous Peking Vase," Richard supplied in a mocking tone, "said vase having been presented to the Duke of Sanford by Queen Victoria for his valiant defense of the British legation during the Boxer Rebellion." He waved one hand expansively out the window in the general direction of Sanford Palace. "The wages of imperialism, Vi, my love."

She closed the guidebook. "You certainly seem to know a lot about Sanford. Did you also happen to know that there are tours of the art collection in the Great Hall every Sunday from ten to three?"

"Actually," Richard said stubbornly, "I was planning on taking you to lunch in Bath."

"Richard, I want to see Sanford."

"Why?"

"Because it's here. Because we're practically on top of it."

"Forget it, Vi. Really. I'll take you to Blenheim if you want. Now there's a real palace—limitless parks by Capability Brown, a library sixty yards long, the English aristocracy at its most conspicuous. I have some connections and I can get us a walk through the grounds and afterwards I can take you down to Oxford."

But Viola, when she got her mind set on something, was not an easy woman to turn aside. A quarter of an hour later, having paid the three-shilling entrance fee, she and Richard were standing in the Great Hall of Sanford Palace allowing a short, bespectacled guide in a black suit to regale them and half a dozen other visitors with a mixture of history and scandal as he pointed out the portraits of the dukes and duchesses of Sanford.

"Beheaded by Cromwell, killed at Culloden, drowned off Madagascar, blood poisoning at Waterloo, disappeared in India during the Great Mutiny, died with wife in dirigible accident while trying to set a world record . . ." The guide pointed to each portrait, listing the disasters with obvious relish. A mutter of approval went up from the crowd, and the woman next to Viola coughed and beat her umbrella on the marble floor in an excited tattoo. This was obviously the sort of thing they'd come to hear. "Gassed at Ypres, led his own Gurkha regiment in a suicide mission and perished with them."

"Don't any of the dukes of Sanford die in their own beds?" Viola whispered to Richard.

Richard shook his head. "Not the family tradition."

". . . went down on the *Titanic* when he insisted on giving his place in the lifeboat to a handsome young lad, perished on the slopes of Everest."

Viola stifled a giggle, wondering how much longer she could listen to all this without laughing out loud. Perished on the slopes of Everest indeed. She looked up at Walter, the tenth (or was it the twentieth?) Duke of Sanford, at his dark hair, pointed nose, and fierce expression, and then lowered her eyes to discover a flesh-and-blood man standing under the portrait who looked so much like the long-dead Duke that all she could do was gape with astonishment.

"Hell and damnation," she heard Richard mutter as he caught sight of the stranger. "I thought they were all in Italy."

"Oh, good morning, Your Grace," the guide said smoothly. "Ladies and gentlemen, we have the good fortune today to encounter the Duke of Sanford himself."

"Hullo there," the Duke said affably. Actually, Viola decided, on second thought—except for the pointed nose—he didn't look like his ancestors at all. Instead of their fierce combativeness, the present Duke had a slack mouth, an indolent chin, and a tiny mustache that seemed to crawl across his upper lip like a caterpillar. In fact, on closer inspection, he was even a little silly-looking, with oversized hands and eyes that reminded her for no good reason in particular of a large, good-natured dog. The Duke waved to the crowd like a man who was used to making speeches from balconies. It was a languid, good-fellowish sort of wave. "Hope you're enjoying the tour," he said, as if the idea of finding people in his house at this hour of the morning had been a surprise he intended to take in good spirits. He laughed a long foolish laugh that clashed gratingly with the lines of sober Sanfords who peered down at him from the walls of the Great Hall. Suddenly his eyes lit on Richard and his mouth fell open. "Good lord, Dicky, what are *you* doing here?"

"Taking the art tour, Bertie." Richard looked at Viola helplessly and then looked around the hall like a man searching for a hole to hide in.

"But good lord, man, you must come up and see Grants."

"Grants doesn't want to see me, Bertie."

"Nonsense. Grants always wants to see you. You're Grants' favorite. Why Harry and I simply pale beside you when it comes to Grants."

"Richard," Viola said, "what's this all about? Who's Grants? Why is he calling you Dicky? What's going on?" Everyone in the tour was staring at them, and the guide was coughing softly into his handkerchief, as if he had suddenly been taken with an attack of asthma.

"It's a mistake," Richard implored. His face was brick red and he looked as uncomfortable, miserable, and exposed as any man she had ever seen. "A case of mistaken identity."

"Mistaken identity indeed." The Duke gave another restless laugh. "That's a good one. I reckon I know my own brother when I see him, Dicky. Now you simply must come up and say hello to Grants or she'll be at me for weeks about it and you know how Grants gets when she turns cross." He shuddered palpably. "Lord, I'd rather go out on Everest and throw myself into a glacier like old Walter up there than brave Grants in one of her *moods.*" Stepping around the velvet cord that separated the family quarters from the hall, the Duke took Richard familiarly by the arm. "Now do be a good fellow, Dicky, and come along."

"Richard," Viola blurted out, "I thought you *loathed* the upper classes." It was a terribly tactless thing to say but the shock of finding out that Richard was somehow related to the Duke of Sanford was so unsettling that later she realized she had been fortunate not to have said something quite a bit stronger. "I thought you were a *Socialist.*"

"Oh, Dicky *is* a Socialist," the Duke said, smiling his silly, easy smile. "No doubt about it. Refuses to take his allowance, won't join a good club, goes to public rallies and makes simply inspired speeches against enterprises in which his own uncles own controlling stock, gives the money from his trusts to the poor and downtrodden workers and all that. Why ever since Dicky ran away from Eton and set up camp in Berlin, half the family hasn't been speaking to him and the other half thinks he should be committed somewhere to spend the rest of his life counting butterflies. Of all of us only Harry takes his political views seriously. Calls Dicky one of the *nouveau poor.*"

"Harry's a fascist," Richard said with a bitterness Viola had never heard in his voice before. "A rotten little fascist who spends his time helping Oswald Mosley turn Britain into Hitler's private game preserve."

"Oh, Harry isn't so little anymore, Dicky," the Duke observed cheerfully. "Actually our youngest brother's put on several stone since you saw him last. Portly, I'd call him these days, rotund, and"—his face suddenly lost its silly look and something somber crept over it—"and rabid, absolutely rabid. You're right about that. Harry's a fanatic. Lord, the boring lectures he subjects us to, Dicky. But then the whole family—with the exception of yours truly—has always been a bit dotty on the subject of politics."

Grants turned out to be Richard's grandmother, Lady Alice, the Dowager Duchess of Sanford, a slender old woman, just under five feet tall, with sharp blue eyes, closely clipped gray hair, and restless, twisted, nicotine-stained hands that never seemed to stop moving. Viola learned later that Lady Alice had once been a suffragette, chained herself to lampposts, been arrested and force-fed in the company of such mythical figures as Emmeline Pankhurst. Now nearly immobilized by arthritis, she was confined to bed, a problem she had solved by ordering the bed moved into the center of the family's main sitting room, where she held forth from it in the manner of a philosopher queen who, knowing that her days are numbered, wishes to get everyone else in shape before she departs.

"Well, Dicky," Lady Alice said as Viola and Richard stepped across the threshold, "it's about time."

"Hello, Grants," Richard said, looking even more uncomfortable than he had downstairs.

"Come over here and kiss me," Lady Alice commanded. "That's one of the few pleasures of being a grandmother, the right to be kissed on demand by handsome young men. Of course now I'm reduced to grandsons, but in my youth I had lovers who were masters of the art." She turned to Viola. "I suppose I'm shocking you, young lady. Well, shocks are good for the system. Keep the blood flowing. Are you shocked? Horrified? Scandalized?"

"Not particularly." Viola was amused. She put out her hand, not knowing if it was proper to introduce herself to a dowager duchess but sensing instinctively that with Lady Alice matters of propriety weren't going to amount to much. "I'm Viola Kessler."

"American?"

"Yes, although I haven't lived in the States for years."

"Good." Lady Alice shook Viola's hand vigorously. "I like the American spirit. Forthright, a little crude but direct. Actually, I always admired your compatriot Carry Nation taking axes to saloon mirrors. Not that I particularly disapprove of drink—a killjoyish, Methodist sort of position if you ask me—but I think I would have enjoyed the sound of breaking glass." She turned to Richard. "You should have introduced us, Dicky, but since you've become a Communist your manners have fallen apart completely."

"A Socialist, Grants. I'm a Socialist, not a Communist."

"Socialist, Communist; the left has always been like the Protestant Churches, forever fragmenting themselves into smaller and smaller sects." Lady Alice picked up a cigarette from a nearby ashtray, took a deep drag, and looked at Viola sharply. "Always distrust anything that ends in 'ist,' my dear."

Viola had to bite her lip to keep from laughing. "I'll try," she promised.

"Sit down, Dicky," Lady Alice commanded. She rooted among the pillows for a moment and retrieved a crushed pack of cigarettes. "Have a fag and a cup of tea and tell me what you've been up to. And while you're at it, say hello to your brother."

Viola looked across the room and noticed for the first time that there was a man sitting at a card table with his back to them. Although she couldn't really see much from this angle, she observed that he was tall and heavyset and that his hair was the same color as Richard's.

Richard sat down and took a cigarette from the pack, lighting it with a heavy, gold-plated cigarette lighter. "Hello, Harry," he called out stiffly.

"Hello, Dicky," the man at the table muttered, without turning around. Viola could hear the sound of the cards as he slapped them down against the green felt.

"Harry, come over here and be sociable," Lady Alice said. "I know you and Richard aren't speaking to each other these days, but in my presence you'll jolly well give up that little affectation or I'll have you both dragged down and shut up in the dungeon until you show better sense."

"Begging your pardon, Grants," Bertie interposed nervously, "but there isn't any dungeon in Sanford Palace." He laughed his silly laugh. "No dungeon at all, actually."

"Well, I'll have one put in then," Lady Alice said, blowing a puff of smoke in Richard's direction. She grinned, old and sharp and dragonlike, and Viola realized with a start that under her dressing gown she was wearing jodhpurs. "Now get over here, Harry, and try not to talk about the pleasures of English fascism for ten minutes. Discuss something neutral with your brother, the weather perhaps. Discourse on the possibility of rain. Surely four years at Oxford should make it possible for you to make several remarks of a purely meteorological nature."

"You win, Grants, as usual." Harry got up, and as he came toward them Viola saw a florid aristocratic face, high cheekbones, a jutting chin, the long, sharp Sanford nose, and a pair of intelligent blue eyes that gleamed with repressed anger. He seemed several years younger than Richard, in his late twenties perhaps.

For the next ten minutes, while Viola looked on dumbfounded, Lady Alice, Bertie, Richard, and Harry discoursed relentlessly on the weather. Would it rain and if it did rain would it continue through midweek? Was a cold snap in the offing? Was too much sun a good or bad influence on the hybrid roses in the formal gardens?

"Good," Lady Alice said at last, briskly consulting her watch, "we have finally managed to have a civilized conversation in this family. If your parents were still alive, they'd no doubt be pleased." She turned to Richard. "Kiss me good-bye, Dicky, and get out of here while we're still ahead of the game." She shook Viola's hand again vigorously. "A pleasure to have made your acquaintance, my dear. Civilizing men is such a task, isn't it? But necessary lest they run completely amok on the planet. Do keep Dicky in line for me, won't you?"

"I'm sorry I inflicted my family on you like that," Richard apologized as they drove on toward Bath. "The fact is, they were all supposed to be in Italy, lapping Grants in the mineral waters of Montecatini to cure her arthritis while my dear brother Harry picked up pointers from his hero Mussolini. If I'd had any idea they'd come back early, I'd have never agreed to stop off there." He grinned at Viola in that appealing, boyish way of his. "So now you know the worst—Richard Stafford, Socialist and composer of England's most forgettable music, is really the second son of the late Duke of Sanford."

There was a long silence as Viola contemplated the scenery, trying to think of what she could possibly say to him under the circumstances. She felt somewhat betrayed by the fact that Richard had deceived her—and everyone else in Berliner Weisse for that matter—but still there was something admirable about the way he had absolutely refused to profit from his family's wealth and social position. On one hand his socialism—complete with shabby shirts and cracked mugs—seemed like rebellious adolescent posing, yet on the other it smacked of true conviction.

Which was the real Richard? She looked over at him, sitting up at the wheel, straight and handsome and absolutely impenetrable. The man was a mystery, she decided. On the outside Richard was as entertaining as anyone she had ever met, easy to be with, intelligent, witty. She was grateful to him for tearing her away from her work and showing her how to have fun; she needed more of that in her life. But on the inside, who knew what he was like?

"Say something, Vi," Richard pleaded. "Don't just sit there thinking what a rotter I've been."

"Nice weather we're having, isn't it?" In retrospect it was a poor time to make a joke. Growing up with Conrad had given her a rather wicked sense of humor that seemed to spring out on its own whenever she got embarrassed or uncomfortable, and at the moment she was definitely both.

"Oh hell and damnation." Richard pulled over to the side of the road so abruptly that she had to catch hold of the dashboard to keep from slamming her head against the windshield. "I've ruined it with you, haven't I?" He turned to her, upset and pleading.

"Richard, what are you talking about?"

"You'll cut me dead the next time you're in London. I know you will. I'll call you up, and some desk clerk will tell me that Miss Kessler isn't in, and that will be the end of it, and all because of my damn family." Suddenly, entirely without warning, he reached out and took her in his arms.

"I love you," he proclaimed. "I've always loved you, damn it. Ever since that first day Jeanne showed up with you at the Cafe Schiller."

"Richard, please." Astonished, she tried to pull away but he was holding her too tightly. "Don't say all this. You're going to regret it. Please."

"I adore you," Richard insisted. "I'm crazy about you. For weeks I've wanted to tell you. You're the most beautiful, intelligent, exciting woman I've ever met in my life, Vi. I see other girls and they look like nothing next to you. Why do you think I haven't gotten married after all these years? Because every time I meet someone all I can think is *she's not Vi.*"

"Richard, please, stop it. I don't want to hear this." She wondered what she'd do if he actually tried to kiss her. They were in the middle of nowhere and it would be a long walk back to the nearest town. She felt an odd sensation in the pit of her stomach and her mouth suddenly went dry. To her chagrin, she realized that she was responding to him physically.

Richard released her suddenly and sat back, his face pale. "You don't love me in the slightest, do you?"

"No," she admitted bluntly. "I don't love you, but I do like you a great deal as a friend." She straightened her skirt, feeling ruffled and breathless and more than a little upset. She was ashamed at herself for getting aroused by him—confused, yet at the same time uncontrollably excited, as if at last something important were happening in her life. The problem was that she'd been keeping too tight a rein on herself since Joseph died; she should have taken Jeanne's advice and gotten herself another man long ago, not let the hunger build up like this. Then she wouldn't be on the edge of ruining a perfectly good friendship. "I want you, Vi," Richard said, his voice thick with emotion. "I know I sound like a lovesick fool, but I want you more than I've ever wanted any woman in my life."

She took a deep breath and folded her hands together to keep them from shaking. It was important—vitally important—that Richard never suspect the sexual feelings she was having for him, feelings that she was frankly ashamed of. There were times when all those years of acting came in handy and this was one of them. By some miracle when she finally spoke she was able to keep her voice cool and steady.

"Richard, I haven't loved anyone since Joseph died." She wanted to explain it all to him, but it seemed impossible. How could she describe her loneliness without implying that she needed someone to share it? How could she make Richard understand that she felt hungry so much of the time yet the thought of any man but Joseph touching her set her teeth on edge? I'm obsessed, she thought, and maybe a little crazy, but I don't love Richard, and I have to let him know that, even if it hurts him so much that it wrecks everything between us.

"Vi," Richard pleaded, "listen, just give me a chance; give me some time to convince you."

"Time won't make any difference, Richard." She moved away from him, feeling more in control of herself, relieved that she was managing to get through this so well, at the same time feeling irrationally and unaccountably disappointed.

"Yes it will."

"Richard, there's just no use to all this. Let's just go on to Bath and forget it ever happened."

"What would it take to make you stay in England?"

"I live in Paris, Richard." She looked away from him, at the door handle, molten in the late afternoon sunlight, at the plaid pattern of the seat covers, not trusting herself to meet his eyes. "Kathe's there. All my friends are there. I have an apartment I like, an acting career."

"But what would it take to make you stay? I know you wouldn't stay for me. I don't blame you for that." Richard smiled a sad, self-mocking smile that touched her despite her resolve to keep him at arm's length. "Richard Stafford, second son and erstwhile composer, isn't much of a lure, I admit, but what would it take to make England more attractive to you?" He brushed his hair out of his eyes and his face colored with a kind of forlorn hope that would have been comic if it hadn't been so very nearly tragic. "How about your own theater, would you like that? You could manage it, control what gets produced, perform whatever plays you liked, assemble your own team of actors. Would that be of interest, Vi? Would that keep you on this side of the Channel long enough for me to convince you that I've got something more to offer you than warmed-over Fabianism and a junior interest in the upper classes?"

The offer was so clearly impossible and so clearly desperate that she felt a wave of pity for him. So Richard loved her that much, did he? The thought was flattering and even touching in a way. She had to admit that she liked the idea of being loved, but except for the pent-up physical desires of a lonely woman, she had nothing to give him in return. At least, she thought proudly, she had the sense not to delude herself into thinking that just because she felt attracted to Richard, she returned his affection.

After ten more almost unbearably uncomfortable minutes, she finally managed to persuade him that anything more than friendship between them was out of the question, and that there was nothing that would change her mind. In silence the two of them drove on to Bath, in silence they examined the Roman ruins, and in silence they drove through the night back to London. All in all, it was as uncomfortable an outing as she had ever been on, and it was with relief that she said good-bye to Richard in the lobby of her hotel. Under ordinary circumstances she would have asked him up to her room for a farewell drink, but given the situation, that seemed out of the question, and she left London several days later wondering if her friendship with Richard really would survive or whether it would be another five years before she saw him again.

Back in Paris, she soon fell into her old routine of rehearsals, performances, and taking care of Kathe, but that was to be a summer of strange reunions, and one of the most unexpected and disturbing was still to come.

13

BERLIN
1933

"Burn Karl Marx!"
"Burn Marcel Proust!"
"Burn Albert Einstein!"
"Burn H. G. Wells!"

The bonfire leapt into the sky with a roar. Grabbing more books, the Nazi students threw them onto the flames and danced around the edge of the fire singing the praises of the New Germany. Pages that contained the greatest poems of Heine curled, browned, and burst into flames. Hamlet's soliloquy turned to ashes; the Bible (written by Jews) caught fire and burned alongside the novels of Gide, the works of Freud, and the autobiography of Helen Keller. Twenty thousand books, looted from the libraries of Berlin, were being fed to the flames. Not since Savonarola, the mad monk, burned the art of Florence in the fifteenth century had Europe witnessed such destruction.

Friedrich stood in front of the Opera House, looking on with satisfaction. At last, Friedrich thought, German culture was being purged; at last the ancestral vitality of the race was being set free. Next would come bonfires of degenerate art: Picasso, Van Gogh, Braque, Cézanne, Matisse, Gauguin, Max Ernst. Soon Aryan artists like himself would no longer be subject to humiliating comparison with the works of Jews and mongrels.

The flames burned higher, and the young Storm Troopers danced more wildly. Their jackets were open, their lips parted slightly, their eyes bright and wild. The barbaric ecstasy of the dancers thrilled Friedrich and excited him, and he longed to join them, but he had a small job to perform first.

Walking over to the bonfire, he stood for a moment shielding his face from the heat, watching the books twist and crumple, watching the print disappear and the covers turn black. Then reaching into his jacket pocket he took out a book—a very particular book that he had brought especially for this occasion. Holding the book up, he read the title one more time, and then he smiled and threw it into the fire with all his might.

"Burn Joseph Rothe!" he yelled.

Theater critic Johannes Wulf lived in one of the most beautiful houses in Berlin. Constructed from red brick and surrounded by a small park of chestnuts, lindens, and oaks, the house contained treasures from around the world: carpets from Persia, brass candlesticks from Peru, priceless wooden statues from Africa, but on the night the Nazis came to take Wulf away all they were interested in was the silver.

"What crime am I accused of?" Wulf demanded as the five Storm Troopers pushed him out of his own front room at gunpoint.

Friedrich, who was in charge of the arrest, smiled and shook his head. "Really, Wulf, I would have thought it was obvious— you shouldn't have given the Schröter Prize to Joseph Rothe; you shouldn't have called Rudolf Hausmann a penguin; most of all you shouldn't have written reviews critical of Goebbels' new Theater of Propaganda."

"But I'm a *critic*," Wulf protested angrily. "It's my job to be critical. Rothe deserved the prize; Hausmann's an idiot; and as for Goebbels' Theater of Propaganda, it's the most boring, pretentious, asinine thing that's appeared onstage since the Emperor Nero forced the Romans to listen to him recite his own poetry."

Friedrich turned to the Storm Troopers. "Take this traitor out in the garden, make him dig his own grave, and then strangle him," he said coldly, "but don't fire any shots. It's late and we don't want to alarm the neighbors."

Back in Friedrich's apartment, Hilde was standing in front of the sink with a towel wrapped around her shoulders, dying her hair blond. The bleach stung her scalp and its fumes burned her eyes, but she gritted her teeth and worked it into the roots of her hair. Thanks to Friedrich, she had just been offered her first movie role, but there was a catch: she had to make herself look more Aryan in time for the screen test tomorrow morning.

Hilde squinted at herself, trying to determine if the bleach was taking effect. The film was entitled *Purity*. If her hair turned blond, and not green or blue or some other ghastly color, she would appear on the screen as a young German student defending her virginity against the assaults of a lecherous Jewish professor.

Damn, Hilde thought, I can't take this anymore. Turning on the tap, she put her head under the faucet and began to rinse the bleach out of her hair, gagging at the smell of it.

Friedrich returned at three in the morning. "So," he said, snapping on the light, "did you do it?"

Hilde sat up in bed, sleepy and yawning. "Yes," she said.

"Walk around," Friedrich commanded, "and let me take a look at you."

Getting reluctantly out of the warm bed, Hilde walked around the room while Friedrich stood in the doorway staring at her. She was naked and it was cold, but she did her best not to shiver. Friedrich always liked a good floor show. Fortunately her days at Leda and the Swan had given her a lot of practice at this sort of thing.

"It looks horrible," he snapped.

"I'm sorry, Friedrich." She wasn't sorry, of course. She was bored. Friedrich always needed these little dramas, and she was willing to give them to him, which was why she had lasted longer than his last three mistresses put together.

Still grumbling about her hair, Friedrich took off his clothes, put on a pair of pajamas, and climbed into bed.

"Tomorrow you'll do it over," he commanded as he adjusted the black nightshade over his eyes. He was having more and more trouble sleeping lately and the least bit of light made him toss and turn for hours. In the mornings he often complained of nightmares. The worst were the dreams in which Joseph Rothe came back to accuse him of fantastic crimes. Hilde could always tell when Friedrich had dreamed of Joseph because he woke up pale and irritable.

Time passed, and Hilde waited patiently. After a while, Friedrich began to snore. When she was absolutely sure he was asleep, she got out of bed, went over to his coat, and began to search through his pockets. Fortunately Friedrich was a heavy sleeper and not likely to wake up, but even so, she couldn't help looking nervously over her shoulder as she memorized the contents of his appointment book. She hadn't been able to get to it for almost a week, so she started at Monday. When she came up to the present and saw the name of Johannes Wulf, the theater critic, Hilde gasped and bit her lower lip. If what she was reading was correct, Friedrich had already paid his visit on Wulf, and it was too late to send a warning.

Jeanne Dufour lived in an unfashionable part of Paris, off the busy Boulevard de Grenelle on a street lined with shoe stores, dry cleaners, and small, undistinguished neighborhood cafes that advertised their daily specials on chalk boards tacked up above rickety metal tables that spilled out onto the sidewalks, making it almost impossible to walk for more than a block without taking to the gutter. Yet, for all the crowding, it was a street Viola always enjoyed, a lively, Gallic street, disorderly and vibrant, full of smells and sights that you encountered nowhere but in Paris. Often she got off a full metro stop early to treat herself to a walk through the neighborhood, but on this particular early June morning she was in too much of a hurry.

The reason for her impatience was a phone call she had gotten from Jeanne at eight o'clock—a ridiculously early hour for Jeanne, who never went to bed before two in the morning, to call anyone. On the phone Jeanne had been unusually uncommunicative and unusually insistent. She had asked Viola to come over to her apartment at once, but had absolutely refused to give a reason, fielding all of Viola's questions with vague references to "a matter of some importance." The only possible explanation seemed to be that Jeanne was in some kind of trouble too terrible to mention, yet she hadn't sounded worried or even upset. As a matter of fact, Viola thought, as she hurried across the Rue de Commerce, Jeanne had sounded particularly cheerful.

Strange. Very strange indeed. Jeanne wasn't given to secrets. Her life, at least as far as Viola knew, was evenly divided between her clients, her married lover, her research in abnormal psychology, and her work with charity patients at the hospital. In fact, Jeanne was so self-contained that Viola often teased her about what a waste it was for her to live in Paris. Since she never went to the opera, to plays, to museums, or even to the Right Bank any more often than she absolutely had to, she might as well have been living in some small provincial town, but now, out of nowhere, she was acting like a spy in a Dashiell Hammett novel.

Negotiating her way around two children who were playing some kind of game in the middle of the sidewalk, Viola headed toward Jeanne's building, a large block of yellow granite whose only claim to style was a brace of plaster cherubs carved over the front door, both of whose noses were half worn away by soot. Thirty seconds later she was ringing Jeanne's bell.

Jeanne threw open the door and stepped out into the hall as if to block Viola's view of the interior of the apartment. There was a grin on her face wide enough to drive through and she was wearing her best summer dress, a plain white linen affair with a low-cut neck and yellow piping on the sleeves—not the kind of thing you'd expect to find her in at this hour of the morning. Her hair, short and cropped close to her head in a way that was now completely unfashionable, had been hurriedly curled around the back of her ears, giving her the look of a French schoolboy bent on mischief. She kissed Viola quickly on both cheeks and grinned even more broadly. "Guess who's here."

"Calvin Coolidge."

"Try again, *cherie*."

"Jeanne, what in the world's going on?"

"Don't be so impatient." Jeanne laughed and all but did a little dance on the doorstep. Her skirt floated out around her legs and she looked younger and happier than Viola had seen her in years. "We've got a visitor from Germany."

"From Germany?"

"From Berlin."

"Quit making her guess," a familiar voice said from inside the apartment. "Have a little mercy on her, Jeannie."

"Hermann!" Viola half ran, half tumbled into the apartment.

"Right"—Hermann stepped forward and clasped Viola in a bear hug—"Hermann himself. Another member of the Teutonic intelligentsia on his way to Hollywood." He ran his fingers through his copper-red hair, making it stand up in the familiar fans on either side of his head. Viola noticed that he was going bald and had put on some weight. Dear Hermann, dressed as usual in stripes and plaids, blues and browns, with a pair of ridiculous pink socks that he probably thought were white. Hermann shifted his weight from one foot to the other and contemplated Viola shyly. "You look great, healthy and all that." His face turned red. "Been doing push-ups?"

"Not to speak of," Viola laughed. Hermann was so invariably tactless when he tried to be gallant.

He touched her arm approvingly. "Great biceps."

"Hermann's left Germany for good," Jeanne announced as she brought out three cups and filled them with coffee and milk.

Viola sat down at the table, hardly knowing what to say next. There were so many things she wanted to ask Hermann, so many things she wanted to tell him. She was surprised at how happy she was to see him. All the bad memories of those years she had spent in Berlin seemed to evaporate in his presence, leaving only the good ones behind. She remembered her first morning at Bluebeard's when he'd teased her about the violets, the wonderful film he'd produced for the opening of *Berliner Ballade*, that time he had given Joseph and her tickets for their honeymoon in Munich. It occurred to her fleetingly that seeing Hermann was a very different experience from encountering Richard, easier and more comfortable, with no disturbing emotions welling up to mar the occasion, but then Hermann was a more comfortable person.

"Everyone with any sense is getting out." Hermann planted himself solidly between Viola and Jeanne, took a deep drink of coffee and his round face was suddenly serious. "Since the Nazis burned the Reichstag and pinned it on the Communists, nothing's stood in their way. As you no doubt know, Hitler's been running the government under an obscenity called the 'Enabling Act,' which means he rules by decree more or less in the style of Attila the Hun."

"Conrad wrote me that in Munich the Nazis burned Joseph's plays in the middle of the street," Viola said, "but I couldn't believe it."

"Oh they did." Hermann patted her consolingly on the arm with his big, soft hand as if to cushion the blow. "And in Berlin too—right in the middle of Unter den Linden in front of the Opera House. It was quite a bonfire. Marx, Freud, Gide, Voltaire—all going up in flames. Joseph was in good company. But the book burning hasn't been the worst of it. The Nazis have started going after all the artists and intellectuals." Hermann hunched his shoulders as if shifting a heavy weight from one to the other. "You can't imagine the insanity of it all; it's as if they're trying to destroy the very best of German culture. Schoenberg, for example, has been dismissed from his professorship at the Academy of Music and told if he comes back to Germany, he'll be cut up into coleslaw. Brecht left the day after the Reichstag burned. Reinhardt, Stern—all gone abroad." Hermann ran his hand through his hair and looked from Jeanne to Viola as if he couldn't quite believe the magnitude of the disaster.

"The French papers are saying that thousands have already emigrated." Jeanne dumped three spoonfuls of sugar into her coffee. "Any truth to it?"

"I'd say, if anything, that's an underestimate." He held his cup out for a refill. "The theater is virtually dead—unless you want to count Goebbels' new Theater of Propaganda, which seems to involve lots of big, burly blond types marching around spouting rhymed drivel about the Fatherland. And as for the film industry, I suspect that for the next twenty years half the major directors in Hollywood are going to have German accents." Hermann paused and looked at Viola and Jeanne thoughtfully. "I don't suppose either of you has heard about Friedrich?"

"We don't exactly keep up a correspondence," Viola said. She took a quick gulp of coffee, not meeting his eyes. "Frankly, Jeanne and I would rather forget he ever existed."

Hermann folded his big square-fingered hands together and parked his chin on them. "Then neither of you would have any way of knowing that Herr Goebbels is about to create a Reichs Theater Chamber, and that he's asked our old buddy to head it up."

Viola was so surprised that she almost spilled her coffee into her lap. "Friedrich head of anything to do with the theater? You must be joking."

"I wish I were."

Hermann ran his finger around the rim of his coffee cup as if reluctant to continue. "The first thing Friedrich did in his new capacity," he said at last, "was to go after Johannes Wulf, the theater critic; had him arrested, so rumor has it. In any event, Wulf has mysteriously 'disappeared.' The official story is that he's gone to Italy for his health, but of course no one believes that."

Viola was stunned. Wulf was an established institution in Berlin—like the Alexanderplatz or the statue of Berolina—someone you always assumed would be there forever.

"Some people say the attack on Wulf was Hilde's idea," Hermann continued. He looked up at Viola, his honest blue eyes full of confusion. "But personally I can't believe that of her." He cleared his throat uneasily. "You see, Hilde's become Friedrich's, uh, good friend."

"You mean his mistress?"

"Let's put it this way," Hermann said. "Wherever Friedrich goes, Hilde goes too. She's at official meetings with him, at rallies, and he stays over at her place maybe four or five nights a week."

"My God." Jeanne looked positively ill at the news.

"Hilde's making quite a name for herself in Nazi propaganda films." In anyone else the comment would have sounded bitter, but bitterness was something Hermann just didn't have any capacity for. He shook his head sadly. "Poor girl. I always liked Hilde a lot, you know. She was a great kid. And now she's gotten plastic surgery and dyed her hair blond to look more Aryan."

Viola tried to imagine Hilde with blond hair and then she tried to imagine her with Friedrich, but her mind balked. It just didn't make any sense. Hilde had always disliked Friedrich. Somehow the fact that Hilde had gone over to the Nazis was the most disturbing news Hermann had brought out of Germany.

Hermann stayed in Paris for less than a week before he left for

Hollywood. At the last minute, as they were seeing him off at the train station, Jeanne and Viola persuaded him to take a few hundred francs to cover his immediate expenses—money which he accepted only on the condition that someday they would allow him to pay it back with interest. He was going to become a famous director, he assured them as he stood on the platform running his fingers through his hair.

Viola hugged Hermann good-bye, thinking what a fine man he was, honest and kind and gentle. If people like Hermann were leaving Germany by the thousands, then who was going to be left? The question went around in her head for days, although she suspected she already knew the answer.

The summer passed, hot and lazy, and near the end of it Viola took Kathe to St. Malo for two weeks to escape the heat. She had just returned, relaxed and ready to launch into the fall season, when she received an extraordinary phone call from London.

"Miss Kessler?" a male voice on the other end of the line inquired. There was a great deal of crackling and static.

"Yes?" Viola put down a pot of steaming hot chocolate and batted at the phone box with her free hand. It was the old-fashioned kind, black and clumsy, mounted on the kitchen wall, with a mouthpiece shaped like a horn. Viola pounded again but the crackling only worsened.

"This is Viola Kessler speaking," she yelled encouragingly into the mouthpiece.

"Ah, Miss Kessler. So good to find you in. Hamilton Carlyle here."

"Good morning, Mr. Carlyle." Now who in the world was Hamilton Carlyle and what was he doing calling her from London at this hour? Viola racked her brains but the name meant nothing to her.

"Who is it, Mama?" Kathe asked, putting the finishing touches on her braids. At nine she was still small and gaminlike, with dark brown eyes and Joseph's glossy black hair, all legs and brown arms and curiosity. On the table in front of her, Kathe's books spilled out of her leather satchel in a messy, disorganized pile. Kathe tolerated school rather than liked it—vastly preferring to hang around the theater watching rehearsals than to do her homework. Even on the best of days, she was usually late for her classes.

Viola shrugged and mouthed the words *I don't know who it is* as she motioned for Kathe to hurry and eat her breakfast. The phone crackled again and then entered a period of calm, as if it had moved into the eye of a hurricane.

"I've never had the pleasure of meeting you personally, Miss Kessler," the mysterious Mr. Carlyle said pleasantly, "but I saw you in *Hedda Gabler* in London this spring. A remarkable performance. Such depth, such feeling. In the last act your Hedda appeared so absolutely driven. I think Ibsen himself would have approved."

"Thank you." Viola wondered what such fulsome praise could be leading up to.

"The truth is," Mr. Carlyle continued, "I have a proposition of sorts to make to you."

"A proposition?"

"A business proposition. I'm the owner and manager of the Arena Theater. Perhaps you've heard of it?"

"Isn't that the theater near Waterloo Station? The one with the stone griffins outside?"

"Precisely." Mr. Carlyle sounded pleased that she had remembered his theater. "The truth is, Miss Kessler, the Arena hasn't been much of a paying proposition lately, what with the economic slump and all that. Oh, we've staged some good, solid productions so far this season—revivals mostly—a bit of Shakespeare, *The Cherry Orchard*, two little experimental pieces by a young American playwright named Henry Arbor, but to be frank, we aren't attracting the audiences we used to."

"So you want to hire me for a performance?"

"Not precisely."

Viola was puzzled. "What exactly do you want then, Mr. Carlyle?"

"Well, Miss Kessler," Mr. Carlyle said jovially, "actually what I want to do is give you my theater."

"I'm sorry," Viola said, "but I'm just not following you. I think we have a bad connection. I thought I heard you say that you wanted to give me your theater."

"That's right, Miss Kessler. That's what I said. I want to give you the Arena. Not the actual physical ownership of the building, of course. I'd want to retain that, continue acting as business manager, but for all other intents and purposes I'd like to put the Arena under your control. It's a fine old theater," Mr. Carlyle continued earnestly, "small but wonderful acoustics—rather like the Old Vic. Frankly, some of the seats need reupholstering and we could use a more modern dimmer board, but other than that it's in top shape, and from a purely artistic standpoint I don't think you'd regret the association."

Viola was stunned.

"Miss Kessler? I say, Miss Kessler are you still there?"

"Yes, Mr. Carlyle, I'm still here." Ever since the Nazis burned the Neues, she had dreamed of having another theater of her own. Viola looked over at Kathe, who was munching her bread and butter. For a moment she gave herself the luxury of imagining what she would do with the Arena—the actors she would select, the plays she would stage, and then she remembered Richard.

Damn it. She frowned and tapped her fingernails against the flowered wallpaper. She should have known there'd be a catch. Strangers didn't just spontaneously dump theaters in the laps of actresses they knew only by reputation. She felt a stab of disappointment. For a minute it had all seemed so easy.

On the other end of the line, Mr. Carlyle coughed uneasily and cleared his throat. "Miss Kessler?"

"Yes?" She stood looking at the phone, trying to sort out her feelings. She wanted a theater of her own, but had Mr. Carlyle called her because he was impressed with her as an actress or had someone purchased his enthusiasm at a stiff price? She remembered sitting in Richard's car listening to his hopeless, embarrassing declaration of love. *How about your own theater?* Richard had asked. *Would that keep you on this side of the Channel long enough for me to convince you?* And now, out of the blue, Mr. Carlyle had offered her the Arena. A coincidence? Hardly likely. Viola took a deep breath. No matter how long she stood here trying to convince herself otherwise, there was no doubt that Richard was somehow behind this offer.

"There's no hurry, you know," Mr. Carlyle was saying, "not in the slightest. I'm only too aware that an actress of your stature would hardly be prepared to pull up stakes and move to London on a moment's notice, no matter how attractive the terms. Repairs could be made on the theater while you fulfilled your present obligations;

plays could be solicited. In fact"—his voice grew confidential—"I think I can assure you that some of our best English playwrights will be clamoring for a showing at the Arena."

Viola considered asking him straight out if Richard Stafford had put him up to this and decided against it. If by some miracle Richard wasn't involved, it would be embarrassing, to say the least, to suggest to Mr. Carlyle that he had been recruited into the role of go-between.

"In the event that modesty has prevented you from being aware of it," Mr. Carlyle continued pleasantly, "I think you should know that in Britain in particular you have a very substantial following, not to mention the respect of the critics to an extent that is, frankly, unusual. Speaking from an economic standpoint, theatrical management is always a somewhat chancy proposition, but . . ."

The only sensible thing to do under the circumstances was to decide not to decide. She'd have to call Richard and have this out with him.

"I'm very interested," she told Mr. Carlyle, "but I'll have to think it over." She spoke of her commitments in Paris, of her friends, her daughter, the problems of relocation.

"I understand." He seemed encouraged. "Yes, of course, by all means. Please take as much time as you need. As I said previously, there's absolutely no rush." He gave her a number where he could be reached, told her several more times how delighted he was at the possibility of having her at the Arena, and then rang off.

After Kathe left for school Viola sat for a long time drinking chocolate and weighing the pros and cons. Everything was in pairs: Notre Dame and Westminster; the National Gallery and the Louvre; Trafalgar Square and the Champs Élysées. She realized somewhere in the middle of her third cup of chocolate that, in addition to everything else, she was excited about the prospect of living in an English-speaking country. She had acted in German and in French, but English, when all was said and done, was the language of her childhood and of her strongest emotions.

She thought of Kathe. What would be best for her—London or Paris? There was obviously no way of telling in advance; however, there was one thing that could be settled immediately. Fifteen minutes later she had succeeded in placing a long-distance call to London.

"Hullo." On the other end of the line Richard's voice was faint, as if he were talking through several layers of thick velvet. "Hullo, hullo. Anyone there?"

"Hello, Richard, it's me. Viola."

There was a brief silence. "Oh hullo, Vi," he said in as guilty a tone as she'd heard in some time.

She had planned all sorts of diplomatic ways to broach the subject, even developed a few tactical backup plans in case her first attempts to assess the situation should fail, but when she heard that guilty edge in Richard's voice they all evaporated.

"Richard Stafford," she yelled into the mouthpiece of the phone, "what the hell do you mean by buying me a theater?" She closed her mouth, absolutely horrified at what she had said. My God, she should buy herself a muzzle. Still, she'd certainly been clear enough. No chance Richard wouldn't understand her after an outburst like that.

Richard must have laughed for a full minute. "Oh, Vi," he said at last, "oh lord."

"Don't pretend you don't know what I mean. I just talked to Hamilton Carlyle from the Arena."

"So you talked to Carlyle?"

"You bet I did."

"Interested?"

"Not unless you absolutely promise me that there are no strings attached to this deal. I have to know that Carlyle wants me because I'm a good actress and not because you twisted his arm."

There was a long silence on the other end of the phone. "It's a business arrangement, Vi," Richard said at last, "and at this juncture it's strictly between you and Carlyle. I swear to God it is. I have to admit that having you in London would be to my advantage, but I swear—on my own personal copy of *Das Kapital*—that there are absolutely no strings attached. I didn't even talk to Carlyle. All I did was have lunch with a few of my old schoolmates—who now are bulwarks of the ruling class—and let it become generally known that you might be responsive to such an offer. After all, you aren't exactly some obscure young actress who is just starting out. Are you aware, for example, that the Prince of Wales is one of your most ardent fans?" She heard a distant chuckle emerge from the receiver. "Lord, old girl, I'd be a fool to try to cash in on your presence over here, wouldn't I? It's all on the up-and-up. Word of honor. Carlyle wants you for yourself alone, and a lucky theater owner he'll be if he gets you."

They talked for ten more minutes, running up an astronomical bill, and at the end of that time she was convinced enough of Richard's total sincerity to wire Mr. Carlyle that she'd be arriving in mid-October to have a look at the theater before she made her final decision.

The trip proved successful. She liked what she saw, and so in mid-January, having packed her things and said good-bye to Jeanne, she moved with Kathe to London to take charge of the Arena.

14

LONDON

1934

"What am I going to do about furniture?" Viola moaned as she unpacked her things. "I have six scripts to read, two rehearsals scheduled, three new sets to approve, and if I don't have lunch with James Birdie some time this week, he's going to start thinking twice about his offer to let me stage one of his plays. Not to mention that I have to enroll Kathe in boarding school and attend some kind of dreadful parents' tea."

"Don't give it another thought," Richard said cheerfully. He was sitting on one of the packing crates drinking a beer, looking cheerful and ruddy-faced despite the miserable midwinter weather. Beside him barrels spewed wood shavings onto the bare floor of Viola's new apartment. The living room was a wilderness of boxes, and where the cooking utensils were was anyone's guess. "I'll take care of getting you a couch and tables and a carpet."

"Richard, that's out of the question. I couldn't possibly put you to so much trouble." Viola peered wearily over the edge of the crate she was unpacking. In one hand she held a small lamp and in the other a paperweight full of glass roses.

"Oh, it won't be any trouble at all," Richard assured her. "The truth is, I rather like poking about in shops. Of course from a political standpoint I believe the possession of furniture represents capitalism run amok, but from a practical standpoint . . ."

"Richard," Viola laughed, "spare me the politics. All I want is something durable and simple that doesn't show dirt."

"I see a couch over here"—Richard pointed to an empty space in front of the windows—"and over there a comfortable chair for you to collapse in after those grueling rehearsals."

She protested for a few minutes more and then gave in and agreed to let him shop for her on the condition that he not spend a penny of his own money. The truth was, she was grateful to Richard for taking on the problem of finding her some furniture. Her apartment was the last thing she wanted to think about—she had more important things on her mind. Her first play at the Arena was going to be a reinterpretation of Aeschylus' *Agamemnon*. The young American playwright Henry Arbor had written it specifically for her, and it contained a few surprises for the British.

Located on Waterloo Road, the Arena Theater had been built in the late eighteenth century by a tallow-chandler with a yen for culture. Its handsome white limestone facade was a merry mixture of stone griffins, Corinthian columns, and swags of amaranth, while inside there were red velvet seats, murals depicting the chandler's beloved Lancashire, and the famous "act-drop," a huge mirror installed in 1821 that reflected the entire audience.

For the first four decades of its existence, the Arena had been a famous spot for assignations of all sorts. Located on the wrong side of the Thames, it specialized in presenting sensational melodramas and revenge tragedies to patrons who were more often than not robbed by highwaymen as they made their way home. Fistfights were common, riots not unknown, and many a London serving girl was rumored to have lost her virtue on the floors of the boxes.

Under Queen Victoria, the scandalous reputation of the theater went into a decline, and it became a temperance music hall, serving coffee and family entertainment. Operas were presented on its stage and, in time, films. There was a long run of Shakespeare before the war, and when Hamilton Carlyle took over ownership in the early twenties, revivals of European classics. By the time Viola came to the Arena in the winter of 1934, it was as staid and unexciting as a pair of sensible shoes.

Within three months she made it scandalous again.

"How could you play Clytemnestra as a *sympathetic* character, Miss Kessler?" a reporter demanded angrily after the first performance of *Agamemnon.* "After all, she murdered her husband!" He had cornered Viola in her dressing room and was taking notes on a large yellow pad, stopping from time to time to fire more questions. "For over two thousand years she's been seen as the villain of *Agamemnon.* So how do you justify making her the heroine?"

"Clytemnestra's husband brought his mistress home to live. He sacrificed Iphigenia—Clytemnestra's daughter—to the gods in trade for enough wind to sail his soldiers to Troy." Viola smiled, enjoying the frenzy she had provoked. "I think that gives Clytemnestra a good reason to do him in."

"The audience was shocked."

"Good, I meant them to be."

"What do you plan to do next? More Greek tragedy?"

"No, a comedy."

"You seem to have quite a range. What's the title of the play?"

Viola smiled. "For the present that's a secret between Mr. Carlyle and me."

On the stage of the Arena, Viola sat at a small table taking tea with Noel Coward. The play was called *Wilde,* and like many comedies it didn't have much of a plot, but it was witty and entertaining and Viola had hopes that the audience would fall in love with it. Most of her hopes centered around Coward. At thirty-five, he was dapper and sophisticated, with a budding mouth, a wide forehead, large ears, and a face that could express comic contempt better than any other face in the world. Thanks to a partially deaf mother, Coward had learned to speak in clipped tones that gave his words a special witty sting. He had written the immensely popular *Cavalcade* only three years ago—not to mention the musical plays and revues that had made him one of the most popular actors ever to step in front of London audiences.

"Do you know the difference between a caprice and a lifelong passion, my dear?" Coward inquired, lifting his eyebrows suggestively.

"Certainly, my love," Viola retorted. "The difference between a caprice and a lifelong passion is that the *caprice* lasts a little longer."

The audience roared with laughter and Viola relaxed. It was a sweet sound. She and Coward sat for a moment relishing it.

The next morning her phone rang ten times before she was awake enough to answer it. Lady Dockett was on the other end of the line, bubbling with her usual enthusiasm.

"You're becoming London's leading lady," Cecily said. "My dear, there's simply no escaping it. What you've done with that theater is a miracle. Noel Coward is one of my favorite actors. However did you snag him?"

"I told Noel he could do anything he wanted," Viola admitted sleepily, "as long as the censors didn't shut us down."

There was a brief silence on the other end of the phone as Cecily took in this piece of information.

"Vi," she said at last, "I'm having another of my little dinner parties on Saturday night, and I'd be ever so pleased if you could make it."

Viola groaned inwardly. "I'd be delighted, Cissy," she said through gritted teeth. At first she had found the constant round of dinner parties exciting, but in the last few months she had come to dread them. The people who came to meet her spoke to her with that dizzy mixture of awe and gushing approbation that rich Americans would have bestowed on a movie star, yet underneath their cordiality was an elaborate system of class distinctions and social rituals that made her feel as if she were living in Tibet. How, she often wondered, did a person make real friends in this city?

"I'll expect you around eleven, after the performance," Cissy was saying.

"At eleven," Viola agreed. The Arena was always in need of money, and she couldn't afford to turn down invitations to places where she might meet future patrons.

Hanging up the phone, she wandered into the kitchen and made herself a hot cup of Bovril. She sighed and wished she had time to slip across the Channel and visit Jeanne; she wished Kathe's vacation wasn't three months away. She was tired of being applauded by strangers and then coming home to an empty house.

"We're going boating on the Thames," Richard announced one afternoon.

"Boating on the Thames?" Viola lifted her head from the script she was memorizing. "But that's out of the question. I've got another play opening in less than three weeks."

"No excuses," Richard admonished. He took her coat and draped it over her shoulders. "You need fresh air, exercise, laughter. Stay inside another minute plugging away and you're going to start looking like Stilton cheese."

"What if I say, 'No, I can't, I'm positively swamped'?"

"Then I'll pretend not to hear you."

"Very well." She put aside the script. "I know when I'm beat." Getting to her feet, she put on her coat. "Bring on the boat, but it had better not rain, because if I come down with pneumonia, Carlyle will have to refund all the tickets."

"You'd play with one lung," Richard teased. "You'd play on your deathbed. Don't try to fool me, Vi. You'd never even *notice* pneumonia."

He was always there, day or night, ready to take her dancing or to dinner; ready to bring her Epsom salts to soak her feet in when she caught cold; ready to make her cups of strong tea and stay up with her as late as she wanted while she railed against the contrariness of actors or the inefficiency of carpenters; ready to persuade her to take an afternoon off; ready to declare that she had been working too hard, pack her bags, and drag her up to Scotland on the crazy theory that she would never really appreciate how eccentric the British were until she had had a look for the Loch Ness Monster.

Before she realized what was happening, he had become her recreation director, her confidante, and her only real friend, and this—despite her best resolutions to the contrary—soon began to have very serious consequences. For no matter how ambivalent she felt toward Richard, he had one great advantage: he was in the right place at the right time.

*   *   *

The right time proved to be a cold, blustery evening in early November. It wasn't raining when she left the Arena but the air was damp and fragrant with soot, and when she looked up the sky was leaden and close, a London sky that seemed about to swoop down and blot out the streetlamps. She walked half a block to the cab stand, her arms loaded with the scripts she planned to read that evening, among which was an early version of Henry Arbor's *Laura*, a play that was to be one of her greatest theatrical successes. That night, however, she had no inkling that she was carrying a good bit of her future in her arms. She only knew that she was tired, cold, hungry, and overburdened, and that if a cab didn't appear soon she would have to sit down on the curb.

A cab finally showed up, moving sedately down the street, its shiny black bumpers smeared with a wavering line of light from the streetlamps overhead. As she stepped off the curb the sky suddenly opened up. Rain fell, not a misty, British rain, but a rain that reminded her of thunderstorms in New York, a sweeping, cold, relentless rain that soaked her hair, dripped down the collar of her coat, plastered her skirt to her legs, and turned her new navy-blue pumps into miniature boats.

Damnation, she thought. She climbed into the cab as quickly as she could, trying to save the scripts, but the cheap leather binders were already dripping rivers of brown dye into her lap. Shivering and miserable, she gave her address to the driver and then sat back and tried to ignore the water dripping down the backs of her legs into her shoes.

When she got home it was still raining in great transparent sheets. Having neglected to bring an umbrella, she was forced to dash from the cab to the portico, a maneuver which left her even wetter than before. Jamming her key in the lock, she fled inside, slogging up the stairs to her apartment. The phone was ringing in the darkness, insistently like a crying baby. Realizing that given the mood she was in she was probably unfit for human contact, she picked it up anyway.

"Hello, Vi?" It was Richard on the other end of the line. "Is that you?"

"Yes, Richard, it's me." She pushed her wet hair out of her eyes, feeling cold and so exhausted that she knew if she didn't sit down soon, she was going to fall down. Switching on a lamp, she looked with dismay at the grimy tracks she had made on her new rug.

"Is something wrong? You sound different." Sometimes Richard's constant worrying over her made her impatient, but tonight she was grateful for it.

"I'm soaked to the bone." She held the phone gingerly, wondering if you could get a fatal electric shock from wet hands on a receiver.

"Poor girl," Richard said sympathetically. "I'll be right over and make you a hot rum toddy."

She slumped down into a chair and waited for Richard, too tired to do anything more than turn on the electric fire and kick off her wet shoes. The rain went on and on, hypnotic and incessant, coating the bricks of the chimney with a cold glaze, running off the shingles in drumrolls, and after some twenty or thirty minutes dripping through the newly plastered ceiling into the middle of her new rose-colored couch. Swearing softly to herself, she struggled to her feet, got a pan from the kitchen, and tried to stanch the flow, but the water was coming down in the most inconvenient place possible—directly on the edge of the arm, which meant that she had to stand and hold the pan if she wanted it to do any good. She was just trying to jockey the couch into a more convenient position, huffing and panting with frustration, when the doorbell rang.

"Hullo." Richard was standing in the doorway with a bottle of rum under one arm, appearing for all the world as if he had just done something heroically aquatic like swimming the Hellespont. He looked her over and clucked his tongue. "You look like a drowned cat, old girl," he said cheerfully. "Why don't you go change into something dry while I boil some water for the toddy? Have any butter?"

"It's in the frig." She gratefully abandoned the pan and the couch to Richard, who deftly repositioned both. In the bedroom she stripped off her wet clothes, throwing them into a heap on the rug. That was one of the advantages of having been so busy that you hadn't had time to shop for more furniture: plenty of places to throw things. Riffling through her closet, she surveyed the scratchy wool skirts and thin silk dresses, thinking that what she really wanted to do was put on her old flannel bathrobe.

Well why not? Richard was old enough to see a woman in a bathrobe, and given the fact that she had had it for the past four years, the cuffs were frayed, and it had three mismatched buttons, it could hardly be construed as an act of seduction to come wandering out in it. The truth was that although she liked stylish dresses and pretty shoes in the public sphere, she relished coming home to dumpy, comfortable things. Peeling off her wet underpants and bra, she threw them after the rest and then reached into her closet and retrieved her robe from the hook next to her summer jacket. The brown flannel was warm and comforting, like a child's security blanket. Giving a sigh of relief, she buttoned up the mismatched buttons, tied the frayed belt around her waist, and padded barefoot into the living room, where Richard had already set out two hot toddies.

"I found a cinnamon stick in the kitchen," Richard said, "so I stuck it in. Nothing like a taste of the Eastern Empire to chase away a British cold, at least for us British. Gives us a jolly sense of imperial power that's most salubrious, like taking a whiff of India."

Viola smiled and lifted the mug to her lips, already feeling better. The toddy was perfect: sugar, rum, butter, cinnamon, and a twist of orange peel. It went down easily, and after she had finished it Richard made her another.

They sat for an hour—maybe more—talking, as they often did, about the theater. Later she vaguely remembered that their conversation had been about Priestley. Richard didn't like Priestley, but she'd defended him, or maybe it had been the other way around.

"What do you think of Baldwin?" Richard suddenly asked, apropos of nothing. Later they both agreed that this was probably the worst introduction to a seduction ever offered by man to woman. Stanley Baldwin became their own private joke, so much so that until the Prime Minister resigned two years later, they both were given to inappropriate fits of laughter whenever his name came up.

"I haven't thought about him much, really." She was feeling a little dizzy from the rum. She put down her mug and looked through the glass coffee table at her bare feet. "He's hardly a Socialist's ideal, I imagine, but he's your Prime Minister, Richard, not mine."

"Viola." There was something in Richard's voice that made her look up. His face was flushed and his eyes bright and pleading. He leaned toward her, such a handsome man, blond and slender as an exclamation point. "I haven't said anything to you for over a year now, and that's a long time to wait."

"Richard, don't; please." She was confused, flattered that he was so persistent, yet some sensible part of her still knew that anything other than running in the opposite direction would be a major mistake. She started to get up, but Richard caught her arm and pulled her lightly down beside him.

"I still love you, you know," he said simply.

"Richard, this just won't work. Nothing's changed." She made a feeble gesture of disentangling herself. "Don't say another word. Really. We'll both regret it."

"Nonsense, Vi." Richard reached out and began to stroke her hair, softly and cautiously. "I worship the ground you walk on. I know that sounds trite, but I'm a musician, not a writer." He grinned. "At least you're not snapping my head off this time."

"No, but I still don't feel—"

"You know what the problem is," he interrupted. "The problem is that we talk too much. That's been my fault, I imagine. I'm an abstract little beggar. Put me in the same room with a beautiful woman and I get so nervous I start babbling about the Depressed Areas Bill or Hindemith."

"It isn't your fault, Richard. It's just that I'm incapable of giving you the kind of affection that—"

"It's time to stop talking," Richard continued firmly. "It's time for me to quit acting the fool. It's time for this, Vi." Richard suddenly took her face in his hands and kissed her, long and hard and passionately. She was shocked by the force of her own response. Taken completely by surprise, she kissed him back. It was exciting, very exciting, as exciting as anything she had let herself feel in years. Richard put the palm of his hand on the back of her neck and pulled her closer. For a moment she thought again of resisting, she thought practical sensible thoughts about all the ways this was a bad idea, but then the excitement of feeling his body so close to hers overwhelmed her again and she moved into his arms.

Richard slipped his hand into her robe, and she felt him draw back for a second with surprise as he encountered her bare flesh. Then slowly he began to run his hand along her sides, around her waist, lightly down the curve of her hips. The robe slipped off her shoulders. She closed her eyes, closed her mind, stopped thinking anything coherent. Her body was like a spring, tense and expectant, and each time Richard touched it the spring inside coiled tighter and tighter. He kissed her for a long time, until there was nothing left in her world but the warm pressure of his mouth against hers. She had a sense of flying into great blank spaces where she saw oceans far below her and on the horizon thin lines of small black birds. She imagined a great stage with gold columns where she stood naked and was applauded by strange men, and all this was disturbing and terribly exciting at the same time.

For a split second she thought of Joseph, how when they had made love she had always been there with him; she thought how with Richard she was fantasizing and how different that was and she tried to stop but she couldn't. Richard drew her down on the couch next to him and erotic images filled her mind, and she was ashamed of these fantasies and at the same time at the mercy of them. When at last she climaxed, it was with a force and incoherence that alarmed her.

For a long time they lay in a tangle on the couch, arms and legs crossed. Outside it had stopped raining and the silence was long and heavy, like a record that had reached the end of the last groove and was still spinning. She opened her eyes and found Richard smiling at her with tenderness and satisfaction; it was a loving, proprietary smile that said once having possessed her, he had no intention of letting her go.

I don't love him, she thought, and then—overcome by guilt and desire—how could I feel such things and *not* love him? Her mind moved in circles, trying to reconcile the contradiction, but it was a confusion she was not to resolve until seven months later when, on a hot spring day in late May, with Kathe as a bridesmaid and Jeanne as maid of honor, she married Richard Stafford, and for a time at least all her misgivings ceased.

15

THE SOUTH
OF FRANCE
1935

Viola stood at an open window looking down at the meticulously tended beach of the Hotel Azur. It was three in the afternoon and brilliantly hot. Beyond the rim of red-and-white umbrellas and well-oiled bodies, a glittering strip of the Mediterranean curved gently toward the horizon.

"Come back to bed," Richard pleaded. He slipped his arm around her waist and tugged her back into the cool darkness of the room. "I'm hungry for you."

"But the sun's shining," she protested.

"Let it go under a cloud." He pulled her down on the bed and began to unhook the straps of her swimming suit. "The beaches are all composed of pebbles and the French loathe us. Let's stay inside this afternoon."

Viola laughed and tried to pull her straps up again but he was too quick for her. Before she knew it her suit was down around her waist and he was kissing her breasts. "Richard," she pleaded weakly, "what are you doing?"

"Following your tan lines to the Orient."

"But we've already made love *four* times."

"Let's go for a world record." He was doing wonderful things to her nipples. Flopping back on the bed, Viola gave in, giggling. Richard nibbled and sucked at her, working his way down her belly toward her crotch.

He was incredibly passionate. She was convinced when he started out that she didn't have an ounce of desire left, but by the time he reached the inside of her thighs, she had changed her mind.

She woke at five and lay in bed trying to remember what it had been like to lie next to Joseph and finding to her surprise that she couldn't. Puzzled, she searched a little longer for the memories of Joseph's arms and breath and flesh the way she might have looked for a familiar pair of worn-out shoes, but the old pain of missing him was gone. My grief is only a spot now instead of an ocean, she thought, a drop ready to dry up, and, Joseph dear, forgive me, because I couldn't go on mourning you forever.

She stretched her bare arms above her head, feeling the strength and youth in them. Only a few weeks ago she had turned thirty-four. Amazing really that she was still so young. For the past seven years she had felt like a woman of fifty or sixty whose life—except for her work—was over. In the space of less than seven months Richard had taken a good twenty years off of her.

She sat up and turned to contemplate this new husband of hers, who was stretched out on his back, his head propped up on the feather pillows, his naked body half eclipsed by the sheets. How she loved him, the slender curve of his shoulders, the rise and fall of his chest, the smooth lean greyhound tautness of his legs and arms. She was drunk with love, silly and foolish as a bride of twenty. She knew her whole attitude toward Richard was excessive, but she had such a damn good time with him. She leaned back and indulged herself in the thought that she would never be unhappy again.

Good lord, she thought with a grin, she really had a bad case. Of course there would be problems. People always had problems. On the other hand, most people didn't have Richard making love to them. She sat for a while staring dreamily at the Mediterranean light coming in through the louvered windows. On the floor, yellow slats of sunshine trembled on the blue-and-white tiles. Everything gave her pleasure these days; everything made her glad to be alive.

During the fall of that first year of her marriage to Richard something happened to Viola's acting that changed it permanently. One night in mid-November on the stage of the Arena she picked up a glass of water. The play was Henry Arbor's *Laura*—the story of a blind girl who falls in love with her father-in-law. Like all of Arbor's plays, *Laura* was a pressure cooker, but in recent years Viola would have felt none of the pressure. She would have played Laura as a passionate young woman, executed every movement of her body, every cadence of her voice with such technical perfection that the audience would have been tricked into believing that she was living the role, but she would have done all this from a distance, efficiently and professionally.

That night, however, something unexpected happened. The emotional intensity that had been lacking in her acting ever since Joseph's death returned. At the moment her hand touched the glass, a metamorphosis took place: she became Laura. By some mysterious mechanism, the love she had for Richard was unexpectedly transformed into Laura's love for her father-in-law, and she felt everything as Laura would feel it: the loneliness and pain of blindness, the insecurity, the guilt, the frustrated passion.

Viola's hand trembled. She tried to drink the water but she couldn't. She tried to say her next line, but she was overcome with emotion. She put her hand to her mouth in a quick, wounded gesture, as if feeling her own lips. Blind, abandoned Laura.

"Thank you," she managed to say at last. The line was nothing, but the effect was electric. The audience was galvanized. She never knew later if they wept, but Arbor insisted that they had.

"All you did was drink a goddamn glass of water, Vi," Henry told her excitedly after the play, "and they were in the palm of your hand. How do you do it, for Christ's sake? You used to be famous the way the Egyptian collection of the British Museum is famous—like some kind of cultural treasure that everyone knew about—but now you're famous like . . ." He searched for a comparison.

"Like Madame Tussaud's?"

"Good lord, no." Arbor was obviously horrified. "You're a con-
summate artist. Don't ever forget that for a minute."

But despite Henry's reassurance, Viola sometimes felt like Madame
Tussaud's, especially when she opened her morning newspaper.
According to the press, Viola Kessler's existence was a dizzy round of
smashing successes and meetings with famous people. Her morn-
ings, the society columns implied, were spent going over scripts with
Henry Arbor, J. B. Priestley, James Birdie, Christopher Isherwood,
T. S. Eliot, and a host of younger playwrights of lesser renown, while
her afternoons were spent rehearsing with the likes of Laurence
Olivier, John Gielgud, and Flora Robson. In the evenings, when there
was no performance, she could be found dancing until the wee hours
with Lady Dockett's set, or laughing gaily in the company of the
Prince of Wales.

All of which was true in a distorted way, but it rather missed the
point. There was no doubt that she had become successful beyond
anything she had ever imagined, but what she remembered most was
not the fame and the parties and the opening nights, but the price she
paid for her career.

The honeymoon with Richard—to put it bluntly—was soon over.

Music crashed and fell, the notes stumbling into each other. There
was a tremendous dissonance of bass, followed by a run of piercing
highs that would have made the hair stand up on the back of Viola's
neck if she hadn't been so used to such things.

"What in the world is that ghastly noise?" Cecily Dockett demanded, shedding her leopard jacket on the sofa and looking around
Viola's living room critically. Cecily was dressed in what Viola
privately thought of as one of her "safari outfits": a tiny hat composed
of the feathers of rare birds, shoes and bag sewn from some hapless
serpent, and a belt of some indeterminate skin (rhinoceros? emu?).
Around her neck she wore one of the famous Dockett lockets, a
massive pendant of diamonds and pearls that swayed between her
breasts with an almost hypnotic quality. "What *is* that hideous
racket?"

"It's one of Richard's new compositions," Viola explained, calmly pouring out the sherry. The crystal of the glasses sparkled in the late afternoon sunlight and the amber liquid was as pale and dry as the rose leaves she had brought from Sanford Palace to keep among her linens. Viola took a sip of the sherry, wishing Cissy would lower her voice, but Cissy—as usual—was in no mood to be diplomatic.

"Richard," she called out imperiously, "hush that infernal racket." There was sudden silence from the other room and Viola heard the scraping of the bench as Richard pushed it back from the piano. "Oh dear," Cissy sighed, waving her gloved hands like the wings of two graceful white birds, "I do hope I didn't insult him, but really, the assault on one's ears is just too extreme." Viola also hoped Richard hadn't been insulted, but it didn't seem likely. Cissy picked up her sherry glass and laughed prettily. "Why can't you convince Richard to do more work along the lines of *Berliner Ballade?*" She hummed a few bars of "Let's Find Someone to Hate" and took a sip of sherry. "Really, Vi, if I'd done something that splendid and now I was spending my time banging away at the piano with my elbows, I'd feel, well"—Cissy leaned forward in the confiding mode—"I'd feel a bit washed up, don't you know."

It was sometime in late November and Viola's bedroom was cold the way only an English bedroom can be cold, so damp that the sheets felt like two clammy bandages wrapped around her chest. Waking suddenly from a disturbing dream, she reached out for the reassuring warmth of Richard's body and found an empty space on his side of the bed. From downstairs the sound of the piano drifted up, muffled by the intervening doors and carpets. She looked at the clock and discovered that it was two in the morning. Now what fit of happy inspiration had gotten Richard up at this hour? Throwing on her new dressing gown (now that she was a married woman again, her old flannel robe had been relegated to the back of the closet), she slipped her feet into a pair of satin mules and tiptoed downstairs.

A band of light was coming from underneath the door of Richard's study. She stood for a moment in the chilly hallway, listening, wondering if she should disturb him. Probably not, she decided reluctantly. If he was in the throes of composing, he'd hardly appreciate the interruption.

Sitting down on the hall rug, she wrapped her hands around her knees and closed her eyes, trying to find some logic or rhythm that she could appreciate, but the sounds were raw and confusing. For some reason the music made her sad tonight. Huddled on the carpet, she became prey to depressing thoughts: a distance was growing between her and Richard. She looked at the closed door. A transparent curtain was gradually coming down, with him on one side and her on the other.

That was ridiculous: she was imagining things, borrowing trouble. Viola rubbed her arms briskly, trying to restore some warmth to them, and decided that she was simply in an off mood. The problem was that she'd been missing Kathe a lot lately, not to mention working too hard. She thought longingly of tropical islands, of waves and palm trees. Perhaps she and Richard should take a vacation to Greece. Was it warm in Greece this time of year?

The music wove a web of disorganization around her; it beat at her forehead like a headache. *Tapering off,* the music seemed to say, *distance, more distance, always more distance.*

She got up and turned her back on the music. Her marriage was fine; she and Richard were just entering a new, more mature stage in their relationship; to think anything else was a betrayal of the love that united them—the love that always would unite them.

Worry the music warned, chasing her upstairs, *worry.* Going into the bathroom, she took two aspirin, went back to bed, and pulled the pillow over her head to drown out the sound of the piano.

"Where are you off to, old girl?" It was December and Richard was sitting on the living-room carpet in his shirt sleeves, playing dominoes with Kathe, who was home for Christmas vacation. The black rectangles lay scattered at their feet and a fire was burning in the fireplace. Viola looked longingly at the cozy domestic scene, wishing that she didn't have to go out in the cold.

"Back to the Arena."

"Why in heaven's name?" Richard laid a double six against its mate and contemplated it with satisfaction.

"Cecily Dockett is meeting me there for a look at the budget for next spring. She thinks she can do another benefit garden tour for the Younger Playwrights Series."

Richard picked up a domino and turned it over in his hand restlessly. His face was pale, his lips tight and thin. "Don't you ever get tired of jumping through hoops for the upper classes like some kind of little trained monkey?"

She stared at him, hardly able to believe he'd said something so deliberately unkind. Biting her tongue, she somehow managed to keep her temper. Maybe he was feeling ill. "I'll be back in an hour," she said, not meeting his eyes. She fumbled for her muffler in the sleeve of her coat. There was a tense silence, broken only by the snapping of the fire.

"Is it my turn?" Kathe asked.

"Yes." Richard picked up the poker and sent a waterfall of sparks flying into the grate. "It's your turn." The dominoes clicked under Kathe's hands. Double six, blank. "Your mama," Richard abruptly informed Kathe, "is a busy, important woman, so the two of us better do our best to keep out of her path."

Kathe smiled uneasily, as if not sure how to take this, a sentiment Viola could sympathize with since she herself was in the same predicament. What was wrong with Richard?

His parting words were like little stabs, and she dragged them with her to the theater and brooded on them the whole time Cecily Dockett was chattering away about roses. A few days later, when she was rummaging around in Richard's desk for some stamps, she came across a sheaf of his music and a letter informing him that it had been rejected by some obscure competition in Scotland. So he'd been turned down again. How humiliating. She read the rejection, marveling at its cruelty: *too obscure and dissonant, derivative in several major aspects, we regret that your present submission is not really up to our standards.* How would she have felt if she'd gotten a review that nasty? No wonder Richard had been so out of sorts, poor dear.

Weeks went by and she soon forgot all about the comment he had made about hoops and monkeys. For her thirty-sixth birthday, Richard—who had known Brecht vaguely back in Berlin—wrote to him to try to persuade him to let the Arena mount a special production of *Mahagonny.* Brecht, who was off in Moscow, didn't even bother to reply, but Viola was touched by the gesture. What other husband in the world would have tried to come up with a present like that?

The Arena prospered, the months passed, King George died, King Edward abdicated, and a new King was crowned at Westminster. Kathe failed ancient history and had to take it over; Eugene O'Neill came from the States to oversee Viola's performance in *Anna Christie* and they all got roaringly drunk together. At Whitechapel Harry was very nearly arrested when the police broke up Oswald Mosley's anti-Jewish march. In Germany Hitler won the election by a landslide and in the States Roosevelt did the same; in Spain a bloody civil war broke out, supported secretly by the Nazis and openly by Mussolini, and in England Viola's life held a slow sense of dislocation that she did her best to ignore.

"Your wife is wonderful, Mr. Kessler. Such amazing stage presence." The American lady waved her punch glass dramatically. The second annual Benefit Garden Tour was in progress honoring the Arena Theater Younger Playwrights Series, and Cecily Dockett had made sure that everyone who might be persuaded to contribute had been lured down to Sanford to see the last of the roses. "Garbo positively pales beside her. You must be very proud of her."

"Oh I am rather," Richard said stiffly.

"You know, Mr. Kessler, Mrs. Kessler is my very favorite actress."

"Ah."

"Oh yes indeed. In America when we think of the British theater, we think of Viola Kessler. I'd like to lure her back home, I really would. Why she'd be a smash in Cincinnati, better than the opera in the zoo."

"Opera in the zoo?" Richard's eyebrows shot up.

"Oh we have opera there *alfresco* every summer, Mr. Kessler. Quite a high cultural experience, only the best singers. You'd love it, Mr. Kessler, if you're the musical type."

Viola, who overheard the whole interchange, was horrified. "I'm so sorry that idiot woman kept calling you Mr. Kessler," she apologized as soon as she could get Richard alone.

Richard drank his punch off in one gulp and refilled his glass. "Is she very rich, old girl?"

"Very. Cecily says that when the American stock market crashed her husband didn't even notice."

"Likely to contribute to the Younger Playwrights and all that?"

"She's already pledged five thousand pounds."

"Ah then"—Richard disposed of his second glass of punch and inspected the roses at his feet—"I suppose I shall just have to put up with her calling me Mr. Kessler then. I mean it would hardly do to quash five thousand quid, now would it?"

"You don't mind?"

"Hardly."

"I think that's very sweet of you."

"Ah well"—Richard refilled his glass—"perhaps I should adopt a name tag like they do at those subscription dancing schools. *HELLO, MY NAME IS: RICHARD STAFFORD*. How does that strike you?" He laughed. "Be a good one, wouldn't it? We could get Bertie in on this too. *HELLO, MY NAME IS: ALBERT EDWARD, DUKE OF SANFORD (COMMONLY ADDRESSED AS "YOUR GRACE")*. Think of the possibilities."

Viola laughed uneasily.

"Hello, you two lovebirds," Cissy called out, bounding up to them. Her dress was emerald green and her great gauzy hat trembled in the breeze like the wings of a monstrous butterfly. "Perfectly smashing party, isn't it?"

"Richard?"

"What?"

"I was just wondering," Viola hesitated, embarrassed. She pulled the sheets up around her breasts and sat up in bed, feeling foolish and vulnerable.

"Wondering what?"

"Wondering if you'd like to make love tonight?" she said timidly.

Richard cleared his throat. "Sorry, old girl, but I've had something of a rough day."

She was disappointed but she understood; he'd started working again and his music was taking all his time and energy for the present. She bent over to kiss his cheek, and he flinched as if he'd been stung. "Good night then," he said, turning away from her. He curled his body into a tight ball so that all she could see was the back of his blue pajamas.

"Good night," she echoed. Her body felt hot and unsatisfied and she felt a silly urge to cry with disappointment. This was ridiculous. Giving up on the idea of going to sleep, she rose from bed, strode into the living room, took a script out of her shoulder bag, and stubbornly began to memorize her lines.

The phone was ringing in the dark and she simply couldn't find it. She grappled at the bedside table and managed to knock over a glass of water. A book hit the floor with a thud. Giving up, she fumbled for the light switch and by some miracle her fingers hit the button.

"Hello."

"Hello, Viola, this is Harry."

"Harry who?"

"Harry Stafford, your brother-in-law."

Richard sat up, bleary-eyed and blinking. "Who is it?"

"Harry, your brother."

"Tell him if he wants us to have tea with Hitler, he'll have to mail us an invitation." Richard looked at the clock. "It's four A.M. for Christ's sake."

She put her hand over the mouthpiece. "He says he needs to talk to you; says it's an emergency."

Richard took the receiver out of her hand. "Good morning, Harry, so good of you to call. I was just lazing about here wondering if you might ring us up." There was a noise on the other end of the line that reminded Viola of a buzzing bee. "What?" Richard said. "When?" In a split second he was fully awake, his whole body tense. Viola had a premonition of disaster. There was another buzzing from the other end of the line. "He was doing what?" Richard yelled.

"What's wrong?" She leaned forward, clasping at the hem of the sheet.

"It's Bertie," Richard said, "killed stone dead in a motorcycle accident."

"Oh no." She had a sudden painful image of Bertie slamming into a tree. Silly, kind Bertie. "I'm so sorry." Plays were full of fine lines for moments like this, but the reality was that there was nothing to be said. On the other end of the phone, Harry seemed to be speaking again. Richard listened for a few seconds.

"Say that again, Harry." His mouth hardened ominously. More

buzzing. Suddenly Richard slammed down the receiver. Viola was so startled that she jumped.

"What happened?"

"Harry just reminded me that I'm now the bloody Duke of Sanford." He got out of bed.

"Where are you going?" She pulled the sheets up around her shoulders, feeling confused. If someone had just called to tell her Conrad was dead, she would have been crying by now, but except for the white spots over Richard's jawbone and the thin, tense line of his lips, his face was a tight, impenetrable mask.

"I'm going downstairs to think for a bit. No need to wait up for me."

"Richard?"

"Yes?"

"Is there anything I can do?"

"Do?"

"To help, I mean."

"Ah well, I rather think not. I mean you can't very well bring Bertie back from the dead, now can you?"

After he disappeared through the doorway she lay awake for a long time, mourning Bertie in her own way and worrying about Richard. Should she go down to him and try to offer him the comfort he'd rejected, or should she let him grieve in his own fashion? Twice she got out of bed and twice she went back. She was just about to get up for a third time and go down to Richard whether he wanted her or not, when she heard the piano, which had been silent for months, crash into life.

As she listened to the music she felt a cold chill creep over her. Richard wasn't playing one of his own pieces. He was playing Tchaikovsky's *First Piano Concerto*.

The whole house seemed to expand, filled by the frantic beauty of the music. Downstairs Richard played on and on like a man possessed. It was a brilliant, frightening performance.

The Crown Tearoom, located near the Monument, was a small, cozy establishment, so exclusive that if your female ancestors hadn't been dropping in at the Crown for tea for the last hundred years or so you didn't have a prayer of finding the place. Despite Cecily Dockett's

directions—which had been detailed in the extreme—Viola got lost
three times before she located the umpromising blind alley that led to
the unmarked door that led to the unremarkable flight of stairs that
led at last to the suffused light, roses, powder-blue rug, and white
tablecloths of the tearoom. Cissy was sitting at a corner table, picking
at a trifle and sipping her tea, wearing a fox stole and a hat composed
of pheasant wings. When she caught sight of Viola she returned her
teacup to its bone china saucer and gave a small worried frown.

"Not up to the mark, definitely not up to the mark," she observed,
kissing at the air on either side of Viola's cheeks.

Viola sat down and helped herself to a cup of tea. "What's not up
to the mark, Cissy?"

"Oh nothing." Cissy dabbed at her lips evasively and spread her
napkin back in her lap. "Well, to be honest, it's just that I *was* rather
struck by the thought that you don't look particularly chipper for
someone who's just become Duchess of Sanford."

"I miss Bertie." Viola poured some milk into her tea and began to
drink it, avoiding Cissy's eyes; she'd told the truth—more or less. She
did miss Bertie, not so much for Bertie's sake as for Richard's. Since
his brother died Richard's state of mind seemed to have taken another
turn for the worse. Lately she had begun to wonder if Richard was
having some kind of mental breakdown. The thought worried her
terribly, but the last person she intended to confide in was Cissy
Dockett, who was famous for broadcasting gossip all over greater
London.

Cissy, however, was not to be so easily turned aside. "Poppycock,"
she said, leaning forward in insistent intimacy, "Bertie was a sweet
fellow, but he was a silly twit, and besides no one mourns one's
husband's relatives all that much—especially when their demise
provides one with a house in Belgravia, Sanford Palace, a title, and a
pile of quid the size of St. Paul's. There must be something else
bothering you. Ah, I have it." Cissy smiled one of her famous
pearl-toothed smiles and puffed the fur stole up around her shoulders. "You're having a love affair with"—she paused like a hound on
the scent of a fox—"Henry Arbor."

"Don't be ridiculous, Cissy."

"Well, if there is something wrong between you and Richard,"

Cissy persisted, "you should have it out with him straightaway. That's my advice."

"Cissy, really!"

"Oh my, I'm so sorry. I seem to have overstepped my limit a bit, haven't I? I didn't mean to hit a sore point."

"You didn't hit a sore point." Viola stripped off her gloves and threw them down on the table. She felt hot, agitated, and constricted. "Let's just change the subject, shall we?" She managed to steer conversation onto safer ground, but long after she left the Crown, Cissy's comment about having things out with Richard stayed in her mind, pricking like a tiny thorn. If things had deteriorated to the point where even Cissy Dockett suspected something was wrong, then the time had finally arrived when she was going to have to talk to Richard about the state of their marriage.

I don't want to do this, Viola thought as she got into a cab, *I don't know how to begin or what to say to him or how he'll react.* The city streamed by: in Piccadilly Circus the Angel of Christian Charity, commonly known as Eros, stood on one foot on a slender column, shooting an invisible arrow into an equally invisible target. Viola sat in the cab trying to formulate some kind of plan, but all the ones she came up with seemed tactless or impractical. *I'll wait,* she decided at last. *I'll give it a few more weeks. Surely a few weeks can't make that much difference.*

But a few weeks, as it turned out, made a great deal of difference. In Spain Franco's troops had Madrid surrounded, and a famous American documentary filmmaker decided to make a movie of the siege. About a fortnight after her lunch with Cissy, Viola and Richard went to a screening of the film, and from that moment on life became so complicated that she felt as if she had been swept up in a tornado.

The hall where the movie was shown was dark and stuffy, filled with uncomfortable wooden chairs and thick, blue cigarette smoke, but it was unlikely that anyone in the audience that evening noticed the discomfort. On the small, silvered screen building after building exploded under the battery of Franco's artillery, wood and windows rising up into the air. Spanish women in black kerchiefs boiled weeds to feed the defenders of the city; a dead mule was cut up to make stew. In the belfries of Madrid, on top of the ruined walls of homes and factories, the republicans lay on their bellies, firing the last of their ammunition. Hopelessly outnumbered, they fought on against incredible odds.

A plane appeared overhead and the camera tilted up to catch the swastikas painted on its sides as it dumped its load of bombs. Children ran for shelter. *NON PASARAN—THEY SHALL NOT PASS:* the motto of republican Madrid was written on the walls of the city in the blood of the wounded.

The film came to a stop, the sound of the projector died, and the lights came up again. There was a round of applause, and a small redheaded man in a brown suit leapt up onstage and delivered an appeal to the audience in a heavy Brooklyn accent.

"Madrid is blockaded," he said, gripping the sides of the podium and leaning forward, "but help is pouring in from all over the world for its brave defenders. A Canadian doctor is setting up blood-transfusion centers; the soldiers in the International Brigades are fighting side by side with their Spanish comrades. But we need more help, more volunteers. Republican Spain is calling out in her hour of need to freedom-loving people everywhere. Answer her call!"

"That was wonderful," Richard exclaimed as they walked out of the theater. His face was flushed with excitement. "Simply wonderful. I think I'll give the Save Madrid Committee some money."

"Good idea." Viola was relieved to see Richard at last take an interest in something besides his music.

The next evening when she came home from the Arena, she found the redheaded man who had spoken after the film sitting in her living room tapping his feet to the flamenco music issuing from the Victrola.

"Meet Mr. Isak Hart," Richard said cheerfully.

"How do," Mr. Hart said, pumping Viola's hand. "The Duke here has just given the republicans two new tanks to smash Franco."

"I mean to give more, too." Richard brushed his hair out of his eyes, picked up a pamphlet with a fist on the cover, and examined it earnestly. "You can't believe the atrocities Franco is perpetrating."

"It's a dress rehearsal for the next European war, Duchess," Mr. Hart said, "take my word for it. As an actress you must know all about dress rehearsals."

"As long as I've come into all the Sanford money, I might as well do something useful with it." Richard put down the pamphlet and smiled contentedly. "And besides, the thought that the family fortune is financing the republicans will drive my dear Fascist brother Harry straight out of his traces."

Every day for the next two weeks Richard closeted himself in his study with Mr. Hart for hours at a time, presumably making plans for his donation to the cause. Viola, who was delighted to see him so actively occupied, was finally able to stop worrying about him and turn her attention to other things. Crazy families were in vogue that year as dramatic subjects and one of her younger writers had just submitted a new version of *Medea* that might have potential if she could just figure out how to stage the climax. In fact, she became so absorbed in the tragedy of the play that when real tragedy came it took her by surprise.

On Monday she came home at one-thirty in the morning to find Richard sitting in the living room drinking a gin and tonic and listening to flamenco music. "Hello, Vi," he said. "I've been waiting up for you." He paused. "The truth is, I've got a bit of news. I've decided to go to Spain to join up with the International Brigade. Isak's got a place all reserved for me." He smiled and drummed his fingers on the table happily. "Surprised?"

"Yes." She could hardly speak. "Yes, I am."

"*Non Pasaran*, and all that." Richard lifted his glass in a toast. "You can give me a hero's welcome when I get back, old girl."

"Richard"—she finally found her voice—"please don't go. You could get killed." She thought of all of his youth and intelligence and talent ending up wasted on some Spanish battlefield, and the thought sickened her the way she might have been sickened to see a forest carelessly burned to the ground or the Turner on their bedroom wall slashed by vandals. "That war isn't some heroic movie. They use real bullets."

"I know that," Richard said, setting his chin stubbornly. "I'm quite aware of that fact."

She could see that she was only driving him to it by her objections, but she couldn't stop. He couldn't go to Spain. It was insane. "Please," she begged. "I can't stand the thought of you getting shot. I know things aren't right between us, but I still love you."

Richard looked at her oddly. "Do you? I wonder. I mean, what is love when you get right down to it? What does love mean to those soldiers who are dying to save Spain from Franco? What does love mean to Bertie, for example, now that his brains have been scattered all along the hedgerows?"

"Richard, for God's sake."

"The problem is, you women look at things differently than a man would. We need honor, adventure, a chance to prove ourselves." He cleared his throat. "As much as I care for you, it's been hard for me to watch your career take off while mine was left behind in the dust. I'm sorry to admit that, old girl, but it's the bloody truth. Perhaps that doesn't sound like one of those fine lines out of one of your plays, but I'm not a writer. I'm just an ordinary fellow who needs something out of the ordinary to do with himself."

A terrible love for him tore at her heart. She saw that he wanted to prove to himself that he was really her equal, and she knew that she would never be able to convince him that no proof was necessary.

It was the second week in November. On Platform C the train that would carry Richard away to Spain was heaving like some great monster about to give birth. Viola stood beside the wheels, dressed in a bright red dress and red hat, because red wasn't the color of mourning and she had promised herself not to mourn, thinking despite that of how much metal and weight there would be between her and Richard in a few minutes, how many miles of unfathomable distance and misunderstanding. Beside her, a few feet to the left of Kathe, Richard stood looking off into the middle distance, his new trench coat billowing in the breeze, blond and clean-cut and handsome, for all the world like some flying ace of the Great War about to depart on yet another noble mission. In less than two years there would be hundreds of thousands of farewells like this made on this very platform, but today it seemed painfully unique.

Five minutes. Three. The train whistled shrilly and some of the passengers on the platform clapped their hands over their ears. Two minutes to departure.

"Good-bye, Uncle Richard." Kathe threw herself into Richard's arms with all the fierce spontaneity of a thirteen-year-old. She hugged him long and hard. "I love you loads."

Richard bent down and planted a fatherly kiss on Kathe's cheek. "Good-bye, Kitty-Katty," he said cheerfully.

"Will you write me?" Kathe begged eagerly, holding on to her new hat with one hand. The skirt of her navy-blue sailor suit blew against her skinny legs and her curly black hair was a hopeless tangle, escaping out of the pink ribbons that held her braids, but her skin had the glow of youth and health and optimism. War for Kathe was something you only read about in history class.

"Righto." Richard pinched her cheek. "Three times a day."

"And tell me about all your adventures in Spain?"

"Every one." Richard turned to Viola with an uneasy grin. "Well, good-bye." He kissed her as he'd kissed Kathe, a friendly, kindly sort of kiss that all but broke her heart, and then, as if at a loss for what to do next, he made a motion as if to climb up into the train.

"Richard." She put her hand on his sleeve. Her gloves felt tight, and her shoes felt tight, and her voice was tight and small in the back of her throat, and if she'd been onstage they wouldn't have heard her beyond the orchestra pit.

"Yes, old girl?"

She wanted to say so much to him. She wanted to tell him that she really had loved him, maybe not as well as she might have, but sincerely and truly. She wanted him to know that parting from him was painful, that she would have done anything to have had things turn out differently, but she didn't know how to begin. "I'll miss you," she said lamely.

"I'll miss you, too, old girl."

Impulsively Viola threw her arms around him and kissed him. "Stay alive," she begged. She pulled at the lapels of his trench coat. "Please stay alive." The train heaved into motion.

"Good-bye." Richard ran for the steps, leapt up, and stood for a moment waving to them. The train clicked and rattled and spewed steam, and then it was gone and there was an empty space so big she felt as if she could get lost in it forever. There was a long silence.

"Mama," Kathe said at last, "are you all right?"

"I'm fine," Viola lied. She looked at the Victorian ironwork of the station, at the trains on the other platforms, at the woman in the stand selling hot tea and newspapers, and she opened her mouth to say something banal and reassuring to Kathe and found herself crying instead.

"Mama." Kathe put a worried hand on her shoulder.

"I have nothing left, nothing," Viola heard herself say. "Nothing."

Kathe put her arms around Viola for a moment and rocked her as if she were the mother and Viola the child. "You still have me, Mama," she said. She patted Viola's hat straight and dried her cheeks with the sleeve of her sailor suit. Then, leading her mother over to the stand, Kathe ordered them both cups of tea so strong and bitter that no amount of milk and sugar could sweeten it.

A month or so after Richard left for Spain, Viola received two letters in the mail. The first, which she tore open eagerly, was postmarked from southern France; dog-eared and soiled, it had obviously been passed from hand to hand before it was mailed, but there was no mistaking Richard's handwriting:

Dear Vi,

Things are in a bit of a muddle here and I can't seem to find my unit but otherwise I am well. I can't say where I'm being sent or what I'm doing, for obvious reasons, but perhaps the censors won't mind if I tell you that . . .

The censors obviously had minded because the rest of the letter had been neatly snipped off. Disappointed, Viola reread the four lines that had escaped the scissors and returned the scrap of paper to the envelope. At least she knew Richard was alive and that he'd reached Spain. That wasn't much, but it was something.

The second letter was a different matter. The envelope was heavy vellum, postmarked Berlin, and addressed to *Her Grace the Duchess of Sanford*. Inside were several sheets of paper embossed with the letterhead of the Theater Chamber of the Ministry of Propaganda, topped by a gold seal featuring two dramatic masks and a large swastika.

My Dear Duchess and dear old friend, the letter began. The handwriting looked vaguely familiar. She glanced down at the bottom of the page to the signature and realized, with a start, that the letter was from Friedrich Hoffman:

It has been all too long since we've seen each other, and yet I have followed the meteoric rise of your career, cheering you on silently from the sidelines from one thespian triumph to another. I know that this letter may come as a surprise to you, since when we last parted company there were some misunderstandings between us, but I hope time has healed them for you as it has for me and that you are left—as I am—with only the pleasant memories of a youth spent together creating the seeds of a new German culture.

I, too, have had my little successes in life. In fact, I am at present in charge of the Theater Chamber of the Ministry of Propaganda, thanks to the generous support of that incomparable genius Dr. Goebbels. As such, it is my pleasure to extend to you an invitation to participate in the fifth annual Reichs Theater Festival Week to be held . . .

Viola skimmed the rest of the letter, full of effusive compliments, references to her as one of the greatest German-speaking actresses of the century and mundane details about expenses, performances, and schedules. This was outrageous. Friedrich must be out of his mind. He had been responsible for both Joseph's death and the burning of the Neues Theater—not things she was likely to forgive no matter how many years went by. Although she hadn't been particularly politically outspoken in the past ten years, even Friedrich should remember her well enough to realize that she hated the Nazis with a passion.

She turned the letter over in her hands, wondering why Friedrich had bothered to send it. Actually, the more she thought about it the more it became obvious that this invitation to Reichs Theater Week was a thinly disguised attempt to use her reputation to give respectability to Hitler's regime, in which case she was certainly not going to dignify it with an answer. Tearing the invitation into shreds, she threw it into the wastebasket. Reichs Theater Week indeed! What kind of German theater festival could you have without Reinhardt and Brecht and Stern and Wulf? Hitler had ripped the heart out of the German theater, which was no doubt why he was reduced to employing flunkies like Friedrich to send out his invitations.

Viola sat at her desk, drumming her fingers angrily and thinking that she would never go back to Germany as long as the Nazis were in power.

It was about a week later when something happened to make her reconsider. She was walking back from the Arena after a matinee, enjoying the spectacle of London traffic, when she felt a light tap on her shoulder. Turning around, she confronted a rather remarkable sight: a woman swathed in a heavy black veil and a large black cape was beckoning to her with such dramatic furtive gestures that even the English—who on principle considered it impolite to notice the existence of anyone to whom they had not been properly introduced—were staring at her.

"Viola, darling," the mysterious woman whispered in German, "it's me, Hilde."

"Hilde?"

"Hilde Krauss. I just got in from Berlin, and I have to talk to you." Hilde turned her head from side to side as if surveying the street. "Somewhere where we won't be overheard."

Viola smiled. How like Hilde to show up unexpectedly after all these years, and how like her to dress herself up so that she was the most obvious thing on the street under the illusion that she was making herself invisible. She suddenly remembered what Hermann had told her about Hilde being Friedrich's mistress and her smile disappeared abruptly.

Hilde evidently saw the change in her face. "Please, darling," she pleaded, lifting the edge of her veil to expose the same heavily made-up eyes and lips that Viola remembered. Hilde winked in a friendly, conspiratorial way. "I know you've probably heard horrible things about me, but I can explain it all."

"Perhaps you'd better start explaining then."

"Please darling"—Hilde looked around nervously—"not here. It isn't safe to talk here."

"Where then?"

Hilde was suddenly practical. "A park bench would be best, one where we'd have a clear view of everyone within earshot."

Viola located them a park bench with the proper requirements. As they sat down she noticed Hilde's hair protruding from under the edge of her hat. To call it blond would have been a kindness. It was more of a bleached-out white, done up on either side of her head in two giant braids. "Hilde, it's something of a shock to see you."

"I know it is, darling." Hilde pushed back her veil and sat down, legs apart, hands on her knees. Her stockings, now exposed, were black net, and she looked, Viola thought, for all the world like Marlene Dietrich in *The Blue Angel,* sitting on a chair in a cabaret about to launch into an encore of "Falling in Love Again"—except, of course, for the fact that Hilde was still looking around like a woman who expected to be picked up by the police at any minute.

"Frankly, you're acting like a spy."

"I am something of a spy, darling." Hilde laughed nervously. "I suppose you heard I'd taken up with Friedrich."

"Yes," Viola said tersely. "I had."

"Well, believe me, darling, it wasn't because I found Friedrich attractive." Hilde made a face. "I have to admit that in my career I've gone out with some pretty unsavory types—mostly to pay the rent and all that—but our friend Friedrich was the most unsavory of the lot. I can't imagine what Jeanne ever saw in him. What that man likes in bed, darling"—Hilde sighed—"you can't imagine."

"No"—Viola was intrigued despite herself—"I don't suppose I could."

"He was useful."

"To whom?"

"I'd rather not say, darling. Just take my word for it." Hilde grinned wickedly. "He can't keep his mouth shut when he's in the middle of you-know-what; he has to brag about everything, and the man's crazy about me, which he should be naturally because . . . well, darling, perhaps we shouldn't go into that." Hilde looked around uneasily and Viola noticed for the first time that there were lines on her forehead and around her eyes that not even heavy pancake makeup could cover. It was a worried, troubled face that didn't go well with the net stockings and the cape. "The fact is, darling, that I've been sent to convince you to come back to Germany for Reichs Theater Week. I'm supposed to reassure you—as an old friend—that you'd be in absolutely no danger, that the Nazis would welcome you with open arms, that Friedrich is chomping at the bit to give you the keys to the city." Hilde tapped her painted nails nervously against the back of the park bench. "But what the Nazis don't know is that I have another message for you—one from your brother."

"From Conrad?" Viola was startled and more than a little concerned. What could have happened to Conrad that had reduced him to sending messages out of Germany via Hilde?

Hilde nodded. "Your brother told me to tell you to come to Munich. He apparently has something important to say to you that can only be said in person."

"Are you telling me Conrad is in trouble?"

"Vi, I'm taking a terrible chance doing this. I'm putting myself in danger, darling, and I'm terrified, so please don't ask too many questions. All I can tell you is that you now have a perfect chance to travel to Germany without arousing any suspicion, and that you should take it."

"Hilde, all this sounds dangerous and ridiculous. How do I know I can trust you?"

"You don't," Hilde said simply. "But I'm going to tell you something that should convince you I'm serious." She took a deep breath. "My grandfather was half Jewish."

"What?"

"Half Jewish, darling. The Nazis don't know it because the father listed on my birth certificate isn't my real father." Hilde tugged at the edge of her veil and looked over her shoulder. "You understand what that means of course?" She lowered her voice to a whisper. "Under the new anti-Jewish laws, my affair with Friedrich is a racial crime. Legally, I'm not even a citizen; I can't work; I can't own property; I can't even go shopping for food except during special hours. If the Nazis knew this, if they even had a *suspicion* of it, they'd deport me— that is if I was lucky. More likely I'd end up in one of those ghastly prison camps they're building all over the place."

Viola was horrified. "My God, Hilde, if you're part Jewish, why don't you get out of that insane country? All sorts of German Jews are coming to London these days. Do you need a sponsor? Money? A place to live? I have a huge house in Belgravia that you're welcome to share."

Hilde shook her head. "No thanks, darling. It's sweet of you to offer, but I'm doing something important in Germany, and I can't make a run for it just yet." She drew her veil back over her face, stood up, and looked around nervously. "I'm frightened out of my mind, but for the first time in my life I'm part of something I can be proud of." She leaned over and kissed Viola on the cheek. "Good-bye. I can't risk talking to you any longer. Go to Germany like your brother is asking you to. If you don't, you're going to spend the rest of your life regretting it."

When Friedrich met Hilde at Tempelhof Airport the next day, he thrust a large bouquet of roses in her arms. His face was pale, he had dark circles under his eyes, and his lower lip twitched slightly. It was a nervous, worn face, a face, Hilde decided, that looked distinctly hung over.

"Did Vi agree to come to Reichs Theater Week?" he asked eagerly.

"It looks good," Hilde told him. She clutched the roses, surprised to see that there were at least two dozen of them. Friedrich had never given her flowers before. Not so much as a tulip.

"Wonderful," Friedrich said. "Good job. Goebbels will be pleased." He took her arm and propelled her toward the terminal. "Come along; I have a surprise for you." He seemed elated and tense and he walked in long, rapid strides. She ran along, trying to keep up with him, wondering what had put him in such a frantic mood. Sometimes he used cocaine. Perhaps another shipment had come while she was in London.

They drove through the streets of Berlin, plunging across traffic, swerving to miss trucks, taking corners at twice the legal speed until at last they came to a beautiful red-brick house set in a small park of chestnut, linden, and oak trees. Hitting the breaks, Friedrich slid to a halt.

"Like it?" he asked, gesturing at the house.

"Yes." Hilde looked at the house, wondering why they'd stopped. "It's lovely, darling."

"It's yours."

"Mine?" She was so surprised, she didn't know what to say. "But how, that is . . . ?"

"Quite simple really." Friedrich waved at the house. "It used to belong to Johannes Wulf, the theater critic, but since Wulf's fled Germany it's fallen forfeit to the Reich. And—through channels I'm not at liberty to describe—I've bought it for you." He sprang out of the car and held the door for her. "Come in and have a look at your new place."

Dazed, Hilde got out of the car and followed Friedrich up the brick path. Inside, Persian rugs carpeted the floor; there were brass candlesticks and crystal decanters on the walnut table in the hall; a huge fireplace; a bedroom big enough to sleep an army.

"Not bad, eh?"

She tried to smile, but the thought that all this had been stolen from Johannes Wulf made her slightly ill. "It's lovely, darling," she lied. "Perfectly divine."

"Come down and see the wine cellar," Friedrich said. He threw open the basement door, and she followed him down the narrow stairs. A single light bulb was burning in a room built of cement and fieldstone. Hilde was surprised to see that there was no wine in sight: only two men sitting at a cheap wooden table. One of the men wore a dark suit; the other had a badly pockmarked face. Between the two men was a strange device: black and square, it sprouted wires and clips.

"I've brought you a visitor, Franz," Friedrich said to the man with the pockmarked face. The man stood up and walked over to Hilde.

"Hello," she said, reaching out to shake his hand.

Taking two quick steps, the man grabbed her and twisted her arms behind her back. Hilde screamed with surprise. The man was hurting her, bending her arms until she felt as if he might break them.

"You bitch," Friedrich yelled. "You rotten little bitch."

"I don't understand," she cried.

"Be quiet! I know all about what you've been doing, you slut."

"Please make him stop hurting me."

Friedrich slapped her across the face. "I said, be quiet." Stunned, Hilde closed her mouth and stopped crying. She stared at Friedrich, terrified. He put his face so close to hers that she could smell the cloves on his breath. "You've been reading my appointment book, haven't you?"

"No, Friedrich, please . . ."

"Don't lie. I saw you. You've been reading my book and warning people when we were coming for them. You warned Eric Stern, didn't you?"

"No." Hilde was trembling so badly she could hardly stand upright. Behind her the man with the pockmarked face put more pressure on her wrists. A sharp pain shot up her arms, making her moan.

"Do you realize what you've done to me, you little bitch? If the

Gestapo got hold of you and made you talk, I'd be ruined." His face swelled with anger, and she flinched, sure he was going to hit her again, but he didn't. Instead he turned away and stormed to the other side of the room. "Fortunately, I have other alternatives." He wheeled around. "So, Hilde, my dear, what we're going to do this afternoon is find out exactly who you've been contacting. You can make it easy on yourself and tell me, or you can be stubborn, in which case Franz and Oskar will persuade you." He motioned to the man in the dark suit. "Oskar."

Picking up one of the wires that protruded from the device on the table, Oskar walked across the room in a leisurely fashion, grabbed Hilde by the chin, opened her mouth, and stuck the end of the wire against her tongue. A jolt of electricity ran through her body, so painful it was like scalding water. She screamed and struggled. "Stop," she begged, "stop, please!" She began to cry uncontrollably as her head twitched back and forth.

"That's enough, Oskar."

The man in the dark suit removed the wire from Hilde's mouth, went back to the table, and sat down. Friedrich walked up and looked at her with contempt. "You're a beautiful little slut," he said, "but if you don't tell us who you've been contacting, you won't ever want to see yourself in a mirror again. Do you want to make it easy on yourself and tell me right now?"

"No," Hilde sobbed.

"You're a stupid bitch," Friedrich snarled. He motioned to Franz. "Throw her in the next room for an hour or so and let her think it over."

For a few minutes Hilde lay on the floor where Franz had thrown her, sobbing with terror, unable to move. Her tongue was burned and swollen, and she felt sick to her stomach. At last she got unsteadily to her feet and looked around. She was in a dirt cellar with exposed beams and rows of crooked wooden shelves. Except for piles of old newspapers, a frayed clothesline, and a rusty bicycle, it was empty.

Limping over to the bicycle, Hilde looked at it blankly, as if it might somehow help her escape. She stared at it for a long time, her mind frozen in terror. The tires had rotted through to the rims and there were cobwebs on the handlebars.

What was she going to do? She had to get out of here. They were coming back for her. She turned away from the bicycle and circled the room, sobbing with fear, searching for a way out, but there were no windows, no doors except the one that led to the next room. She was trapped.

She became frantic at the thought. She had to escape. She would never survive more questioning. She wasn't a brave woman. She was terrified of pain, and if those men out there touched her one more time with that wire, she would tell them anything they wanted to know. And she knew so much: she knew about the network that was smuggling marked people out of Germany; she knew the names of the printers who forged the documents; she knew the addresses of some of the houses where the refugees were hidden.

For some indeterminate period of time she sat with her back against the wall, staring in horror at the door, waiting for Franz to reappear and drag her off for more torture. The clothesline hung above her, limp and moldy, a few wooden pins clinging crookedly to the far end. More and more often her eyes came back to it.

She could hang herself.

The thought made her shudder. She didn't want to die. She wanted to be outside in the sunshine. She loved being alive.

But if she was dead, they couldn't hurt her.

She pushed the thought out of her mind, terrified by it, but it came back.

She'd be safe.

No she wouldn't, she'd go to hell. She was a Catholic; suicide was a mortal sin. And she didn't want to die.

She closed her eyes, but all she could see was Oskar sticking the electrical wire against the end of her tongue. Gasping for breath, she opened her eyes again. That was just the beginning. They would have other surprises waiting for her, things too terrible to think about. They would mutilate her, torture her for hours, perhaps rape her, and in the end she would talk, she would betray her friends.

Nearby, a broken fruit jar lay on its side, full of dirt and spider webs. Impulsively, Hilde picked it up. Hanging was horrible. She couldn't bring herself to do it, but a crazy girl at Leda and the Swan had once told her that slitting your wrists hardly hurt at all.

Death was safe; death was the only way out. Shivering with fear,

Hilde took a deep breath, closed her eyes, and before she had time to change her mind she drew the jagged edge of glass across her left wrist. It hurt badly, more than she'd expected, and she had to bite her lower lip to keep from crying out. Blood ran down her arm and onto the floor.

Dropping the broken jar, Hilde leaned back against the wall, feeling faint. She didn't have the courage to slash her other wrist, but it didn't matter. She had cut deeply and well.

By the time Franz and Oskar came back to get her, Hilde Krauss was dead.

16

BERLIN

1938

Viola hated everything about Nazi Germany from the moment she stepped off the plane. The sky was an ambivalent blue, studded with small curdled clouds and bordered with Nazi flags, hundreds of them, flying from every niche of the terminal, draped from the control tower, snapping in the wind along both sides of the runway. As soon as the crowd caught sight of her trumpets blared and a red carpet snaked out of the gate, rolled in her direction by a team of blond men in brown shirts. She stopped halfway down the steps and stared at the spectacle in disbelief.

"Willkommen!" the rug rollers chanted in unison, snapping to attention and raising their arms in the Nazi salute.

"Welcome, great German actress!" a chorus of uniformed schoolchildren echoed obediently. As Viola took a reluctant step onto the red carpet, four earnest-looking young women hurried forward and began to scatter roses and violets in her path.

This was ridiculous. She looked at the flower tossers, dressed in clumsy pseudo-Bronze Age costumes, and she had to bite her tongue to keep from breaking into uncontrollable giggles—not that it was funny; it was horrible, grotesque. She'd heard about these Nazi spectacles from friends, but you had to see them to get a feeling for the banality of evil that lurked under the surface: the children in military uniforms, the insane precision of the way men moved in unison like some kind of demonic glockenspiel. If you put this act on the stage in any sane country, the audience would hiss it into oblivion.

She walked contemptuously down the carpet, trying to dodge the roses. At the other end a short man in a plain brown suit was eagerly rocking back and forth on his heels. She took three more steps and there was a sudden, unnerving silence as every person in the airport—with the exception of herself—snapped to attention and raised their right arms.

Actually, on closer inspection, it was obvious that the man in the brown suit wasn't raising his right arm either, for the very good reason that he didn't have one. Viola realized with a shock that he must be Friedrich, but how could he be? The man suddenly broke into a smile and hurried toward her. The nose, she thought, the eyes are right but there's something wrong with the nose; it's not Friedrich's; it's too little and snub and my God I think he's had it operated on and . . .

"Viola, my dear friend," said Friedrich—for there was no doubt once he spoke that it was indeed Friedrich. He embraced her effusively. "Welcome to Germany, welcome to Reichs Theater Week, welcome to the most wonderful experiment in human history." Flashbulbs popped around them, blinding Viola.

"Hello, Friedrich." Under the new layer of fat, Viola could feel his old body, sticklike and rigid, the inflexibility of his backbone, the familiar scent of cloves on his breath. She remembered Joseph, and it was all she could do to permit Friedrich to touch her. This was going to be a rotten week, she realized, even more rotten than she had imagined. She tried to recall something good about Friedrich that might make his presence more bearable, but all she could come up with were the sets he had painted for *Berliner Ballade:* the tilted doors, the bleeding Christs, the disembodied heads. I have to be civil, she told herself, not warm but at least decent because Friedrich is in charge here and no matter how much I might dislike him, if I don't remember that I could get myself—and maybe Conrad and Angela— into some real trouble. Friedrich always did take offense quicker than anyone on earth, and these Nazis don't fool around. Resisting the urge to flinch, Viola returned Friedrich's embrace and somehow managed to smile. That smile was the first of many bitter compromises she made with herself that week.

Friedrich stepped back and surveyed her with a cheerful, precise smile of his own, obviously satisfied. Then he turned to three women who were beaming nervously at Viola. Dressed in an expensive, understated way, they wore fashionable suits with padded shoulders, tasteful hats, and tailored blouses that would have made them equally at home in London or Paris. Well, what had she expected? Monsters decked out in jewels confiscated from the Jews?

"My dear Viola," Friedrich was saying, "this is such an honor for us all. Permit me to present several of the brightest lights of the contemporary German stage—Fräulein Gottlieb, Fräulein Leonhardt, and Frau Vahlen."

Viola shook the hands of the actresses, thinking that it was interesting that she had never heard of any of them. Were they Nazis, too, or were they just third-rate actresses, chosen because they looked Aryan? Back in London the rumor was that the way you became a leading lady of the Berlin stage these days was to bleach your hair and invite an important Nazi into your bed.

"So pleased to meet you, Duchess."

"So happy to have you here."

More flashbulbs popped, so many that Viola began to wonder if she was going to spend the rest of her trip half blinded.

"Such a pleasure, Duchess." Fräulein Gottlieb pumped Viola's hand excitedly. "I've admired you for ever so long." She was a heavyset, blunt-jawed woman with tiny blue eyes and white-blond hair done up in a coronet of braids. "My little sister is also quite a fan of yours. She has your picture pasted up on her mirror and she made me absolutely promise to get your autograph."

"You must be tired," Friedrich interposed smoothly, taking Viola's arm. He led her into the terminal and out the front door to the curb to a shiny black Mercedes decorated with more flags. Viola realized with horror that she was about to enter Berlin behind an escort of police on motorcycles.

"Friedrich . . ." she protested, but it was too late; the sirens had already started up and the cavalcade was getting under way. Giving up, Viola climbed into the car and sat wedged in between Frau Vahlen and Friedrich, wondering if she looked as foolish and embarrassed as she felt. She was overtaken by a sense of powerlessness. I've put myself into Friedrich's hands, she thought; that's a mistake, but how big a mistake?

The drive seemed to take forever, through crowds who appeared so curiously indifferent to the screaming of the sirens that Viola got the impression they were accustomed to the sight of convoys of black cars being rushed through the streets. From what she could see through the window over Frau Vahlen's shoulder, Berlin looked good, even prosperous. The streets were cleaner, the prostitutes were no longer plying their trade on the corners of the Kurfürstendamm, the beggars she remembered so vividly were nowhere in sight, and in place of the unemployed men and women who had once occupied every park bench, there were crowds of brisk, well-fed-looking Germans going about their business.

Still, for all the outer prosperity of this city, there was definitely something ugly in the air. When she left Berlin, it had been a brilliant, dangerous place full of extreme contrasts, more alive than any other city in Europe. Today as she rode through the familiar streets, past the vacant lot where the Neues Theater had once stood, past the empty building that had contained the Cafe Schiller, everything felt clean and lifeless, as if the Nazis had turned the whole town into a perverse sort of museum. Viola thought of the stories she had heard in London of the Jews of Berlin, driven from their homes, living like wild animals in the Grünewald, and a shudder ran through her. The feeling of being trapped pressed down on her more every block, and she wished with all her heart that she had never agreed to come. But then she thought of Conrad and was filled with determination again.

Friedrich cleared his throat. "You're no doubt noticing how things have changed," he said.

"Yes, I was actually." Viola tried to keep the sarcasm out of her voice, but it wasn't easy.

"We've made such marvelous advances," Friedrich observed complacently. He opened a silver case embossed with a swastika and offered everyone cigarettes, Italian with gold bands around the tops. "Six million were unemployed in 1933, and now every honest German man who wants to work is snapped up in a minute. The factories are going full blast night and day." He's gotten pompous, Viola thought; he speaks like a man who's reading a prepared speech. She wondered if this was Friedrich's usual tone of voice or if he'd adopted it for her benefit. She tried to remember how he'd spoken in the past, but all she could remember was his diatribe the day he'd torn apart the sets for *Berliner Ballade*. "And of course," Friedrich continued affably, "you also must have noticed the extraordinary number of young children. The birth rate is at an all-time high, a fact which reflects the optimism of the German people." Friedrich smiled and leaned so close to Viola that the scent of cloves was almost overwhelming. "Frau Vahlen here is the mother of five herself. In fact, the Führer is thinking of creating a Medal of Honor for especially prolific mothers."

Frau Vahlen flushed with pleasure. She was a delicate woman, with gray-green eyes and a small, pointed chin that gave her a shrewd look. She sighed, fluffed her short red hair with the palm of her hand, and leaned confidentially toward Viola. "I understand you, too, have children, Duchess."

"Yes, a daughter, fourteen."

"Just the age of my oldest." Frau Vahlen smiled in a phony way that put Viola's teeth on edge. "It isn't easy combining a career in the theater with motherhood, is it?"

"No," Viola admitted stiffly, "it isn't."

The conversation moved on to safer grounds: the upcoming events of Reichs Theater Week, the technical difficulties of staging such a large number of productions, the excellent weather that Berlin was enjoying this spring. After about ten more minutes of driving, the Mercedes came to a halt at the gate of one of the most beautiful houses Viola had ever seen: two stories of brick, mellowed to a soft red by age; rows of curved windows, a sweep of perfectly tended lawn, and a small park of magnificent trees—linden, chestnut, and giant oak—their boughs tangled into a leafy arch over the walk.

"Your home away from home," Friedrich quipped, jumping out of the car and holding the door for her. "A poor thing now that you have Sanford Palace at your beck and call, but the best we can do I'm afraid and"—he smiled archly—"you must admit that it's a step or two up from your old room at Bluebeard's."

Viola looked at the house, at the trees and the lawn and the red bricks, and wondered privately who the Nazis had seized it from and what the price tag was going to be for staying in it, but the price—if there was one—was well concealed. Friedrich conducted her inside, where everything was even more beautiful than it had been outside: the light from the leaded windows cast diamonds on the hardwood floors, there were deep blue Persian throw rugs scattered in just the right places, vast bunches of flowers in crystal vases, an antique fireplace big enough to burn an entire tree in.

"Make yourself at home"—Friedrich waved at the opulence with studied casualness—"and tomorrow morning, after you've had a chance to rest, I'll drop by and take you over to the new theater."

"The new theater?"

"Oh how lovely," Fräulein Leonhardt exclaimed, "she doesn't know. Oh how lovely of you to surprise her with it."

"Herr Doktor Goebbels has had an entirely new theater built for Reichs Theater Week," Friedrich announced proudly. "It's monumental, constructed on the Roman style, and it seats ten thousand."

"Marble, basalt—rest rooms everywhere." Fräulein Gottlieb clapped her hands together excitedly. "So much better than those crowded, dirty playhouses."

"It sounds like a football stadium." Viola realized she was being tactless, but she couldn't stop herself.

"Oh it is," Fräulein Gottlieb said, obliviously, "just like a great, wonderful stadium. I can't tell you how rewarding it is to act in a place that gives proper *scope* to one's emotions."

"But how does anyone hear in a place like that?"

"Loudspeakers," Fräulein Gottlieb supplied cheerfully.

Viola realized to her dismay that she was evidently scheduled to perform a scene from *Laura* in a football stadium. "Whatever happened to Stern's theater?" she asked. "Is there any chance I could perform there instead?"

"Oh you mean the Kallmann Theater," Friedrich said with a quick laugh. "Oh it's still there, of course, but it wouldn't be large enough for the crowds we're expecting." He cleared his throat uneasily. "It isn't Stern's anymore, you know. Stern is—"

"Gone," Frau Vahlen interrupted briskly, "so of course there was no question of him continuing to run the place."

"Of course not," Fräulein Gottlieb agreed. "I believe he left Germany in '33."

"This house—" Fräulein Leonhardt began.

"I think the Duchess would like some time to herself," Friedrich interrupted, putting a restraining hand on Fräulein Leonhardt's shoulder. Fräulein Leonhardt closed her mouth so quickly that Viola got the distinct impression that whatever she had been going to say about the house was not very likely to be repeated on a subsequent occasion.

Reichs Theater Week proved to be an elaborate, depressing experience. Viola had hoped to see Hilde while she was in Berlin, but Hilde was apparently off shooting a film in Austria. Few foreigners had accepted the invitation to the festival, which meant that the majority of the pieces were performed by the new crop of German actors represented by Fräulein Leonhardt, Fräulein Gottlieb, and Frau Vahlen—most of whom, Viola decided privately, couldn't have gotten a role in a high school play under ordinary circumstances. The sets were ponderous, the newly constructed theater a nightmare of echoes, and although she received a standing ovation and over twenty minutes of enthusiastic applause after her performance of *Laura*, she was never convinced that anyone in the audience had actually been able to hear her.

The most disturbing part of the festival were the plays themselves. In the twenties Berlin had been the theatrical center of the world; now, as far as she could tell, the German theater was a national disgrace. Ever since last year, when Goebbels had banned art criticism and replaced it with something called "art observation," the censors had evidently been having a field day. There was a prohibition list that went on for pages and pages: to perform a play by Brecht or Ibsen was unthinkable. Shakespeare had been sanitized to the point where the only one of his works regularly presented was *As You Like It*. In a fit of delirious insanity Charlemagne had been banned from the stage as a "race-alien" (as Fräulein Gottlieb pointed out, he was, after all, a Saxon); Cromwell, who was rumored to be one of Hitler's favorite historical figures, was the subject of no less than five of the plays presented, and Viola got so tired of watching the various actors impersonating him rant against Charles I that it was all she could do to keep from falling asleep in her seat.

Compared to the propaganda plays, however, Cromwell was a delight. For hours at a time during that interminable week, the stage was taken up by choruses of blond German males marching about spouting patriotic homilies in blank verse. But one of the worst moments of all came on Friday when Frau Vahlen took her on a tour of the Kallmann Theater.

It was a beautiful spring morning, and the birds of Berlin were singing under a sky so blue and deep that it looked like a chip of polished turquoise. The theater was resplendent, the stone facade sandblasted to a glittering white, the doors freshly gilded, the ticket kiosk repainted to resemble a fantasy out of the Arabian nights. The only sign of Nazi influence was the red flag that fluttered gaily in the wind over the main entrance. Frau Vahlen conducted Viola to the office of the new manager of the Kallmann, a bland-looking man whom she introduced as Herr Speemann.

"Such a pleasure to finally meet you, Duchess." Herr Speemann shook Viola's hand. "I'm sure you don't remember me, but we were once actually on the stage at the same time."

"We were?"

"In Stern's wonderful production of *Faust*. You played Margarete, and I was only a humble extra." He handed her a rectangle of tastefully printed poster paper, topped by two dramatic masks and the ever-present swastika. "I thought you might enjoy looking at the playbill for our fall season."

Viola read the playbill and saw that the entire output for the Kallmann for the fall of 1938 consisted of farces, operettas, plays by third-rate Party playwrights, and puppet shows. She thought of Eric Stern's brilliance, of the artistic integrity of his work, the uncompromising courage and honesty with which he had produced even the least important of his plays, and she felt sick at what had been done to his theater. For that matter the whole of Germany was giving her a sick feeling in the pit of her stomach, and if it hadn't been for Conrad and Angela, she would have left that very afternoon.

Munich was a relief after Berlin, not that the Nazi presence there was any less. The Nazis, as Viola remembered all too well, had gotten their start in the beer halls of Munich, but she had never actually lived there so the memories were less painful. Then, too, there was something lighthearted about the city that seemed to persist even under the grimmest conditions. Maybe it was in the sound of the Bavarian accent or the shoulder-clapping *gemütlichkeit* good cheer of the people, but whatever it was, Viola sensed it as soon as she stepped off the train, and it made her feel almost normal again.

Conrad and Angela were waiting for her on the platform, holding bunches of lilacs. Viola saw them before they saw her, and she experienced such an intense pang of happiness at the familiar sight of the two of them that she felt like yelling at the top of her lungs or turning a handspring. Pulling a handkerchief from her purse, she waved it up and down.

"Con, hey, Con, over here!"

"Sis!" Conrad caught sight of Viola and his face broke into a huge welcoming smile. Running toward her, he enveloped her in a bear hug, lifted her off her feet, and whirled her around, to the amusement of the other passengers who were disembarking from the train. She clung to him, unable to speak. Seeing Conrad made her realize how desperately lonely she'd been these past months since Richard left for Spain. I might not have a husband these days, she thought as she embraced Conrad, but at least I still have a brother, and as long as I have a brother I have a family, and thank God for that because Kathe is wonderful but she isn't enough and I need Conrad and I love him and I've been a fool to wait so long to see him again.

Depositing her back on the platform, Conrad held Viola at arm's length and inspected her. He had become thinner instead of fatter, something she never would have predicted. Nearly forty now, he had taken to wearing gold-rimmed glasses, which gave his gray-blue eyes a meditative expression. There was something weary about his face that worried her.

"You look wonderful," Conrad said. He smiled and kissed her on the forehead. "Not a year older." He kissed her again and she had a sense of being wrapped in the warm blanket of his love and concern. Conrad turned to Angela. "I think my little sister's found the fountain of youth."

"It comes from not living in Nazi Germany," Angela retorted, briskly piling the lilacs into Viola's arms. She, too, had changed: her hair had gone almost completely gray and—well, it was hard to pinpoint, but if someone had asked her, Viola would have said that Angela seemed restless, as if she were expecting something unpleasant to happen at any minute.

Conrad's smile faded and he looked around with the same hunted expression Viola had seen on Hilde's face. Two boys dressed in the uniforms of the Hitler Youth were running past, yelling and laughing, bare knees pumping, black ties flapping in the wind. A rather bored-looking Nazi officer, SS death heads prominently displayed on his shoulders, waited beside the ticket office under a huge poster that featured a worker and an engineer clasping hands. "Don't say that so loud, Angela, *Liebling*," Conrad pleaded.

Angela pushed her sensible brown hat down on her head and grimaced. "Sorry," she apologized tersely.

Conrad and Angela's house was unusual to say the least. Built on a lot next to the Kessler brewery, it was a sweeping experimental construction of glass and concrete that looked, Viola privately thought, like a large airplane waiting on the runway for clearance to take off. Since the brewery had been designed to resemble a medieval castle, the two buildings faced each other like combatants across a narrow strip of green grass and Angela's neatly tended flower and vegetable gardens.

It was after dinner and they were sitting in three comfortable overstuffed chairs looking out the front window at the brewery, the turrets of which were turning a light pink in the sunset, a sight that made Viola feel a bit as if she were living in the middle of a German fairy tale. She looked over at Conrad, drinking him in, feeling completely content. She would come back to Germany more often, she promised herself, Nazis or no Nazis; she would sit in this same chair, making small talk with Conrad and Angela, feel the peace and the comfort of their presence. She wondered for a moment what would have happened if Mama and Papa hadn't died so young.

Perhaps they would have all been together now in this very room. The thought was sweetly painful, and she felt nostalgia for everything that was good, and kind, and commonplace.

"Business is booming," Conrad observed, extracting a mechanical pencil from his vest pocket and toying with it thoughtfully. She said something about how nice it was that the brewery was doing so well and there was a long, gentle silence, punctuated by the ticking of the clock on the mantel. After a while there was a light knock on the door and a maid entered bearing coffee and cakes on a silver tray. Angela poured the coffee and passed out the cakes on little china plates decorated with strawberries. For a moment they were all absorbed in the dessert.

"Vi." Conrad put down his coffee cup and folded his fingers into a nervous lattice. "I wish this could just be an ordinary visit." Here it comes at last, she thought, whatever it is that's so important that Con could tell me only in person, and I hope to heaven that whatever it is I'll be up to it, because from what I've seen of Germany it could be almost anything, and if Conrad is in any danger, I'm not going to take it well no matter how hard I pretend.

Conrad cleared his throat. "I've missed you a lot over the past years," he said. "I don't know if you could tell that from my letters. I'm not very good at expressing my feelings in writing, and then there were obvious reasons why I couldn't say straight out what was going on. I always understood, of course, why you didn't want to visit Germany, and I don't blame you for it." He picked thoughtfully at a crumb of cake. "Things get worse here every day and frankly—as much as I've wanted to see you—I wouldn't have sent that message through Hilde if there'd been any other way, but there wasn't." He paused awkwardly. "The problem is that now that you're actually here, I keep thinking that I should forget the whole thing. I keep thinking"—Conrad leaned forward earnestly—"that Viola's the only sister I have. Why should I involve her in this? Last night I lay awake all night trying to think of another way, but we've already tried other ways."

"And they haven't worked," Angela interjected. "Three times we sent the information out of Germany secretly and all three times it just disappeared, like it had been swallowed up. Not a line in the foreign press, not a word on the radio."

"What information?" Viola had the feeling that she had gotten lost in the conversation. Conrad looked at Angela and Angela put down her knitting and looked at Viola unhappily. "You've heard of the prison camps?" she asked in a tight voice.

Viola nodded. "Just about everyone's heard of them by now. They were built when Hitler came to power in '33 as I remember—a dumping place for leftists, dissidents, and the like, or so the British papers claim—all except the Fascist papers, which say that the camps put people in 'protective custody,' but of course no one believes that."

"Were you aware," Angela said quietly, "that my father was one of the architects who designed Dachau?"

"Oh my God." Viola didn't know what else to say.

Angela stood up and walked briskly across the room to the bookcase. "I have a copy of the blueprints." She took out a folder, opened it, and spread it on the table in front of Viola. Viola looked at the blueprints, not understanding them. There seemed to be a lot of long, low buildings surrounded by a fence. Angela shut the folder brusquely. "We calculate that at present there are about thirty thousand people in camps spread out all over Germany. Most don't get out once they get in—except for the ones with money. The SS sells the rich ones back to their relatives for a stiff ransom—if they're not Jewish."

"As you can probably imagine, conditions are hard." Conrad pushed a cake crumb around on his plate and stared at it as if trying to make it disappear. "Some of the people who are sent to the camps are old and a lot of them die of natural causes."

Angela jammed the folder of blueprints back into the bottom shelf of the bookcase. "And some of them die of unnatural causes." There was something in her voice that sent a chill up Viola's spine.

"What do you mean 'unnatural causes'?"

"They're murdered," Angela said bluntly.

"You mean executed?"

"No, murdered. By the SS, sadistically, for no reason. Some-times"—Angela hesitated—"they're tortured first."

"How do you know that?" The room suddenly seemed cold, and when Viola stared out the window the brewery no longer looked endearing; it seemed ominous and shadowed, like a fortress.

"You forget about Papa." Angela smiled bitterly. "I have special connections, you see. I go over to Papa's house and I hear the commander of Dachau and his friends bragging to each other when they've had a little too much to drink, and then there are other ways Conrad and I have of getting such information, ways internal to the camps themselves that we can't talk about, not even to you."

"The anti-Nazi resistance in Germany is small, Vi"—Conrad put both hands on the table and leaned forward, his eyes bright with enthusiasm—"but it's growing. There's a student group in Munich, for example, that calls itself—"

"I don't think we should name names," Angela interrupted. "The less she knows, the less trouble we get her into."

"That's true." Conrad sat back. "Forget what you just heard, Vi. You don't need to understand how this works, but there is something we do need you to do, that is if you're willing." Viola opened her mouth to answer, but Conrad stopped her before she could speak. "Take your time; think it over; it could be dangerous."

Viola thought it over. She tried to imagine what it must be like to be penned up in one of those camps at the mercy of the SS: it must be like hell, she thought, no it must be something beyond hell. "Con," she said after a long silence, "you know better than anyone that politically speaking my life has been like a roller coaster. I've taken stands and not taken stands; I've spoken out and I've run scared. For years I've been wrapped up in my career—no, why not tell the truth?—I've been *hiding* in my career. I'm somewhat ashamed to admit it, but when the Nazis tried to terrorize me, they succeeded. Joseph's death and the burning of the Neues frightened me away from anything to do with making public statements, but that was nearly ten years ago. Times are changing, and lately I've been having the feeling I'm ready to change with them. Richard is off in Spain fighting the Fascists; you're here in Germany resisting the Nazis. I can't see myself sticking my head in the sand much longer. I hate what I've seen here. It's loathsome and violent under a sugar coating, and I don't see how anyone with any shred of decency could remain silent about it." She paused. "I suppose what I'm trying to say is that you've picked the right time to ask me whatever it is you're going to ask me. So tell me what you want me to do."

Angela stood up, face flushed, eyes shining. "Good," she said. "I told Conrad you'd say something like that." Walking back to the bookcase, she seized a large atlas by the spine and shook it briskly. A small square of white paper fluttered to the floor. Bending down, she retrieved the paper and carried it over to where Viola was sitting. "This is what we have for you. It's a list of the names of forty people who have died in the camps of 'natural causes.' "

The handwriting on the list was so small, Viola had to strain to make out the notation beside each name. What she read shocked her so much that she had to read the list again to convince herself that she hadn't made a mistake.

"This is incredible." She looked up at Conrad and Angela, appalled. "I can hardly believe it. Why"—she pointed to one of the names—"this man is one of the most distinguished scholars in Germany. I read in *The Times* that he'd died of a heart attack, but here it says that he was strangled to death."

Angela nodded. "Emil Hagen, a professor who took issue with the Nazi ideas of racial purity. Cause of death listed on his certificate— heart failure. Real cause of death, as you said, strangulation." Angela pointed to other names. "Walter Kerr, a journalist who wrote an article critical of the Strength Through Joy Movement. Cause of death listed on his certificate—pneumonia. Actual cause of death, concussion sustained while being tortured. Anna Osten, a gymnasium teacher who objected to the burning of books—raped and beaten to death. Sister Lise Baur, a nun who refused to turn over the feeble-minded patients in her care to 'special facilities'—beaten and then shot."

"This is fantastic." Viola felt her stomach turn over as she read the list.

"That's just the problem," Conrad agreed. "It *is* fantastic, so fantastic that no one in the civilized world—by which I mean the world outside of Germany—can believe it. Innocent people tortured and killed for no reason. What journalist is going to be willing to stake his reputation on such a story? Three times we sent this list to the foreign press and each time they looked at it and said to themselves, 'This is a fable made up by the German Communists or whatever to discredit the Nazis.' That's why we need your help."

"We want you to take this list back to England, Vi." Angela's voice was level but dark eyes were pleading. "And we want you to take it back in your head, memorized, so the Gestapo won't find it in your luggage. You have an international reputation. You're a famous actress. Not only that, you're the Duchess of Sanford. If you say this kind of thing is happening in the camps, maybe someone will finally believe it."

Viola took the list from Angela's hand and read it for a third time, thinking of the danger taking such information out of Germany might involve. *Beaten . . . shot . . . strangled:* despite what she had just said about being ready to take a political stand, the words were frightening. She tried to measure her own courage. Just how afraid was she? Very, she decided, but the more she thought about it, the more she realized that she couldn't know about something like this and not do whatever she could to expose it.

"I'll do it," she told them. "I'll recite this thing from the rooftops of London if necessary, and I promise you that this time someone will listen." She would waste no more time thinking about the consequences. Conrad and Angela were perhaps the two most decent people she had ever known; if they were willing to risk their lives, then she was too. "As for memorizing the list, that shouldn't be a problem. I've always been a quick study."

"Good." Angela nodded, obviously relieved. "Excellent."

Now that she'd made the decision to help, Viola felt calm. Then a new fear suddenly took hold of her. "But what about you two? Surely you aren't going to stay in Munich. I mean"—Viola contemplated the list uneasily—"giving me this kind of information must put you in terrible danger."

"It does," Angela said quietly, "but we can't leave."

"But it would be so easy." Viola turned to Conrad. He and Angela couldn't stay in Germany, it was unthinkable. A dark sense of foreboding came over her. "You're my relatives," she pleaded, "and I occupy a privileged position with the Nazis at the moment. It's disgusting, I loathe it, but that's the price I had to pay to see you. If you put in for permission to visit me in London, I'm sure I could get Friedrich Hoffman to have your visas approved. You could leave with no questions asked, you could—"

Conrad put his hand on her shoulder, stopping her in mid-sentence. "It's no good, Vi," he said soberly. "I'm sorry. I know you're worried about us. I expected you would be, but try to see it our way. If people like Angela and me leave Germany, who's going to be left to resist?"

"There is one thing you could do for us," Angela said.

"Anything." Viola was so upset at the thought of abandoning the two of them in Munich that it was all she could do to keep from demanding that they leave with her on the next train. She put her hand on Conrad's arm. I love him, she thought, and I love Angela, too, and the Gestapo will kill them if I let them stay behind, and I can't lose them both, not now, not just after I found them again.

"Give us your passport," Angela said quietly.

"My passport?"

Angela nodded. "You can report it lost when you get back to Berlin and the embassy will issue you a new one."

Viola got up, walked over to the table, picked up her purse, opened it, and extracted her passport. "I'm not going to ask you why you want this, Angela," she said, handing the passport to her, "but please be careful." Her hand trembled and her voice broke. "I love you both so much, if anything were to happen to you . . ."

"Nothing's going to happen to us," Angela said firmly, putting the passport in the pocket of her dress.

"I'll come back at Christmas," Viola promised, trying not to think about what might happen in the intervening months. She looked at Angela's plain, honest face, at Conrad, whose eyes were so much like Papa's, and she felt such pain, such fear for both of them, that she could hardly speak.

Conrad took her hands and held them in his. "Maybe we'll see each other at Christmas," he said, "and maybe we won't. But I want you to promise me one thing, Vi. Whatever happens to Angela and me, make this list of atrocities public."

She took the train to Berlin the next morning, reported her passport lost, and got a temporary replacement so quickly that it was slightly unnerving. When she returned to the house in the late afternoon, she noticed a large, black car pulled up in the circular driveway. The maid, a young round-cheeked Swabian woman, met her in the entry hall, pale-faced and frightened.

"I think it's the police, madam," the maid whispered in a trembling voice, wiping her hands on her apron.

"Who?" Viola stared blankly at her, not understanding.

"The Gestapo."

Viola's mouth went dry and she put one hand against the frame of the door to steady herself. Her first thought was of Conrad and Angela, of the list of names she was carrying in her purse. She cursed silently to herself: what a fool she'd been not to tear that list to pieces; how could she have carried it back to Berlin right into a trap like this? She'd planned to get rid of it this evening, after she'd reviewed it one more time, and now it was too late. If I try to destroy it now, she thought, the maid will see me and report me and maybe scream and they'll come out here into the hall and get me and maybe the list too. Behind her the leaves of the lindens and the oaks rustled in the afternoon breeze. The lawn was smooth and quiet. Viola briefly considered turning and running, but that was obviously out of the question. She wouldn't get a hundred yards, and besides, there was nowhere to run to. All of which left only one alternative.

Squaring her shoulders, she walked into the living room, where two men in trench coats were standing on one of the blue Persian rugs waiting for her. They looked up at the sound of her footsteps, but their faces were blank, like pieces of white paper. She clutched guiltily at her purse. The list inside it seemed to weigh a hundred pounds. She imagined that the two men noticed the gesture and once again she had an urge to run. This wouldn't do. She had to say something normal.

"May I help you, gentlemen?" Somehow, by a miracle, she managed to keep her voice level. The word *gentlemen* stuck in her throat.

"Frau Viola Kessler, Duchess of Sanford?" one of the men demanded without preamble.

"Yes," Viola said. "I'm Frau Kessler." She pressed her fingers together to keep her hands from trembling. "What can I do for you?"

Without another word the tall man handed her an envelope. The warrant for her arrest, no doubt. She took the envelope, very nearly dropping it in the process. What would they do next? Drag her into the Mercedes and take her down to the police station? Or would she get some kind of special treatment reserved for visiting foreigners, a session in a back room maybe? She wondered if she'd betray Conrad and Angela. She prayed silently that she wouldn't. In her hands the envelope felt heavy, as if it were filled with lead. She opened it. There was a huge gold seal, an evil-looking eagle grasping a sheaf of swastikas.

DR. AND MRS. JOSEPH GOEBBELS REQUEST THE PLEA-
SURE OF THE PRESENCE OF THE DUCHESS OF SANFORD
THIS EVENING AT 8:00 P.M. AT THEIR SCHWANENWERDER
ESTATE . . .

"Herr Doktor Goebbels saw you in *Laura*, gracious lady," the tall man supplied, "and he's crazy about actors, and as all Berlin knows, your presence, your talent, the genius of your—"

"Goebbels is inviting me to his house?" She sat down on the couch and began to laugh so hard she almost went into a choking fit. "You mean you came to deliver an *invitation?*"

The two men looked at her as if she'd gone mad, which in a sense she had. "Yes, gracious lady," the tall man said in a cautious tone of voice. "What reply shall we give?"

She somehow managed to get her hysteria under control. Folding her hands together, she looked at the two men, at the black gloss of their shoes, the incomprehension on their faces. She was almost drunk with relief and all she could think of was how easy it would be to call a cab and order it to take her to the airport. Even Nazi emigration officials would hardly dare stop a famous actress with a reservation and a valid ticket. On the other hand, rudely refusing an invitation from a highly placed official of the Reich could get Conrad and Angela in serious trouble. For a few seconds she weighed her own feelings against the potential danger. The idea of shaking Goebbels' hand was completely repellent, but as much as she wanted to leave, it wasn't worth the risk.

"Tell Doktor Goebbels I accept," she told the two men.

After they left, after the black Mercedes was definitely gone from the driveway and she was alone again, Viola went upstairs to her bedroom, tore the list of forty names into tiny pieces, and flushed it down the toilet. Sitting in front of the mirrored dressing table, she took the pins out of her hair and placed them in a neat pile beside the bottles of expensive French perfumes that had come with the room. Then she began to brush her hair: forty strokes on one side, forty strokes on the other. With each stroke she silently recited a name.

Schwanenwerder, one of Goebbels' many country estates, was located a short distance from Berlin on an island in the Wannsee. Under different circumstances Viola might have found it beautiful, but the vast expanses of lawn, the pavilions, formal gardens, and the fleet of pleasure boats rocking at anchor at the dock sent a cold chill up her spine. All this, she thought, has been looted from some German who made the mistake of crossing the Nazis.

As the Mercedes pulled smoothly to a stop, a servant hurried forward to open the door. Everything seemed organized like clockwork, and Viola, who had somehow managed to convince herself that she might be the Goebbelses' only dinner guest, was immensely relieved to see that she had been wrong. A large party of some sort was in progress, complete with a gigantic bar and, outside, a sumptuous buffet. The cream of Nazi society was evidently being amused at Doktor Goebbels' expense: women in long gowns and jewels were standing about laughing and talking to men in formal evening dress; couples were dancing to a familiar tune that she recognized after a few minutes as the popular "Lambeth Walk."

Inside, at the foot of a spiral staircase, a slight, round-shouldered man with a prominent nose and thin lips stood beside a rather pretty matronly-looking woman whose blond hair was swept back exposing a broad forehead topped by a widow's peak. Viola recognized the man from newspaper photographs as Goebbels and she felt an odd sensation, part disgust and part curiosity. So this was the twisted genius who had sold Hitler to the German people? She examined him, looking for some outer signs of this, and was disappointed to discover that there weren't any. Except for a tiny chin, and deep-set eyes that gave him a brooding, unhealthy appearance, Goebbels looked quite ordinary. But he wasn't, of course. Viola thought of Joseph, and it was all she could do to extend her hand. Flashbulbs popped, and she blinked, taken by surprise.

"Ah, Duchess"—Goebbels smiled affably—"this is such a pleasure. Permit me to introduce my wife, Magda."

"How do you do, Duchess," Frau Goebbels said. Her hand was

cool and limp, and she extended it wearily, as if she had already shaken her quota for the evening.

"You're a very impressive actress, and a very beautiful woman." Goebbels gave Viola an appraising look of badly concealed interest that—considering the fact that his wife was standing beside him— was unsettling. "It's a pity we can't persuade you to stay here in Germany." More flashbulbs popped.

"You must come back again next year," Frau Goebbels observed without enthusiasm.

Goebbels clasped Viola's hand and patted it in a way that she found repulsive. "And you must tell the world the truth about Germany."

"What's that, Herr Doktor?" Viola started, caught off guard.

"Why that the German people want peace, of course," Goebbels said. "The foreign press distorts things so badly." He sighed and released Viola's hand. "You must tell them that."

Viola thought that Goebbels would be rather surprised to learn exactly *what* she was planning to tell the press, but she managed to keep any hint of it out of her face.

"I hope you've enjoyed your visit with us, Duchess," Frau Goebbels said languidly.

"It's been very interesting," Viola replied with as much enthusiasm as she could muster. "I wouldn't have missed it for the world."

Goebbels gave her a sharp look, and she could see that he wasn't fooled. Dropping her hand, he wished her a good flight and turned to the next guest.

17

Viola stayed in Berlin one more day for the closing ceremonies of Reichs Theater Week, and then she flew to London. All the way across Europe she wondered why Goebbels had bothered to summon her to Schwanenwerder. Considering the fact that Germany had recently annexed Austria, his statement that the German people only "wanted peace" was unconvincing to say the least, and even if he had wanted such garbage conveyed to the British people, there were dozens of more appropriate channels he could have used. On the other hand, the Nazis did have a record of trying to convert famous people to their cause. They'd certainly chosen the wrong celebrity this time, she thought grimly.

It was a long drive from the airport, and she spent most of it thinking how good it was to be back in London, but when she finally climbed the steps to the Belgravia house Viola found a surprise waiting for her that drove all other thoughts out of her mind: in the living room Grants sat on the sofa reading a Graham Greene novel.

Beside her a nurse in a white uniform was mixing up some kind of pink liquid in a glass.

"Grants!" Viola was so startled that she dropped her coat in a pile on the floor and just stood there staring. In all the years she had been acquainted with Richard's grandmother, she had never known her to travel more than a few miles from Sanford Palace.

"Hello, Viola." Grants put her book on the table next to the couch, took the pink liquid from the nurse, and drank it cautiously. "I've been expecting you for hours."

"The plane was delayed," Viola stammered.

Grants looked at Viola oddly. She seemed different, nothing like her usual self. The old snap and fire had gone out of her, and she appeared a good ten years older. Something's wrong, Viola thought. "You aren't the fainting type, are you?" Grants demanded abruptly.

"No." The question was so strange that Viola wondered if Grants could have possibly had a minor stroke or something of the sort. "Why do you ask?"

"Dicky's been wounded in Spain." Grants held out a tattered yellow envelope. Her hand was shaking slightly, and if Viola hadn't known her better, she would have said Grants was on the edge of tears. "Now don't go neurasthenic on me; it was weeks ago and the wound wasn't serious." Grants tried to smile but it didn't come out particularly well. "By now he's probably out of hospital and back on the battlefield pretending to be Cardigan at Balaklava. I blame myself. I never should have let his nanny read 'The Charge of the Light Brigade' to him when he was a boy."

The joke was hollow and unconvincing, a piece of bravado thrown in the face of disaster. Viola took the envelope out of Grants' hand and tore it open. The letter had been written by an American nurse named Gladys Johnson, and it said simply that Richard had received a shoulder wound, that it wasn't serious, and that he was making splendid progress. The date on the letter was March 23.

"You'd have thought they could have sent us a telegram," Grants said wearily, "but I suppose the wire service out of Madrid isn't functioning."

Viola sat down and tried to make herself understand that Richard had been hurt. I still love him, she thought. I don't care if he was a fool to run off to Spain, I still love him, and I should be there with him, but that's impossible and there's nothing I can do, and what if he isn't wounded but dead and this Gladys Johnson is lying. The week she had spent in Germany had made her suspect everything. She read the letter again, trying to force more information out of it but there wasn't any more information to be had. *Shoulder wound.* Richard's shoulders were smooth and she had put her head on them more times than she could count and the thought that one of them had been torn up by a bullet made her sick.

"There's nothing we can do, of course," Grants observed, echoing Viola's thoughts. "Leave it to Dicky to make sure of that." She folded her knotted hands together in a gesture of grief and frustration. "He shouldn't have gone," she said in an old, petulant voice. "If you ask me, his place is here with you, especially at a time like this."

There was something in Grants' tone that made Viola look up from the letter. "What do you mean?"

"You really don't know, do you?"

"Know what?"

Grants shook her head. "I was afraid of this. That's why I came up from Sanford. Why it's been my role in life to be the bearer of bad news in this family is beyond me, but that seems to be the way it is." She gestured to the nurse. "You can go now, Miss Simmons."

"Yes, madam." The nurse left the room, closing the door behind her.

There was a brief, uncomfortable silence.

"Well," Viola said, "what else is it that I'm supposed to know?"

"This." Grants picked up a newspaper from a pile that was lying on the coffee table and handed it to Viola. "It came out yesterday afternoon. Amazing how rapid modern communications are. The photos must have been flown in directly from Berlin, but then the Nazis wouldn't have spared any expense, would they?"

Viola looked at the front page of the paper to find her own face staring back at her. It was an excellent likeness of everyone concerned, especially Goebbels.

VIOLA KESSLER TOURS GERMANY

the caption read. Grants extracted another newspaper from the pile. This one, a tabloid, was obviously a publication of the British Union of Fascists. Viola looked at the photograph of herself shaking hands with Goebbels and for a minute she was so angry that she could hardly read the headline that screamed out in four-inch letters from the top of the page:

GREAT GERMAN ACTRESS COMES BACK TO THE FATHERLAND

Reprinted under the photo was a long article taken from the official German press, laced with what purported to be quotes from Viola about the wonders of Nazi Germany.

"Harry brought this piece of trash around last night," Grants said. "I gather that the picture of you with Goebbels was in all the papers by this morning."

"It's a lie." Viola was so angry she could hardly speak.

"I never doubted that for a minute," Grants said, "but it's a disaster all the same. People who don't know you are going to think you're a Nazi sympathizer."

"Listen"—Viola crumpled the newspaper and threw it to the carpet—"there's something you need to know. When I was in Germany I paid a visit to my brother, Conrad, and his wife." She told Grants about everything: Angela's connection with Dachau, the list of forty, the reception at Schwanenwerder.

Grants' face grew more animated. She tapped her cane on the carpet and her eyes snapped. "Hire a hall," she suggested suddenly, interrupting Viola in mid-sentence.

"Hire a hall?"

"You've obviously been framed, and the only thing to do when you've been framed is to make a public statement and clear yourself." Grants leaned forward. Her face was flushed with color and she looked more like herself again. "You're a woman of spirit and courage, my dear, and the Nazis are going to rue the day they ever invited you to Germany. Tell the world about those forty innocent people they've murdered." The old warhorse has heard the call to battle, Viola thought. The idea was comforting; Grants was a friend who'd stand by her and, not only that, Grants knew what she was doing. Viola had an urge to go over and give her a hug, but she knew Grants would pretend to be annoyed if she did any such thing.

"On second thought," Grants observed, "you don't need to hire a hall. You've already got one—the Arena. So all you need to do is invite in the press and defend yourself."

It was a good idea, Viola thought. She began to go over the practical details: the capacity of the theater, announcements in all the newspapers, posters, calls made to the right people. Would Mr. Carlyle object: Probably not. She thought of Isak Hart. Perhaps he had a mailing list he could lend her.

"Ring up Cissy Dockett," Grants suggested. "The woman's spent half her adult life putting on charity events. If there's a meeting to be publicized, Cissy will know how to do it." Grants looked at Viola fondly. "I rather envy you, you know."

"I don't feel much like a proper subject of envy."

"Ah, but you are. Here we are, poised on the brink of another war, with our idiot Prime Minister placating Hitler, and you get to play Joan of Arc." Grants pulled briskly at the bell cord to summon the nurse. "If I could walk, I'd be up there at the podium with you."

"We'll rally round you, simply *rally*." Cecily Dockett wrung her hands one way and then wrung them the other, as if she were having at a fine linen handkerchief. "But, Vi, my dear, it couldn't have happened at a worse time what with all this war scare."

She leaned forward and the diamond locket around her neck swung back and forth, sending chips of light scudding over the powder-blue rug and white tablecloths of the Crown Tearoom. "Do you realize that at this very minute plans are actually being drawn up to *evacuate* London? Barrage balloons are in the making, and gas masks." Cissy frowned and stroked at her fur stole. "They're actually going to issue us all gas masks if things get any worse. Can you imagine how I'd look in a gas mask, Vi? Ghastly, I should imagine. Rather like a praying mantis or something of the sort."

"But you'll see that the posters get printed," Viola insisted, "and you'll handle the publicity?"

"Of course," Cissy said. "I'm your friend, aren't I? I never believed this ghastly smear for a moment, Vi, not for a minute. Why I told Maureen Norwood only yesterday that I didn't know how you'd managed to get your picture in the papers with that horrid little man but that we'd all just have to wait for you to come back from Germany and ask you before we went jumping to any conclusions. And Maureen agreed—she hardly knows you but she knows you're married to Dicky and that's all she needs to know. You may have trouble with the general public, Vi. I mean, my dear, I do hope you aren't planning to go on the *stage* or anything until this all clears up because there's a certain class of people who—well, enough said, rotten fruit perhaps, if you follow me—but your own will simply *rally*."

"My own?"

"Let's not be coy, Vi." Cissy retrieved her alligator bag and stood up. "As an American, you may be able to forget from time to time that you're the Duchess of Sanford, but I assure you no one else does." She kissed Viola on both cheeks, enveloping her in a cloud of expensive scent. "I'm not only going to print up those posters, I'm going to assemble you a crowd the like of which London hasn't seen since the coronation."

Cissy was as good as her word. Five days later Viola stood at the makeup table in her dressing room at the Arena examining a roll of posters that had just arrived in the morning mail. The posters, printed in bright reds and blues, sported the famous picture of her shaking hands with Goebbels with a giant black X drawn through it.

> *HEAR VIOLA KESSLER*
> *DUCHESS OF SANFORD*
> *REVEAL THE TRUTH ABOUT THE NAZI*
> *CAMPAIGN OF TERROR*

In the same package was a note from Cissy informing Viola that by the time she received them they'd be plastered on every lamppost and blank wall in London. *I didn't know exactly how to refer to you, Vi,* Cissy wrote. *On one hand, the public knows you as Viola Kessler, and on the other—well as you can see, I've compromised a bit with the proper nomenclature, but I think the general effect is perfectly smashing.*

Viola agreed. Smashing indeed. She examined the posters with satisfaction, thinking that she ought to send one down to Sanford to Grants. She was just in the process of rolling them back up into the cardboard tube when there was a knock on the door.

"Come in," she said automatically. Her dressing room was an informal office of sorts and people dropped by all the time.

"Hullo, Vi," an all too familiar voice said. Viola whirled around to find her brother-in-law, Harry Stafford, standing in the doorway contemplating her with an unpleasantly cordial smile. "Mind if I come in?"

"Yes," Viola said, "I do mind, Harry." She realized that she should have expected this visit, but for some reason it took her by surprise. "I'd rather you just left. I can't imagine that we have anything to say to each other."

"After what I read in the papers," Harry observed, "I rather thought we were soul mates."

"Well think again." It always amazed her how much Harry looked like a dissolute version of Richard: heavy where Richard was slender, the same blue Stafford eyes looking out from under drooping lids.

"Nice place you have here." Harry pushed aside a rack of costumes and sat down on the bench, so close to Viola that their knees almost touched. Taking a cigar out of his pocket, he bit off the end and chewed on it thoughtfully. "Fact is, this isn't a social call. I have a bit of a message for you, high-level communication and all that."

"A message from whom?" Viola turned her back on Harry, sat down at the makeup table, picked up her brush, and began to brush her hair. In the mirror she could see him toying with the hem of one of her costumes.

"A message from the Polliwog," Harry said.

Viola paused, brush in mid-air. "What are you talking about, Harry?"

"Don't tell me you don't know his nickname. I thought everybody who had ever been to Germany had heard his nickname."

"Whose nickname?" She was losing what little patience she had left.

"Why Goebbels' nickname, of course," Harry observed affably. "If you'll think about it a minute, you'll realize that in German it's a pun. *Polliwog*—a little thing that's made up of a big head and a huge tail—

or to be more precise . . ." He said a German word that was obscene. There was a short silence during which Viola's heart began to beat rapidly. She felt an odd, congested sensation, as if all the blood in her body had suddenly rushed to her brain. "Herr Doktor Goebbels has a message for you." Harry cleared his throat.

"What sort of message?"

"He wants you to know that it's all up with your brother and sister-in-law, cat's out of the bag, so to speak."

Viola turned to confront Harry. "What did you just say?" Her mouth was dry with fear. She tried to swallow but her throat felt as if it had closed up.

"Don't look at me that way, Vi." Harry chewed uneasily on his cigar and made a poor attempt at a smile. "I'm just the message boy."

"Are you telling me that Conrad and Angela have been arrested?"

"By the Gestapo." Harry nodded. "Three days ago to be exact. Rotten affair, but then they shouldn't have been meddling where they had no business, you know. Our German friends don't take kindly to meddling. Fact is, old girl, the good Herr Doktor Goebbels specifically asked me to impress upon you the fact that the spectacle of a 'great German actress' making statements against the Reich could have unhappy consequences."

Viola put the hairbrush back down on the dressing table and made a monumental effort to keep her voice level. She felt like screaming at Harry or raking her nails across his simpering face, but that would hardly help Conrad and Angela. "What sort of 'unhappy consequences,' Harry? Just exactly what do you mean?"

"Ah well," Harry said uneasily, "I think I'd rather leave that to your imagination, Vi. Let's just say their situation could become very delicate, uncomfortable perhaps. Yes, I'd say it could become quite uncomfortable if, for example, you were to go through with this, uh, ill-advised speech you're planning to make."

"Are you telling me that my brother and Angela are going to be tortured by the Gestapo if I speak out against the Nazis?"

"Ah well"—Harry looked at his cigar—"I didn't say any such thing, you know. But people do fall ill under these conditions, Vi."

"Goebbels would execute them, wouldn't he?"

"Yes," Harry said bluntly, "he would, and I'm afraid it wouldn't be a pretty execution. Now if you'd like to see them released, it might be a good idea for you to show some public enthusiasm for the Reich—attend a rally or two with me, for example."

"Harry," Viola said, "get out of here. You may be Richard's brother, but as far as I'm concerned you're a piece of unspeakable slime."

"I'm just doing what I believe in," Harry protested primly. He got up. "I have a right to my opinions, you know." He stopped, blocking the doorway. "Think it over, and I'm sure you'll see the logic of it all. Besides, Hitler's the wave of the future."

"Not my future," Viola snapped. "Now get out."

"You'll come around in time," Harry promised. "I guarantee it."

"Oh dear," Cissy moaned when Viola telephoned an hour later with the news. "This is a disaster. The posters are up everywhere, and I've already contacted all the papers. Did you say your brother and sister-in-law have actually been *arrested?*"

"By the Gestapo." Viola was so upset, she could hardly speak. She thought of Conrad and Angela and a sick sensation swept over her. How would their death certificates read? Heart failure? Pneumonia? It was a morbid thought but she couldn't put it out of her mind. Cissy was still going on about what a disaster this was, but Viola hardly heard her.

"Of course your friends will still *rally* about you, Vi," Cissy was saying, "but the general public—well I mean, how will it look? If you don't make that speech, why you'll have to go into retirement."

"What?"

"I said if you don't make that speech—"

"But I *am* making the speech, Cissy. I have no intention of canceling." It was the hardest decision Viola had ever had to make in her life, and her voice trembled as she said it.

"But your brother and sister-in-law?"

"I've thought it over, Cissy." She paused and took a deep breath. "For the last hour, ever since that bastard Harry walked out the door, I've been examining my conscience, and I've come to the conclusion that Conrad and Angela would want me to go ahead with this. I think my brother knew that he and Angela didn't have much time left. Before I left Munich he made me promise that whatever happened to the two of them, I'd make this list of atrocities public." Her voice broke, but she forced herself to continue. "The truth is that if the Gestapo has them, then they won't escape no matter what I do."

"You poor dear," Cissy said, "you sound *so* upset. This is all too ghastly for words."

"I'd give anything to get Conrad and Angela out of Germany, but I can't. No one can. They're brave, fine people and I love and respect them for what they did. That list of names is obviously something they were willing to make public at any cost, and if I back out, I'll be failing them. If they're going to die, I'll be damned if I'm going to let them die in vain. But I have to admit that I hope Goebbels will reconsider. I intend to bring international attention to the fact that they've been illegally arrested and imprisoned. From what I saw in Germany, even the Nazis care about world opinion."

"You sound so logical, so brave," Cissy said. "I simply don't understand how you're managing to surmount all this, but if you're absolutely determined to go through with it, I'll send off the rest of the announcements posthaste."

"Do that," Viola said. She hung up the phone and sat for a moment looking at it. I may sound logical and brave, she thought, but I'm not. She wondered for the hundredth time if she'd made the right decision; she wondered again if this was what Conrad would really want her to do. She felt tormented, unsure, and vulnerable. Putting her head down on her arms, she thought of Conrad and Angela in some Gestapo prison cell, of Richard, who was so far away in Spain. She was lonely and afraid, but one thought consoled her: she believed—with every ounce of her being—that truth always had more power than lies.

Three days later she sat grimly on the stage of the Arena as Cissy stood at the podium introducing her to the crowd of photographers, reporters, and journalists. Every newspaper in Britain must have sent a representative, and it was a daunting sight to see so many cameras and microphones. Of all the audiences she had ever played to, Viola thought, this was going to be the hardest.

"After she speaks," Cissy was saying brightly, "the Duchess will be happy to take questions from the press, but we would ever so appreciate it if you gentlemen could hold your inquiries until then."

"Excuse me," a voice whispered. Viola felt a tap on her shoulder and turned to find Maureen Norwood, Cissy's bosom friend, peering through an opening in the curtain just behind her. "I know I shouldn't interrupt you at this point, my dear," Maureen apologized in a sotto voce voice, "but the man who delivered this said I had to give it to you before you spoke." She handed Viola an envelope. "He was frightfully insistent, said it was an emergency. I do hope he wasn't some kind of crank."

Viola took the envelope from Maureen with a feeling of foreboding and ripped it open. A small piece of charred wood fell into her lap. The note was short and brutal. All it said was:

REMEMBER THE NEUES? IF YOU SAY ONE WORD AGAINST US, BITCH, IT WILL HAPPEN AGAIN. THERE IS A MAN IN THE AUDIENCE WITH A BOMB. IF YOU MENTION THE BOMB TO THE REPORTERS, IT WILL GO OFF. IF YOU TRY TO SPEAK IN PUBLIC ANYTIME, ANYWHERE, YOU SLUT, YOU WILL DIE.

My God, the Fascists were going to bomb the Arena! Viola sprang to her feet just as Cissy was saying, ". . . and now I give you Viola Kessler."

This was a bluff. It had to be. She should walk straight to the podium and tell the press that there'd been a bomb threat. There'd be no time after her announcement for the bomber to set off his bomb and get away unharmed. The Fascists weren't crazy enough to blow up one of their own just to silence her.

She started toward the podium.

But what if this wasn't a bluff? What if they had found a man crazy enough to blow up the whole theater and himself along with it? The old fear of fire hit her suddenly in the pit of the stomach, bringing her to a sudden halt.

Fire. Sheets of flame. Gasoline. She remembered the Neues burning around her, the explosion, the screams, the panic. For an instant she imagined it all happening again: heard the incendiary bomb going off, saw the reporters trampling each other to escape, saw the Arena going up like a torch. It was her worst fear, her nightmare.

IF YOU SAY ONE WORD AGAINST US . . .

She looked out at the crowd. The audience was applauding and Cissy was gesturing for her to take the podium. What kind of chance was she willing to take? Was she willing to bet hundreds of lives on the idea that British Nazis were more sane than German Nazis?

Her hands were shaking and her mouth had gone dry. Suddenly she had no doubt the Nazis meant what they said. Somewhere in this audience there was a madman with a bomb. Who was he? Where was he? She looked around, and rows of bland, white British faces looked back at her. He could be anyone, anywhere.

She couldn't chance it. She couldn't mention the bomb. It was too dangerous. She'd have to get through the next ten minutes as best she could, and then tell the press afterward what had happened. She walked up to the podium and turned to face the audience.

The applause stopped and the reporters waited expectantly. She stared at them, afraid to say anything that might provoke the bomber. There was a restless shuffling of feet. "Well, get on with it, Duchess," one of the reporters called.

Still she said nothing. "Vi, dear," Cissy hissed in a loud stage whisper, "don't just stand there like a statue."

A man stood up in the second row. "Miss Kessler," he said, sympathetically, "I understand you have something to tell the press about the campaign of terror in Nazi Germany."

"No," Viola said.

"What!" There was consternation.

"You didn't come here tonight to defend yourself against the charge that you are a Nazi sympathizer?"

"I have nothing to say."

The consternation turned to pandemonium. Flashbulbs popped, reporters crawled all over each other to get closer to her.

"Are you a Nazi?" they yelled.

"No comment."

"Do you support Hitler?"

"No comment."

"Are you Goebbels 'bosom buddy'?"

"No comment." She wanted to yell the truth, but she was trapped. One word from her, and they might all die, but they didn't know that. They fell on her with their questions like a pack of dogs, and to every one she gave the same answer:

"No comment."

"Vi." Cissy was dumbfounded. "What in the name of God are you doing? You're destroying yourself." She tried to take over the podium, but Viola held her back. For a second the two women wrestled for the podium, and then Cissy gave up and began to cry.

That was the picture that appeared the next morning on the front page of almost every paper in Britain: Cissy bedraggled and outraged, hat askew, standing beside a silent Viola under the headline:

DUCHESS OF SANFORD REFUSES TO DEFEND SELF AGAINST CHARGES OF FASCIST SYMPATHIES.

"Bomb threat, eh, Duchess?" Daniel Farnsworth, editor of the *London Clarion*, flicked a few inches of cigar ash into his coffee cup and looked at her sympathetically. His paper was supporting Stalin, the Spanish Civil War, equal rights for women, London transit strikes, and the organization of Marxist-Leninist study groups. It had a circulation of about a thousand.

"Yes," Viola said firmly, "a bomb threat."

"And that's why you didn't speak out?"

"Yes, I have a copy of the note here. I've already given the original to Scotland Yard."

The editor inspected the note and frowned. "Nasty business," he said. "We'll print this on page one along with a story about why you can't talk in public. In my opinion, Duchess, the Fascists are framing you."

"And the List of Forty?"

"I'll print that, too, of course, although frankly if it were just our German comrades being tortured, our readers would find it more interesting. But don't worry. I'll see that this list gets made public. Time someone blew the whistle on those murderers."

"And the story about how my brother and sister-in-law have been arrested by the Gestapo?"

"Page one. Never fear."

She shook his hand and thanked him. Of the six editors she had called on in the past week, Mr. Farnsworth had been the only one willing to listen to her. For the vast majority of the British, the name Viola Kessler had become inexorably linked with Goebbels. She had lost all credibility; she was tainted; she was that bloody Duchess of Sanford who was soft on Hitler.

Nothing she did over the next few months seemed to be able to stem the tide of misinformation. The article in the *Clarion* had no noticeable effect. Audiences boycotted the Arena and attendance fell to almost nothing on the nights when she appeared. It soon became clear that if the theater was going to survive, she was going to have to stop acting altogether and do something less public, such as directing.

Meanwhile, the words of the note haunted her. Terrified, she bought fire extinguishers and put them in every room of her house. At night she awoke shaking. The next fire could happen at any minute. The bomb could be anywhere; it could explode at any time.

But of all the griefs of that terrible spring, there was one that overshadowed even her fear of fire. It arrived at Sanford Palace on a bright, sunny day in the form of an envelope bearing two Spanish stamps and no return address.

"Open it," Grants said. "Open that bloody thing and tell me what it says." They were in the east rose garden and Grants was propped up in a wicker wheelchair—a huge Victorian sort of contraption with a sunshade and giant rubber-rimmed tires. Grants brushed her hair out of her eyes and her mouth trembled. Dressed in her favorite pair of jodhpurs, with a riding whip under her arm, she hardly looked the part of a grandmother, but there was something old and fragile in her face that Viola had never seen before.

Viola opened the dog-eared envelope and pulled out the letter.

Dear Mrs. Stafford, the American nurse had written, *I am sorry to inform you that . . .* " With a cry of grief, Viola threw the letter to the ground. She would never see Richard again; he was dead of blood poisoning, buried somewhere in Spain.

"Viola," Grants exclaimed, "what is it? What's the matter?"

Seizing Grants' riding whip Viola began to lash out at the roses. "I hate war! I hate death!" she cried passionately. "It's a goddamn waste! Oh, Richard!" Dropping the riding whip to the ground, she began to sob. Rose petals littered the path in front of her, and the bushes were bare stems. Everything was waste, she thought, waste and destruction.

With great effort Grants leaned down and picked up the letter. "Dicky was a good boy," Grants said softly. She fingered the white square of paper and tears came to her eyes. "But a fool to go off to Spain."

Viola nodded, too grieved to speak.

Politics had widowed her for the second time.

BOOK
FOUR

THE
MAGIC
BOX

18

PARIS
1940

It was early May, the last spring before the war came to France, and Paris was at its most beautiful. The chestnut trees tossed their blossoms prodigally into the Seine; the air was delicate as a vanilla wafer; the bridges of Paris seemed to bend over the water with extra grace; the flying buttresses of Notre Dame looked like the decorations on a giant stone confection, and in the gardens of the Tuileries and Luxembourg red and gold tulips spread their petals to seduce the pollen-booted bees.

Yet in the Joie-Verte nightclub, May was passing, as it always did, almost unnoticed. In the Joie-Verte there were no seasons, no day or night for that matter; the smoke and the conversations were the same, summer or winter, spring or fall. In the Joie-Verte the most famous chanteuses of Paris sang their endless, haunting songs of love and betrayal, looking at the audience with world-weary eyes, a technique which conspired to create an atmosphere *"fanée"* as the French put it, an atmosphere redolent with the philosophy that life is a meaningless, randomly tragic, rather boring affair—all of which was a pose, of course, since the French—although they hate to admit it—love life more than most peoples.

On this particular May evening Kathe Rothe, sixteen years old and attending school in Paris for the semester, sat at a small round table in the Joie-Verte trying to look twenty with only moderate success. To the left of her a slender, darkly handsome Frenchman with long tapered fingers sat drinking a glass of good red wine and pretending to listen to Edith Piaf, who was standing at the center of the tiny stage, hands on her hips, belting out a ballad in a voice mixed with passion and gravel. Actually the truth was that Henri Lagarde—for that was the Frenchman's name—hardly heard Piaf, primarily because he was obsessed with Kathe, whom he had known now for exactly forty-eight hours, and whom he had decided, rather impulsively, was probably the grand passion of his life.

Henri studied Kathe's profile, the wet gloss of her lips, the neat turn of her ankles, and he felt an ache that came partly from his groin and partly from his heart. Kathe was an enigma, Henri thought. She wasn't American, or English, or French, or—thank God—German, although she spoke the languages fluently enough to tell good jokes in all three. She wasn't a stylish girl; the couturiers and the shopkeepers in the fancy boutiques that lined the Rue de Rivoli would have thrown up their hands in despair at the sight of what she was wearing tonight: a plain white linen dress with yellow piping on the sleeves that was at least five years out of fashion, and which Henri had good reason to suspect Kathe had borrowed from her Tante Jeanne. Nor was she beautiful in the classic sense: her dark black hair was chopped off just below her ears, giving her the look of an inquisitive schoolboy; her cheekbones were high and delicate, but her lips were just a little too full. Add to this her eyebrows, which nearly met in the middle of her forehead, a nose that jutted out a fraction too much, and a stubbornly square chin and you had a remarkable face, but not the kind men were usually taken by.

Yet Henri was indeed taken by Kathe. Twenty-two years old and a graduate student of anthropology at the Musée de L'Homme, he already considered himself something of an expert on women. Kathe Rothe, in his opinion, was exceptional, perhaps even sensational. She was practically a baby, absolutely naive, and undoubtedly a virgin, and yet she radiated an unconscious sensual quality that had kept Henri up most of last night contemplating ways to get her alone. Not that he should really, if he had any sense. Mademoiselle Jeanne Dufour, the girl's godmother, was Henri's mother's best friend, thus the penalty for seducing Kathe would undoubtedly be a family fight of the first order.

Henri drank his wine and told himself that he should go home and take one of those cold baths that the good Jesuit fathers in his *lycée* had always been suggesting. By French standards Kathe Rothe was a *jeune fille*—that is to say, too young and off limits. She might be intelligent, witty, and physically sensational, but she was untouchable; she was going back to England in a few weeks, and if he had an ounce of brains he would be thinking about the international situation, the possibility of a German invasion, his thesis, or some other important topic instead of mooning over her.

Kathe, for her part, was conscious of Henri's admiration, but she was trying to ignore it. In England boys her own age from the neighboring boarding school had occasionally asked her out to tea, given her bashful kisses on the forehead, and stuttered so much when they tried to make conversation with her that she had decided that this whole man-woman thing was highly overrated, but the French were so different that it was—well, to tell the truth, it was embarrassing. Kathe, who had lived in Paris as a child, had thought she knew the Gallic temperament inside out, but the difference between being ten and sixteen was something she hadn't foreseen. She had been in Paris since January and she still didn't quite know what to do when strangers accosted her on the street and offered to buy her drinks or sat staring at her the way Henri was staring at her this very minute—like he was hungry and she was a *baba au rhum*.

Studiously not looking at him, Kathe sat on the hard wooden chair, leaning slightly forward, chin on her hands, eyes bright with excitement, drinking in every motion of Piaf's body, every shift in her amazing voice. What stage presence the woman had, what a sense of drama. The songs were reasonably good, but it was Piaf who made them spectacular, putting her own imprint on them with the kind of easy self-assurance that any professional actress would have envied. An involuntary sigh escaped Kathe's lips. She wished Mama could be here drinking French wine and listening to this performance; it might cheer her up a little. She'd had been so sad since Uncle Conrad and Aunt Angela disappeared and Richard died in the Spanish Civil War. Three quarters of London seemed to think she was some kind of Fascist, which outraged Kathe, but adults were idiotically stubborn once they got hold of misinformation. Not only was Mama suffering unjustly, but for the first time Kathe could remember, she wasn't acting. She'd more or less retired from the Arena and was down at Sanford Palace most of the time taking care of Grants, who could hardly get out of bed these days. Naturally retirement wasn't something Mama was taking gracefully, and Kathe didn't blame her. Oh, Mama bore up well enough under it, never complained, but the two of them had always been close, and Kathe could see by her face that she was seriously unhappy.

Kathe wrinkled her forehead, lost for a moment in thought. Mama was such a wonderful person, but she never seemed to be able to keep her life in order. When Kathe was grown up—which wouldn't be long now—she intended to do a lot better. For one thing, she was never going to get mixed up in politics. She knew all about Uncle Conrad and the List of Forty, and the reasons why Mama couldn't make public speeches, but Kathe had no intention of ever getting herself into a similar situation. Papa—whom she still remembered with painful nostalgia—had been killed because of his political beliefs, as had dear Uncle Richard, and her Mama's life had been more or less wrecked by the same thing, so as far as she was concerned, it didn't even pay to read the newspapers.

Second, Kathe thought, she wasn't ever going to get married. Marriage was obviously a mistake, especially for a woman who wanted a career, which Kathe definitely did. What kind of career she wasn't entirely sure yet. She'd always thought it would be acting, but lately—after watching the troubles Mama had gone through—she'd begun to question if the price you paid for success in the theater was too high. Besides, who could compete with Viola Kessler? As Uncle Richard had always said, Mama was a hell of a hard act to follow. Lately Kathe had been leaning toward botany. Now there was a secure field: you'd never find plants hissing you off the stage or sending you hate mail. Plants, Kathe thought, knew their place, which was more than you could say about most people.

The music suddenly came to an end, and Piaf made her exit to a crash of applause. The air in the Joie-Verte began to hum with conversation, most of it, naturally enough, about the possibility of France getting into the war, a topic that had been on everybody's mind since Hitler invaded Norway. Kathe heard the words "Maginot Line" uttered with conviction. Remembering her vow not to mix in politics, she tried to close her ears, but it was more or less impossible.

"Paris will never fall to the Huns," the man at the next table was loudly declaring. "The Maginot Line will hold; it's the most extensive system of permanent defenses since the Great Wall of China."

"Well, Kathe"—Henri put down his wineglass and raised his voice above the din—"what next?"

Kathe pursed her lips thoughtfully. She appreciated the fact that Henri had offered to take her around Paris. When Tante Jeanne had first suggested that she go out with the son of one of her friends, Kathe had been dubious, but Henri had proved to be polite, knowledgeable, and even attractive. Of course, since she was never going to marry, this last quality didn't matter, unless she began to take lovers like George Sand or Isadora Duncan—something she might consider when she was an old woman of thirty or so and had her career really under way. "Is Piaf singing again this evening?" she asked. She didn't want to miss a moment of Piaf—not even if she ultimately decided to become a botanist.

"I don't think so," Henri said.

"Then how about taking a walk?"

"What Mademoiselle wishes," Henri said, gallantly helping her into her spring coat, "Mademoiselle gets."

"I rely on the bravery and vigilance of the French Army," the man at the next table was proclaiming with drunken fervor.

"This phony war is getting on my nerves, *cheri*," the woman next to him snapped, "so could we please stop talking about it."

Yes, Kathe thought, could we please. Mama hadn't wanted to let her come to Paris this spring because of the worsening international situation, but the plan for her to spend a semester living with Tante Jeanne had been in the works for years. Kathe had begged and pleaded, and promised Mama that at the very first sign of France getting into the war she'd come home. She actually had gone back to London after Hitler invaded Denmark and Norway, but a few weeks later, when things calmed down again, she'd managed to persuade

Mama to let her return to finish out the school year. France had the strongest army in Europe; Hitler was moving east, not west. Still, it made Kathe nervous to hear everyone in Paris chewing over the inevitability of war with Germany.

Outside, the moon was a clear half-circle in the sky. Henri walked rapidly, swinging his arms. Kathe lagged a little behind him, feeling slightly tired and a little dizzy from the wine. For some reason the conversation she had overheard in the cafe stayed with her, growing into an anxious lump at the base of her throat. She tried to banish it from her mind, but it hung on. Kathe listened to the sound of their footsteps echoing on the cobblestones. *A German invasion is just around the corner*, the echoes seemed to say.

"You know," Kathe confided impulsively to Henri as the two of them turned into one of the side streets that bordered the Joie-Verte, "I keep having the feeling that my life is, well, more or less in a mess." She laughed nervously and pulled at her gloves.

"Why is that?" Henri asked sympathetically. He wondered if Kathe had any idea how beautiful she looked in the moonlight. The pale glint of it in her black hair was like a streak of molten silver, and her face was so pale it was like marble, only marble that breathed and moved.

Kathe was hesitating, not sure how to explain exactly what was bothering her. "Well for one thing," she admitted, "my mother's very unhappy." She had a dim sense that she was talking too much and too intimately, but the wine had loosened her tongue. "And then there's all this war talk."

"It's not just your life that's in a mess," Henri observed. "It's the world in general."

"I suppose that's true," Kathe agreed. For some reason the thought was comforting. They walked for another block, past closed store-fronts and gutters filled with rainwater. Kathe tried not to listen to the echoes of their steps, but they were still there, still speaking of war. At the next corner she stopped and turned to Henri. "Are you frightened?" she asked him bluntly.

"Frightened of what?"

"Of the Germans. In London, during the Munich crisis, they put up barrage balloons and evacuated people. I even got issued my own gas mask." Kathe laughed uneasily. "I keep thinking that maybe

Mama was right; maybe I should go back to England again and forget about taking my final exams."

"Oh don't." Henri seemed taken aback by the suggestion. "There's no danger, really, at least not at present." He described the Maginot Line, explained how well France was protected—all of which Kathe had heard before, but it was reassuring to hear it again.

"Then you think we're safe here?" She waved at the empty street, at a lamppost, at Paris in general.

"No one can say for sure," Henri admitted. "Hitler's an unreasonable type, but to my mind it's unlikely he'd take on the French Army when it's obviously at least as strong as anything he could throw at it." They walked for eight more blocks as Henri explained in detail the difference between French and German armaments, the various diplomatic pressures, the forces that might start or prevent a German invasion. Kathe listened to him, fascinated by the depth of his knowledge. She was flattered that he treated her so much like a grown-up, consoled by his repeated assurances that it wasn't necessary for her to go back to London. Only later, as she lay on the guest bed in Tante Jeanne's apartment, did it occur to her that she had spent almost half the evening talking politics—quite a bit, she thought ruefully, for a girl who had promised herself a lifetime of ignorance on the entire subject.

But Mama hadn't had the benefit of Henri's reassurances. When Kathe came home from school a few days later, Tante Jeanne was waiting for her with a cable from London.

> KATHE DEAREST
> COME HOME AT ONCE. INTERNATIONAL SITUATION WORSE. CISSY SAYS CHAMBERLAIN ABOUT TO RESIGN AND GERMANS MAY ATTACK FRANCE AT ANY MINUTE. COME BACK WITHOUT DELAY. LOVE MAMA

Tante Jeanne read the cable over Kathe's shoulder and gave a small sigh. "I suppose you'll have to go, *cherie*." She sat down on one of the comfortable chintz-covered chairs and gazed at Kathe sadly. Tante Jeanne was a thin, wiry woman, full of energy, always reading the latest psychiatric journals, or cooking gourmet meals, or running off to the hospital wearing her red beret and carrying patients' files slung over her shoulder in a leather school bag like a *lycée* student. Most of the time it was hard to remember that she was nearly forty; Kathe often felt like Tante Jeanne was more of an older sister. In fact, they behaved like sisters: wearing each other's clothes, exchanging shoes, sitting up at night to giggle endlessly over silly jokes that only the two of them found funny. Kathe had even cut her hair short because that was the way Tante Jeanne wore hers—a practical style, they both agreed: just shake yourself dry in the shower, no fuss or bother. But at the moment Tante Jeanne didn't look like a sister at all; she looked like a middle-aged woman who was miserable about the prospect of losing Kathe's company, and that worried Kathe because—next to Mama—Tante Jeanne was the person she loved most in the world.

Kathe reread the cable and then folded it up and stuck it in her pocket. Since it was obvious that she was going to have to leave for London immediately, she couldn't think of anything to say to comfort Tante Jeanne. She could invite her to come along, of course, but Tante Jeanne would never leave her patients, not even for a long weekend, so the prospect of her agreeing to come to London on the spur of the moment was dim.

"Who's this Cissy that Viola mentions?" Tante Jeanne asked after perhaps a full minute of uncharacteristic silence.

"Cissy is Lady Dockett, one of Mama's friends. Her husband, Lord Dockett, is something or other in the government and he gets all kinds of forewarnings about what's going to happen, through diplomatic channels or something like that."

Tante Jeanne grinned, amused despite herself. "You don't know what position this Lord Dockett holds?"

"No," Kathe admitted.

"My little babe in the woods"—Tante Jeanne clicked her tongue sympathetically—"here you are in a country about to go to war and you pay no attention to what's going on, do you?" She got up briskly. "Well, in that case, I'll just have to take care of you. Have you got any money?"

"About twenty pounds." Kathe felt a little silly about not knowing what Cissy's husband did exactly, but she knew enough to know that if Cissy said there was going to be a German invasion, then it was very likely true. The idea, which hadn't seemed real up until now, was suddenly frightening.

"We'll book you a reservation on the boat train for tomorrow morning." Tante Jeanne walked over to the phone and called the ticket bureau but there were no reservations to be had until the eleventh—two days away. She hung up the receiver looking worried. "You could get trapped if Hitler pulls another of his Blitzkriegs," she told Kathe, "but there's not much we can do about it except drive you to Normandy, and besides the fact that we don't have a car, even if we borrowed one, I don't think you could get across the Channel any faster." Tante Jeanne shrugged her shoulders. "It seems that a lot of people are suddenly leaving France."

"It's only two days," Kathe said bravely. She tried to tell herself that nothing important could possibly happen in two days.

"True"—Tante Jeanne nodded—"it's only two days." Her face relaxed slightly and she impulsively came up and gave Kathe a hug. "And it will be good to have you here for a bit longer. So the only thing left for us to do is not to worry between now and then." Tante Jeanne smiled and it was like sunlight breaking through an overcast sky. She had a way of controlling her moods that, from Kathe's perspective, was practically awe-inspiring. "And now," Tante Jeanne said, "I've got another message for you. Guess who called? Henri Lagarde. He wants you to go on a picnic with him tomorrow."

"Henri wants me to go on a *picnic?*"

"I can tell he's completely *fou d'amour.*" Tante Jeanne winked. "The boy's falling in love with you, so watch out for him."

"Henri couldn't be falling in love with me," Kathe protested, embarrassed. "Why he hardly knows me."

Tante Jeanne shook her head. "What you know about men, *cherie,* I could put in my thimble and still have room for my finger."

The next day, sixty kilometers from Paris, at precisely two-thirty in the afternoon, Henri Lagarde kissed Kathe Rothe. Kathe always remembered the exact time because it was her first real kiss, and she had just happened to look at her watch a few seconds earlier because she wanted to make sure they got back to Paris in time for her to pack. They were sitting on a blanket spread out on the grass near a pond that was half covered with water lilies. They had just finished a picnic lunch of crusty bread, creamy cheese, a white wine that had tasted like grapefruit, and the cheese pie Tante Jeanne had made for them, a fat crusty concoction with bacon and onions. Kathe was looking at the shiny green leaves of the lilies spread out on the surface of the water when, all at once, without warning, Henri stopped right in the middle of a sentence and kissed her. It was a long, hard kiss that practically took her breath out of her body, and she could taste the tartness of the wine on Henri's lips and that made it seem even more exciting and abandoned. Kathe immediately thought of a perfume ad she had once seen: a woman with her hands still lingering on the keys of a piano swept up in the arms of a man who had all but dropped his violin, kissing her with forbidden kisses (because you could just tell that her husband or father or whoever was in the next room). It was probably strange to think of a perfume ad while you were getting your first kiss, but that's the way modern life was, Kathe decided. You read about everything before you experienced it.

Henri pulled away suddenly. "I'm sorry," he said. "I shouldn't have done that."

"Why not?" Kathe asked, licking her lips thoughtfully. Having been kissed once, she was eager to try it again.

Henri stared at the pond, not meeting her eyes. His face was flushed, and he looked as uncomfortable as Kathe could ever remember a man looking. She followed his gaze. A turtle was sunning itself on a rock, and under the water Kathe could see the long shadows of fish. "You're too young," Henri said in a low voice.

"I am not." Kathe was offended at the idea that he was taking her for a child. "I've been kissed before, you know."

"You have?"

"Loads of times." She neglected to tell him that the kisses had never strayed below her forehead. "By lots of boys."

Henri looked encouraged by the thought. "Care to be kissed again?"

"You bet," Kathe said brashly. "Only don't stop so fast this time."

Leaning forward, Henri put his arm around her waist and drew her to him. She could feel the warmth of his body through his shirt and the soft prickles of his beard. She'd never felt a beard before; all the boys she knew were too young to grow them. Henri began to kiss her, gently pushing her backward at the same time. She felt the triangle of his tongue, the hard ridge of his teeth, the open space of his throat, and it was all very exciting. Kathe let him lay her back on the blanket. Her arms and legs felt tepid and limp, as if they had suddenly been filled with warm water. She kissed him back enthusiastically and a tingling sensation began to move up the backs of her legs.

Henri was breathing hard. He kissed her again and again, and then, all at once, he stuck his hand into her blouse and began to fondle her breasts. Kathe felt her nipples harden and she was overwhelmed with a desire to get even closer to him. Arching her back, she pressed against Henri, lost in his kisses. His hands kept working at her breasts and she began to lose track of everything but the feel of him against her. Overhead the sky was a milky blue. She could see the black limbs of a tree, hundreds of white apple blossoms and tiny green buds.

Henri took his hand out of her blouse and Kathe decided, with regret, that he'd gotten tired of touching her breasts, but then Henri probably did this sort of thing all the time, so it probably wasn't as exciting for him as it was for her.

"*Je t'aime*," Henri whispered.

Kathe wasn't sure if an answer was expected so she decided not to say anything and just go on with the kissing. She was fairly sure that she didn't love Henri, at least not with the kind of love you read about in books, but she certainly liked the way he was kissing her. She let her mouth drift into his, and a tiny moan involuntarily escaped her lips. Henri seemed to take the moan as a signal. Putting his hand on Kathe's leg, he slid it quickly up under her skirt.

"What are you doing?" Kathe sat up, embarrassed and confused. She pulled down her skirt and glared at Henri.

"Making love to you, *cherie*," Henri stammered.

"Well I didn't like that last part."

Henri stood up, went over to the apple tree, and gave it a good solid kick. "I knew you were too young," he said grumpily.

"Maybe we had just better go home." Kathe put on her shoes and picked up her sweater. She felt suddenly deflated, as if somehow the afternoon were wrecked and it had been her fault.

Henri came back, sat down beside her on the blanket, poured out what was left of the wine, and drank it in a single gulp. "Look," he said, "I'm sorry. I really am. I got carried away. You're very beautiful, you know."

"I am?" Kathe examined the grass stains on the palms of her hands and wondered how anyone could call her beautiful.

"Do me a favor," Henri pleaded. "Don't tell your Tante Jeanne about this or she'll tell my mother and Maman will give me one of her famous three-day lectures."

"Certainly," Kathe said generously. "I wouldn't think of telling." She grinned, her sense of humor restored at the thought of Henri being scolded by his mother like a little boy. "Besides," she admitted, "I liked the kissing part just fine."

Henri leaned over and gave her a chaste kiss on the nose. "So we're friends?"

"Of course," Kathe nodded. "No hard feelings."

Henri rose unsteadily to his feet. "I think I should take you home now," he told her. He was obviously rather drunk. He looked at Kathe strangely and she wondered if he was going to start leaping in her direction again. "Maybe when you're older . . ." He didn't finish the sentence.

"Maybe what when I'm older?"

"Maybe you'll come back to France," Henri said sadly. Kathe could tell that he really did care about her. Henri put on his jacket and began to pick up the picnic things, stuffing the leftovers into the saddlebags of his motorcycle, folding the blanket into a pillow for Kathe to sit on. He helped her climb onto the seat and position her feet on the pegs. When he tried to start the motorcycle, he nearly knocked it over.

"Are you sure you can drive?" Kathe asked, feeling a little worried. She looked at the chrome handlebars of the motorcycle, at the two narrow tires and the polished chain guard.

Henri assured her that there was no problem, that he could drive the motorcycle in his sleep if he had to. "The only thing intoxicating around here," he said gallantly as he kicked the engine to a start, "is you, my dear."

From the back of Henri's motorcycle the French countryside seemed to dip and sway and then right itself. Kathe hung on to

Henri's waist feeling exhilarated and a little frightened as they took the curves one after another, smoothly and a shade too quickly. Wheat and cows blurred together, the thatched houses were like ratchets, bobbing up along the hedgerows and then sinking back into oblivion. A château with a gray slate roof appeared for a moment in front of them in the distance and then slid to the left and out of the line of Kathe's vision like a block of gelatin on a tilted plate. She felt Henri's body shift with the weight of the cycle and she tried to move along with him. It's like a dance, she thought, like a dance on two wheels, with Henri leading and me trying not to do anything clumsy to upset things.

She was booked on the boat train for eight the next morning, and by this time tomorrow she'd be in London. Kathe was just thinking about this and about how good it was going to be to see Mama again, when all of a sudden she felt the motorcycle heave sharply to the right. Clutching at Henri, Kathe looked up in time to see a stone fence coming straight at them. She opened her mouth to yell to Henri to look out, but there wasn't enough time. With a sickening crunch, the front wheel of the motorcycle collided with the stones and Kathe was thrown up in the air in a long arc. It was a terrifying flight and she must have screamed, but later there was no memory of the moment her head hit the ground, only a blinding pain and then unconsciousness.

There was a sudden silence, broken only by the croaking of a few frogs. After a minute or two, Henri opened his eyes and discovered that he was flat on his back looking up at the sky. He lay for a moment in the muddy ditch, dazed and confused. Above him he could see the wheel of the motorcycle spinning, the spokes flashing in the afternoon sunlight.

Henri took a deep breath and it burned in his chest, making him wince. I must have broken a rib, he thought. Staggering to his feet, he looked around for Kathe, and to his horror he saw her stretched out on the grass about ten meters away. The blue skirt of her dress was muddied and torn and there was blood all over her face.

"Kathe," he yelled, but Kathe didn't move. My God, he thought, I've killed her. Ignoring the burning pain in his side, he limped over to Kathe, knelt beside her, and felt frantically for her pulse but couldn't find it. Kathe's skin was clammy and her arm was limp and boneless.

Henri dropped Kathe's hand and contemplated her body with disbelief. She was dead. He'd murdered her on his damn motorcycle. He looked over at the hateful machine, twisted and crushed like a giant insect, the shiny chrome handlebars protruding from the mud. He'd been a fool ever to take her on it; she was such a beautiful girl, good and delicate and kind and he would never forgive himself for this terrible waste of her life. Henri hadn't cried since he was a small boy, but putting his face in his hands, he began to sob with grief and guilt. After a few seconds he got control of himself again. Wiping his nose on the back of his hand, he looked around, glad that no one had witnessed this moment of weakness.

Turning back to Kathe, he bent over her and gave her a farewell kiss on the forehead. He was just about to pick her up in his arms and take her body to the police or somewhere—he hadn't exactly figured that part of it out—when Kathe made a small sound.

Henri stared at her, stunned. She wasn't dead. *Mon Dieu*, the girl was alive. Henri felt almost crazy with happiness at the thought. Putting his ear to Kathe's chest, he listened for her heartbeat and found it this time, weak but steady. She was alive but unconscious. Of course. What a fool he'd been not to realize that in the first place. Henri sat back, so relieved that he almost felt ill. The rational part of his mind, which seemed to have been partially paralyzed by the accident, gradually began to function again. It was a good thing he hadn't moved her, he thought. When you moved people who had been hurt, sometimes you hurt them more. Henri tried to remember what you were supposed to do in a case like this, but he drew a blank. There was something about elevating the feet. Gently turning Kathe over on her back, he placed several stones under her feet and added his jacket for padding. Then he recalled that you were also supposed to keep accident victims warm. The blanket he and Kathe had picnicked on was lying in a wad next to the motorcycle. Retrieving it, Henri spread it over Kathe, tucking it under her to keep her off the wet ground as much as possible. He examined her closely and decided that he had done as much as he could. The wound in her scalp had stopped bleeding of its own accord, and now that he had straightened out her skirt and covered her up, she appeared to be resting peacefully.

The road was infrequently traveled so there was no use waiting for a car to come along. He had a vague memory of having passed a farmhouse not long before the accident. He'd go back to the farm, he decided, and get help. If they had a telephone, he'd call a doctor. Then he'd get the farmer to hitch up the cart and come get Kathe. Maybe the farmer would even own a car or a truck. Peasants owned things like that these days, especially the rich ones.

Getting to his feet, he limped away, turning back several times to reassure himself that Kathe was still lying quietly under the blanket. The road was hot and dusty, rutted with old wheel tracks and littered with small sharp stones. After a few minutes it was all he could do to concentrate on walking. His broken rib hurt more with every step he took and frequently he had to come groaning to a stop and steady himself for a few moments on a fence or tree trunk while the pain subsided.

The farmhouse proved to be less than a kilometer away from the site of the accident, but it probably took him at least forty minutes to get there. When he finally turned into the farm yard, past the familiar mound of manure and clucking chickens, he was so exhausted that if it hadn't been for the thought of Kathe lying injured in that field, he would have stopped at the barn, found a pile of hay, and collapsed.

The house was constructed of stone, half thatched and half roofed in the modern fashion, whitewashed so that it appeared almost unbearably bright in the afternoon sunlight. Henri shaded his eyes and looked around but there was no one in sight. A deserted swing rocked gently in the wind under a tall tree, and two geese lay complacently in the dust in front of the door.

"Hello," Henri called out, "is anyone home? Hello, there's been an accident." There was no answer. Now that was strange. The farmer might have been out in the field, but usually in these places the women of the family were around, cooking and tending the animals and children. If it had been Sunday, they might all have been at Mass, but it wasn't Sunday.

Henri took a few more steps and stopped to listen. He now distinctly heard the sound of a radio issuing from the open windows. Odd, he thought, very odd. What's a peasant family doing listening to the radio on a fine, sunny day like this? Walking up to the door of the house, he tried it and found it open. Inside it was dark and cool and it took a minute for his eyes to adjust. There was a rustling sound and Henri saw that in the far corner three women and a man were standing in stunned silence, looking at a small radio from which the voice he had heard was issuing. The man, a farmer, was dressed in wooden clogs and a mud-splattered blue smock. Incongruously, he held a rake in his hand, as if he had hurried in from the barn without bothering to put it aside. An older woman, whom Henri took to be his wife, stood with her arms around two girls who were obviously her daughters. The man's face was solemn and all three women looked as if they had been crying.

"Excuse me," Henri said, "there's been an accident down the road and—"

"Germany's invaded Belgium and Holland, monsieur," the farmer interrupted, turning abruptly to face Henri.

"What?" Henri stared at him, dumbfounded.

Patriotic music suddenly issued from the radio. The farmer's wife drew her daughters closer. She looked at Henri, her plain, work-worn face streaked with tears. "The Germans will never beat us, monsieur," she said simply. "*Vive la France.*"

19

Kathe woke to the sound of the short-wave radio, a low trilling hum that she hoped to God couldn't be heard by the neighbors. With a sigh of resignation, she sat up in bed and waited for the noise to stop. If it had been any ordinary sound keeping her awake, she would have spoken to Tante Jeanne about it, but in theory she wasn't even supposed to know that the radio existed—part of Tante Jeanne's plan to protect her from the consequences if the Germans discovered it.

Reaching out in the darkness, Kathe fumbled for a light. The tiny guest room was stuffy and hot, as tightly sealed as a canvas bag, all the summer breezes and every ray of moonlight excluded by the heavy blue curtains that hung at the windows. Finding the switch, she turned on a small lamp and looked at the clock. It was almost 3:00 A.M. She wondered how long Tante Jeanne had been at the radio. Less than five minutes, probably; it was dangerous to be on the air much longer than that. The Germans were spending a lot of time and energy trying to trace these clandestine broadcasts.

Leaning forward, Kathe listened intently for footsteps, voices, car doors closing, any warning of a raid, but the only sound was the whistle of the radio. Wiping the perspiration off of her forehead, she ran her fingers through her hair. At the hospital they had shaved a small part of her head so they could bandage the wound in her scalp and she was still a little self-conscious about her looks. Not that it mattered all that much what she looked like these days, considering that her desire for attention from the opposite sex was at an all-time low.

Kathe poured herself a glass of water from a cut-glass carafe and took a long, slow drink. The water was tepid and slightly stale, like the air in the room. As she drank she found herself thinking about Henri. Henri was nice enough, but she no longer cherished any romantic notions about him. In the past few weeks he had probably brought her a hundred francs' worth of flowers with an apologetic air that made her feel sorry for him, but as for feeling anything else— well, when a man has managed to bring your head into collision with a stone wall, it rather dampens your passion for him. A vase of those flowers was wilting in the summer heat at this very moment, peering out of the shadows at her from the far corner of the room: roses and tulips and a burst of baby's breath that gave off a heady, sweet scent mixed with the odor of slow decay.

Kathe was becoming conscious of a dull pain in her temples. For a moment she sat absolutely still, trying to convince herself that she wasn't going to get another one of the headaches that had plagued her ever since the accident, but the slow throbbing in her temples persisted like a drum being beaten in time to her heart. Damn it, she thought, not again.

The worst part about that stupid motorcycle accident was that it had trapped her here in Paris and made her useless into the bargain. Kathe thought of the days following the collision when she had drifted in and out of consciousness. Even when she'd finally come back to reality to discover that the Germans had invaded France and the whole world was at war, she had been seized by sudden bouts of vertigo and blackouts that had made it hard for her to sit up, much less travel. If it hadn't been for those blackouts, she and Tante Jeanne could have simply gotten into a car and driven to Spain, and by now they'd both be safe in London. At the very least she could have been doing something useful instead of lying in bed while everyone else was out risking their lives. Kathe suddenly felt a lump of homesickness in her throat and had a silly urge to cry. She missed Mama badly; she wanted to be back in London, well and safe, instead of lying here awake in this oven of a city with a splitting headache waiting for the Gestapo to break down the door.

Now that was a melodramatic thought if she'd ever had one. Kathe ordered herself to relax, but between the sound of the radio and the throbbing in her temples, it wasn't easy. Her thoughts kept drifting back to the events of the past few weeks. She thought of all the things she wasn't supposed to know about: the secret group Henri and his friends had formed to get information to the Free French in London, the whispered phone calls, the downed British flyer who had been staying with Madame Lagarde, Henri's mother, while the group tried to think of some way to smuggle him out of France.

What incredible risks they're all taking, she thought. It's almost as if they're making up being spies as they go along. How in the world are they going to keep from being caught by the Germans? Kathe thought of Henri again, of Madame Lagarde, of Tante Jeanne and the old woman who ran the religious artifacts shop who she suspected was acting as their letter drop, and any possibility of sleep disappeared in a new wave of anxiety. None of them had any sense. In a way that was brave and wonderful, and if she'd been reading about all this in a novel, she would have probably thought it romantic, but lying here in the dark she found their blind heroism frightening. Everyone she cared about in Paris seemed to be running recklessly toward the edge of a cliff, urging each other on with cries of "*Vive la France.*"

In the next room the radio suddenly gave out a final sigh and then ceased, and all at once it was so silent that Kathe could hear herself breathing. Tante Jeanne's footsteps echoed in the hallway as she made her way wearily back to her own bedroom. I wish I didn't know so much, Kathe thought with a shiver, and yet . . . The thought floated up unbidden from the bottom of her mind that even though she was frightened, she had never felt so alive.

About four days later Madame Lagarde showed up unexpectedly at the apartment. Madame Lagarde was a soft, dreamy sort of woman with comfortable hips, a small mustache, and short fleshy hands that often made Kathe wonder how she could have produced a son as handsome as Henri. Yet despite her look of lazy self-indulgence, Madame Lagarde was brilliantly efficient, a true patriot, and per-haps—with the possible exception of Tante Jeanne—the most sensible of the entire group.

She was accompanied by two worried-looking people: a man whom Kathe recognized as André Buisson, the young playwright who had been writing anti-Nazi tracts for the group's clandestine printing press, and a small chic woman who was dressed head to foot in green: green hat, green dress, green shoes, even green-tinted silk stockings. Kathe, who was sitting at the table putting together a jigsaw puzzle, dropped a handful of pieces and stared at the woman so hard that later it made her blush to think how star-struck she must have looked. The woman, Mathilde Chaillet, was an actress from the Comédie-Française and her face was plastered on every kiosk in Paris. Having a mother as famous as Viola Kessler should have made a person indifferent to such things, but Kathe was so excited by the thought that she was actually under the same roof with Madame Chaillet that she impulsively rose to her feet, managing somehow to knock the entire puzzle onto the parquet floor. The pieces made a terrible rattling sound and Madame Lagarde looked around quickly to find Kathe on her hands and knees scrabbling to pick them up.

"The girl should leave the room," Madame Lagarde told Tante Jeanne. "She shouldn't hear this."

Kathe was so embarrassed, she could have sunk through the floor. Mumbling apologies, she hurried out of the room, still clutching pieces of that stupid puzzle in her fist.

Sitting down on her bed, she put her hot cheeks in her hands and tried to convince herself that everyone was a fool once in a while and that Mathilde Chaillet was so famous she probably hadn't even noticed someone as unimportant as a sixteen-year-old girl. On the other side of the door she could hear low voices rising and falling. A serious conversation of some sort was in progress, not that that was anything new. People were always arriving at all hours of the day and night to have long, whispered conversations with Tante Jeanne. Kathe picked up a book and tried to read, but the voices distracted her. She was curious about why Mathilde Chaillet was sitting in Tante

Jeanne's living room. Except for attending an occasional play, Tante Jeanne had no connection with the French theater, so obviously this mysterious visit must have something to do with the group.

Kathe realized she was tempted to eavesdrop. Now that was a ridiculous thought. Madame Lagarde had sent her out of the room to protect her. Kathe turned a page in her book and looked at it without seeing it. A musical female voice drifted in from the other room, full, rich, and operatic. Mathilde Chaillet was speaking like a woman unaccustomed to secrecy. Kathe heard the words *terrible danger*, the words *life and death*. That was too much, even for her. Dropping her book softly onto the mattress, she tiptoed into the hall and pressed her ear against the living-room door.

"You have to do something to stop this." Mathilde Chaillet leaned forward, her eyes glowing with passionate intensity. Under the brim of her green hat the actress' small, pretty face appeared flushed with excitement, like some exotic rosy blossom. "I plead with you as French patriots. I beg you. The most terrible consequences could ensue. Dozens of lives are at stake at the Comédie-Française alone. If the Nazis even began to suspect that—"

"No details for heaven's sake," Madame Lagarde interrupted, holding up her hand. "Have some sense of discretion. Anyone could be a police informer, even me."

"But the head of the Reichs Theater Chamber is going to be here in *two days*," Mathilde protested, "two days. *Mon Dieu*, I'd be discreet if I had time, but I don't have the time."

"You're sure it's Friedrich Hoffman they're sending?" Jeanne asked in a tight voice.

"We're absolutely sure," André Buisson replied. He was a good-looking boy with quick green eyes who had an awkward habit of shrugging his shoulders when he got excited about something. "Madame Chaillet's sources are impeccable. It seems all those patriotic demonstrations—the spontaneous singing of the 'Marseillaise,' Edith Piaf appearing wrapped in the tricolor, that near riot last week when Pétain's name was mentioned onstage—have got the Nazis stirred up. Hoffman's being sent here with orders to root out subversive activities in the French theater. That means the Jews, of course, but not only the Jews. I don't mean to be melodramatic, ladies, but once this Hoffman starts poking around in the theater, he'll trace those anti-Nazi flyers we've been handing out with the playbills straight to our door."

"This Herr Hoffman's coming to Paris from Berlin to conduct a *purge*," Mathilde said. "He'll have people in the theater arrested and questioned and some of them will break down and tell him what he wants to know." Her voice wavered. "He's a ruthless man."

"I know," Jeanne said grimly.

"You must *do* something," Mathilde insisted.

"Frankly," Madame Lagarde demurred, "we don't have the apparatus to do anything. We're not some kind of underground army, madame."

"We can't help you." Jeanne shook her head. "It's impractical."

"Impractical! Am I talking to French patriots or am I talking to a pack of cowards?"

"I'm sorry you feel that way about it," Madame Lagarde said sharply.

Mathilde rose to her feet, shoving back her chair. She picked up her purse and stood confronting them. *"Bon soir, mesdames."* Her voice dripped with contempt. "The French theater will take care of itself." She walked out, slamming the door behind her.

There was a long silence. André Buisson coughed. "Well," he said quietly, "what now?"

"Is Chaillet out of earshot?" Madame Lagarde asked.

"Yes."

"Then I say we have only one choice." Madame Lagarde paused. "We have to stop this Hoffman somehow."

"But how?" Jeanne asked.

"Kill him," André Buisson suggested in a low voice.

"You can't be serious."

"I'm completely serious. As far as I'm concerned, he's a criminal who deserves execution."

"But if we kill him," Jeanne protested, "what good would it do? Be reasonable, André. They'd only send someone else in his place, and the repression would be worse than ever. I happen to read history—it's a hobby of mine. Do you know what happened when the Party of the People's Freedom assassinated the Tsar of Russia in the 1880s? They were exterminated to the last man, that's what happened."

"If you're afraid to get involved, then leave it up to me."

"I don't think Jeanne is talking about a lack of courage," Madame Lagarde interposed. "I think she's talking about having some common sense, André."

"The hell with common sense. I say we should make the Germans pay, show them that they can't come in here and screw around with us."

"Lower your voice, for God's sake," Jeanne pleaded.

"If we shot Hoffman, it would be a symbolic act," André insisted. "It would give people something to rally around."

"We can't afford symbolic acts, André," Madame Lagarde said sharply. "Don't be a hothead."

"I say we should shoot Hoffman."

"And I say we should distract him, play for time, put him off the scent."

André snorted with impatience. "Just how do you propose to do that, eh?"

"That," Jeanne said, "is what we have to work out. So if you'll just sit down and be reasonable, we can get on with the discussion."

Kathe had heard far too much. Taking her ear away from the door, she retreated quickly back into the guest room.

Friedrich Hoffman liked Paris. He liked the wide boulevards, the soft serpentine grace of the Seine, the Opera, where French angels of ambiguous gender presided over the muses of music, art, and drama, but most of all Friedrich liked the idea that Paris now belonged to the Reich. Once, at the age of fourteen, he had accompanied an aunt to France to see a specialist in some female disease or other, and when the two of them had arrived in Paris, dusty and exhausted, Friedrich had been overwhelmed by the beauty of the city, which seemed so feminine compared to anything he had seen in Germany. He and his aunt had spent a long afternoon visiting the Louvre, and it was there that Friedrich, intimidated by the endless rooms of great paintings, and humiliated by the thought that he knew so little about European culture, had decided to become an artist.

Now, as Friedrich sat in a box in the Théâtre du Cours watching a performance of *Antigone,* he had a sense of having returned in triumph. Those paintings in the Louvre belonged to Germany now, as did Notre Dame, Sainte Chapelle, and even that decadent bit of ill-conceived *Kitsch*, the Eiffel Tower. Friedrich Hoffman, who had once walked down the boulevards feeling small and inferior, was now Herr Friedrich Hoffman, head of the Reichs Theater Chamber, and he could ride in state past the Arc de Triomphe in his own private car and admire the swastika flying from the flag pole.

Filled with a pleasant sense of his own power, Friedrich smiled archly at his companion of the evening, the Countess de Beauville, a beautiful woman of thirty-two whose ash-blond hair sported a tiara of diamonds, any one of which would have supported Friedrich for a year in his struggling artist days. The Countess smiled back and fanned herself coquettishly with her program. After the performance, Friedrich thought, he would take her back to his suite and sleep with her and then summarily dismiss her. Because she was a collabora-tionist, he had nothing but contempt for the Countess, but because she was beautiful he desired her, and what he desired these days, he took.

"I will resist you, and your tyranny," Antigone was telling King Creon in a loud, rather melodramatic voice. The actress had turned to address her speech to the audience, a stance that Friedrich found rather annoying. "I will follow my conscience; you can arrest me, torture me, even kill me, but where I fall, a thousand others will rise in my place."

Really, Friedrich thought, the French were so unsubtle sometimes. How in the world did they imagine that anyone with a particle of sense wouldn't understand that this play was a thinly disguised call to resistance? *A thousand others will rise in my place,* indeed. Not if the Reichs Theater Chamber had anything to say about it, they wouldn't. Friedrich consulted his program once again to check the name of the idiot who had made this so-called translation of the Greek classic. Probably a Jew, Friedrich thought; it would take a Jew to do something so perverse as this mutilation of Sophocles. Well, he would simply have to have this fellow arrested, along with the actress who was playing Antigone, the director, and the theater manager, unless the manager agreed to avoid such trash in the future. Then he would have to get to the bottom of these scurrilous anti-Nazi tracts that were being passed out with the playbills. Friedrich had been commended by Goebbels for the way he had cleaned up the Austrian and Polish theaters, and he planned to do an equally thorough job with the French. With a little luck it should take no more than a few weeks, not that he was in any hurry to leave Paris.

The play continued as the actors harangued the audience with ill-disguised patriotic fervor. Ultimately Antigone committed suicide, which as far as Friedrich was concerned should have been a lesson to anyone planning resistance but which probably wasn't, judging by the reaction of the audience. When the final curtain fell, people rose to their feet clapping and yelling. In the balcony women were crying openly and Friedrich's ears were assaulted by distinct cries of *"Vive la France!"*

This was intolerable. Friedrich sat stonelike and unmoving, staring at the stage and making plans.

"A terrible play," the Countess de Beauville laughed nervously as they walked out into the warm August evening. "Really, if one must perform *Antigone*, Euripides' version is so much more *cheerful*."

"Ah"—Friedrich smiled at her condescendingly—"but then you must understand that this kind of performance is symptomatic." He smiled a second time at the beautiful, lavishly dressed women and uniformed German officers who stood on the steps of the theater, waiting to flutter in his aura like moths about a light. It was pleasant to hold court this way, to be the object of flattering compliments, to be able to count on rapt attention whenever he spoke. The Nazi elite of Paris were here, and for the moment at least, he was the conqueror of the conquerors.

"What do you mean 'symptomatic'?" a pretty redheaded French-woman asked in a tone of hushed awe.

Friedrich waved at the Théâtre du Cours, taking in the gilded tips of the iron balconies, the stone cherubs, and wreaths of limestone laurels. "The French theater is rotten with Jewish decadence and cultural Bolshevism and as a result it concentrates on death instead of life, sickness instead of health." For five or six minutes Friedrich spoke without interruption, holding forth in a brilliant, twisted way on what he repeatedly called "cultural cancers." "A theatrical perfor-mance is meant to bring joy to the people," he concluded, "and when it brings suffering instead then it's bacteria which, like all dangerous organisms, should be eradicated."

When he stopped speaking he had the gratifying sense that if he had been on the stage, he would have been applauded. The Countess de Beauville licked her lower lip as if she had just tasted something sweet and intoxicating.

"He's a genius," the little redhead exclaimed breathlessly.

Friedrich dismissed the compliment with a modest wave of his hand. "I'd be happy to discuss this in more detail, my friends, but the hour is late." He took the Countess' arm. "Come along, my dear," he said. The walk down the steps of the theater to the waiting Mercedes had something of a processional quality to it, Friedrich and the Countess in front, the others following docilely behind, voicing their regrets that Herr Hoffman had to depart so early.

Friedrich stepped to the sidewalk and began to walk toward the curb. He saw his chauffeur throw open the door of the car with a flourish and snap to attention, and then, out of the corner of his eye, he saw the young man on the bicycle. The man was wearing a black beret and a black leather jacket and he was riding rapidly up the street, crouched forward, legs pumping. Bicycles were common on the streets of Paris these days, since gasoline rationing had been imposed, but there was something about this one that struck a discordant note. As the bicyclist approached he suddenly reached inside his jacket. Instinctively, Friedrich stepped back, but he was a fraction of a second too late. The man drew out a gun and fired straight at Friedrich three times. Friedrich felt a horrible pain in his arm. The Countess screamed. He clutched at her and fell to the pavement, leaving a long smear of blood on her white satin dress. *The bastards have killed me*, he thought. Somewhere in the midst of the pain he heard the satisfying sound of his bodyguards' machine guns barking into action.

The night of the shooting of the head of the Reichs Theater Chamber became famous in the annals of newly born French Resistance as the night of the first great Gestapo sweep of Paris. As chance would have it, Karl Oberg, head of the Gestapo in France, had been standing on the steps of the Théâtre du Cours not more than ten meters behind Friedrich when the shots rang out. After chewing out the bodyguards for killing the assassin (who might very well have been persuaded to talk), Oberg walked over to the corpse sprawled in the gutter by the overturned bicycle and personally searched through the dead man's pockets. He hadn't expected to find anything useful, but to his surprise he came up with a small stub of green cardboard that had been caught in the lining of the man's jacket.

Oberg looked contemptuously at the stub, which was clearly imprinted with the words "Comédie-Française: Complimentary Pass." With a lead like this, his men would probably be able to come up with the identity of the assassin. Behind him, two French doctors who had been in the audience were frantically attending to Friedrich, who lay bleeding on the pavement, but the death or survival of Herr Hoffman was not Oberg's concern. As head of the Gestapo in France, he felt personally humiliated by this blatant attack, committed in his very presence.

What idiots, Oberg thought. Disgusted at the amateurishness of the attempt, he handed the stub to his aide.

"Find out who gets free passes to the Comédie-Française," he ordered. Oberg paused for a moment. "And search the premises of anyone else who's given us the slightest reason to suspect them of anything, no matter how minor."

The aide snapped to attention. "Yes, sir," he said. "At once, sir."

"I don't care if you have to put half of Paris in jail." Oberg looked disdainfully at the dead assassin. "The time for playing games is over."

Kathe was sound asleep in Tante Jeanne's guest room, curled up around a pillow, dreaming of London. In her dream she was walking through Trafalgar Square with Mama and they were feeding the pigeons when suddenly a knocking woke her. Kathe sat bolt upright in bed. Caught in the seam between waking and sleeping, she wasn't sure for a few blank seconds where she was.

"*Open up in there*," a voice barked in French. "*Police*." My God, Kathe thought, it's the Gestapo. Her first thought was to escape through the open window, but it was a five-story drop down to the street. The knocking increased in volume; Kathe sat frozen in panic, not knowing what to do. She heard the sound of Tante Jeanne hurrying to the door.

"*Jeanne Dufour?*"

"*Yes?*" Tante Jeanne's voice was tight with fear.

"I have orders to search your apartment."

"But, monsieur—"

"Stand to one side." Kathe heard the sound of boots pounding on the parquet floor. Suddenly her bedroom door was thrown open, and a blinding beam of light caught her full in the face. She put up her hands in defense, blinking and terrified.

"There's a girl in here." someone said in German.

"Well, bring her out."

"Please," Kathe begged. Somehow there was an added horror to the fact that she couldn't see the man behind the flashlight. A rough hand grabbed her by the shoulder.

"Up, you," he ordered in broken French. Kathe was jerked roughly out of bed and pushed across the bedroom into the hall. In the living room the front door was standing open. Tante Jeanne stood next to it, facing a large man in a brown suit; she was barefoot and in her nightgown and she looked frightened. A German soldier in the dreaded black uniform of the SS was training a machine gun on her, while two others were searching the apartment, slashing pillows with their bayonets, pulling out drawers and dumping the contents onto the floor, even inspecting the blank backs of the pieces of Kathe's jigsaw puzzles. Kathe thought of the radio concealed behind the bathroom wall and felt sick with fear.

"Who are you?" the man in the brown suit demanded, pushing Kathe into a chair. He was large and red-faced, his French perfect, without a trace of an accent. "There's only one person legally registered to occupy this apartment."

"Leave the girl alone," Tante Jeanne pleaded. "She's my niece, visiting me from Arles, and she's just a child."

The man shot Kathe a look that made her want to curl up with humiliation. She tugged at the hem of her nightdress, trying to cover herself. "She doesn't look like a child to me," he said.

Tante Jeanne made a motion as if to come over to Kathe, but the soldier with the machine gun stopped her by poking the barrel into her chest. One of the soldiers gave the Nazi salute and handed the man in the brown suit a packet of stamped papers that Kathe, with a sinking feeling, recognized as the ones Tante Jeanne had bought for her a few weeks ago. The man inspected the papers and then thrust them in Tante Jeanne's face. "Do you expect me to be fooled by these clumsy forgeries?" he yelled. "The girl isn't any more French than I am. So I ask you one more time, who is she?"

"Her name is Marie Rollan and she's a French citizen," Tante Jeanne insisted stubbornly. The man reached out and slapped Tante Jeanne brutally across the mouth. "One more lie, and I shoot you."

"I'm Kathe Rothe," Kathe yelled, "and you can stop hitting her because I'm an American citizen, so you might as well hit me instead." She tried to sound brave but her voice was shaking and all she could think of was Tante Jeanne, whom she couldn't bear to see that man beating, and the radio concealed in the bathroom, which by some miracle they hadn't found yet.

"So you're an American citizen, are you?" The man thrust his face into hers, his eyes gleaming with triumph. "What are you doing here in Paris?"

"I was visiting," Kathe stammered, "and I got caught when the war broke out."

"You can tell a better lie than that."

"It's the truth, I swear it."

"She's telling the truth," Jeanne pleaded. "I'm a family friend. She was staying with me and she got into an accident and couldn't travel."

"What kind of accident?"

"A motorcycle accident." Kathe could hear the soldiers searching her bedroom. In a minute they'd be in the bathroom, where the radio was hidden behind the tile wall over the tub. She gazed nervously at Tante Jeanne and Tante Jeanne shot her a warning look.

The man in the brown suit pointed his finger at Kathe. "Get dressed," he said. "I'm taking you in."

"Please," Tante Jeanne begged, "don't arrest her. She's been sick, and she hasn't done anything, I swear it."

"Be quiet," the man said, "or I'll arrest you too." He caught Kathe by the arm and pulled her to her feet. Just then one of the soldiers entered the living room. "Find anything?" the man in the brown suit demanded.

"No." The soldier shook his head. "Just a lot of books." So they'd missed the radio. Kathe was so relieved she felt dizzy.

The man in the brown suit gestured at Kathe. "Watch her while she gets dressed," he ordered. "Sometimes these idiots hang themselves."

"I have no intention of committing suicide," Kathe protested. "Please let me get dressed by myself."

"Shut up," the man in the brown suit snapped. "You've got no choice in the matter. Now get in there and put on your clothes or I'll take you in in what you're wearing."

"Do what he says, Kathe," Tante Jeanne pleaded. "Just do what he says for God's sake."

Crimson with embarrassment, Kathe went into her bedroom and got dressed in front of the young soldier, who stared at her all the while. Her hands were shaking so hard that she could hardly do up the buttons on her dress. She tried not to think about what being under arrest by the Gestapo meant, but visions of prison cells and torture kept running through her mind. I know too much, she thought. Her mouth went dry with fear. She bent over, pretending to adjust her shoe, trying to hide her face from the soldier, knowing it must have guilt written all over it. I shouldn't have listened at the door; I shouldn't have been so curious. Tante Jeanne tried to protect me but . . .

"Hurry up." The man in the brown suit appeared at the door. "We haven't got all night."

In the living room Tante Jeanne was standing where Kathe had left her, looking white and strange. Impulsively, Kathe ran over and threw her arms around her. "I'll be all right." Kathe tried to sound optimistic, but she could hear the hollow bravado in her voice. She felt Tante Jeanne's shoulders shake and realized that this woman who was brave enough to sit up night after night sending clandestine radio messages out of France was crying.

Tante Jeanne gave her a passionate hug. "I'll never forgive myself for this. Oh my God, Kathe."

"Let's go." The man in the brown suit took Kathe by the arm. There was no use trying to resist. In a daze, Kathe let him lead her out of the apartment. The street was absolutely deserted except for two police cars, which sat at the curb, motors purring. Kathe was thrust unceremoniously into the back seat of the first police car. Now, she supposed, she would be taken to Gestapo headquarters and interrogated.

She shivered although the night was hot. The man in the brown suit and one of the soldiers climbed into the front seat of the car.

Another soldier wordlessly entered the back and sat beside Kathe, gun held rigidly in front of him. As the cars pulled away from the curb, no one said a word.

The cars glided through the silent streets of Paris, past the Parc du Champ-de-Mars, across the Pont Alexandre III, with its elaborate statues staring blindly into the night. In the few weeks they'd occupied Paris, the Germans had filled the city with a snarl of white wooden street signs in their own language. Kathe read the signs and tried to steel herself for the ordeal to come, but all she could think of was the sound the man's hand had made when it struck Tante Jeanne's face. The memory of that sound put her teeth on edge and made her sick with apprehension. I'm not at all brave, she thought; I'm a coward and I don't want to die. The thought of dying brought tears to her eyes. She looked out the window at the Champs Élysées, and never had it seemed so beautiful to her. Please God, let somebody get me out of this, she prayed incoherently.

The cars stopped at the Gestapo headquarters on the Rue de Saussaies. Grabbing Kathe by the elbows, the soldiers marched her into the building and thrust her into a large, windowless room that contained several chairs, a bench, and a table. A woman was sitting on one of the chairs, her face buried in her hands. She was wearing a faded brown dress and shoes that were splitting apart at the seams. The woman looked up at Kathe and shook her head sadly. "Another one caught in the net. Ah, you poor thing." She extended her hand. "I'm Valerie Cusset," she said, "and I've been here for hours watching them come and go."

Kathe shook her hand. "How do you do," she muttered automatically.

"I'm doing as well as could be expected considering I'm terrified." Valerie pointed grimly to a bench in the corner. "But that one over there isn't doing so well."

Kathe looked in the direction she had indicated and realized that there was another woman lying on the bench, knees drawn up to her chest. The woman was dressed in what appeared to have once been a blue linen suit, although the skirt was ripped and one sleeve was pulled half off at the shoulder. The woman's body twitched almost imperceptibly.

"What's wrong with her?" Kathe went over to the woman and started to touch her and then drew back in horror. "Oh my God, she's got cigarette burns on her face."

"The Gestapo took her away and tortured her," Valerie said flatly, "and then they dumped her back in here to die. I expect they're going to do the same thing to me."

"Oh my God."

"Before she passed out she told me she hadn't talked." Valerie went over to the woman and looked at her lovingly. "She was brave."

Kathe was so frightened that she couldn't speak. She sat down on the edge of the bench and looked at the woman in the blue suit. The woman was about Mama's age. "Can't we do anything for her?" she finally managed to say.

Valerie shook her head; her eyes were bleak. "No, we can't even do anything for ourselves."

So there really was no hope. Terrified, Kathe put her face in her hands and began to cry. After a few seconds she felt Valerie put a comforting arm around her. "Go ahead and cry, girl," Valerie whispered. "I'd cry, too, if I had any tears left."

"Georges," the woman on the bench moaned. "Georges, where are you?" She turned restlessly, flailing her arms. Kathe and Valerie ran over and held her to keep her from falling to the floor. "Georges, my darling. The dinner will burn. Turn down the stove. Put the baby back to sleep."

"She's delirious," Valerie said grimly. Taking a cotton handkerchief out of her pocket, she mopped at the woman's brow.

"Georges!"

Holding the woman by the shoulders, Kathe looked into her face, horrified at what she saw there. The burns covered the woman's cheeks and forehead and most of her chin; her lips were torn and bleeding, her neck and arms terribly bruised.

"Let me go!" the woman screamed, staring at them with terrified, sightless eyes. Arching her spine, she pulled out of their grasp, quivered, and fell back. Then the panting began—low and terrible, as if she were drowning. For an hour or more Valerie and Kathe stood by helplessly as it went on and on. The woman's chest heaved, her head rolled from side to side, her breathing became faster, thicker.

"Georges . . . Madeline . . . Maman . . ."

It was unbearable to hear, terrible to watch.

Suddenly the woman sighed and relaxed. Her hands went limp, her face placid.

"She's better." Kathe stroked the woman's hand gently, afraid of waking her again.

Valerie put her ear to the woman's chest. "No," she said quietly. "She's not better. She's dead."

They folded the woman's arms across her chest and covered her face with Valerie's handkerchief. Time passed, and with every second Kathe grew more desperate and terrified.

For hours they sat with their arms around each other, speaking very little, jumping at every sound. Keys rattled in locks, doors slammed, the sound of traffic filtered in through the walls. Finally they heard footsteps; the wooden door flew open and two men in SS uniforms marched into the room, accompanied by a man in a blue work smock. One of the SS men motioned brusquely to the body on the bench. "Take that out of here," he ordered.

Hurrying forward, the man in the blue smock picked up the dead woman, threw her body over his shoulder, and left without once looking at Valerie or Kathe.

"Valerie Cusset, on your feet."

Valerie stood up and confronted them bravely, but Kathe could see she was trembling. "Good-bye, Kathe," she said. "If you get out of this place, tell my mother I love her. Her name is Madame Bernard Cusset, 86 Rue—"

"Silence." The soldier pushed the barrel of his pistol into the small of Valerie's back and shoved her out of the door, slamming it behind him.

Stunned by how quickly Valerie had been taken, Kathe went back to the table and sat down. Her head ached, her hands were shaking, and she felt as if she might be sick. She was more afraid than she had ever been in her life. She wondered what they were going to do to Valerie. She tried not to think about it.

More time passed, blank and terrible. She waited alone for what seemed like days, and then she heard footsteps again. The SS men reentered the room.

"Kathe Rothe, on your feet."

Her knees felt like jelly. She stood, clinging to the edge of the table, wondering if she was going to black out from fright. The room, which had been her prison, now seemed like an island of safety. She thought of Mama, of Tante Jeanne, of Henri. She thought about the ordinary wonderful things of life: fresh coffee, sunshine, flowers. She was only sixteen. She wanted to live to be a hundred.

"Move," the SS man commanded, sticking his pistol into the small of her back.

She moved.

The German officer sat at a large elaborately carved wooden desk, smoking a cigarette and reading a sheaf of papers in a manila folder. To his left was a silver-framed photograph of a plain-looking woman with two children. Kathe looked at the photograph, thinking that it was obscene for a man who tortured people to have such a picture on his desk. She was dizzy from fear and hunger, nauseous and desperate and terrified.

The officer finished reading and put down the folder. "Your name?" he demanded.

"Kathe Rothe."

He pursed his lips and flicked a few centimeters of ash off of his cigarette with an abrupt tap of his index finger. "It's a familiar name."

She was startled. "It is?"

"Yes." The officer inspected her closely, running his eyes across her body as if he were undressing her. "I have the feeling I've heard the name before. Can you tell me why that might be?"

"No," Kathe said, shrinking back into the chair.

"That's a pity"—the officer shook his head—"because in that case we'll have to question you until you remember."

Kathe could see he was about to return her to the guards. Terrified by the thought of what they would do to her, she tried desperately to think of a reason why her name might sound familiar to him. "My mother's a famous actress," she offered. "Very famous. She used to act sometimes under the name of Viola Rothe, although for years now she's been using her maiden name."

"Oh?" The officer looked at her with vague interest. "And what would that be?"

"Viola Kessler."

"Where does she live?"

"London."

"Kessler and Rothe are both German names. Any relatives in Germany?"

"No." Kathe thought with a shudder of her own dual citizenship, of Uncle Conrad and Aunt Angela and what the Gestapo would probably do to her if they discovered she was related to them.

"Is this famous actress mother of yours Jewish?"

"No. She's the Dowager Duchess of Sanford." She felt ashamed of herself for trying to trade on her mother's title, but she didn't have any choice. She had to keep this man from turning her over for interrogation.

The officer made some notes on a pad and then reached out and pushed a button on his intercom. Two SS guards appeared. "Take her back to the holding room," the officer ordered, gesturing toward Kathe. Without looking up, he went on writing.

The day dragged on and Kathe waited in the empty room. Around dinnertime a soldier brought her a bowl of watery soup and a hunk of bread, which she didn't have the heart to eat. Then there was more waiting, an infinity of boredom and fear. Exhausted, she tried to sleep, but the bench was hard and she kept imagining she heard footsteps. Sometimes she wondered what Tante Jeanne was doing, and sometimes she wondered what Mama would do if she never came home, but mostly she sat staring at the walls in numb desperation, waiting for the guards to return for her. Ultimately she must have dozed off, because the next thing she knew she was being startled awake by the sound of the door opening.

"Mademoiselle Rothe." The man in the brown suit stood in the doorway, flanked by two guards. "Please come with me." His tone was cordial in a way that sent chills up Kathe's spine. Rising unsteadily to her feet, she picked up her purse, not knowing what to say, but nothing seemed to be expected. The man in the brown suit led her outside to the curb, where a police car was waiting. "If you'll promise not to cause any trouble," he said, gesturing in the direction of the guards, "we can dispense with these."

"I promise," Kathe agreed weakly. She wondered what kind of trouble he imagined she could possibly cause. The man dismissed the guards and climbed in the back seat with her.

"Cigarette?" He held a gold case out to her.

"No, thank you." She sat as far away from him as she could, trying to understand what was going on. Was the Gestapo releasing her? Was she being taken to another prison? None of it made sense. They drove down the Rue du Faubourg St. Honoré, entered the Place Vendôme, and abruptly pulled to a stop. Kathe stared blankly out the window at the blue canopies and pots of orange trees. They were parked in front of the Ritz, perhaps the most famous hotel in Paris.

The man in the brown suit opened the door. "After you," he said. It wasn't a request; it was a command.

Kathe got out and stood for a moment on the cobblestones looking at the jaunty blue canopies of the hotel snapping in the wind. Surely this was some kind of cruel joke; surely in a moment he would order her into the car and drive her back to the Rue des Saussaies.

"Come along," he said, taking her by the elbow. Like a person in a dream, Kathe allowed herself to be led into the lobby of the Ritz. Luminously beautiful paintings hung on the walls, and the carpet was soft and luxurious under her feet. At the end of a hallway she could see a glassed-in porch filled with tropical plants and chairs upholstered in blue velvet. The lobby was empty except for the desk clerk, who took one look at the man in the brown suit and quickly averted his eyes. Striding across the lobby, the man stopped in front of the elevator. He saw the look of surprise cross her face and smiled in a way that made Kathe feel as if she had bitten down on an ice cube.

They took the elevator to the third floor, got off, and walked down the corridor. Pausing for a moment, the man in the brown suit extracted a small notebook from his pocket and consulted it. Then he led her to the door of Room 303. Straightening his spine as if coming to attention, he gave two crisp knocks.

"Come in," a voice commanded sharply in German. The man opened the door and Kathe found herself in a large, sunny room. A small dark-haired man with cold eyes lay on the bed, propped up with bolsters. The man's arm was in a sling and there appeared to be bandages wrapped around his chest.

"Hello, Kathe," a familiar voice said. Startled, Kathe looked past the wounded man and saw, lolling in a blue velvet armchair, none other than her step-uncle, Harry Stafford. "I suppose you're surprised to see me, aren't you?" Kathe stared at her step-uncle, too shocked by his presence to reply. Uncle Harry coughed and folded his hands self-importantly across his paunch. He was wearing a white linen suit and gleaming white spats, but his face was heavy and unclean-looking. "I said, I suppose you're surprised to see me here."

"Yes," Kathe somehow managed to say. "I am."

"Well, that's easily enough explained." Uncle Harry coughed again and twisted at the large gold ring he wore on his second finger. Kathe noticed that the ring was inset with a swastika of diamonds. "You see when the war officially broke out, a rather nasty bit of legislation called Section 18B of the Emergency Powers Act was taken out of mothballs and amended—called for the rounding up and imprison-ment of British Fascists and all that. Strictly unconstitutional, of course, but I could see that my own country no longer had a place for me so I just took French leave—literally. I slipped over to France and volunteered my services to the Germans. I'm going to do English radio broadcasts out of Berlin, try to shake some sense into our fellow countrymen." Uncle Harry nodded in the direction of the man who lay on the bed. "Herr Hoffman here has all but promised me the job, contingent on the approval of Goebbels, of course."

Kathe turned back to the man on the bed; she tried to convince herself that the name Hoffman was just a coincidence, but one look at the bandages made any such belief impossible. This was obviously Friedrich Hoffman, the head of the Reichs Theater Chamber, the man Tante Jeanne, Madame Lagarde, and André had been talking about, the one they'd said was going to conduct the purge of the French theater. This was the Friedrich Hoffman whom André Buisson had threatened to kill.

My God, she thought, looking at the sling and the medicines piled up on the night table, André tried to kill him and failed. She thought of Tante Jeanne, of the midnight raid on the apartment, of the soldiers who had dragged her away into the night. Kathe had imagined that they'd been after the radio, but this was a hundred times worse—attempted assassination of a Reich official. The consequences were unthinkable.

"Where's Tante Jeanne?" She blurted out the words before she could stop herself. "What have you done with Tante Jeanne?"

"Tante Jeanne?" Uncle Harry looked puzzled.

"She's talking about Jeanne Dufour," Herr Hoffman supplied in surprisingly good English. "Your step-niece was apparently staying at Mademoiselle Dufour's apartment when our men chanced on her." He turned to Kathe with disconcerting cordiality. "You mustn't worry about Mademoiselle Dufour. She's already been notified of your release."

"Notified of my what?"

"You've been released," Uncle Harry said, "thanks to the intervention of Herr Hoffman here. You should be thankful that you have an uncle who knows the right people."

"By the way," Herr Hoffman said with a thin, tight-lipped smile, "Madame Dufour and I are old friends. Did she ever tell you that?"

"No." Kathe looked away, not meeting his eyes. "She never did. I don't know anything." The question made a prickle of fear run down her spine, but she managed to keep her voice neutral. So she was being released, and Tante Jeanne hadn't been arrested; it was a miracle. She thought with a pang of André Buisson, who must have died without talking, and hoped his death had occurred before the Gestapo got to him.

"Well, whatever you knew or didn't know is beside the point," Uncle Harry interposed. "The point is that your mother's been a nervous wreck. I gather she sent dozens of frantic cables around the time of your accident—before communications with the Continent broke down, of course—and it was all Grants could do to keep her from coming over to France to get you." He regarded Kathe accusingly. "Really, my dear, you should have let the authorities know where you were; this silly concealment—"

"Was completely unnecessary," Herr Hoffman interrupted smoothly. "Germany may be at war with Britain, but we are not at war with the Duke of Sanford's step-niece." He paused and contemplated Kathe thoughtfully. "Actually we've had the Gestapo out looking for you ever since the Duke notified us that you were missing. Unfortunately your uncle couldn't supply your address, things between your mother and him being—as you know—strained. In any event, we're sending you back."

"Back?" Kathe stared at Herr Hoffman, praying she'd understood him correctly. There was something about the way he was crouched among the blankets and bandages that reminded her of a spider spinning a web.

"Back to England. You'll fly to Lisbon and then connect with the regular London flight." Herr Hoffman smiled again. It was a cold, mechanical smile. "You can tell your mother for us that anytime she'd like to come to Germany the door is open. A great German actress should act in her own tongue, yes?"

"And in the future, my girl," Uncle Harry warned, shaking a fat, admonishing finger, "try to stay out of trouble."

Kathe left France on the next flight to Lisbon.

Three weeks later, at one in the afternoon, Friedrich came in person to Jeanne's apartment to settle an old score.

"Go underground," Natalie Lagarde begged Jeanne on Wednesday. "It's only a matter of time before you're arrested."

"But I can't leave my patients at the hospital," Jeanne protested.

"You're a fool. I could get you forged documents. You could join the Resistance in the south."

"They let Kathe go; I'm not in any danger. André was shot before he could talk. The Gestapo isn't looking for me."

"Mathilde Chaillet has been missing for five days."

"Mathilde has a lover who lives in Chartres. She's always running off to see him."

"Jeanne, listen to me—get out of Paris."

"My patients *depend* on me, Natalie. I have responsibilities. I make three broadcasts a week to London. How long do you think it would take to install an aerial in another apartment? Not to mention the problem of moving the short-wave radio and building a hiding place for it."

"Jeanne," Natalie said grimly, "you're going to regret this decision." She sighed impatiently, picked up her shawl, and wrapped it around her large shoulders. "Henri and I are leaving tonight for the south, and I wish to God you'd come with us."

Two days passed uneventfully, and then on Friday, while Jeanne was in the middle of eating her lunch, the Gestapo came for her.

Brakes squealed and car doors slammed. Jeanne threw down the psychology journal she had been reading and ran to the window. The first thing she saw were two black cars pulled up on the sidewalk, then the German soldiers, then the guns.

She drew back from the window and stood for a moment with her back pressed to the wall, gasping with fear. She knew now that Natalie had been right—she should have gone underground.

She heard the soldiers pounding on the door, the voice of the concierge shrill with fear. She had to do something. A weapon—she needed some kind of weapon to defend herself.

Running into the bathroom, she pulled out a loose tile and opened the secret door behind the tub. The short-wave radio lay wrapped in a black cloth. Beside it was a revolver. Seizing the revolver, Jeanne stuffed it into the pocket of her dress. It was heavy and made a huge, unsightly lump. *Mon Dieu!* Why hadn't she planned something in advance! The German soldiers would see the gun the instant they walked in the door and probably shoot her on the spot if she tried to reach for it. Throwing the revolver back into the hole, Jeanne slammed shut the cover and paused for a split second to wipe her handprints from the white tiles.

She could hear the boots of the soldiers on the stairs and in seconds they would be at her door. Running out of the bathroom, she darted into the kitchen and picked up the only weapon she really knew how to use: a sharp carving knife. Holding the knife behind her back, she went into the living room and stood facing the door.

Leading the German soldiers up the stairs, Friedrich waved them to a halt and gave himself the pleasure of knocking on Jeanne's door. It wasn't a hard knock, because his arm was still sore, but it was most satisfying. She didn't answer, of course. He hadn't expected her to. Most of the time when the Gestapo came for people, they tried to pretend they weren't home. They stood in their apartments, holding their breath, as if perhaps the Germans might go away, or else they ran to their windows to escape. But no enemy of the Reich ever escaped through a window, and the Gestapo never went away.

"Try the door," Friedrich commanded, stepping aside. Sometimes there was resistance, even from the Jews, none of which was ever reported. If Jeanne were armed, Friedrich had no intention of standing in the way of a bullet. More likely, he would find her cowering in a corner.

One of the soldiers stepped forward and tried the knob.

"Locked, Herr Hoffman," he reported.

"Well," Friedrich said impatiently, "what are you waiting for?"

The soldier saluted, turned his rifle around, and slammed the butt of it against Jeanne's door. The lock gave with a splintering sound, and the door swung open. On the far side of the room, Jeanne was standing with her back to the wall. Her hair was longer than it had been in Berlin, and her face had a few extra lines in it, but Friedrich was pleased to see that she hadn't changed much. He was also pleased to see that she looked completely terrified.

"Hello, Jeanne," he said. "Remember me?"

"Friedrich!" She stared at him like he was a ghost.

"That's right. Friedrich." He clicked his heels. "At your service." He waved to the soldiers who had followed him into the apartment. "Go out in the hall," he commanded, "and wait for me there; I have some special business to attend to." Gestapo soldiers were used to "special business." They left obediently, and Friedrich shut the door. He stood for a few seconds, looking at Jeanne, savoring her fear. For twelve years he had been imagining this moment, and he had no intention of rushing it.

He smiled and helped himself to a sip of her wine. "Rather quiet, aren't you? Overwhelmed by the pleasure of seeing me again after so long a time, *Liebling?*"

"You bastard," Jeanne said in a trembling voice.

"You should try to be more pleasant," Friedrich said, putting down the empty wineglass. "Mathilde Chaillet didn't die nobly crying *'Vive la France.'* She fell all over herself telling us about your little group, about the radio in the bathroom, about your friendship with André Buisson." He took a few steps toward her. "I know everything, you see."

"*Salaud.* You murdered Joseph and Hilde."

"Hilde committed suicide, Jeanne, but what does it matter? In a few minutes you'll be on your knees begging me to set you free. You don't believe me? Well, let's review your situation. Outside that door are five soldiers with guns. One word from me and they'll take you down to the Rue des Saussaies for interrogation. Do you have any idea what that means? I see from your face that you do." He sat down in her armchair and put his boots up on her hassock. "Come here," he commanded. "We have unfinished business."

She stood rigidly, arms behind her back, glaring at him.

"Well, if you won't come to me, then I'll just have to come to you." Getting up, Friedrich strolled across the room. She shrank back as he approached her.

"Gotten shy, haven't you? You weren't so shy when you dumped me for someone else, were you? Oh no, then you were ready enough. But I think I'm going to like having you this way. Don't look so self-righteously horrified, my dear. I'm not going to rape you. I'm a civilized man. We're going to do it in comfort in your bedroom, and it's going to be the best lay you've ever had, and you're going to tell me that at least a half a dozen times." He smiled. "If you're very, very convincing, I might just decide to take you back to the Ritz for a few days."

He moved closer. He could smell her perfume now, the same brand she had worn in Berlin, and she was trembling. "Good," he said, "very good." He was getting excited. "I've waited a long time for this."

Jeanne gripped the handle of the carving knife and tried to stop shaking. She was frightened and repulsed, and the thought of him touching her made her skin crawl, but she forced herself to wait. She was going to get only one chance and she didn't want to miss. If Mathilde Chaillet had talked, there was no way she was going to get out of this alive, but she could at least take him with her.

Friedrich leaned forward and touched her lightly on the cheek, and she flinched as if he'd struck her. "Relax, my dear," he said. "We're going to do this very slowly." Putting his arm around her shoulders, he drew her to him and bent to kiss her. For a second she smelled the cloves on his breath and felt the pressure of his lips against hers, and then she drew the carving knife out from behind her back and stabbed him in the stomach as hard as she could. He screamed and reeled back, and she pursued him, stabbing him again.

"You bitch!" he yelled. "What have you done?" He fumbled for his gun and fell, clutching at the lace tablecloth. Dishes and books crashed to the floor. Throwing away the bloody knife, Jeanne stood over him, triumphant.

"*Salaud!*" she yelled, and then the German soldiers burst through the door and shot her where she stood.

Jeanne died instantly, but it took Friedrich over a week. His large intestine had been perforated, and the wound turned septic. He developed peritonitis, gangrene. On the day of his death the other patients in the ward stuffed their ears with cotton to blot out the sound of his shrieks.

"Hilde!" he screamed, clutching at his burning bowels. "Joseph! Jeanne! Put out the fire!" At the end he died in such terror that the French nurses whispered to each other that the head of the Reichs Theater Chamber had seen the devil.

20

LONDON
1940

The Luftwaffe pilot banked the bomber and came in low, avoiding the huge silvered barrage balloons that floated in the moonless darkness. He and his crew had flown a bombing mission over London every night from the seventh of September to the thirty-first of October, and they were half drunk with exhaustion.

The British were crazy, he thought. Without the Americans, they didn't have a chance to win this war, and yet they went on, night after night, taking the bombing: fifty-five nights in a row. Fifty-five nights, and they still showed no signs of surrendering.

He surveyed the burning city with a practiced eye. Their target for this evening was Waterloo Station. Following the dim black ribbon of the Thames, he flew over Vauxhall and Lambeth, but before they made Westminster Bridge the antiaircraft guns started up. Cherry-red tracers streaked through the air and spotlights probed the darkness. One of the spotlights caught the bomber, pinning it like an insect.

"Das Spiel ist aus!" the pilot thought. Fleeing to the east, he signaled the bombardier to push the release switch. The bomb bay opened, spewing out dozens of deadly eggs, just as the British ack-ack guns blew the German plane out of the sky.

Viola sat bolt upright in bed, startled by the concussion. That last hit was too close for comfort, she thought. I should have taken cover when the air-raid sirens went off, but they go off every night and you can't hide forever.

Fumbling for her robe and slippers, she got up and went to the window. Since Richard's death she had moved from the house in Belgravia to a small apartment a few blocks from the Arena. The Belgravia house belonged to Harry now, and even though he was in Germany betraying his country, she didn't want to live among his things. Henry Stafford, Duke of Sanford—it made her ill just to think of Harry inheriting Richard's title. Richard, thank God, had left her well provided for. If it wasn't for Grants, she would have been happy to forget that the Staffords had ever existed.

She pulled back the blackout curtains and looked in the direction of Waterloo Station. The skyline was ruddy with fire, but that was nothing new. After nearly eight weeks of German bombing, much of London already lay in rubble. Viola stood looking at the sky, thinking of the many famous landmarks that no longer existed: the Guildhall was in ruins; six million books had burned to ashes on Paternoster Row; the Burlington Arcade was totally destroyed, and St. James's, Piccadilly—Christopher Wren's favorite church—was a gutted shell. But St. Paul's still stood, and Westminster Abbey, and the Houses of Parliament. And Big Ben still tolled the hours.

She was snapped out of her reverie by someone pounding frantically on the downstairs door. Running out into the darkened hall, she plunged down the steps and pulled the bolt to find Hamilton Carlyle standing hatless and agitated on her front porch.

"The Arena's burning!" he yelled. "Took a direct German hit!"

"Oh no!" Without stopping to put on a coat, she plunged past Carlyle and began to run in the direction of the theater. Perhaps something could be saved: costumes, sets, the account books, anything. A block away, the street was littered with rubble. Viola heard the fire before she saw it, a great roaring sigh, a terrible crackling.

Rounding the corner, she saw the remains of her theater. The windows had all been blown out; the stone griffins knocked into the gutter, the cornices and granite amaranth leaves pulverized. Fire fighters stood in a whirlwind of steam and smoke, aiming their hoses at the flames.

She stopped and threw up one hand to shield her face from the heat. There was going to be nothing left when this was over: the stage where she had given some of her best performances would no longer exist; the curtain that had risen on *Laura* and *Wilde* would be a pile of ashes; even the iron frames of the seats would melt. She looked on, desperate and helpless, as the Arena burned.

After a time Carlyle came up behind her and put one hand on her shoulder. "There's nothing we can do," he said, "but at least no one was in the building when it was hit. The night watchman took cover when the warning blew."

"Thank God," Viola said. For she remembered the Neues all too well tonight, and if she or anyone else had been inside, she would quite probably have gone out of her mind from fear.

The Arena burned and burned until it was only a pile of smoking rubble. She stood in the cold wind watching numbly, until the fire fighters gave up, packed their hoses, and left. It seemed to her that her theatrical career was finally and definitively over.

Trembling, she walked over to the ruins and poked at them with the toe of her house slipper. Then she sat down on the curb and began to cry.

"You're getting chilled," Carlyle said softly. "Let me walk you home." He helped her to her feet.

"Home?" she said. She felt as if she had no home. The Arena had been a second mother to her, and like everything she loved, it had been consumed by fire.

The air-raid sirens were going off again as they had for the last six months, cutting through the dark, fogless night with whoops of alarm. Kathe could feel them vibrating in her bones as she ran toward the nearest tube station clutching her gas mask. *Take cover*, they commanded, *take cover!* Kathe was frightened, but not panicked. After you had been through one or two raids, you got to know what was coming: first the wail of the sirens, then the drone of the German planes, then the whine of the falling bombs, the explosions pounding London like a giant fist, making the ground tremble under your feet as you crouched in the shelter, and finally—that most blessed sound on earth—the All Clear. For eight solid months the Luftwaffe had been bombing London in a campaign designed to drive the British to surrender, but, Kathe thought with grim pride, it isn't working; we're hanging on, and Hitler has gotten us mad, and that's the mistake that's going to lose him this war.

Thinking about how the Germans were going to lose the war made her feel more in control of the situation, which was a good thing, because she wasn't quite sure where the entrance to the tube station was, and unless she found it soon she was going to be in serious trouble indeed. By some happy chance the tunnels that housed the underground transport system had been constructed far under the streets of London, and since the first days of the Blitz, last September, thousands of people had regularly been taking refuge in them. The catch was that in order to take shelter in a tube you had to know where an entrance was, and with the blackout in full swing that wasn't always easy. Kathe, who had been staying at the flat of a friend, didn't know the neighborhood. Her friend was off dancing in the concrete-reinforced underground cabaret of the Savoy Hotel and had left only the vaguest directions, which Kathe should have known better than to accept, but she had been tired after a hard day at work and the grueling trip across town in a bus so packed that it had been impossible to do anything but hang from one of the bars and look enviously at the people who had managed to get a seat, so she had listened with half an ear to Janet's directions and then, like a perfect idiot, had fallen asleep.

Result: she was lost. She stopped for a moment and tried to get her bearings and then hurried on, ignoring the cold April wind. The street, which was easy enough to negotiate by daylight, was as dark as the inside of a closet. There was no moon tonight, only stars blotted out here and there by a sprinkling of small, rapidly moving, grayish clouds. For a second, in a brief interval between the wails of the sirens, she heard the terrible, monotonous droning of the first German planes, followed almost immediately by the ack-ack guns in the park starting up. The red tracings of antiaircraft fire cut through the sky; the noise of the guns was deafening, but to Kathe, as to most Londoners, it was a sweet sound. It was good to know they were going to give the Germans a taste of their own tonight.

Tripping over the curb, Kathe stopped again, swearing to herself as she tried to disentangle the heel of her shoe from a crack in the pavement. Damn those shoes. They were completely inappropriate. She should have put on her slippers, but when the air-raid sirens had gone off she had grabbed the first pair she'd come across. As it was, she'd been lucky to find her dress in the dark. Taking shelter in your nightgown—as she knew from previous experience—could be cold and unpleasant, although so many people were reduced to it these days that it was no longer embarrassing.

She pulled at her heel awkwardly as the planes droned closer. Of course she could have just kicked off the shoe, but shoes were hard to come by these days and running barefoot over the broken glass that littered the streets was dangerous. Besides, after you'd been through eight months of air raids you tended to develop a sense of invulnerability. She knew the German bombs regularly killed hundreds of people, of course, but her mind had long ago stopped accepting the fact as anything that had to do with Kathe Rothe. Like a battle-seasoned soldier, she had become irrationally convinced that she was in no danger, even though the screaming sirens and drone of the bombers warned otherwise.

Freeing her heel at last, she ran in what she hoped was the direction of the tube station. She was just rounding a corner, panting with exertion, when she heard a sound that made the hairs stand up on the back of her neck. It was the banshee-like whistle of a falling German bomb. Always before the sound had been blocks away, muffled and indistinct, but now, she realized to her horror, it was directly overhead. I've had it, she thought; I'm going to be blown to bits. As the bomb hit she ducked, instinctively burying her head in her arms. There was a flash of greenish-orange light, followed by a shock that threw her to her knees. Dust filled her lungs and eyes and something wet and cold splashed over her, soaking her to the skin.

She coughed and rubbed the grit off her face, realizing with amazement that she wasn't hurt. She was in one piece, sitting on the pavement in a pile of rubble, covered with white gummy bits of plaster. Beside her a water main had ruptured and was spewing up like a fountain, treating her to a freezing shower. The street was no longer dark. About two hundred yards away a large apartment building was burning, sending up copper-colored tongues of flame. Kathe sat stunned, watching people running to pull out the injured. The entrance to the tube station was now clearly visible half a block away.

The water from the broken main drenched her skirt and legs and turned her hair into a wet tangle. After a moment she became aware that she was shuddering with cold. Getting to her feet, she checked herself again for damage and discovered that, except for a few skinned places on her knees, the only casualties seemed to be her dress and shoes. Just as she was heading toward the burning apartment to offer help, another German bomb came screaming through the sky. There was a tremendous explosion somewhere in the distance and a fountain of fire rose up in the center of a curl of black smoke. No longer feeling in the least immortal, Kathe ran as hard as she could for the entrance to the tube.

The stairs were steep but she took them quickly, hanging on to the rail for balance. At the bottom people were sleeping by the hundreds: men, women, and children mixed in a tangle on the platform, pillowed on bundles and suitcases, their white faces dull and unhealthy-looking in the dim glow of the emergency lights. Kathe picked her way carefully among the bodies to an unoccupied space, wishing she had a blanket or at least a coat.

Rubbing her hands together to warm them, she looked around for something to cover herself with but there was nothing, not even a newspaper. With a sigh of resignation, she sat down on the cold floor with her back to a large poster that warned against careless talk. At this distance underground, the German bombs sounded like the rolling of distant thunder. A baby cried and then stopped, hushed by its mother. Kathe shivered and folded her arms across the wet bodice of her dress. Closing her eyes, she drifted off into a restless sleep.

An hour or so later she woke to find herself covered with a warm coat. A few feet away a man was sitting cross-legged on the platform, smoking a cigarette and regarding her with friendly concern. He was about twenty-five, slender and compact, with dark curly hair, dark eyes, olive-tinged skin, a Roman nose, and full lips that made him look vaguely Mediterranean.

"Hello there," the handsome stranger said in an American accent. "Looks like you took a near miss."

"Yes." Kathe sat up and yawned, stretching her arms over her head. Her whole body ached, and she felt monstrously hungry. "I did rather."

"Bombed out of your house?"

She shook her head. "No, just caught on the run." She realized suddenly that the man was in his shirt sleeves, which undoubtedly meant she was wearing his coat. For some reason the thought embarrassed her. Blushing, she removed the coat and held it out to him. It was a light, expensive tweed; in the inside collar was a black silk label which read *Harvard Square Clothiers*. "I should give this back to you," she stammered stiffly. "Thank you very much. It was most kind."

"You looked like a drowned cat," the stranger observed cheerfully. "Sure you're warm enough without it? Personally, I'm a human furnace—raised in the wilds of Boston where only the hot-blooded survive—so if you want to keep that coat awhile longer, it's okay by me."

"It's not necessary," she insisted, forcing the coat on him. "I'm just fine, thank you." She was suddenly acutely conscious of how she must look to him in her ripped, plaster-smeared dress, muddy shoes, and damp, snarled hair. The man took the coat and extended his hand.

"I'm John Duke—actually Giovanni Duccini, but as my major professor, Giles Venable, never tired of pointing out to me, that's no name for an aspiring diplomat these days. I'm in the diplomatic service, you see, attached to the American Embassy here but with orders to keep my suitcase packed in case they want to send me into the steppes of Russia or whatever, so the Duccini had to go, although I still keep a carton of spaghetti under my bed to remind myself of my humble origins."

"How do you do." She shook his hand, amused at the way he went on about himself so unselfconsciously. "I'm Kathe Rothe."

"A pleasure, Miss Rothe." John shook her hand enthusiastically. "What do you do when you're not dodging German bombs?"

"I work as a clerk in a factory that makes altimeters for the planes that shoot down the German bombers."

"There's a neat justice to that." John smiled pleasantly. "How's the work?"

"Exhausting and pretty boring," Kathe admitted, "but at least I'm doing my bit. The hardest thing to get used to was the idea of being such a prime target. During the time when the Germans were doing all those daylight raids, everyone—myself included—was pretty scared. The factory had been painted with camouflage—you know, the usual green and buff—which was supposed to delude the Germans into thinking we were a park or something of the sort, but we all kept expecting to get an incendiary bomb in our laps. It hasn't happened, thank God. In fact, the worst problem so far has been the girls who work on the assembly line getting their hair caught in the machines."

John looked at her with that same expression of pleasant interest. "You know, I wouldn't have taken you for a secretary."

"Actually, everyone told me I should be a nurse or drive an ambulance like all the debutantes do, but I had this romantic idea I'd be doing more good at the factory. The truth is they were desperate for a girl who could type and that's my one real talent. My grandmother—she's my step-grandmother, really—taught me the touch system. She's an old suffragette who believes that every self-respecting woman should learn a trade. Before the war broke out I'd intended to be an actress or a botanist; I hadn't decided which." She really didn't know him well enough to rattle on like this, but there was something about the easy way he kept smiling at her that made her feel relaxed and confiding.

"An actress, eh? That's an exciting profession."

She nodded. "It runs in the blood. My mother's an actress, or rather she was an actress. For years she ran a theater called the Arena, maybe you've heard of it?"

"All I've heard of is the Windmill."

"That makes sense. The Windmill is the only theater in London open these days, but the Arena was much better—artistically speaking. The problem is, the Arena took a direct hit a few months back . . ." Kathe paused, remembering the broken walls, the burned beams, and the pained expression on Mama's face.

"That's too bad," John said sympathetically.

She shrugged. "There was nothing to be done about it, but it was especially hard on my mother, even though she was more or less retired at the time. She said the Arena was the second theater she'd had burned out from under her, and she was beginning to wonder if maybe she was a bit cursed or something." Kathe smiled. "Of course that didn't stop Mama for a second. She has more energy than any three people I've ever met. The day after the Arena burned she went down to Sanford—that's my grandmother's place—and started turning it into a home for refugees. She's got all sorts there—mostly Jewish families along with some Poles, some Norwegians, and about sixty children from the East End who nobody else wanted to take in."

"Your mother sounds like a remarkable woman."

"Oh she is. I admire her no end, and we get along beautifully."

"I wish I could say the same thing about my mother." John took a pack of Camels out of his pocket and offered Kathe one with a graceful motion. There was something balanced about his entire body that made her wonder if he had been an athlete. She accepted the American cigarette gratefully, thinking of the horrible flannel-tasting domestic brands she occasionally smoked. As John lit the match she found herself wondering if he had a ration card like everyone else or if the Americans had their own supply system going. The thought that he might be someone who still ate chocolate and drank real coffee gave him an aura of incredible wealth, like a prince in a fairy tale. "My mom's always on my back," John observed as he lit her cigarette and then his own.

"On your back about what?"

"Well, it's embarrassing really." He grinned. "She's one hundred percent Italian, you see, even though she's second-generation, and all she can think about is grandchildren. She keeps telling me I should settle down, marry some nice Catholic girl and start a family. I try to tell her that this is no time to have kids. Mama, I say, there's a world war going on and the U.S. is going to be in it in no time, and besides, I want to see the world first, and Mama just pulls this black shawl around her head like she was in Sicily or something and moans that she never should have let me accept that scholarship to Harvard because all those atheist professors put the crazy idea in my head that there's something in the world more important than the family. It's all very dramatic, like something out of an Italian opera."

"What does your father say to all that?"

"Nothing. He's dead, has been ever since I was three. I'm the only son, so that's why I come in for so much of the Italian mothering bit." John looked vaguely uncomfortable for the first time since the conversation began. Kathe was just trying to think of something appropriate to say in return when she heard the familiar wail of a siren. John's face brightened instantly. "Say," he said, stubbing out his cigarette, "isn't that the All Clear?"

Kathe listened for a moment. The sound was faint but unmistakable. "Yes," she agreed. "I think it is."

"Wonderful sound," John quipped brightly, "like Mozart to my ears. Did I tell you I play the violin?"

"No, you didn't." Kathe got to her feet and began to brush off her skirt, but the plaster dust was stuck to the fabric like glue. At least she hadn't gotten her stockings torn, for the very simple reason that she no longer owned a pair decent enough to wear in public. She inspected her shoes with a sinking feeling. A few hours ago they had been black, but at the moment they were a sickly brownish white, as if she had waded through a mixture of mud and white paint.

"Oh I do play," John was saying, "terribly; sounds like a cat being eviscerated."

Kathe laughed. "I imagine you aren't all that bad." She was grateful to him for distracting her from her dress and shoes. The man has a sense of humor, she thought, which is rare these days.

"After my freshman audition," John continued, "the conductor of the Harvard Orchestra informed me that the only thing I should carry in a violin case was a machine gun."

"That sounds rather mean."

Richard nodded. "Harvard's a brutal place—boot camp for the world, I call it." He smiled at her as if they shared some sort of wonderful secret. "Survive there and you can survive anywhere." All around them people were struggling wearily to their feet, putting on their coats and picking up their bundles. John and Kathe walked toward the stairs. A draft was blowing down the tiled passage, bringing the scent of smoke and dust.

"Say." John stopped and turned to her. "How are you getting home?"

"I'm walking. It's only a few blocks from here. I was staying with a friend when the raid happened."

"A female friend?"

Kathe was a little shocked. "Of course."

They walked up the stairs and out into the cold April wind. The sky was clear now, the stars bright and hard like little points of metal. Somewhere in the distance there was still a wail of sirens, but it was a good wail, the kind that said the German raids were over for the night.

"Mind if I ask you how old you are?" John said abruptly.

"I'm seventeen."

John grinned. "That's a relief. When I first saw you asleep over there I took you to be about fourteen. You were all curled up like a sleepy kid." He hesitated. "Say, how about me walking you home?"

Kathe was flustered. "Janet's place isn't very far away, only a few blocks, so there isn't any need, that is . . ." She looked at him standing there in the dim light, handsome and solid and so obviously interested in her, and she trailed off weakly into a self-conscious silence.

"If I don't walk you home, we have a problem." John's voice was low, almost tender.

"What sort of problem?"

"Well here I am, a perfect stranger whom you met by accident in the tube, and I know how girls are. They always want to make sure strangers are harmless before they go out with them, so my plan was to walk you home, being as harmless and charming as possible, and then when we arrived to ask you out to lunch."

"I couldn't possibly," Kathe stammered, awkward and suddenly shy. "I have to work."

"On Sunday?"

She was embarrassed to realize that tomorrow was indeed Sunday and that she had half the day free. "Well, I don't know, that is . . ."

"Say yes. You won't regret it, I promise." His enthusiasm was almost boyish, Kathe thought, and yet when she had been talking to him in the station he had seemed so self-contained and adult, so much a man of the world. "Please."

"Well . . ."

"I'll take you to a real restaurant and ply you with steak and chocolate cake and Burgundy. They don't count ration points at restaurants, you know."

"You have to be joking."

"I'm perfectly serious. Civilization is falling apart, so we might as well enjoy what remains while we can."

Kathe thought guiltily of her friends, most of whom were trying to exist on a few ounces of rationed meat and horrible reconstituted potatoes, but this American was so sincere, so charming and it had been so long since she had tasted steak. Her mouth was actually watering, which was embarrassing but predictable after weeks of eating sausages that tasted like sawdust—"I think I can make it."

"Good." John sounded quite pleased. He took her arm in a proprietary fashion and began to walk briskly down the street, dodging stray bricks and hunks of plaster in the dark by some kind of instinct. Kathe decided that he definitely must have been an athlete of some sort in college. She would have said rugby only they didn't have rugby over in America and he was too small for their brand of football. In any event he must have had eyes like a cat, because they got all the way back to Janet's block of flats without once tripping or losing their way.

"Good night." John shook her hand gently, almost as if caressing her, and Kathe felt an odd sensation pass up through her arm and into her chest, a sort of tingling, as if she had grabbed hold of a live wire.

"Good night," she muttered, turning to unlock the door. She was thrilled and a little nonplussed. She had known this man for only a few hours and she was already attracted to him. What in the world was going on?

"You won't forget about lunch?"

"What time?" She put her key in the lock and opened the door into the dark hallway. A vague wartime smell of cooked cabbage and musty raincoats assailed her.

"I'll come by for you about eleven."

"Fine, I'll see you at eleven then." She gave him her home address and then walked quickly into the hallway and shut the door behind her, blotting out the shadow of his body silhouetted against the night sky. This is silly, she thought as she groped her way up the unlighted stairs—a bomb-shelter romance. This war's making everyone crazy; nobody can hang on to the old standards because they don't make any sense anymore, and the more the bombs fall the more you find yourself wanting to get as much out of life as you can, but I shouldn't have agreed to go out with him.

Upstairs in the bedroom, she stripped off her dirty dress and kicked her shoes into a pile in the corner. I'll call him and tell him I can't make it, she thought, and then she realized that she wouldn't be able to call him because she didn't know his phone number. The thought that she had to go to lunch with this John Duke tomorrow whether she wanted to or not made her ridiculously happy. Curling up under the blankets, she fell into a heavy, dreamless sleep.

"Cream?" John asked. It was one o'clock in the afternoon of the next day and he and Kathe were sitting lazily in the restaurant of the Chadwick Hotel lingering over cups of real coffee after a lunch that had included two steaks, boiled new potatoes, and half a dozen miraculous spears of fresh asparagus swimming in cheese sauce.

"Thank you." Kathe took the silver pitcher and poured cream into her coffee cup, a lacy delicate bit of Coalport decorated with Chinese flowers and gold bands. The cup looked as thin as an eggshell, and the cream was rich and thick, and as she poured she had a sense of having been magically transported to another world where there was no Hitler and no Blitz, just long sunny afternoons when people sat about eating fine meals and making bright conversation.

Yet if she lifted her head and looked across the restaurant, there were indications even here that the enchantment was of a temporary nature. In the first place, nearly every man in the room and many of the women were in military uniform. In the second place, shortages had made the bill of fare odd even here: rabbit, canned tuna crepes, and dried meat were all on the menu, neatly disguised by French names that somehow made them sound more appealing; and in the third place, they were eating, not in the famous dining room of the hotel with its French windows and nineteenth-century murals, but in the basement in a concrete-reinforced bunker of sorts which no amount of white tablecloths and soft rugs could completely disguise. Still, Kathe was content: she had eaten steak for the first time in months; she was full, happy, and in the company of a very interesting, handsome foreigner who seemed to like her a great deal, and she was enjoying herself thoroughly.

"I want to tell you all about myself," John said abruptly, putting down his coffee cup with a clink.

"Why?" Kathe looked up from her coffee, a little surprised.

"Because . . ." He hesitated, put his chin in his hands, rested his elbows on the table, and stared at her strangely. "Because, crazy as it probably sounds, I think I'm falling in love with you."

Kathe stared at him, mildly appalled. "You can't be serious."

"Oh, but I am. I truly am."

"But you hardly know me," she protested.

"I know enough to know that you're beautiful and smart and brave." John leaned forward earnestly. "A man would have to be a fool not to see that in the first five minutes."

"Please." Kathe was getting uncomfortable. "You sound like one of the R.A.F boys on a twenty-four-hour leave. They're always telling you that they love you and that you should make them happy men before they go back to defend King and country."

"The difference between the R.A.F boys and me," John said with quiet sincerity, "is that I mean it. Personally I've always believed that you can tell within the first few seconds if you can love someone or not, and the rest is just marking time. I know that this probably sounds like some kind of line, but when I saw you asleep in that tube station all covered with dust, looking like you'd survived hell, I thought, this girl is a possibility, and when I talked to you I knew it was definite."

"But even if that were true—which I'm not by any means convinced it is—something so important shouldn't be rushed."

"I agree with you completely." John nodded. "But rushing seems to be my only choice. I haven't told you this, but the bad news is that in ten days I have to leave the country."

Kathe was irrationally disappointed. To cover her confusion, she picked up her coffee cup and toyed with it aimlessly. The gold band around the rim sparkled under the overhead lights and she could see the shadow of her own thumb through the thin china. "Where are you going?" She tried to make her voice light, but she couldn't meet his eyes.

"I can't tell you."

"Oh." Ever since she had returned from France, Kathe had been seeing posters all over London warning that careless talk cost lives. If John couldn't tell her where he was going, then that was the end of it.

"Had we but world enough, and time"—it was said softly; he reached across the table and took her free hand in his. "This coyness, Lady, were no crime/ . . . An hundred years should go to praise/ Thine eyes, and on thy forehead gaze/ . . . But at my back I always hear/ Time's wingèd chariot hurrying near. . . ."

"You're quoting Marvell." Kathe laughed nervously, thinking she should disengage her hand but not really wanting to.

"I'm an educated man." John smiled. "That's one of the advantages of having gone to Harvard. I'm also third-generation Italian, born of poor but honest parents, a liberal Democrat who believes FDR is next to God, a man of modest means and immodest ambitions. I don't cheat on my taxes, I pay all my bills the day they come due, I speak three languages besides English, and someday I shall be wealthy and famous and when that happens I will want you by my side."

Kathe pulled back her hand. "You're making fun of me."

"No I'm not." John took her hand back again. "I'm just a love-struck, awkward American without an idea in the world how to go about courting in so short a time the most wonderful woman I've ever met. In fact, I spent all of last night wondering what you thought of me and feeling completely helpless to do anything about it. I wondered, for example, if you thought I was a coward because all the other fellows over here are in uniform and I'm not. I wanted to tell you that I'm doing my bit. I can't give details, but the work I do is important—even rather dangerous at times." His face was flushed and eager. "I'm not a shallow person, Kathe."

"I didn't think you were."

"Well, that's a start at least." John dropped her hand and sat back.

"Ten days from now you're going to be completely in love with me. I'm warning you ahead of time."

"That's big of you." Kathe laughed, uneasy at being the object of such a sudden passion, yet—despite her better judgment—she was intrigued. There was no denying the fact that this kind of attention was flattering, especially when you were seventeen and had been spending most of your free time volunteering to work extra shifts at the office. "What makes you think I'd be interested?"

"Instinct. Destiny."

"I don't believe in destiny."

"Neither do I, but it's true just the same. You and I were meant for each other, like . . ."

"Ham and eggs," she supplied playfully.

John look mildly offended. "That's not a very romantic comparison."

Kathe giggled at his discomfort, thinking that, really, the whole situation was comic. "I'm a sensible girl."

"You *were* a sensible girl," John assured her gravely. "Your sense is all in the past tense, Kathe my love, but you just don't know. it yet."

John, as it turned out, was right—her sense was in the past tense. Three days after that first lunch together, Kathe began to think that maybe she really was falling in love with him; in five days she was sure, and by the end of that first crazy week, she was lost. Falling in love with John was a confusing, exhilarating, thoroughly unsettling experience, but no matter how much she tried, she didn't seem to be able to be reasonable about it. This is rash, she would tell herself sternly; this has got to stop. When he calls next I won't even answer the phone. Then the phone would ring and she would nearly break her neck getting to it.

In many ways during those ten days she became a stranger to herself. When she asked why she loved John, what possible reason she could have for feeling such emotions for a near stranger, her mind felt oddly paralyzed, or worse yet some trite phrase would pop up. When she tried to push herself further, she came up against a fund of emotion so intense that it was almost frightening.

Work and friends faded into the background; she slept poorly, dreamed of John incessantly when she wasn't with him, and soon found herself walking around London giddy and slightly dazed, as if love had dropped out of the sky like the German bombs, landing squarely on top of her and blowing her life apart. Meanwhile, John went on telling her about himself: about his Sicilian grandmother, who liked to listen to soap operas, about the first Christmas of the Depression when he had gotten nothing but a pair of socks, about his crazy uncle who thought Mussolini was the reincarnation of Christ, about his toy soldiers and his Harvard philosophy classes and his dream of being an ambassador someday, about anything and everything until she began to feel that he wasn't a stranger at all but someone she'd known for years. She, in turn, told him how difficult it was for her to remember anything about her childhood in Germany; she described her grief over her father's sudden death, the terrible loneliness she had felt when she and her mother moved from Paris to London, her fears of not being as talented or as beautiful as her mother, the pain of the motorcycle accident, the terror of being interrogated by the Gestapo, the near miracle of her return from France, and John listened to it all gravely and afterward, each time, he took her face in his hands and kissed her with such tenderness that it was like coming home at last.

"Kathe?"

"Yes, John?" It was ten o'clock in the morning of the ninth day, and after another night of marathon conversations they were sitting in his flat making a breakfast out of jars of odd delicacies from Fortnum & Mason's: pickled corn, caviar, tiny preserved tomatoes the size of her thumb, smoked salmon, cheddar cheese, and Bath Olivers. For almost a week he had been going to exclusive shops where ration points weren't required and buying her amazing treats, even though she had repeatedly begged him to stop, protesting that he must be using up his entire salary on her. He had given her bars of chocolate, silk stockings, books of poetry printed on thick creamy paper, even real coffee, and now he was holding still another gift, a small brown-paper parcel about the size of a cube of butter.

"I want you to have this." John placed the parcel in her hand and gently closed her fingers around it. His voice had a strange timbre to it, and when she looked up she saw that he was regarding her anxiously. How I love his face, she thought, his dear face. Really, she was over the hill about John Duke. Hefting the parcel, she balanced it on her palm. It was about as heavy as one of the small bolts the workers in the factory put into the altimeters. "What is it?" she asked, examining it with curiosity.

Instead of answering, John leaned over and kissed her lightly on the lips. It was an odd, trembling kiss, as if he were frightened, but Kathe couldn't imagine that, since he was quite simply the bravest man she had ever met. Only last night they had been forced to take refuge in an Anderson—one of the small curved-roof, kennel-like shelters the government had handed out free in September. They shouldn't have been out at all, of course, but it had been a foggy night and they had both agreed that the Germans wouldn't be able to find London, much less bomb it, but the raids had started anyway, and there they'd been, caught in the dark with a family of five, packed cheek to elbow. About twenty minutes into the raid, they had taken a close hit and the mother of the family had become slightly hysterical, crying that she couldn't take this anymore, and that it had gone on long enough, and that it was time the Blitz stopped— sentiments Kathe completely agreed with. John had been wonderful. In a calm voice he had explained that the Andersons were constructed so that they could survive anything short of a direct hit, and then he had started amusing the children, telling them stories and whistling bits of popular songs to them, and now he was trembling and she couldn't imagine why. Hesitantly, she tore open the brown paper. Inside was a small blue box with a gold crest stamped on the lid, and inside the box was a ring.

"Good heavens," Kathe exclaimed. The ring was gold, about a quarter of an inch wide, intricately worked with flowers, ivy, and birds. She turned it over in her hands, thinking that it was absolutely beautiful and that she couldn't possibly accept it.

"Like it?" John asked eagerly.

"Yes, of course. It's perfectly gorgeous, but—"

"It's an antique," he interrupted, "eighteenth century. Some high-born lady in love with one of Bonnie Prince Charlie's cavaliers might have worn it. Here, put it on." Taking her left hand, he slipped the ring on her third finger. "It fits," he exclaimed delightedly. "I thought it would."

Kathe looked at the ring and then at John. She didn't much like what she was going to have to say next. "John"—she took off the ring and handed it to him firmly—"it's beautiful but I can't take it."

He looked shocked, as if she had slapped him. "Why not?"

"Because it's much too expensive and, well, frankly it's too much like a wedding ring."

"But that's just the point."

"What do you mean that's just the point?"

"Oh damn it, Kathe"—John smiled wryly—"I'm making a real hash out of this, aren't I? Here I've gone and sprung this thing on you without any explanation. What I meant to do was to ask you first, but believe it or not, I'm something of a shy fellow. I mean, I've never done this before, you know, and at the last minute I lost my nerve and just handed you the ring."

"John"—she looked down at the table, suddenly overcome with shyness—"is this some kind of proposal?"

"Of course." He looked immensely relieved. "That's just what I've been trying to say. Will you marry me? There, it's out. Well, will you?"

Kathe felt an odd thrill. My God, she thought, he really means it, but it's completely crazy; I love him and he loves me, but we've known each other for only nine days and . . . Her mind spun, thinking that maybe it was possible, and then thinking that no, it was completely impossible and she was a madwoman to consider saying yes even for a moment. "No, John"—the word came out of her mouth of its own accord. "I'm sorry. I can't." She felt oddly disappointed, as if he were the one refusing her instead of vice versa.

"But you have to marry me," John insisted. "You don't love anyone else and you never will. Take my word for it."

"People don't get married after they've known each other only nine days."

"Before the war maybe that was true, but now things are different. War always has done crazy things to people and this one is no exception. The fear of death brings out the life force; birth rates go up. Look at history if you don't believe me. Kathe"—he took both her hands and kissed them—"please, listen. One of my buddies just got married, and he and his girl had known each other only *two* days."

"Your buddy and his girl were fools, then," Kathe said stubbornly.

She had the feeling that if she began to waver the slightest bit, it was going to be all over.

"God knows I'd love to court you for years, I told you that the first time we had lunch together, but we don't have years. Look, you're the only woman in the world I've ever wanted to marry. The truth is, I feel married to you already. Please, Kathe, don't let this chance slip away from us."

"John, I'm sorry. I just can't."

He dropped her hands and sat back. "Isn't there anything I could say to make you change your mind?"

"No," she said gently, "nothing."

"Would you at least take the ring?"

"John . . ."

"Please. It would mean so much to me to know that you had it while I was away. I don't ask you even to think of it as an engagement ring if the thought bothers you. Just think of it as a souvenir, a little bit of me left behind." He made a poor attempt at a smile. "I wouldn't want you to forget me, you know."

"I could never forget you."

There was a brief silence. Picking up the ring, John slipped it back on her hand. Kathe let him do it without protest. "I'm coming back for you," he said. "You can count on it, and when I do I'm going to marry you." He kissed the ring, and then her fingers, and her wrist, and the back of her hand. "I love you. I know those words have been said a million times by people who only half meant them, but I'm saying them as if I were the first man ever to discover them. I love you, Kathe Rothe."

"I love you, too, John." She was moved. Lowering her face to his, she kissed him lightly on the mouth. "When you get back, I'll be here."

"You know," he said with a faint grin, "it's no use if you go and marry some other fellow because you'll just have to leave the poor guy when I get back." He caught her face between his hands and kissed her hard and long. "I want you to remember me," he whispered.

"I will." He kissed her again and she felt breathless and excited.

"Promise," he commanded, kissing her again and again hungrily, "promise you'll wait." He had been kissing her for days, but these kisses were different. They were desperate, passionate kisses, and somehow the desperation of them made them all the more exciting.

Kathe kissed him back. "I promise." Her body suddenly felt light and unattached to the ground, as if she had reached out and caught hold of a passing train. John lifted her off her feet, scooping her into his arms. Bending forward, he rocked her for a moment as if she were a child, kissing her eyelids and lips. Then he carried her toward his bed.

"John . . ."

He closed her mouth with more kisses. "I want to make love to you, Kathe."

"But we can't," she protested weakly.

"Why not?" He put her gently down on top of the blankets and began to unbutton her dress. She knew she should put up her hands to stop him, but her arms felt like lead. I want him, she thought. I wanted Henri a little, and no one since Henri, and I thought maybe the motorcycle accident had changed my feelings about that sort of thing forever, but it isn't true. I want John, he's made me feel alive for the first time in months, and I love him, I really do, and still I shouldn't because he's going away and it's dangerous and what if I got pregnant, but if I don't make love to him now, I might never get the chance because although neither of us has mentioned it out loud we both know he may get killed, and my God if he died and I never made love to him, I think I'd spend the rest of my life regretting it.

The buttons ran from her chest to her knees. As John undid them Kathe could feel herself flushing with embarrassment. She put up her arms to cover her breasts and looked at him pleadingly. She was excited and trembling, thinking that she wanted to make love to him and at the same time thinking that she wanted to tell him to stop. "Have you ever done this before?" he asked gently.

"No." She shook her head, feeling shy and awkward. "I'm a bit of an amateur."

"Don't worry." John stroked her hair softly. "Just relax. We won't do anything you don't want to do." He tucked her under the sheets and lay on top of her, kissing her some more, and gradually she began to relax again. After a bit he sat up and took off his own clothes. Kathe opened her eyes and then closed them again quickly. It was strange to see a naked man and yet at the same time it was a beautiful sight. John's arms were lean and slender, and there were tiny tufts of dark curly hair on his chest. Lifting up the sheets, he crawled under with her.

The shock of pleasure when his naked body touched hers was tremendous. She had read books that described lovemaking, but they had been poor, clinical reports of the actual experience. John pulled her close to him, and she felt his breath, the warmth of his flesh, smelled the scent of the soap in his hair. She was dazzled. She had never suspected, never even imagined, anything could feel so good.

"This may hurt a little," he said quietly.

"What?"

"Sometimes it hurts a little the first time." He kissed her on the nose tenderly. "But you're brave. I knew that the first time I saw you in that tube station."

"I am brave," Kathe agreed. She wondered how much it was going to hurt but she needn't have worried. John spent a long time caressing her, so long that she lost track of what she was doing and where she was, and when at last they made love it was almost painless.

Afterward she wept a little in his arms.

"Are you all right?" he asked.

"Yes, only it was so moving."

"The best part is the second time."

"We're going to do it again?" She was surprised.

"Again and again, darling," John said, "as many times as you'll have me." He began to caress her all over again, and this time, as he had promised, it was different. This time there was no pain at all, only a long tunnel of pleasure and excitement and at the end of it the mystery of his body, the dark quiet center of him spread over her like a black coat. The first time she had cried out in pain; this time she cried out in pleasure and fell back spent and exhausted in his arms. "I love you."

"I love you," he replied.

She had the feeling that somehow they should have invented other words to mark this moment, but there were no other words. She lay still for a few minutes, then turned to John and kissed him.

"You like it?" he asked.

"Yes. It's the best thing since"—she hesitated, at a loss for words—"since breathing."

"Glad you like it." John smiled. "I invented it myself, a Duccini special." Laughing, they embraced.

21

The next twenty-two hours were completely crazy. They made love a great deal—Kathe lost track of how often—and each time it seemed to her that they came closer together. Occasionally they managed to get out of bed long enough to eat or take a warm bath or once to turn on the radio and sit like an old married couple in each other's arms in front of the electric fire listening to the evening news. Since they had last bothered to pay attention to the outside world, Greece had been invaded and the Germans had entered Salonika. Lying in John's embrace with her head resting on his shoulder, Kathe thought, guiltily, that it all seemed rather distant. It was a mood that couldn't possibly last, yet she clung to it, not daring to look at a clock. The night of the ninth day passed in a sweet haze. John was full of plans, some serious, some playful. Kathe would come back to Boston with him to meet his mother; he would forget about being an ambassador and become mayor of New York instead, since New York was a better place for her to pursue an acting career.

They would have five children and three dogs and live in an apartment with a view of Central Park.

The hours passed slowly. Sometime around three in the morning she fell asleep at last, curled in John's embrace, feeling happier and more secure than she could ever remember feeling. When she woke the blackout curtains had been pulled aside and sunlight was streaming into the room through the water-spotted windowpanes, making little prisms of color on the white sheets. For a second she lay in perfect contentment listening to the sound of water running in the bathroom. It sounded as if John might be shaving, and somehow being witness to this small domestic detail of his life made her feel as if she were indeed his wife. She thought lazily of the hundreds of mornings that she would wake up to the same sound, and then suddenly it was all over and time had started up again, not gradually but with a sickening lurch that left her dizzy and suffering. My God, she thought, this is it—this is the day he leaves.

"John," she called out, sitting up in bed. She felt panicked, afraid somehow that he had already left, although that was obviously ridiculous. He appeared at the door, razor in hand, and she realized with a shock that, except for putting on his shirt and tie, he was already dressed. I'm actually going to have to let him go, she thought. For the first time the idea was real to her. She gripped at the sheets and an odd feeling seized her, as if she were about to fall into some dark, unpleasant place.

"Are you okay?" he asked.

"I'm fine." She tried to speak with bright affection but it was such a weak parody of her earlier happiness that he wasn't deceived. Putting down his razor, he strode across the room and folded her in his arms. Kathe leaned her head against his chest; there was a comforting smell of after-shave lotion and soap and the warm scent of his body. For a moment she almost recaptured the sensation of being protected by his love. Yet in a few minutes he would walk out the door. The thought hit her in the pit of the stomach and she suddenly felt as lonely as if he had already left. Tears ran down her cheeks and dripped comically over her chin, and she felt ridiculous and sad and abandoned. "Damn it"—she wiped the tears out of her eyes quickly with the back of her hand, wishing she were braver and wondering what he must think of her—"I know I'm being childish, but I just can't stand it."

John chucked her under the chin. "Say," he said gently, "I thought you Brits had a monopoly on the stiff upper lip."

She tried to smile but the corners of her mouth were trembling. "My upper lip isn't very stiff at present, I'm afraid."

"I adore you," he said, "I'm absolutely crazy about you." He kissed her again, got up, went over to his closet. Except for a shirt, tie, and suit coat, the closet was empty. Removing the shirt from the hanger, John put it on, then retrieved the tie and put that on too. Kathe watched the whole performance in stunned misery.

"Are we having breakfast together?" she asked in a small, reproachful voice that she was immediately ashamed of. What in the world was wrong with her? She was acting as if he was to blame for leaving her, but he had told her from that very first lunch at the Chadwick that this moment would arrive. Still, she had had no idea parting with him would be so painful.

John shook his head gravely. "No, I'm afraid there isn't enough time to eat. My plane leaves at nine."

"I could go to the airport with you," she immediately volunteered.

"It isn't open to civilians, Kathe."

"Oh." She knew better than to ask questions.

John sat down on the edge of the bed and took her hands in his. "Besides," he continued, "I want to remember you just like this, naked between my sheets, all your beautiful pink curves and luscious unmentionable parts tucked away and waiting for me." The thought made Kathe smile despite herself. "There," John said, "that's better. I hate good-byes, to tell you the truth. They have a taste of mortality to them that sticks in my craw. In fact I don't even want you to see me go." He put his hand on her face and gently closed her eyelids. "I love you," he whispered.

"I love you too," Kathe said.

"Keep your eyes closed, my darling, and think of last night." He kissed her quickly on the lips and then she felt him get up and the bed was light and empty. There were some rapid, busy sounds: the thump of the suitcase being closed, hurried footsteps, the terrible finality of the door closing behind him. Kathe opened her eyes and everything in the apartment was like it had been before—the sunlight, the white sheets, the empty wine bottle on the table—only John was missing. Running over to the window, she looked out just in time to see him climbing into a cab. Dear God, she prayed silently, gripping the windowsill, let him be safe, let him come back to me healthy and whole.

She watched the cab until it was out of sight. The street was blank to her, like a white page, and the brick buildings looked empty and cold. After a long time she turned and walked numbly back to the bed. The sheets were in a tangle from their lovemaking the night before, and the blankets had fallen onto the floor in a heap. Automatically she began to make the bed. Picking up one of the pillows, she impulsively lifted it to her face. The pillow still smelled of John. Somehow that was too much to bear. Sitting down on the edge of the bed, she buried her face in the pillow and wept for all the long, lonely days ahead.

His first letter came to her apartment a week later in a thin blue envelope postmarked Lisbon. She tore it open with trembling hands and devoured it as if it were food. For three pages he told her how much he missed her and loved her. He didn't mention what he was doing or where he was going, of course, but she had expected that, and just hearing from him was enough to make her sing to herself as she walked to work. The next week passed quickly, and on the following Wednesday a second letter arrived with a blurred postmark that she couldn't make out, although she spent an inordinate amount of time trying. It was only a single page, and John's handwriting looked blotted and uneven, as if he had been trying to overcome the effects of a moving bus or a bouncing airplane.

> *My dearest,*
> *I had a queer dream last night. In the dream an angel came to me and offered to let me into heaven, and I asked him, "Does it include Kathe?" and the angel hemmed a bit and then admitted it didn't. "Forget it," I told him. "Heaven without Kathe wouldn't be worth the trip." I know all this sounds hopelessly romantic, but that's the state I'm in about you. Take care of yourself until I come home to you.*
> *I love you forever,*
> *John*

Kathe read and reread the letter until she had it memorized. Then she folded it, laid it away carefully in her dresser drawer and waited for another, but the third week went by without a word, as did the fourth and fifth. Obviously he had gotten wherever it was he was going and was too busy to write. Still, as the days passed and spring gave way to early summer and no thin blue envelope was dropped through the mail slot in her door, she began to become impatient. On the second of June she impulsively called up the main post office to make sure that there had been no confusion about her address, and they listened to her with polite sympathy. Was Miss Rothe getting any mail at all? She had to admit that she was. Then there was no chance her mail was being misdirected. Perhaps, the postal clerk suggested diplomatically, the problem lay elsewhere. The war was making such a snarl of foreign correspondence. No one knew how many letters were lying at the bottom of the Atlantic at this very moment, courtesy of the German U-boats.

For three more weeks Kathe bore the lack of letters bravely, and then panic set in. In late June, shortly after the German invasion of Russia, she began to scan the papers frantically for news about remote places. Perhaps John was in Siberia or China or South America. Perhaps he had been sent to some remote island where there was no mail service; perhaps he was doing something so secret that he had been absolutely forbidden to contact her. As the weeks passed and no letter arrived, her anxiety grew almost unbearable. She developed odd rituals of loneliness, eating little and sleeping poorly. At night before she went to bed, she would pull out John's two letters and read them over to herself. He sounded so devoted, so passionately in love with her; it just didn't make sense. Why wasn't he writing?

The days went slowly and terribly, each one a little worse than the next. One morning in early July she got up and looked at herself in the mirror and saw a thin, harried woman with lusterless hair and tired eyes. Startled, she instinctively put the palms of her hands against the glass to try to erase the image, but it stared back at her like a ghost. I'm not well, she thought; something's terribly wrong. The idea that she might be seriously ill frightened her. Missing John was one thing, but dying for him was quite another. Walking into the living room, she impulsively picked up the phone, called a doctor, and made an appointment.

*   *   *

It was late July and in the Great Hall of Sanford Palace the dukes of past generations were looking down at a children's dormitory. Viola paused in the doorway, listening with amusement to the humming that issued from the sixty white iron beds. Although lacking a great deal of its former splendor, the hall was on the whole a much more cheerful place these days. After nearly a hundred years of musty magnificence, the heavy red velvet drapes had been pulled down, wrapped in muslin bags, and banished to the attic, letting in the first real sunlight the hall had seen since the reign of Queen Victoria; the oriental rugs (a gift from a long-dead Indian raja) had been rolled up and stored against the day when sixty pairs of small muddy feet no longer ran in and out of the wide doors. In place of the neoclassic statues, pale Elizabethan tapestries, and hollow suits of armor, sixty real flesh-and-blood children between the ages of four and six lay taking their afternoon naps, girls at one end of the hall, boys at the other, all sleeping peacefully.

At least they were supposed to be sleeping peacefully. Viola smiled at the sound of the whispering voices. When you had sixty young children on your hands, the likelihood of getting them all to take a nap at the same time was about equal to the likelihood of it snowing in midsummer. Still, the dormitory was as quiet as could be expected. She took a quick survey of the premises and was satisfied with what she saw. Ian and Patrick weren't locked in mortal combat; Bella (who was forever homesick) wasn't sobbing into her pillow, and Nigel hadn't thrown up his lunch. A good start to the afternoon.

She contemplated the row of beds, thinking that after years of running a theater full of temperamental actors and directors, establishing a shelter for children had been relatively simple. She loved the work, it gave her great satisfaction, and it couldn't have come at a better time. With her career at a standstill, the war in full swing, and the Arena reduced to a pile of rubble, she had been heading for a nasty depression when Grants had come up with the suggestion that they turn Sanford Palace into a shelter for the children who were being evacuated from the London slums. From the moment she agreed to the idea, she hadn't had the time to be depressed.

Well, actually, that wasn't completely true. She still had days when she felt achingly lonely, days when she would have given anything to be on the stage again, but the shelter tended to get her through those bad times. She was even becoming increasingly aware that the children were giving more to her in some ways than she was giving to them. Sixty children from the worst slums in London needed her to make sure they had something hot to eat and something warm to wear, and that was enough to keep her going, at least for the present.

Leaving the hall, she strolled aimlessly for a few minutes and then turned in the direction of the east rose garden. The grounds were a mess these days, with all the younger gardeners off in the military, but she hardly noticed, having other things on her mind. Milk was in short supply again and drinking glasses were almost impossible to obtain. Then there was the perpetual question of whether to make jam or use the children's sugar ration to buy it ready-made. If they made jam, they could use the pears from the orchard, but would the children eat pear conserves? Viola paused in front of a rose bush and examined it idly. Half a dozen magnificent shocking-pink roses exploded in the hot summer air like the spray from a petrified fountain. The scent was sweet and almost overwhelming, with a faint suggestion of spice and musk. She was just thinking how amazingly well the roses were doing on their own when a movement caught her eye. Looking up, she saw her daughter walking across the vast expanse of lawn, suitcase in hand.

"Kathe," she called out, "whatever are you doing here?"

Kathe approached and put down her suitcase, looking as tired and bedraggled as Viola could ever remember her looking. Her face was white and there were deep blue circles under her eyes. "Hello, Mama," she said. She clasped her hands together nervously, and Viola saw with a pang that her fingers were thin and unsteady. "I suppose I should have phoned ahead to let you know I was coming."

Viola looked from Kathe's thin hands to her drawn face and felt a wave of motherly anxiety. The girl looked as if she hadn't been eating, hadn't been sleeping either for that matter. A cloud passed over the sun and Kathe shuddered. It was an odd, unhappy gesture that made her seem for a moment like an old woman instead of a girl of seventeen. "Darling, what's wrong?" She walked briskly over to Kathe and put her hand on the girl's forehead. "Are you sick?"

"Not exactly." Kathe sat down on a iron bench and stared at Viola sadly. "I've quit my job," she said in a flat voice.

Viola was relieved. "That isn't such a disaster. London isn't the safest place on earth, you know, nor the healthiest, and Grants and I would love to have you here—"

"That's not all," Kathe interrupted. "There's more." Suddenly, to Viola's surprise, she hid her face in her hands. "I'm a bloody fool," she moaned.

She sat down beside Kathe, taken aback by this unexpected outburst. "Darling, what could be so bad?" She put her arm around Kathe's shoulders, wanting to protect the girl from whatever was bothering her but not knowing how to begin. She had always felt such a fierce love for Kathe, but Kathe was so stubbornly independent, and she didn't like to play the role of interfering mother. "Nothing could be that terrible," she said encouragingly.

"Oh yes it could." Kathe sat up abruptly. Her cheeks were streaked with mascara and her lips had a pale, blotted look.

Viola began to worry in earnest. Kathe complained so rarely; she was so determinedly brave and cheerful that she couldn't imagine what could have put her in such a state. Still, the war was doing strange things to people. London had been badly bombed and Kathe no doubt had seen some terrible sights. Rumors had come to Sanford of people buried alive in the rubble, of burned children and terrible devastation. There was no telling what Kathe might have witnessed. "Do you want to talk about it?" she asked gently.

"I'm not sure." Kathe bit her lower lip and frowned. "I came down here to tell you, but now that I'm here I don't think I can." She looked at Viola uneasily and then looked down at the tips of her shoes.

Viola took a deep breath. This was obviously going to take some tact on her part. "I can't imagine you telling me anything that I wouldn't do my best to understand," she said quietly.

"I know that," Kathe said. "That's part of the problem. You're always so darn understanding, Mama. I feel so clumsy compared to you, like you're a swan and I'm some kind of lumbering elephant who just goes blundering ahead, only this time I think I may have blundered too far, and I'm afraid if I tell you how far you'll lose all respect for me, and I don't think I could take that on top of everything else."

"Kathe," she said firmly, "there's absolutely nothing you could tell me that would make me think badly of you."

"Truly?"

"Truly."

There was a long silence. Kathe seemed to be thinking it over. "I suppose," she said at last, "I'm going to have to tell you sometime anyway." She smiled weakly. "It doesn't hide well."

"What doesn't hide well?"

"Being, uh"—she colored uncomfortably—"oh hellfire, Mama, I'm pregnant. I thought I was sick, you see, so I went to the doctor and he gave me the verdict. Actually I got the happy news from the doctor's assistant. You should have seen the look on her face. It had the words *fallen woman* written all over it. 'We see so much of this kind of thing these days, miss,' she said. I know I shouldn't have let her make me feel ashamed, but she did."

"How did it happen?" Viola's mind was spinning in a hundred directions at once.

"Oh, the usual way." Kathe smiled weakly. "You see I had this bloody stupid fling with an American, a ten-day wonder of an affair that I thought was true love. In fact"—her voice trembled alarmingly—"I still think it's true love, only John's gone off and doesn't write and I'm scared and . . ."

"There, there." Viola patted the girl awkwardly. "Are you absolutely sure you're pregnant? Sometimes there are false alarms, you know."

"I saw the doctor two weeks ago. There's no doubt about it." She looked at Viola miserably. "I suppose you must think I'm a complete disgrace."

There was a short silence. Viola cleared her throat. What she should say next was obvious, but she found it difficult to begin. "Well," she said, "I don't think you're a disgrace, and even if I did it would be pretty hypocritical of me considering my own history." She took Kathe's hands and held them tightly in hers. "Darling, I'm going to tell you something I've never told anyone, something that only a few people alive know." She paused. "This is hard to admit after all these years, even to you, but I suppose I'm still a little old-fashioned. The truth is, when your father and I were married I was already pregnant with you. So how could I blame you for doing the same thing? It wouldn't be reasonable, you see, that is . . ." She stopped, suddenly embarrassed at the peculiar way Kathe was staring at her. "I suppose what I'm really trying to say," she concluded awkwardly, "is that I love you, and I don't intend to judge you, and I'll help you get through this any way I can."

"Mama"—Kathe looked immensely relieved—"you never cease to amaze me. You were really pregnant with me when you married Papa?"

"Yes." Viola nodded. "And I never regretted it, not even for a minute, and I never would have, not even if Joseph hadn't married me. I know what it's like to be in love, you see."

"It's terrible," Kathe exclaimed passionately, "the worst thing on earth."

"And wonderful too."

"Yes," Kathe agreed, "being in love is terrible and wonderful, and I'm glad it happened and sorry it happened, and I'd give anything to go back and erase it all, and at the same time I don't ever want to forget him."

"I know exactly what you mean," Viola said. "It may sound crazy, but after all these years I'm still angry at Joseph for dying and leaving me to raise you all alone, and yet if by some miracle he showed up, I'd take him back in a minute."

Kathe pressed her hand. "Mama," she said, "I can't tell you how much it means to me that you understand."

They sat for a moment longer, side by side, looking silently at the roses. A pale-winged butterfly paused on one of the blossoms, beat its wings a dozen times, and then moved on, blown across the brick-bordered beds like a scrap of yellow paper. "You must be tired from the trip," Viola observed after several minutes.

"Yes." Kathe nodded. "I am." She sighed wearily and got up from the bench, brushing the rose petals off her skirt. She's going to need a lot of sympathy and understanding in the next few months, Viola thought. There are things in store for her that she can't possibly begin to imagine.

October 21, 1941.

Kathe repeated the date to herself because it was the only way she could hang on to any sense of time. She had gone into labor at 11:40 A.M. Statistics were comforting: she had type O positive blood; she was five foot three inches tall, wore a size six shoe; she was in pain, but all pain ended sooner or later. She squinted and tried to turn her head. A hand caught her deftly under the chin, steadying her. She took another deep breath and more gas hissed out of the rubber mask the midwife was pressing over her face. The gas filled her nostrils and throat with a medicinal smell.

"Breathe deeply and count to ten, please," the midwife said firmly. She was a large elderly woman with bluish hair wrapped in a sterile kerchief.

Kathe lay back, and began to breathe and count, but the numbers were clumsy and hard to arrange in any satisfactory order. The gas was like a balloon taking her away from all pain. The midwife's face shrank into a pink-and-white blur the size of a sixpence. One, two, Kathe thought, three, four . . .

As she reached four John suddenly emerged from the overhead light and looked down at her, his hair curled and wet, as if he'd just stepped out of the shower. He was wearing an odd suit made of blue silk so he must have been in China after all. He smiled and Kathe smiled back.

I love you, he said, stroking her hair. She tried to lift her hand to his face, but her arms weren't working correctly. *My darling wife,* John said. He kissed her and his breath smelled like cinnamon so he must have been in India after all.

"I'm so glad you've come back to England, John," Kathe said happily. She felt her lips moving and heard her own voice, far away and dim, but John was still smiling at her so it must not matter. "I've been waiting and waiting for you all these months. When no letters came, I thought maybe you'd forgotten me, but I knew in my heart that you'd never forget me and oh, my darling, I've missed you so." She tried to touch him, but he was like water. "Give me your hand please," she begged. "Let me hold it, because I'm scared and the baby is coming too soon and I did my best to stop it, but there's nothing I could do and it hurts so much."

And I asked the angel, does heaven include Kathe, and he said . . .

"John, that's not really you talking, that's your letter."

So I told him to forget it . . .

"John, are you really here? Please. I'm in pain, and I'm so frightened. Don't play tricks on me." She reached for his hand again, and just then the pain came in a great solid wave, blotting out everything else. Her body coiled and fought to expel what was in it. She cried out and there was a long interval of fear and confusion. When she came back to awareness, John was gone. There should have been a baby crying, but instead there was silence. I've gone deaf, she thought incoherently.

"Miss Rothe, can you hear me?" The midwife's voice came from a great distance. "It's all over, and you're going to be just fine. You're in splendid shape."

"Hurts," she said thickly. The rubber mask was clamped back over her face. She smelled the medicinal smell of the gas and just as she was about to give in to it, she remembered that there was a very important question she'd forgotten to ask. "How's the baby?"

"I think we should talk about that later when you're feeling better," the midwife said, washing something in a basin. Kathe could hear the clink of metal against ceramic; the gas made it sound like a string of tiny bells.

"Please tell me how my baby is," she pleaded. She was beginning to feel very frightened by the silence.

The midwife turned, holding a shiny glass and metal syringe. Her eyes were full of pity. "I'm going to give you an injection now, Miss Rothe. It's a sedative."

"I said *how's the baby?* Please tell me, please . . ."

The needle stung in her vein. For a moment she fought the sedative; then there was only a long dark blankness full of slow, troubled dreams.

When Viola came into Kathe's room three hours later, she found Kathe awake and sitting up in bed in her old blue housecoat, staring out the window at the falling leaves. Viola stood in the doorway looking at the girl for a moment, thinking that she was young and strong and would survive this blow but that for a while things were going to be very hard for her. Kathe lifted the metal pitcher beside the bed and poured herself a glass of water. Her face was pale and sad, and she drank slowly. Putting the glass back down on the table, she ran her finger around aimlessly in the wet ring, not meeting Viola's eyes. For a moment neither of them spoke. "Hello, Mama," Kathe said at last.

"Hello," Viola said. "How are you feeling?"

"Pretty rotten." Kathe looked down at her hands and her voice trembled slightly. "The baby's dead, isn't it?"

"Yes." Viola sat wearily on the edge of the bed. "It was born too early." She wanted to say something comforting, but she couldn't think of anything. What comfort could there possibly be for something like this? Reaching out, she took Kathe in her arms and held her. Kathe curled up like a child, hiding her face in Viola's sweater.

"Was it a boy or a girl?" she asked.

"What does it matter, darling?" Viola said gently.

"I need to know."

"Why?"

"I just need to. Please, Mama."

"It was a boy."

There was a long silence.

"That baby was all I had left of John," Kathe said at last in a strange voice. "I loved him so much and now I've got nothing. I've lost him, and I've lost the baby. I've lost everything."

Viola stroked the girl's dark hair that was so much like Joseph's. "Kathe," she said quietly, "do you remember that day Richard went away and I told you that I had nothing, and you told me I still had you?"

"Yes," Kathe said, "I remember."

"Well, you still have me, sweetheart. We still have each other."

For a long time they sat holding each other. Outside a still breeze was blowing the leaves off the trees, piling them along the edges of the walks, filling in the empty fountains. Somewhere, in some distant part of the building, Viola could hear the laughter of small children and she wondered if Kathe could hear it too. Gradually she became aware that Kathe was crying.

"My baby boy died," Kathe said softly. "Even though he was never really alive, I loved him, and if he'd lived, I would have named him John."

"Kathe, for God's sake try to stop thinking that way."

"I'll try, Mama, but I doubt if it will do any good."

"Promise me you'll try."

"I'll try." There was another long silence. "Mama," Kathe said at last, "how do you go about getting over something like this?"

"I don't know, darling." Viola stroked Kathe's hair and looked out the window at the falling leaves. "I only wish I did. I think . . ." She stopped, overcome by her own emotions. "I think every woman has to do it in her own way."

22

NEW YORK

1947

"So, what, please, is your name?"

Kathe put up her hand to shield her eyes from the lights and looked out into the dark hall where fifty of the most promising young actors in New York sat on rows of wooden folding chairs waiting to watch her audition. "Kathe Rothe," she said firmly.

"Hmmm." Lee Strasberg adjusted his heavy horn-rimmed glasses and contemplated her application intently. A short, balding man with big ears, blue-gray eyes, and a stubborn chin, he was filling in this morning for Robert Lewis, who usually taught the advanced class. Lewis, according to his secretary, was at home with his throat wrapped in flannel, nursing a bad case of laryngitis, a turn of events that had come as a disappointment to Kathe, who had been looking forward to meeting him. Mr. Strasberg cleared his throat. Once a member of the famous radical Group Theatre of the thirties, he spoke with a slight accent that gave whatever he said an exotic sound. "So who recommended the Actors' Studio to you, Miss Rothe?"

"Mr. Lang."

"Hermann Lang, the producer of *Comanche?*"

"Yes, sir." Kathe tried to ignore the rows of students in blue jeans and baggy shirts who sat staring at her, but it wasn't easy. The hall in the old Union Methodist Church on West Forty-eighth Street was a dreary, unpromising room that looked as if it would have made a good setting for a rummage sale, and she felt very English and very out of place in her new black suit and silk blouse. It was ironic that she had come dressed to the nines to make a good impression only to discover that the students at the Actors' Studio did their best to look like applicants for relief packages. Perhaps the fact that America was so unscathed by the war had given them all some kind of guilt complex.

"So Mr. Hermann Lang recommends you. Very fancy," Mr. Strasberg was saying. "It's not every day we get one of his protégées. How do you come to know him?"

"He's an old friend of my mother's," Kathe mumbled, embarrassed.

"Speak up, please," Mr. Strasberg said.

"A friend of my mother's," Kathe yelled. Her voice bounced off the walls of the studio with a tinny sound that made her want to sink through the floor.

"She's who, your mother?"

"Viola Kessler." It was out at last. She had promised herself this very morning before she took the train into New York that she wouldn't admit under any circumstances that her mother was Viola Kessler, intending to get a place in the Studio on her own merits or not at all. Mr. Strasberg, however, seemed to have no intention of handing her a place just because her mother had been a famous actress. He peered over his glasses at her critically, inspecting her from head to toe.

"Viola Kessler's daughter, eh? So what have you got for us this morning?"

"I'm going to do a monologue from the third act of *Nina*, the Henry Arbor play that just won the Pulitzer Prize." She looked at the students. "As most of you probably already know, it's the scene where Nina has been abandoned by her father, who has remarried, a young woman half his age. She's jealous, of course, and—"

"Don't tell us, show us," Mr. Strasberg interrupted, leaning back his chair. "Well, go ahead. We're waiting."

Kathe took a deep breath and looked around at the bare platform that served as a stage. There was a small wooden table flanked by a couple of folding chairs, an ashtray, and a potted plant that looked as if it had died weeks ago. Sitting down on one of the chairs, Kathe pulled the pins out of her hair one by one. Her hair fell down around her shoulders, partially hiding her face. Reaching over, she pantomimed putting two slices of toast into a nonexistent toaster. She moved wearily—for the character, Nina, was always tired—but the truth was she was terribly excited, so much so that it was all she could do to concentrate on her lines. Fortunately, she knew them cold. For the past month, ever since she'd decided to audition for the Studio, she had been practicing this scene, driving Anna and Erwin Reiter crazy by her habit of repeating her lines at odd moments. Mr. Reiter was another old friend of her mother's, a former German actor who now worked in the offices of Levitt and Sons, the developers who were building the giant housing tracts in Nassau County. When they heard she was coming to the States, Mr. Reiter and his wife were kind enough to offer her a place to stay, and she'd repaid them by muttering the monologue from *Nina* morning, noon, and night.

"Father isn't coming," she said, looking at the door, "and I don't suppose he'll ever come again. I was so good to him, taking care of him for all these years since Mama died, and he never noticed." She felt stiff for a moment, as if she were reading the words from the script, and then by some transmutation that she never quite understood, the stiffness disappeared and she was absorbed in the scene, working at it from every angle. Getting up, she walked over to the dead plant and picked off a leaf.

"I was like a flower," she continued, picking off another leaf, "like a flower when I was around him, like a lily or something, and now I'm all dried up, an old nothing, and I suppose it's going to be like this forever, him gone and me dry and nothing left. And that girl he's married, all she wants is his money—"

"Scene," Mr. Strasberg called out suddenly.

"What?" Kathe looked around, surprised to have been interrupted.

"Stop, please."

"What's wrong?" She came to the edge of the stage. "Did I do something wrong?"

"Just about everything, I'm afraid. You were acting very slickly and competently, Miss Rothe, but that's all you were doing—acting. There was no feeling, no emotional recall."

Kathe felt humiliated. "I'm sorry," she mumbled, "but I don't know what you mean."

"You need *context* for a monologue like that." Mr. Strasberg pointed his finger at her. "You need to feel what Nina was feeling; you need to know what had happened to her before she came onstage—what she ate for dinner last night, what she dreamed, whether she washed out her stockings in the sink and hung them in the bathroom or hid them in her closet to dry."

"How could that make any difference?"

"It makes all the difference in the world."

"Oh," Kathe said, "I see." But she didn't see at all. Mr. Strasberg's critique struck her as dictatorial and slightly insane. Know where Nina dried her stockings indeed. She started to step down from the stage.

"Not so fast." Mr. Strasberg waved her back. "That bit with the plant was a nice touch. I don't mean to discourage you. There's something very intriguing about your presence onstage, but you need more training. Perhaps the scene would work better if you had a partner."

Now Kathe was really confused. "But it's a *monologue*, Mr. Strasberg."

"That's just the point. A monologue is really a dialogue between the actor and an invisible person—in this case Nina's father."

"Oh." Kathe stood irresolutely, wondering how in the world she was going to turn Nina's monologue into a dialogue.

"Marlon." Mr. Strasberg waved to a dark-haired, handsome boy in a white T-shirt. "Go on up there and improvise with Miss Rothe."

"Okay." The boy ambled up on the stage as if his entire body were joined together by ball bearings. "Hi," he said.

"Hi," Kathe said.

"Marlon is one of Kazan's finds," Mr. Strasberg said.

"So what do I do?" Marlon asked.

"Just sit there and be her father."

"You want me to talk?"

"No, just sit there."

"I don't see how this is going to do any good," Kathe objected.

"Try it," Marlon suggested. "The guy knows what he's doing." Sitting down at the table, he folded his arms and contemplated Kathe stonily. It was really rather eerie having him there, she decided, certainly a far cry from doing the scene alone.

"Well," Mr. Strasberg said, "what are you waiting for?"

Kathe sat down at the table, trying not to look at Marlon, who was somehow managing to radiate indifference. "Father isn't coming," she stuttered, "and I don't suppose he'll ever come again. I was so good to him, taking care of him all these years since Mama died." She felt something black and nasty to her right. Looking over, she saw that Marlon had changed his indifference into rage. It was frightening really, as if he were about to jump out at her and hit her. She could feel every bit of energy in the room being drawn to him like a magnet, and yet if she'd been asked to describe how he was doing it, she would have been at a loss: he hadn't moved, the expression on his face hadn't changed, and yet he seemed so threatening that it made the hairs on her arms stand up. She fumbled her next lines, thinking that he must be some kind of genius.

"Scene," Mr. Strasberg yelled. "That was much better."

"But I blew my lines," Kathe objected.

"Right." Mr. Strasberg seemed pleased. "That shows you were feeling something." On the opposite side of the table Marlon had once again become a pleasant fellow with a warm grin. Kathe stared from him to Strasberg, thinking that she was definitely out of her depth.

"So where have you studied?" Mr. Strasberg asked briskly.

"In London at the Kessler School for the Performing Arts."

"With your mother, I take it?"

"Yes."

"Been in any productions?"

"A few small roles. Frankly I decided only recently that I really wanted to do this professionally. I've been in, uh, conflict about what to do with my life. I thought for a while I was going to be a botanist. I even went up to Cambridge for a few terms, but I'm just not made for it. There's too much petty detail and not enough appreciation of the beauty of the plants and . . ." She stumbled to a halt, embarrassed, wondering why in the world she was telling him all this when it was obvious that he had already decided that she wasn't up to the Studio's standards.

"A botanist, eh," Mr. Strasberg chuckled. "For me it was wigs."

"I beg your pardon?"

"Wigs," Mr. Strasberg said. "I started out in the Human Hair Novelty Company as a bookkeeper. So this is good you study science. The more life you live before you come to the stage, the more life you give your characters. You want my honest opinion, Miss Rothe? You aren't ready for the Studio yet."

"Oh." Even though she'd known it was coming, she still felt the blow. Stepping down from the platform, she retrieved her raincoat from an empty chair in the first row. "Thank you for letting me take up your time," she said stiffly.

"Time"—Mr. Strasberg waved his hands—"time is nothing." He leaned forward, his round face intense and slightly luminous, as if someone had switched on a light behind his cheeks. "You could be a good actress if you could only *feel*. You're frozen."

"Frozen?" Kathe was taken aback.

"I'm not saying you're frigid. How should I know this? But something isn't connected. Such a pity in such a young girl, so pretty, but there's a big blank space inside you"—he spread his arms—"like this. You've been hurt, yes?"

Kathe nodded impulsively, and then was terribly embarrassed. Mr. Strasberg remained nonplussed. "So," he continued, "we've all been hurt. So what? You want to be an actor, then getting hurt is necessary, only you can't close down. You have to *use* the pain. When you can feel your own emotions, Miss Rothe—feel them in public the way you did up there with Marlon—come back and try again."

Don't call us, we'll call you, Kathe thought. Mumbling her thanks, she hurried out of the hall feeling insulted, humiliated, and disappointed. Before she reached the door two young actors were already up on the stage doing the balcony scene from *Romeo and Juliet*. Outside on West Forty-eighth Street at eleven-thirty in the morning it was so dark that most of the delivery trucks had turned on their headlights, so bitterly cold and miserable that the few pedestrians who hurried along the sidewalks walked with their heads down, like swimmers braving a heavy surf. Pulling the collar of her raincoat up around her neck, Kathe threw back her head and took deep gulps of the icy air. Sleet stung her cheeks and lips. So she was frozen, was she? Well the hell with Mr. Strasberg. Waving away a cab that miraculously appeared out of the storm, she stomped off across town, ignoring the fact that her new suede pumps were turning to mush. She didn't need the Actors' Studio. So what if she wasn't admitted. She had plenty of connections. She could always go back to London and get parts just by mentioning her mother's name. And if that wasn't enough, Hermann Lang had a successful musical running this very moment.

At the corner of Broadway and Forty-eighth she turned toward Times Square, still steaming. At Forty-fourth, half a block from Sardi's, tourists were standing in line in front of the Oxford Theater to buy tickets to this evening's performance of *Comanche*. So what if it was a silly musical about cowboys and Indians, Kathe thought obstinately. It was entertaining—no *Oklahoma!* maybe, but definitely a hit—and if she asked Hermann, he would probably give her a part in the chorus. As she stood across the street, stubbornly contemplating the flashing red-and-gold marquee and the tourists' blue, pinched faces, she suddenly had a realization: Mr. Strasberg was right. She fought off admitting this to herself, but the thought kept coming back that there really was a frozen place in her; there had been ever since she'd lost the baby, and no matter how much she tried to run away from that old pain it was still there and it was true, and Mr. Strasberg had been smart enough to pick it out the first time he saw her act.

She suddenly felt humble and a little frightened. Hurrying back to Times Square, she hailed a cab. Inside the air was musty and overheated and the windows were covered with steam. As the driver edged through traffic, Kathe stared blankly ahead, lost in thought. I'm like a jigsaw puzzle with an important piece missing, she thought. She put her hand over her heart and was reassured to hear it beating quite normally, but she felt lonely nevertheless, and sad and rather lost.

A week later Kathe stood in a residential section of the Bronx looking up at a seven-story building of weathered yellow brick. She started to cross the street, reconsidered, and stepped back up on the curb. Not yet, she thought; think it over some more. If you're going to make a fool of yourself, at least plan ahead.

The day was cold and sunny with a wind that cut through her gloves, numbing her hands. As she pulled up the collar of her coat and pressed her chin into her muffler, she was suddenly struck by a feeling of pity for her younger self. Five years ago it would have meant so much to her to be standing here with John's address tucked into her purse. She thought of the endless letters she had written to the U.S. State Department inquiring about him, the money she had spent calling every Duke and Duccini in the Boston phone directory, but there had been a war on and no one would tell her where he was, or even if he was alive. For an entire year after she lost the baby she had kept trying, hitting dead end after dead end, and with every failure the love she had felt for John became more painful, like a piece of glass working its way through her skin. By the time she turned nineteen she had begun to believe that she was being punished for ever having allowed herself to feel. Slowly, day by day, her emotions had died inside her until finally she had closed her heart, promising herself never again to try to find him. She had kept that promise until the day before, when, after nearly a week of mulling over Strasberg's criticisms, she had impulsively decided to call the Harvard Alumni Association in Cambridge. Five minutes later she had John's address. That's all it had taken: one long-distance phone call, forty-five cents, and five minutes of her time.

Clapping her hands together to warm them, she stared nervously down at a gutterful of cold water that glittered golden in the pale November sunlight and then back up at the building. She was beginning to feel something like stage fright, which was absolutely ridiculous. She had gotten over John long ago—at least in any way that really mattered. In the last five years she had built a whole new life, made new friends, developed new interests, even briefly found herself another lover—a Swedish mathematician at Cambridge who had wanted to marry her. John had faded from her memory like a photograph left out in the light. Still her mind went on inventing excuses for not going up to his apartment, and not very good excuses at that.

She took a deep breath. The facts, she told herself impatiently, were simple enough to be faced without all this mental subterfuge.

Fact number one: her affair with John had been a piece of wartime craziness that had had such painful consequences that if she thought of it at all, she only thought of it with regret. Fact number two: on the other hand, it had become clear to her since her unsuccessful audition for the Actors' Studio that the affair had damaged her. She'd loved John so much and lost him in such a strange, inconclusive way that she had evidently suffered an amputation of sorts. Thanks to him, one of her emotional legs had been cut off, rather neatly, with a good anaesthetic. The question at hand was: could the leg be reattached? John probably wasn't completely responsible for the vacuum that was crippling her work. Would seeing him again put her back in contact with the emotions she needed to move an audience? Maybe yes, maybe no; maybe she was indeed about to wound herself beyond healing.

On the other hand, what did she have to lose? If she lurked out here any longer, those women on the park bench across the street were probably going to report her as a burglar. She pulled the pearl-tipped pin out of her hat and reanchored it firmly. She was five years older, six pounds heavier, her hair was longer, and John probably wouldn't even remember her name. Squaring her shoulders, she crossed the street and entered the building.

The first thing she saw was the elevator, a massive brass cage decorated with fleurs-de-lis and sporting an OUT OF ORDER sign. The stairs, in contrast, were plain concrete, clean, ugly, and utilitarian. Taking them two at a time, she arrived out of breath and rather exhilarated at the fifth floor. The hall was dim and overheated in the usual American way, carpeted in dour blue and brown squares. Everything was dull, proper, and relentlessly middle class—at least by English standards. She found it strange that John had ended up in such a place. He'd had such expensive tastes and such extravagant plans: mayor of New York, ambassador to the Court of St. James's. How could a man who had once lectured her on the aesthetics of medieval church windows live with such a rug?

Walking resolutely toward the light of a small rectangular window at the far end of the hall, she passed the doors to apartments 501 and 502. Number 503 was decorated with a polished brass knocker in the shape of a lion's head. The lion was grinning inanely, as if it had just finished off an especially tasty zebra. Now that was another incongruous touch. As far as she could remember, John had hated anything precious. Grabbing the lion by its mane, she brought it down with a resounding thud.

There was a brief silence followed by the sound of someone walking toward the door, and a female voice said with distinct exasperation, "Well it took you long enough!" The door was thrown open and she found herself face-to-face with a pretty young woman holding a baby. The woman wore a blue cotton housedress; her black hair was tied back from her face with a red ribbon, her eyes were dark and velvety, and she had a vaguely foreign look.

"Oh," the woman observed, obviously surprised, "you're not the delivery boy after all."

"No," Kathe stammered, "I'm not."

The woman shifted the baby to her other hip. The baby, who was wearing a blue knit top and a large white diaper, clutched at her with sticky hands that appeared to have been smeared with grape juice. "So what can I do for you?" the woman asked. The baby attacked the chain she wore around her neck and extracted a large gold cross from between her breasts. "No, sweetie," the woman admonished the baby gently, "not now." The woman looked up at Kathe and shrugged apologetically. "He's always wanting to nurse, and he doesn't understand about strangers. I never saw such a hungry kid."

"Excuse me," Kathe said, feeling a little bewildered. "I think I have the wrong apartment. I was looking for a Mr. John Duke."

"Oh you've got the right place," the woman said cheerfully. "I'm Mrs. Duke. Giovanni isn't here now, but he's gonna be back soon. He ran out to the store for some beer and some Gerber's baby beets for Emmanuel. The kid eats beets like they're going out of style."

Kathe knew she should say something, but she was speechless.

"Say," Mrs. Duke said, inspecting her solicitously, "you okay?"

"Yes," she mumbled awkwardly, "I'm fine. That is, you see, I'm an old friend of John's and . . ."

"An old friend?" Mrs. Duke positively beamed with hospitality. "Say, why didn't you say so in the first place? Come on in. I just baked some cookies. You can have some while you wait." She smiled, exposing a row of pretty white teeth. "Us skinny girls don't have to worry, but when we get old, *Mamma mia*, watch out! You like cookies?"

"Thank you but I have to go, that is . . ." Kathe began to back away. It was all too obvious that this visit was a major mistake, but Mrs. Duke was too fast for her.

"Come on in," Mrs. Duke insisted, catching her by the arm. The baby reached over and wrapped his small grubby fingers in Kathe's hair, making escape difficult. "Giovanni would never forgive me if I let one of his friends get away. What did you say your name was?"

"Kathe Rothe," Kathe stammered.

"You can call me Candy," the woman said amiably. "Everyone does. So where do you know Giovanni from?"

"London." Giving up, Kathe allowed herself to be led into the living room. A large yellow couch dominated one entire wall. Littered with books, newspapers, embroidered pillows, toy trucks, balls of yarn, and a half-eaten banana, it looked like some kind of exotic animal that had died on the blue carpet. In front of the couch was a small marble coffee table, incongruously beautiful, with scrolled legs and delicate bird-shaped feet. Plopping the baby down beside Kathe, Mrs. Duke headed for the far side of the room. "Do me a favor and watch the kid while I get us some coffee," she called out over her shoulder as she disappeared into what was presumably the kitchen.

Kathe looked around at the room, feeling increasingly uneasy yet curious. The walls were covered with framed pictures of Italian landscapes and saints. On a low table by the window a large radio stood flanked by about thirty pots of African violets, all in full bloom. Candy Duke obviously had a green thumb.

Candy reappeared with two small cups of coffee on a wooden tray and a plate of Italian cookies. "Dig in," she said. She took a powdered cookie, broke it into pieces, and fed part of it to the baby. "Emmanuel loves this stuff."

Kathe took a cookie and bit into it. There was a hint of almond mixed with lemon.

"So where are you staying?" Candy inquired. "If you need a place, we can put you up."

"Thank you," Kathe said, feeling acutely uncomfortable at the suggestion, "but I'm staying with family friends in Rockhaven." Calm down, she told herself. The woman can't read minds.

"Rockhaven's on Long Island, isn't it?"

"Yes."

"Nice place, Long Island." Candy sighed and fed the baby another scrap of cookie. "Someday, when they make John president of the company or something, I wanna move out there so Emmanuel can see more trees. A kid needs trees, you know?"

My God, what if John had told her about their affair in London? Men did that kind of thing all the time. "Excuse me," Kathe stood up abruptly, "could I use your bathroom?"

"First door to the left down the hall," Candy volunteered.

Kathe switched on the light, threw several handfuls of cold water on her face, and inspected her reflection in the mirror. What in the world was she doing here? John could come in at any minute, creating a situation that would be awkward to say the least. The only thing to do was to go back out in the living room and excuse herself, pleading an appointment. When you get yourself into a mess, Kathe Rothe, she told her reflection, you don't do it halfway, do you?

On the way back down the hall she stopped. The bedroom door was ajar, and she could see two framed photographs sitting on a walnut dresser. She hesitated for a moment longer. Then, pushing open the door, she walked quietly across the gray carpet, knowing that if Candy discovered her, she would feel like a complete fool, yet she was unable to resist the temptation to see what John looked like these days. The larger of the two photos displayed Candy in her wedding dress, beaming out from a vast lace veil that all but hid her face. She looked very young and very happy. Beside her was a small snapshot of John, his dark hair curling out from under a wool cap, and in the background a battered white rowboat and the smooth horizon of a lake. He seemed content, as if life had been good to him, but she imagined that she could still see some of the old restlessness in his eyes, as if he would never completely settle anywhere. The picture gave her an unexpected pang. She picked it up and looked at it for a long time, thinking about those ten days they had spent together in London. No doubt things had turned out for the best, and yet it all seemed such a waste somehow.

Feeling sad, she put the picture back down on the bureau and turned away. She was just about to leave the bedroom when a piece of parchment in a gold frame caught her eye. It was a marriage license—one of the elaborate, decorative sort filled with golden cherubs and intertwined hearts. Impulsively, she stepped over and read it:

> LET IT BE KNOWN THAT
> ON THIS SECOND DAY OF JUNE
> NINETEEN HUNDRED AND THIRTY-NINE
> AT THE HOLY REDEEMER CHURCH OF BOSTON
> CANDICE MARIA FARINI
> AND
> GIOVANNI EMMANUEL DUCCINI
> WERE JOINED IN HOLY MATRIMONY . . .

The second of June, nineteen hundred and *thirty-nine?* She reread the date but it stayed the same no matter how hard she tried to make it come out differently. When she met John in London he had already been married for *three years!* Furious, she stalked out of the bedroom, feeling the pain of betrayal so intensely that it was all she could do not to scream at Candy, who was, she realized, only another of John's victims.

"Oh, hello," Candy said, looking up from the baby. "I thought you'd gotten lost."

"I'm sorry," Kathe said, picking up her coat, "but I have to leave."

"But you just got here."

"I'm sorry," she insisted, "but I have to go somewhere right away." She put on her coat, not meeting Candy's eyes. Somewhere in the background she could hear her entire past breaking up.

Candy looked disappointed. "I'll tell John you stopped by."

"Yes," Kathe said politely through gritted teeth. "Do."

Outside, the air was cool against her cheeks and the street was mercifully deserted. Well at least she finally knew why John had stopped writing to her. He had lied to her, seduced her, and played her for a fool, and it had taken her five years to discover the fact. Reaching into her purse, she took out his address, wadded it into a ball, and threw it into a trash can. Good riddance, she thought. The subways ran every half hour this time of day. If she hurried, she might be able to make the next train.

As she walked through the park, sending clouds of pigeons scattering in her path, she had a sense of seeing it all for the first time:

the sleek, glittering necks of the birds, the rusted iron benches, the candy wrappers, and long dry grass polished and smooth as bamboo. Her whole life up to this moment had been built on a lie, and now that that lie was gone she felt abandoned and angry and liberated and a little frightened, and if she had been asked to say which feeling was the strongest, she would have had to admit that it was still the feeling of having no feeling at all.

23

NEW YORK
1948

Hermann Lang's office was located above Sardi's restaurant, so close to the Oxford Theater that if he wanted to see how his latest musical was doing, he only had to stick his head out the window, but on this particular morning in early May he had other things besides box-office receipts on his mind. Ten minutes ago Kathe Rothe had walked into his office to spill out her guts to him, and he was listening to her now with that sympathetic intensity that always endeared him to his friends. Hermann had learned a lot since those days back in Germany when he had been an aspiring film director cranking the camera for silent vampire movies. Although he would always be more comfortable-looking than handsome—barrel-chested, balding, possessed of a pair of sweet blue eyes that peered out from behind heavy horn-rimmed glasses—he had learned to make the best of his appearance, wearing neatly tailored suits instead of the striped shirts and plaid slacks he had favored back in Berlin. More important, he had mastered the art of producing to the point where it had become an entertaining game instead of a miserable struggle. At the age of forty-six Hermann could tell a successful script from a flop by reading the first ten pages; he could soothe enraged actors who were convinced that their dressing rooms had been designed to insult them, pacify temperamental directors who wanted to use real elephants and man-eating lions for authenticity, sweet-talk the musicians' union, and keep entire chorus lines of underpaid dancers from walking out when the salary checks didn't arrive on time. But most of all over the past fifteen years since he had fled from Germany to America, Hermann had learned to listen. He was doing that now, expertly, his round body hunched forward over a desk that looked as if it were serving as a dump for every spare piece of paper, stale sandwich, depleted ballpoint pen, and empty coffee cup in Manhattan.

"I'm just drifting, Hermann," Kathe was saying. "When you gave me that bit part in *Comanche* I thought I might get my feet back on the ground, but it's only made things worse." She frowned, young and sincere and very beautiful in a black turtleneck sweater that made her look like a cross between a bohemian from the Village and a novice who had taken some kind of vow of chastity, which in an odd way, Hermann suspected, wasn't far from the truth. He was struck once again how much the girl looked like her mother, even though she was dark and Viola was blond. Whenever he talked to Kathe—which he did at least once a month—something pinched at his heart. He had been very fond of Viola and Joseph during their Berlin days, and there was something about Kathe—a unique combination of her mother's passion and her father's reckless idealism—that made him remember a world he had spent the last fifteen years trying to forget.

"I'm not complaining, God knows." Kathe twisted at one of her silver bracelets. She was—he thought about it for a moment—twenty-four. A good age to plunge into life, but a dangerous one; he knew from long experience that sometime between twenty-two and twenty-five a lot of young actresses got tired of the fight and gave up. "I'm grateful you gave me that part in *Comanche*, really I am, but it's a taste of the theater without really being the theater, if you know what I mean. I get to dance, sing a little, spend fifteen minutes a night pretending I'm a real actress, but the truth is I'm just not getting anywhere—not with my career or my life either for that matter. I feel"—she gestured expansively—"like I'm treading water. Every six weeks or so I go back to audition for the Actors' Studio and they tell me the same thing—that I'm frozen up emotionally."

"The Studio." Hermann shook his head. "Always the Studio. It owns the theater, this Studio? There aren't maybe five hundred producers and would-be producers within maybe a mile radius of here? You have to be Brando?"

Kathe grinned for the first time since she'd walked into his office. "I don't think I'd look all that good in an undershirt, Hermann, but that's the general idea. Yes, I have to be Brando."

"This is a crazy girl I have in front of me, yes?"

"Yes." Kathe nodded stubbornly. "A hundred percent crazy. Obsessed, willing to do anything to get up there onstage and *feel* something for once."

Hermann sighed and sat back. This wasn't going to be easy. "Look," he said kindly. "I'm not going to give you compliments. For compliments you're too smart. You want me to tell you that tomorrow Kazan is going to fall all over himself to give you a part? Sorry. Life doesn't work that way, especially since you don't let me put in a word for you. Such a stubborn girl you are." He shook a friendly finger at her. "But you keep making the rounds and auditioning, and sooner or later you'll get something. Maybe not Blanche Dubois, but something."

" 'Something' just isn't good enough."

"So you want the moon, yes? And maybe the galaxy thrown in for good measure? Ambition." He shook his head. "So full of it you are, just like your mother. She would have walked through hell for a good part, your mother would have. She did in fact, and where it got her I don't need to tell you."

"What about Hollywood?"

Hermann had known this was coming ever since she walked in the door. "So Hollywood, what about it? It's a place."

Kathe leaned forward, her dark eyes troubled. "Seriously, Hermann, do you think I should go out there and give it a try? I keep telling myself that it's either do that or go back to England, but frankly"—she laughed nervously—"I don't fancy the idea of coming home like the prodigal daughter and admitting to Mama that I couldn't make it on my own."

Hollywood, Hermann thought, would eat her alive, but if he told her that, she would very likely think he was just a cynical old man. Warning the young was a dangerous occupation. "Well," he said, choosing his words cautiously, "it's, I suppose, a possibility, but if it's my advice you're asking, I'm telling you that for you it's *Scheissdreck.*"

"I beg your pardon? What?"

"Some things"—Hermann grinned—"I don't translate." He looked around his office, at the posters of the films he had directed, the musical comedies he had produced. His whole career was stuck to the walls. Interspersed with the posters were stills of Christina Hagerup—known to the world as Christine Bergen—beautiful, blond, Norwegian Christina, whom he had made into another Dietrich, married for a time, and then divorced amicably. Christina hadn't been much of an actress, not even half as good or as sensitive as Kathe, but Hollywood had taken its toll on her nevertheless. Watching it grind so much of the happiness and simplicity out of Christina had been an enlightening experience, one that had sent him back to Broadway. Money, even when it came in six-digit packages, wasn't compensation enough for what the film industry could do to a beautiful woman once it got its hooks into her. "Do something else, *Liebling,*" he said. "You go out there and—snap"—he made a breaking motion with both hands—"Goldwyn and his pals will make your backbone into a pretzel and eat it with their beer."

Kathe frowned anxiously. "But what other alternatives are there, Hermann? I mean, here I am, hanging out in New York, living with the Reiters, baby-sitting Erwin, Jr., on Sundays, and watching my career go down the drain. Frankly, I'm not even sure anymore if I have talent. So what do you suggest? Extensive psychotherapy? Secretarial school? A lobotomy to finish off what's left of my feelings? I feel all washed up."

Hermann repressed a chuckle. "So impatient. Such ants in the pants. More and more you remind me of your father. Tell Joseph Rothe to slow down and like a freight train the man would take off just to show you he could do it. Your mama's the same way. 'Relax, Vi,' Hilde and I would say to her, but Viola never knew the meaning of the word."

"By the time Mama was my age," Kathe said passionately, "she was working with Eric Stern, playing Nora and Clytemnestra and

Antigone, and what am I playing?" Her face turned red and her dark eyes glittered. "I'm playing a girl who square dances with half a dozen other girls yodeling about the joys of kissing cowboys under the stars." She stopped suddenly. "Oh rats, Hermann, I didn't mean to insult you. *Comanche*'s a wonderful musical."

"It's a piece of junk"—Hermann shrugged—"but ask me if I care. It entertains, yes? It brings in the money? Someday I'll do some serious theater again, but meanwhile I laugh all the way to the bank."

"Tell me frankly," Kathe demanded. "Do I have what it takes or don't I?"

"Ask your mother."

"That's just the problem." Kathe sighed in a way that would have been comic if she hadn't been in such deadly earnest. "Mama's always been more or less dotty about me. She'd tell me I was the next Bernhardt even if I couldn't walk across the stage without tripping over my own feet, but you're totally tactless."

"*Danke schön.*" Hermann laughed.

"You're sweet, Hermann, I don't mean to say you aren't—but when you've got something to tell me, you don't pull punches."

Hermann was irrationally pleased. "So you want my frank opinion?"

Kathe's face paled slightly. "Yes," she said stubbornly. "I do."

"Well, then . . ." He paused and considered for a moment, weighing her performance in *Comanche* and trying to calculate what she might be able to do if she had a part with some substance to it. "Hermann Lang's frank opinion is that you have talent."

"As much as Mama?"

"That question," Herman chuckled, "I'm too old and too wise a man to answer. Anyway, who can tell at this point? You're young, yes? You go in one direction"—he gestured to the right—"and maybe you become another Helen Hayes or Katharine Cornell." He gestured to the left. "But you go the way you're going now, and pffft."

"Pffft?"

"Nothing." Hermann picked up a paper clip and flicked it expertly into an empty coffee cup. "You act but it stays like a machine, your acting. No heart. No *Seele.*"

"Oh." Kathe's face fell. "In other words, Strasberg was right?"

"Yes," Hermann said, knowing there was no way to soften the

blow. "For once maybe he was. He looked at you and he saw the truth. What can I say?"

Kathe tried to smile but the corners of her mouth wavered. "I guess I asked for your frank opinion and got it." She started to get to her feet. "Thanks for telling me."

"Hold on." Hermann waved her back into her chair. "That's not all."

"There's more?" She looked at him apprehensively.

"Maybe you don't want to hear any more, yes?"

"Shoot," she said gamely, sitting back down.

Hermann got to his feet and took a few steps across the room. This was the hard part and he wasn't sure how to begin. "So," he said, "we talk frankly some more. First"—he waved a large finger at her—"let me tell you like a Dutch uncle that you've got to stop comparing yourself to your mother. You love her, of course. We all love Mama. But you use that love like a weapon. Always you're attacking yourself with it; always you're making Kathe less than she is. So you go here; you go there; you act a bit, and then you don't act a bit. A pleasure this isn't to say to you, *Liebling*, but you don't stick to anything. Up on that stage there's only half of you. And where's the other half? Thinking of Mama, that's where."

Kathe swallowed and looked down at her hands.

"You want me to stop, you say the word."

"No, go on. I hate to admit it, but this is making a lot of sense."

"You know," Hermann said, "you've got guts. Most girls would be crying by now."

"I've been through some nasty times," Kathe said quietly. "The tears dried up quite a while ago. So go on. What else is wrong with me?"

"Almost nothing," Hermann said.

"Almost nothing?" She looked surprised.

"Right. In here"—he pointed to her chest—"there's such a little thing wrong. Like a tiny gear with the teeth worn off. And there's so much good—you're a fast study, *Liebling*." Hermann smiled and readjusted his glasses, pleased that he was honestly able to tell her she was talented. "You deliver your lines like—how shall I say?—like Heine's poems—nice rhythms, soft when soft is needed, hard when the play asks for hard. And do I need to tell you you're pretty? I think not. I think this you already know. So onstage you look good. Maybe this shouldn't be important, but it is. In the audience all the men are thinking, this is the woman for me—or at least that's what they'd be thinking if not for that one little gear, the one"—he struck his chest—"here."

A shadow of hope spread over her face that was very touching. "What can I do about that one gear, Hermann?"

"You can start by thinking of Christine Bergen." He put up a hand. " 'Christine Bergen?' you're thinking. 'The man's gone crazy.' But there is so much that you don't know. When Christina and I started working together in '38 she couldn't act. Not her way out of a paper bag, as the Americans say. Put her in front of the camera and maybe you think you've got a dressmaker's dummy. Nice legs, nice profile, but she talks and you're supposed to be crying only you're laughing instead and so is the whole crew."

"But Christine Bergen's a fine actress," Kathe objected. "She's one of the best. I saw her in *Africa* and it gave me chills. That scene where she walks alone into the desert after her French lover wearing her high heels and singing was incredible. Everyone in the theater was cheering."

Hermann shrugged. "We did a hundred and twenty-five takes to get that scene."

Kathe looked slightly horrified. "You're kidding."

"So we wasted a lot of film. But she got better. You want to know the reason why?"

"Why?"

Hermann pointed to himself. "She worked with me every day. I taught her how to feel. I'm not a romantic-looking man, I know this. I don't stimulate great feelings in women." He smiled. "I'm not Don Juan, but I think I know something about the human heart. So I made a class of it for Christina." He chuckled. "Too good a class maybe, since we ended up married."

"I knew you'd been married to Christine Bergen but I had no idea you were her teacher."

"Christina mostly taught herself. She was always a smart woman." Hermann suddenly felt embarrassed, as if he had done something boyish like stand on his head to impress her.

Kathe frowned, as if she were mulling over what he'd just told her.

"Hermann," she said after a rather long silence, "do you think you could teach me the way you taught Christina?"

"You wouldn't want me for a teacher, *Liebling*."

"Why not?"

"Because"—he grinned—"I'm a tyrant. There's the yelling—I yell; and sometimes I turn red and swell up like a frog; for my blood pressure this wouldn't be so great. Here"—he pointed to himself— "you see Clark Kent, but if I try to teach you how to act, it would be King Kong."

"I can't imagine you ever yelling at anyone, Hermann." Kathe bit her lower lip thoughtfully. "And even if you did, I'm willing to take the chance." She smiled suddenly, and it was like a wave of sunlight entering the office. "What would I have to do to convince you?"

"It's not a good idea," he said, feeling himself weakening.

"Oh yes it is; it's a great idea." She got up, obviously excited. "You say I have one little gear out of order. Good, then fix it for me. In return I'll do anything you want."

"Anything?"

"Anything."

He thought it over and was surprised to discover that he was tempted. "Even television?"

She looked slightly horrified. "You mean those little dim seven-inch boxes they're selling at Macy's for $179.95?"

"So now it's a little box, but tomorrow who knows?" He laughed. "Yesterday Mr. Sardi goes on some godawful program called *Home on the Range* and makes crepes in a chafing dish. This, I admit, isn't high art. But in a year, maybe less, you're going to start seeing first-run plays on that little box, and when that happens I'm going to need actresses."

"Actresses? I don't understand."

"So," Hermann said, "I'm telling you my secret. I'm going to produce plays for television. Now you think the fancy Broadway stars are going to be interested? You think they're going to stake their reputations for the peanuts I'll be able to pay? Forget it. That's where you come in." He paused. "You say you're willing to do anything? If you really mean it, let's make an agreement." He paused again. "On second thought, maybe this is a bad idea."

"No it isn't," Kathe pleaded. "Please go on. You said we should make an agreement. What kind of agreement?"

Hermann sat back for a minute. He always took extra pains to make sure that people knew what they were agreeing to, having learned the hard way that if he didn't, bad feelings were bound to result. "It would be a real commitment," he said after a short silence. "I'd teach you like I taught Christina. If we got no results, fine. You'd go back to your mama and tell her you'd decided to learn shorthand. If we got results . . ."

"Please, Hermann." Kathe leaned forward, face flushed, eyes bright with excitement, and the thought occurred to Hermann that she was going to look stunning in close-ups. "Don't stop now. I can't stand the suspense. What if we got results?"

"Then you'd agree to take a role in, say, ten of my productions." He chuckled. "At a reasonable salary."

"Ten plays?" She laughed with surprise. "You can't be serious."

Hermann spread his hands on his desk and looked at her intently, trying to gauge how serious *she* was. "I'm planning to do two plays a month on alternate Monday nights. You know what's on television on Monday nights these days? Boxing, the weather report, films on how to mow your grass."

Kathe looked stunned. "That's an amazing proposition. If I hear you correctly, you'll be doing ten plays in not much more time than it takes to rehearse two for the Broadway stage, and you want me to agree to be in all of them?"

"There's nothing amazing about it." Hermann smiled. "I'm just a very practical man. That little box is going to eat up talent the way a boa constrictor eats rats. So are you interested?"

Kathe thought for a moment. "Yes," she said gravely. "I am. Very. It sounds a little crazy, but I guess by this time you must know what you're doing, and frankly I don't see how I can lose." She held out her hand. "You've got a deal." Her touch was firm and light, like a small bird caught in his palm.

For about five more minutes they discussed the details of the lessons—times, dates, how he would coordinate them with his schedule—and she was gone, leaving behind her the faint scent of spring flowers. Hermann spent about half an hour more sitting at his desk. Then, impulsively, he got up and did a rather strange thing.

Walking down the hall to the men's room, he locked the door behind him and stared at himself in the mirror. What he saw was a big man in his mid-forties with a fringe of thin, copper-colored hair, large blue eyes, a small flat nose, and a round, friendly face. He looked, he decided ruefully, rather like a teddy bear. The idea that he had agreed to teach Kathe to feel seemed ludicrous. He ran his fingers through his hair, making it stand up in tufts on either side of his head, and took a deep breath. One thing was certain: it promised to be an interesting spring.

A week later at two in the afternoon, Kathe arrived at Hermann's large, rambling apartment on Central Park West for her first lesson, feeling excited and a little apprehensive. She had no idea what was in store for her as the elevator bore her toward the sixth floor, only an exhilarating sensation of forward motion, as if she were about to embark on the Trans-Siberian Railroad or set off down the Amazon with only a pack of matches and a can of beans. Ringing the bell, she was startled to see Hermann's round, friendly face appear immediately, like a jack-in-the-box. He stared at her with an air of pleasant surprise, and she experienced a momentary attack of anxiety. Surely he was expecting her? Surely she'd gotten the time right? But in Hermann's presence, as she was soon to discover, it was hard to be anxious for very long.

"So come in, *Liebling*," he said, throwing open the door and waving hospitably, "so come in. The great experiment is about to begin, yes?"

Kathe went in, feeling reassured. Hermann was muffled in a huge blue sweater decorated with white and red reindeer, which she decided gave him the air of being a cross between a Laplander and a Swedish playwright. The elbows of his jacket were patched with leather, and he exuded an aura of homey, masculine comfort. Relieving her of her coat, he conducted her briskly down a long, bright hall lined from floor to ceiling with bookcases. He seemed so cheerful and businesslike that she began to relax. This is going to work out, she thought.

Settling her on a vast brown leather couch next to a flourishing potted palm, Hermann walked over to a bank of records that stretched the entire length of one wall. Kathe looked about, surprised to see that everything was in meticulous order. From the condition of Hermann's desk, she had imagined he would live in a labyrinth of old newspapers, dust, and half-eaten salami sandwiches, but the room was spotlessly clean, flooded with sunlight, and decorated with posters and framed photographs from the productions Hermann had worked on. To her left Nosferatu, with four-inch fingernails and vampire fangs, leaned over a frail lady in a white dress as if he had designs on her neck. To her right Viola and Hilde stood with their arms thrown around each other, looking hopelessly young as they kicked up their feet and sang something from the original production of *Berliner Ballade*. Below them Christine Bergen appeared—wearing the low-cut evening gown from *Africa* that had provoked the wrath of the censors—plastered (there was no other word for it) against Robert de Preux, the French actor who had played her lover and who was now her husband. Last of all—positioned modestly in a corner behind a lamp with a green glass shade—was a glossy photograph of Hermann smiling from ear to ear as he accepted the Gilbert and Sullivan Award for *Comanche*.

"So now," Hermann commanded, gently lowering the arm of the record player onto the spinning record, "you will listen, yes? Not just with the ears, but with the entire body. With the arms you will listen, and with the elbows, and with the stomach."

"What?" Kathe was startled out of her examination of the photographs. "Are we starting?"

"Maybe you're not ready?" Hermann lifted the needle off the record and glared at her comically. "Maybe you want I should make you tea? I warned you—King Kong, I said. Mr. Simon Legree at your service. As the Americans say, I don't mess around. You come; we start." He shook a finger at her. "No pussyfooting, *ja?*"

"Yes, sir." Kathe grinned, feeling amused at his attempt to look so stern. "Should I salute you?" she asked mischievously.

"From time to time," Hermann chuckled. "Now I shall repeat my instructions. You will listen to this music with your whole body, not forgetting"—he pointed to her right side—"your liver"—he pointed to her forehead—"your pineal gland, and, most important"—he pointed to her chest—"your heart."

"What about with my brain?"

Hermann lifted his eyebrows. "The brain," he said, "is for the serious actor an imprecise organ. Like the stick of a blind man, it taps along giving only echoes of the human heart. Very pretty, yes? I quote from Johannes Wulf, the great German drama critic who spoke out against Hitler and was foully murdered for it, Wulf who awarded your father the Schröter Prize in '27. You have maybe read Wulf?"

"No," Kathe admitted, feeling a little abashed. "I haven't."

"So"—Hermann waggled his finger at her again—"we shall be having homework. And now, on with the music—Schubert's Arpeggione Sonata in A Minor." The heavy black disk with the yellow German label whirled around under the tip of the needle, and the sound of a piano flooded the bright, high-ceilinged room. After a few seconds the piano was joined by a cello. Kathe sat back against the cushions of the couch, one blue jean-clad leg thrown over the other, closed her eyes, tilted back her head, and tried to follow Hermann's directions but it was hard going. The music was beautiful but slippery: painful and almost unbearably tragic at first, then quick and passionate, running away from her like water rushing out across a flat beach. After about a minute Hermann stopped the record and started it from the beginning.

"Listen," he said. "The shift. You're getting it, yes? The transition moves from here"—he touched his chest—"to here." He touched the base of his throat.

"Frankly," she admitted, "I don't know what you're talking about."

"So"—Hermann didn't seem surprised—"this I expected. Consequently, we shall do some more listening."

For the next half an hour he played the same sixty seconds of music for her, over and over, until she became convinced that he had gone a little crazy on the topic. At last he stopped. Walking out of the room, he came back bearing an ordinary paper Dixie cup, creamish white, banded in blue. Placing the cup on the coffee table in front of her, he contemplated it for a moment happily, like a man who had unearthed a great treasure.

"I want you to pick up that up," he said, pointing to the cup. Kathe started to reach for it. "'No," he said none too gently, catching her hand in midair, "not like that."

"How then?" She was beginning to feel a little exasperated. She had expected him to teach her how to feel, and instead he was teaching her to pick up paper cups. No doubt he knew what he was doing, but she wished he would come out and tell her what he wanted instead of playing guessing games.

"I want you should pick it up like the music," Hermann said cryptically.

"What do you mean like the music?" She tried to imagine picking up the cup as if she were a cello and failed utterly.

"The music"—Hermann waved his hand, taking in the entire room—"fills everything. It has space and weight, yes? It is a great sadness and a great realization."

"A realization of what?" she asked. She wondered if she should talk to him in German. Maybe in German she would understand him better. Perhaps this was all a problem of translation.

"Ah that," Hermann said, pouncing on the cup and holding it out to her, "is what you must tell *me*." He put the cup back down on the table. "Pick it up like your lover is in the next room," he suggested.

Well as least she could understand that. She picked up the cup and cradled it gently.

"No," he yelled. "No, that's not it! That's too trite. You don't rock this cup like a baby. You fill it with all the past of this love affair, with all the future, with the pain and the thought that maybe you don't want to go in there and make love to this man and maybe you do. You fill it with if he is married or not married, and if he is good or bad to you, and if you fear him or trust him."

This was too much. Kathe exploded with laughter. "That's a pretty tall order for a Dixie cup, Hermann," she giggled.

Hermann looked slightly hurt. "So," he said, "you want maybe to quit?"

She shook her head. "No, I'm sorry. It's just that I don't think I understand what you want."

Hermann sat back and folded his arms across his chest. "What I want is nothing; what you want is everything. This you will learn in time. Now try again."

For about an hour she picked up the cup and put it down again, trying vainly to do what Hermann wanted and feeling more and more inadequate. At the end of the session she was surprised to discover that he seemed pleased.

"Not so bad for a start," he said cheerfully, crumpling the cup and tossing it into the wastebasket with an expert flick of the wrist. "You'll come back Wednesday."

"Wednesday?" She was aghast. "I thought we were going to do this once a week."

"We do it three times a week," Hermann said. "This you need, I tell you frankly, or nothing will happen." He got to his feet and suddenly he was kind, pleasant Hermann again instead of the tyrant of the lessons. "So, *Liebling*, until Wednesday then?" He patted her on the shoulder in a friendly fashion. "You did okay"—he smiled— "very okay. The little gear isn't as broken as I thought. This should be an encouragement, yes?" He began to take books off the shelves and pile them in her arms. "Some light reading." He winked. "Stanislavsky's *An Actor Prepares*, Keats' essay on *Negative Capability*, a biography of Eleonora Duse, Johannes Wulf's *Critique of the Moscow Art Theater*, and"—he ran a finger down a line of small green volumes and pounced on one of them like a cat cornering a mouse—"the *Poetics* of Aristotle." He led her toward the door with a satisfied expression. "Just to give you something to do until we meet again on Wednesday."

"Smell a violet," Hermann commanded. It was June and six stories down, on the other side of the street, Central Park had become a mass of shining green leaves under an implacable sun. Kathe wiped the sweat off of her forehead and tried to give the impression that she was smelling a violet—not a rose, or a lily, or a carnation, but a violet. If Hermann had taught her one thing over the past month, it was to be specific.

"Good," Hermann purred. "Very nice. Now you are smelling chicken soup."

Without moving a muscle she imagined herself in a kitchen. On the range was a pot of chicken soup, fragrant with dill and rich with chicken fat. She saw the lemon-colored broth, the weight and volume of the carrots and onions, the transparent green of the celery.

"Now you are tasting it."

Dipping an invisible spoon into an invisible bowl, she tasted the soup. Salt, she thought, sweet dill on the back of my tongue, warm homey stuff, good for me. The conjuring up of the soup was so complete that her stomach growled loudly.

Hermann laughed. *"Gut gemacht!* Bravo!" Kathe flushed with pleasure. "So," he demanded, lifting a questioning finger, "what are you learning from this?"

Kathe sat back against the familiar brown leather cushions of the couch and pursed her lips. She was wearing a bright yellow sundress that fluttered in the breeze, and her bare arms were brown from a recent weekend spent at Jones Beach. She looked, Hermann thought, much too beautiful to be spending the afternoon indoors. "I'm learning," she said cautiously, "that emotion is connected to memory."

"Ha. This is undoubtedly true. And what else are you learning?"

She paused and frowned, thinking back over the experience. "I think," she said hesitantly, "that Stanislavsky was right. An actor can't force himself to feel on cue, but he can begin to conjure up feelings by concentrating on remembered sensations."

"By concentrating on objects, *ja?"*

"Yes"—she smiled one of those brilliant smiles of her that always made Hermann feel as if she had handed him a bouquet of roses— "by concentrating on objects."

He looked away, unable to meet her eyes. She obviously trusted him completely, but lately he had begun to wonder if he deserved that trust. Over the past few weeks he had become aware that he was having some rather peculiar feelings toward Kathe Rothe. Well, to be honest, they weren't peculiar feelings at all. The truth was, he was dangerously close to falling in love with her—which, of course, would be a disaster. I'm too old for her, he thought. She thinks of me the way she would have thought of Joseph if he were still alive, as a kind of father. The admission made him a bit melancholy. He stared at a spot of sunlight on the rug, wondering if he had come to that time in life when men made fools of themselves over young girls. Since his divorce from Christina, he had felt lonely from time to time, but this was a different kind of temptation. Kathe was far from ordinary. She was, he thought, quite amazing: beautiful, talented, with a sharp mind and a quick wit, but—more important— he could feel the passion in her, lurking under the surface, waiting to be released.

"Hermann," Kathe asked, "is something wrong?" She was contemplating him with a puzzled air, as if wondering why he had suddenly fallen silent.

"No." He looked up, feeling vaguely embarrassed. "I am only thinking, *Liebling*."

"About what?"

"I am thinking that now the time has come for you to take the next step." He took a deep breath and told himself that if he was going to play Pygmalion, he might as well do a thorough job of it. "For four weeks," he said, "we have been doing exercises; now it is time to do theater." He got up, went over to the bookcase nearest the window, and extracted a thin black notebook with dog-eared pages. "Here I have an English translation of *The Wailing Wall*. You've read it, yes?"

"No." Kathe shook her head. "What is it? A play?"

Hermann took a deep breath. "Yes—or rather, no. A complete play it's not. Only two acts were finished." He hesitated, hoping that what he had to say next wouldn't startle her too much. "Your father was working on it when he died. In fact, when your mama gave me this copy, she said she thought maybe the Nazis found out about it and that was part of the reason why they murdered him. Such a smart man, your papa. He could see into the future like he had telescopes for eyes." Hermann looked at the black notebook; after nearly twenty years he had never found another friend as good as Joseph Rothe. "It's about the Jews," he said softly. "Your papa imagined them banding together with the Communists and assassinating the Nazi leaders. This in 1928."

Kathe had turned absolutely white. "I didn't know this existed." She shook her head, amazed. "Mama never told me."

Hermann sat down, opened the notebook, and spread it out in front of her. "So now," he said, "you know. Now we do some theater."

"You want me to do a scene from this?" She pointed at the notebook. "Bang, just like that, out of the blue?"

"Bang." Hermann nodded. "Act Two, Scene Two. The heroine, Esther, has just found out that her lover has been shot. Do I need to tell you that when I think of Joseph this scene gives me what the Americans call 'the creeps'? My flesh it makes crawl. Esther is feeling many things—fear and sorrow, anger at the Nazis, a desire for revenge she is feeling, and too—strange as it sounds—she is feeling anger at Hans, her lover, who has betrayed her and left her by dying.

That was Joseph's genius, to put in all the parts of the human heart. In Joseph's plays no one was ever completely good or completely bad."

Kathe stood up abruptly. "I'm sorry, Hermann," she said, "but this isn't going to work. I know what you're trying to do—you want me to use my feelings for my father to fuel the emotional memory for this part, and I'm grateful, really I am, but you see"—she paused and looked at him oddly—"you see, I don't feel anything about my father. I know I did once; I can even remember feeling upset and abandoned when he died. I was just a little girl, and I must have cried for weeks about it, but today when I try to feel some of that sadness there's just a big blank."

"A blank?"

"Like ice." Kathe shivered and clasped her bare arms around her chest dramatically. "No, worse than ice. I go back and rummage around in my mind and there's nothing. It's like an empty attic."

"Read Esther's lines anyway," Hermann suggested. "What harm can it do?"

"I'll be rotten," she insisted.

"So be rotten. I should care?" He settled back in the overstuffed chair and adjusted his glasses.

She could see that he wasn't going to take no for an answer. Giving in, she picked up the notebook and quickly skimmed the lines. Esther's soliloquy was a fine piece of drama, she could see that at once. She felt a tiny thread of pain. Too bad her father had never gotten to finish this play.

"Well?" Hermann said. "You are waiting, maybe, for a contract?"

Taking a deep breath, she plunged in. For about five minutes Hermann let her read without interrupting her, and then he held up his hand.

"Stop," he said. "You tell me you will be rotten, and this— unfortunately—is a promise you are keeping."

"Rats, Hermann"—she threw down the script in disgust—"what did you expect?"

"Take a minute," he chuckled. "That was the motto of the Group Theatre in the thirties, you know. Take a minute and try to remember a time when you felt what Esther is feeling—anger and fear, abandonment, the kind of love that cuts the heart like a sharp nail, and remember"—he waved a finger at her—"to concentrate on the objects."

She closed her eyes and ran through all the times in her life when she had been hurt and angry. She tried to remember objects, but her father's death seemed to have taken place in a space without them. Had Berlin had parks and apartments and streets and flowers in 1928? If it had, you couldn't prove it by her. Well then, how about the time she lost the baby? Surely that was painful enough. She grappled with the memory, but that, too, was a blank—or rather not a blank but a pencil sketch without colors. She knew, of course, that she'd been at Sanford Palace; she could even remember that awful afternoon when Mama had come into her room with the news, but it was all like the transcript of some distant event. She opened her eyes to find Hermann staring at her expectantly. "Damn it to hell," she exploded, throwing the script to the floor, "I can't do it, Hermann. I just tried to remember what was maybe the worst moment of my life, and there's *nothing* there."

"What was it, this worst moment?" He contemplated her calmly from behind his glasses.

"When I was seventeen," Kathe said, "I gave birth to a baby that died. I'd had an affair with an American, who as it turned out"—she laughed bitterly—"was married. Smart, yes? It was perfectly horrible, but the most horrible part is that I can't even remember how horrible it was."

Hermann's face changed to a look of profound sympathy. Getting to his feet, he walked quickly over to Kathe and put his arm around her shoulder. "What you are telling me is very intimate," he said gently. "Tomorrow or the next day maybe you will be hating me for having told me this, so to keep that from happening I will now tell you something in turn. When one person confesses, the other must too. I will tell you something very wicked I once did that I regret greatly."

Kathe was so astonished, she didn't know what to say. "Hermann," she stammered awkwardly, "I don't see how you could have ever done anything wicked. You're not the type."

"When I was in Germany," he said softly, "I betrayed a man."

"Who?" She drew back.

"Johannes Wulf, the great critic. One afternoon some of Friedrich Hoffman's thugs showed up on my doorstep. You met Friedrich in France, I believe, so you know what his friends would be like, yes? They demanded to know where Wulf was."

"And you told them?" Kathe was horrified.

"No." Hermann shook his head. "Of that level of evil I hope I'm not capable."

"Then what did you do?"

"I told them I didn't know Wulf. I denied him. Such a good man—kind and generous and a friend of mine—and out of cowardice I denied him. I think sometimes of that place in the Bible where Peter betrays Christ." Hermann's saucer-blue eyes were sad, and he shook his head. "Of this I am deeply ashamed." He removed his arm from her shoulder. "So now we both know the worst about each other, yes? We have traded pains and it has been a long afternoon and I think you must be tired."

Kathe looked down at the black notebook, feeling ashamed of her outburst. Hermann had been through so much; what were her troubles compared to his? He had a courage she lacked. He felt his pain and took responsibility for it, whereas she floundered around, complaining and out of touch with herself. She wondered if he thought of her as a hysterical child. It would serve her right if he did. She tried to think of something she might do to redeem herself in his eyes. Bending over, she picked up the notebook. "I could try the part of Esther again," she offered.

"No." Hermann shook his head. "I think you have tried too hard. I think this is enough."

"Are you giving up on me, Hermann?"

"No, *Liebling*." There was something in his voice that made her look up from the script, but behind his glasses his face was once again cheerful and inscrutable. He gestured to the notebook. "Take this back to Rockhaven with you and memorize Esther's soliloquy and next time we try something different." Walking her to the door, he ushered her out of the apartment briskly, as if he had a whole afternoon of appointments ahead of him.

How odd, Kathe thought, as she stood on the curb waiting for a bus. He sounded as if he were about to say something else important to me, and then he reconsidered. He was so patient, more than she deserved, despite his threats about being like King Kong, painfully self-critical, honest to the core, more likely to hurt himself than someone else. Hermann, she thought, would never lie to her. Now that was an admirable quality. Also—the thought came unbidden—he was cute. What a silly word. She blushed, glad no one could read her mind. She wondered what in the world Hermann would think if he knew she was having such thoughts about him.

"I can't take this any longer," Kathe complained one torrid afternoon, crumpling into a heap on Hermann's couch and looking at him irritably. Her hair was sticking to the back of her neck, the skirt of her cotton dress was sticking to her legs, and she felt hot, miserable, and foolishly vulnerable for someone whose main problem seemed to be that she wasn't open to her own emotions. "I'm not saying that you're not doing a good job with me, Hermann, but I think"—she pointed melodramatically to her forehead—"that my brains have fried inside my skull. It must be a hundred and ten out."

"It's ninety-eight, actually," Hermann chuckled. He hated air-conditioning and wouldn't have it in his apartment, and Kathe was perversely annoyed that he was so cheerful, but then Hermann was almost always cheerful. The man was inhumanly good tempered.

"Good lord," she exclaimed, grabbing a magazine and fanning herself with it. "I'm just not used to these American summers. I was raised in London, remember? The city of warm beer and cold fog. We call it summer when we can go outside without turning blue." She threw the magazine back down on the coffee table, got up, and paced around the familiar living room.

"So," Hermann said, "you want to go to the beach, yes?"

"Yes." She nodded vigorously.

"I am thinking"—Hermann waved dramatically—"that it is useful this heat. I am thinking that maybe it will melt down barriers. The heat maybe will open you up like fire opens solder. In such summers the passions boil, many murders take place. Sorry, no beach today."

"That's all very comforting, Hermann." She flopped back down on the couch and contemplated him with sweaty self-pity. "But what if I die?"

"That," he chuckled, "is a chance we will have to take." He sat down across from her in one of the overstuffed armchairs and adjusted his glasses. "So where were we? Ah, I remember. I was about to tell you about a new idea I came up with last night. In the heat I don't sleep so good. So I get up, I have a cold beer, I think, and a revelation comes into my noodle."

"You're actually going to go on with the lesson, aren't you? It's an inferno in here, the leather on the couch is melting, the windows are turning liquid, but you're going on."

"You expected maybe a holiday? I warned you—Simon Legree."

"All right, master," she sighed, grabbed her hair, and pinned it up on top of her head, thinking that if she had to perish she might as well do it in as much comfort as possible. "You win. What's the idea?"

Hermann contemplated her soberly. "I think," he said at last, "that it's whales you've been fishing for when it should have been those little fish—I can't remember the English name for them—but on crackers they taste good."

"Sardines?" Kathe prompted.

Hermann nodded. "Exactly. You should be fishing for sardines."

She crossed her legs, uncrossed them, shifted to a cooler part of the couch, and thought longingly of how nice it would be to be having a drink in the air-conditioned lobby of the Biltmore Hotel. "Care to translate?" she said, wondering what sardines had to do with anything. The problem with Hermann was that half the time he talked in metaphors.

"A big emotion," Hermann explained, "can be too strong for an actor to work with. Like a steam shovel, it can tear up everything. I sent you looking among the big emotions when what I should have done was send you looking among the little ones. For this, I apologize."

She thought over what he had said and found it intriguing. "Do you mean I should look for a little memory?"

"Precisely." Hermann beamed at her. "For a small betrayal you should search for a small pain. I think you should be looking for a painful moment you spent with a stranger—a quick moment like the beat of an eyelash. Here, I think, you will find the objects, and when you find the objects, the feelings, too, you will find."

Kathe pursed her lips and thought it over some more. "Well," she said after a short silence, "it's an interesting idea, and I think I have just the moment."

"So"—Hermann shrugged—"you're waiting maybe for the Second Coming? What is it, this moment?"

"It happened back in Paris, in 1940, when I was arrested by the Gestapo."

Hermann's face clouded. "Your mama wrote me about that," he said. "This was not so good a time for you."

"Well, it wasn't so bad a time for me either—not half as bad as it was for some people." Kathe leaned forward, no longer feeling the heat. Her eyes were bright and small wisps of hair hung down around her face. "I was scared out of my mind, of course, but in the end, thanks to my step-uncle Harry—who was, by the way, a bloody traitor—they let me go, even shipped me back to London. The point is, while I was at the Gestapo headquarters in Paris waiting for them to interrogate me, I think I had the kind of experience you say I should be looking for."

"Don't tell me any more." Hermann put up his hand to stop her. "Feel the moment, and when you think you have it, try to say Esther's soliloquy from *The Wailing Wall*."

Kathe sat back and closed her eyes the way she had done perhaps a dozen times in the last three weeks. Always before she had tried to summon up something important, but this time it was just a little thing: a room in which she had spent perhaps twelve hours. There had been a bench, she thought. A long bench. She tried to conjure it up, and to her delight the bench materialized in front of her, clumsy, with thick uneven legs. She imagined running her hand down the back of it. There had been a series of nicks along the top edge, a molding, and a spiral at each end; it had been made out of some heavy wood, oak perhaps, and it had smelled like varnish—

Suddenly the memory exploded in her mind, and she was sixteen again, back in that windowless room on the Rue des Saussaies gasping for air and terrified. In front of her a woman was sitting at a table with her face buried in her hands. The woman looked up and shook her head at Kathe sadly. *Ah, you poor thing*—the words rang in Kathe's mind as clearly as if she were hearing them for the first time—*I'm Valerie Cusset, and I've been here for hours watching them come and go.* Kathe opened her mouth. She wanted to yell at the woman that the Gestapo guards were going to kill her; she wanted to beg her to fight and run, but the past was sealed off and all she could do was watch.

Valerie Cusset pointed to a bench in the corner—the same bench that Kathe had first imagined, only now there was a body on it: a woman in a blue linen suit with her knees drawn up to her chest and cigarette burns on her face.

This was too much, too terrible. She had forgotten about the death of the woman in the blue linen suit, blotted her out of her mind as if she had never existed. Kathe felt a shiver run through her entire body. She clenched her fists and then, suddenly, she was crying in great, gasping sobs through gritted teeth. She opened her eyes to find herself sitting on Hermann's couch. "My God," she cried, agonized by the memory, "I'd forgotten all about those women. They were both strangers, but one was kind to me and one died right in front of my eyes, and it was horrible, so horrible that I had to forget about it." She knew she sounded incoherent, and she tried to stop crying, but she couldn't.

Hermann leaned forward. "Say Esther's lines," he commanded.

"You have to be kidding." She stared at him through her tears, not believing she could have heard him correctly.

"Say them."

"I couldn't. Not to save my soul. Not now."

"Are you an actress or just a girl who maybe wants to outdo Mama?"

"Leave Mama out of this, Hermann." She stood up, suddenly furious.

"Say Esther's lines."

"I have a personal crisis and you want me to cannibalize it? You want me to *use* my memory of those women? That's disgusting." She pointed her finger in his face. "Hermann Lang, you're the most insensitive, stupid, dictatorial, unsympathetic person I've ever had the misfortune to meet, and I'll tell you something else . . ." She sputtered to a stop and glared at him. "You never made a decent film or produced a decent play, and what you know about acting wouldn't fill a rat's ass."

"So you hate me. So what. Say the lines."

"You want me to say the lines?"

"*Ja,* I want you to say the lines."

"Then I'll say the lines, but after I say them I'm walking out of here and never coming back."

"Such a threat. All night I'll cry. So walk out. But say the lines first."

Almost too incensed to speak, Kathe took a deep breath and launched into Esther's soliloquy, throwing the words at him as if they were daggers. It was a furious, totally brilliant performance. Kathe spoke the last sentence and then closed her mouth, and stood looking at Hermann, stunned at what he had provoked her into doing.

"Bravo," Hermann yelled, "bravo." Jumping to his feet, he ran over and threw his arms around her. "There is power in you, *Liebling*. Always it has been in you, but you never expressed it before." Taking her face in his hands he kissed her. It was a surprising kiss, so passionate that it left her dizzy. "I love you," he said, kissing her again. "What you will do to an audience! Such an actress! Such a miracle you are!"

24

Two days later Kathe dropped by the Actors' Studio to make an appointment for another audition.

"Can you be ready in half an hour?" The secretary arched her eyebrows and bit the tip of her pencil. "The girl we had scheduled just called to say she wasn't coming. She claims flu, but if you ask me, it's an attack of cold feet."

"Half an hour?" Kathe gasped. "Did you say *half an hour?*"

"Right." The secretary nodded. "You want the slot or not?"

Kathe could feel herself panicking. Usually it took at least three weeks to get a chance to audition. She paced from one side of the tiny office to the other, her mind racing wildly. How could she go out there in front of all those hot-shot young actors on such short notice? They'd grind her to mincemeat; they'd eat her alive. Her hair was a mess; her blouse had coffee stains on it; her lipstick probably looked like it had been applied by touch. What if that last session with Hermann had been a fluke? What if she froze up and made a fool of herself? Go onstage on half an hour's notice? She'd rather walk barefoot across hot coals; she'd rather go swimming with sharks.

"So?" The secretary tapped her pencil impatiently on the edge of the desk. "What's the word?"

Kathe took a deep breath. "I'll do it," she said impulsively.

"What part?"

Kathe thought for a moment. What part did she have down cold? What lines did she know so well that she couldn't possibly forget them? "I'll do a scene from *Hedda Gabler.*"

"Nice." The secretary wrote something down in her book. "Eva Le Gallienne just died in that part at the Cort. So how could you do worse?"

"Thanks for the encouragement." Kathe was seized by an urge to strangle her. "You don't know how comforting it is to hear you say that."

The secretary smiled cheerfully. "Don't mention it," she said, waving Kathe in the direction of the auditorium. "I'll scare up someone to feed you the cues."

In the auditorium the houselights were on and a few spectators were already lounging in the chairs eating sandwiches and chatting. They looked at her without curiosity; by now she was more or less a regular feature at the Studio: the young actress who never quite made the grade. Climbing up on the stage, she sat down in a wooden folding chair, closed her eyes, and put her hands over her face. She searched her memory for something appropriate to the character of Hedda, but there was nothing there. I've frozen up again, she thought. Agreeing to do this audition on such short notice was a big mistake, and I'm going to make an idiot out of myself. She took a deep breath and tried again, and then, all at once, she saw it: a letter in a thin blue envelope postmarked Lisbon; a letter full of lies and deception, false love and terrible pain.

Twenty-five minutes later, Kathe stepped down from the stage a full-fledged member of the Actors' Studio. She had given a strong, passionate interpretation of Hedda Gabler, one that had been received by a round of enthusiastic applause, given it so effortlessly that she felt a little stunned. It was, she thought, like walking out into the sunlight after years of living in a cave. As she moved through the audience receiving congratulations, she saw that she was no longer the young actress who never made the grade. Indifferent only a little while ago, the faces of the other Studio members now shone with respect, even envy.

"You were great."

"A wonderful performance."

"Hedda's a hell of a role."

"Great job, Rothe. I didn't know you had it in you."

"Welcome aboard."

Muttering thanks and shaking hands, Kathe passed through them in triumph.

The next day she was scheduled to take another class from Hermann at noon, but at ten o'clock she was still standing in her bedroom in Rockhaven, dressed only in her slip. The small mirror above the dresser reflected a pretty young woman with curly black hair, smooth skin, and quick, intelligent eyes, her oval face turned toward the light in Madonna-like repose, marred only by an upturned nose and a slightly thoughtful expression, but the serenity was all an illusion. At this precise moment Kathe was experiencing an unfamiliar emotion, quick and sharp and a bit intoxicating. Was it happiness? she thought. Yes, definitely. Pride? Yes, that too. But there was something else in it—something powerful and subtle that she couldn't quite put her finger on.

How odd, she thought. She ran her tongue around her lips exploring the feeling, thinking that perhaps this was the flavor of awareness, then smiled at her own metaphor. What a bad poet she'd make. Still, put it any way you wanted, something was going on inside her, something exciting and a bit unnerving. Putting down a box of hairpins, she placed her fingertips on the mirror and rested her forehead against the cool, silvered glass. Last night she had such amazing dreams; pieces of them were still swirling around in her mind. For the last five years or so she had awakened from sleep remembering nothing, and now, almost overnight, that had all changed. They had been exhilarating dreams, rich with plots and symbols, the kinds of dreams that would make plays in themselves, and they had come spontaneously, with no effort on her part.

I owe it all to Hermann, she thought. My God, the man's worked some kind of miracle on me. He's a genius; he's wonderful. She felt a dizzy, irrational sweep of love for this man who had taught her so much. It was a feeling, she realized, that had been coming on for months. For several seconds she stood there possessed by the thought of him, and then reason took over.

Wait a minute, she thought. Hold everything. I'm not really in love with him. This is just an attack of gratitude. Hermann taught me how to reach my feelings, and I gave an audition that knocked Kazan's socks off. I got applauded and praised and treated like the prodigy of Forty-eight Street; so who wouldn't be grateful for something like that? But love? That's another matter, girl. That's serious stuff. I have to be sensible about this. Hermann's twenty-four years older than I am; he's old enough to be my father. Rats, that's probably the basis of this feeling.

She shrugged and turned away from the mirror, feeling unaccountably disappointed. Young woman seeks father figure—how classically Freudian. It was almost embarrassing to be such a textbook case. You want to play Electra, she told herself sternly, then go to the library and check out a copy of *The Libation Bearers*, but don't drag Hermann into this. She thought with a shudder of how close she'd come to running off half-cocked and telling him she adored him. My God, she would never have been able to look him in the face again.

The train for Manhattan left in fifteen minutes. Slipping on her dress and shoes, she grabbed her purse and hurried out of the house, down the sidewalk, past the Reiters' wildflower garden, past the green lawns of suburbia, littered with tricycles and abandoned toys. Her heels clattered on mica-speckled concrete. There were bread trucks, milk trucks, women in bathrobes poised at front doors calling to children in cowboy suits that came complete with tooled leather boots and miniature gun holsters. She thought of America, of its richness and strangeness. Such a prosperous country, and yet the people often seemed so lonely to her. Or perhaps she was the lonely one.

A bit of milkweed down floated in front of her, a white disconnected tassel that danced from polished car to polished car until, swept into an invisible updraft, it disappeared. Some lines of poetry came back to her, memorized long ago at the boarding school Mama had sent her to when they first moved to London: *I wandered lonely as a cloud.*

Would she be lonely without Hermann?

Be reasonable, Rothe, she told herself sternly; stop thinking about him. But she didn't feel reasonable, not in the slightest, and the harder she tried, the less reasonable she felt. That day she went through the exercises stiffly, without feeling. It was by any standard a poor performance, and Hermann commented on it.

"There's something on your mind," he said. "Okay, deny it; I should care. But one look at you, and I know the cat has consumed the bird. You want to tell me you're not going to take any more lessons from me now that Lewis and Kazan have given you the Studio seal of approval? So go ahead. I can take it. Do I own you? No. By the Thirteenth Amendment to the Constitution, the Americans have outlawed slavery. Mr. Legree can retire."

"I wasn't planning to quit my lessons with you," Kathe said, unable to meet his eyes. She looked down at her hands, at the tips of her shoes, at the oatmeal-colored carpet Hermann kept so neatly vacuumed.

"What is it then? Yesterday you finally get admitted to the Actors' Studio so I expect you to dance in here like Pavlova and knock over some of my furniture. Instead I see a performance written by Kafka."

"I think maybe I'm running a fever." It wasn't a lie, not exactly. She did feel as if perhaps she was getting sick, but it was the wrong move. Hermann disappeared into the kitchen and returned bearing a cup of tea so bitter that when she tasted it her mouth felt like someone had filled it with oak galls and cotton.

"An old German remedy," he said, patting her on the arm. He sat over her, making solicitous noises until she had drained it to the dregs. When she left he pressed a bag of herbs on her and advised her to keep her feet warm and avoid drinking milk.

For three more weeks the lessons with Hermann continued on schedule, and the tension built in Kathe until she felt as if her emotions were being stretched into tiny wires that vibrated every time he looked at her. She had, she told herself, every reason to be happy: she could drop by the Studio now any time she wanted; she was being treated with respect by other actors; she was even making progress in her interpretation of Electra, a role she had chosen to practice to remind herself of the reality of her situation. Yet every three days when she boarded the train to go back to Rockhaven, she felt a stab of disappointment, as if something should have happened that hadn't. The trip would seem unusually long and tiring and at the end of it she would walk the six blocks from the station past manicured lawns, pure-bred dogs, and men in sport shirts pushing gasoline-powered mowers, and the sight of all this wealth and antiseptic neatness would oppress her, and she would find herself wondering once again if perhaps she should go back to London.

Then one night near the end of August she didn't return to Long Island. Instead she walked from Pennsylvania Station to Fifth Avenue; up Fifth to 110th Street; across 110th to Central Park West; and then down Central Park West, past the park, with its streetlights round and white like blooming carnations on black posts; past buses and horse-drawn carriages, and the yellow smears of taxis. It took hours but she was unaware of the passage of time. She simply walked and walked until her legs felt as if they were no longer part of her. Once it rained lightly in a feathery mist that swept across the sidewalks and streets, transforming the asphalt into a long black mirror. Turning her face up, she let the warm rain fall on it. She felt happy and a little crazy, but oddly enough she also felt as if she finally knew what she was doing.

When she arrived at the familiar green awning of Hermann's building, she stopped, knowing that this was the goal she had been heading for all the long, wet evening. Taking the steps two at a time, she walked up all six floors to his apartment and pushed the doorbell so hard she broke a fingernail. It was not the most diplomatic time to be ringing doorbells. It was, in fact, two in the morning. There was a long silence, then the sound of footsteps.

"Who is it?" Hermann called out sleepily.

"It's me, Kathe." The madwoman, she thought, the crazy lady; the woman who has been walking all over Manhattan.

"Kathe?" He threw open the door and stared at her, astonished. "So what is it? An emergency?" He waved her into the apartment, looking worried. She walked into the living room, walked around it, walked from one side to the other. She couldn't seem to stop walking.

"Sit down," Hermann pleaded. "You're making me dizzy."

"Hermann," she said, "I have to level with you."

He looked startled. She sat down and tried to calm herself but her mind went on walking. "I don't know quite how to put this, but a few weeks ago a door opened up inside me." She pointed to her chest. "I can feel everything—the good and the bad. It's like a beehive in here." She leaned forward, willing him to understand. "It's the emotional memory, you see. It's done something to me."

"So," Hermann said, "this is good, yes? But to announce this you have to come in the middle of the night?"

"I'm sorry, I know it's a crazy hour, but I'm exploding, blowing up." She got up, sat down again, walked her mind back and forth until it came to the stopping place. "I've got to tell you."

"Tell me what, *Liebling?*"

She took a deep breath and plunged ahead recklessly. "I have to tell you that I love you." Her words were like bits of glass; they broke in the room with a ringing sound followed by a long silence. Hermann stared at her in a very peculiar fashion.

"This is gratitude I'm hearing," he said softly. "Because you get into the Actors' Studio you feel happy and being young you get confused."

"It isn't just gratitude." She shook her head stubbornly. "I already thought of that. I'm not denying that I'm grateful to you, but it's more than that." She sat back and folded her arms across her chest. "So tell me straight out—do you love me too? I've thought you did from time to time, you know, from the way you look at me and you're so good to me, but maybe I'm imagining things and just making a fool out of myself. Well if I am, I have to know. It's all right, Hermann. Just lay it on the line. You can be as blunt as you want. I'm ready to take it."

"This is a dream, yes?" Hermann grinned uneasily. "Like a tiger you come to my apartment and pounce on me in the middle of the night. Such luck no man has. So this isn't real. Soon I will wake up; the alarm clock will be ringing, the phone will be ringing."

"This isn't a dream. I've been trying to get up the courage to say this to you for weeks."

His face suddenly became sober. "Then this is very serious." He cleared his throat uneasily. "You say an emotional door has opened for you. Good, let it open, but I think it will close again—at least this part of it. You're young and pretty, and pretty young women, they love quick and they forget quicker. This is what the books call infatuation."

"I doubt that," Kathe said stubbornly. "I doubt that very much."

"You do, eh? Well in that case I make a speech—no smart man would make a speech at a time like this, but a smart man I never pretended to be." He sat back. "The speech goes like this—I think we should forget about love."

She was bitterly disappointed but not surprised. "Oh," she said, crumbling back into the couch. "Then you don't love me. I'm sorry, I really am—to have put you through this." She felt like crying but she was too proud.

"So who said I don't love you?"

"I suppose you love me like a daughter."

"No, *Liebling,* not like a daughter."

There was a long silence. She stared at him, feeling extremely confused. "I don't understand," she said at last. "I really don't."

Hermann picked up her hand, kissed it, and put it back in her lap. He looked sad. "It's simple," he said gently. "I want to make love to you; any man would. This you know, yes? But if I made love to you, I would also want to marry you. This is old-fashioned of me, I know, but I am not pretending to be up to date. For me love means marriage, and this is a problem." He sat back and looked at her sadly. "You see, my marriage to Christina was very painful. With you, too, with someone there was pain. Do I avoid women because of this pain? Mostly I do. I am not so proud of this. Perhaps it is cowardly. But I have my work; I have my life. With you, there would, to be honest, be a great risk. You're so young." He waved. "Like sunlight—here one minute, then gone."

Kathe thought it over. "Hermann," she said, taking back his hand. "Listen, I can't honestly promise you that we'll stay together forever. Life to me has always seemed like some kind of game of chance run by a god who's always changing the rules, but I can promise you that I care about you more than I've ever cared about anyone except maybe Mama. I may be young, but I've been through a lot. I'm not flighty." She paused, trying to find the right words. "It may not be very diplomatic of me to mention this, but I want you to know that

I'm not going to run off the first time some younger man makes a pass at me. I'll try my best to be good to you and faithful. I guess what I'm trying to say is that I know there's a risk, but I want to take it." She leaned forward and kissed him. "You see, I do love you. Really I do."

Hermann took her in his arms. "This," he said, "is an amazing speech; this is as much as any man could ask for. *Ich liebe dich;* I love you, sweet Kathe." She put her arms around his neck, trembling but determined. She was very happy and more than a little frightened. "So we make love now, yes?" Hermann asked. She nodded weakly, not trusting herself to speak.

"Scared?" he whispered gently.

"Yes."

"So who isn't?" He unbuttoned her blouse and kissed her bare shoulder. "Ask me how long I've loved you."

"How long?"

"So long. Since you were a little girl back in Berlin. That was the love for a child, yes? And then, when you came into my office for the first time I saw my Kathe had become a woman, and I began to feel a different kind of love."

"So long ago?" She was amazed.

Hermann smiled. "So long ago." He kissed her and then he kissed her again, as if kissing were the beginning and end of what he was going to do. Little by little her nervousness began to disappear and she relaxed against him, feeling safe in his arms. He was moving so slowly, with such patience, that it was like being gradually submerged in warm water. For perhaps half an hour she thought of nothing at all except how good he felt to her. Her mind wavered on the surface of time and sank to the bottom, where everything was infinite and sensual, like a row of white stones along a beach. Then there was movement, a rush of tides and a shifting of bodies and she suddenly had a sense of the passion in him: dark and vast and warm. At the same time, like a light floating on the surface, there was his care for her pleasure, his patient attention. He seemed filled, she thought, with a great, kindly force.

With surprise she recognized that this must be what love was really about. She thought about John. She had loved John, she couldn't deny that, even now, but John had drained her. His ecstasies had been sharp and self-centered, but Hermann was like the earth: he fed and nourished. Then all at once he was an avalanche coming down on her, and she moved under him, swept away by passion, not knowing where he was taking her, and he covered her, buried her in his love, and she knew that together they had arrived at a place beyond words.

25

NEW YORK
1949

"Get those damn fish moving," Hermann yelled from the control booth. It was the first Monday of 1949 and *The NewCo Television Theater* was just about to go on the air live before an estimated audience of 750,000. Or maybe it was four million. No one really knew how many people were out there staring at the little seven-inch screens that flickered in the darkness of living rooms all over America. "So you're waiting maybe for a fishing license?" Hermann's face turned red and his glasses slid down his nose on a sheet of sweat. "The fish," he pleaded, "where are the fish?"

A stagehand inspected the large glass aquarium that sat on a table in front of camera number one. The aquarium contained fifty gallons of water, a NewCo Watch ("You'll Know If It's Newco!"), and six tropical fish. The idea had been to televise the fish swimming in front of the watch to show how water resistant it was, only the fish were nowhere in sight.

"I think the fish got cold feet," the stagehand yelled. "They're kinda all clumped up at the bottom of the tank."

Hermann looked up at the monitor and groaned. Thanks to the poor resolution of the black-and-white screens, the water was invisible. Viewers were about to be treated to the sight of a watch hanging in space, ticking away merrily. The entire point of the commercial was going to be lost. Above the monitor the second hand of the clock swept relentlessly toward nine o'clock. "So throw rocks at them," he yelled. He was only supposed to be producing the show, but as usual he had ended up directing it, casting it, and writing most of the script. "Pick them up and throw them in front of the watch. Don't just stand there, *Dummkopf.*"

The stagehand hesitated for a few seconds, then, rolling up his sleeve, he reached into the tank and began groping around for the fish, but the delay proved fatal. With a burst of violins, *The NewCo Television Theater* came on the air, treating viewers to the sight of a watch ticking in front of a hairy arm, decorated, Hermann noted despairingly, with a tattooed heart and the word *Mother*. Groaning again, Hermann quickly punched in a close-up of the face of the actor who was doing the commercial, but that was no better. The actor was staring at the tank in horrified fascination. Suddenly, realizing he was on the air, the actor mouthed the word *shit*, then broke into a broad smile and launched into his spiel.

Up in the control room, Hermann sat back and took a deep breath. *The NewCo Television Theater* was off and running, and if there weren't any lip readers in the audience tonight, Hermann thought, they just might survive until ten o'clock.

"Good evening, ladies and gentlemen," the actor said cheerfully, fingering his wide tie and staring into the camera with pop-eyed enthusiasm. "Do *you* know what time it is? It's NewCo time! The NewCo watch—made to run even when the going gets rough. On land, sea, or in the air, *You'll Know If It's NewCo!* And now, our evening's presentation—Kathe Rothe, Burt Lawson, Frank Roberts, and Jason Crebs in a special television adaptation of that great French novel by Gustave Flaubert, *Madame Bovary.*"

Ten feet to his right, Kathe, dressed as Emma Bovary, stood looking out an imaginary window, waiting for her doctor husband to return from an emergency house call. Her makeup was melting, and she was having trouble breathing under the relentless glare of the lights, but these were inconveniences she hardly noticed anymore. Like a prize greyhound, she was poised and waiting for the red light on the camera to go on, signifying that her performance was being broadcast out over the airwaves. In the last five months she had performed not in ten plays, as Hermann had originally suggested, but in thirteen out of the twenty NewCo performances, and at this point they were all a bit muddled in her mind. She had dim memories of doing *Jane Eyre, Of Human Bondage, The Princess of Cleves, Crime and Punishment, The Death of Ivan Ilych, Tom Sawyer,* and—on one occasion that she would have preferred to forget—a sixty-minute version of *War and Peace.* The only thing the plays had in common was that they were all classics in the public domain. *The NewCo Television Theater* wasn't big on paying for the rights to things—not when the salary of the two poor suckers who were saddled with the job of producing a script a week came to something under three hundred dollars a month.

Five, four, three, two, one. The theme music ended and there was a moment of silence. As the floor director pointed at her, the red light on the camera came on, winking away in the darkened studio like a tiny eye. Kathe felt an almost electric burst of excitement. She looked at the round glass lens, peering at her like some strange cyclops, and suddenly she could feel a great, invisible audience hanging on her words. Opening her mouth, she spoke her first line.

Up in the control booth, Hermann watched her on the monitors, feeling proud and quite foolishly in love. Kathe had a real genius for television. Not every actress could play to a bundle of cables and hot lights and sweaty men in overalls as if she were playing to a packed house. He picked up a yellow number-two pencil and tapped it happily on the edge of the control panel. She was making the play come alive. She was Emma Bovary, and such a beautiful Emma. Such a wonderful face. He surveyed Kathe's high cheekbones, dark eyes, and full sensual lips, thinking of how sweet she had looked this morning when he woke up beside her. She conveyed such an unusual combination of wholesomeness and allure. Who would ever have thought she'd look so good in front of a camera.

Hermann leaned forward, his finger poised over the buttons on the control panel. He felt content and very lucky. As he waited for the next cue, he wondered idly what Flaubert would have thought of Kathe's performance. Not much, probably. If Flaubert had been out in the audience glued to a TV set, he probably wouldn't have recognized his own novel, and if he had, he would have had apoplexy. *Madame Bovary* was a spicy story of adultery and illicit love affairs, but like all spicy stories, it had to be laundered for television. Emma Bovary's problem tonight wasn't sex but money—or rather the lack of it.

Hermann punched in another close-up of Kathe's face and wondered if he would have wanted her doing love scenes under any circumstances. Ridiculous as it might sound, he was jealous of every man who came near her—not that she gave him any cause—but it appeared to be some kind of animal instinct. If anyone had tried to touch her, he would have cheerfully torn them apart. An interesting sentiment, he thought, for a middle-aged man. He adjusted his glasses, punched in another cue, and grinned. I'm such a tiger, he thought.

He turned back to the control panel, coordinating the three cameras with the deftness of a juggler, and for a time he had no more leisure to think of anything else. The images tumbled over each other like water racing out of a dam, flowed into anywhere from 750,000 to four million minds, and then disappeared into the night and were lost forever. As usual, minor disasters punctuated the hour, but Kathe played through them, ad-libbing, never skipping a beat. Cues were missed, doors stuck, actors entered a fraction of a second too late, but she plowed ahead, turning in a memorable performance. Still, no matter how well she acted, chances were there would be no reviews the next morning. Television plays rarely got more than a line in the *Times*. They were, Hermann thought, an expendable commodity.

At nine forty-five he began to relax. It was a good night as live television went, an excellent night. No one had gotten sick, no one had fainted, the sets hadn't fallen over. In fact, things were going so well that as the final five minutes approached he began to feel confident that *Madame Bovary* was going to be a minor masterpiece of sorts. There was only one bit left to do—Emma's suicide—and what, he thought, as he brought up camera number three on Kathe's profile, could possibly go wrong with that?

Down on the floor, Kathe was thinking the same thing. The desk that contained the bottle of poison stood ready and waiting, wheeled on by stagehands during the last NewCo commercial. For a few minutes she wandered around, pantomiming hysteria. Emma had come to the end of her ability to endure. She was lost, half-crazed, desperate. At exactly the right moment she strode over to the desk, threw open the drawer, and prepared to take out the bottle, but the drawer was empty. Stunned, she stared at the cheap plywood lined with checkered shelf paper trying to make the bottle materialize. The poison had to be there. She had to kill herself with it.

Turning her back to the camera, she rummaged around frantically, but all she came up with was a gum wrapper and a discarded pencil. My God, she thought, this is a disaster. I'm supposed to kill myself; if I don't, none of this will make any sense, but there's no poison. Where's the damn poison?

There was only one possible answer: the propman had forgotten to put the bottle in the drawer. So what should she do now? Time was running out. She thought of four million people staring restlessly at her back thinking, *Why doesn't she get on with it?* Panicked, she groped for some way to kill herself without the poison. She could strangle herself. Yes, that was it.

She looked up at the remote recesses of the ceiling twenty feet above her and realized strangulation was out. She wasn't wearing a belt, and besides, there was nothing to hang a rope on. So what should she do? Take out the desk drawer and beat herself over the head with it? She bit her lower lip to keep from laughing, and something caught her eye. On the far side of the set, just behind the desk, there was an open window. Fine, she thought, great. She'd throw herself out of the window. Emma Bovary leaps to her death. Not exactly what Flaubert had written, but better than taking off her shoes and trying to beat out her brains with her high heels.

Mastering her panic, she turned toward the camera, threw the audience a look of suicidal desperation, and then wheeled around and hurled herself through the window. Unfortunately, the sill was only a foot above the floor, but she had been prepared for that. Sliding on her belly, she lay flat among the cables, praying that her behind didn't show. In a far corner, crammed behind a pile of scenery, the live orchestra struck up with a moan of violins. The sweet sound of the end theme reverberated through the studio, and all the red lights went out simultaneously. *The NewCo Television Theater* was off the air.

Picking herself up off the floor, Kathe inspected the bruises on her elbows. She was dead tired, exhausted, and elated. She felt as if she had drunk fifteen cups of coffee; she felt as if she might die any minute. She was getting the best experience an actress could ask for—she was killing herself. Television was insane and wonderful and somehow she'd gotten through another Monday night. Stumbling off the set, she wandered in the direction of the closet that sometimes served as a dressing room for as many as fifteen actresses. Sitting down at the dressing table, she slathered cold cream on her face and began to remove it with Kleenex. It was ten-fifteen and her work day was over. She was free to go home with Hermann, have a cup of warm milk, curl up next to him, and beg for a foot rub.

Ah, the romantic life of a television star, she thought, grinning at her reflection. Tomorrow at eight in the morning she had to be back at the studio to begin rehearsals for next Monday's show—that is if she lived until tomorrow.

Through most of the rest of 1949, Kathe flourished, fueled by Hermann's love and the sort of fevered excitement she had formerly associated with forest fires, volcanic eruptions, and the sinking of large ships. By the time summer rolled around, she had done fifteen more plays, and *The NewCo Television Theater* was loaning her out to other networks for an occasional guest appearance. By fall she had clowned with Milton Berle on NBC, performed an excerpt from *Nina* on Ed Sullivan's *Toast of the Town*, and even taken a ride on Mr. I. Magination's magic train. Then in late November, a quarter of an hour before she was scheduled to perform *Cleopatra*, a short man in a blue suit appeared unexpectedly at the door of her dressing room.

"Good evening, Miss Rothe," the man said, laying a heavy black briefcase on her makeup table. "I've come to offer you your own show."

"I beg your pardon?" She put down a tube of brown greasepaint and stared at him blankly. She was wearing a black wig, several pounds of fake gold jewelry, and an Egyptian headdress that made her feel like her neck might snap off, and she was mildly annoyed at the interruption. Most of the time she was more than willing to yield to the crazy pace of television, with its impromptu script changes and endless technical squabbles, but several months ago she had managed to persuade everyone that the final fifteen minutes before she stepped in front of the cameras were sacred.

"I'm Jack Gordon from CBS," he said, sticking out his hand and shaking hers. His grip was cool, and he smelled faintly of talcum powder. "We want to give you your own show, put you in a slot on Friday nights at nine, right after *Man Against Crime*. We were planning on calling the show *The Kathe Rothe Hour*—that is if you agree." He smiled, exposing a row of brilliantly white teeth. "Contract to be drawn up at your convenience."

"My own show?"

"Right."

"But what would I do?" Kathe stammered.

"Well," Mr. Gordon said pleasantly, "we had in mind some kind of combination of variety and drama—short sketches, excerpts from first-run plays, interviews with Broadway stars, musical numbers from the most popular shows, and perhaps even a weekly look behind the scenes. You'd be the hostess, wear pretty dresses, tie everything together, and of course you'd act." He cleared his throat. "The truth is, though, we don't so much care what you do, as long as you do it well and do it fast. We want you to go on in two weeks. We put this other show on in October, two famous comedians who bombed so bad you could hear it from here to China. We're jerking them off before the sponsor puts out a Mafia contract on us. Comedians"—he shrugged—"the way television eats them up I don't have to tell you. It's like the Roman Coliseum."

"You're telling me you want me to do a show in *two weeks?*"

"Twelve days to be precise." Mr. Gordon smiled. "Friday after this. Well, how about it?"

"It's crazy," Kathe said. "You must be out of your minds over there at CBS."

Mr. Gordon shrugged. "It's television. So, are you interested?"

"Of course I'm interested. What actress in her right mind wouldn't be interested in having her own show, but I think it's impossible."

"Possible, smossible." Mr. Gordon shrugged again and smiled cheerfully. "Forget the difficulties. We're not asking for something that will win you a Nobel Prize. All we're asking is that when we turn the camera on, you do something interesting, something that will sell the sponsor's product."

Kathe thought for a moment. This was the most insane proposition she had ever heard, but that was the way things were these days. Television was so young and so hungry for material that scouts from the newly born networks walked the streets hauling in entertainment. There was Kuda Bux the Eastern Fakir, who purported to read minds; Ted and Amy Barrie, the blind tap dancers; the kindergarten class that spent Sunday mornings acting out Bible tales. Only last night she had seen a contestant on *The Amateur Hour* play "The Star-Spangled Banner" on a set of venetian blinds. Could she be any worse than that? Obviously, if she turned this down, Mr. Gordon would just go out and find someone else. On the other hand, if she accepted, she would have an hour a week to bring whatever she wanted into four million living rooms. What kind of actress in history had ever had an audience that big?

"What kind of run would I be looking at?" she asked cautiously.

"The usual." Mr. Gordon tapped the tips of his fingers together as if listening to distant music. "Starting December 2 you'd be in to us for fifty-two consecutive shows. To be perfectly frank, we could cancel you at any time, but Paley thinks you'll go over big. After you were on Sullivan's show, the phones at CBS nearly rang off the wall."

Kathe pursed her lips and thought some more. "Sounds pretty good."

"Oh it is. A sweetheart of an offer if I do say so myself. So do we have a deal or don't we?"

"Sure," Kathe said impulsively, shaking Mr. Gordon's hand, "we have a deal—on one condition, that is."

Mr. Gordon leaned forward, like a cat about to pounce on a mouse. His small brown eyes glowed. Here, Kathe thought, is a man born to negotiate. "What condition?" he purred smoothly.

"I have to talk this offer over with Hermann Lang. He's been producing most of the *NewCo* plays, and even though my contract happens to be up for renewal this month, I can't just walk out on him. Besides"—she cleared her throat and attempted to look business-like—"we have a close working relationship. I feel that I owe much of my success as an actress to Mr. Lang." Not to mention much of my happiness, she thought; not to mention that I'm crazy in love with the guy, but Mr. Gordon doesn't need to know that, although from the look on his face I suspect he's already guessed.

"So take Lang with you." Mr. Gordon picked up the tube of greasepaint, spun it in a circle, and looked up at Kathe with the air of a man who had all the angles covered. "Lang's got a great rep. What he's been doing for this poor excuse for a network, CBS would go down on its knees to get him to do. You need some leverage to pry him away? You can tell him from me that, subject to your approval, he can have a free hand—no sponsor interference, no big boys telling him how to call the shots. Just him and you, a honey of a budget, and an hour a week of some of the best time we've got."

"It's that easy?"

Mr. Gordon nodded blithely and licked his lips. His tongue was pink and slightly conical. He was a well-fed man, a man who obviously knew how to woo anyone, male or female, if the payoff was high enough. "It's that easy. You want Lang to produce your show, you got him"—he snapped his fingers—"like that. In fact, anyone you want, you got. Except dwarfs. Those turkey comedians used dwarfs, and we got lots of mail from people who thought it was heartless."

"How long do I have to think this over?"

"Take all the time you want." Mr. Gordon smiled a wide, generous smile and spread his arms as if entreating her to come aboard. "Take all night; take until tomorrow morning at eight. I'm not worried. I know you'll see it's in your best interest to accept." He pulled a silver fountain pen out of his shirt pocket and wrote his phone number for her with a flourish.

"Fine." Kathe accepted the paper from him and stuck it in the corner of the mirror. "I'll call you by eight then." I'm a maniac, she thought. I've virtually committed myself to a schedule that makes *The NewCo Theater* look like it's being done in slow motion. Twelve days. If Hermann decides to go in on this with me, where can we get a script writer? Where can we get musical numbers? Where can I get a dress that won't look like I bought it from the Salvation Army? She felt time slipping out from under like a badly anchored rug, but it was a rather exciting sensation.

"Welcome to CBS," Mr. Gordon said, shaking her hand all over again. "You're about to become a very famous lady. Now if you decide to do this—which I have no doubt you will—we'll need the first script in eight days at the outside so we can run through the technical cues—the usual format—commercial breaks; no graphic violence; no sex; no live animals over, say, thirty pounds. You want to interview someone, you tell us his name and we'll get him for you if we can, but don't count on it. Broadway stars are a cinch, especially if they've just opened in a new production, but film stars won't touch us with a ten-foot pole. So who would you like to start with?"

Gordon crossed his arms and looked at her expectantly. She could tell he was intentionally trying to snare her into planning shows, but even though she saw through him, the temptation to think about what she'd do with that hour on Friday nights was too great to resist. "What about T. S. Eliot?" she suggested.

Mr. Gordon looked at her blankly. "T. S. Eliot?"

"The American poet who lives in England."

"A poet?" Mr. Gordon shuddered visibly. "The kiss of death. Look, I'll try to borrow you Sid Caesar from NBC."

It was Kathe's turn to look blank.

"Caesar's funny," Gordon said, "trust me. He'll probably jump at the chance. He just started working a Saturday-night slot which—since everyone is out at the movies—is the kiss of death."

"It seems," Kathe observed, "that in television there are rather a lot of kisses of death."

"You said it." Mr. Gordon retrieved his briefcase, picked up his hat, and headed for the door. "So I'll hear from you by eight tomorrow, yes?"

"Yes, by eight."

"Good." He smiled a vast, radiant smile. "Great. Paley is going to do handsprings. You're the best thing on television. Two shows, maybe three, and you'll have the American public eating out of your hand."

Kathe tried to tell herself that he was just flattering her, but his words made her feel warm and happy. The best thing on television? Ridiculous. She could bomb out in six weeks. She sat for a moment, staring into the mirror, trying to decide how she felt about having a show of her own. Well on one hand she felt as if she'd been run over by a freight train, and on the other hand she felt a little drunk. She imagined the next fifty-two weeks. What was at the end of the ride?

Fame? Obscurity? She realized with amusement that she hadn't even asked Mr. Gordon what CBS was planning to pay her.

Suddenly she jumped up, smeared on the last of her makeup, and thrust her feet into her sandals. The Egyptian headdress made a sudden dive for the floor. Clutching at it, she burst out of her dressing room and hurried toward the control booth, ignoring the usual last-minute panic that was sweeping through the studio. She had five minutes before *The NewCo Television Theater* went on the air, and she wanted to spend at least three of those minutes finding out what Hermann thought of the craziest, most exhilarating scheme she'd ever heard of.

Trans-Atlantic Cable to Miss Viola Kessler
10 Spencer Court
London, England
December 2, 1949

DEAR MAMA SURVIVED DEBUT OF KATHE ROTHE HOUR
WITH NO MAJOR DISASTERS STOP CAMERAMEN LAUGHED
SELVES SICK HOPE TV AUDIENCE DID SAME STOP LOVE
YOU LOVE YOU LOVE YOU STILL REELING WITH IT ALL
STOP KISSES KATHE

Trans-Atlantic Cable to Miss Kathe Rothe
87 Lancelot Drive
Rockhaven, New York
December 3, 1949

CONGRATULATIONS DARLING STOP SEND KINESCOPE
OVER AS SOON AS POSSIBLE SO I CAN SEE MY GIRL IN

*ACTION STOP VERY PROUD OF YOU VERY HAPPY FOR YOU
LOVE MAMA*

*Kathe to Viola
January 4, 1950*

*DEAR MAMA CBS GOT TEN THOUSAND PIECES OF MAIL
ABOUT LAST SHOW AND I AM GOING TO BE IN LIFE
MAGAZINE STOP POWER OF TELEVISION BEYOND BELIEF
STOP FEEL LIKE AM BECOMING AMERICAN INSTITUTION
LIKE KLEENEX STOP HERMANN AND I BOTH DELIGHTED
BUT HOW DO YOU HANDLE OVERNIGHT FAME STOP IT
ISN'T ALL BAD BUT ITS A LITTLE UNNERVING STOP MISS
YOU STOP KISSES KATHE*

*Viola to Kathe
January 5, 1950*

*DEAR KATHE SARAH BERNHARDT ONCE TOLD ME THAT
BEST WAY TO HANDLE FAME TO IGNORE IT STOP PROBA-
BLY GREAT ADVICE BUT SEND ME TEN COPIES OF LIFE
ARTICLE ANYWAY STOP LOVE AND KISSES MAMA*

*Air letter to Miss Viola Kessler
10 Spencer Court
London, England
January 10, 1950*

Dear Vi,

*Don't bother to be jealous of the stamp on this letter because Acapulco
isn't all it's cracked up to be. It's crawling with insects, the water is
salty, there's no decent nightlife, and every time I walk out the door I
get sand in my shoes—not to mention that the fish here are big, surly,
and hungry-looking. I never should have let Jean-Claude persuade me
that getting back to nature was a good idea, but what can one do when
one is involved with a lad whose idea of the height of intellectual
achievement is a good tan?*

*Nevertheless, by hiding in my hotel room and refusing to venture out
in the sun, I've managed to complete a rewrite of* The Kindness of

Strangers. *Perhaps you remember it in its previous incarnation? Well it's changed quite a bit, as you'll see.*

I'm sending a carbon to you by air mail, but God knows when it will arrive. The Mexican postal service is, shall we say, primitive, especially in this godforsaken corner of the country.

Be a dear and give it a read, will you?

> Yours in perpetuity,
> Henry

Air Letter to Henry Arbor
148 Bleecker Street, Apt. 3C
New York, New York
February 6, 1950

Dear Henry,

I've just canceled the next two planning sessions for the play I'm supposed to be directing to finish reading The Kindness of Strangers, *and all I can say is that I think you've outdone yourself. Lucile is one of the best roles for an actress that I've come across in the past twenty years. You've given her everything—passion, intelligence, and the kind of love for that no-good husband of hers that makes you want to take her into protective custody until she comes to her senses. Has anyone told you lately that you're a hell of a writer?*

Now for the bad news—I think the first act still needs some work. The death of Lucile's mother just isn't presented strongly enough for my taste. Other than that, all I have are a few minor suggestions about dialogue and pace. I'm mailing the script back to you with my comments, so keep an eye out for it. As I recall, the last time I sent a script back to you some kids stole it to use as homeplate for a baseball game.

Sorry to hear about Jean-Claude's abrupt departure. Kathe wrote that you returned from Acapulco with a bad case of sun poisoning. My favorite cure for sun poisoning is baking soda in a tepid bath, but when I mentioned your plight to Cissy Dockett, she said to tell you to force down a couple of stiff shots of scotch. Shall we lay bets on which remedy you'll choose?

> Affectionately,
> Vi

Kathe to Viola
February 7, 1950

DEAR MAMA THANKS FOR BIRTHDAY PRESENT STOP BA-
ROQUE PEARLS GREAT ON TV BECAUSE DONT READ HOT
ON LIGHT METERS STOP HERMANN GAVE ME RING STOP
LOVE KATHE

Viola to Kathe
February 8, 1950

DEAR KATHE RING EXCLAMATION POINT WHAT KIND OF
RING STOP PLEASE CLARIFY STOP IS THIS AN ENGAGE-
MENT WE HAVE HERE STOP LOVE YOUR INTENSELY CURI-
OUS AND SNOOPY OLD MOTHER

Kathe to Viola
February 9, 1950

DEAR INTENSELY CURIOUS AND SNOOPY OLD MOTHER
YOU BET ITS AN ENGAGEMENT RING STOP I FINALLY GAVE
IN AND AGREED TO BECOME MRS HERMANN LANG STOP
DOES MARRIAGE TAKE ALL THE ROMANCE OUT OF THINGS
STOP PLEASE REPLY STOP AM SO DIZZY IN LOVE WITH
HERMANN I CANT TIE MY SHOES BUT MUST ADMIT AM
STILL GUN SHY ABOUT GOING THROUGH WITH IT STOP
LOVE KATHE

Viola to Kathe
February 10, 1950

DEAR KATHE THIS NO QUESTION TO ASK POTENTIAL
GRANDMOTHER STOP BUT SERIOUSLY MARRIAGE TO
YOUR FATHER HAPPIEST TIME OF MY LIFE STOP IF YOU
LOVE HERMANN THEN ADVISE YOU GO AHEAD WITH
WEDDING STOP LIFE A RISKY BUSINESS AT BEST BUT
HERMANN A REAL TREASURE STOP LOVE MAMA

Henry Arbor to Viola
February 11, 1950

DEAR VI JUST GOT YOUR LETTER STOP IF YOU WANT THE PART OF LUCILE ITS YOURS STOP CAN NOW ADMIT THAT SENDING YOU SCRIPT WAS ALL PART OF PLOT TO GET MY HANDS ON YOU AGAIN STOP LOVE HENRY

Viola to Henry Arbor
February 13, 1950

DEAR HENRY I RETIRED YEARS AGO STOP BUT THANKS FOR THE THOUGHT STOP ITS TRULY A GREAT PLAY STOP BEST OF LUCK WITH IT STOP LOVE VI

Henry Arbor to Viola
February 15, 1950

DEAR VI YOU CANT TURN THIS PART DOWN STOP I WROTE IT FOR YOU STOP PLEASE AT LEAST THINK IT OVER STOP ON BENDED KNEE HENRY

Viola to Henry Arbor
February 18, 1950

DEAR HENRY IM TEMPTED BUT THE ANSWER IS STILL NO STOP VERY SORRY STOP THANKS AGAIN FOR OFFERING PART OF LUCILE TO ME STOP UNDER DIFFERENT CIRCUM-STANCES I WOULD SNAP IT UP STOP LOVE VI

Kathe to Viola
March 23, 1950

DEAR MAMA HAVE GREAT NEWS STOP YOU ARE COMING OUT OF RETIREMENT STOP EXPECT YOU IN NEW YORK IN TWO MONTHS TO STAR IN HENRY ARBOR PLAY KINDNESS OF STRANGERS STOP HERMANN PRODUCING STOP ARBOR SAYS YOU WILL WIN HIM SECOND PULITZER STOP ALL ARRANGEMENTS MADE REHEARSALS TO BEGIN JUNE 1 STOP REVISED SCRIPT FOLLOWS BY MESSENGER STOP LOVE KATHE

Special Delivery Letter to Miss Kathe Rothe
87 Lancelot Drive
Rockhaven, Long Island
March 26, 1950

Dear Kathe,

I just got your cable, darling, and needless to say it was quite a surprise. The idea that you and Hermann and Henry would take the time and trouble to hatch up a plot like this is very touching. In fact, when I opened the envelope and read what was inside I actually started crying, which just goes to show you that I'm still something of a sentimental old fool. I've been sitting here all day staring out the window, trying to write a reply, but I keep crumpling up the letters and throwing them away. You see, I want you to know how much I appreciate what you've tried to do for me, and yet the simple fact is that, although I'd give my eyeteeth to play Lucile, I can't accept the part.

I know this is going to be a disappointment to you and Henry, and it no doubt seems terribly ungrateful to Hermann as well, since he so obviously put this production together as a wedding present, but I think all three of you underestimate the trouble it would cause if I accepted. It's not that I've lost my courage—I still have plenty—and it's not that I don't want to act. Although I've been happy teaching and producing, I've spent the last ten years longing for the smell of greasepaint and the applause of an audience the way a drowning man longs for oxygen, but, frankly, I've tested the water over here several times and I know for a fact that people still associate me with the Nazis.

You know I was completely cleared of any complicity—as do all my friends and most of my professional associates—but the problem is that the general public doesn't know this.

I realize that must seem incredible—after all, it was a matter of public record, but the problem is that the newspapers printed the truth on page twelve while they printed the story of my supposed collaboration on page one. Then, too, even though Richard's brother Harry died in the bombing of Berlin, everyone still remembers him as the traitor who broadcast anti-British propaganda during the War. Harry was quite famous, you know, for his remark that if the King wanted to stop the Blitz he should hold a Black Mass in Westminster Abbey and solicit the help of Satan since only the Devil could save London. That's not the kind of thing people ever *forget, and they still associate me with him, and the long and the short of it is that, taken all together, my name has never been fully cleared.*

I'll come over for your wedding, darling, and play the proud Mama, but that's the only role I can play, I'm afraid. I can't tell you how moved I am that the three of you cooked up this ruse to lure me out of retirement. You are the finest daughter a mother could have, and I pass the torch on to you knowing that you'll carry it better than I ever did. So as I creep into a genteel old age this will be my satisfaction.

Please give my regrets to Hermann and tell Henry that I agree that The Kindness of Strangers *is going to win him another Pulitzer. I think he should try casting Katharine Cornell or Laurette Klemens in the role of Lucile.*

All my Love,
Mama

Kathe to Viola
April 1, 1950

DEAR MAMA WHATS THIS GENTEEL OLD AGE RUBBISH STOP GET YOUR ASS OVER HERE STOP HERMANN AND I THRIVE ON TROUBLE AND HENRY SAYS IT WILL SELL MORE TICKETS STOP IF YOU DONT COME WE WILL COME AND GET YOU STOP THIS IS NO APRIL FOOLS JOKE STOP LOVE KATHE

Viola to Kathe
April 2, 1950

DEAR KATHE I WARN YOU THAT IF YOU THREE MAKE THIS OFFER ONE MORE TIME IM GOING TO ACCEPT IT STOP LOVE MAMA

Kathe to Viola
April 3, 1950

DEAR MAMA HENRY IS DEPENDING ON YOU AND HER- MANN AND I ABSOLUTELY REFUSE TO TAKE NO FOR AN ANSWER STOP THEATER HIRED COSTUMES IN WORKS SEE YOU SOON STOP LOVE KATHE

Viola to Kathe
April 4, 1950

DEAREST KATHE YOU WIN STOP WILL ARRIVE MAY 28 TEN
AM BRITISH AIRWAYS FLIGHT 122 TO BEGIN REHEARSALS
STOP AM GETTING HAIR CUT LOSING TEN POUNDS AND
ALREADY HAVE LINES MEMORIZED STOP LETTER THICK
AS WAR AND PEACE FOLLOWS STOP OH MY DARLING IM
SO HAPPY STOP THANK YOU FOR BEING SO STUBBORN
STOP ALL MY LOVE MAMA

Viola's first hint of what was in store for her came approximately two minutes after British Airways Flight 122 touched down at Idlewild. There was a moment of silence broken only by the hum of the air-conditioning system and the chime that indicated the pilot had turned off the seat-belt sign, and then the pack of reporters who had been waiting behind the gate vaulted over the wire fence and charged toward the plane.

"Good heavens, Miss Kessler," the red-haired stewardess said, gaping out the window, "it looks like another American Revolution out there. I think the Yanks have gone balmy. Maybe you should just sit in here and wait until they settle down."

Viola stood up, gathered her purse and her copy of *The Kindness of Strangers*, and shook her head stubbornly. "I rather expected something like this," she told the wide-eyed stewardess. Squaring her shoulders, she waited until the other passengers had disembarked, and then she walked briskly out of the plane to face the press.

The first reporter to reach her was a thin man in a brown suit. Skidding to a halt, he thrust a microphone in her face. "Miss Kessler," he demanded, "is it true that you once performed for Hitler?"

"No," she said passionately, "it isn't true. I never saw Hitler except in a newsreel, and if you bothered to keep track of what was going on in the world, you'd know that I was officially cleared of any—"

"Miss Kessler," another reporter interrupted, "there's a rumor that Senator McCarthy tried to keep you out of the United States because you once lived in Berlin with a pack of Commies. Care to comment on that?"

"He did indeed, but it just so happens that I'm a United States citizen. Whether I once lived with Communists or a herd of promiscuous pandas is irrelevant. I have the same rights every other citizen has, and I think that question reeks of—"

"Are you a Fascist or a Communist?"

"—witch hunting, guilt by association, and an irresponsible—"

"Why won't you answer my question, Miss Kessler?"

"I am answering your question. I said—"

They pushed up against her, climbed over each other, shoved and yelled and jostled as she stood there stubbornly, clutching her purse in one hand and the script in the other. Come on, she thought, do your worst. She discovered that she was actually beginning to enjoy herself. Too many years out of the action, she thought, makes a woman rusty. She hadn't felt so alive since those days back in Berlin when Joseph was writing his political plays and nearly every performance ended in a riot.

Smells assailed her: tobacco, after-shave lotion, sweat-soaked shirts, the acrid odor of spent flashbulbs. What a crew. Where had these people come from? American reporters had always impressed her as being a polite, rather well-educated lot, but this group seemed to have escaped from an asylum for the criminally excitable. She cast a quick glance over her shoulder at the astonished face of the stewardess who had fed her Cornish pasties and hard candies all the way from Heathrow. The poor girl seemed to be in shock. Probably wasn't used to watching her passengers being mobbed. Good-bye British politeness, boredom, and afternoon tea. Hello American rudeness, excitement, and the survival of the fittest. It was good to be home, and if they could dish it out, she could dish it right back.

Turning on the reporters, she faced them without flinching. A few backed off a bit, as if impressed, but the questions kept coming like machine-gun fire:

"Miss Kessler, how do you feel about the accusation that by performing in *The Kindness of Strangers* you're wrecking Henry Arbor's career?"

"I think that's a statement cooked up by critics jealous of Henry's talent and—"

"Are you aware that veterans' groups and members of the Jewish community are planning to protest your appearance?"

"I had been warned that it was a pos—"

"Miss Kessler, is it true that captured German documents show you worked against the Nazis, not for them?"

My God, a sympathetic question. Viola was so surprised that she was temporarily rendered speechless. She stared at the reporter—a short man in a gray hat—wondering where he had come from.

"Is it true," he persisted, "that all of this is being blown out of proportion?"

"Yes, it's true. Thank you for asking that question. I was never a Nazi sympathizer, never. On the contrary—"

"Miss Kessler, over here, Miss Kessler. Our readers want to know how it feels to be the mother of a famous TV star? Are you jealous of your daughter's success as an actress—I mean considering how poorly your own career has been going?"

What an amazingly nasty question. Viola felt the blood rush to her face and the adrenaline course through her body the way it had back in Berlin in '25 when the audience had thrown stones at her during the first act of *Gas Mask*. She opened her mouth to inform the woman in no uncertain terms that her relationship with Kathe was nobody's business but her own, but she might as well have been trying to talk underwater for all the good it did.

"Miss Kessler, is there any truth to the rumor that Hermann Lang, your daughter's fiancé, bought this part for you to clear your name?"

"Why haven't you performed professionally for the last ten years, Miss Kessler?"

"What do you think of Alger Hiss?"

"Where do you buy your shoes?"

"Why won't you tell the American public whether you're a Fascist or a Communist?"

Viola gave up. It was hopeless. They weren't giving her time to answer, and even if she had managed to reply to half of these questions, they were too busy putting their own words into her mouth to listen.

"No comment," she said, attempting to push her way through the reporters, but she might as well have tried to walk through a brick wall. They closed in around her, someone stepped on her left foot, her hat was knocked off her head and trampled. She folded her arms across her chest and stopped trying to move forward; it was an odd sensation to be caught up in the middle of so many people, but if they were trying to scare her, it was having the opposite effect.

"What do you mean 'no comment'?" a large man in a blue-and-white seersucker suit demanded, flourishing a notepad. Half a dozen more microphones were thrust on her; flashbulbs popped like corn; a newsreel film crew took up position on the runway and the camera began to grind away, following her every move.

She smiled pleasantly, aware that dozens of cameras were catching her face. It was a professional smile—the kind that made her skin glow, her hair seem more golden, reduced her age by fifteen years, and looked good from the balcony, but anyone who knew her well would have seen the snap of impatience in her eyes.

"Thank you so much for welcoming me back to New York in this extraordinary fashion," she said, beaming at them with relentless goodwill, "but I really have no more comments at this time." Kathe was supposed to be meeting this plane. Where the hell was she? She looked toward the terminal, hoping to see Kathe, and was rewarded by the sight of her daughter running full tilt across the runway carrying a huge bouquet of roses. Diving into the reporters, Kathe began to flail at them with the bouquet.

"Let me through; get back; get away from her," Kathe yelled. Rose petals flew everywhere, blood-red and yellow and white, raining down onto the brims of the reporters' hats, sticking onto their lips and notepads and camera lenses. The stems of the flowers emerged from the white tissue paper, slick green, beheaded. Stripped of their thorns by one of Manhattan's most expensive florists, they weren't much of a weapon, but thornless or not they stung. With little comic yelps, the reporters broke ranks, letting Kathe through.

"Mama," Kathe said, throwing herself into Viola's arms. Kissing and hugging and laughing and weeping, they embraced each other as the cameras clicked and the flashbulbs popped. It was a memorable picture, and by morning it would undoubtedly be on the front page of every major newspaper on the East Coast.

As the cab pulled away from the terminal, Kathe tilted her head back and began to laugh. She tried to stop, but the more she tried, the harder she giggled. Her eyes watered and her chest heaved. She looked helplessly at Viola and then at the rose stems, which lay limply on the floor, still wrapped in the torn white tissue paper.

"You looked like you were going to eat those reporters alive, Mama."

"What about you? Attacking those poor people with a bouquet. Such manners."

"They deserved it."

"They certainly did."

"Still"—Kathe caught her breath and sat back—"it isn't all that smart to offend the press."

"No"—Viola grinned—"it isn't, but it was a great moment."

"Prime," Kathe agreed, "absolutely prime."

Viola inspected her hat—or to be more precise, her former hat. Once a pretty concoction of summer straw and flowers, it had been squashed into a dirty rectangle with protruding wires. The sight of it was a little sobering. "How much trouble do you actually think we're in for?" she asked. The reality of the situation was just beginning to sink in, and somehow—even though this was America, with its skyscrapers and fast highways and intolerably bright sunlight—she couldn't help feeling anxious about bomb threats.

"It's hard to say." Kathe shrugged. "Hermann's arranged for you to rehearse in seclusion, and he's hired some security guards, but we all think that's probably not going to be necessary. You know how the Americans are—fanatical but with short memories." She gestured at the cars that sped along beside the cab. "One day they're all excited about an issue, and the next day they can't remember it ever existed. There'll undoubtedly be a protest of some kind when *Kindness* opens at the Oxford, but with a little luck it will be a small one. By that time the issue of what you did or didn't do in Nazi Germany could be as dead as the flying-saucer craze."

"That's all very encouraging, but after being descended on by that wolf pack at the airport, I'd like to get my side of the story out to the press as soon as possible." She twirled the trampled hat jauntily on one finger. "Otherwise, my millinery bills are going to be astronomical."

Kathe cleared her throat uneasily. "Actually, to tell you the truth, Mama, we already tried to do something along that line, but the results weren't all that great."

Viola let the hat fall back into her lap. "What happened?"

Kathe frowned. "Nothing important really. It just didn't work very well, that's all."

"Darling, you may be a good actress, but you've always been a poor liar. Tell me what happened; I'm not made of glass. Whatever it is, I can take it."

"Well," Kathe said reluctantly, "you'd warned us in advance that there might be trouble, so at the first sign of this Nazi stuff coming up Hermann hired the best publicist he could find, a woman named Julia Dancer, who works for big-time movie stars like Judy Garland. This Mrs. Dancer was good, very efficient, and she convinced some of the more responsible papers like the *Times* to print the whole story—complete with excerpts from the documents that cleared you, but some of the others decided to go for your throat. Don't ask me why. I suppose uncovering Nazi actresses sells subscriptions. Anyway, a few of them did the worst thing possible." She paused. "I hate to be the one to tell you this, but they printed the story about how you denied all the charges that you were a collaborator and then, above the story, they reprinted that picture of you shaking hands with Goebbels."

"Oh no." Viola leaned forward, horrified. "They didn't, they couldn't have."

"They could have and they did." Kathe smiled grimly. "But don't panic; the situation isn't all that bleak. A lot of important people have come out in your favor. The president of the Manhattan branch of Hadassah, for example, made a public statement saying that after examining the evidence, she believed you were innocent, and most of the unions are behind you. So I'd say that at this point New York is divided into two camps on the topic, neither of which is speaking to the other. Still, as Henry predicted, it's selling tickets. We've already had about five hundred requests, and we haven't even gone into rehearsals yet. Anyway," she concluded, "don't think about it any more than you have to, because there's nothing you can do."

They rode in silence for a few minutes as Viola tried not to think about the fact that a magazine containing a picture of her shaking hands with Goebbels had recently been for sale at every newsstand in Manhattan. It was, to say the least, a disquieting thought. She searched for some way to change the subject. "How's Henry reacting to the idea of his play becoming such a hot political issue?" she asked at last.

"Lapping it up, I'd say." Kathe looked relieved. "The man loves scandal, Mama. He's spent his whole life wanting to be like Hemingway only he doesn't hunt, doesn't fish, is scared stiff of bulls, and thinks Central Park is a wilderness area. Now he has a chance to play the tough guy, and he's exploiting it for all it's worth. He's taken to wearing black turtlenecks and motorcycle jackets to parties, smoking nasty-smelling cigars, and discoursing on artistic freedom. He wants to see you, by the way—this afternoon as a matter of fact."

"I was planning to go to the hotel and sleep for the next twenty-four hours," Viola sighed, "but what Henry wants at this point, I suppose Henry gets. By the way, has Henry got a new boyfriend or is he still mourning Jean-Claude?"

"Henry has droves of new boyfriends. They flock around him like flies around honey. Jean-Claude is probably eating his heart out this very minute wishing he'd stuck around long enough to get in on the notoriety. By the way, Henry sent Hermann and me a wedding present, one of our more unusual, although, God knows, we've gotten enough strange things. The fan magazines broke the story of our engagement about a month ago, and ever since viewers have been mailing in presents by the boxcar load—toasters, salad bowls, silver-plated gravy boats, even a praying hand-towel rack that glows in the dark, but Henry's gift tops the list for pure weirdness."

"What was it?"

"A TV planter."

"A what?"

"A television set with the screen taken out and replaced by Boston ferns." Kathe grinned. "I think this is a none too subtle expression of Henry's opinion of television." She leaned forward suddenly and grasped Viola's hands. "Mama," she said softly, "you're here, aren't you? You're really here."

"Yes, darling." Viola nodded, "I'm here."

"I've missed you," Kathe said simply.

Viola was very moved. She looked at Kathe and then out the window at the skyline of Manhattan, jagged and beautiful as a western canyon. Papa, and Mama, and Conrad were gone, but New York and America had endured. There was something balanced and beautiful in that thought, and she rested in it for a while, holding Kathe's hands. She thought, too, of *The Kindness of Strangers* and how good it would be to act again, and how she would overcome the present trouble, turn the hate of the audience into love, and make the part of Lucile come alive for them—how she would finally play an American heroine and how much satisfaction that would be to her and how she should have done it long ago. She loved this country, she realized. She might even move back—to New York, or perhaps to California.

"What are you thinking about, Mama?" Kathe asked. "You look like you're a thousand miles away."

Viola leaned over and kissed Kathe on the cheek. "I was thinking," she said softly, "how—despite everything—how very good it is to come home."

Although Viola remained on edge, the month of rehearsals went by without incident, *The Kindness of Strangers* took shape, and the scandal seemed to subside and then disappear, pushed off the front page—as Kathe had predicted—by more important news like the opening of the Brooklyn-Battery Tunnel. For Viola this was a happy time. Working onstage again nourished her, and she began to remember things she had almost forgotten: the thrill of picking up a cue with perfect timing, the pleasure of inhabiting a character, the satisfaction of expressing a wide range of emotions. And when she wasn't working on the play there was always Kathe's wedding to be organized—a silly, motherly occupation, perhaps, but one she found she thoroughly enjoyed. Weddings, after all, were bits of theater in their own right; the origin of the theater itself was in the church, and so, as she and Kathe visited florists and planned the reception, she told herself that nothing so dramatically expressed the uniting of two people as a wedding, and this had an almost magical effect, turning what might have been an onerous chore into a way of expressing her love for Kathe and Hermann.

June passed into July, and on the fifteenth *The Kindness of Strangers* opened to a sold-out house.

Scene: A darkened bedroom in a small town in Mississippi. The room is hot and speaks of sickness and death. LUCILE DESAINTS, a woman of thirty-nine, sits beside her mother, who is in the last stages of a long illness.

    LUCILE: Mama? Mama, can you hear me?

Viola leaned forward over the actress who was playing the dying mother. Her body was coiled like a spring, tense and concentrated. She had worked on this part of the play for days, trying to get a sense of looking into a small, dark window. That window, she told herself, was the eternity of the dying woman, but Lucile wouldn't know that. She would see only the constriction and barely sense the vastness on the other side; she would be upset, and frightened, and the audience would have to feel that fear and claustrophobia from the moment the curtain rose. She'd learned from long experience that you had a minute, three minutes at the most, to establish a character, but if you could do it, if you could capture the audience at the very beginning, they'd be yours for the rest of the play. At least half this audience, however, was in no mood to be captured by anyone.

"Go back to Germany."

"Fascist!"

The first catcalls came seconds after the play began. Viola tried to ignore them, but they sent little thrills of fear rippling up her spine. The actress who was playing the dying mother opened her eyes and looked up at Viola with a worried expression.

"What the hell's going on?" she whispered. Since this was a nonspeaking part, she was young and inexperienced. Her eyes were wide, and Viola could tell she was on the verge of getting up and bolting off the stage.

"Stay in character," Viola hissed. "Lie there and play dead." Under any other conditions it would have been comic to be having a conversation with a corpse.

"Fascist!"

"Pipe down over there, will you?"

At least some members of the audience wanted the play to continue.

"I fought a war to get rid of people like her!"

"And I paid money to hear this play!"

There were more catcalls, more cries for order. Someone yelled the first obscenity. A rotten orange flew through the air and hit the foot of the bed. The actress who was playing the dying mother jumped and there was laughter.

"Curtain! Bring down the curtain! Get that Nazi out of here!"

"Somebody call the police."

"Screw you, buddy. I'm a veteran, and I won't have that Nazi up on that stage." More rotten fruit spattered around Viola, mixed with eggs and other sorts of filth. She struggled to go on with her lines, but the audience was on its feet now, yelling. Stubbornly, she persisted. From the sound of it, the audience was dividing into two camps.

"Let her say her lines."

"Get her off the stage."

"This is America. We have freedom of speech here."

"Six million Jews died in the camps."

Goaded beyond endurance by that last remark, Viola got up and stormed to the footlights, her eyes flashing dangerously.

"I'll have you know," she yelled, "that my husband was murdered by the Nazis, my own brother died in Dachau, my sister-in-law—"

"Shut up."

"Let her talk."

"I worked for the German Resistance. I smuggled out one of the first lists of people who had been tortured and murdered. I risked my life and my reputation and—"

"The Germans shot my only son," a woman in the front row yelled. "They executed my Willie."

"I'm sorry. I know how you must feel, but we all lost people we loved in that war. I wasn't to blame. I was completely cleared of any—"

"Look at this!" The woman held up a newspaper, and Viola saw with a sinking feeling the picture of herself shaking hands with Goebbels. "Shame, shame on you."

"Please," Viola pleaded, "listen to me. I can explain—"

"Explain it in hell."

There was more commotion, and suddenly everything came apart: fistfights broke out in several places simultaneously, women screamed, the audience lunged forward as if they were about to rush the stage. Viola made one last attempt to yell above the din.

"Please," she begged, "don't do this. Can't you see what you're doing? Please . . ." But it was too late. Reason had been lost somewhere and all that was left was animal chaos and bitter passions. Frightened, the stage manager ordered the curtain brought down. It fell in front of Viola, just missing her, a mass of dusty gold velvet. For a moment she stood looking at it, unable to believe that the play was over before it had started. She could still hear sounds of rioting on the other side, and she wondered if the audience was going to destroy the Oxford Theater the way the Brownshirts had destroyed the Neues.

This is America, she told herself. Things like this don't happen in America. But it had happened, and as she turned to walk offstage she had the feeling that perhaps she was making her final exit, and she would never act again.

"I can't believe it." Kathe stormed into Viola's dressing room, her face white with anger. "I just can't believe they did that to you, Mama."

"Well they did," Viola said. "I know I said that I expected there to be trouble, but to tell you the truth, until it happened I never really believed it could be so bad." She knew she should take off her makeup but she didn't have the heart to.

"I hate them." Kathe paced across the room. "They were vile, absolutely vile."

"Not all of them were against me, and the others were just misinformed." Viola shook her head. "What could you expect? Some of those people lost their entire family—children, parents. It's a wonder, really, that they aren't even more insane with grief."

"How can you be so understanding?" Kathe whirled on her. "How can you just sit there and take it? You're a superb actress, and they've wrecked your career. And for what? For nothing. Because they're too dumb to read the back pages of the newspapers; because they'd rather deal in prejudice than truth. The Allies may have won the battle, but fascism won the war."

Viola leaned forward, her face sober and earnest. "Don't ever say that, not even in anger. There's no comparison between New York and Nazi Germany. You're very young. You don't understand that the problem is that even in a functioning democracy like this one people would always rather feel than think. That's what keeps the human race in so much trouble. Five thousand centuries of recorded history and not one of them without a war. Does that look like the record of a reasonable species? Let's just face reality, darling. My career as an actress *is* over. Well, so what—I can still produce; I can direct; I can teach. I don't plan to abandon the theater or curl up and die or suddenly become one of those old ladies who wander around muttering to themselves. I just can't appear on the stage."

"I don't accept that."

"I'm afraid you have to. No theater owner in his right mind would ever let me into his building."

"Hermann *owns* the Oxford Theater, Mama. Of course he'll let you back in here. He'd book you in another play tomorrow."

"Yes," Viola said, "I suppose you're right. I suppose Hermann would do that for me, but you see I wouldn't let him. Hermann was always a good friend—not to mention that he's about to be your husband. I couldn't let him take a financial risk like that. All that crowd did tonight was riot, but next time they could very easily burn this place to the ground. Take my word for it—I've seen it happen before. I'm too big a liability."

"The hell you are, Mama. I'm not letting this rest."

"You know," Viola said thoughtfully, "the one quality I've always appreciated most about you is your stubbornness. Joseph was like that. I'm stubborn myself, but not that stubborn."

"Great," Kathe said, "it's good to know I run true to form. Hereditary stubbornness sounds like a fine quality to me, and I intend to exploit it to the fullest." She came over to Viola and put her hands on her mother's shoulders. "I'm warning you right now that I don't intend to let you go back to London without completing at least one performance of *The Kindness of Strangers*."

"What are you planning to do?"

"Prove your innocence, Mama."

Viola shook her head. "Sweetheart, that's very touching, but it's not possible."

"Why not?"

"Because people won't listen, and even if they would, everyone who knew anything firsthand is dead—Conrad, Angela, Hilde, even Friedrich, who was probably responsible for blackmailing me. All that are left are captured German documents. Those documents cleared me beyond a doubt—they were even published in *The New York Times*—but people aren't interested in documents. They'd only listen to a witness, someone who'd been there, a member of the old Munich network, for example. But the Nazis, you see, were very thorough. They shot everyone even remotely connected with the network. They'd have shot me for that matter, but I had the good fortune to be in London when they got around to tidying up. So you see, it's hopeless."

"Nothing," Kathe said stubbornly, "is ever hopeless."

"Don't do this to yourself," Viola pleaded. "Don't break your heart on this. It isn't worth it."

Kathe folded her arms across her chest. "Yes it is. I won't see you slandered like this. I love you, Mama, and if it costs me my own career, I'm going to see your name cleared."

"What do you mean, if it costs you your own career?" Worried by the expression on Kathe's face, Viola got to her feet. "You aren't planning to do anything rash, are you?"

"Yes"—Kathe nodded—"I certainly am."

"What?"

"Tune in tomorrow for further details."

"What does that mean?"

"It means," Kathe said, "that I have just had a superb, if not to say brilliant, idea."

"Which is?"

Kathe smiled cryptically. "If you want power, then go where the power is."

"Oh, you mean write a letter to the President or something like that?" Viola was surprised to discover that she was disappointed that all Kathe had to offer her was an aphorism.

The next night was a Friday and *The Kathe Rothe Hour* went on the air as usual at nine o'clock. In the newspapers, which had begun listing the programs for the infant medium, viewers were informed that this evening Miss Rothe would interview Laurette Klemens, a young understudy who had recently stepped into the role of Anne Boleyn in *Anne of a Thousand Days*, and whom critics had acclaimed as one of the more promising young talents of the season. At nine o'clock sets were duly tuned to CBS—some six and a half million it was estimated, since *The Kathe Rothe Hour* was an extremely popular program and the new coaxial cables had recently linked up the East Coast with the rest of the country. Also, since the program was being broadcast on radio frequencies, there were at least that many more people hearing the show.

For the first few minutes nothing in the least extraordinary occurred. The theme music—a lively Viennese waltz—played, and Kathe Rothe came whirling out of the white door with the star on it dressed, as always, in a gown that made millions of American women sigh with envy. Tonight it was especially stunning, flared at the hips, covered with tiny sequins that—although you couldn't see color, of course—gave the impression of being gold or perhaps silver. This fashion show was a part of the program Kathe had agreed to reluctantly, but the sponsor had been dead right. It was a big hit; it got the audience's attention, and that, after all, was the purpose of an opening.

Pausing beside the white couch, Kathe rested her hand lightly on the back of it and smiled at the audience. Anyone who had been looking closely would have seen that it wasn't her usual smile, that there was an extra glint to it.

"Welcome," she said smoothly, "to the Kathe Rothe Hour." Camera number one moved in, red light blinking, to get a good shot of her smile. Her next line was to be "Tonight I have a very special guest for you—Laurette Klemens," followed by Miss Klemens' entrance, but Miss Klemens never got in front of the cameras that night because instead of saying her next line Kathe stepped forward and, to the confusion of everyone in the studio, began to make a speech that wasn't in the script.

"Ladies and gentlemen," she said firmly, "I have something very important and very personal to talk to you about this evening. Last night my mother, Viola Kessler, opened at the Oxford Theater in Henry Arbor's play, *The Kindness of Strangers* . . ."

There was a gasp from the studio audience as they realized what was happening, and then a silence you could have dropped a mountain into.

"What the hell is she talking about?" the panicked floor director hissed into his headset. "Was this stuff added at the last minute or something? What are the camera cues? What are the light cues? When does Klemens come in? For Chrissake, is there anybody up there minding the store?"

Up in the control booth, Hermann was staring at the monitors in horrified fascination.

". . . however my mother never got to complete that performance because the minute the curtain went up she was unfairly attacked by members of the audience who were under the false impression that she once had ties with Hitler." Kathe paused and looked directly into the camera. "I am here to tell you that that is a lie. My mother, Viola Kessler, is not nor has she ever been a Nazi sympathizer. . . ."

"Pull the plug on her, H.L.," the engineer begged Hermann. "She's going crackers on national TV."

Hermann waved him aside. "Let her talk."

"You can't do that. Christ, H.L., the sponsor's going to have a fit; Gordon will cut you up and eat you for breakfast."

"So I should care. Give me a close-up on number three."

"Jesus H. Christ, everyone's gone bats around here." The engineer did what he'd been ordered to do, and Kathe's face filled the screen.

"Viola Kessler worked *against* the Nazis; she loathed them and everything they stood for. In 1928 they murdered my father, Joseph Rothe; in 1938, at great personal danger, Viola Kessler brought one of the first lists of atrocities out of Germany. Her brother, my uncle Conrad Kessler, died in a German concentration camp, as did his wife. My mother loved her brother as much as a sister ever loved a brother, but even while the Gestapo was holding him hostage she still would have spoken out had not the British Fascists threatened to bomb any theater in which she made a public appearance. Viola Kessler is a heroine, not a collaborator. I say that not only as her daughter, but as a person who knows firsthand what sacrifices she made. I myself was involved with the French Resistance . . ."

She went on speaking of many things—of betrayal and trust, of love and ethics, of what freedoms were worth giving your life for, and all the time Hermann kept the camera on her. It was a beautiful, eloquent speech, which would no doubt destroy both their careers in television, but he didn't care. He was proud of her for making it, and more than a little awed by her courage. Never, he thought, had she looked more beautiful.

At the end Kathe stretched out her arms. "I beg anyone who can clear my mother's name to come forward," she pleaded. "Captured

German documents confirm every word I've said this evening, but people don't listen to documents, they listen to other people. There are so many decent, innocent Germans who came to this country after the war to find safety and freedom, surely there must be someone out there who can tell the world the truth about Viola Kessler. Whoever you are, wherever you are, I beg you to come forward. Next week I'm going to have my mother on this show." She dropped her arms to her sides and stood, looking brave but very alone, in front of an invisible audience of millions and a live audience of five hundred. "And I promise you that the truth *will* be told."

There was a moment of silence and then thunderous applause from the studio audience.

"Cut!" the floor manager screamed.

"Cut," the engineer begged, "please, H.L., cut away from her now before she goes completely cuckoo."

Hermann took one last look at Kathe's face on the monitor. Her eyes were bright with emotion, but her chin was set stubbornly. She'd known exactly what she was doing. She's got guts, he thought. What a wife she'll make, but remind me never to cross her. Sighing, he signaled for the cut. For the next forty minutes he had no idea what they'd do, run commercials maybe or show an old movie. Time, that demon of television producers, no longer concerned him.

27

At nine o'clock on that same Friday evening, Albert Sachs had been sitting in his landlady's apartment in Harlem watching television for the first time in his life. At first glance he had not been particularly impressed with the new invention. The screen, he decided after a few minutes, was too small and too dim; he had hoped to see something on the order of a movie, but instead he found himself straining to peer into what looked like a glass tank full of dirty gray water. Sachs, who had once been a photographer, was sensitive to fine shades of black and white, and he had an almost physical revulsion to anything that was out of focus or poorly framed, but Zelda Johnson, his landlady and proud owner of the set, was so happy with her purchase and so delighted to see it working that he politely refrained from telling her his opinion of her new toy.

"Isn't Kathe Roth wearing a fine dress," Zelda sighed. "I'd go a long way for a dress like that." She took a sip of Pabst Blue Ribbon beer and put her feet up on the red-velvet hassock. "That woman wears party clothes all the time. Do you think she goes to parties all the time or just on the TV?" Zelda rested a slender, brown hand on Sachs' knee and smiled at him. She was a widow in her fifties, and she and Sachs had been occasional lovers for the past two years in a comfortable sort of way that suited both of them.

"I should think she only gets dressed up for these performances." Sachs inspected the screen critically, trying to make out some of the background details, but except for a white couch and a door with a gold star on it, everything was a bewildering maze of little pulsing dots. "It would be uncomfortable for her to walk around in a dress like that, Zelda. It's too elaborate."

"It's fine by me," Zelda said. She gave Sachs an affectionate pat on the knee. "Enjoying yourself, honey?"

"Yes," Sachs lied politely, "television's very interesting, an entirely new form of communication."

"Want to go down to the Lyme Spot after the show's over? I hear Billy's gonna do a set or two."

"Really? Billy's back from Chicago?" Sachs brightened considerably. The Lyme Shop was a small jazz club three blocks away. Billy, Zelda's son by her first marriage, was a superb clarinetist, the best Sachs had ever heard. Ever since Sachs was a boy in Munich he had been passionately fond of American jazz; when he emigrated to America after the war he had moved to Harlem to be close to the brilliant race of people who had invented it, and he could think of nothing he would rather do with an evening than spend it at the Lyme Spot with Zelda, eating salted peanuts, drinking chilled beer, and listening to Billy and his friends improvise. Sachs was just savoring this prospect when Zelda tugged at his sleeve.

"Say," she said, "will you listen to that."

"To what?"

"To Kathe Rothe. She's talking funny." Zelda leaned forward and turned up the volume. "Lord," she said, "just listen to her."

Sachs turned his attention back to the television set, and what he heard made him forget all about going down to the Lyme Spot.

Her brother, my uncle Conrad Kessler, died in a German concentration camp, Kathe was saying, *as did his wife . . .*

At the mention of the name Conrad Kessler, Sachs went pale and clutched at the arm of the chair so hard that Zelda turned to see what was the matter with him. His face had gone completely white and he was staring at the television set like he'd seen a ghost, and for a moment she was worried that he was having some kind of heart attack, like the one that killed her first husband.

"You okay, honey?" she asked.

"Please, Zelda," Sachs begged, "be quiet."

On the television screen Kathe Roth was talking on and on about Germany, where Albert had once lived, and Zelda decided that maybe it was giving him the willies.

The show ended rather suddenly and a commercial came on for an electric refrigerator. The woman selling the refrigerator appeared a little shocked, as if she hadn't expected to be on the TV so early in the evening, but she went through all the usual motions of opening the door to show off the milk and vegetables, and pointing out the freezing compartment. Albert just sat there without saying a word, looking like someone had died or something.

"Zelda," he said at last, "can I use your phone? I have to make a call."

"Sure," she said good-naturedly. "Help yourself."

Sachs got up and started toward the kitchen, but he got only as far as the hall. Sitting down on a straight-backed chair near the coat closet, he buried his face in his hands.

Zelda hurried over to him and put an arm around his shoulders. "You aren't having chest pains, are you?"

"No." He opened his eyes and blinked. "I'm just fine." He got to his feet and gave her a kiss on the cheek that was friendly enough, but his face was drawn and sober.

"You look like you just seen your own death," Zelda observed.

Albert opened the kitchen door and stood for a moment on the threshold, shifting from one foot to another like someone was sticking pins into him. "Don't worry about me," he said, and then he disappeared into the kitchen to make his call.

Half an hour later, after no less than a dozen unsuccessful attempts, Albert Sachs got through to CBS and asked to speak to Kathe Rothe. He didn't get Miss Rothe, he got her secretary instead. The secretary—who had already taken over a hundred calls so far that evening—almost hung up on him, but fortunately Sachs persuaded her to hear him out, and it was a good thing she did because what he had to say proved very interesting indeed.

Kathe sat on the white couch facing Viola as the cameras moved in and out around them, restless and huge, like great metal birds of prey. A mass of cables lay on the floor: thick snakes of rubber and insulation and wire designed to carry every word and gesture to an audience that CBS estimated was larger than any other in the brief history of television. A week had passed, the sponsor had been pacified, it was nine o'clock, and *The Kathe Rothe Hour* was once again about to go on the air.

Kathe looked at her mother, sitting across from her, beautiful beyond her years in a pale gray dress, her hair swept away from her face, and a rush of pride overcame her. Mama had guts. She was now about to defend herself in front of an audience of fifteen million people, and she still managed to look calm. She wasn't of course. Before the show she'd been a mass of nerves, but you couldn't see it in her face, and that, Kathe thought, was an admirable quality, one she wished she'd inherited more of.

"You're on in ten seconds," the floor director warned.

"Ready, Mama?" Kathe reached over and squeezed Viola's hand.

"Ready and waiting, darling."

"Nervous?"

"You bet."

"I love you."

"I love you too."

"Here goes."

The theme music filled the studio and the lights came up.

"Welcome," Kathe said smoothly, turning toward camera number one, "to *The Kathe Rothe Hour*." Tonight, they had all agreed, there would be no entrance through the gold-starred door, no designer gown or flash of jewels. There would only be the mother and the daughter and, Kathe thought, the truth. For a second she almost faltered, frightened by the sudden realization of how many invisible eyes were on her, but she caught herself and went on with her opening speech, looking straight into the camera without flinching. This was the strange and intimate game of television: to be as close as any friend or lover to millions of people, to enter their living rooms and their minds, to strip your soul bare and yet never know until days later how they had reacted. And yet there was such power here; she could feel it even now swelling up around her, invisible and electric, flowing out across the darkness of the continent with each word she uttered, and she felt intoxicated by it and a little frightened. "I have the pleasure of having with me tonight Viola Kessler, who—as most of you already know—is my mother." She turned back to Viola. "Welcome, Mama," she said simply.

"Thank you," Viola said. The camera moved in on her face, and up in the control booth Hermann noted with satisfaction that the lighting was perfect. Caught by three small spots, Viola's blond hair glowed around her head like a halo. She was forty-nine, Hermann calculated quickly, and yet she looked about thirty-five at the most—which shouldn't have mattered of course, except in the ruthless world of television it did.

"Mama," Kathe said, "I think we should dispense with the pleasantries and get right down to business. You've come here tonight to answer charges that you were once a Nazi sympathizer." She leaned forward. "Well, were you?"

"No," Viola said firmly. "I wasn't."

"How do you expect the people out there to believe that? Of course I think you're telling the truth, but I'm your daughter. I could be deluded or prejudiced or simply unwilling to face the facts. So what evidence can you give the people of this country that you didn't collaborate?"

Viola spent ten minutes explaining about the captured German documents, photographs of which were projected onto the screen. Her voice was level but Kathe could hear the edge of tension in it. Still, it was a thorough, convincing speech—or rather it would have been convincing if those on the other side of the issue had been in any mood to be convinced. At the end Viola fell silent and looked at Kathe as if she weren't quite sure what to do next.

"That's all the evidence?" Kathe asked.

"All."

"And how many times before have you told people these same facts?"

"A dozen times at least."

"And have they listened?"

Viola nodded. "Yes, some have, but for the most part the issue's too explosive. People hear me and at the same time don't hear me; in other words, they're confronted with the evidence, but they ignore it. And I'm not sure I can blame them for that."

"Do you expect those people to listen to you tonight?"

Viola shook her head. There was resignation in her face and a glint of stubbornness. "No," she said, "I'd like to think that tonight would be different, but to tell you the truth, I doubt it. Scandal is always much more appealing than facts; scandal is exciting, facts are dull. I think that these accusations are something that I'm going to have to continue to live with, just as I've been living with them for the past twelve years."

"There are no witnesses who could confirm what you've just told us?"

"None."

"You're sure of that?"

"Positive. They're all dead."

There was a moment of silence. Kathe took a deep breath. "Mama," she said, taking Viola's hand in hers, "I have a surprise for you."

"A surprise?" Viola started visibly. Maybe this was a mistake, Kathe thought, maybe I should have told her in advance, and yet I wanted this reaction. I wanted her to be surprised, to be innocent and startled, and if this was cruel of me, then God forgive me, but the television audience has to see that this isn't something she set up in advance. They have to see that Mama's human.

"Mama, have you ever heard of a man named Albert Sachs?"

"No." Viola looked blank. "I haven't."

Kathe gestured toward the door behind her. "Mr. Sachs, will you please come onstage?" The door opened and a thin, rather ordinary-looking man in a wrinkled blue suit came out in front of the cameras. Kathe felt a thrill of excitement. It was an odd feeling, like stepping up to the edge of a steep cliff. "Mr. Sachs," she said, "will you please tell the audience who you are?"

"Certainly." The man turned toward the studio audience. "Good evening, ladies and gentlemen," he said with a faint German accent,

"I'm Albert Sachs. I was born in Munich, but now I'm an American citizen."

"How long have you been in this country, Mr. Sachs?" Kathe squeezed Viola's hand, but she didn't dare look at her.

"Five years," Sachs said. "I came right after the war."

"Why did you come here?" Kathe leaned forward slightly, her face serious and pale under the hot lights.

"I came here for freedom," Sachs said simply. "I know this sounds old-fashioned to Americans, this idea of coming somewhere to be free, but for me it was everything. I had been in prison, you see."

"In a concentration camp?"

Sachs shook his head. "No, in an ordinary prison. I had a small photography business in Munich—I did weddings, graduation pictures, and the like—and then in '38 I started forging passports and false documents for the Resistance. I'm still not sure why I took the risk. I wasn't ever the kind of man who had been interested in politics, but there seemed to be so much dirty business going on, and after a while I couldn't just stand by and do nothing." Sachs shrugged. "In any event, I began working with a group that called itself the Munich Network, so I should have been sent to Dachau or one of the other extermination camps, but the ridiculous truth is that the Nazis didn't catch me for working with the Munich Network."

At the mention of the Munich Network, Kathe felt Viola's hand grip her own.

"They caught me in the first year of the war for forging ration cards," Sachs continued. "The cards were for families that were in hiding, but they didn't discover this either. They thought I was an ordinary criminal—miracle of God, a black marketeer—so they put me in a regular prison."

"What happened then?"

"Nothing," Sachs said matter-of-factly. "It was a long sentence, and it probably saved my life. I was in that prison for the duration of the war. There wasn't much to eat toward the end, but it was bearable. By the time the Americans came through and liberated us, all that was left of Germany was a pile of rubble; everyone I'd worked with in Munich had been shot by the Nazis; my family was dead. So I emigrated."

"Mr. Sachs"—Kathe turned to Viola—"do you recognize the person who is sitting here beside me?"

Sachs scrutinized Viola's face. "Yes"—he nodded—"I never met her, but I recognize her from her passport picture. She's Conrad Kessler's sister." He stopped, as if suddenly overcome with emotion. "Excuse me," he said, "when I say the name Conrad Kessler it's a painful experience. Conrad was one of the heads of the Munich Network; he was a very fine man. He was rich; he owned a big brewery, and he could have sat out the war in peace, but he had too strong a conscience and he . . . I heard that they tortured him terribly . . . I heard . . ." He faltered to a stop. "Excuse me, but I owe Conrad Kessler my life and I can't speak of what happened to him without a terrible anger that I pray God every day to take out of my heart."

Sachs suddenly strode across the stage and grasped Viola's hand. "It's an honor to meet the sister of such a brave man," he said passionately. "You look like your brother. I thought of that when I first saw your picture, how you and Conrad had the same look on your faces. He used to bring me passports to alter, you see, and one day he brought me yours. He said you'd given it to him, and I thought even then that the sister was like the brother, willing to risk herself. I remember your passport because it was American, and American passports in those days were like gold. Do you know what we did with it? Did anyone ever tell you? We used it to get a man named Hans Schmidt out of Germany. Schmidt later organized an underground railroad for the Jews."

"I didn't know," Viola stammered. "Conrad never lived long enough to tell me, but thank you, thank you for letting me know."

Sachs turned back to Kathe. "I'm sorry," he apologized, "I can't say this all calmly. I know I should; I know this is a television show, but you see it's all still alive inside me. I'm not a poet; I can't put it into words, but"—he pointed to Viola—"I'm angry that she's suffered this way. I would have come forward sooner only I didn't make the connection between her and Conrad until last week. She should never have had this trouble. She's a brave woman. Because of her thousands of people are alive who would otherwise be dead." Sachs turned to the audience. "I'm not a highly educated man; there's a lot about life I don't understand, but I believe we were put on earth to help one another no matter what the cost. I believe that this is what it means to be human. I don't say she's a saint; there were many like her who risked their lives to help complete strangers, but I say that she's good and generous, and I admire her courage."

No one who saw Sachs that night ever forgot the look on his face, and no one ever forgot the sight of Kathe and Viola, hugging each other, oblivious of the cameras. The studio audience applauded and cheered, the cameramen applauded, the engineers in the control booth applauded, and in the darkness millions of unseen people applauded as well. For a few seconds, caught up by the flickering images, they were all united across three thousand miles and forty-eight states. It was a rare moment in the history of television.

Three days later *The Kindness of Strangers* reopened at the Oxford to begin a long successful run, and four weeks after that, with Viola looking on proudly, Kathe and Hermann were married.

As Kathe lay in Hermann's arms on their wedding night, she thought over her past. She was, she realized, content for the first time. As for the future, it seemed to open in front of her like a narrow path through a field of blooming flowers: twisting, unpredictable, but always beautiful, she thought, always filled with the grace of summer.

BOOK

FIVE

ATLANTIS

28

SANTA MONICA, CALIFORNIA 1975

The sunlight crept through the French doors of the small apartment on Wadsworth Street, paused at the row of Boston ferns in shiny ceramic pots, then flowed across the handwoven Zapotec rugs, glittered off.the seashells, made shadows on the white stucco walls, and fell at last on the face of Mandy Lang, who was sleeping sideways in a tangle of turquoise and gray sheets. At the age of twenty-one, Mandy was a lovely sight: her white-blond hair was spread out around her face in a curly tangle like a lion's mane, and the sheets had fallen back exposing a pair of small, strong shoulders. She had slender hands, delicate wrists, a square chin, and Kathe's high cheekbones and full lips. She also had, to her despair, Hermann's freckles, hundreds of them, peppered over the bridge of her nose and across her cheeks like grains of sand.

A few minutes passed and the sunlight grew brighter, turning from lemon-yellow to gold and then to a blinding blue-white. Mandy stirred restlessly, put up an arm to shield her face, and opened her eyes. They were amazing eyes, sea-blue and rather brilliant, with green centers that often made people accuse her of wearing colored contacts, but the most striking thing about them was their frankness. Mandy might have done much better in the movie industry if she'd only had a beautiful face, but she radiated an intelligence and determination that often threw directors for a loop. The truth was that even though she looked good on camera, they didn't know what to do with her.

Mandy blinked, squinted at the sunlight, and then moaned and dived under the sheets. Sleep, she needed sleep. Please God, no lawnmowers; please no disco music from the apartment upstairs. It was ten o'clock in the morning, but she hadn't gotten home until well after five because after she'd finished her waitress job at the No Satisfaction Cafe over on the Strip, she'd let Ted Van Dusen talk her into driving around with him to find a good location to shoot the next sequence of *Waiting for a Break*. A mistake, Mandy thought, curling her face into the crook of her arm, a definite mistake. Ted's father had been a famous prosecuting attorney, and Ted had inherited his tenacity. When Ted got his teeth into a project he never let go. He was only a student at USC, but he was treating this twenty-minute film of his like it was *Citizen Kane*. They'd driven from one end of L.A. to the other—from the Hollywood Hills halfway to San Diego. She even had a vague memory of stopping outside Disneyland while Ted and his roommate, Peter, discussed the possibility of getting permission to shoot the next set of interviews on the Mark Twain steamboat, which was a quixotic project if she'd ever heard of one because Disneyland never let anyone with a professional camera within a hundred yards of the front gate.

Putting her head under the pillow, Mandy rooted her way back into the darkness. Her eyes closed, her breathing became regular, and her body relaxed, and then just at that moment when pleasantly colored blobs of paisley were beginning to float through her mind, the alarm clock went off with a buzz that brought her straight up. Sputtering with frustration, she batted at the darn thing but it went on buzzing until she got up, stumbled around behind the night table, and pulled the plug out of the wall. What day was it? she asked herself groggily. Friday, right? So why had she set the alarm? She stood barefoot and naked for a moment, trying to remember what might have possessed her. Work? No, she wasn't due back at the No Satisfaction until eight tonight. An appointment with her agent? No such luck. Had she been planning to call Central Casting? No she hadn't. Perhaps she had a lunch date with a famous producer who had seen her in that deathless bit of cinema *Sunlotion* and who—able to see beyond the surfer beach blanket idiocy of the script—had noticed that she was a woman of talent and perspicuity? She stood with the electric cord in her hand and allowed herself the luxury of imagining the conversation that would take place at the bar of the Beverly Wilshire.

My dear Ms. Lang, the producer would say respectfully, offering her a glass of organic orange juice laced with vodka, I first saw you in the film version of Comanche *when you were only a child, and I've been following your career with interest ever since. Your work in commercials for Kal Kan cat food and Pepsi had a certain* je-ne-sais-quoi *quality to them, and as an extra in* Sunlotion *you projected an intellectual freshness that made me hardly notice that you were wearing a string bikini the size of a postage stamp, but it wasn't until your deathless—or should I say deadly—performance as a day player in* Slash and Slash Again *that I became aware of the full range of your talents. That scream, Miss Lang, coupled with your amazingly sensitive delivery of the line "Don't stab me, stab my roommate," has convinced me that you are the new Hepburn. Here is a contract for six films. As for salary, name your price anywhere in the seven-figure range.*

She grinned, tossed the end of the clock's cord on the bed, and headed for the bathroom, feeling considerably cheered by the fantasy. She remembered now why she'd set the alarm: her mother had called yesterday and said she wanted to stop by for a visit on her way out to the LangRothe studios in Burbank.

After brushing her teeth with the last of the Crest, she took a hot shower, blew her hair dry, drank a cup of Celestial Seasonings peppermint tea, and wolfed down a cold English muffin. Then, tossing one of the pillows onto the floor, she sat down, crossed her legs in the full lotus, and began to meditate. It was a routine she followed for twenty minutes every morning, and although she sometimes felt a little silly repeating a mantra to herself, it was a relaxing thing to do. Besides, she hadn't paid for the mantra. She'd gotten it out of a book. That was one of the advantages of a Yale education: for a mere $11,000 dollars a year they taught you how to find things in a library.

For the next twenty minutes she disappeared into a place where there was nothing to worry about. This was often the only quiet part of her entire day, and Mandy made the most of it. When she was finished she opened her eyes slowly and sat for a moment looking around her apartment. There was only one room, long and more or less rectangular, with a high ceiling and a scuffed parquet floor that she intended to get around to stripping someday. The room looked neat, but that was only because yesterday she'd had one of her rare fits of tidiness and thrown everything movable into the closet.

She surveyed the place with a satisfied feeling. Nowhere she'd ever lived had ever been so much her own, not even the room she'd grown up in. One whole wall was taken up with her books and her record collection. There was a shelf of plays, a shelf of cultural anthropology, two shelves of film history and criticism, some sociology, some philosophy, three large unabridged dictionaries: Spanish, German, and Zapotec, and a row of dog-eared science-fiction paperbacks that she liked to take down to the beach on those days when everything else seemed too overwhelming.

The other wall was covered with posters and photographs, neatly displayed in black wooden frames bought on sale at Woolworth's: Christine Bergen smiling in sultry splendor on the cover of a press packet advertising the film version of *Berliner Ballade;* a program from the opening night of *The Kindness of Strangers;* Grammy Viola as Queen Elizabeth, regal in a vast starched ruff and red wig; Daddy, perspiring and beaming in a pair of white shorts, tennis racket poised, ready to swoop down and smash the ball across the net; Mom and Mrs. Van Dusen on a holiday in Ensenada, decked out in Mexican sombreros the size of the Hollywood Bowl; a small snapshot of Mandy herself, costumed as a Peruvian priestess, taken when she was a sophomore in high school.

Mandy inspected the Peruvian priestess photo with affection, remembering the play Ted and Peter had written for her. Now what had it been called? *Death of the Inca*, or had they settled on *The Secret of Machu Picchu*? Funny how you forgot things like that, but it was no wonder really: they'd written and performed at least a dozen plays between their freshman and senior years. Thanks to the three of them, Kagan Preparatory School had been a real theatrical hotbed. Too much of one, in fact. She'd gone off to Yale with unrealistic expectations and done everything there was to do: acted, built sets, written scripts, done summer stock in upstate New York, even found time to write a paper on the theatrical nature of Zapotec religious rituals. And acting classes, had she taken acting classes! At Yale, in New York, in Chicago, even in London for a summer from none other than her own grandmother, and then she'd come back out to California prepared to make it big in the movies, and she'd hit a brick wall.

Mandy frowned, uncrossed her legs, and got to her feet. In L.A. nobody cared if you were a trained actress. Why couldn't she get that through her head? Who cared if she'd gone to Yale to study drama? She might as well not have gone to college period for all it mattered. Look at Ted's buddy, Kevin: Kevin had dropped out of USC his freshman year, hung out on the Strip, got lucky, made one appearance as a teenage drug addict in a forgettable made-for-TV movie called *Andy's Family*, and his phone had never stopped ringing. Her résumé, on the other hand, read like a thesaurus of failure: commercials; gigs as an extra in grade Z surfer movies. And the one time she had swallowed her pride and gone to her parents, she had ended up on television in a bit part so embarrassingly stupid that she still turned red when she thought about it.

So don't think about it, she told herself. Getting up, she dumped a heap of blues records on her stereo, put on a pair of faded Levi's and a turquoise tank top, and tossed three days' worth of dirty dishes into the sink. The records whirled on the turntable and low-down, get-down, funky blues blared out of the speakers: Driftin' Slim singing "Somebody Hoo-Doo'd the Hoo Doo Man"; B. B. King, Bessie Smith, Dr. Longhair. She danced around between the table and the sink, singing along, feeling the energy of the music running up her backbone. She loved the blues; it was sexy stuff, powerful, and the lyrics were about ten times as good as most of the junk that made the pop charts these days.

Plunging her hands into the soapy vat of Joy, she washed the dishes vigorously, scrubbing out the cups and arranging the flatware on a dry towel at the edge of the sink, and then, in honor of her mother's visit, she began to make a coffee cake from a mix. She worked quickly, as if the work were a drug that might help her forget how frustrating it was to be going to waste, and gradually the work and the music put her in a more hopeful frame of mind. She was naturally optimistic and it was hard for her to stay unhappy for any length of time, even when there wasn't much to feel happy about.

Mandy looked out the window at a black-chinned hummingbird that was sucking nectar out of the fuchsia bushes that grew along the side of the apartment building. It was February and the rest of the country was snowed in, and here she was watching a hummingbird. She loved L.A. She loved Olvera Street, with its endless variety of Mexican crafts and exotic sweets; she loved the La Brea Tar Pits and Rodeo Drive, the brashness of the Strip and the view from the Hollywood Hills at night that still awed her the way it had when she was ten. This was her town, and no matter how many times Grammy Viola wrote to her urging her to come to London, she was convinced she belonged here.

Putting the cake into the oven, she took a cup of tea outside and sat in the courtyard on a redwood bench enjoying the sunshine. The palm trees cast feathered shadows on the brown adobe tiles and the air had a fresh, salty flavor to it. I've been getting too discouraged lately, she thought. I'm too obsessed with my film career, or rather my lack of a film career. I need other interests. I need a lover or a hobby or another line of work altogether. I can't wait around forever hoping to be discovered. It's frustrating; it's stupid; it's straight out of Joan Didion. So what will I do about this intolerable waste of my talents?

She thought it over for a moment, and then she stood up, grinning, and went back inside. She knew what she'd do; she'd do what she always did when she was faced with an important decision: she'd procrastinate.

Walking over to the bookcase, she pulled out a battered copy of *The Best Science Fiction Stories of 1972*. Her mother wasn't due for another forty-five minutes, and the nice thing about living in Santa Monica was that when life burdened you with existential angst, the beach was only a few hundred yards away.

An hour later Kathe sat at Mandy's round oak table drinking decaffeinated coffee from a large, slightly cracked pottery mug. Although she no longer looked like the glamorous Kathe Rothe who had swept out of the white door with the gold star, the years had been kind to her. Her dark hair was streaked with gray and there were clusters of wrinkles around her eyes, but in the right light it was hard to imagine she was over fifty: she was wearing a red sleeveless dress that brought out the color in her cheeks; her chin was firm, her eyes were quick and bright, and there was an elastic, almost childlike quality to her body. Not to mention, Mandy thought, that Mom had enough energy for any ten people.

"Coffee cake?" she said, offering her mother a slice. The cake was covered with walnuts and brown sugar, and it was only slightly burned, which—considering that she'd forgotten it was in the oven— was a piece of pure luck.

"Thanks." Kathe took a large piece of cake and bit into it without flinching. Mom was good about things like that. Mandy could remember a time when she'd made a batch of cookies for her as a Mother's Day present and had forgotten to put in the sugar; Kathe had eaten at least half a dozen of them with aplomb, and it wasn't until years later that Mandy found out her mother had been cheerfully consuming something that had tasted like salty cardboard.

Mandy ate a piece of the coffee cake and decided that it wasn't too bad. Leave it to Pillsbury to make these things idiot-proof. They sat in companionable silence for a while, drinking coffee. Outside, the palm fronds clattered, and an occasional motorcycle roared by heading for Ocean Front Walk, where all the real action was.

"So, Mom," Mandy said, flicking at some cake crumbs with her fingernail, "out with it."

"Out with what?" Kathe looked up innocently from her coffee.

"You know what. Come on, I can feel you over there agonizing over interfering in my life. What is it that you can't quite bring yourself to say?"

Kathe grinned. "Not bad at mind reading, are you?"

"I took a course," Mandy said, "by correspondence. Lesson number one said that when your mother appears on your doorstep before noon and looks at you with loving desperation for more than three consecutive minutes, she's got something on her mind."

"Raising an intelligent daughter has its drawbacks." Kathe put down her coffee cup. "You're not easy to sneak up on, so I'll be blunt. Your dad and I talked it over again, and we still want to help you. Specifically we want to help you get your career off the ground. I know we've been over this a hundred times, but we keep hoping you'll be more reasonable on the topic. Not," she added hastily, "that you aren't a reasonable person on all other topics, but on this one, frankly, you're as stubborn as—"

"As you, Mom," Mandy supplied with a wicked grin.

"Yes," Kathe admitted, "as stubborn as I am. Curse the DNA that gave you that trait. Do you know how much trouble it's caused me?"

Mandy sighed and gave another flick at the cake crumbs. "I was afraid you were going to bring this up again. What can I say?"

"How about saying yes?"

Mandy shook her head. "I can't. I'm Don Quixote, remember. I like to tilt at windmills; I have this crazy idea that I can make it on my own. Okay, so I live in fantasy land. I admit it. But at least it's my fantasy land." She brushed the cake crumbs into a small pile and frowned. "It's a simple matter of self-respect. Does that sound pathetically idealistic? Well maybe it is; maybe I'm an anachronism— *Brontosaurus idealisticus*—a member of a nearly extinct species that blossomed in the late sixties—but that's me, and even though it's hardly a convenient way to live one's life, I'm stuck with it."

Kathe took a deep breath, sat back in her chair, and looked at Mandy as if she didn't quite know how to respond. "Darling," she said after an awkwardly long silence, "please be reasonable. You and I both know that the entire entertainment industry runs on personal connections; I'm not saying this is a great state of affairs, but it's reality. If your father hadn't helped me when I was your age, I never would have made it. You can be another Anne Bancroft, and if you don't know the right people you could very well spend the rest of your life as a dress extra. What kind of a career is that for a young woman with your talent? LangRothe produces a sizable hunk of prime-time television." She leaned forward, pleading, "You want to meet Lucas? Your father knew him when he was making *THX 138*. Brando? He and I were at the Actors' Studio together. Spielberg? Altman? Lily Tomlin?"

"Please," Mandy begged, "stop. I feel like you're reading to me out of *The Filmgoer's Companion*."

There was another awkward silence. "I'm sorry," Kathe said at last. "I don't know what comes over me." She smiled apologetically. "It's my maternal instinct, I suppose. You've always been such an independent little cuss, ever since you were a baby. You'd think I would have gotten it through my head years ago that you had to do things your own way, but, frankly, at the moment it's not a pretty spectacle. You keep beating your head against the wall and you won't take anything from us—not a connection, not a dime. Oh in some ways it's a great quality, and I suppose I should admire it in you. You're strong-willed, persistent to a fault, nobody's fool, and you're smart and you're pretty and I'm proud to be your mother, but sometimes I feel like you're drowning and I'm sitting by in a life raft watching you struggle."

"Mom," Mandy said gently, "let's just change the subject." She ran her fingers through her blond hair until it stood up around her head in a tangle, and suddenly she looked very tired and pale and vulnerable. She isn't eating right, Kathe thought. She's overworking herself; she's at the end of her rope; she's lonely and she's discouraged, and there's not a damn thing I can do about it except shut up and drink my coffee.

Outside, the black-chinned hummingbird was still hovering over the fuchsia bush and the sky had turned blue and milky as a glass marble. Kathe sat for a moment in silence, thinking how much she loved Mandy and what an enigma she was.

Mandy always thought of the Sunset Strip as a kind of demilitarized zone. Unincorporated, and hence unrestricted by the laws that governed the rest of Los Angeles, it had always been a place where nearly anything went, the stranger the better. In the thirties and forties it had been the pulsing night heart of the city, home to famous clubs like Ciro's and the Mocambo. Bogart used to drop by the Strip for a few stiff ones after a hard day of playing tough guys for Jack Warner, as did Carole Lombard and the other blond bombshells of the era, and despite the fact that Sunset Boulevard was now cluttered with Ramada Inns, Budget Rent-A-Car lots, and billboards the size of Cleveland, it still retained, in Mandy's mind at least, some aura of those decades when a river of black limousines flowed nightly between banks of glittering lights.

At present the Strip was mainly taken up with rock clubs, among which was the No Satisfaction Cafe, where she worked six nights a week from eight in the evening to two in the morning, passing out

Sunset Strips and Rolling Stones—which were merely steak sand-wiches and baked potatoes—and toting pitchers of beer and carafes of wine to the customers who mobbed the place to dance themselves into a state of exhaustion on the nights when there was music, and to laugh themselves into hysteria on the nights when there wasn't.

The No Satisfaction was an unusual place for two reasons. Number one: unlike the Troubadour or the Comedy Store, it didn't specialize in any particular form of entertainment. One night you might find an up-and-coming band on the stage, blaring out rock loud enough to make your ears bleed; twenty-four hours later a young comedian might be going through his routine, and the night after that a jazz combo would be softly moaning away, soothing people into leaving decent-sized tips.

Thanks to Max Tull, who'd bought the place five years ago from a big-time hash dealer who was now serving a life sentence in a Turkish jail, the No Satisfaction was one of the best showcases for new talent in L.A., and for that reason it attracted a mixed crowd: established stars like Linda Ronstadt and Woody Allen; young actors hungry for a chance to touch the hems of their garments; plus fans, agents, writers, gawkers, dope dealers, and tourists. There was a saying that you could get anything you wanted at the No Satisfaction, except, of course, disco. Max hated disco; he spat on it; he called it the most forgettable collection of vacuous crap since the invention of Muzak—an opinion that Mandy concurred with completely. In fact, she often thought that if she'd been waiting tables at a disco club she would have gone completely out of her mind.

The second unusual thing about the No Satisfaction was the decor, if that was the right word for it. Remodeled sometime in the late sixties, the club had a kind of classic acid-rock ambience. For a start, two of the walls were completely covered with crazy, Day-Glo murals, and not just little murals either but vast, frenetically detailed visions that looked like a cross between a *Furry Freak Brothers* comic book and a Hieronymus Bosch painting. Mandy had spent a good deal of time trying to make out the subject of those murals, but even after a year and a half she remained puzzled and mildly disturbed by them. The other two walls were movie screens, designed for a light show that no longer took place. In the sixties, as Mandy understood it, overhead projectors had flung images of colored oil on those screens and old W. C. Fields movies had played silently to the accompaniment of strobe lights and cuts from *Sergeant Pepper.* Now Max tended to keep them blank, except when, seized by some odd impulse, he projected television programs on them. It was always a little disconcerting to look up and see a blurred, twelve-foot Gerald Ford beaming down at you, but over the months Mandy had gotten more or less used to it.

Tonight as she sat at a back table taking her break, she was so lost in thought that she didn't even notice what was going on around her—which was by anyone's standards considerable. Up on the stage Kevin Darrow was playing the electric flute, using some kind of amplification device that he'd made by cannibalizing three or four old stereos. Kevin's music was clear and almost sweet, but Kevin was neither. He was a darkly handsome, brooding man in his early twenties, with pale green eyes and a narrow face that reminded her a little of a cat. Mandy wasn't overly fond of Kevin: he was cynical and more than a little crazy, but he was a talented actor and an even more talented musician. Also, to be fair, there was a soft streak to Kevin which could at times be endearing. For example, he seemed quite devoted to Mayumi Kennedy, his steady girlfriend—not devoted to Mayumi the way any other man would be devoted to a woman—but devoted nevertheless.

Mayumi was standing by the stage now, literally at Kevin's feet, looking up at him proudly. Part Irish, part Japanese, she was from Salmon Creek, Oregon, of all places. Like Mandy and Kevin, Mayumi was an aspiring actress, and you'd have thought with all that heavy waist-length black hair, delicate features, and almond-shaped eyes, she would have gotten somewhere by now, but the movie industry had decided that this wasn't the year for Asian ethnic types. Monsters were in—large white sharks preferably. No one actually came out and said this, of course, but Mayumi had gotten the message. At present she wiled away her days selling leather purses to the rich at Gucci's on Rodeo Drive, but recently she'd been threatening to have an operation on her eyes to make them look more Caucasian. Mandy had spent untold hours begging her not to, but Mayumi's confidence had been badly undermined in the past few months, not only by her lack of work but by Kevin, who since his recent success on television had been acting like he was Mick Jagger.

Mandy looked down at the untouched Sunset Strip sandwich in front of her and frowned thinking of the conversation she had had with her mother this morning, which had upset her more than she cared to admit. Around her the nightly cruising was going on as usual, passing from table to table like a slow cake walk. The young actors who had just made a hot movie sat in chummy groups, leaning back in their chairs, and laughing so hard that you could see the whites of their teeth. They were the ones who drank the most and left the biggest tips. Around them the not-so-famous circled: the would-be playboy bunnies, the girls from Fresno, the boys from little towns over in Nevada that no one had ever heard of, laughing, and exaggeratedly casual, dressed in clogs and crammed into tight jeans and flimsy tank tops, half of them high on something, all of them hopeful and desperate. The famous young superstuds looked them over at their leisure, wondering what was in it for them if they let these losers sit down at their tables; and sometimes they smiled back and gestured, and connections were made, while outside the silver Porsches and red Maseratis and custom four-wheel-drive jeeps stood waiting to carry them off to another club, or a party in one of the luxury suites of the Château Marmont thrown by somebody even more famous, or simply to whisk them away to a more private part of the night where the payments of sex and love and hero worship being tacitly offered at the No Satisfaction could be more easily collected.

Kevin finished his set and stood for a moment, looking out at the parade with an enigmatic, vaguely cynical smile. Then he pulled a bandanna out of his back pocket, lovingly wiped the fingerprints off his flute, and put it away in the hand-tooled leather case he'd had custom made over in Tijuana. Walking to Mandy's table, he sat down and looked at her like she was the most attractive woman on the face of the earth.

"Hi," he said smoothly, "what's happening?" It wasn't really a question so Mandy didn't bother answering it. Instead, she pushed her untouched Sunset Strip in his direction.

"Want it?" she offered. "Not that a big TV star needs free handouts, but I hate to see food go to waste." Was it her imagination or did Kevin flinch when she called him a big TV star? Perhaps he was having one of his rare attacks of modesty this evening. If he was, he recovered in record time.

"Sure, thanks," he said, smiling a slow, sexy smile. Kevin was one of those men, Mandy thought, whose eyes leaked sex like balloons leaked helium. Picking up the sandwich, he began to eat it, still managing to look suave and on top of things. Quite an accomplishment when your mouth was full of steak, lettuce, and tomato sauce. Mandy had to admit that Kevin really was attractive. He had a kind of bad-boy look to him that made you want to protect him, and there was a sensual quality to his smile that made something flutter inside her even though she knew it was all complete bullshit and that Kevin came on out of habit to anything female that crossed his path. Maroon Kevin on a desert island and he'd try to seduce the sea gulls.

Mayumi came up and sat down beside him, and Kevin put his hand on her neck without taking his eyes off of Mandy.

"Hi, Mandy," Mayumi said cheerfully. "How's it going? Anyone leave you a fifty-dollar tip yet?"

"Not yet." Mandy took a sip of beer and smiled warmly at Mayumi, whom she sincerely liked. "But I still have hopes."

"I ran into Ted and Peter today." Mayumi put her elbows on the table and leaned forward, her face flushed and happy. She was wearing a light blue dress, thin and clinging, with a gold belt and gold earrings, and she looked very beautiful—a fact that almost every man in the place except Kevin seemed to be noticing. "Ted told me to tell you that he's decided where he wants to film the next sequence of *Waiting for a Break.*"

"Don't tell me"—Kevin waved his sandwich dramatically—"let me guess—Mann's Chinese Theater, and he's going to have Peter pose in Norma Talmadge's footprints."

"No." Mayumi shook her head. "He wants to do it at Venice Beach."

"That's convenient." Mandy ran her fingers through her hair and took a swig of beer. "Venice is in my backyard, so to speak."

"There's one little catch." Mayumi grinned. "He wants to do it at dawn."

"Dawn? You have to be kidding."

"I wish I were, but no such luck. Ted told me to tell the two of you that we're all supposed to assemble tomorrow morning at six-thirty sharp."

"My brain doesn't function at that hour," Kevin objected.

"Why not have us meet at sunset and pretend it's dawn?" Mandy said practically. "After all, who would know?"

"Ted's a fanatic on the subject." Mayumi picked up a scrap of shredded lettuce and ate it thoughtfully. "He spent maybe fifteen minutes giving me a lecture on how the slowly increasing light will symbolize the radiant future of our prospects, or something of the sort. To tell the truth, I didn't follow him when he got into the details, but I did come away with the impression that he woke up this morning convinced that this was the one and only way for him to end his movie. When I tried to suggest others he looked at me like I was the kind of person who'd rewrite *King Kong* and leave out the gorilla."

"Why do I do these things for him?" Kevin said. "What is it about my ex-roommate that makes me want to drag my body out of bed at some ungodly hour just to satisfy one of his whims? Has the man stolen some of my fingernail clippings? Do I think he's going to be another von Stroheim or Welles? None of the above, but"—he smiled winningly—"I'll be there—dead of course, unable to move, a zombie, my body racked with early morning remorse—but I'll be there. That is"—he turned his full attention to Mayumi—"if somebody wakes me up."

Mayumi blushed and smiled and looked as if he'd handed her an Oscar, and Mandy felt sorry for her and a little annoyed and at the same time touched. All Kevin had told Mayumi was that she would probably be occupying his bed tonight, and she'd accepted it as a grand compliment. How blind, she thought, were the arrows of Eros, and what was it about Kevin that made a good 75 percent of the women who came within ten feet of him turn into jelly-kneed groupies? He's got charisma, she decided; he radiates heat; the guy's like an atomic power plant going full throttle all the time. She realized suddenly that if Kevin didn't destroy himself, he was going to be a big star someday. It was an unnerving thought.

Kevin finished off the sandwich and licked his fingers slowly, as if enjoying the sensation. "Want to go to a party?" he asked.

"Sorry." Mandy got to her feet and looked at the cafe, which was filling up with people. The air was hazy with blue smoke, and Cheryl, the only other waitress, was rushing from table to table, dispensing beer like a madwoman. "I have to work until two. We're short tonight. Susan called in sick again, and Max is on a rampage about flakiness and absenteeism."

"Come on," Kevin pleaded, "you don't know what you're missing. It's up in the Hollywood Hills in a house designed by Pierre Koenig. The view alone will knock your eyes out of your head, not to mention that there's a swimming pool the size of the Pacific Ocean, and I have it from a very reliable source that Dustin Hoffman's going to be there in the flesh and maybe Led Zeppelin, plus"—he winked knowingly— "other delights too numerous to mention."

"Thanks," Mandy said, shaking her head, "but I've never been big on that sort of party." She knew what that wink meant, and although it would no doubt be very interesting, and she was tempted, she had enough sense to know that she'd be better off going back to Santa Monica and curling up in bed with a good book.

North of Los Angeles, crammed between the Pacific Coast Highway and the ocean, the Malibu Beach Colony was one of the most expensive strips of private real estate on the planet—at least that was Kevin's impression, although he'd never bothered to look it up to make sure. Take his house, for example—well, it wasn't really his, he was just house sitting it for the winter; the actual owner was a producer from NBC, a friend of his mother's who was off in France trying to evade California's community property laws—but take it anyway. Dark and musty, with bedrooms designed for midgets, walls you could stick your hands through, and a foundation slowly being eaten away by the surf, it probably would have been condemned if it had been located anywhere else. Instead, it would rent out this summer at the height of the season for something along the lines of $20,000 a month.

As Kevin sprawled indolently on the leather sofa staring out of the picture window at the place the ocean would have been if it hadn't been too dark to see it, the thought that he was occupying a room worth roughly $30 an hour gave him a perverse sense of power. The party had been a bust: no Dustin Hoffman, no Led Zeppelin, no anything worth mentioning except a cocaine bar that had come complete with silver straws and a guy in a white jacket to set up the lines, but Kevin didn't care. He had Malibu to come home to. So what if most of the famous film people were moving on to even more exclusive pastures these days. So what if you couldn't walk out on the beach anymore and count on running into Burton and Taylor and Fonda and Polanski. Malibu was still, as his agent never tired of pointing out, the best address in the world. It was the kind of place that convinced people you were a force to be reckoned with, and at the moment, Kevin thought darkly, I need as much help as I can get.

The memory of the bad news his agent had laid on him this morning came over him suddenly like a black cloud. He shifted uneasily, trying to get comfortable, but despite the overstuffed cushions and dozens of plump pillows, he felt like someone had just tossed him onto a hot griddle. Sitting up, he checked out Mayumi, who was draped out on the rug, drinking tea and staring at the fire. The fire crackled in the grate, converting the oak logs to white ash, and somehow this was also a depressing sight. I'm letting myself get too bummed out, Kevin thought. He reached into the pocket of the jacket he'd bought at Monsieur on Rodeo Drive, found it empty, and then reached into another pocket.

"Eenie, meenie, miney, mo," he said, pulling out two capsules, one red, one yellow. Descending to the carpet, he picked up the small round Japanese cups, dumped the remains of the tea back into the pot, put one capsule under each cup, and moved them in a large, scuffing circle. The shag of the carpet rose up under his hands like the hair on a cat's back, green hair with flecks of blue in it. "Pick a cup, any cup," he said to Mayumi.

"What are they?" Mayumi said softly. She was sitting with her arms crossed around her knees, wearing a pair of stereo headphones. Inside her mind, the Doobie Brothers were singing away full blast. At least that was Kevin's best guess from the scraps of music that were leaking out.

"That's the fun of it." Kevin took the earphones off of her head like he was uncorking a bottle. "One's speed, and one's a downer, but I can't remember which is which. I buy them by the bag like jelly beans, and you pay your money and you take your choice." He gave the cups another twirl. "It's the old shell game."

Mayumi turned over the nearest cup, picked up the red capsule and balanced it in the palm of her hand. She had a reluctant expression on her face, and Kevin suddenly felt sympathetic and protective. "You don't have to take it," he said reassuringly, kissing her neck. "It's just for fun, that's all."

Mayumi's entire body relaxed and she smiled a sweet, trusting smile. "It's okay," she said softly, pushing her long silky black hair back from her face. Kevin thought of her breasts underneath her blue dress, small and crumpled like golden flowers, of the delicate pinch of her waist and the smooth curves of her hips. Mayumi poured herself a cup of cold tea, put the red capsule on the tip of her tongue, and washed it down. She was so beautiful, like some kind of shy, half-wild animal, a deer maybe or a small bird. In a half an hour or so they would be high, and then he would lead her into the bedroom and stretch her out on the producer's white satin sheets, and make love to her for a long time, very slowly. Turning over the remaining cup, he picked up the yellow capsule and lobbed it into his mouth like a piece of popcorn.

About an hour later Mayumi lay on the brass bed in the master bedroom, floating in her own private space. She tried to open her eyes, but her lids felt heavy and soft like strips of satin. Kevin was making love to her and she wanted to see him, but she was drifting somewhere in a lazy place, where moving so much as a finger was a major effort.

Kevin's flesh seemed to go on forever, like a giant rose petal. She curled into him, sank down deeper and deeper into his skin until she felt like she was at the bottom of a well. Somewhere, up there on the surface, she could feel him swimming over her whole body, stroking her breasts, running his hands down her sides, feathering the insides of her legs with the tip of his tongue, but it was all very far away.

"Sweetheart," he muttered. She felt him catch her foot and bite lightly at the instep, but the bite was painless and distant and all it did was make her laugh. She laughed some more at herself laughing, rolled slowly from side to side under him, as if she were a sailboat rocking at the Malibu pier, and then suddenly everything was very sexy and exciting, as if tiny lights were attached to the tips of her breasts and they were blinking off and on, and Kevin was flicking the switch. There was a scramble of legs and arms, and they were a ball of fishing line tangled up, a human pretzel, a handful of soft pink wool, and she was right up on top of the roller coaster where she liked to be, and there was a steep hill in front of her and a set of golden tracks that glittered blindingly all the way down to the bottom. By the time she realized that the golden tracks were nothing more than the brass bars at the foot of the bed, she was too tired to do anything more than bury her face in Kevin's shoulder and go to sleep.

Sometime later, she wasn't sure exactly when, she woke to find Kevin sitting bolt upright staring off into the darkness. The fog had lifted and the beach outside the window was a streak of tarnished silver, barely visible.

"Are you okay?" Mayumi asked. Kevin looked at her silently, his eyes green and glittering. Since he didn't seem inclined to reply, Mayumi got up and went into the kitchen to get herself a glass of orange juice. She drank her juice and stood in front of the sink for a minute thinking of the party and its aftermath. The view from the Hollywood Hills had been great, but she wished they hadn't gone because five minutes after they'd arrived Kevin had been taken in tow by a very pretty redhead from Oxnard who had seen him on TV and who had been awestruck, to put it mildly. Mayumi knew she was probably too tolerant of Kevin's habit of picking up women wherever he went, but she also knew that she didn't have a prayer of reforming him and if she wanted to go on seeing him she was going to have to put up with it, so she tried to put up with it with a certain amount of grace, although now that he was becoming famous that was getting harder. Still, oddly enough, in her own way, she supposed she was satisfied. He always came back to her no matter what he did or who he did it with, and if that wasn't ideal, at least it was reliable.

When Mayumi got back to the bedroom Kevin was still staring off into space. He got the speed, she thought, and I got the downer. Reaching out, she touched him lightly on the shoulder. His skin was cold and tense, like vinyl, and she wondered how many milligrams of the stuff he still had in him. He jumped as if she'd startled him, but he didn't seem annoyed—just unhappy and a little frantic.

"I've got to get a decent role soon or it's all over," he said suddenly, coiling up his body like a spring and then uncoiling it again. "Something with class, something directed by someone who isn't an idiot. I'm on the edge of making it big, right on the edge, but it could go either way." He chewed on his lower lip and tapped his fingers against the bedpost. "Do you know what my agent told me this morning?"

"No," Mayumi said, sliding across the sheets and putting her arm around his shoulders, "what did he tell you?"

"He told me I didn't get that part I was up for."

Mayumi didn't know what to say. She stroked his bare shoulder consolingly.

"The director said I was perfect for the part"—Kevin picked at the flocked wallpaper with the tip of his fingernail—"and then he said that he'd decided for financial reasons to go with a star, someone with a big name who'd pack them in at the box office. So they gave the part to Pacino. Okay, so Pacino will be good, I'm not denying that, but I would have been better. I would have put my heart and guts into that part. The problem is, people don't make movies these days; conglomerates make movies. No one wants to take any risks; all they care about is the goddamn bottom line. And my agent said something else; he said I was getting stale and that I had to make a movie soon before people forgot I existed. One made-for-TV gig doesn't make a summer, he said. Very cute, right? He just sat there in his godawful pink-and-blue Hawaiian shirt and $3000 worth of gold chains and implied that everything was going to fall apart if I didn't get on the stick. I could be nothing, he said, a six-week wonder and this town is full of six-week wonders." Kevin clenched his fist so hard that Mayumi could see his fingernails digging into his skin. "You know what I think of when I hear something like that? I think of breaking glass, I think of tidal waves, I think of nuclear holocaust. I think maybe I should get a new agent."

He talked on and on, getting up to pace across the room and then coming back to bed. When he was in the bed she massaged his back, trying to calm him down, but once he started talking, he didn't seem to be able to stop. She listened patiently, nodding from time to time and making sympathetic noises. Tonight, though, he went on longer than usual, and he was particularly pessimistic. From what she could tell, he seemed to believe his entire career was on the line, and that worried her.

Four hours later Mandy Lang sat on the beach next to a pile of film equipment waiting for the sun to come up. A few feet away—hung over, half asleep, and looking like they'd just refugeed out of a burning city—Mayumi and Kevin lay on a space blanket next to Peter Karp, who was snoring lightly, mouth open like a hole waiting for a golf ball. Mandy yawned, unscrewed the thermos she'd brought from home, and poured herself a cup of peppermint tea. The metal cup was hot and hard to hold, and she shifted it gingerly from one hand to the other. Around her the Pacific Ocean was slapping against the shore, the fog was lifting in smoky scarves, and Venice was taking form—blue and bleary at six-forty in the morning, deserted, Mandy thought, and oddly innocent, as if it had just emerged from the ocean complete with sidewalk cafes, joggers, and metal trash cans.

She took a sip of the tea and gazed sleepily out over the pinkish-gray sand, swept into Zen gardens by the Department of Parks and Recreation, past Mayumi, Kevin, and Peter, to Ted Van Dusen, who was striding briskly through a grove of palm trees in the general direction of Ocean Front Walk, that famous strip of concrete that ran along the beach tying Venice to Santa Monica. Empty now and deceptively tranquil, the walk seemed poised and waiting for the skateboards, ten-speed bikes, giant tricycles, unicycles, rickshaws, wheelchairs, roller skaters, panhandlers, chess champions, retired rabbis, tourists, jugglers, fire eaters, weight lifters, hucksters, sword swallowers, and families out for a weekend stroll. By noon it would resemble the San Bernardino Freeway at rush hour, which was fine as far as she was concerned. She knew that tourists often found Venice overwhelming, but personally she enjoyed the weekend circus. We Angelenos, she thought, are a sociable people; we like to amuse ourselves in packs.

She sat back, dug her bare toes into the cool sand, and watched Ted reach the walk, pull a light meter out of his pocket, make some mysterious adjustments, pace back and forth, and stare up at the sky. He was a tall, broad-shouldered young man who walked in firm, long strides as if he were making his way up an invisible mountain.

Dressed in his usual uniform—a red-and-blue-checked flannel shirt, safari vest, high-topped waffle stompers, and faded jeans—Ted looked like he should be out in some wilderness area splitting wood or skinning a deer. Not that he would ever kill a deer or anything else for that matter. He was a member of Friends of the Earth and Green Peace, and he considered hunters in the same category as people who ate dolphin steaks for breakfast.

Mandy took another sip of tea and wondered, as she often did, just what it was that made Ted tick. She'd known him all her life. The Van Dusens were next-door neighbors and Ted's mother and father had been like a second set of parents to her, but she still found Ted mysterious and a little maddening—especially recently. He'd always been complex, like a jigsaw puzzle with a thousand pieces that didn't quite fit into any known pattern. When he hiked he crashed through the forest like a moose, toting a fifty-pound pack as if he didn't know it was on his back. He swam like a sea otter, pitched the meanest curve ball she'd ever tried to hit, and could paddle a sea kayak so far and so fast that if you were in the back of the boat trying to keep up, you'd be seized by an urge to drown him. Yet at the same time, lurking just beneath his Davy Crockett act, there was the Ted who wrote poems and plays; the Ted who gave what little money he had to every good cause, animal or human; the Ted who in the past eight months had taken to staring off into space, sad and preoccupied, as if he were remembering something he would rather have forgotten—although Mandy couldn't for the life of her imagine what that something could be.

She sighed and took another sip of tea. Hopeless, she thought, absolutely hopeless. Sometimes she felt like she had no perspective on Ted at all. She didn't even know if he was good-looking or not, something she knew instinctively about every other man she met. On film he looked attractive, perhaps even handsome: his eyes were a pale blue-gray; he wore his brown hair a little long, tousled, as if he'd just gotten up out of bed, and he had the square jaw, straight nose, and oval face of movie heroes from Ted Mix to Cary Grant, yet in real life—this morning for instance—there was nothing flashy about him, nothing to make your heart skip a beat. Then again, he was so much like a brother to her that she probably didn't see him as other women did. Ted had certainly had his share of relationships, a whole string of them. Not that he was like Kevin. Kevin made a play for anything with double X chromosomes, whereas Ted didn't really seem to be interested in anybody. His women always found that out sooner or later and moved on, which was a pity really, because Ted was her oldest buddy and best friend, and she hated to see him going to waste.

Up on the walk, Ted turned in place, exposing the white Ping-Pong ball hemisphere of the light meter to all points of the compass. Mandy imagined the red needle rising with the sun: gray sky, white sky, pale yellow sky. Suddenly Ted froze and peered at the meter. "The light's right!" he yelled, hightailing it back across the sand to the camera, a heavy, black metal Mickey Mouse-eared antique on loan from USC. Beside it lay a battered Nagra tape recorder, connected by an umbilical cable so lips would move in time to sound. Real film crews didn't bother with such things. They had radio microphones and vibrating crystals and cameras that descended from the sky like angels.

Mandy sprang to her feet, feeling a pulse of excitement, which was silly really, considering that this was only a student film. Still, Ted was taking it all so seriously. She could easily imagine him waving his arms and summoning up dressing rooms, generators, helicopters, reflectors, dollies, cranes, and all the other paraphernalia of a big studio.

"Mayumi first," Ted called out cheerfully, swinging the camera over to the left where Mayumi, Kevin, and Peter lay sprawled out on the blanket. He played with the zoom lens, looking for the right shot in a nervous way that told Mandy that he, too, was excited. "Remember, My," he said, "I want your life story in fifty words or less."

Mayumi moaned, sat up, and rubbed her eyes. Her hair was pressed into fuzzy little coils, her face was pale, and she was wearing a pair of cutoffs and one of Kevin's old T-shirts emblazoned with the words *I Survived Sunset Strip*. "I look a mess," she objected, and indeed, Mandy thought, she did.

"So look a mess," Ted said encouragingly, zooming in on her face. "Waiting for a break in this town is a messy business. It wears you down, right? So look worn, look human. That's what this movie's all about. But however you look, do it fast before we lose the light." He turned to Peter, who had come up to the tape recorder and was crouching over the reels like a sleepy chipmunk. "Rolling?" he asked.

Peter switched on the tape recorder. "Rolling," he said, peering up through the thick lenses of his glasses. Peter had been Ted's roommate for the past three years, and they'd developed a kind of rapport that Mandy, for one, found slightly amusing. No two people could have been less alike. She'd known Peter ever since her freshman year in high school. The son of a nuclear physicist from Cal Tech, he had always dressed in what she privately labeled "haute nerd": wrinkled white shirts, shiny black pants, dirty tennis shoes, and belts so narrow that you had to turn sideways to see them. But for all that, she found him an extremely likable guy, even attractive. He had an IQ of about 180, a wicked sense of humor, and maintained a finely honed ironic perspective on his ambition to become an actor. Someday, Peter insisted, Woody Allen would realize that by hiring Peter Karp he could make himself look like Clint Eastwood. On that day, Peter claimed, his career would take off. Gorgeous blondes would pursue him; his dad would forgive him for majoring in film instead of physics, and he would spend the rest of his life eating expensive French pastries, winning Oscars, and screwing like a squirrel. Peter was always hungry and always horny, or at least he had been for the nine years Mandy had known him.

"Clapboards," Ted called out from his perch behind the camera.

Walking over to the battered metal suitcase that held their equipment, Mandy picked up the wooden clapboards, stepped in front of the zoom lens, and slapped them together. "Scene One, Take One, Venice," she yelled for the benefit of the Nagra. This film was definitely a group project.

"Go for it," Ted told Mayumi.

"Okay"—Mayumi settled down and crossed her arms over her bare legs,—"here goes nothing. My name is Mayumi Kennedy and I'm from Oregon." She stopped, as if she'd come to the end of her spiel.

"Go on," Ted prompted from behind the camera.

"What should I say?" Mayumi leaned forward, looking shy and uncomfortable.

"It doesn't matter," Ted said kindly. "You can't go wrong. Just tell us anything. Tell us about your parents."

"My parents? You have to be kidding. Who would be interested?"

"Trust me," Ted said. "I'll make it interesting when I do the editing."

"Well, okay." Mayumi settled back and her delicate face suddenly seemed to harden a little. "Remember you asked for it. My parents are a nice topic. My father's an alcoholic Irish lumberjack and my mother's a Japanese-American who spent her childhood in an internment camp out in Nevada." She pushed her hair out of her eyes and looked at the camera wearily. "I won a beauty contest in high school—Miss Redwood. Funny, right? They gave me a crown and everything, and I thought, well, if I'm so pretty, maybe I can go down to L.A. and make a fortune in movies and come back and take my mom away from this bum who beats her around when he's worked his way to the bottom of his daily bottle. A real practical plan. I've been here almost two years and the closest I've gotten to the movies is a job I had selling popcorn." She closed her mouth abruptly. "That's all," she told Ted. "There's more but what's the use? I'm a living stereotype. I'm laughable."

There was a moment of uncomfortable silence as the four of them stood looking at Mayumi with sympathy and not particularly well-concealed pity. Mayumi suddenly colored with embarrassment and turned away. "I screwed up, didn't I?" she said to no one in particular.

"No," Ted said gently, "you were great." He turned around, as if erasing the awkwardness of the moment, and began setting up for the next shot: taking another light reading, getting Peter to play back the tape so he could make sure there wasn't too much background noise; blowing the invisible motes of dust off the lenses with a round rubber thing that looked like a small plunger.

Standing back, Mandy watched Ted work against time as the sky brightened behind him. He'd been sensitive to Mayumi's embarrassment and tried to distract everyone's attention from it as soon as possible, but she'd also noticed that when Mayumi broke down at the end of the interview he'd kept the camera running. She wondered if she broke down, if he'd keep the camera on her, too, recording every tear and hesitation. She wondered if this was a cold-blooded thing to do or the mark of a talented filmmaker. Was Ted really in tune with the people around him these days or had he changed into someone she hardly knew? For some reason she imagined a helicopter shot of the beach: the five of them crouched in the sand like savages and the camera glinting up on the tripod above them like an idol. Strange rituals and human sacrifices, she thought, and just what *is it* that has Ted Van Dusen so preoccupied?

May, Mandy thought, reaching over the sink and ripping April off her calendar: ice plant in bloom, no more rain until October, an end to the mudslides, and thirty more days of waiting tables and waiting for a break. On the stereo Professor Longhair was singing "Rockin' Pneumonia," and the apartment vibrated along with him, glasses dancing on the shelves, the spider above the door rocking in its web. Mandy danced around the room and then out the door into the courtyard to surprise the hummingbird, and she might have danced down to the beach to see the maypole that the beach people had put up at the Santa Monica Pier only just then, as her bare feet were tapping their way across the tiles, she heard her phone ringing. Running back inside, she turned off the stereo and picked up the receiver.

"Hello," a familiar voice said, "Mandy? This is Tammy."

"Hi, Tammy." Mandy sat down on the floor, crossed her legs, and put the phone on her lap. No need to have silenced the Professor.

Tammy Watkins was her agent, and she called regularly once every two weeks or so to tell Mandy that there wasn't any work to be had. Like the Professor had just said, it was a mean ol' world and life was all rock 'n' roll gumbo—not that Tammy didn't try, but no one seemed to be in the market for a blue-eyed actress whose most important role had been playing a housewife in a Kal Kan commercial. "What's up?" she asked Tammy hopefully. "Has Kubrick called for me yet?"

Tammy laughed her 15 percent on-the-track-of-something laugh. "Better than that, sweetie."

"Really?" Mandy leaned back against the bed and looked out the French doors at the palm trees.

"Guess who did call asking about you," Tammy said cryptically. Mandy closed her eyes, imagining Tammy's flaming-pink sweater, her gold earrings, the picture of Diane Keaton on her desk placed there to convince new clients that she was in the know. *To Tammy with Love*, the inscription read. Who might have called Tammy today begging for Mandy Lang, actress extraordinaire?

"Roman Polanski? Ingmar Bergman? John Huston?"

"Get serious, sweetie," Tammy admonished. She sounded a little miffed, and Mandy heard her candy-red nails tapping away on the other end of the line sending out Morse code messages about taking life for something more than a game.

Mandy scratched her bare shoulder and put her feet up on the rungs of the closest chair. Time to be polite and mollify Tammy, who did the best she could considering Mandy gave her nothing to work with—except talent, of course—which no one much wanted, which was a liability like big ears or a crooked nose or a bad complexion. "To tell the truth, Tam," she said, stretching and yawning, "I haven't any idea who'd call for me unless it was the Kal Kan people wanting me to do another of my immortal cat feedings."

"Try Jane Crews," Tammy said.

"What!" Mandy jumped to her feet, nearly knocking over the chair. "Jane Crews? You're kidding. What did she want?" Jane Crews was one of the only important women directors in Hollywood. Come on, she thought. Sober up, Mandy. You're suffering from auditory hallucinations. "The director?"

"No"—Tammy was witty this morning—"the plumber."

Jane Crews—the name was mythic. Crews not only financed her own films, she was the best director of women since Cukor, or so the young actors said down on the Strip at the No Satisfaction when the beer got flowing. Eccentric, difficult, brilliant, temperamental, and weird; a recluse; lives by herself in a house in the Hollywood Hills with a pet eagle and a pack of Dobermans if you wanted to believe the rumors. "What did she want?" Mandy grabbed the telephone and carried it from one side of the room to the other. "What did she say?"

"Calm down," Tammy said. "In fact if you're not sitting down, sit, because I've got news for you. She wants to see you at three on Monday."

"Monday!" Mandy sat down on her bed, stood up, and sat down again. "Did you say Monday?"

"Right. At her private fiefdom up in the Hollywood Hills."

"Why," Mandy said, "why me?" A warning bell rang in her mind. This had to be a false alarm. Directors like Jane Crews just didn't go around calling up out-of-work actresses. Crews must have been trying to reach Fritz Lang, or Charles Lang, or Lana Lang. Superman's girlfriend could fly through the air. What could Mandy do? Feed cats; wear a bikini; scream on cue; recite all of *Hamlet*. Was it likely Jane Crews had a need for any of these talents? "How did she get my name?" Mandy pleaded. "For God's sake, Tammy, how did she even know I exist?"

"Well," Tammy said cheerfully, "your friend Ted Van Dusen evidently got her to take a look at that student film of his—don't ask me how. Anyway, Crews told me that the film was strictly amateurish, but that she'd been looking for a group of young, unknown actors. And there were the five of you, sweetie, sitting on the beach, pouring out your hearts or something as I understand it, and Crews went ape over it. You know how directors are, especially the good ones—they're all crazy. Crews, it seems, has some cockeyed theory that on-screen reality reflects off-screen reality, and she's been beating the bushes for a group of friends. She must have said the words *group of friends* twenty times. 'Are they buddies?' she kept asking me, and I kept saying yes, you were all bosom buddies. And then she got around to telling me she was doing a new film—which I'd suspected all along, of course. Something called *The Plunge*. Don't ask what the script's about because she wasn't about to confide that to a mere agent. She just said that she's casting, and she wants to talk to all five of you, pronto."

"Casting?" Mandy tried to make herself understand that Jane Crews wanted to see her because she was casting a new film. The whole idea had the flavor of a miracle. She stiffened, waiting for the buzz of the alarm clock that would smash her back into a life where nothing ever happened.

"Right," Tammy said, "casting. Sounds promising, doesn't it, sweetie?" She laughed a pearl-studded laugh that spoke of percentages and money and maybe a trip for Tammy Watkins to Palm Springs. "By the way," she added, "can you swim? *The Plunge* sounds like a swimming movie to me."

"Sure," Mandy said eagerly, "sure, of course. I can swim like a fish. I was even on the girls' swim team in high school. I specialized in the side stroke." She laughed, feeling a touch hysterical. Swimming reminded her of Esther Williams, but no—Crews had class. *The Plunge* wouldn't be a water ballet; it would be something serious. A woman marooned on a desert island maybe—like *Swept Away* only less brutal. She imagined a stretch of white sand and herself in front of the camera walking into clear blue water—Italy or the Caribbean or Lahaina in Hawaii where the whales played. She imagined working with Mayumi, and Ted, and Peter, and Kevin. She knew she was getting her hopes up prematurely, and she tried not to, but she was drunk with happiness.

"How about diving?" Tammy said.

"What?" Mandy started out of her reverie.

"On further thought, *The Plunge* sounds like a swimming *diving* movie, so can you dive or can't you? Level with me, sweetie. An agent has to know these things."

Some of Mandy's elation disappeared. "I couldn't dive at gunpoint," she confessed. "I'm terrified of heights. Just going up a stepladder makes me dizzy."

"Well don't tell Jane Crews that," Tammy cautioned. "Say you've been diving all your life." She gave Mandy the address and hung up, wishing her luck. For a few seconds Mandy sat looking at the phone, too stunned to move. Then, leaping to her feet, she went to her closet and began dragging out her clothes and piling them on the bed. Monday was only a few days away, and she had to figure out something to wear that would make Jane Crews know that she was right for the part—whatever it was.

Five days later the whole gang sat in Jane Crews' private screening room watching the diving sequence from Leni Riefenstahl's famous documentary, *Olympiad*. Up on the screen perfect human bodies kept diving through the air in slow motion, rising and falling on an invisible tide. Arms formed exquisite arcs, legs pulsed with strength, shadows flew out into space, spread like the wings of great eagles. All of which would have been stunning, except that there was something wrong. Mandy leaned forward, past Mayumi, who was slumped in her seat biting her fingernails, and tried to decide what bothered her so much, but before she could work it out the film ended abruptly and Jane Crews snapped on the lights. They were bright lights, full-spectrum fluorescent, and Mandy found herself blinking and slightly disoriented.

"Riefenstahl filmed that in '36," Crews announced, striding up to the front of the room. She folded her arms across her chest and looked at the five of them as if considering what to say next. A rather intimidating woman in her early forties, Crews had a triangular face, a long sharp nose, and brown hair, cut off just at the nape of her neck. Nearly six feet tall, she stood up straight, as if capitalizing on every inch of her unusual height. But it was her eyes, Mandy thought, that were her most striking feature. Small and bright blue, they gazed out at the world with knife-like precision, intelligent, cynical, never missing a trick. Mandy had decided the first moment she laid her own eyes on Jane Crews that she never wanted to cross her or try to win an argument with her. The only thing that kept Crews from being completely overwhelming was her smile. It was a surprisingly pleasant smile, and it redeemed her face.

Crews unfolded her arms. "As you perhaps already know, *The Olympiad* was made on the occasion of the Berlin Olympics." She paused. "Well," she demanded, "what did you think of it?" There was an awkward silence as Kevin looked at Mayumi, Peter looked at Ted, and Mandy looked at no one in particular. "Come on," Crews prompted, "this is a test." She rubbed her hands together briskly. "Look," she said, "let's get this straight—I don't bother to give ordinary interviews. They're a complete waste of time, full of bullshit and false posturing. Not that I'm blaming you; all actors posture. But I haven't got time for crap like that. I want to know who you are and what you know, and I want to know that fast because lately my time has been worth money. So I'll ask you again. What did you think of *The Olympiad*?"

No one said anything. We're blowing it, Mandy thought. This woman wants an answer. She swallowed hard and held up her hand like she was in school, and immediately felt ridiculous.

"So," Crews said, "you have a theory?"

"I liked it," Mandy said bluntly, "and at the same time, to tell you the truth, I didn't like it."

"Hmm"—Crews seemed interested—"why not?"

Encouraged, Mandy searched for some way to explain her reaction. "It was pretty, but soulless," she said. "The divers were great, but they lacked individuality; they were like Greek statues stamped out in a souvenir shop." She began to get carried away with her own analysis. "I'm no film critic, but I watch a lot of movies, and I noticed something else—most of the shots were taken in silhouette—framed against the sun or the water. If you ask me, Riefenstahl distrusted ordinary physical reality. Her film was out of touch," she concluded, gesturing toward the empty screen, "sentimental as a basket of kittens and at the same time insidious." She stopped, feeling suddenly embarrassed at her own speechifying. Who was she to tell Jane Crews that the movie she had just shown was unpleasant? Great going, Lang, she thought. The perfect way to get a job from this woman. Peter and Kevin were glaring at her, and even Mayumi and Ted looked upset. If there was an award for putting your foot in your mouth, Mandy decided, she'd just won it.

Crews contemplated her silently, lips pursed. "You're right. *The Olympiad* is insidious," she said at last. "You're absolutely right. Riefenstahl's work is beautiful but, it's—how shall I put it"—she frowned—"metaphysically wicked." She paced back and forth in front of the screen as if temporarily taken up by the idea. "It's Fascist art, and Fascist art is always hollow at the core. Before I can consider working with you people, I have to make sure you know the difference because, you see, what I want to do in *The Plunge* is get that same beauty with some guts and some political content. What kind of political content? Ah, that, my friends, should be interesting.'' She turned abruptly and ran her eyes over the five of them. "I tell you straight out that I'm not a Communist, but if there was a blacklist in Hollywood today, I'd be on it. I fit no known category. I'm part Populist, part feminist, part Luddite, part aesthete, and part mule. I'm hell to work with and worse than hell to cross, but I make great movies." She chuckled. "Odd sort of screen test, isn't this? But then I've already seen all of you on camera, and I'm quite interested in you as a group—that is if you can learn how to do the flying. I'll tell you right now at the outset that I'm against stunt shots—not absolutely, after all I don't want to get you killed—but you'll have to do the bulk of the flying for real."

Flying, Mandy thought. Did she say *flying?* What the hell was she talking about? There was a puzzled silence as the five of them looked at each other in confusion. Crews, unfortunately, was either too wound up to notice or just plain didn't care. "I suppose logically if I want to out-Riefenstahl Riefenstahl I should make another movie about diving," she was saying, "but diving doesn't interest me, and it's too easy to break your neck, so I looked around." She waved her lanky arms dramatically. "I asked myself what sport was the most like diving; what sport let people fly through the air; what sport would look great on film; what sport was dangerous, beautiful, dramatic, colorful, graceful, and took some skill instead of merely strength, and by the time I got through all that, there was only one possibility—hang gliding." She pounced on the words happily.

The effect must have been very satisfying from her viewpoint: Mandy gaped at her, too shocked to speak; Kevin turned pale; Ted fell back in his seat, and Peter muttered "Oh no!"

"Hang gliding?" Mayumi said in a small, choked voice. "You mean like those guys who jump off mountains wearing bamboo wings?"

"Aluminum and Dacron wings to be precise," Crews said briskly. She sat down abruptly in the front row and slung her legs over the arm of one of the seats. "Anyone want a cup of coffee before I go into the details?" She looked around at their white, startled faces as if enjoying the result of her revelation. "No? Well then, the plot's quite simple. I'll give you all copies of the script before you go, but let me outline the basic story. A group of kids takes up hang gliding. It's the sort of sport that tempts you to show off once you get good at it, and one of them shows off and has a fatal accident, and the others begin to blame each other for it. All sorts of tensions arise—some of them sexual—to the point where they start to sabotage each other's equipment. It's a sort of a *Lord of the Flies*, a real fall into evil, if you see what I mean."

They stared at her dumbfounded.

"Well," Crews said, "having heard that, are you still interested? By the way, I'm not promising to cast you in these parts. Frankly I've been looking at some other groups of young actors, and I haven't made up my mind yet. But having passed the *Olympiad* test, you're in the running—that is if you want to be."

Mandy wanted to say something, but for once she was absolutely speechless. She felt bowled over. Hang gliding! She'd seen those idiots jumping off the cliffs and soaring out over the Pacific a thousand feet up in the air. It was crazy, dangerous, scary; the kind of things ex-surfers with a death wish did when they got bored dodging great white sharks. Crews might as well have told them she was making a film about atomic energy and that she wanted live volunteers for a real nuclear blast.

"Well?" Crews demanded impatiently. "Are you on this bus or off it?"

"On," Kevin blurted out eagerly.

"On," Mayumi echoed.

"Sure," Ted said bravely, "it sounds great."

"Count me in." Peter started to get up and then he sat down again in a heap. "Hang gliding?" He laughed nervously and adjusted his glasses. "I always wanted to learn to hang glide, Ms. Crews. Yes, ma'am. Hang gliding's been one of my life's ambitions."

Mandy tried to say something, but her mouth felt like it was full of sand. She thought of cliffs with piles of sharp-pointed rocks at the bottom. Aluminum and Dacron wings? She tried to imagine herself putting on a pair and shuddered. Surely she wasn't contemplating throwing herself off a precipice dressed like a high-tech bat? She should confess to Crews that she was acrophobic, but if she did, she'd blow it for everyone else. They'd never forgive her, and maybe she'd never forgive herself. She was being offered a crack at a major role in a feature film. How often did that happen? She gritted her teeth and clenched her fists. I've got to tell her yes, she thought. Yes is the only possible answer.

"Well?" Crews leaned so close, Mandy could see the fillings in her teeth. "How about you?"

"I'm on," Mandy said impulsively. She snapped her mouth closed, not believing she'd actually agreed to do something so insane.

Crews studied their faces as if waiting for one of them to crack and try to back out, but nobody did. She swung her feet off of the arm of the chair and stood up, looking mildly impressed. "I've been hang gliding ever since '69 when Bill Bennett opened up the first school here in California, and I've got a Master Rating," she said, "so if I do decide to go with the five of you, I'll be teaching you myself. Of course, if any one of you can't make the grade, then we've got a whole different ball park. You're hired as a group, you act as a group, and if any one of you screws up, you leave as a group. I believe in collectivity—do any of you know the meaning of the word? It's the missing element in American life. Not complete collectivity, of course. I'm not about to try to make a movie by consensus. The five of you will be the collective, and I'll be your absolute dictator. Like I said, I fit no known political category. Think you can take that? Good. Too much for you? Well then, let me know now and save us all a lot of trouble."

She walked over to her seat and picked up a pile of black folders. "I have all your résumés here. Pretty pathetic. None of you has much of a track record—except for Kevin—but frankly I like that. It gives me more slack. To tell you the truth, I hate stars. They're too temperamental, and they aren't hungry enough. I like to work with unknown actors whose asses are on the line—not to mention that I suspect that if I want the five of you, I can get you at bargain-basement prices. Well, doesn't anyone have any questions?"

Mandy closed her eyes and tried once again to imagine herself leaping off a cliff with a pair of Dacron wings tied to her back. The very thought made her whole body prickle with terror. She felt a warm hand encircle her own, and when she opened her eyes Ted was leaning over the back of her seat, looking at her with concern. "It's okay, Man," he whispered, "you're doing great; just hold on, and I'll help you."

"I'll break my neck," Mandy whispered back. "I can't hang glide." She was almost in tears. "Damn it, Ted, this is the best role I've ever come close to, but you know how I've always been about heights. One look over the edge of a cliff, and I'll go nuts."

"Say"—Crews turned, her eyes sharp and probing—"is there some problem over there?"

"No," Ted said quickly, "no problem at all." He squeezed Mandy's hand, hard.

"Good"—Crews nodded—"I'm glad to hear it." She went around and shook all their hands ceremoniously. When she got to Mandy she gave her a long, searching look and then turned away and went back up to the front of the room. "I'll be in touch with your agents," she said, dismissing them. "Who knows. Maybe we'll all meet again."

Kathe and Hermann sat in their kitchen at a round oak table eating scrambled eggs and reading the *Los Angeles Times* in that kind of silent companionship enjoyed only by people who have been having breakfast together virtually every morning for the past twenty-five years.

Reaching out with his right hand, Hermann located a piece of toast by feel, and without lifting his eyes from what he was reading began to munch on it, scattering crumbs in small dry showers all over the front of his maroon robe. Over the years he had lost virtually all of his hair, but other than that he was in the best physical shape he'd been in since those days back in Berlin when he'd spent hours walking from one job interview to another, too poor to ride the trolley car and too proud to hitchhike. Rudy Van Dusen's sudden death, seven years ago, had— quite frankly—put the fear of God into him: he'd lost fifty pounds, taken up tennis, stopped smoking, stopped eating salt, and even cut down on animal fats, which was why his toast was lightly brushed with margarine instead of smeared with the butter he would have much preferred. Devouring the last bit of crust, he leaned forward intently and reread something on the second page of the paper.

"Looks like we're actually out of Vietnam for good," he said thoughtfully.

"Um," Kathe said, turning the page of her piece of the paper. The word held a multitude of meanings: disapproval of the war, relief that it was finally over, a personal dislike of violence—all of which Hermann heard and registered. He knew Kathe so well by now that he could tell from a lift of her eyebrow what her opinion was on any given topic, and sometimes he didn't even need that. They read in silence for five or ten minutes more and then, outside, a car door slammed and rapid footsteps crunched over the gravel.

"Say"—Kathe looked up, surprised—"you don't suppose that's Mandy, do you?"

"At 9 A.M.?" Hermann grinned and ran his hand over his head as if redistributing the ghost of his hair. "I think this is unlikely, *Liebling*."

But for once he was wrong. A few seconds later Mandy herself appeared in the doorway, looking elated and slightly frazzled.

"Hi," she said.

"Hi, honey." Kathe waved at the food. "You want some breakfast?"

"Sure." Mandy sat down and helped herself to the eggs and toast. She drank a cup of coffee quickly, wiping the cream off her upper lip with the back of her hand. All her movements were hungry and excited, and both Hermann and Kathe could tell that she had news for them, but they knew her too well to press her for it. Finally she sat back. "I've got a part in a film," she announced.

"Really?" Hermann put down his paper and smiled a smile that stretched from one of his ears to the other. "This is good news. So what kind of part?"

"Jane Crews has cast me in one of the main roles in her new feature," Mandy said, casually toying with the salt shaker. "It's called *The Plunge*." She looked up and grinned. "Surprise."

"Jane Crews!" Kathe jumped up and gave her a hug that nearly knocked her off her chair. "Darling, how wonderful! Congratulations!"

Hermann shook her hand and then pulled her into a bear hug. "So my daughter becomes a star," he said, kissing her on both cheeks. "So it's the big time at last, eh?" They laughed and embraced and laughed some more.

"There's only one catch," Mandy said at last, sitting back down in her chair, red-faced and breathless.

"What's that?" Kathe asked.

"I have to know why I'm acrophobic."

"What?" Hermann and Kathe stared at her blankly.

"I have to know why I'm so afraid of heights. That's one of the reasons I came out here this morning. I wanted to tell you the news, and I wanted to ask you if you had any idea why I turn to jelly every time I get more than five feet off the ground." Mandy leaned forward earnestly. "I know it sounds silly, but I absolutely have to know. Usually people work this sort of thing out with years of therapy, but I don't have years. In fact, I figure I have something less than a week before I have to take my first hang-gliding lesson."

"Hang gliding?" Hermann looked puzzled. "What's that?"

"Flying," Mandy supplied reluctantly, "with Dacron wings. That's what the movie's about—hang gliding."

"Sounds dangerous," Hermann said, puffing out his cheeks.

Kathe was pale and silent. She knew perfectly well what hang gliding was, and she wanted to beg Mandy to have no part of it, but she forced herself to keep her mouth shut.

"So," Mandy said, running her fingers through her blond hair until it stood up around her face in a halo, "do either of you have any idea why heights scare me?"

Hermann shrugged. "Always, I think, you were afraid. Most little girls when you swing them up over your head, they laugh, but you would scream, so this I didn't do with you more than once or twice."

"Mama," Mandy said, "do you know why?"

Kathe looked down at her breakfast plate, at the cold eggs and half-eaten toast, and her face was suddenly very sober. "I think you got it from me, to tell you the truth."

"From you?"

"Yes." She looked up at Mandy, reluctant, wondering how much to tell her. "Phobias seem to run in the family. Your grandmother is afraid of fire—for good reason—and as for me, I've always been terrified of heights and I suppose I passed that fear on to you—not intentionally, of course, but you were such an intelligent child, you knew I was afraid even before you could talk. When you were a baby I was frantic that you would roll off your changing table if I took my hands off you even for a second, and later I couldn't sleep nights because I was sure you were going to fall out of bed. I must have kept you in a crib until you were nearly four, and then there were other incidents—like the time you climbed the orange tree or that afternoon when you got up on the roof to play Wonder Woman. Can you remember any of this, honey?"

Mandy took a sip of coffee and frowned thoughtfully. "No." She shook her head. "It's all a blank."

Kathe closed her eyes and saw Mandy, age five, balanced fifteen feet in the air on a slender branch, grasping for the sweet oranges that hung like magic globes just out of her reach. She saw Mandy laughing and happy, proud of herself for climbing so high, and then she saw herself running out of the house, her face a mask of terror, screaming, *"Get down! You get down out of that tree right this second, young lady!"*

"No, Mama!" Suddenly frightened, the child had climbed higher, retreating behind the leaves, looking down at her with a white, startled expression on her tiny face. Kathe had wept and begged, pleaded with the stubborn little girl.

"Come down; it's dangerous; you could fall and get hurt; come down, baby, please come down." And at last Mandy had given in and come down.

"Promise me you'll never climb another tree." She had known even then that she was being irrational but she couldn't help it. *"Promise,"* she had begged, hugging Mandy. And Mandy had promised.

But a week or so later she had put on her Wonder Woman pajamas, tied a bath towel around her neck, and climbed out her bedroom window. A neighbor spotted her and called Kathe.

"Your daughter's up on the roof."

"I can fly, Mama!" Mandy had yelled as she balanced on the edge of the rain gutters. The blue bath towel had flared out behind her, throwing her off balance for an instant, and Kathe had gone sick with panic. This time when Mandy refused to come down she called the fire department and the police, and when Mandy was finally back in her bedroom, safe and elated at having created so much excitement, she gave her the only serious spanking of her life.

Kathe opened her eyes and looked at Mandy, who was still waiting expectantly on the other side of the table. "I couldn't stand to see you more than five feet off the ground," she admitted. "I'm sorry. I know I should have kept my fears to myself, but I simply wasn't capable of it—especially when you were a small child. For the most part, I think

I was a pretty good mother, but this fear of heights was my Achilles heel." She paused and took a deep breath.

"You see, when I was just a little girl, only four years old, a man— a stranger—swung me around in the air, and although I wasn't particularly afraid at the time, later the experience haunted me and . . . it's silly, really. It was so long ago; I can't imagine why it bothered me so much."

"What your mother isn't telling you," Hermann said quietly, "is that the man who swung her around was a Nazi, and he was threatening to kill her."

"My God," Mandy said.

Kathe shrugged. "It was years ago, but for some reason it stuck, and I'm sorry I infected you with it. I never mention it to anyone—in fact, Hermann may be the only person who knows how frightened I get at the prospect of climbing a mountain or even looking straight down out of a second-story window. But at least you don't seem to have it as badly as I do. Haven't you noticed that I almost never fly anywhere—not even back to London to see your grandmother? I love her and I miss her, but I haven't been back more than two or three times in the past twenty-five years, mainly because whenever I fly I have to take so many tranquilizers I can hardly function. That's one reason your dad and I moved from New York to Los Angeles. Until 1957, because of the earthquake danger, there was an ordinance that no building in L.A. could be over thirteen stories." She smiled weakly and pressed Mandy's hand. "And frankly, honey, even that's about twelve stories too high for me."

"Have you ever been able to do anything about it?"

Kathe shook her head. "No, I'm afraid I haven't. To tell you the truth, I haven't tried very hard. After all, a fear of heights doesn't come up particularly often when you're in a television studio." She paled slightly, picked up her fork, and poked at her eggs. "Mandy, listen, I know I shouldn't say this but I have to. Please be careful. Please. Crews has a reputation for pushing her actors over the edge." She laughed weakly. "What a horrible pun. What I mean is, Crews doesn't seem to have any normal fears. I won't say she has a death wish, but if you read about her, you begin to wonder if she knows she's mortal. She races motorcycles, goes whitewater rafting, hang glides. She was on that mountain-climbing expedition to Nepal a few years ago when two women were killed trying to scale a glacier. She may not have any phobias, but she doesn't seem to have any healthy fears either, and she expects her actors to feel the same. I'm terrified that she's going to put you into dangerous situations just to satisfy her own directorial ego. I know I can't ask you to pass up this part, but I wish you'd at least think it over some more. The thought of you hang gliding makes me ill. You could be crippled or killed, darling, and I love you so much . . ." Her voice trailed off and she looked at Mandy helplessly.

"Mama," Mandy said gently, "don't worry so much."

"I can't help it," Kathe said. "I'd rather see you wait tables until you're old and gray than let Jane Crews convince you that you can become a star by jumping off a cliff."

"Mama, please try to understand. I have to take this part. Believe me, I don't like the idea of jumping off a cliff any more than you do, but I have to take it. It's my first real break."

Kathe was silent for a moment. Her mind raced with conflicting emotions: she wanted Mandy to be independent, but she didn't want her to run off blindly on her own and get hurt. She didn't want to be an interfering mother, but she wanted Mandy to listen to her. She was proud of Mandy, and frightened for her, and she loved her, and she was angry at her for being so stubborn. But the anger had to be swallowed, and the fear put in its place, because when your daughter was twenty-one you couldn't send her to her room. You had to send her out into the world.

"Darling," she said firmly, "I apologize for being such a worry wart. You're a grown woman and I have total faith in your judgment. If you want this part, then I'll do everything I can to support you in it."

"Really?" Mandy's face glowed with relief.

"Really." Reaching out, Kathe embraced Mandy and kissed her on the cheek. "Knock 'em dead, kiddo," she said cheerfully. She may not have been in front of a camera since live television went the way of the saber-toothed tiger, but she was still one hell of an actress.

"Phobias," Peter said, consulting one of the ten books that lay spread out on the desk in front of him, "can be treated in three main ways."

"Well," Ted said, "go on. Don't keep me in suspense. What are they?'' He folded his arms, lay back on his bed, and looked at the USC pennant on the wall, and then at the picture of Mandy that stood on his dresser. Mandy didn't know he had a picture of her, of course. He had taken it from one of the frames of *Waiting for a Break,* and sometimes he felt foolish about having it planted on his dresser like a shrine, but he couldn't bring himself to put it away somewhere more private. He liked her face to be the last thing he saw before he went to bed; he liked to wake up to her. He had—as Peter never tired of putting it—a bad case.

Ted contemplated Mandy and thought, as he often did these days, that she was the most beautiful woman he had ever encountered. The irony of it was that, until about eight months ago, he hadn't known she was beautiful or that he was in love with her. She had been so familiar that he'd taken her for granted—good old Mandy, his buddy and childhood friend, always there like the sky or the air he breathed. Until last fall he hadn't even suspected she was the reason other women bored him, the reason why, hard as he tried, he could never keep a relationship going for more than a few months. This blindness had been stupid, and it had caused him years of unnecessary pain. He had worried about his capacity for intimacy; he had wondered—despite all evidence to the contrary—if he was gay. He had done crazy things like drop out of college his freshman year and go hitchhiking around South America, running from himself and a string of fine women whom he couldn't seem to care about with any intensity. He had actually thought he might be incapable of love, and this had made him feel sad and lonely, and he had wondered how someone who cared so much about nature, who felt so passionately about whales and eagles and the soul-tingling sweep of the untouched wilderness could feel only friendship for the women he slept with. And then one day, hiking by himself in the San Gabriels, he had had a revelation: he wasn't incapable of love, he was in love, and he had been ever since he was six, and the woman he loved was his best friend and—and this was the bad part—she had absolutely no feelings for him at all except those of a sister. This realization had put him in a different kind of pain: disorienting, intense, exciting, and hopeless, and the more Peter tried to convince him to do something about it, the more he stubbornly clung to his silence and pride and timidity, until by now if Mandy herself had threatened to tear his tongue out unless he confessed what was wrong, he wouldn't have told her.

Turning away from the sight of her face, Ted directed his attention back to Peter, who was waiting, with his usual patience, for him to return to earth. Peter had been very understanding through all of this, an attitude which Ted appreciated. Ted sometimes felt that he was making a complete ass out of himself over Mandy, but if Peter thought so too, he was too good a friend to mention it.

"So"—Peter cleared his throat—"as I was saying, the first method of curing a phobia is gradual deconditioning." He tugged thoughtfully at the plastic pen case he kept clipped to his shirt pocket and peered up over the rim of his glasses. "Which more or less means we could slowly accustom Mandy to the idea of going up higher and higher, and help her build a sense of security. For example, we might actually get a stepladder and have her climb it a step at a time. Every time she started feeling afraid, she'd go back to the next lowest step. After a while she'd probably be able to climb to the top without experiencing vertigo or any of her other symptoms. Then we could take her up to a second-story window, a third-story window, a skyscraper, a mountain, a crop-dusting plane, and given enough time, chances are she'd feel so secure that heights wouldn't bother her much more than they bother you or me."

"What amount of time are we looking at here?" Ted asked.

"Well"—Peter frowned—"I'd say, given how badly heights scare her, gradual deconditioning would take maybe five months."

"So that's out of the question."

"I'm afraid so, and the next method—therapy—is even worse. To work out an irrational fear like acrophobia, Mandy would have to go digging around in her subconscious for God knows how long—a year, five years." Peter grinned. "Woody Allen, for example, claims to have been in therapy for his entire adult life. Maybe he's just kidding, but the fact remains that therapy is for people with lots of time and money and the belief that talking to someone at fifty bucks an hour can cure all the ills the psyche is heir to—an opinion that I, personally, don't hold." Peter scratched his head. "Which leaves method number three."

"Which is?"

"You aren't going to like this one, not the way you feel about her."

"Try me," Ted said. "She needs this part; we need her to get it. At this point I'd be willing to do almost anything to help her—swim raging rivers, battle lions." He grinned. "I seem to have a penchant for melodramatic fantasies of heroism where Mandy's concerned, but I mean it. I'd do anything."

"It isn't a question of you doing anything," Peter said, "it's a question of *her* doing something. The third method of curing a phobia is what the French usually call '*la methode dure*,' which can be roughly translated 'the hard way.' Basically what it amounts to is burning out all your circuits by putting yourself in a situation so terrible that everything else seems like small potatoes in comparison. For example, if you were claustrophobic, you might let someone shut you up in a coffin for a few hours, or go caving, or deliberately jam an elevator between floors and turn off the lights. If you were afraid of snakes, you'd take a hike in the Amazonian rainforest or get a job extracting the venom from rattlers or something of the sort. It's also called 'counter-phobic behavior.' Most people do a little of it from time to time—ride roller coasters, that sort of thing—but for people with real phobias it has to be extreme. With Mandy, for instance, it probably wouldn't do any good just to park her in front of an open window and make her look down at the sidewalk. We'd have to put her in some real danger—or at least convince her she was in real danger."

"You mean force her to scale a cliff face or dangle her from the top of a fire tower?"

"Well"—Peter closed the book and stared at Ted reluctantly—"yes, that's about it."

"You're right," Ted said, "I don't like it; I don't like it at all. You're saying we have to terrorize her."

"No," Peter objected, "she has to terrorize herself. She has to feel this fear of heights as intensely as possible, until she panics and blows a gasket. After that hang gliding should be a piece of cake."

"How long would this take?"

"It could happen in a few minutes, in no time at all. That's the advantage."

"Could it do her any harm?"

"I'm not a psychiatrist," Peter said, "but from what it says in these books, I think one of two things could happen—her phobia could get better or it could get worse."

"Worse!" Ted sat up in bed and looked at Peter in disbelief. "You actually mean to tell me we might make her *worse?*"

"Well," Peter said, "if we put her up somewhere high, she may not be able to overcome her fear. She may freeze up there and have to be carried down. It happens to people all the time—they try to climb a cliff and the next thing you know they're clinging to the wall and a helicopter has to come pluck them off. Cats are the same way; they climb up trees and then are too afraid to climb down. But Mandy's tough, and if I were betting money on it, I'd bet she'd scream her head off, and then she'd get mad about the whole thing and do what she had to do." He paused. "Of course, afterwards she might never speak to us again."

"It sounds rotten," Ted said, "scaring her like that."

"We wouldn't be doing it without her permission," Peter countered. "So we wouldn't be doing it *to* her, exactly. We'd be doing it *for* her and we'd do it only if she gave us her complete consent."

"Her complete consent, huh?"

"Right." Peter nodded. He began to pile the books into a neat stack at the side of the desk. "We tell Mandy everything except the precise details of what we're going to do. We warn her that it's going to be terrifying; we promise her that she won't get hurt, and then we ask if she wants to give it a try. If she does, fine. If she doesn't, then we phone up Jane Crews and tell her we're backing out of the deal now, before the contracts are signed. Crews can always find another five suckers willing to break their necks for her." Peter grinned. "To tell you the truth, I'm not wild about learning to hang glide. I wouldn't say I have a phobia but"—he tapped his chest—"I've grown rather attached to this overweight, pudgy little body of mine, and if it gets snapped in half, I'd rather have the snapping done by some ravenous brunette in a denim miniskirt whom I've driven crazy in ways too pleasant to be mentioned in polite society."

That night in San Bernardino, Kathe had a bad dream:

The baby was falling and she couldn't catch it. She ran around under it with her arms outstretched as it plunged toward her, but every time she moved the baby moved, and she knew she was going to miss, and she knew the baby was going to hit the rocks. The baby was falling and she couldn't stop it. The baby was . . .

She woke up shaking and breathless. The bedroom was dark and beside her Hermann lay wrapped in a light blanket, snoring peacefully. What a horrible nightmare, Kathe thought. Sliding quietly out of bed, she went into the bathroom, turned on the faucet, and splashed cold water on her face.

It was only a dream; it wasn't real. No baby was falling. She didn't believe in premonitions.

Mandy came to a flat place in the trail, paused, and looked around warily. The bear went over the mountain, she thought, as did Mandy Lang, but was the bear acrophobic? That, my friends, is the question of the day. Taking off her yellow baseball cap, she fanned herself with it nervously. So where was the precipice? Nowhere in sight? Good. Let's not rush things. To her right she could feel the wind tugging at the chaparral, the kind of wind that blew up from deep, blue valleys, but, as Ted had promised, everything was mercifully cloaked by the brush that rose to form a dusty green barricade between her and a view that—had she caught a glimpse of it—would probably have sent her gibbering back down to the safety of Kevin's jeep.

Distract yourself, she thought. Think of Kevin and Mayumi up ahead there, getting blisters from their new hiking boots. Think how silly Kevin's fifty-buck walking stick is and what a tenderfoot he looks like slamming it into the ground like he was traversing a glacier or taking on Mount Everest. Think of Ted and Peter, lugging along behind with Peter moaning for drinks of water and trail munch and cursing the day he was born. But don't think of what the four of them have in store for you when you finally get to the top of this mountain.

She ran her fingers through her hair, pushed up the sleeves of her blue cotton shirt, and tried not to think about The Plan. Be practical, she thought, be cool, pretend you're strolling on Ocean Front Walk. Close your eyes. Hear the waves. Does your nose need more sunscreen? But it wasn't any use, and there weren't any waves, and she was thousands of feet above sea level, and her body knew that even if her mind tried not to.

Turning abruptly, she started up the trail again, walking fast past clumps of Indian paintbrush and bunches of purple lupine. A few more minutes passed. There's no alternative to this, she told herself sternly, putting one foot in front of the other, but her mind kept looking for one. She imagined sheer cliffs, and drop-offs, and clawing at granite with her fingernails as her feet slipped out from under her, and she was seized with a childish urge to sit down and refuse to go on, which was perfectly idiotic, because she was doing this of her own free will, and it was going to be safe and harmless and good for her, the way bitter medicine was good for you when you had a cough.

They continued hiking for another half an hour or so, and gradually she began to calm down. The trail twisted on and up and got steeper, until she was walking almost nose to ground, bent forward under a pack that was at least fifteen pounds too heavy. It was hard, absorbing work and nothing bad was happening: no glimpse of sheer trail edges, no sign that they were about to plunge off the end of some giant cliff like Wily Coyote in pursuit of Roadrunner. At last, some time around noon, the world started to level out again, the chaparral got shorter and more Munchkin-like, and they arrived at a small, bowl-shaped meadow filled with tall grasses, orange poppies, and large flat boulders.

"Hold up," Ted called to them. "This is where we have lunch."

Mayumi and Kevin stopped, threw themselves down on the ground, and began to drink out of Kevin's canteen. Mandy took off her pack, opened it, extracted half a dozen plastic bags full of food, and arranged them on a flat boulder. After she finished unloading her pack, she started in on Kevin's and then Mayumi's, feeling amused and a little embarrassed. It was ridiculous how much they'd lugged up here: turkey sandwiches dripping with avocado, three pounds of coconut-carob trail munch, a dozen oranges, carrots the size of bananas, tubs of gourmet potato salad, a round of creamy ripe Brie that smelled like damp gym socks, Armenian cracker bread, a bag of Famous Amos Chocolate Chip Cookies (Peter's favorite), and enough beer and mineral water and cans of Pepsi to quench the thirst of a platoon. Ted was going to take one look at this stuff and laugh himself sick. She could recall him setting out on three-day backpacking trips with not much more than a few strips of beef jerky and a bag of Spirulina.

But when Ted appeared he didn't say a word of reproach. He just sat down and began to eat, silent and thoughtful. Mandy tried to eat, too, but there was growing tension in the air. She spread some Brie on a cracker, lifted it to her mouth, and then put the cracker back down on the boulder. Mayumi nibbled at an orange; Kevin stirred a plastic spoon around in the potato salad. Only Peter actually seemed hungry, but then if the end of the world had been announced, Peter probably would have sent out for pizza. The day Peter didn't eat would be the day they were really in trouble.

Mandy sat back, picked a blade of grass, and studied it intently. "How much farther is it?" she asked Ted in as casual a voice as she could manage.

Ted popped the tab on a can of Pepsi and drank it without looking at her. "We're here," he said.

"Well," Peter burrowed into the cookies and came out with a large broken one, "that's a relief. I was just about to inform the rest of you that if you wanted me to continue on this death march you were going to have to carry me." He laughed nervously and crammed the cookie into his mouth, and there was an awkward silence.

"What do we do now?" Mayumi asked.

Ted finished off the Pepsi, put the empty can inside his pack, got to his feet, and picked up the coil of rope he'd carried all the way from a saner altitude. "I'll be back in about twenty minutes," he announced. He looked at Mandy as if he wished she would tell him that she'd decided not to go through with the whole thing, but having come this far, and climbed this hard, she wasn't about to back out, so she just pressed her lips into a smile and told him that he'd know where to find her when everything was ready. Then she spent a bad twenty minutes wishing she was back in Santa Monica.

Everyone else seemed equally nervous. Kevin got up, paced over to the edge of the meadow, and stood looking out into space. Peter pulled his hat over his eyes and pretended to be asleep, and Mayumi sat on a boulder toying with the cap to the canteen. After a while she came over to Mandy and slipped an arm around her waist.

"You know," she said gently, "if you don't want to do this, you don't have to. We'd all understand and we wouldn't think any less of you."

"It's okay," Mandy said stubbornly. "It's fine, just fine."

"Sure?" Mayumi frowned, and little wrinkles curled across her forehead.

"Positive." But she wasn't positive, and when Ted came back without the rope she almost told him so, but she caught herself in time.

"Ready?" Ted asked, planting both hands on his hips. He looked her up and down, and she could see something strange in his face, pity maybe or some other emotion, only it was hard to tell exactly what it was except that it was intense.

"Sure." Mandy make a weak attempt at a grin. Now or never, she thought, ten seconds to launch and counting, and here goes nothing. "What was it those ancient Roman gladiators used to say before a match? 'We who are about to die salute you.' "

Peter turned pale and flicked cookie crumbs off his lap. "If that's a funny remark," he said to the boulder, "I don't get it."

"She's being brave," Kevin snapped. "For chrissake, Pete, show some tact for once."

"Well excuse me," Peter said.

"Look," Ted pleaded, "let's not all get bent out of shape about this, okay?" He turned to Mandy. "Say the word, Man, and we'll get on with it."

"The word," Mandy said.

"Okay." Ted paused for what seemed like an eternity. "Well," he said at last, "as you remember, the plan we worked out goes something like this. First we blindfold you so you can't get frightened too early on." He gestured toward the far end of the meadow. "There's a cliff just beyond those bushes over there." Mandy felt a little stab of fear go through her at the word *cliff*. "And what we're going to do is tie a good strong hank of rope around you and lower you down to a ledge. It's a pretty wide ledge, so there's really nothing to be afraid of, and besides, you'll be tied to the rope and I'll be on belay so you wouldn't be able to fall if you wanted to. When you take off the blindfold, the view is going to be, uh, well, rather spectacular."

"Oh," Mandy said, and she would have said something else, only under the circumstances there didn't seem to be anything else to say.

"You'll have to climb back up the cliff," Ted said.

"Will it be hard?" She couldn't believe that she was actually asking him if it was going to be hard to climb up a sheer cliff face.

"Not too," he said encouragingly. "It's not a chimney or even an expert-level grade; there are a lot of handholds and outcroppings, the granite isn't crumbling, and if you get into any real trouble, we can always pull you up with the rope. In fact, if you weren't so afraid of heights, you probably wouldn't have any trouble with it."

"There's no danger," Peter said, putting a hand on her shoulder, "none at all. It's the kind of thing the Sherpas do before breakfast to work up an appetite. Of course you're not a Sherpa and we're a long way from Nepal, but . . ." His voice trailed off as he tripped, as he often did, over his own metaphor. "You'll be just fine," he concluded, patting her awkwardly.

"What Peter is trying to say," Mayumi supplied, "is that we all love you and we wouldn't let you get hurt. You know that, of course, but I thought you might like to hear it again."

Mandy could feel their friendship weaving a safety net around her, and suddenly she felt that yes, she was going to be able to do this and that it would be fine and that there was really no reason to be afraid. It was an intoxicating feeling and she had a silly urge to laugh, which was part relief and part hysteria. "Come on and blindfold me, you creeps." She folded her arms across her chest, planted her feet firmly on the earth, and gave them a brave grin. "Let's get this circus over with."

Mayumi took the bandanna out of her hair and handed it to Ted, and Ted folded the bandanna and laid it gently across Mandy's eyes. She felt the dusty darkness of the printed cotton and the twist as he tied it into a knot behind her head, and then she felt the four of them leading her forward over the uneven ground, supporting her, Kevin on one side, Ted on the other, Mayumi in front and Peter behind, saying things like "Watch your step here" and "There's a rock to the right" and "Just a little further," and if she'd wanted to she could have peeked around the edges where the sunlight lay in a molten line and where even now she could see the yellow and orange glow of the poppies, but she didn't want to look, and she was thankful that they had thought to bring her here in darkness.

"Lift your arms, Man," Ted said quietly. Wind tugged at her shirt and blew her hair and played across her skin. She lifted her arms and felt a rope being tied around her chest and around her legs. "How does it feel?" Ted asked, tugging on the lines.

"Fine," she told him. "It feels fine." Oddly enough, she was no longer afraid.

"Take a few steps forward and then sit down," Mayumi said, taking her by the hand. Mandy took a few steps forward, sat down, and felt her feet dangle into space. She was on the edge of the cliff now and she should have been terrified but she wasn't. I must not be afraid of heights after all, she thought. I must just be afraid of *seeing* heights. How strange.

"All set?" Kevin asked.

"Sure," Mandy said. "Fire away."

She felt someone lift her up—Ted probably—and then she was hanging from the end of the rope, swinging gently and descending, and she almost laughed because she felt like an angel in a Christmas play coming down from the sky. She imagined them above her, playing out the line hand over hand, and still she felt no fear. Then her feet touched bottom, and she heard the crunch of gravel, and the line went slack suddenly and she heard a strange whipping sound, and then there was only silence and the feeling of vastness all around.

"Mandy." Ted's voice had an odd ring to it, she realized later, but she didn't hear that at first. "Mandy, don't move."

"Okay," she said obediently, and she stood there, relaxed, waiting for orders like she was standing in her own living room, and she marveled at her own courage and thought that this was going to be easy after all.

"Take off your blindfold," he said. "Do it slowly, okay?"

"Sure." She reached up and slowly pulled the bandanna off her eyes and discovered that she was facing a fairly steep slope. It was rather handsome really: yellowish and white, flecked with moss and tiny clumps of grass, and a few stray poppies. She'd once had a calendar from The Nature Company and the entire month of July had been a picture of a rock face just like this.

"Mandy," Ted said, "can you hear me?"

"Of course I can hear you." She looked at the slope intently, trying not to think about what she'd see if she turned around. There might be a black hole behind her, but here it was solid granite. "What next?"

"I'm sorry to tell you this . . ." Ted paused. "But we have a problem."

"A problem?" The word shocked her slightly, as if a small rock had fallen from the top of the cliff, and for the first time she felt a wave of vertigo that sent her heart racing. Reaching out, she grabbed on to an outcropping to steady herself. "What kind of problem, Teddy?"

"We lost the rope, Mandy."

"Lost it?" She didn't understand—or rather she didn't want to understand, so she just echoed his words and kept looking at the wall.

"It went over the side with you," Ted explained. "You aren't tied into anything anymore. In other words—" He stopped abruptly. "Look, don't freak out, don't panic, and whatever you do, don't look down. Just start climbing up the slope. You can make it. Believe me. And when you get close enough we'll give you a hand."

"Get another rope," Mandy said quietly, gripping the stone outcropping. "Lower me another rope, and I'll tie it around my waist." She suddenly felt the empty space ballooning out behind her like a vacuum, sucking her toward the edge. They had to lower her another rope because without another rope she could fall off into that nothingness and die. Her logic was pristine; none of them could refute it.

"There isn't another rope," Ted explained. "The one we lost was the only one we had."

She grabbed at the rock so hard she scraped her hand. "No," she said. "I don't believe that."

"Mandy." Ted's voice was pleading. "Try not to get excited. That ledge you're on is about three feet wide. If you get tired, you can sit down for a while before you start climbing. But try not to look over the edge."

"Come get me."

"We can't come get you. There's no way."

"How the hell could you have let that rope drop?"

"Mandy"—Mayumi's voice, almost in tears—"please, listen to Ted. You've got to keep it together and start climbing."

"You idiots, you stupid idiots." She knew it was insane to stand here abusing them and yet part of her couldn't believe that they'd been so careless. She felt angry with them and angry with herself for ever having agreed to something so witless, but she had agreed and there was no getting around it. Fumbling at her waist, she tried to untie the useless rope, but her hands were shaking and the knots were too tight and all she managed to do was tangle them further. What a harebrained scheme. Why did she always let other people talk her into things? Perfectly safe, huh? Something the Sherpas did before breakfast, huh? She must have been out of her mind. Well if she got out of here in one piece, one thing was certain: she'd never climb any higher than the first rung of a stepladder, and if she stayed acrophobic for the rest of her life, well, great, fine, she wouldn't mind a bit.

She gave another impatient tug at the knots, and then she made a major mistake: she turned her head. A few feet to her left the ledge came to an abrupt end, jutting out into an immense emptiness. She saw a vast blue valley thousands of feet below, and a circling hawk, and her eyes were drawn down in horrified fascination to a dry gulch dotted with tiny trees like the trees on a toy train set. She gasped and her heart skipped a beat, and then the fear came—not an ordinary fear, but a primal, animal panic that sent her clutching at the cliff. Cowering on the ledge, she looked down and down, and the world seemed to rock under her.

Maybe she screamed; maybe she didn't. She never knew. She only knew that her mind went blank with terror, and when she came back to herself again, her whole body was shaking. New waves of vertigo swept over her one after another, leaving her dizzy and nauseous and so frightened, she felt as if she were going to die. Covering her face with her hands, she closed her eyes, but the fear went on and on, and she couldn't stop it, and the panic kept building inside her. Calm down, she told herself, stop hyperventilating, you're going to faint, you're going to fall if you faint, calm down—but she couldn't calm down or think, and when she tried to pray she couldn't do that either.

"Please come get me," she pleaded. "Kevin, Ted, Mayumi, Peter, please don't leave me here." But no one came. She broke down, cried, beat her fists on the rocks until they bled, and she knew dimly that none of this was doing any good and that she was hysterical but the terror was so awful it ate away at her and whispered to her that she was helpless, and the more she tried to fight it, the worse it got.

Then slowly, for no obvious reason, the fear began to recede. Gradually she stopped crying. She lifted her head and heard a voice calling her name.

"Mandy, Mandy, can you hear me?"

"Help me," she yelled up at the voice. "For God's sake, help me."

"Mandy, you've got to climb."

"I can't."

"You've got to. You can't stay there forever."

Some rational part of her realized that the voice was Ted's, and that he was right. She had to climb off this ledge by herself; there was no alternative. Biting her lower lip, she closed her eyes and forced herself to move backward, inch by inch, until she felt the cold granite of the rock face pressing against her spine. She sat for a moment, clinging to the solidness of it. She was possessed by a desire to survive. I can do it, she told herself; I got myself into this, and I can get myself out of it. Did she really believe that? Yes—no—maybe—but what did it matter? She had to try; she had no choice.

Turning with agonizing caution, she grabbed the nearest outcropping, pulled herself to her feet, and stood there sweating and trembling, trying not to look down. It was frightening to stand, and another wave of dizziness came over her. She clutched at the outcropping to steady herself, and her hands slipped. The world reeled and dipped and her stomach turned over. She'd been wrong; she wasn't going to be able to make it back up the slope after all. If she tried, she'd fall, and yet what choice did she have? It would be dark in a few hours, and the longer she waited, the more exhausted she'd get.

"Climb," Ted begged, "please climb."

Gritting her teeth, she took one hand off the outcropping, wiped the sweat off her palm, and then did the same thing with her other hand. Getting a firmer grip, she pulled herself up, and as she did so the toe of her left foot fell into space and rock crumbled under her, and for a second she tottered on the edge, and then she was on another, smaller ledge like the one she'd just left. It was much worse up here than it had been down below, but she knew if she thought about it, she'd start to panic again, so she willed herself not to think.

Grabbing the outcropping just above her, she repeated the process. The useless rope dangled like a tail; gravel pattered down behind her and fell off into silence. She crawled upward a foot at a time, digging her fingers into the side of the slope until they bled. Once she grabbed for a rock and it fell out from under her hand and she slid backward, clutching at the grass and mud, and ended up breathless and trembling on the ledge she had just left, but she kept on climbing, knowing if she stopped even for a minute the panic would overpower her again. Gradually the sky above her widened, spreading out from a small patch to a deep, blue bowl, and then at last she saw them—Kevin, Mayumi, Peter, and Ted—peering over the edge of the cliff at her, their faces paler than the pale clouds above their heads.

"You're almost up," Ted yelled. "Just a little more, Man. Just a little farther." She climbed toward them, trying to think of solid ground and an end to this horror. The poppies along the top of the cliff dipped toward her in a yellow-gold fringe, and at the center of each one there was a tiny black cross. She rose above the poppies and saw a flat expanse of mud and stones carpeted with long grass and chaparral.

"You're safe," Ted yelled. "You made it, Man. Thank God, you made it." He reached down a strong, brown arm for her, and she pushed his hand away angrily because she'd made it on her own and didn't need his help. It was a crazy, irrational gesture that she never would have made if she'd been in her right mind, and as she did it she lost her balance.

"Mandy!" Ted yelled.

She grabbed at the edge of the cliff, clutching at grass and mud and loose gravel, and then she fell backward, out into nothingness. The fall was horrible and sickening; it ripped the breath out of her lungs, and she screamed and grabbed at the cliff face again as it tumbled out from under her hands, and she knew she was going to die, and then, suddenly, there was a snap that almost jerked her arms out of their sockets, and she found herself dangling at the end of a rope a few feet below the underside of the ledge.

Her body swung to the left and to the right, back and forth like a pendulum, and she just hung there and let herself swing, too stunned to move, and when she finally caught her breath and looked up, Ted was rappelling down the slope toward her.

Hitting the ledge with both feet, he ran to the rope, bent forward, grabbed it, and pulled her up. He caught her under the shoulders and dragged her onto the ledge.

"Mandy," he said, taking her into his arms and kissing her, "Mandy, darling. It's okay. It's okay. You were tied in twice." He kissed her again and again, long and hard, and held her like he was never going to let her go. "I'm sorry," he said incoherently, "we had to do it, you see. We had to make you think you were in danger. But you weren't, never, I swear it. You were tied to a piton, do you understand? A metal spike. I hammered it into the face of the cliff under the ledge myself, and I swear it could have held an elephant. I knew you wouldn't be in any state to notice that; I figured you'd believe me when I told you you were on your own, but you couldn't really have fallen." He stroked her hair and her eyes and her cheeks, and she saw to her astonishment that he was crying. "I love you," he said. "Say something, please. Don't just look at me like that."

She tried to say something but she couldn't so she buried her head in his shoulder and touched his cheek with the palm of her hand and closed her eyes and let him kiss her some more, and part of her knew that things would never be the same between them again. She felt so many different emotions that she couldn't sort them out, but two things were clear: she wasn't angry at him, and when she opened her eyes again and looked down the cliff at the blue valley and the dry gulch and the toy trees, she was only a little bit afraid. The fall must have burned the terror out.

I died, she thought irrationally, and I can't die twice, and I'm safe forever, and I'm standing on the roof of the world, and, my God, it's beautiful.

That night, back in Malibu, Mayumi woke up to the sound of the garbage disposal grinding away in the kitchen. Putting on her robe, she staggered in and found Kevin standing over the sink dumping pills down the drain.

"I'm cleaning up," Kevin announced. He pulled out his silver stash case and tossed about five hundred dollars' worth of cocaine after the pills with a grand gesture, and then threw in a bag of dope. Mayumi slipped her arm around his waist and stood with him as the water swirled and the disposal sucked the seeds and stems and leaves and blue and red and yellow capsules into oblivion. "These little recreational vehicles of mine were about the only things left that could screw it up for the five of us," he said, turning off the water. He was excited and his eyes glittered and he kept searching his pockets for more pills but his pockets were empty. "After what Mandy went through today I decided the least I could do was chuck this shit and see what it's like to go straight for a while. Like *Leave it to Beaver* probably, but I'll adjust. I'll buy polyester shirts; I'll join the Rotary Club; I'll take up bowling."

Mayumi reached out and touched the empty sink with the tip of her finger. The enamel was cold and clean and blank, like a white page of paper. "Did you get rid of your entire stash?" she asked in an awestruck voice.

Kevin grinned. "Well, to tell the truth, I did keep back a small lid of prime Acapulco Gold for high holidays. I mean I'm not getting born again or turning into a Mormon or anything like that. It's just if I blow this movie, I'm dead in the water, not to mention that if I show up on the set stoned, Jane Crews is going to sniff it out like a German shepherd."

"I'm glad you're doing this," Mayumi whispered. "Really."

"Don't be too glad," Kevin protested. "When I do something Boy Scout-like I'd rather not have it noticed. I mean, if I get the feeling I'm being too wholesome, I have this overwhelming urge to go out and counter it—screw myself sick, score some acid, drink seven bottles of Romilar cough syrup. This is primarily a symbolic gesture and more dope is only a phone call away."

"But you won't make that phone call?" Mayumi looked at him hopefully.

"Who knows?" Kevin said. "Probably not." The smile faded from his face and he was suddenly deadly serious. "I think I'm going to need some help with this. Will you help me? I mean, if I get a yen for some nose candy, will you remind me that I'm on a diet?"

"Sure," she said. "Of course."

Kevin contemplated the empty sink for a moment with a sad, slightly abandoned look on his face. "You know," he said, "I'm not actually sure I can go through with this clean-up campaign, and that really scares me."

"You can do it," Mayumi said.

"Right." Kevin nodded. "I can do it. Just keep telling me that."

Four days passed. At eight in the morning on the following Monday, Ted's phone rang. Fumbling for the receiver, he clutched it to his ear and sat up in bed. "Hello," he mumbled sleepily.

"Hello," Mandy said. "Could you come by? I have to talk to you." Her voice was oddly formal, like she was asking him to subscribe to a magazine or buy a six-week course in aerobics.

Ted was suddenly wide awake. "Talk to me about what?" he said. He hoped he sounded innocent, but she'd known him all his life and the chances of her believing a "Who me?" act were slim.

"I'd rather talk to you about it in person," she said tersely.

Ted winced. This was not a good sign. "Okay," he agreed. "I'll be right over." He wanted to say something suave and witty, but the best he could manage was a nervous laugh. He knew of course what she wanted to talk to him about: he probably should have apologized on the spot for kissing her, but how do you apologize convincingly for something you aren't sorry for? He'd spent the last four days debating whether or not to call her—not because he was too cowardly to face her, but because if he said anything to her it would have to be another *I love you,* and he kept thinking that would only make things worse. Now it was too late for apologies; from the way she'd asked him to come over, she sounded as if she felt he'd taken advantage of a very emotional situation, and if she did, he was in big trouble. Mandy was no one to play for a sucker. He'd known that ever since they were ten and he'd tricked her into taking over his paper route by pleading an attack of appendicitis. When she'd discovered he was faking she hadn't said anything, she'd simply gone out and neatly disassembled his bicycle and it had taken him the better part of a month to find all the parts. As for kissing her, he'd never meant to do it, but he'd gotten carried away by the excitement of hauling her back up on the ledge and the fear of seeing her fall in the first place, and something had come over him, and he was sorry that it was going to cause trouble, but he also felt excited and happy, which might have been a macho reaction, but wasn't the kind of thing he felt like begging forgiveness for.

"By the way," Mandy added, "I seem to be more or less over my acrophobia. I went up on the cliffs the other day—the ones at Palos Verdes—and just stood there watching the hang gliders take off, and I only felt a little dizzy, which is an improvement to say the least."

"Good," Ted said, "that's wonderful." Perhaps there was a chance that she wasn't out after his scalp. Being naturally optimistic, he allowed himself to hope.

"See you soon," she said and hung up.

Getting dressed was never much of a problem under ordinary circumstances, but for the next ten minutes he wandered around his room incapable of deciding the most basic things—like should he wear his blue socks or his gray ones. Finally he simply reached out and threw on whatever came to hand, jammed his feet into his favorite pair of Mexican cowboy boots, gargled a glass of Peter's mouthwash, and headed out the door. Half an hour later he was ringing Mandy's bell, feeling like he was about to climb a rock face without a rope or pitons.

Mandy answered the door wearing a faded pair of jeans, a stained yellow tank top, a blue bandanna around her hair, and a pair of yellow rubber gloves. Somehow, despite those ridiculous gloves, she looked completely beautiful and Ted felt his heart do a small flip into his throat when he saw her. The way he reacted to her drove him crazy, but he couldn't seem to control it. Around all other women in the world he was Mr. Cool—in fact, he practically had to beat them off with sticks—but Mandy turned him into an abashed, clumsy, inarticulate adolescent. I'm acting like a damn puppy dog, he told himself, but it didn't do any good.

"Come on in," she said, waving him across the threshold, "I'm in the middle of cleaning the oven." Not only was this not the most romantic statement in the world, it was definitely bad news. Mandy, to the best of his knowledge, had never cleaned an oven in her life except when she was moving out of a place and wanted to get back the damage deposit. In fact, she never did housework at all if she could avoid it. She preferred to let things silt up in a graceful way until she ran out of cups or plates or so much dust collected that it began to endanger one of her precious records. Her cleaning fits were whirlwind affairs, frantic and unstoppable and almost always correlated with severe emotional upset. The last time Ted had seen her do something of this magnitude was when his father died seven years ago. He'd come over the day after the funeral, bummed out, wanting to talk to her, and found her down on her hands and knees in the kitchen, sobbing as she stripped the wax off the linoleum.

"Make yourself comfortable," she said. "I'll be done in a minute." She went over to the stove and stuck her head inside and began scrubbing away. Ted tried to make himself comfortable as she had suggested, but it was an impossible task. The sight of her wringing out sponges and chopping off bits of burned casseroles gave him chills. Whatever she had to say to him was going to be very heavy indeed.

Finally she finished and tossed aside the gloves, but instead of sitting down and telling him whatever it was she had on her mind, she spent another ten minutes pacing around the kitchen lining up the spices in the spice rack and going for invisible fingerprints on the cabinets until he couldn't stand it anymore.

"Sit down," he begged.

"What?" She looked up from buffing the chrome on the refrigerator as if she'd forgotten he was there, but he could tell she hadn't, not by a long shot.

"You said you wanted to talk to me about something." He took the dust rag out of her hand, led her over to the bed, and sat her down. After he did it he realized that this wasn't the most appropriate place to have a conversation of this sort, but the apartment was small and her chairs were so wobbly that he always felt like they were going to collapse under him, and it was too late to suggest that they sit at the table because calling attention to the fact that they were on the bed would make him look like he was a first-class creep with only one thing on his mind, so he sat down next to her, as far away as possible. "What's up?" he asked.

Instead of answering, Mandy pulled the bandanna off her hair, shook it out, and just sat there staring at him with a really weird expression on her face. "I have to ask you a question," she said at last.

"So ask." Ted tried to smile, but he felt like his face was cracking so he canned it. "Really," he said, "go ahead, ask."

Mandy got to her feet and then sat down again. "This is really embarrassing," she said, and she looked like she might cry. Ted felt terrible, but he didn't know what to do except apologize and some sixth sense told him it was too early for that, so he just sat there until she found her tongue again, which she did of course, because only Krazy Glue could keep Mandy's mouth shut once she'd made up her mind to say something. "Darn it," she said, "there's just no diplomatic way to ask this, so I'll be blunt. When we were up on that ledge the other day and I was freaking out, you started kissing me." She paused and shot him a look that could fry eggs at a hundred yards. Oh no, Ted thought. She did think he'd taken advantage of her, and he was in for it. He steeled himself for the blow, but what she said next was: "And you said you loved me, and what I want to know is, did you mean it?"

He wasn't at all sure he'd heard her right. "Did I mean it?" he echoed idiotically.

"Yeah." Mandy rolled up the bandanna and slapped it against her hand and looked down at the tips of her sneakers like maybe she was thinking of getting them resoled. "Did you mean it when you said you loved me?"

Ted briefly considered the possibility of denial, but he knew he couldn't bring it off. "Yes," he confessed, "I meant it." This was the

hardest sentence he had spoken in twenty-one years, and he immediately wanted to take it back because Mandy's face got very pale, and
she kept looking down at her shoes.

"Rats," she said. "I was afraid you'd say that."

"I'm sorry," Ted stammered. "I can't help it. I never meant for you
to find out. I know it must seem crazy to you. After all, we've been
friends ever since we were kids and I never once came on to you
before, and I swear to God I had no intention of ever telling you, but
I lost it when I saw you hanging from that rope even though I knew
you were perfectly safe. My feelings exploded and I couldn't control
them, and I apologize, Man, because I know you think of me as a
brother and nothing else, and that this is no doubt a major drag for
you and—"

"Wait," she interrupted, "don't apologize."

"Don't apologize?"

"No." She looked up with one of the strangest expressions on her
face he'd ever seen. "The fact that you're in love with me isn't the
problem."

"It isn't?"

"No," she said in a small, shy voice. "The problem is that well, to
tell you the truth, I think maybe I feel the same way about you."

Ted gaped at her open-mouthed. "What?" he stammered.

"I think I love you."

"That's wonderful. That's absolutely wonderful." He couldn't
believe it.

"I'm not sure it's wonderful at all." She sat back and ran her fingers
through her hair. "I mean, look at it this way, we've been friends all
our lives, right? We lived next door to each other for seventeen years
and we're practically brother and sister. You taught me how to ride
my first bicycle—when I was how old?"

"Seven," Ted supplied. He was in shock.

"So I'll level with you." She folded her arms across her chest. "I'm
attracted to you. To tell you the truth, I'm surprised I am, but I am.
I used to look at you and not even know if I thought you were
good-looking or not, but since you kissed me, I've been seeing you in
a different light. This confuses the hell out of me; it makes me wonder
if I've gone a little nuts. I'm not sure about my own feelings and I'm

scared to death of blowing our friendship. I feel so vulnerable right now. I'm lonely; I haven't got a boyfriend—I haven't even wanted one in a long time—and I'm not sure I have much of a career either. Even though we've got the job with Crews, I'm not convinced I'm up to it. I keep comparing myself to my mother and my grandmother and every time I do I get cold feet. I keep thinking that maybe all I'm good for is Kal Kan commercials and bit parts and that I can't act— much less hang glide—and that I'm going to screw it up for the four of you."

He started to tell her she was a wonderful actress, but she stopped him. "Please," she begged, "let me finish, because if I don't get this all out in one breath, I'll never be able to say it. I'm trying to warn you that I'm afraid maybe my feelings for you are coming out of loneliness or hormones or insecurity, and that if we got involved with each other, I might come on all hot and heavy and then realize it had been a mistake. I have to confess that I've done that sort of thing before." She looked at him with such pain and confusion that he wanted to take her in his arms right then and there. "I've been hard on men," she admitted, "and I'm not particularly proud of it."

"If this is true confession time," Ted said, "I don't exactly have a great record myself in that department."

Mandy smiled for the first time since he came in the door. "That," she said, "is certainly true."

"So, I agree—we're both flakes; we both love 'em and leave 'em. Not that we mean to, but we're both unreliable when it comes to relationships." He took a deep breath and plunged ahead. "That just gives us something else in common. Only this time it's going to be different."

"You think we have a chance?"

"My God, yes, of course. Look what we've got going for us." He leaned forward, wanting so much to convince her that it was painful. "We know each other inside out; we like the same music, the same books, even the same kind of pizza for chrissake." He took her hand and she didn't pull away.

"You don't think we'd end up hating each other?"

"Not a chance."

"I can be a real pain."

Ted chuckled. "I know that, Man. Believe me."

She sat quietly, holding his hand. "Well," she said at last, "I guess if you really do understand what I mean, then . . ." She paused and looked up at him and the corner of her mouth trembled slightly. "I'd be willing, to take the risk that is, as long as we were always friends, because you're very important to me, Teddy, and I couldn't stand it if we weren't friends."

"Is that a yes?"

She nodded and squeezed his hand. He put his arm around her and there was an awkward silence. The refrigerator hummed and water dripped into the sink, and the electric clock on the night table clicked and sputtered.

"Mandy," he said after a few minutes, "there's one more thing."

"What's that, Teddy?"

He cleared his throat, feeling mildly embarrassed but determined to start off right with her because she was so important to him—"the next logical thing for us to do is make love, not now," he added hastily, "but sooner or later. And the thing is, well, I don't want to seduce you."

"Seduce me?" She looked as if she might laugh.

"I'm sorry," he said awkwardly. "I know I must sound like some kind of prig, but what I mean is, I want you to tell me when you're ready. I don't want you to ever feel like I've imposed on you or taken advantage of you or anything like that, and if you reconsider and decide it's all off, then please tell me that, too, and I'll take it"—he grinned uncomfortably—"like a man."

Mandy gave him a very strange look. "You want me to decide when we make love?"

"Definitely."

"You are a strange and wonderful man, Ted Van Dusen. Believe me, no one else has ever said anything like that to me before."

"I don't intend to ever be like any of the other men you've known, because they were obviously too stupid to hang on to you."

Mandy smiled and then she laughed. "This is for real? You mean it?"

"Yes. Absolutely."

"Well, well." She got up, walked over to the other side of the room, and stood for a moment looking out the double doors that faced the courtyard. Finally she turned around and walked back to the bed.

"How about now?" she said.

Ted was surprised to say the least. "Now?"

"Look, I'm not very skilled at making the first move, so you'll have to forgive me if I don't do it suavely, but I figure we might as well get this over with." She grinned and blushed. "Just listen to me. I sound like I'm proposing an execution." She sat down beside him. "This has to be the worst seduction job ever performed."

"Not necessarily." Ted felt a mild burst of panic. "But are you sure now's the time? I mean I was planning to court you for a few weeks—candy, flowers, dinners for two, the whole bit."

"I'm nervous," she said softly. "I'm scared as hell, Teddy. If we spend weeks building up to this, I'll be a complete wreck. And besides . . ." She stopped talking and looked at him very sweetly. "Could you please kiss me?" she said.

He didn't need any more of an invitation. Folding her in his arms, he kissed her long and hard, and she put her arms around his shoulders and drew him closer and kissed him back.

"I really do love you," she murmured.

"And I love you, Mandy."

They kissed again and he could feel her growing excited. He wanted to touch her breasts and her bare shoulders and her neck, and hold her and caress her all over, but he didn't want to rush her so he went very slowly. Her skin was wonderful, like a long, soft sheet of velvet, and he explored it reverently. She curved beautifully everywhere, hips and shoulders and arms and legs, and she tasted sweet and he was overwhelmed with the desire to protect her and care for her, and this was a new feeling for him. He held her very close until he could feel she wasn't afraid anymore. Then he took off her clothes and stretched her out on her blue-and-gold flowered sheets, and kissed her navel and her thighs and the soft mound of hair between her legs, and every part of her, and he was lost in her, and he thought that if he never touched a woman for the rest of his life, he would be satisfied with this moment, that having Mandy in his arms was more happiness than a man had any right to expect, and that he loved her like he'd never loved anything, not even the wilderness.

*   *   *

The dunes ran into each other in soft brown mounds, curving into low slopes that glittered in the hot afternoon sun. A photographer could no doubt have had a field day with them, but on this particular June afternoon Mandy was too absorbed in fighting a fifty-pound hang glider to appreciate the sensual lushness of the landscape. For almost a week now she had been trying with every ounce of her being to learn this so-called sport, and she was getting—why not admit it?—nowhere.

Gritting her teeth, she grabbed at the control bar, and the wind caught under the edge of the glider and threw her on her ass. She struggled up, grabbed again, and the same thing happened. The wind, she thought grimly, was having fun. Picking herself up, she looked at the turquoise wings and aluminum tubing, wishing it would all vanish in a puff of smoke or fall apart or fly off by itself. Learning to hang glide was the hardest thing she'd ever done in her life. It was as tedious as washing dishes, as exhausting as digging a ditch, and as frustrating as—well she couldn't think of *anything* as frustrating as learning to hang glide except maybe trying to bail out the ocean with a teaspoon.

A few yards to her left Jane Crews stood on a small ridge of sand, hands planted on her hips, shaking her head and looking amused, impatient, and annoyed in that order. "Hump that glider back up the hill and try again," she ordered Mandy, "and this time don't grab on to it like it was a goddamn life preserver. You can't *pull* yourself up into the air; you have to get enough ground speed up to get some lift."

Go to hell, Mandy thought, but she picked up her glider for a third time and was just about to start up the hill when Kevin came crashing and flopping down from the top and nearly did a nose dive into her lap. "Watch it," Crews yelled, jumping back and waving her arms. Her face was red and her eyes bulged; she looked positively apoplectic. "Watch where you're flying for chrissake! These gliders cost *money*. One bent strut and they're trash."

Kevin extracted himself from his glider, spit out a mouthful of sand, pulled off his helmet, and contemplated the red-and-black Dacron wings with loathing. "This thing sucks," he growled. "I could get higher by jumping."

"Sucks!" Crews yelled. "Why you unappreciative little twerp, that's a classic Rogallo wing with a cambered keel, dog-eared deflexors, and the best battens money can buy." She waved her arms passionately and looked at the glider like it was her best friend. "It's a brilliant piece of engineering. I'd have given my eyeteeth to have had one of those back in '69. The problem isn't the glider, the problem is *you*."

"Bullshit," Kevin yelled.

"If you don't like it," Crews yelled back, "you know what you can do with it."

This was the fifth yelling match Kevin and Crews had gotten into in the past hour, and Mandy paid no attention to it. Hoisting her glider up on her shoulders, she turned it cautiously until the wind lifted it just a little. An inch too far and she'd be on her back again. Keeping an eye on the flapping wings, she began the trek back up the dune.

"You could fly like a bird if you'd quit screwing around!" Crews was yelling.

"Yeah," Kevin yelled, "right, like a goddamn ostrich!"

Mandy lost her footing in the sand, stumbled back, and nearly toppled over. The control bar was an aluminum triangle that bit into the insides of her arms and made her feel like she was about to dislocate both elbows. She shifted it back and forth trying to find a comfortable position, but there were no comfortable positions. The damn thing weighed a ton and her arms were falling off and this was the fifteenth time she'd struggled back up the hill, and so far she hadn't gotten more than ten inches off the ground. What an idiot she'd been to worry about heights. She looked up at the dunes, which sloped gradually down toward her like a child's sand pile. There was a mild breeze blowing and nothing in sight but salt grass, sun, and five sweating, awkward would-be actors laboring under the eye of the merciless Ms. Crews. No cliffs, no ridges, no melodramatic plunges through space: the worst acrophobe in the world couldn't get upset under these conditions.

At the top, Mayumi, Ted, and Peter were sitting on the control bars of their gliders, trying to keep them from blowing away as they consumed the last of the Crunchy Granola bars.

"How's it going?" Ted asked, glancing up from his lunch of oatmeal, honey, and sand.

"I hate hang gliding," Mandy proclaimed, flopping down beside him. "I'm never going to be able to get this thing off the ground."

Ted grinned and stroked her hair. He was always touching her, smoothing her down like a cat. They had been lovers for eight days, five hours, and thirty-three minutes, and they were ridiculously happy, even now in an eighty-degree sun, with sore backs and aching legs. Mandy leaned against his shoulder and some of her frustration disappeared. Overhead, the wings of their gliders fluttered in the wind, dancing and pulling as if they wanted to take off by themselves. The gliders really were pretty to look at—that is if you weren't slogging up a hill with one of them. The sails, dyed brilliant hues of red and green and turquoise, had a grace to them that reminded Mandy of Gothic cathedrals and spiderwebs.

Ted shielded his eyes from the sun, leaned back against his glider, and watched Kevin's progress up the slope. Kevin was moving sideways now like a crab, with Crews at his heels bellowing advice. There was a lull, and then the wind coiled in a playful gust and sent Kevin on his back under his glider, kicking his legs like an overturned turtle. It would have been funny if all of them hadn't just been in the same fix. "There's a nasty rumor that some people actually do this for fun," Ted said.

"They must be brain-damaged," Peter observed.

"You've got to take some risks!" Crews was yelling.

Risks, Mandy thought. Who needs them? Crews is nuts.

Crews stomped up the sand dune past Kevin, who had somehow managed to right himself again. "Get the lead out," she yelled at the four of them. "What do you think this is, a picnic?" She came closer and gave them her general-inspecting-the-troops glare. "Mandy," she said, pointing. "On your feet."

Wearily, Mandy got up. This wasn't fair, she thought. She'd only just sat down. It was Mayumi's turn. But "fair" wasn't in Crews' vocabulary.

"Get your ass over here," Crews commanded, "and bring your glider with you."

Holding the glider over her head, Mandy wobbled over to the edge of the dune. Crews ran one calloused finger along the guide wires and grunted. It was the kind of sound that could have meant approval or contempt, or even indifference for that matter. Mandy tried to get a look at her eyes, but the wraparound sunglasses she was wearing were the one-way window kind.

"Go for it," Crews said, gesturing at the downhill slope. Folding her arms across her baggy designer T-shirt, she waited.

Here goes nothing, Mandy thought. Taking a deep breath, she lifted the glider over her head and ran as fast as she could down the slope. The wind tugged at her, throwing her off balance, blowing her hair into her eyes, taking the breath out of her lungs, and the glider lurched and dipped and lifted with a long, rolling sigh.

She was a good twelve feet off the ground before she realized she was flying.

That night in San Bernardino, Kathe, Hermann, Ted, and Mandy celebrated over a bottle of Schramsberg champagne.

"You flew," Kathe said, toasting Mandy, "and I'm so proud of you. You're a braver woman than I'll ever be." She meant every word of it. She still worried about the hang gliding, of course. She'd probably never get over that, but she was sincerely proud of Mandy's courage and determination. It amazed her slightly that she had managed to produce such a daughter.

"She's a bird," Hermann said, rubbing his bald head happily, "my girl is a human bird. Wonder Woman should step aside."

Ted laughed and put his arm around Mandy, drawing her close. "It gave me hope to see her up there," he said. "I was beginning to think none of us was ever going to get off the ground."

Mandy sat at the table looking happy and triumphant. Her face glowed and her eyes shone.

I made the right decision, Kathe thought, as she sipped her champagne. I'm not such a bad mother if I do say so myself.

The Plunge was shot in less than seven weeks. When the last frame was in the can, Jane Crews disappeared into her studio to spend fourteen hours a day editing the rough footage; putting it together, taking it apart, and generally driving herself crazy. About once a week the whole gang went out to Madame Wu's to eat shrimp-fried rice and try to second-guess what the film would look like by the time she was through with it. Kevin was convinced Crews was doing something along the lines of *Endless Summer;* Ted thought maybe a hang-gliding version of *Jaws* was in the works, and Mayumi was convinced they were in for a remake of *Gidget*. Crews could be doing anything in there, Peter insisted as he stuffed his mouth. Better not to think about it at all. Pass him the soy sauce; pass him the tea; pass him, he begged, some hemlock.

Peter had a point. The days crawled by with impossible slowness, summer turned to fall, and as Crews remained sequestered in her studio Mandy found herself biting her fingernails down to the quick and waking up in the middle of the night wondering if *The Plunge* was going to be a work of substance or a surfer movie with wings. There was nothing they could do except wait. Their careers were in her hands. It was, they all agreed, the most nerve-racking period they'd ever been through.

In September, when Viola wrote that she was coming over from England for a three-week visit, Mandy drove up to Crews' house, cornered her in her studio, and begged her to set up a screening of the rough cut.

"Are you crazy?" Crews snapped. "I never show anyone an inch of unfinished film. Let her come to the premiere."

"My grandmother's seventy-four years old," Mandy pointed out, "and she doesn't get over here that often, and besides, she can't come to the premiere because she's committed to open in London in November in a revival of *Suddenly Last Summer*."

"*Suddenly Last Summer*?" Crews brightened. "That's a nice, vicious play. I always did like Tennessee Williams. Is Madame Kessler going to descend from the air in a gold elevator like Hepburn did in the movie version?"

"I don't know," Mandy begged, "but please show her *The Plunge*. It would mean so much to her to see me in something that didn't involve cat food."

Crews went over to the coffee machine, poured herself a mug of French roast, and sat for a long time staring at her moviola. In fact, she sat for so long that Mandy began to wonder if she'd forgotten she was there. "I must be crazy," she said at last, "because I'm going to say yes. But I want you to know I'm committing this piece of rank insanity only because I've admired Viola Kessler ever since I was seventeen and cut school to see her in *The Kindness of Strangers*. That woman can act. So I'll set up a special screening of *The Plunge*, but only you two get to see it. No one else. Sorry if that puts you in a tight spot with your buddies, but if one word gets out to the press about what's on that screen I want to know exactly who to come gunning for. Get the picture?"

"I get the picture," Mandy said.

"I mean it," Crews persisted. "You don't even tell Ted, not even when the two of you are jumping around in bed together playing horny chipmunks." Tact definitely wasn't Crews' strong point.

"I understand," Mandy promised. "My lips are sealed."

"They better be," Crews warned, "or I'll have your head on a platter."

Which was how it came about that a week later Mandy found herself sitting next to Viola in Crews' private screening room watching *The Plunge*. The projector clicked and the untimed print danced past the light, and up on the screen the Pacific Ocean appeared, stretching out to the horizon, smooth and glassy, broken only by a fringe of surf breaking on the beach at the base of a sheer cliff. It was a slightly sickening shot, high and vast and held for so long that you felt as if you were falling straight into the center of it. Suddenly the camera zoomed in on the cliff, and Mandy was revealed, poised on the very edge, holding a great, delicate turquoise hang glider that beat and fluttered above her like a gigantic kite. Before you could get used to the sight of it, she ran a few steps and with a smooth, forward movement lunged into space, caught the wind, and rode it, rising in long, dizzy turns.

"My God," Viola whispered, gripping her hand, "you don't mean to say you actually *did* that! It looks positively suicidal."

Kevin jumped next, then Ted, then Mayumi, and last of all Peter, and for a few minutes the five of them rode the currents, dipping and soaring hundreds of feet above the ocean like a flock of great, brilliantly colored birds. Mandy recalled what hell it had been to film this scene, how exhausted they'd been doing one take after another— worrying about the wind, and turbulence, and whether or not they'd be able to carry it off without crashing into each other in midair—but there was no trace on the screen of the pain, only laughing faces, effortless turns, and a grace beyond imagination. Jane Crews, she decided, was one hell of an editor.

The movie continued for about forty minutes, relentlessly beautiful.

In the final frames Peter caught an updraft and rose quickly—too quickly if you knew anything about hang gliders. In real life, of course, he never would have shon off like that, not if he'd had an ounce of brains. He'd have had a variometer strapped to his wrist to tell him that he was getting sucked into the sky at something along the lines of 800 feet per minute; he'd have known that those innocent-looking cauliflower-shaped clouds above him indicated that he was rising into a thermal that could engulf him and throw him out of control, but this was fiction, and Peter was Icarus and so he went on rising and laughing until suddenly everything went haywire. Without the slightest warning he seemed to hit an invisible wall and his wings collapsed. Thrown sideways, he began a horrible nose-dive straight toward the earth. Crews had edited brilliantly. It took forever, and even though Mandy knew for a fact that the person falling wasn't really Peter but a stuntman and master hang-glider pilot, she still felt ill at the sight of that spinning, careening plunge. You saw Peter crash into the ocean (by this time it wasn't even a stunt-man but a dummy, but there was no way you could know); the yellow wings of his glider floated on the surface for a moment, and then they sank and there was nothing left, not even a trace.

Suddenly the projector stopped and Crews flipped on the lights. "That's it," she announced. "That's as far as I've gotten."

"Amazing," Viola said. She looked quite pale.

"With all due respect, Miss Kessler," Crews said, "I'd rather you didn't tell me what you thought of it at this point. You see, I have a vision of what I want the final cut to look like, and if I get any feedback this early on it only confuses me." She was amazingly polite, conducting them to the door, shaking Viola's hand and telling her how honored she'd been to meet her. Mandy had never seen Jane Crews on her good behavior before, and it gave her quite a bit of satisfaction to watch the director turn into Grammy's awkward, awestricken fan. She left with the impression that Crews had been on the verge of asking for an autograph.

They made an interesting pair as they ambled through the surf getting their feet wet. They were the same height, had the same build, the same upturned nose, the same habit of swinging their arms as they walked, and if one of them hadn't been twenty-one and the other over seventy, people might have taken them for twins.

"What did you think of *The Plunge?*" Mandy asked, bending over to inspect a ribbon of green seaweed.

Viola paused, picked up a shell, examined it, and tossed it back into the ocean. Her hair had gone gray, but there was a playful snap to her eyes and a fairness to her skin that made her look healthy and slightly athletic, as if she spent most of her days jogging up and down beaches instead of standing around in drafty theaters. "Well," she said briskly, "to tell you the truth, I'm not sure what I thought. I suppose the thing it did best was scared the bejesus out of me. I kept thinking that as soon as Kathe and Hermann found out what you were up to they should have locked you in your room and posted guard dogs around you. I only have one granddaughter—whom I love very much—and I rather enjoy the idea of finding her in one piece when I come over to pay her a visit. I still can't believe you actually jumped off that cliff, and, by the way, I thought you were afraid of heights."

Mandy grinned and kicked at the seaweed. "I was, Grammy, but I got over it."

"It wasn't a bad film." Viola smiled mischievously and sent another piece of shell skipping out over the water. "And it was fun to see you in action. I'm not prejudiced, of course, but frankly I thought your leap into eternity was the best thing I'd seen on the screen since Lillian Gish nearly went over Niagara Falls on a hunk of ice in *Down East.*"

Mandy laughed. "I wish Crews thought that."

"And," Viola continued, skipping another shell, "I have to admit that the movie had some some of the qualities of a good Greek tragedy—at least as far as it went. That plunge your friend Peter took was pure *hubris* getting smacked down by the gods." She watched the shell career across the water in four solid leaps and disappear between two waves. "It may turn out to be quite interesting by the time Ms. Crews is done with it. She looks like nobody's fool."

"Crews is amazing," Mandy agreed. "*The Plunge* isn't even edited, and she already has another script in the works. Writing it herself, of course, in her spare time, although how she can have any spare time is beyond me. In fact, if I didn't know for certain she hated drugs, I'd say she was on amphetamines. But no, she just manufactures her own speed in her armpits or something and goes right on rolling along like a freight train. It's practically inhuman."

"What's the subject of this new film written by the inhuman and infamous Ms. Crews?" Viola chuckled.

Mandy shook her head. "I don't know really. She's so closed-mouthed. But from a few hints she's let drop I gather the plot centers around some kids who go skin diving in Mexico and get shipwrecked. Peter's convinced it's a remake of *Robinson Crusoe*."

"Do you have a part in it?"

"Maybe."

"What does 'maybe' mean?"

"It means that if *The Plunge* does well, I probably have a part, and if *The Plunge* bombs, I'll be back at the No Satisfaction slinging Sunset Strips and Rolling Stones, but I'm hoping for the best."

"Always a good tactic," Viola agreed, bending down to scoop up another shell.

"If I do get the part," Mandy suggested, "maybe you'd like to come pay me a visit on location. Mexico is full of shells."

"Shells, eh?" Viola's face lit up. She'd been crazy about collecting shells for at least three years now, and today she hadn't found even one worth keeping. You had to go south for the fine ones, to places where the water turned bright blue and was so clear you could see your feet when you stood in it.

"I had a friend who came back from Isla Verde last year with a hundred and fifty sand dollars," Mandy said temptingly. "Not to mention a *Fusinus ustulatus* and a superb *Lyropecten nodosus*." When Viola had taken up shelling as a hobby, Mandy had gone to the Yale library and read everything she could get her hands on about the subject, an act Viola had found rather touching.

"A *Lyropecten nodosus*, eh?" Viola smiled. "You're speaking my language, kid. Maybe I can get away. After *Suddenly Last Summer* finishes up, maybe I'll just schedule myself another little vacation." They walked on for a few minutes in silence, enjoying the sunshine and one another's company. Mandy thought how much she always enjoyed her grandmother's visits, and Viola thought that there was no place she'd rather be than here on the beach with Mandy. After about a quarter of an hour more of drifting aimlessly, Viola wandered over to a piece of driftwood, sat down, put her chin on her hands, and gazed out at the ocean. Pacific waves had a different rhythm than the waves that lapped up against the shores of England; they rolled in great ridges, softly, like ripples in blue-gray silk.

"Tired, Grammy?" Mandy asked, settling down beside her companionably.

"A little," Viola admitted. She ran her hands along the polished white surface of the log thinking how she loved the way the ocean shaped the things it touched. Time, she thought, polished down the human soul the same way, until only the essentials were left. One of the essentials in her own life was Mandy, and she was grateful to simply sit here beside her. She looked over at the girl, who was drawing aimlessly in the sand with a stick and tried to remember what it had felt like to be twenty-one. She'd been so in love with Joseph at that age; Mandy from all reports was heading in the same direction. I'm happy for her, Viola thought, and I hope she's spared all the pain. She wondered how an intensely curious and snoopy old grandmother could find out the exact state of affairs without seeming to intrude. "How's Ted?" she asked casually.

Mandy colored slightly and went on poking at the sand. "Just fine," she said.

Viola tried to shut her mouth, but she was absolutely incapable of not asking the next logical question. "Any plans?"

"Plans, Grammy?" Mandy grinned. "Whatever do you mean?"

Viola laughed. "Not very subtle, am I?"

"No," Mandy giggled. "You're certainly not. Say," she said, tossing down her stick, "how about you? I hear Mr. Carlyle's still giving you the rush."

Caught in the act, Viola thought. She waved an indifferent hand and tried not to blush. "That silly old man proposes to me once a year like clockwork," she protested. "I don't encourage it, but what can I do?"

"*And* I hear Lord Dockett's been falling at your feet," Mandy teased.

"Don't be silly. Ever since Cissy died, the poor man's been inconsolable."

"That's not what the rumor mill's reporting on this side of the Atlantic."

Viola grinned sheepishly. Trying to sneak anything past Mandy was a losing proposition. "Very well, I admit it. Larry is interested in me, poor soul. I think it's a symptom of senility."

"You know"—Mandy's eyes gleamed wickedly—"I think you need a younger man."

"A younger man?" Viola was surprised. "How much younger?"

"Oh, about twenty-five, say." She pointed to a chunky fellow in a tiny swimming suit who lay sprawled out on the beach perfecting his tan. "Like that one over there. I mean, face it, Grammy, only a guy like that can keep up with you."

"Amanda Rothe Lang! What a thing to say to your decrepit old grandmother!"

Jumping to her feet, Mandy fled laughing, and Viola pursued her, bending over to scoop up a fistful of sand and fling it at her. "Come back here, young lady; come back here and show a little respect for age!"

Anywhere else in the world the sight of a seventy-four-year-old barefoot woman in a blue linen suit pursuing a young girl in faded jeans might have turned a few heads, but on Venice Beach it took more than that to rouse the sunbathers. They ran for thirty yards or so, and then Viola collapsed in a breathless heap and Mandy came back and fell down beside her, and they lay there in perfect kinship, sprawled out on the sand side by side, laughing helplessly.

Mandy always remembered that day at the beach, mainly because of its sweet anonymity. Three months later *The Plunge* was released, broke box-office records, and became the second most popular cult film of the decade. From that moment on, except when she was in her own house or the house of a friend, she never had another minute of real privacy.

33

PLAYA AZUL,
MEXICO
1976

It was nowhere. It was south of Texas and north of Palenque and east of ugly Pemex oil fields that smoked and burned and sent black smoke spewing out over the ocean, but the smoke never got that far. It had a jet port for tourists but no first-class hotel; a volleyball court without a net; three doctors, two lawyers, a mayor, and about two hundred families who lived on fish, coconut oil, rice, mangoes, and Coca-Cola. The children wore tattered blue-and-white school uniforms and carried their books slung over their shoulders in bags woven of sisal, and when the gringo film crew came out in the morning to load their equipment into their helicopters, the oldest ones would gather in a circle around them and beg for chewing gum and news of John Travolta.

"This," Kevin declared, putting his bare feet up on the bamboo railing of Playa Azul's only authentic cantina, "is the life." Out on the beach a flock of brown pelicans rose into the air and skimmed over the water. This, the birds echoed, is the life indeed. Infinite fish;

plenty of room to mate; no offshore drilling; only blue water and sun and palm trees and crazy gringos who travel thousands of miles to eat shrimp, get turista, and make movies.

"This is the life," Mayumi agreed. Her face was so badly sunburned that it looked like she'd spent the last seven weeks on a griddle, but makeup covered that nicely so she didn't complain. Every day two dozen yellow roses arrived for her from L.A., courtesy of a producer from Warner Brothers, so the rumor went, but Mayumi wasn't saying. She put the flowers in water or gave them to the children or handed them out to the crew one by one, and she smiled a cryptic smile as much as if to say to Kevin that she didn't really care that he had left her months ago for a rock star named Tiina Zaap. A woman who built her entire career around a name with double letters couldn't be much competition, even if she did wear miniskirts that came up to her navel and lace body stockings and had her picture on the cover of *Rolling Stone*. Mayumi had been in *Time* and *People*—the whole gang had for that matter—so who was Tiina Zaap that Mayumi should get bent out of shape about her?

Mandy drank her beer and contemplated Kevin and Mayumi with amusement. Still couples die hard, she thought, and whenever Kevin says something like *This is the life* Mayumi will be seconding him and agreeing with him, on automatic pilot after all those years of being his personal yes woman. But they're friends despite everything, which is more than Ted and I would be if he left me for some rock star. I'd rip his lungs out; I'd tear out his heart; I'd put a contract out on him. I wouldn't, of course. I'd just go into a genteel decline and cry. Thank God there's no need for that; thank God our relationship's survived all this hype. No thanks to the fan magazines and scandal sheets. "IS HOLLYWOOD'S SWEETEST YOUNG COUPLE ON THE ROCKS?" subtitle: "THE LANG GANG'S BEST BANG: WILL IT LAST?" Yuck. Sentimental drivel; near pornography. There've been so many rumors about us, so many reporters trying to crawl into our bedroom, it's a miracle we're still speaking, still in love.

She took another sip of lukewarm beer, reached across and grabbed Ted's hand, and squeezed it. He looked up from his book: Prescott's *The Conquest of Mexico*. "Siesta time?" He winked. He was wearing an embroidered Mexican shirt and he had a beard, a red beard—

surprise. Back in L.A. she'd never imagined Ted's beard would be red. Pancho Villa. She grinned—he lacks only the cartridge belt. His hands were dear to her, as were his wrists, his arms, and the rest of him. She felt a languid wave of lust and love pass over her. Behind him the ocean sparkled metallically.

"Siesta time coming up." She grinned and stroked his wrist. Their room was a whitewashed cubicle with a concrete floor, rusty screens, and two double beds that Ted had lashed together with rope, and they had spent seven happy weeks there lying in each other's arms and staring up at the ceiling fan.

"Such lovebirds," Peter said. He pretended to be disgusted but she could tell that he approved. He beamed at them and pushed up his phantom glasses—phantom because he'd gotten contact lenses and didn't wear real glasses anymore. He was eating greasy fried potatoes that looked disgusting, a plate of black refried beans sprinkled with white cheese, a pork chop, a piece of baked yucca, and a sliced-cabbage salad, and the salad was sudden death, and he knew it and Mandy knew it and everyone in the cantina knew it, but Peter wouldn't listen to reason, which was why he had spent two of the past seven weeks in the infirmary where the nurses sterilized their needles with tequila and bats hung from the ceiling while Jane Crews threatened and fumed and filmed around him, but there was no reasoning with him. Mandy watched him eat his slaw. Hello turista, she thought, and is there any paregoric left? A teaspoonful maybe. She'd take it over to his room this evening even if he hadn't developed any symptoms yet, because they had a shoot to do tomorrow, a sailboat to capsize out on Isla Seca, sixty miles southeast of here, and it was a long helicopter ride, and helicopters and turista were a fatal combination.

Mayumi picked up a paper napkin and fanned herself with it. The air stuck to them, wet and hot and sweet. Out on the beach in front of the cantina naked children were playing in the surf, singing the theme song from *Jaws* and lunging at each other and laughing. *Tiberones!* they yelled. *Cuidado!* Mayumi put down the napkin, lifted up her hair, pulled a pencil out of her purse, and skewered it on top of her head in a French knot. The skin below her ears was golden and smooth like the inside of a seashell.

"So when's your grandmother showing up?" she asked Mandy.

"Tomorrow night." Mandy smiled absently and picked at the label on the beer bottle, scratching off one of the red X's.

"Will we be back from Isla Seca in time?"

"I hope so. I can't quite remember when her plane's coming in. I'll have to take another look at the letter she sent me. It's a miracle it got through, really, considering the mail service around here." Mandy thought of Grammy Viola stepping onto the cracked concrete landing strip, wearing a flowered dress maybe, or since it was cold in London a wool suit that would be too warm. She thought of the shells she'd already found: a Lace Murix, an *Astra longispina*, and one she couldn't identify, bubble-shaped with small brown stripes. She'd give them to Grammy instead of flowers, put them in her hands and tell her there were hundreds more on the beach at Isla Seca. Grammy in a bathing suit and floppy hat striding across the sand making discoveries with Mandy beside her—it was a wonderful image, one that made her inordinately happy.

"The fleas," Peter was saying to Kevin, "are like vampire bats!"

"They haven't been so bad lately." Mayumi turned toward him, fanning herself with the napkin again, a band of sweat on her forehead, eyes lided and sleepy. "Not since Jane had that special bug repellent flown in from Mexico City."

"Fleas caused the bubonic plague."

Kevin scratched his bare chest. "You're getting overly bent out of shape by this, Karp."

"They're miniature sharks."

A silly, pointless conversation, yet Mandy enjoyed it. Fleas and food and what Crews was going to do next: the texture of their life here. And a good life it was, as Kevin had noted. A very good life. In some ways she was going to hate going back to L.A., even though it meant hot showers and edible salads.

A slight breeze blew off the water, rustling the fronds of the palapa as they sat, elbows planted on the wobbly wooden table among puddles of beer, arguing amiably. The day droned to a close like a fly, and all that was left on the table was a plate with a pork-chop bone on it and half a dozen empty brown bottles.

After a while they got up, one by one, and wandered off. Ted and Mandy headed back to their room with their arms around each other;

Mayumi went to look at tide pools; Kevin wandered over to the local pool hall to shoot a game or two, and Peter began a long letter to a French film star named Nicolette Rameau. Night fell, calm and velvety, and the mosquitoes hummed at the screened windows, and if the stars looked particularly indifferent that evening, scattered in the tropical sky like chips of polished steel, no one noticed, not even Mandy, who slept all night in Ted's arms, dreaming peacefully of nothing in particular.

At three o'clock the next afternoon Mandy sat in a sailboat off the coast of Isla Seca, going nowhere and glad of it. Isla Seca, *the dry island* in Spanish: palm trees, sand, mangroves, no potable water, sixty miles from Playa Azul with a helicopter pad on the beach. The end of the earth, Mandy thought, leaning up against the mast of the sailboat. Well, almost the end of the earth. From where she was sitting the island was only a speck on the horizon, floating a few inches below Ted's right shoulder; beyond it was a rim of crashing surf that marked the edge of the reef, and beyond that nothing but blue ocean until you got to what? Cuba? Florida? West Africa? She tried to remember a puzzle map she had had as a child, but she was too exhausted and the colors smeared and blurred in her mind, and she couldn't even recall if this part of Mexico faced east and west or north and south. Her hands were skinned raw, there was salt in her throat, and her hair looked like seaweed. Mayumi slumped, Kevin had his eyes closed, Peter was picking at his sunburn, and Ted was not working the rudder as he was supposed to, although he was faking it nicely. On strike, she thought. Shut it down. We've drunk enough ocean for one afternoon.

Overhead, Jane Crews hovered in helicopter number two, nick-named "The Flying Lady," doing an increasingly accurate impersonation of Attila the Hun. "Tip that goddamn boat over," she yelled through her yellow bullhorn. "What the hell are you waiting for?" She stood in the hatch, hands planted on her hips, frowning. God is wroth, Mandy thought. God is about to kick ass. It was three in the afternoon and a storm appeared to be brewing, and they were supposed to be killing Kevin for the fifteenth time, or was it the sixteenth? She'd lost count. Anyway, that was what it said in the script: ATLANTIS: Scene 123: Sailboat capsizes. Jonah (aka Kevin) drowns.

Only the problem was, the boat wasn't capsizing because the five of them had just rebelled and were taking a break. Becalmed, headed into the wind, sails luffing. Look, Ms. Crews, we're helpless. Can't do a thing about it. Sorry.

"I don't believe this," Crews yelled. "What's going on down there? An idiots' convention?"

Mandy giggled hysterically, Peter belched, and Kevin swore and slapped at the boom.

"Slave driver!" he yelled.

"What was that?" Crews lowered her mirrored glasses in their direction, but she couldn't tell what they were doing, of course, because she was too high up.

"He said the boat won't tip," Ted lied, waving his arms, relinquishing all responsibility for the *Jolly Roger*, rented from a couple who wintered in Playa Azul. A pretty boat, but not going anywhere if Crews knew what he meant. The engine of the copter slugged at the damp air, blowing his words out to sea and chopping them to shreds.

"What?" Crews yelled.

"We've got terminal stability down here, boss," Peter yelled. He pulled some Reese's Peanut Butter Cups out of the plastic bag he kept tied to his waist. Snack break. He passed them around and sent half a piece over the side to astound the parrot fish.

"Jibe!" Crews bellowed. "And stop laughing. I can see your grins through the telephoto lens and you're all supposed to be terrified, get it? *Terrified*. Do I have to spell it out for you?"

"Great idea." Peter swallowed half a Peanut Butter Cup. "Have her spell it; stall for time." He made an obscene gesture, but low and sneaky, because Crews was famous for her revenges and he was no fool.

"Jibe." Ted grinned. "Jibe? It seems to me I've heard that term before somewhere, but I can't quite recall what it means."

The wind sprang up a little and the sun went under a cloud, and about a hundred yards away a school of flying fish broke the surface and then plunged back into the ocean. Beneath them the reef sloped off, dotted with brain coral, and reindeer coral, and bright red fire coral that burned your hands if you accidentally touched it. Peacock flounders, Mandy thought, hanging out on shelves of rose-colored coral; schools of blue and yellow cow fish; parrot fish with pink and green fins—everything lazy and laid back and taking its own time, including us. She scratched a flea bite on her ankle and fed some more line to Ted, who was doing something to the sail to keep them from moving.

Kevin looked at the sky, licked his finger, and held it up to test the wind. "With a little luck," he said, "we could be in for a hurricane."

"Very funny," Ted said, "and I really don't like the look of those clouds." He stared at the piece of red yarn that hung from the mast and then up at the helicopter. The yarn, which was a wind indicator, kept changing direction. Mandy wondered what would happen if they sailed off into the sunset, but it was over sixty miles back to Playa Azul and Crews would no doubt pursue them, and besides, they had a contract, not to mention that they were working on points, and if *Atlantis* was a success, they stood to make hundreds of thousands of dollars. Still, there were some things that money couldn't buy, like the energy to capsize a boat when you'd already done it fifteen times. Ted tilted the tiller a few degrees to the left and the sails fluttered and the boom swung and they went nowhere in a most satisfactory fashion. Picking up the end of the nearest rope, Mandy tied it into a bowline knot just for practice. Yo, ho, ho and a bottle of rum, she thought, we're off to Treasure Island and Crews is Captain Hook.

"Hey, you down there!"

They ignored her.

"Hey, I'm talking to you!"

Mayumi sighed. "If we don't turn this boat over soon," she warned, "Crews is going to go into her Caligula act."

"We're stars." Kevin yawned and stretched. "We can do as we damn well please. What's she going to do? Replace us?"

"Hey," Crews yelled, "are you acting down there or growing moss? Your little conversation is costing us all three hundred dollars a minute."

"She has a point," Peter observed.

"Hmmm," Kevin said. "Three hundred dollars a minute, huh?" He looked past Mandy with cash-register eyes.

"Maybe . . ." Mayumi said.

"Yeah," Kevin agreed. "Maybe. After all, that's a lot to pay to screw around."

Ted shrugged. "Well, I suppose we might as well jibe. I mean she isn't going to stop, is she?"

"Jibe!" Crews yelled. "Jibe, damn you!"

"Jane is such a sweet-tempered lady." Peter grinned. "I'd like to fix her up with a soul mate—Godzilla maybe." He tied his plastic bag back to the drawstring of his swimming suit and wiped the chocolate off his lips. Rest time was over.

Ted sighed, drew in the line, and tightened the sails. The boat pranced and leapt and cut through the water. Mayumi stood up and waved at the copter. "We're going to jibe," she yelled.

"So do it," Crews bellowed, and the copter hovered in close like a big insect. Mandy grabbed the side of the boat to brace herself. The wood was salty and slick, cool to the touch. She liked capsizing: the sudden turning, the rush of water, plunging down under the boat. There was some danger to it, some excitement, and it was quiet under there because even Crews hadn't figured out how to yell at you when you were six feet below the surface. The boat rocked and tepid bilge sloshed against her bare ankles. The air was heavy and slightly sweet; she imagined she smelled salt and kelp and mangrove swamps and the sting of fresh ozone. Ride 'em cowboy, she thought, as she watched Ted getting ready. Here we go again. *Kevin Dies: Take Sixteen.*

"Okay," Ted said, "we're all set. Everybody remember to duck when the boom swings across." He touched her lightly, only the tips of his fingers, but it said so much. "Ready, Man?"

"Sure," she told him. The mast rocked from one side to the other and the sails sang in the wind and her hair blew in her fce. They went faster, picking up speed, heading for Cuba. It was Cuba—she remembered that now—Cuba on the other side of the horizon: Castro and rum and big fat cigars.

"Jibe oh!" Ted yelled. He pushed the tiller away from his body, and the boat bucked, spun around in its own wake, and flipped over like a pancake, throwing the five of them into the ocean. Sputtering and coughing, Mandy rose to the surface to find everyone safe and treading water, except Kevin, who was submerged and holding his breath as instructed. The boat floated on its side, sails dragging. Grabbing for the keel, she rested on it, trying to look shipwrecked, while Crews flew back and forth overhead filming the scene from all angles.

"Great," Crews bellowed through her bullhorn. "I liked that take. Good job. Nice jibe. Frankly, I didn't think you little suckers had it in you."

Kevin broke the surface, spouting like a whale. "Do I have to die a seventeenth time," he yelled, "or is it a wrap?"

"It's a wrap," Crews yelled. "Turn that sorry excuse for a boat back over and anchor it inside the reef. I'm heading back to Playa Azul to put the stuff I just shot on the 5:20 flight to L.A."

Fun and games, Mandy thought. It's going to take at least an hour to bail this boat out, get the sails stowed, and load the gear. She wondered fleetingly if they were going to make it back to Playa Azul before dark.

An hour later Mandy was in helicopter number three on her way back to home base. To her left, Kevin and Mayumi lay sleeping in an exhausted heap on a pile of life jackets. To her right, Ted was sitting with his bare feet propped up against a stack of film equipment reading *The Conquest of Mexico*, Peter was fooling with a Rubik's Cube, and Zack Blumberg, the soundman, was winding up his cables. It was a quiet, rather domestic scene, dominated by the chopping of the propeller overhead, but otherwise unremarkable.

Of course if she had looked out the window she could have seen an endless expanse of clear blue water mottled by underwater reefs and banks of clouds piled on top of one another in pinkish-gray columns, but she had flown this same route eighty-four times in the last seven weeks, so she no longer looked out the window much. There were no landmarks until you were almost to the mainland, and the ocean, although beautiful, grew boring after a while, and besides, she had other things on her mind at present, or, to be more precise, one other thing: namely a quarter of an inch of black graphite that was stuck in the sole of her foot just below her big toe. The graphite had formerly been part of a sea urchin spine, and now it was a painful little needle that produced an unpleasant twinge whenever she stepped on it. Nothing serious, but certainly inconvenient.

Leaning forward, she tilted her foot until it caught the light, doing a kind of Caribbean yoga that had become all too familiar. Sea urchins, she thought, nasty little beasts. Sneaky too. Always lying in wait where you least expect to find them. I should have been more careful but I was in a hurry to get back. She probed for the spine tip with her fingernail and winced. The Japanese, so she'd been told, ate these things on rice—not the spines but the soft glop in the middle. She tried to imagine sitting down to a meal of sea urchins topped with soy sauce and ginger, or whatever they put on them. Inedible, she thought, useless to everyone but themselves, and what was it like to live the life of a sea urchin anyway? Pleasant, probably. You just sat there on your hunk of coral waiting for the sea to bring you a nice, tasty foot—bare preferably, although those spines were so sharp they could go right through the bottom of a rubber flipper.

She probed again, catching the top of the spine between her nails, but before she could pull it out it broke off. Well, that was par for the course. This was perhaps the tenth time she'd had to extract one of these little suckers from her body. Still, that was one of the hazards of working around a reef. She could have been a miner and gotten black lung or worked in a chemical plant and had her genes mutated. Count your blessings, she thought, going for the spine again.

Zack looked up from his cables. "Want a pair of tweezers?" he offered.

"Sure," Mandy said gratefully. "Thanks."

He opened a metal toolbox-like contraption and began rooting around in it, sorting through hanks of wire and transistors and switches. A big, solid man with a black beard and a shovel-shaped face, Zack was almost homely but good-tempered in that obsessed-with-technology soundman way of his. He never said much, and Mandy hadn't gotten to know him very well during the shoot because he mostly hung out with the technical part of the crew, drinking, playing cards, and discussing things like resistors, crystal sync, and the Cincinnati Reds, which were something of an obsession with him. Then, too, there was always an invisible social barrier between the cast and the crew, although who was on top of the heap was a matter of opinion. Soundmen sometimes talked to extras, but by unspoken tradition they left the stars pretty much alone. Mandy didn't like that much, but she'd learned to live with it.

"Hmmm," Zack murmured. He dug into the recesses of his box, came up with a pair of needle-nosed pliers, discarded them, and dug some more. How he ever finds anything in that mess, Mandy thought, is a mystery. Voltammeter, solder gun, more cable. "Will these do the trick?" Zack asked, holding up a small pair of steel tweezers.

"Thanks," Mandy said. She took them from him and bent back over her foot, frowning intently.

Ted looked up from his book. "Want some help?" he asked.

"Sure." She threw her leg across his lap. "Tell me when it's over."

Ted stroked her ankle. "If I take the thorn out of your paw, you'll have to love me forever."

"Don't press your luck." She grinned.

He wrinkled his forehead, inspected the spine from all angles, and then made a plunge at it, tweezers in hand.

"Ouch!" Mandy said.

"Got it." Ted held up the tweezers, displaying a tiny piece of black graphite. Ridiculous that something so small could cause so much pain, and she was just about to tell him that when the helicopter suddenly lurched to the right, throwing her into his arms so hard that she banged her chin against one of the metal struts and saw stars.

"What was that?" She picked herself up, rubbing her chin, and felt a bite of fear in the pit of her stomach.

"I don't know," Ted said in a shaky voice. "Turbulence, I guess." Mayumi and Kevin were awake, sitting bolt upright, and Peter, pale and sick-looking, was holding his Rubik's Cube. The insides of Zack's tool kit were scattered all over the floor, rolling around under their feet. Another lurch, to the left this time, and metal suitcases flew through the air, cameras crashed down, lenses shattering, and cables went skidding into each other.

"Put on your life jackets!" the pilot yelled.

"Oh God," Mayumi moaned. Kevin reached out and put his arm around her.

"Put on your goddamn life jackets and fasten your seat belts and stay calm!"

Leaping to their feet, they grabbed life jackets and began putting them on, slipping their arms through the orange canvas, tying the straps under their legs, bumping into each other and helping each other, all too terrified to say anything. The cabin began filling with black smoke. Mandy coughed and gagged and clutched at Ted, as if he could somehow keep them from falling. She fastened her seat belt, wondering if she was buckling herself into a death trap. What would happen if they crashed? Would the helicopter float? Sink like a stone? It had pontoons, she told herself. If they crashed into the ocean, they'd get out somehow.

Ted grabbed her hand so hard it hurt. "I love you," he said. "We're going to be okay. Just hang on."

Overhead, the rotary blades skipped a beat, made a choking sound, and skipped again. Suddenly they stopped. There was an instant of silence, and then the helicopter took a sickening plunge. Mandy felt her whole body tug against the seat belt, pulled up and out, and she screamed and clawed at the side of the cabin, trying to find something to hang on to, and the terror was like nothing she had ever felt before. It lasted forever, and then, without warning, the motor coughed and turned over, and the blades started up again and they leveled out.

She was shaking so hard she couldn't think. The inside of the cabin was a mess, and if they hadn't been buckled in they would have been part of it, and for a second no one could move or say anything. Mayumi sobbed softly, hands over her face. Kevin was bleeding from a cut that ran all the way across his forehead, but they were all alive and no one seemed seriously injured and it was a miracle.

Ted threw back his head and laughed. His pale blue eyes sparkled and he looked drunk with relief. Mandy opened her mouth to say something to him, but no sound came out. She leaned forward to hug him, to kiss him, to celebrate, and the tips of her fingers had just touched his shoulders when the motor stopped again for the second and final time.

The helicopter froze for an instant and then plunged straight down, spinning wildly. This time there was no last-minute reprieve—just confusion and terror, and at the end nothing but fire.

Salt water was washing into Mandy's nose and mouth, burning her throat, and it tasted of blood. She couldn't breathe and she was panicking, coughing and spitting and begging the man who was holding her to let her go, fighting him, not understanding why he wanted to suffocate her; he had to let her go for the sake of God, give her air, but she was too weak to make him do it.

"Hold still," he said sharply. "Don't struggle, damn it."

She opened her eyes, or rather her eyes blinked open, and she saw that it was Zack who had his arm around her. "Zack," she said, "why . . ." Another wave washed over her, taking her by surprise, and she choked and spit, and the salt stung, and suddenly she was very frightened because something terrible must have happened, but she couldn't remember what it was.

"Easy now," Zack said gently. He tightened his grip, and she realized that he was hauling her through the water, only why was she in the water? Her head hurt; she was confused and disoriented. Maybe she was drowning and he was saving her. She tried to kick to help him, but her left leg hurt. Everything hurt. She would have floundered, but his arm supported her. The waves were small and choppy, littered with oil and wreckage, bits of aluminum suitcases, hunks of metal, an incongruous Styrofoam cup. Fifty yards away a small green boat floated, bobbing up and down, only it wasn't a boat because it didn't have any inside. It had two pieces of jagged metal sticking up above it like masts and it was . . .

A pontoon.

Oh Jesus, the helicopter must have crashed and broken up and they were swimming through the remains of it. She felt sick with fear. She tried to remember the accident, but there was only a blank spot; a piece of her mind was gone. Then an image came to her: black smoke and gagging and silence. The motor. Of course, that was it. She remembered now that the motor had stopped. And then she remembered that it had started again. But if that was true, why was she here? What had happened? She was scared because she couldn't remember. How could she not remember, and where were Mayumi and Ted and Peter and Kevin? She lifted her head and tried to find them, but there was only the wreckage and the pontoon and the waves. The sun lay on the horizon in a fiery, quivering ball, and in the distance something orange floated in the water, which could have been a person in a life jacket or a body or only more trash or . . .

"Take it easy," Zack told her. "Try to relax. You're exhausting yourself."

She closed her eyes and gave up, and her mind took a dizzy sick spin into nothingness again, and she wasn't sure what happened next, but she must have fainted because the next thing she remembered they were beside the pontoon, hanging on to it, and it was tilting, threatening to topple over on them. She tried again to remember the accident, but she felt too confused to do anything but cling to the pontoon. Her lip was cut and it throbbed. She spit out some blood. Pink stained the foam.

"Come on," Zack was saying, "I can't do this alone. Try to help yourself up." He had caught hold of the pontoon and was trying to push her up over the edge, and it was tipping even more, threatening to throw her back into the ocean, and she kept slipping off because it was round with a raised metal seam down the center with the two metal struts sticking up into nothing, sheared off at the end where they'd once been attached to the body of the helicopter. Grasping for one of the struts, she managed somehow to get a grip on it and pull herself most of the way out of the water. She crawled forward on her stomach, cutting the palm of her hand on a sharp edge of metal. The cut stung and she licked at it and hung on with her other hand, and the pontoon settled under her a little and listed crookedly.

She looked over her shoulder and saw Zack, a foot or so below her, treading water.

"I'm going to tie you on with my belt," Zack said.

"Why?"

"Because you might faint again."

"I fainted?"

"Yeah, you did, twice. Don't you remember?" He looped his belt around her waist and lashed her to the nearest strut. His arms were long and skinny, tanned from the wrists down, white from the wrists up, like fish bellies. She felt scared. Had she fainted? She couldn't remember. But then she couldn't remember a lot of things. Best to take his word for it. "Don't lean too far forward or you might tip this thing over," he warned. "Do you understand?"

"Yes, Zack, yes, I understand." She sounded so sensible, which was amazing, because the truth was, she was very frightened and getting more frightened every minute.

Zack turned and began swimming away, taking long steady strokes. The waves rolled him from side to side. He rose to the top of a swell, turned his head, waved to her. She sat on the left side of the pontoon, with her feet dangling in the water, and watched him disappear between the troughs and then reappear again, his head dark and slick like the head of a seal, and she tried to think, and little by little she fought off the fear enough to notice that the sun had set, and that there was something wrong with her left leg. Broken probably. It should be hurting but it wasn't, at least not very much, and that was a bad sign. The thought occurred to her that she must be in shock. She looked for Zack and didn't see him. Her hands were trembling badly. She folded them in her lap and laced her fingers together, but they went on shaking. It was beginning to get dark.

Suddenly she felt very alone.

Then Zack was back, thrashing through the water awkwardly, towing Ted by the collar of his life jacket. Ted's arms floated out to either side, Christ-like in an incongruous Hawaiian shirt with dancing girls and ukuleles on it. His head lolled, he was limp as a sack of sand, and he kept sinking feet first and Zack kept trying to lift him up.

She felt such relief at the sight of Ted that she nearly wept—how could she have forgotten him, even for a moment—and then fear again because where *were* the others? It was terrible not to be able to remember. Had they died in the crash? She had an awful, shameful thought: if only one of them had survived, then thank God it was Ted. God forgive her, but she couldn't help it. She loved him so much. She wanted to dive in the water and help Zack, but she knew she was too weak. "Is he alive?" she yelled. Ted had to be alive. She willed him to move, but he didn't. He only lay there floating on his back, white and helpless. A wave washed over his face but he didn't cough.

"Of course he's alive," Zack said. He swam closer with his precious cargo. "Would I bother with him if he wasn't?" Zack paddled around to the far side of the pontoon, caught Ted under the shoulders, and hefted him up. Ted's life jacket made him an awkward burden. "Grab him," Zack told her.

She grasped Ted eagerly, pulled him toward her, and as she wrestled with him, her leg began to throb, sending darts of pain up her hip that made her gasp and bite her lower lip, but she didn't care because Ted kept slipping out of her hands, and she couldn't think about anything else until he lay safely on the pontoon beside her. His wet shirt clung to his body, and there was a large bruise on his forehead.

Move, she thought. Say something. Open your eyes. You're okay. But Ted just lay there. She bent down and looked into his face, and then she cradled him in her arms and put her head to his chest and heard his heart beating. Impulsively, she kissed him. His lips were warm and salty. She kissed him again and all at once something broke inside her and she was crying and laughing and saying his name. "I love you, Teddy," she was saying. "Can you hear me?" She touched his forehead, pushed aside his wet hair, rubbed his hands to warm them. He was unconscious, who knew how badly hurt, maybe paralyzed, but alive, in her arms. "Teddy." She embraced him and she felt such love for him, and she knew that if they got out of this alive she would love him forever. "Teddy, I'm here. I'll take care of you. It's okay. You're going to be okay."

"Help me get his feet up out of the water," Zack said gruffly, but there was compassion in his eyes for the two of them. He pushed Ted's legs up on the pontoon; she caught them and tried to keep them from slipping off again, but his body, no longer buoyed by the water, was heavy, and it slid about, nearly dragging her over the edge.

"Get a better grip on him," Zack panted.

She gritted her teeth and pulled Ted up higher, and the pontoon righted, balanced, and it was easier. She wanted to tie him but there was nothing left to tie him with, and then she felt a tap on her ankle and Zack was reaching up, handing her some strips of white nylon, and it wasn't until she had Ted securely lashed to the second strut that she realized Zack had cut the harnesses off his own life jacket.

"How can you go back for the others that way?" she asked him.

There was a long silence.

"Zack, I said how . . . ?"

"I heard what you said."

"Aren't you going to try to find them?"

"No."

"Why not?"

"Because it wouldn't do any good."

She refused to understand. "What do you mean it wouldn't do any good? How do you know that?" She looked out over the water and saw only fuel oil, wreckage, and bits of plastic. The waves rolled silently through the twilight, right out to the horizons on all four sides. "Kevin!" she yelled. "Mayumi! Peter! Where are you?"

"Stop that," Zack said sharply. "It won't do any good. They aren't going to answer you."

But she went on yelling.

"Sit back and save your breath."

"Please," she begged, "tell me what happened to them. Where are they? Please, Zack."

"Let's not talk about it, okay?"

She pleaded; and then her pleading turned to desperation.

"Well, okay then," he said reluctantly, looking only at the pontoon. "If you have to know, they drowned and so did the pilot."

"They drowned?"

"Yes, they drowned."

"I don't believe you!" she yelled. She didn't mean to yell at him, but she couldn't stop herself. "They couldn't have drowned. They could swim, all of them. We were making a goddamn *skin-diving* movie. We could all swim, even Peter."

"Get ahold on yourself, Mandy."

"Where the hell are they? Tell me!"

"Listen to me." Zack grabbed her ankle and shook it. "They never had a chance to swim, understand? It was the seat belts. That copter burned and then it sank fast, filled up with water, and they were on the low side. I only had time to get the two of you out. I threw you out the hatch, and I threw Ted after you. Then it was all over. The copter sank and there was nothing left, just some junk and an oil slick. I almost went down with it trying to cut Mayumi out with my Swiss Army knife. She was struggling. It wasn't pretty. You're lucky you're alive, so get hold of yourself or you're going to tip over that pontoon and drown."

He let go of her ankle, and she sat back, ashamed of herself. Zack had saved her life and she was yelling at him, and she must be out of her mind or in shock, and, oh, Mayumi, she thought, Mayumi, Mayumi, Peter, Kevin. She tried to calm herself, but she felt such terrible sadness.

She ran her fingers through her hair, reached over the edge of the pontoon, scooped up some water, and threw it on her face. The water was warm and smelled of fuel. Later, she told herself, cry later. Zack was right. She was lucky to be alive. Grief overwhelmed her again, but she fought it off. She had to keep it together. Ted was unconscious. He was depending on her. She had to be logical, useful, in control of herself. She looked down at Zack and the thought occurred to her that he might slip out of his life jacket, and if he did, and he started to drown, she'd never be able to save him because he was too big and heavy.

"Come up here," she told him. She stretched out her hand, being useful.

"No," he said stubbornly, and backed away until there were several feet of oily water between him and the edge of the pontoon.

She stared at him, completely surprised by his reaction; she couldn't believe he was refusing. What was this, some kind of macho game? "Zack." He swam back some more. "Stop it!" she commanded. "Stop swimming away from the pontoon. Are you crazy? Listen, you're the one that has to get ahold on himself. You saved Ted and me, now get up here and save yourself."

"I can't," he said, and he paddled back some more so she couldn't touch him.

"Why not?"

"Mandy," he said quietly, "it's like this. I weigh maybe a hundred and eighty pounds, and if I get up on that pontoon with the two of you, I'm going to swamp it. So I'll just float and hang on to the edge until we're rescued."

"You're kidding. It's dark. They might not spot us until morning."

"Couldn't be more serious."

"But what about sharks? There are sharks in these waters, Zack, remember?"

"Forget the sharks. What sharks? Who sees any sharks?" He smiled crookedly, but it wasn't a happy smile; it was shaky and scared and she couldn't let him do this.

"I want to take turns with you," she insisted stubbornly. "You're right about the pontoon swamping, I can see that. So we'll take turns holding on to the edge."

"You try it," he threatened, "and I'll swim away from here so fast you won't know what hit you. You could pass out again any minute. You had a concussion. Got any idea what that means? Well, I do. I was a medic in 'Nam, and I've seen things that, well never mind what I've seen, this is no time for war stories, but if you have any idea of going over the side and playing Miss Florence Nightingale, then stuff it because you don't do it, understand?"

Finally his face softened. "I'm sorry to talk to you so rough, but I'm a little weirded out. I'll be okay, really. I'm pretty tough."

"Zack, please, isn't there anything I can do for you?"

"No, but thanks all the same." He paused. "Well," he said in an uncertain voice, "there is one thing."

"What's that?"

"Hold my hand and talk to me," he told her. "I know that sounds strange, but I think I'm hurt pretty bad, and I'm afraid I might pass out."

"How badly are you hurt, Zack?"

"Bad," he said. "The whole lower part of my body is burned and I'm just starting to feel the pain." He clutched her hand and put his face against the side of the pontoon.

"Zack," she pleaded.

"Don't ask me to come up there," he warned. "I mean it, Mandy. Don't even ask."

An hour or so after sunset it began to rain in light, gauzy sheets. Mandy was just in the process of straining to catch the last drops on her tongue when she heard a familiar sound.

A helicopter was approaching from the west.

No, it couldn't be. She was delirious, imagining things. She held her breath, but the sound grew louder. The helicopter was not only real, it was coming closer. My God, she thought, we're going to be saved! Half crazy with joy and hope, she clutched Zack's hand and struggled to an upright position.

"Here!" she croaked hoarsely, waving her free arm. "Here we are!" Her voice was weak, her arm a dim gray line, the pontoon green and invisible in the darkness. She looked around, desperate for something she might use to attract attention. If only she had a light, a dry match, even a white sheet.

"Here," Zack was yelling, "over here!" He pounded on the pontoon with his fist. "Down here, damn it!"

They screamed at the top of their lungs for several minutes, but their voices were swallowed by the drone of the motor and the lapping of the waves. As if taunting them, the invisible helicopter flew directly overhead, hovered for an instant in the clouds, then passed on without stopping. Horrified, Mandy heard the beat of the blades grow fainter.

"No," she begged, "please, don't go. We're here. We're here. Please come back, please. At least help Ted."

"It's no use," Zack said grimly.

"But they can't leave," she insisted stubbornly, "they can't, they can't." She knew she was raving and that it wasn't doing any good, but she couldn't stop. It was too cruel, too unbearable. Clinging to Zack's hand, she began to cry in fear and anger and frustration.

Mandy lay on her stomach, feeling the pontoon rise and fall under her. It was even darker now and the sea was getting rough, throwing her from side to side in a way that was sickening. Her throat ached and her tongue felt swollen and the pain in her leg had spread to her hip and back. Still, there was nothing she could do to make herself more comfortable, so instead of thinking about it, she tried to think about Ted. Ted was in worse shape than she was, and it was making her crazy with worry. He was still breathing, but he didn't move or make a sound. She wanted more than anything in the world to get him to a hospital, where he could be taken care of, but the three of them had been drifting through the dark forever on this damn pontoon, and she didn't have anything to make his suffering easier, not even a Band-Aid.

The only thing good that had happened in the last two hours was the rain.

The pontoon bucked, and she winced and bit her lower lip. She kept thinking that if only it had been light, maybe the pilot would have seen them—but on the other hand, if it had been light, they would have had to reckon with the sun. She was afraid of the sun. It was a new fear but strong. If they were still on this pontoon when the sun came up tomorrow, it was probably going to kill them, because there was no shade and no water except salt water. If she had to go through a whole day without a drink of water, she might go out of her mind. She was already running a fever and was dizzy, and once she had imagined Ted had turned over and smiled at her and they had started kissing and she had come to her senses only at the last minute and realized it was a hallucination.

"Mandy," Zack whispered. He hadn't spoken for a long time, not since they had both been forced to admit that they weren't going to be rescued. The sound of his voice snapped her awake. She sat up on one elbow and peered down into the shadows, trying to see his face. She licked her lips and tasted salt. They were swollen and hurt.

"What is it, Zack?"

"You know . . . I was thinking I'd like some . . . beer or some ice. . . . Could you pass some of . . . the ice down here?"

His request sent chills up her spine. "Zack, what the hell are you talking about? We don't have any ice." She shook his hand. "Are you okay?" Silence. "Say something." More silence.

"I'm fine," he said at last. "I'm sorry. I think . . . I sort of lost it there for a minute." She felt reassured by the tone of his voice. It was stronger, and he was making sense again, or at least something close to sense. Under the circumstances, it was best not to analyze too closely.

"You're sure you're okay?"

"I'm okay."

She put her cheek back down on the pontoon and tried to relax, but her whole body ached and she felt light-headed and out of control. There was a pause. The waves slapped and retreated, and the sky looked very close. She lay there, holding his hand, not thinking of much of anything.

"Mandy," Zack said after a long time.

"What, Zack?"

"I was lying. I'm not okay."

She sat up abruptly, startled and frightened. "What do you mean you're not okay?"

"It hurts bad."

"Can I do anything for you?"

"Don't let go of my hand."

"I won't."

"Promise?"

"I promise, Zack."

"I already . . . blacked out once, and I think I'm about . . . to do it . . . again."

"Zack, don't! Try to hang on."

"The pain . . . it's . . . bad . . . real bad."

"Zack, please, I know it must be terrible, but fight it, please, Zack. For God's sake, please fight it. You can't pass out."

"Mandy, I think—"

"Don't think! Just stay awake. You have to stay awake. Do you hear me, Zack?"

Silence.

"Zack?'

More silence.

"Say something," she begged. "You can't pass out. I won't let you. Zack? Say something. Let me know you're still conscious. Can you hear me?" She shook his hand, but it was limp. "Damn it, Zack, wake up! Say something. Please. Please, Zack, don't leave me."

A wave hit the pontoon and he began sliding away from her, out into the darkness. She grabbed him harder, digging her nails into the palm of his hand. "Zack!" she yelled. She reached down with both hands and shook him, but he didn't respond.

"Help me," she cried, "somebody help me," but there was no one to help her. Another wave hit the pontoon and she almost lost hold of him. She clung to Zack and tried to think, but she couldn't. She could only feel, and what she felt was fear and determination and a sort of bullheaded stubbornness that rose up from the pit of her stomach. I won't let go of him, she thought. I just won't.

"You aren't getting away from me this easily, Zack," she told him. She got a good grip on his shirt. "I won't let you leave me, do you understand? I'm going to hold on to you until we're rescued. It isn't so hard, holding on to you. You're floating. All I have to do is keep awake and keep you here next to the pontoon. I'd bring you up and take your place if I could, now that you can't object, but you're too heavy, you see, so there really isn't any choice, but don't try to get away, Zack, or I'll come in after you, I swear I will." She went on talking to him—explaining and pleading and promising him that she'd never let him go.

After the first hour or so, she must have gone a little crazy because she lost all sense of time. All she knew was that she was holding on to Zack, and that if help didn't come soon, they were both going to die.

34

MORNING

Viola woke to the ringing of the phone. Sitting up, she fumbled
groggily for the receiver. She had fallen asleep fully dressed; her eyes
burned and her head ached, and she was exhausted and almost sick
with anticipation.

"Miss Kessler?" a gravelly voice inquired. It was Jane Crews.

Viola took a deep breath and looked at the cheap red-and-blue
bedspread decorated with gaudy palm trees. Above her the electric
fan was beating the air, and pale morning sunlight was streaming in
through the windows revealing the naked ugliness of the room: the
spots of mold on the walls, the broken tiles and peeling window
sashes. There was only one question she wanted to ask Crews, but
she was afraid to voice it.

"Miss Kessler?"

"Yes, yes, I'm here." She closed her eyes and leaned back against
the pillow, squaring her shoulders for the possible blow to come. "Is
there any news yet?"

"Great news," Jane Crews said triumphantly, but there was pain in her voice. "Wonderful news. Mandy and Ted and Zack were found this morning about half an hour after sunrise, floating about thirty miles off the coast. I just got word from the helicopter pilot that he's bringing them in."

"They were found, you said they were found!" She was overwhelmed with joy, crazy with excitement. She sat up, got to her feet, walked over to the window, and looked out at the ocean. She laughed and cried and felt wonderful and moved and relieved and not quite in her right mind. "How is Mandy? Is she hurt?"

"She's fine. She's dehydrated and exhausted, of course, and she has some cuts, and maybe a dislocated hip, but nothing serious."

"And Ted?"

"He was evidently knocked out for a while, but he's come around. He's a little out of it, but the pilot said it looks like he's going to be okay. Zack was burned in the crash, but he's alive and he's probably going to make it. I've made arrangements to have all of them flown back to the States as soon as they get here, and I've got two doctors on standby. The insurance company flew in a medical unit from L.A. last night, and they're taking care of everything. Zack's going straight to the burn center in Houston."

"And the others?"

There was a long pause. "No sign of them, but we're still looking." There was grief in Crews' voice, the kind of grief that left little room for hope.

That was sobering. Viola sat back down on the bed. "Mandy's alive? She's not badly hurt? You're sure?"

"I just told you, she's fine. It's a miracle."

"Yes," she repeated softly, "it's a miracle." She hung up the phone and put her face in her hands. Mandy, she thought. Mandy, darling, I was so afraid I'd lost you. She had never loved anyone as she loved Mandy, she realized, not Kathe, not Conrad, not her mother, not even Joseph. She wondered what it meant to have such strong feelings for another human being, and she wept with happiness and relief and grief for Mandy's friends, who were probably dead.

After a while she dried her eyes, got up, and went over to the mirror. Silly old fool, she told her reflection. What would Mandy think if she saw you like this? Blowing her nose, she put on some powder and lipstick and carefully erased all signs of tears. Taking off her wrinkled clothes, she slipped into a fresh dress, picked up her purse, and started for the door.

She paused, hand on the knob. Wait a minute, she thought. I've forgotten something. Now what is it? She looked around the room, at the unmade bed, the empty water glass, the television set that received only static, trying to jog her memory, and then she saw what she had forgotten, lying on the night table right where she had left it.

Walking briskly across the room, she picked up the small pearl button, tossed it into her purse, and hurried down to the beach to meet the helicopter that was bringing Mandy back to her.

35

A small cabin cruiser left the bay at ten in the morning, carrying three passengers and a curious cargo. The cargo was flowers—hundreds of them, packed under strips of wet burlap to keep them fresh. The passengers were Ted and Mandy, with Jane Crews at the helm.

They said very little to each other as they headed southeast out into the Gulf. Mandy and Ted stood at the rail most of the time, holding each other's hands and looking quietly at the ocean. They had been married less than a month and gold wedding rings gleamed on their fingers.

In the last year a lot of things had changed. Mandy had left films for the stage and was presently starring in a revival of Henry Arbor's *Laura* that had gotten good, if not spectacular, reviews. Her agent wasn't speaking to her, the media was ignoring her, and over lunches at the Beverly Wilshire the movers and shakers of Hollywood shook their heads and told each other that she was out of her mind to give up such a promising career, especially after the Oscar nomination, but Mandy didn't care. That night she had spent on the pontoon had made her see that life was too short not to do what you wanted, and at present she wanted to act in front of live audiences. Maybe sometime in the future she would go back to the movies, maybe she wouldn't. Meanwhile, she had Ted and she was happy, and that was all that mattered.

As for Ted, he hadn't exactly left the movies, but at the moment he was writing a script for Jane Crews, one that had every likelihood of getting produced, especially since Crews had somehow managed to salvage *Atlantis*. Everyone had expected her to abandon the film after the accident and collect the insurance money on it. In fact, the critics had all predicted that even if she was able to come up with a final cut that made sense, the movie would be box-office poison, but—as usual—the critics were wrong. After Mandy and Ted recovered from the accident, Crews had persuaded them to do two weeks of retakes—not in Mexico, but off the coast of Santa Monica. Then, cloistering herself in her studio, she had spent nine months working and reworking the raw footage.

Released in December, *Atlantis* had played to packed houses, walking off with seven Oscar nominations, including one to Zack for best sound. Crews' enemies said that by making the film into a memorial to the dead members of the cast and crew, she had exploited the accident shamefully; her admirers said that she was a genius and that it was a fitting tribute to her beloved colleagues. But whatever anybody said, the fact remained that she could pretty well write her own ticket these days.

The cabin cruiser plowed southeast for about an hour as Crews consulted dials and charts. The sea was glassy, with small waves. Overhead a few white, cauliflower-shaped clouds moved lazily toward the west. Around eleven Crews turned off the motor and they drifted to a stop.

"Are we here?" Ted asked.

Crews nodded. "I think so," she said. "I'm no expert at this and we aren't sure of the exact location, of course, but as nearly as I can tell, this is where they picked you up."

Mandy looked at the ocean, trying to see something familiar in it, but it looked like all the other miles of water they had crossed this morning. "We drifted of course," she said.

Crews nodded. "Of course." She went over to the flowers and began pulling the strips of wet burlap off them. The petals burst forth in a cascade of colors—red poppies, purple violets, daisies, camellias, carnations, chains of begonias and orchids, fuchsias, and iris, and lily of the valley, and narcissus, and a great basket of nameless tropical flowers that they had bought at a stand in Playa Azul. "Here," Crews said, handing Mandy a wreath laced with white orchids.

Mandy held the wreath thoughtfully for a moment, and then cast it into the sea. "Good-bye, Peter," she said. "I'll miss your jokes as long as I live."

"Good-bye, Kevin." Ted threw a wreath of red roses over the rail. "Good-bye, my friend."

"Good-bye, Mayumi." Mandy cast a wreath of pink roses into the water, and her voice broke. "I'll always love you."

Crews threw in a wreath for the pilot, David Collins, and there was a long silence. They stood quietly for a moment, watching the four wreaths bob up and down on the waves. Then they turned and began to cast the cut flowers into the water. In less than five minutes the vases and boxes were empty, and they were floating in a sea of flowers.